Go the Way Your Blood Beats

Foreword by E. Lynn Harris

EDITED AND WITH AN INTRODUCTION BY

SHAWN STEWART RUFF

An Owl Book
Henry Holt and Company   *New York*

Go the Way Your Blood Beats

An Anthology

of Lesbian and Gay

Fiction by

African-American

Writers

Henry Holt and Company, Inc.
Publishers since 1866
115 West 18th Street
New York, New York 10011

Henry Holt® is a registered
trademark of Henry Holt and Company, Inc.

Library of Congress Cataloging-in-Publication Data
Go the way your blood beats: an anthology of lesbian and gay fiction by African-American writers/foreword by E. Lynn Harris; edited and with an introduction by Shawn Stewart Ruff.—1st ed.
p.   cm.
1. Gays' writings, American.   2. American fiction—Afro-American authors.
3. Lesbians—United States—Fiction.   4. Gay men—United States—Fiction.
5. Afro-American gays—Fiction.   6. American fiction—20th century.
I. Ruff, Shawn Stewart.
IN PROCESS   96-4905
813.008′0920664—dc20   CIP

ISBN 0-8050-4736-0
ISBN 0-8050-4437-X (An Owl Book: pbk.)

Henry Holt books are available for special promotions and premiums.
For details contact: Director, Special Markets.

First Edition—1996

Designed by Kate Nichols

Printed in the United States of America
All first editions are printed on acid-free paper. ∞

1   3   5   7   9   10   8   6   4   2
1   3   5   7   9   10   8   6   4   2 (pbk.)

Due to limitations of space, permissions appear on pages 542–544.

FOR MOONEY—I REMEMBER.

Contents

BAD BLOOD

BEHIND CLOSED DOORS

BLOOD, SWEAT, AND TEARS

HEARTACHE

HEMORRHAGING

BASHERS

GO THE WAY YOUR BLOOD BEATS

Foreword

E. LYNN HARRIS

While in Los Angeles on a speaking engagement, I had a wonderful experience. It was at a church—a large church in South Central—headed by a progressive ministry. There were lots of teenagers, male and female. Nothing unusual about this—except that many were gay or bisexual. "I feel as though I know you," several of them said. I couldn't believe it. So open, so confident—and in a church!

I've thought about this experience often, and these kids are extraordinary to me. Honesty and truth have become priorities, maybe because in terms of my own sexual identity they didn't always seem possible. As a young adult, about the same age as these South Central teens, I read James Baldwin's *Giovanni's Room* in a dim, dusty corner of the library, trying to find my place in the world, or, at the very least, in Little Rock, Arkansas. I remember thinking that I felt as though Baldwin knew me through his words, knew the feelings I had but did not quite understand. Even though Baldwin was an invisible mentor to me, guiding me from boyhood to manhood, from dreamer to writer, securing my place in the world, I don't imagine that I had, at that age, the courage to speak my truth so eloquently, and so publicly, as those remarkable young people before me.

Life on the road has been full of many such surprises. Faced with the prospect of touring as a "gay" author, I didn't at first know what to expect. I'm always amazed at how open and honest people are. I was with a writer who recently shared with me that his sister had come out as a lesbian after being married. Many tell me that they use *Invisible Life* and *Just As I Am* as a means of coming out to their parents and other people they are close to. Telling your family you're gay is not easy. There are many indications that Black families don't talk about homosexuality, and when they do they don't necessarily do so in constructive ways. I'm fortunate that my family has always been very supportive. The only time my mom and I came close to talking about sexuality, she said to me, "You're my baby, and I love you no matter what." I think the bottom line for parents is that they want the best for their children. I'm sure that my mom would prefer that I weren't gay—not out of any particular homophobia on her part—but due to the fact that, like any mother who wants the best for her children, she doesn't want me to suffer any kind of injustices because of any aspect of my character—particularly my sexuality. Last year I took her on tour with me to San Francisco. Someone asked her, "What do you think of all this?" She said, "I'm very proud of him, I've always been proud of him." I hold on to that.

In African American–owned bookstores, the ladies that come to my signings don't really ask a lot of questions about sexuality. What's been rewarding to me, and what makes me feel hopeful, is that they're asking questions about the characters. They say that once they're reading the novel, they forget that a character's gay or bisexual. In Washington, D.C., I had an incredible crowd that was predominantly heterosexual women and men, and they asked questions about MamaCee in *And This Too Shall Pass* and other characters. Afterward, the bookstore owner said that it was like a block party atmosphere. I'd like to think that straight African Americans are viewing gay and lesbian lives in a more positive way. By that I mean they're getting away from what they may be repulsed by in sexual activity. I always ask the question when I do radio shows: Why, when we're talking about gay and bisexual issues, does sex always come up? I think what's happened with my books is that people have gotten into the characters, and they've seen that even though lesbians and gays are different, we have so many similarities as oppressed people in general. We're all in search of love, we're all in search of peace—those things that'll make us happy.

I've had a couple of situations where I've spoken to all-women bookclubs, and the women said that *Just As I Am* made them mad. "I couldn't put it down, but it made me mad." I've told them that it's okay to be angry, but I also told them that they have to create an environment in which truth is the only thing that's worth dealing with. My impression from the women I speak with is that so many times they ask the right questions about sexuality but they don't hear the response. Sometimes they expect so much out of men that if a man were gay or bisexual, he wouldn't feel totally comfortable in sharing that, because he'd feel he hadn't lived up to the expectations of what a man is supposed to be—which, in my opinion, means being responsible. Part of that responsibility is having the integrity to tell the truth.

I love speaking at colleges. Every experience has been tremendous. One in particular stands out, where a professor stood up and said that one of her students was very distressed when I said during an earlier talk that rumors suggest Langston Hughes was gay. The young man admired Hughes and was offended by my comment. Later, after this outing, the young man in question came up to me and said, "I didn't want to come to this lecture, but I was forced, and I'm glad I did. I liked what you had to say." When I asked him what made him upset in the first place, he shared with me the story of a cousin he grew up with. He said he came in the house and found his cousin with a dude and it freaked him out. He was very angry. When I asked him why, he said, "We were boys. We ran women. And then he turned gay. I felt betrayed." I asked him what he was going to do, how would he handle this? He told me that he was going to call his cousin and tell him that he was sorry. He understood that maybe we don't choose to be gay.

Not every experience on the road has been great. There is always that fear, justified or not, that someone's going to ask negative questions, or say negative things. My fear was realized recently in Philadelphia, where I was doing a Black call-in radio show. I had done this show before when I toured for *Invisible Life.* But this particular day the calls were really quite negative. Callers nastily asked why I was on the show. One caller said: "I don't understand. They sent all the white slaves back to Africa, this isn't a part of our African heritage." Another said: "You're on the *New York Times Best Seller List* and you're successful because the white man don't see you as a threat." As disheartened and angry as I was, I tried to remain calm. I said people are entitled to their opinions. Then I said, "It wasn't white people that made me gay. If so, when did this happen? Are whites sneaking us out late at night to convince us that we're gay? Who's teaching gays and lesbians to be gay?" After the show I was so disturbed that I canceled a later interview. I hadn't felt that kind of venom before. However, I did a signing at a bookstore in Philly the next day, and so many people came out— about three hundred. Several came up to me and said that they'd never heard of me before, but they liked the way I handled myself on that radio show, and that Philadelphia is not like those people who called in.

The road has also allowed me to learn a lot about myself, too, and my own prejudices and misconceptions. A very beautiful woman I was talking to told me that she was lesbian, and I said, "But you're so attractive." I should have known better. I do now. Sometimes when taking questions from the audience I have to check myself. Not too long ago, in Miami, there was a Black guy with his hand raised who looked very straight and very angry. I passed him over a number of times, but he kept his hand up. When I finally did call on him, I was surprised. He was gay. He came across as being very sweet and honest, saying that books helped him deal with his sexuality.

A slightly similar situation happened in New York last summer, only this time it was in a social situation and the person was a writer I admire. He was very cold, very unfriendly. I was surprised by this. Months later, I saw him in another social situation, and he came over, grabbed me, and said, "I've got to apologize to you. I was chilly to you when we met. I need to tell you why: I thought this woman had brought you over to meet me to see if I knew you. I thought she was calling me out. I am living an invisible life." I told him I understood.

But it made me sad. I can't tell you how many times men and women, especially men, come up to me and ask me how does it feel to be so open and honest with my life? They look at me with such longing in their eyes. Sometimes they'll say, "I wish I could live like that." Then they give me all the reasons they can't.

All of us always need to tell the truth about who we are, because so often when people say that they love us, who they love is the person they *think* we are. Truth earns respect. Acceptance comes in waves; truth is everlasting.

The themes I have shared here—love, self-acceptance, misconceptions of gay and lesbian life, bigotry—are ties that hold this important collection together. These finely and thoughtfully crafted works of fiction show how necessary it is for us—gay, lesbian, bisexual, or straight—to understand and to love one another as best we're capable.

E. Lynn Harris
Atlanta

Acknowledgments

Thanks to all the wonderful authors whose talents abound in these pages. I admire you all.

To Tracy Sherrod, my editor, for enthusiasm, chutzpah, and support.

To Victoria Sanders, my agent.

To Laurie LaRose, my girl Friday, for the smart help.

To Miranda Ottewell, my copyeditor, for an impeccable job.

Introduction

You don't have to read literature by gay and lesbian writers to read meaningfully about homosexuality. Amiri Baraka's brilliant short story "The Alternative" proved that point to me several years ago. In it, a motley crew of young Black men are moaning over the boredom of life at college, when one of them tells the others he has spotted their dormmate with a faggot. Seeing this as an opportunity not to be missed, they go stand outside the door of their neighbor, jeering and heckling as they overhear and watch through the keyhole the two men making love. On an obvious level the story plays to types: Both gay characters are "theater," limp-wristed sissies; the straight boys are dangerous, gang-prone, inner-city youth. But then comes the moment when type flips on itself, and the rough boys, who almost without their being aware of it are aroused by what they are watching, turn against one another, their masculinity suddenly at issue.

Early on I didn't intend to use this story. My agenda was set: I planned to historicize and contemporize lesbian and gay fiction, and provide a context in which to describe the tradition of African-American gay and lesbian literature while setting the precedent of marrying the two. Cutting a swath from the canon of African-American literature gives a certain gloss to our writings as being part of the African-American literary tradition. The juxtaposition of Alice Dunbar Nelson, Wallace Thurman, and even James Baldwin with successful contemporary writers such as Randall Kenan, Jacqueline Woodson, and Carolivia Herron allows the older writers' works to be read in an appropriate context, while providing a kind of genealogy of gay and lesbian literary fiction. Ideas and themes are suddenly traceable, and a story that seems casually violent, like Dunbar Nelson's "A Carnival Jangle"—in which a young woman dressed as a man for Mardi Gras is mistaken for a "sweetheart"—becomes a terrible testimonial about the fate of those who dare to be different. Published in 1895, it seems quite at home beside emerging writer Bennett Capers's short story "The Truth of the Matter," in which a journalist, on the trail of a murder mystery in a small Southern town, finds at the center of the crime a troubled gay man so scorned by the community and so traumatized by the tragedy surrounding him that he refuses to speak.

I couldn't get Baraka out of my mind, though. As I sat compiling the contents, not only did I find myself scribbling his name but also jotting down the names of others as I remembered, say, a passage from Toni Morrison's *Song of Solomon*, where Milkman, on his quest for Pilate, ends up in Danville, Virginia, and experiences every homosexual person's nightmare: being called out and attacked. Or remembering that effeminizing portrait of Bledsoe in Ralph Ellison's *Invisible Man*. And Gayl Jones's evilizing of lesbians in both *Corregidora* and *Eva's Man*. Then John Edgar Wideman's erotic hostess in "The Statue of Liberty"; Richard Wright's desperate crossdresser in "Man of All Work"; and Darryl Pinckney's worldly uncle in the hilarious *High Cotton*. The more I thought about it the more convinced I was that many of these works belonged in this collection.

Each of these writers, and many more that I researched but couldn't possibly have included lest this book be thousands of pages, have commented upon the lives of gays and lesbians— some with charity and insight, some with unmitigated rage, and some, it seems, accidentally. For instance, in the Toni Morrison excerpt, Milkman's sexuality is not in dispute. Though he appears fancy to his attackers, it is his impertinence that inspires them to violence. There is no fiercer way to insult a man than to question his masculinity. In Richard Wright's dialogue story "Man of All Work," an unemployed laborer falls into dire straits when his wife, after giving birth, is too ill to work. The solution to his problems is a want ad for a housekeeper. Dressed in his wife's clothes he applies for the job and is immediately hired. He quickly learns that there's more to the job than was advertised when he is forced to fend off the advances of the master of the house.

If there was any doubt in my mind that the collection should be open to all African-American writers, Langston Hughes, Countee Cullen, and Wallace Thurman eased it. All were allegedly homosexual. None were out—possibly not even to each other. In fact, except for Hughes, all were married and, if anything, lived as closeted bisexuals. Even the Harlem Renaissance's enfant terrible Richard Bruce Nugent was married. But like the man he admired most, Oscar Wilde, he was out. Including Thurman and Nugent meant that literature, not the sexual orientation of its writers, had to define this collection, with bisexuality and homosexuality as literary themes my guiding principle.

For the title I turned to James Baldwin and an interview he did in 1984 with the *Village Voice* called "Go the Way Your Blood Beats." He said: "The best advice I ever got was from an old friend of mine, a Black friend, who said you have to go the way your blood beats." To go the way your blood beats means to live life instinctively, intuitively, with integrity and an awareness of consequences, and without self-deception. I knew I wanted this collection to adopt that insouciant phrase as creed—as, indeed, words to live by—as well as to encompass and embrace as much as could appropriately fit here. I wanted it to breathe and sigh. I wanted it to think and feel. To love. To need. To lust and to fuck. To laugh, to pray and fear and cry, to be outraged, afraid, to lose and win, to bleed and age, and to die, be missed and mourned. Each of the stories I selected have desire in common. Each contemplates a moment of telling confusion over identity and self-meaning, with protagonists who fall into the fires of conflict and either rise above it, or crash and burn.

"Wet Behind the Ears," the first section, explores the dynamics of sexual identity as a defining moment that separates the individual from others. I selected three stories that in some ways chart the journey from innocence to the loss of innocence, highlighting that moment of chaos. The first story, Gayl Jones's "The Women," is about a young girl's budding sexuality and her mother's lesbian relationships; how her mother's sexuality becomes a catalyst for the girl to lose her virginity, to prove to herself that she is not lesbian. In James Baldwin's ironically titled "The Outing," two young male lovers are on a church picnic, when one, tempted by a prized girl, abandons the other. Johnny, the abandoned one, is hurt, but his love for his capricious friend, hence his love for men, resigns him to a kind of despair, while his oblivious lover hints at a future of deceit, abandonment, and disappointment. "Meredith's Lie," my own contribution, explores the fault line of deception in the lives of three middle-class teenagers, each of whom spins a web of lies to be accepted by the others. When Meredith discovers her pianist boyfriend kissing another man, in despair and for revenge she turns to the Stanford bound, all-American athlete her parents approve of. At war with herself, Meredith must choose between her pride, her heart, and saving face.

The disapprobation of family in particular, and society in general, is, to be sure, at the center of much of gay and lesbian angst. For the next section, "Blood Is Thicker Than Water," I've selected four stories that are very self-consciously aware of the bonds of blood, and the price exacted. In the first, "What Has Been Done to Me," Jacqueline Woodson's protagonist has forced herself to accept a gift of a trip to New Orleans with her mother. While sitting in a bar having cocktails and acting more like girlfriends than mother and daughter, an asphyxiating tension rises between them when the mother sees a man who reminds her of her ex-husband and makes light of and distorts details about the breakup of her marriage. The daughter is violently upset by this, precisely because these details compose an indissoluble pain, at the root of which is a sexual assault by her stepfather. In Charles Harvey's disturbing story "To Taste Fire Once More," the middle-aged main character has literally split himself into two people. At Sears, where along with his mother and aunt he has gone to have the car repaired, one emboldened half of him contemptuously observes the other stuck between the two grizzled and cross old women. As one half remembers his own story—that his father was murdered by his mother and aunt—it helplessly merges with the other half. In Becky Birtha's "Ice Castle," Maurie is a performing poet and very much attracted to a young, privileged white woman who attends one of her readings. The two begin what looks like a courtship, until the Christmas holidays interfere and Maurie leaves to be with her own family. Among them, her delicate standing in the world is realized when her father bemoans and condemns a young gay man, and thus her own lifestyle. Bruce Morrow's "Near the End of the World" pays homage to AIDS. Mel, Jr. has traveled to Los Angeles to spread his father's ashes in the Pacific. For days he hangs out on the beach, plagued by dreams of being choked by vines and reliving nursing his father to the grave. Nearly paralyzed by fear, he meets and befriends a curious white woman who helps and, without knowing what is wrong with him, comforts him.

In "Bad Blood" I've selected three stories that maddeningly stretch the boundaries of relationships by exploring homosexuality as a deliberate act of betrayal. In addition to the Amiri Baraka and Bennett Capers stories, I've included Randall Kenan's masterful "Run, Mourner, Run." Dean, the white protagonist, is hired to seduce the town's richest Black man. Unaware of the motives for his hiring, he succeeds in helping to bring about this powerful man's undoing when the man who hired him, along with a gang of locals, crashes in on the unlikely couple in bed together. Dean soon discovers, though, that the joke is on him.

The four works in "Behind Closed Doors" are steeped in desire—remembered, fantasized, or acted out, with each suggesting not the sexual crapulousness of homosexuals but rather the desperate, neurotic, self-destructive behavior that outlawed desire can create. In Richard Bruce Nugent's elliptical prose poem "Smoke, Lilies and Jade," Alex, the protagonist, floats along in a state of semiconsciousness, randomly appearing in and out of moments—a funeral, his mother's home, walking along dark streets. One evening while out walking, he encounters a white man he calls Beauty and has sex with him. This stranger becomes the succulent subject of not only Alex's desire but his love. In "The Statue of Liberty," by John Edgar Wideman, a white woman, apparently neglected by her husband, becomes erotically obsessed with a Black man who jogs by her house. One morning he is accompanied by a Black woman, and the fantasy adjusts accordingly. In Sapphire's thrashing piece "There's a Window," a sexual encounter between two women in prison distills a kind of terribleness and hopelessness that stolen intimacy can't dissipate. And in Samuel Delany's orgiastic novel *The Mad Man,* from which "The Place of Excrement" is excerpted, a postdoctoral student is on a quest to uncover the mysterious murder of an important Asian philosopher by a male hustler, and is having an extraordinary amount of sex along the way.

"Blood, Sweat, and Tears" explores sexual ambiguity, as well as situations controlled by circumstances that produce suspect outcomes. In addition to Richard Wright, I've included a relatively unknown Harlem Renaissance author, Maude Irwin Owens. Published in 1932 in *The Crises,* "Bathesda of Sinners Run" is the vaguest of the Harlem Renaissance stories. It is about the trials and tensions of a saintly healing woman who administers to an impoverished community that consists mostly of divisive women who do not understand why she doesn't lay down with men. There is a palpable lesbian sexual tension just beneath Bathesda's saintliness that threatens to shatter her resolve to be apart from her vulgar charges. At the end we see Bathesda above it all—sexless, sanctified, and adored—masculinely gliding forward toward acceptance by the community. In the excerpt from Alice Walker's *The Temple of My Familiar,* the main character is actually a long dead father whose tribulation is being told by his son. The father worked for a white man whose son had become his best friend. Later, as adults, the friend begged for sex with him. Caught in the crisis of loyalty and the threat of possibly being lynched, the father complies. However, he never forgives the young white man nor himself for doing it, and comes to detest anything suggesting homosexuality.

In "Heartache" love is a many splendid and splintered thing. Using the stories and excerpts included here, I wanted to look at love not as a happily-ever-after ending, but as the complex, frightening, and ofttimes disappointing event that it can be. The object of love is a harmless liar in Brooke Stephens's "Just Friends." A woman finds herself friends with a man who, in the course of their relationship, lives a homosexual life without admitting to it, not even in the end when he dies of AIDS. In Wallace Thurman's *Infants of the Spring*, the grandiloquent Raymond is in love with himself. In Carl Hancock Rux's hallucinatory "Asphalt," the love obsession is with a ghost. The main character, Racine, is emotionally splayed by a life of constant transience as he searches for the answers to questions of who he is and why his mother abandoned him to foster homes. In Cary Alan Johnson's "Obi's Story," a memory of love can neither be forgotten nor ignored. Stu, a young American sent to Africa on a Peace Corps mission falls in love with Obi, a beautiful Nigerian Stu meets at an orgy at the home of a wealthy white homosexual. All is going well until Obi falls in love with Stu's best friend—a woman—and Stu flees to the States, heartbroken.

"Hemorrhaging" focuses on abuse—physical, emotional, sexual, intellectual. In this section, I wanted to explore how the course of self-doubt and destruction is set, by examining situations that program gays and lesbians for self-hatred. In the Orian Hyde Weeks selection, "Dissimulations," Star, the main character, hasn't seen her brother in years and comes home for the holidays expecting that he has gone off to fight in the Persian Gulf War. He hasn't left, though, and what ensues is a struggle in which she threatens to mouth to everyone that he molested her when she was a young girl. In Gloria Naylor's "The Two," excerpted from her novel *The Women of Brewster Place*, a lesbian couple is found out by the neighbors and become the object of ridicule and contempt. Frightened and unable to deal with the adversity around them, the two begin quarreling between themselves, with one wanting to run and the other to stay and fight. In Audre Lorde's excerpt from *Zami: A New Spelling of My*

Name, the young lesbian Lorde mourns the loss of a troubled young woman who kills herself. And in Catherine McKinley's "Afro Jew Fro," the protagonist reflects on her young life, her complex relations with her family in general, and a young cousin in particular, who, called sissy by their peers, prepares her to defend herself against the heterosexual world.

"Bashers" looks at violence and how vulnerable gays and lesbians are. In addition to the Toni Morrison excerpt from *Song of Solomon* and Alice Dunbar Nelson's "A Carnival Jangle," I've included an excerpt from E. Lynn Harris's *Just As I Am* and a short story called "Babylon" by emerging writer Max Gordon. In the Harris excerpt, Raymond, the main character, returns to his alma mater for a fraternity reunion, only to hear about a young pledge's suicide attempt after being humiliated by his rush brothers. Raymond is divided on his response: Should he condemn the action and risk exposing himself, or should he remain silent? In Gordon's story, a seven-year-old boy on any given school night between the hours of three and five A.M. can be found at a local convenience story playing video games. One morning, rushing to get home before his parents awaken, he witnesses the murder of a gay man. The event stuns the boy into a kind of awe-inspired silence, a silence that knows no conscience, no guilt, no compassion.

For the last section, "Go the Way Your Blood Beats," I chose two short stories and a novel excerpt because each explores, in some way, the plethora of individual expression—one with great difficulty, the other two effortlessly. In Artress Bethany White's story "Undressing Lady J.," a young woman is confused and concerned about her bisexual appetite. While browsing in a Brooklyn bookstore, she finds a package of letters addressed to one Lady J., a mysterious woman presumably endowed with wisdom. The young woman becomes convinced these letters will help her in her sexual dilemma. She buys the letters and once home casts a spell that conjures up Lady J. Reginald Shepherd's miscegenous story focuses on a young Black man from the Bronx visiting his college best friend at his parent's wealthy home. Racial inequities pit the protagonist against the environment, so that even as he enjoys it he resents it. When the best friend's lover shows up and the two fight and have sex constantly, the protagonist becomes almost righteous in his contempt for these white boys. But at the heart of his resentment is a longing to be loved, to feel safe, not so much as a gay man, not even as Black man, but as a man. In Carolivia Herron's rapturous prose poems "Epithalamion," acceptance isn't just a given, it's required. Whether between two men, two women, or a man and a woman—love is divine. Excerpted from her novel *Asenath*, the three chapters are used as one to celebrate the relationship between love, love choices, and the human capacity to love.

Love, indeed, is what matters in the end. I hope what has been posited in this anthology is the idea that difference should be celebrated, that love should be cherished. James Baldwin was asked in the *Village Voice* interview whether Black people are more open to homosexuals because of our long history of suffering. In response he said, "Black people don't have a heightened capacity for tolerance or acceptance in its truest sense. . . . There is a capacity in Black people for experience, simply. And that capacity makes other things possible. It dictates the depth of one's acceptance of other people. The capacity for experience is what burns out fear."

"Won't it hurt you?" I said

"Not unless it's square," he said. "Are you square?"

"Could be," I said.

"Let's see," he said.

> —Langston Hughes,
> *Sex Silly Season*, March 25, 1963

Being women together was not enough. We were different.
Being gay-girls together was not enough. We were different.
Being Black together was not enough. We were different.
Being Black women together was not enough. We were
different. Being Black dykes together was not enough. We
were different.

> —Audre Lorde,
> *Zami: A New Spelling of My Name*

Wet Behind
the Ears

GAYL JONES

◎〜◎

The Women

I was three years old when the first woman come. My mama
had just get the divorce from my daddy. Miss Maybell
was the first woman. Miss Maybell Logan. She lived up on
Douglas Street and had a mustache. All us children used to
point at her and make fun a her cause she had a mustache. But
the grownups didn't. I guess they had just got used to it. Miss
Maybell Logan used to come sometimes and spend the night.
I used to wonder why she come and spend the night when she
got her own house. She used to go in the bedroom with mama
and sleep where my daddy used to sleep. My mama always
couldn't get to sleep when Miss Maybell was there, cause she
be tossing and turning all night. I'd get scared sometimes
and hide under the covers. When my daddy was there, in the
mornings, while it was still dark outside, my mama would
let me go in the bedroom and climb in the bed and sleep between the two of them. But when Miss Maybell was there,
mama wouldn't let me sleep between the two of them. I was
scared of Miss Maybell anyway. I didn't want to get in bed
with them. In the morning, Miss Maybell would look at me
with her mustache, and then she would leave. Miss Maybell

kept coming till I was five, and that's how I remembered her since I was three. And then when I was five, my mama and Miss Maybell have a fight, but I didn't know what the fight was about, and then Miss Maybell didn't come no more. It was just like when my mama and daddy have the fight, and then my daddy didn't come back.

I asked my mama, "Why Miss Maybell don't come no more?"

"She a bitch's whore."

Something else happened when I was five, before Miss Maybell left. My cousin Freddie who was ten come up to stay with us three days cause his mama have to go up to Michigan for a Baptist convention. My mama put Freddie on the couch in the living room to sleep. The second night Miss Maybell come. She act like she didn't like to see Freddie there. She just look at him with her big mustache and call him "funky pants" like she call all little boys. I didn't know what she call little girls because my mama wouldn't let me hear it. She just say, "Winnie here," and Miss Maybell wouldn't call me what she was going to. Miss Maybell didn't leave cause Freddie was there. Her and my mama just went on in the bedroom and close the door. Miss Maybell just say, "Pet, I'm sleepy early." My mama name Gertrude, but Miss Maybell always call her "Pet."

Freddie grin up at Miss Maybell while she in the room but when she leave he call her "pussy woman." I ask him, "What that mean?"

"It mean she got a pussy mouth."

"What that mean?"

"It mean she a pussy willow."

"What that mean?"

"It mean what I hear my mama say. It mean she a woman that want to be a man."

"She is a man. Got whiskers."

"Naw, she got a mustache."

"Woman don't got a mustache."

"Your mama got one."

"Naw she don't."

"Only it so little you caint see it."

"Naw I caint."

"When you grow up you goin' have one."

"Naw I won't."

"Only it be so little you won't be able to see it. Just like your mama. When you grow up you gonna be jus' like your mama."

"Naw I won't."

"Live with her, don't you?"

"Yeah."

"Be like her then. My mama say you be like the company you keep."

"Then you be like your mama too."

"No, I be like my daddy."

"I ain't got a daddy."

"You got a fake fucka daddy."

"What that mean? I'ma tell."

"She be mad if you go in there."

"Then I'ma tell tomorrow."

"I be left tomorrow."

"Tell her way 'fore the cock crow."

Freddie laughed.

"Mustache Woman still be in there then. Ain't got no cock to crow."

"Miss Floyd keep chicken next door. She keep chicken and a big red rooster. He crow ev'ry morning."

"How old you?"

"Five."

Freddie didn't say nothing.

"How old are you?"

"Old enough to crow."

"I'm old enough to crow too."

Freddie laughed. "You ain't even old enough to cackle."

"I'm old enough to do what you old enough to do."

"Born 'fore you was."

"Naw you wasn't."

"My Mama Daddy did it 'fore your Mama Daddy did it."

"Did what?"

"Do what they do in there. Only ain't nothing goin' happen in there."

"What they do in there?"

"Wont me to show you?"

"Yeah. They be mad if we go in there."

"We ain't goin' in there. What y'all got in y'all's basement?"

"Nothing."

"Show me what you ain't got."

"You goin' show me what they do in there?"

"You know when we get back."

We have to go outdoors to get into the basement, and then when we get there, I ask, "You wont me to turn on the light?"

"Don't need no light."

"How we see?"

"Don't need to see. Our eyes 'just in a minute."

"What she keep in here?"

"Some old rugs over on the floor. That about all."

"Get over on the old rugs. I show you what they been doing ev'ry time she come here."

He raise my dress up and take my panties down and then he was doing something to me but I didn't know what he was doing. I wont to get away but was scared to scream cause my mama'd come down here and then Miss Maybell'd come down here and see we doing what they been doing, and then he did it. And then he put his hands down there and wipe it on my dress, but I just sit there. He say, "Cover up your ass 'fore you get a cold pussy." I pull my panties back up, and pull my dress back down and still just sit there.

"We better be going," he says.

"I don' wanna go."

"Your mama wonder where we at. If she come out the pussy room." He laugh.

"Aw'n care where we at."

He grabs me by the arm and I don't say nothing, but let him take me up the stairs with him, and he keeps saying, "They feelin' pussy, that's what they doing. They feelin' pussy. They feelin' titties. You ain't got none." Then he hush up when we go in the house. And then he say when there ain't nobody there, "See, they ain't come out the pussy room. We better go bed." Then he let my arm go. "Go bed with you if I had my own house," he says and then he go in the front room where he sleep, and I climb into bed and keep all my clothes on.

"Where Freddie?"

My mama in the kitchen cooking breakfast. Miss Maybell wa'nt there like she always wa'nt.

"His mama come and got him early."

"Aw."

"What you do to your dress?"

"Slep' in it."

"You know better'n that."

"Yes'm."

"Go take it off and I wash it. You be big enough to be going to school soon."

"I big enough to do it now. I jus' ain't old enough."

"Awright, put on your little jumper and then come and get your eggs while they still hot. Wash you up later."

I put on my jumper and then came back and eat my eggs while they still hot.

After a while, my mama said, "You quiet. What you and Freddie find to do las' night?"

"Nothing. We just go straight on to bed. Like y'all done. When his mama come get him?"

"Right after seven. He was up bright and early like he know she was coming. Maybell open the door. She always get up 'fore the cock crow. . . . You finished? You better go wash up."

"Yes m'am."

Little after that Mama and Miss Maybell have they fight. I didn't know where they have their fight, cause they couldn't had have it in the house because I never did hear them fighting, and then all a sudden, Miss Maybell just weren't coming anymore and when I ask mama, mama call Miss Maybell that bad name, and then mama didn't talk about Miss Maybell no more. Miss Maybell still live in that little house up on Douglas Street, and all us children still point at her and say, "They goes the mustache woman."

The next woman that my mama have in the house was name Fanny. Fanny Bean have pretty skin like milk and cocoa, and her hair have waves in it. I liked Fanny Bean. Fanny Bean would smile at me but never speak to me. My mama said Fanny Bean was shy. Fanny Bean was a little woman. My mama said Fanny Bean was twenty-seven and taught in school. I liked Fanny Bean. Fanny Bean was an old maid school teacher who didn't have a husband and came to live with us. That was still before I was old enough to go to school. Fanny Bean would smile at me but wouldn't talk to me. My mama said that was because Fanny Bean didn't know what to do with little children. She taught grown-up children in school. Sometime when Fanny Bean was on her way to school, she would fix my breakfast, but wouldn't talk to me. I never talk to Fanny neither, but I still like Fanny. Fanny have skin like milk and cocoa. Fanny sleep in the room where my mama sleep because my mama said there weren't enough room in the rest of the house. I didn't ask her why couldn't Fanny sleep where Freddie sleep. Fanny stayed with us till I was old enough to go to school. When I asked my mama, "Why Fanny Bean ain't here no more?" she say, "Fanny Bean a bitch's whore."

◎∕◎

When I was old enough to go to school, my mama said she was going to work in the tobacco factory. She said now that she didn't have Fanny help pay the bills, the alimony just weren't enough, not with me starting in the first grade. I asked her why she going to work in the tobacco factory, stead of some place else. She said she was going to work in the tobacco factory because she didn't wont to be fucking around no white woman's kitchen and she said, "If you got to work for The Man, least you can work some where where you don't come in contact with him personal." I asked her what she was going to do there. "Sort tobacco. Only they probably have me down there mopping till I learn what I'm s'pose to do and then they probably say I ain't learned what I'm s'pose to do when I'm s'pose to do it, just so they can keep me down there mopping. And then they have they summer layoffs. And then prob'ly the next year they have me sort tobacco."

When I started in the first grade my mama took me down to the schoolroom and then she told me to be good and then she went to the factory. The teacher take me and sit me in a chair in the back of the room cause there weren't no chairs in the front of the room, and then the teacher went up to the front of the room and ask the children what nursery rhymes they knew and then she played them on her piano and have all the children sing nursery rhymes. I didn't sing. I sit in the back beside another little girl in the back of the room.

"What your name?"

"Retta Pace."

"Winnie Flynn."

"Win Flynn."

"How come you ain't singing?"

"Don't know what they singing."

"I know what they singing. I just don't want to sing. Mama said she goin' teach the alfbet."

"Yeah."

"I know it already. Cept write it down. She teach to sing it firs."

"I don't know it."

After the teacher finished singing the nursery rhymes, she taught the children how to sing the alphabet. She have skin like milk with a little bit of tea in it. Retta Pace sing. Retta have skin like coffee with chocolate syrup in it. I didn't sing. When the teacher get through teaching them to sing the alphabet, she come to the back of the room and bend down to me.

"Why aren't you singing? Don't you know it yet?"

"I know it all ready. I want a learn how to write it down."

"I have to hear you sing it first."

"I know it all ready."

Miss Fletcher go back to the front of the room. They sing the song again but I still don't sing.

Miss Fletcher say, "Winnie will have to stay after school and sing for me."

I say to Retta, "My mama come and get me."

Miss Fletcher say, "No talking."

After school when all the desk chairs empty except mine Miss Fletcher come back to the back of the room and say, "Now will you sing."

"I want to learn what I don't already know."

"Well, then, talk them for me."

"Do you know Miss Fanny Bean up to the big school?"

"Yes, she teaches at the high school, doesn't she?"

"My mama sleep with her."

Miss Fletcher don't say nothing.

"My mama sleep with you too."

I ran out the room.

That evening a man bring my mama a note from school. It said that they have transferred me into Miss Dalton's class. She older, and more experienced with difficult children. My mama ask me what did I do wrong the first day. I say, "Nothing." My mama say I had to done something. I say, "Miss Fletcher a white lady, ain't she?" My mama say she wasn't white, she was just real light.

The next day I didn't mind being moved over into Miss Dalton's room. By that time they got off singing the alphabet, and start writing it down.

The next day at recess, I see Retta standing over by the sliding board. When I come over, Retta say, "I heard you said something bad and nasty to the teacher and they put you outta school."

"They didn't put me outta school, they just move me over to some other room. What the white lady do today?"

"What white lady?"

"Miss Fletcher. I call her the white lady but mama say she ain't white just real light."

"Nothing. She told us to bring in tablets tomorr'."

"We start writing this morning. Miss Dalton ain't even got a piano in her room. She a old lady, kinda tall, an' dark."

"Miss Fletcher the music teacher. Tha's how come she got a piano. This morning some big third-graders come in to get they music lesson."

"Aw."

"What you say to her?"

"Nothing."

"Had to been something."

"You too young to hear."

"Old as you."

"Naw you ain't."

"How old are you, Win Flynn?"

"Six."

"I be seven. Jan'ary. When you be seven?"

" 'cember."

"Olderner."

"Naw y'ain't. Mama said it don't matter how old you are. What you know. She say I act old'ner some people fourteen. She call me her little lady."

"So. You prob'ly fast with boys."

"Naw ain't."

"Yes y'are."

"I said ain't."

"You see that girl over there."

"Where?"

"Girl got the good hair."

"Yeah."

"Her mama keep her and her sister locked up in the yard behind a white fence and keep a dog in the yard and won't let no boys come inside the yard. Anytime a boy come he have to stand outside the fence and talk. Her sister ten. I stand outside the fence and talk too cause I'm scared the dog."

"What's her name?"

"Bev'ly Carp'ter. She say don't like you and don't want to play with you cause she say you fas' with boys."

"How she know if I am if I ain't?"

"Cause her sister ten and your cousin Freddie 'leven and he stand up at the fence and talk."

"Tell her kiss my black ass."

"Awww."

"Why you still standing here?"

"Aw'no."

"I thought you be go tell Bev'ly what I said."

"I ain't a tattle."

"You in'cent?" I ask.

"What?"

"In'cent. You ever had a boy?"

"What?"

"Come on over here by the fence. . . . You ever had a boy put it in you?"

"Put what in me?"

"His *thing*."

"Naw."

"I bet you don't even know what being fast mean."

"Yeah I do."

"I bet you don't even know what he got that you ain't got."

"Yeah I do."

"I bet you ain't never seen it."

"Naw. But I know what it look like. Debby seen it. She got a brother. She told me what it look like. So. I bet you ain't never seen it neither."

"Naw I ain't never seen it, but I had it put in me."

"How you have it put in you an' ain't never seen it?"

"It was dark. Couldn't see nothing."

"How come?"

"I was raked when I was five. You know how they talk about on the radio how such an' such a girl get raked."

Retta laugh. "They don't say raked they say raped."

"Thought you didn' know nothing."

"Know what I hear."

"Know what I hear. Know what I do too."

"Who raped you?"

"My cousin Freddie."

"Mama say that's call 'cest. Somebody kin to you do it to you. Say it's bad."

"Anybody do it to you bad. Thought you didn't know nothing."

"Know that."

"You in'cent?"

"I ain't never had it put in me. Seen it neither. Hear about it."

"I bet you don't even know how they put it in you. I bet you don't even know what you s'pose do."

"Naw."

"Flap your legs open just like a book. And then he put it in you."

"Your mama know?"

"Course she know. She got me. You got to do it firs."

"What you get?"

"Nothing. I ain't ol' enough. You got to have titties firs," I say.

"Debbie Allen got titties."

"That mean she been doing it all a time. Got to be leas' thirteen."

"She in the third grade."

"She ain' ol' enough."

"Your mama know you been doing it?"

"I didn't did it but once. Then I didn't do it. *He* did it."

"Your mama know he do it?"

"Naw. Cept day after she was washing clothes and come in and ask me how come my panties got blood on 'em and I say I didn' know and then she say, 'You too young to bleed' and then she don' say nothing else and then after that she just be call me her little woman."

ⓔ✑

When my mama started working in the tobacco factory, she started bringing different women home. I never get to know them because it seem like each time they was different and they would come late in the evening just about when it was my bedtime and my mama would say, "So-in-so got to stay the night cause she ain't got no place to stay tonight." I remember once some woman came and then left real quick cause I hear the woman say, "I didn't come here for this." And my mama say, "Don't you come shaking your ass at me like you got something down there I wont." And then the woman left. There was other women.

Once I ask my mama if my friend Retta from the school could

stay over the weekend cause her mama was going up to Detroit to the Baptist convention. My mama say, "We ain't got enough room."

"She can sleep with me."

"Your bed ain't big enough."

"She littler than me."

"Well, awright."

Retta's mama bring her over the next Friday evening and bring her little weekend bag. Retta's mama sat on the couch in the front room and talked for a while with my mama.

"I certainly do appreciate this Misses Flynn. I didn't have nobody take Retta. I even got them to let me off from work, and then find ain't nobody take Retta. All the Baptist women out the church goin', so couldn't get one of them. I certainly do 'preciate this."

"Where you work?"

"Out the narcotics farm."

"Least ain't no white woman's kitchen. I tell everybody stay out them white woman's kitchen. All them addicts, though. You like it?"

"Naw, not especially. Actually, I caint stand it. At first I thought it be interesting, you know, only one of two like it in the country."

"Other one over somewheres in Texas, ain't it?"

"Uh-hum. You know, Billie Holiday was out to this'n."

"Was she?"

"You know, when she was goin' through all that stuff. Friend of mine, used to work out there 'fore I did, said she seen her too. Look real bad."

"I can imagine."

"Skin coming off her."

"I can imagine."

"I ain't had to seen nothing like that though myself."

"How long you been out there?"

"Six months. Work with the dieticians."

"Yeah."

"It's this other stuff going on out there I don't like."

"What other stuff?"

"Well, they got the women se'grated from the men."

"Yeah."

"I'm in 'ere with the women. Got people standing on top of chairs and stuff. Now 'at ain't so bad. It's this other stuff got me lookin' for someplace to go. Don't mean it literally, I stay there."

"What other stuff?"

Retta's mama screw up her nose. "You know, women hugging on each other. Guess when you in a sit'ation where you ain't got nothing else, like them women in them prisons too you hear about, you get that way. But it just ain't right. I don't think it's right. Do you think it's right?"

My mama don't say nothing, she just let Retta's mama go on talking.

"Well, what got me was this one woman come up to me pulling all on me and say, 'I been trying to go wid Gertrude but Maggie go wid her. I'm scared to go up an' tell her. Can you go up and tell her I wanta go wid her too.' I just tell her I don' even know Gertrude, and try to shrug her on off and go on about my business what they pay me for."

That night Retta slept in my bed with me. She was little and skinnier than me, so we fit together all right. My mama said that she woulda let one of us sleep on the couch if we wanted to but that she was entertaining some guests that night. I said we didn't mind cause Retta said her mama didn't turn all the lights out at night in they house and she was scared of the dark if she was by herself. Then my mama said, "Then it work out just fine, won't it."

"They be guest from the fact'ry?" I ask.

"Yeah. I be have two hussies over. One of them prob'ly get so drunk she 'bout down need the couch."

When me and Retta was alone and all the lights was out I ask Retta, "You scart?"

"Naw. You scart?"

"Naw. I ain't never scart a what I caint see in the dark. See it, then you be scart a it."

"I be scart a it e'n if I don't see it."

"You a scarty cat. You a scart pussy."

"What that mean?"

"Pussy another name for a woman, or a girl. Like I heard mama say to this woman, 'Pussy, don't be that way. Don't be that way, pussy.'"

"Aw."

We laughed.

"If I'da said 'You got a scart pussy' I been talking about your thing."

"Aw, *I* know it."

"You don't ack like it."

"Yeah I do. . . . What you doin'?"

"Trying to feel pussy. Let me feel it. I don' think you know what you got down there."

"Yeah I do."

"Let me feel it then."

"Okay."

It was soft and smooth with no hair on it.

"Feel good, don't it?"

"Yeah."

"Cept I ain't s'pose to be doing it."

"Why not?"

"Boy s'pose to do it."

"I wouldn't let a boy do it."

"Yeah you would."

"Naw I wouldn't."

"When you grow up."

"Don't know if I would when I grow up."

"Then you be a queer donut."

"Naw I won't."

"Yes you will."

"Naw I won't."

"I let a boy do it when I grow up. Wouldn't let a girl do it though."

"You doin' it."

"Cept we dif'rent. We *little* girls. When you git titties you ain't suppose to let a girl do it. That mean you queer. I ain't goin' be queer."

"I ain't either."

"You said you was."

"Naw I wasn't."

"Yeah. You ain' goin' have nothing but pussy feelers."

"Feel yours."

"Be a pussy feeler same thing."

"Caint feel mine if I caint feel yours."

"I ain't through yet. Smooth down there. Still feel good, don't it?"

"Yeah. Wanna feel yours?"

"When you get growed, you gonna have hair all over down there."

"Naw I won't."

"Yes you will."

"Naw I won't."

"Your mama does."

"Naw she don't."

"Ast her."

"If I ast her she wouldn' tell me. She ast me who I been talkin' to."

"Mean your mama a scart pussy too."

"Why?"

"Scart to talk to her own girl child about sex."

"Naw she ain't. Told me I be bleeding down there when I got be about twelve. Told me in front a my daddy too."

"So. I been bleeded. Cept it ain't come on strong yet. I probably be bleeding 'fore you be bleeding."

"Naw you won't."

"Yeah I will."

"Debbie sister bleed. Somebody say, 'See that girl. She bleed every month.' I didn' know what they talking about. Thought it was something bad. Went home and ask my mama and tha's when she told me."

"See."

"See what?"

"Had to tell you. Wouldn't a told you if she didn' had to."

"Yeah she would."

"Naw."

"Feel yours."

"Okay."

Mine didn't have no hair on it neither.

"Feel good to your hand too, don't it?"

"Yeah."

<hr />

Before Retta's mama came to get her to take her home, Retta said, "Maybe Mama let me come stay overnight with you sometime she ain't goin' up to the Baptist 'vention."

But Retta's mama never did let her come back and spend the night with me. We still was best friends at school though, until we got in the six grade and Retta and her mama and her daddy moved up to Columbus, Ohio. So we never did know who started bleeding first. I started after I was halfway through the six grade, and my mama have to put paper towel down there till she get the right sized Kotex cause I was so skinny.

When I was halfway through the six grade that was when I saw what I wasn't supposed to see. I got up in the part of the night that was close to morning to go to the jar. We didn't have a bathroom in them days and my mama kept the slop jar in a little room next to the kitchen. When I got to the little room next to the kitchen I heard some woman say, "I parked my car round to the back door."

Then I heard my mama say, "Goodnight, honey. Goodmorning, ain't it?"

Then I didn't hear nobody say nothing, and peeped around and saw my mama standing up in the back door kissing some big woman, and then I didn't go to the jar, but went on back to bed. I get under the covers and say, "I ain' goin' be like my mama when I grow up. I ain' goin' be a bitch's whore." Then I just waited till I hear the back door slam and my mama come back through the house before I go try the jar again.

It wasn't until I was fourteen that I went out on a date with my first boy. But I didn't go out with him anymore because he kept wanting to kiss me and I didn't want him to and everytime he call I would say, "I'm goin' work on my science club project," and then I hang up the telephone. He had taken me to the movies and had put his arm around my shoulders so that his hand dangled down so that he could feel my titties through my clothes. I didn't know what else to do so I had let him do it.

Once after I didn't go out with him anymore I was sitting in the school cafeteria by myself. After Retta left, I didn't make any more girl friends. Some of them tried to get friendly but I wouldn't get friendly back. When I was sitting in the cafeteria by myself this boy came over. He was chocolate-colored and had paper doll eyes. He say, "You still working on your science club project?" He grinned. He had crooked teeth. I didn't say nothing.

"Mind if I sit here?" he ask.

"Naw, it's free."

He sat down. He was heavyset, but not fat, and looked older than he was, but I knew he was just fourteen too.

"Lew said you wouldn't go to the bowling alley with him las' week cause you was working on your science club project."

"You Lew's friend, or the whole world know?"

"We hang around together sometimes."

"Aw."

"You keepin' company?"

"Keepin' yours."

"You know what I mean, you going with anybody?"

"Naw."

"Wanta keep my company? Is, if you through with your science club project?"

"Turned it in."

"Well?"

"I don't know."

"You cold, ain't you?"

"Naw."

"Don't say nothin' to nobody, do you?"

"Say somethin' to me I do."

"You know Alvin Davis?"

"Yeah, he in my Citizenship class."

"He say he saw you come down the street with your head all in the air, wouldn't speak."

"Didn't see him. Air where it b'longs."

"You cute too, ain't you?"

"Naw."

"You okay. Pie all you havin'? Make you fat. Some people think just eat dessert, don't make you fat, but it do."

"Sometimes I don't even have any lunch. I just go stand down in the girls' bathroom till the lunch period over."

"You on a diet?"

"Naw."

"Mama said if you go on a diet 'fore you get grown mess you up when you get grown."

"I ain't on a diet. Sometimes a lot of people make me nervous, and then I don't know nobody to sit with."

"Sit with me. Cept you ain't said we be keeping company yet. Lot of people make me nervous too, but I just come on in sit down anyway. Don't talk to boys. Don't talk to girls neither. You kinda funny, but don't know what kind of funny."

"There's some girls that stand down in the bathroom sometimes and smoke. Sometimes I talk to them."

"You smoke?"

"Naw. You?"

"Naw. Bad for you."

"Yeah."

"Bad for you 'fore *and* after you get grown."

"Yeah."

"You talk to anybody else? I mean talk talk."

"Talk when I got somethin' to talk about."

"Talk in class?"

"Naw. Ain't got nothin' to talk about in class."

"You look like you talk in class."

"Talk when they ask me a question. Talk on the blackboard. Talk on a paper when they give a assignment."

"You okay."

I didn't say nothing. The bell rang that meant lunch period was over.

"We be keepin' company," he said.

I got up and left without saying nothing.

The next time I saw him I was sitting on the rock fence outside school. It was recess. He just come walking by. He walked over where I was. He didn't sit down.

"Sitting by yourself again," he said.

"Yeah."

"Didn't ask what your name was. Didn't tell you mine."

"Winnie Flynn."

"Garland Morton."

Then he just walked on away.

I didn't go back in the cafeteria any more because I didn't want him to come over. I didn't know why I didn't want him to. I'd stand down in the girls bathroom with the girls that smoked, and sometimes they'd talk to me. But most of the time they didn't talk to me, they just look over at me, and I look back over at them. One of the girls was dark chocolate and sixteen and looked like a woman but was in the same grade I was in. What made her look like a woman was that her hips were round and wide and she wore straight skirts. The other girl was the color of milk coffee and had long black straightened hair. Sometimes the milk coffee girl would bring her lunch down in the bathroom and eat it there, but most the times they didn't eat lunch either. The milk coffee girl looked like she knew what to do with boys, but whenever she talked to me she never talked about what she did with boys. I didn't know what we talked about after we got through talking about it. The dark chocolate girl looked like boys had been doing things to her but she didn't know what they were doing.

"Want a cigarette?" milk coffee asked.

"No thank you. I don't smoke."

"Wish I didn't." Then milk coffee smiled.

I smiled.

Milk coffee had little bumps on her face but she had a lean firm face and I thought she was pretty. She looked old too because she had a shape that made her look like a woman too. Sometimes her eyes were dark underneath even when she didn't put makeup around her eyes.

"Want to go sit outside after I smoke before the bell ring? They goin' be coming in checking the bathroom see who's smoking somebody said."

Milk coffee and dark chocolate put out their cigarettes.

"Have to start smokin' in the stalls," dark chocolate said.

"Then they see the smoke comin' up over the stall," milk coffee said.

Think you burning pussy, I thought, but didn't say it out loud.

"Just say your pussy hair caught on fire, you try'n to put it out," dark chocolate said.

Milk coffee didn't say anything. Then she said, "They ask you how it do that."

"Tell 'em you been givin' out too much pussy," I said. They looked at me like I was bad, and made me feel bad, and then milk coffee said we better go outside if we was going to go outside before the lunch bell rang. Dark chocolate said she rather stay in the bathroom. Me and milk coffee, who say her name was Shirley, went outside and sat on the rock fence till the bell rang. We didn't say anything to each other, just sat on the fence and watched the people that passed by. Then when the bell rang we went different ways to our lockers to get our books.

"You been avoiding me or somethin'?" Garland asked.

He caught up with me when I was on my way home from school.

I looked over at him but didn't say nothing.

"Saw you sitting over there with that girl today. Wouldn't speak. Get with some girl don't want to speak."

"Didn't see you. If I see you I speak."

"Where you live?"

"Breathitt."

"I live up in the project."

"Aw."

"Walk you home?"

"Guess."

"If you don't want me to, just say so, I walk over to th'other side the street."

"That be silly."

"I mean if you don't want me walk with you."

"Don't make me no difference you walk with me."

"Say it like that I just well cross over the other side."

"I didn't mean it like that. Street's free. You be walking on the street."

"Wouldn't be coming this way didn't see you."

"Aw."

"Want to go to the show Saturday?"

"What's on?"

"I don't know. Jus' ask you you wanta go. The Lyric show."

"Naw, I be busy."

"Doing what?"

"Work."

"What kind of work?"

"School work."

"Bet you ain't got enough school work go over the whole weekend."

"Do."

"I get mines done evening, through. Ain't got another science club project?"

"Naw. Other work."

"Why you don't want to go?"

"No reason."

"Scared I try something?"

"Naw. Wouldn't let you."

He grinned. "Scared you try something?"

"Naw."

"Why won't you go?"

"No reason."

"Ask why."

"Cause I don't want to. Don't like the show."

"Come visit you?"

"Mama don't like nobody come on Saturday cause she be waxing the floor."

"Come sit on your porch then."

"Don't like to sit on the porch."

"Come take you for a walk."

"Said I don't like to go nowhere much."

"Didn't."

"I don't."

"Aw, come on. You cold, you know that."

"I live over cross the street. I guess I cross over. See you around school."

"I be over there one these days, surprise you. Surprise your mama too."

I didn't say anything. I just crossed over to the other side of the street.

"Who that boy I seen you with?"

"Aw, some boy at school."

"What's his name?"

"Garland Morton."

"Any kin to John Morton?"

"Don't know."

"Used to go to school with John Morton myself. Might be his boy. Prob'ly have one about your age."

"Don't know."

"Got a lot a homework?"

"Yes m'am."

"Your supper's in there on the table. I ate mine a ready. Told Alice I be up to see her. Be back 'fore it gets dark."

"Yes m'am."

"You go on in and eat 'fore it gets cold."

"Yes m'am."

"Be bout two hours."

"Yes m'am."

Mama went out the door and I went in to get something to eat.

When I finished eating I heard a knock on the door. I didn't know who it was and wondered why whoever it was didn't ring the bell.

When I got to the door I opened it and Garland was standing out on the porch, outside the screen door. I didn't open the screen door.

"Can I come in?" he asked.

"My mama ain't home."

"What diff'rence that make?"

"I don't think she like me having nobody here, 'specially boy when she ain't at home."

"I don't see what diff'rent it makes. Aw, come on let me come in. When you spect your mama back?"

"She said she be gone two hour. That was bout a half hour ago."

"I be gone in a hour, a half hour. I just come to visit you cause you wouldn't let me visit you if I didn't come."

He started twisting the knob of the screen door, but it was locked.

I said, "Aw, awright," and opened the screen door. Garland came in.

"You got a nice house," he said.

"If you don't got to live in it."

"Your mama keep things around."

"What-nots."

"Yeah, my mama got those around too. She paint pictures and put them up on the wall. Daddy tell her take 'em down. She say she don't like look at the bare wall."

"Aw."

I sat down on the couch, and he sat down beside me.

He said, "My mama paint up all her own furniture too. She don't never keep it the same color the store got it. She always paint it up herself and call herself being creative."

"Aw."

"Give me your hand."

"Why?"

"Just want to hold your hand."

I gave him my hand.

"Got nice sof' hand. Bet you don' wash dishes."

"Yeah, I wash dishes. You?"

"Naw. Mama do. I told her I ain' goin' do what a woman do. Didn't tell her like that. She be slap the shit out a me if I did. I tell her I empty the garbage 'stead, wash down the outdoor windows or something."

"Aw."

"You know I don't mind the way you say aw. Don' want to be bothered with me, tell me to go, but don' go 'Aw' me."

"Don' have nothing to talk about."

When he put his hand on my leg I didn't say nothing. I was thinking of my mama gone to visit Miss Alice that live down the road. She probably be more than two hours.

He started feeling my leg at the knee and then moved almost up where the crotch was. My legs felt warm all inside. Then he put his hand on my crotch feeling me, and then he was kissing me and feeling me through my panties. And then he said, "Let's get out the front room."

"Where?"

"Where you sleep."

We got up and I started in my room, but changed my mind, and take him into my mama's bedroom. Then I lay down on my mama's bedspread, and let him get on top of me.

JAMES BALDWIN

The Outing

Each summer the church gave an outing. It usually took place on the Fourth of July, that being the day when most of the church-members were free from work; it began quite early in the morning and lasted all day. The saints referred to it as the "whosoever will" outing, by which they meant that, though it was given by the Mount of Olives Pentecostal Assembly for the benefit of its members, all men were free to join them, Gentile, Jew or Greek or sinner. The Jews and the Greeks, to say nothing of the Gentiles—on whom, for their livelihood, most of the saints depended—showed themselves, year after year, indifferent to the invitation; but sinners of the more expected hue were seldom lacking. This year they were to take a boat trip up the Hudson as far as Bear Mountain where they would spend the day and return as the moon rose over the wide river. Since on other outings they had merely taken a subway ride as far as Pelham Bay or Van Cortlandt Park, this year's outing was more than ever a special occasion and even the deacon's two oldest boys, Johnnie and Roy, and their friend, David Jackson, were reluctantly thrilled. These three tended to consider themselves sophisticates, no longer, like the old folks, at the mercy of the love or the wrath of God.

The entire church was going and for weeks in advance talked of nothing else. And for weeks in the future the outing would provide interesting conversation. They did not consider this frivolous. The outing, Father James declared from his pulpit a week before the event, was for the purpose of giving the children of God a day of relaxation; to breathe a purer air and to worship God joyfully beneath the roof of heaven; and there was nothing frivolous about *that*. And, rather to the alarm of the captain, they planned to hold church services aboard the ship. Last year Sister McCandless had held an impromptu service in the unbelieving subway car, she played the tambourine and sang and exhorted sinners and passed through the train distributing tracts. Not everyone had found this admirable, to some it seemed that Sister McCandless was being a little ostentatious. "I praise my Redeemer wherever I go," she retorted defiantly. "Holy Ghost don't leave *me* when I leave the church. I got a every day religion."

Sylvia's birthday was on the third, and David and Johnnie and Roy had been saving money for her birthday present. Between them they had five dollars but they could not decide what to give her. Roy's suggestion that they give her underthings was rudely shouted down: did he want Sylvia's mother to kill the girl? They were all frightened of the great, rawboned, outspoken Sister Daniels and for Sylvia's sake went to great pains to preserve what remained of her good humor. Finally, at the suggestion of David's older sister, Lorraine, they bought a small, gold-plated pin cut in the shape of a butterfly. Roy thought that it was cheap and grumbled angrily at their combined bad taste ("Wait till it starts turning her clothes green!" he cried) but David did not think it was so bad; Johnnie thought it pretty enough and he was sure that Sylvia would like it anyway; ("When's *your* birthday?" he asked David). It was agreed that David should present it to her on the day of the outing in the presence of them all. ("Man, I'm the oldest cat here," David said, "you know that girl's crazy about me"). This was the summer in which they all abruptly began to grow older, their bodies

becoming troublesome and awkward and even dangerous and
their voices not to be trusted. David perpetually boasted of the
increase of down on his chin and professed to have hair on his
his chest—"and somewhere else, too," he added slyly, whereat
they all laughed. "You ain't the only one," Roy said. "No," Johnnie said, "I'm almost as old as you are." "Almost ain't got it,"
David said. "Now ain't this a hell of a conversation for church
boys?" Roy wanted to know.

The morning of the outing they were all up early; their father
sang in the kitchen and their mother, herself betraying an excitement nearly youthful, scrubbed and dressed the younger children and laid the plates for breakfast. In the bedroom which
they shared Roy looked wistfully out of the window and turned
to Johnnie.

"Got a good mind to stay home," he said. "Probably have
more fun." He made a furious gesture toward the kitchen. "Why
doesn't *he* stay home?"

Johnnie, who was looking forward to the day with David and
who had not the remotest desire to stay home for any reason and
who knew, moreover, that Gabriel was not going to leave Roy
alone in the city, not even if the heavens fell, said lightly,
squirming into clean underwear: "Oh, he'll probably be busy
with the old folks. We can stay out of his way."

Roy sighed and began to dress. "Be glad when I'm a man," he
said.

Lorraine and David and Mrs. Jackson were already on the
boat when they arrived. They were among the last; most of the
church, Father James, Brother Elisha, Sister McCandless, Sister
Daniels and Sylvia were seated near the rail of the boat in a little
semi-circle, conversing in strident tones. Father James and Sister
McCandless were remarking the increase of laxity among God's
people and debating whether or not the church should run a
series of revival meetings. Sylvia sat there, saying nothing, smiling painfully now and then at young Brother Elisha, who spoke
loudly of the need for a revival and who continually attempted
to include Sylvia in the conversation. Elsewhere on the boat
similar conversations were going on. The saints of God were
together and very conscious this morning of their being together

and of their sainthood; and were determined that the less en-
lightened world should know who they were and remark upon it.
To this end there were a great many cries of "Praise the Lord!" in
greeting and the formal holy kiss. The children, bored with the
familiar spectacle, had already drawn apart and amused themselves by loud cries and games that were no less exhibitionistic
than that being played by their parents. Johnnie's nine year old
sister, Lois, since she professed salvation, could not very well
behave as the other children did; yet no degree of salvation
could have equipped her to enter into the conversation of the
grown-ups; and she was very violently disliked among the adoles-
cents and could not join them either. She wandered about,
therefore, unwillingly forlorn, contenting herself to some extent
by a great display of virtue in her encounters with the unsaved
children and smiling brightly at the grown-ups. She came to
Brother Elisha's side. "Praise the Lord," he cried, stroking her
head and continuing his conversation.

Lorraine and Mrs. Jackson met Johnnie's mother for the first
time as she breathlessly came on board, dressed in the airy and
unreal blue which Johnnie would forever associate with his fur-
thest memories of her. Johnnie's baby brother, her youngest,
happiest child, clung round her neck; she made him stand, staring in wonder at the strange, endless deck, while she was introduced. His mother, on all social occasions, seemed fearfully
distracted, as though she awaited, at any moment, some crush-
ing and irrevocable disaster. This disaster might be the sudden
awareness of a run in her stocking or private knowledge that the
trump of judgment was due, within five minutes, to sound: but,
whatever it was, it lent her a certain agitated charm and people,
struggling to guess what it might be that so claimed her inward
attention, never failed, in the process, to be won over. She talked
with Lorraine and Mrs. Jackson for a few moments, the child
tugging at her skirts, Johnnie watching her with a smile; and at
last, the child becoming always more restive, said that she must
go—into what merciless arena one dared not imagine—but
hoped, with a despairing smile which clearly indicated the im-
probability of such happiness, that she would be able to see
them later. They watched her as she walked slowly to the other

end of the boat, sometimes pausing in conversation, always (as though it were a duty) smiling a little and now and then considering Lois where she stood at Brother Elisha's knee.

"She's very friendly," Mrs. Jackson said. "She looks like you, Johnnie."

David laughed. "Now why you want to say a thing like that, Ma? That woman ain't never done nothing to you."

Johnnie grinned, embarrassed, and pretended to menace David with his fists.

"Don't you listen to that old, ugly boy," Lorraine said. "He just trying to make you feel bad. Your mother's real good-looking. Tell her I said so."

This embarrassed him even more, but he made a mock bow and said, "Thank you, Sister." And to David: "Maybe now you'll learn to keep your mouth shut."

"Who'll learn to keep whose mouth shut? What kind of talk is that?"

He turned and faced his father, who stood smiling on them as from a height.

"Mrs. Jackson, this is my father," said Roy quickly. "And this is Miss Jackson. You know David."

Lorraine and Mrs. Jackson looked up at the deacon with polite and identical smiles.

"How do you do?" Lorraine said. And from Mrs. Jackson: "I'm very pleased to meet you."

"Praise the Lord," their father said. He smiled. "Don't you let Johnnie talk fresh to you."

"Oh, no, we were just kidding around," David said. There was a short, ugly silence. The deacon said: "It looks like a good day for the outing, praise the Lord. You kids have a good time. Is this your first time with us, Mrs. Jackson?"

"Yes," said Mrs. Jackson. "David came home and told me about it and it's been so long since I've been in the country I just decided I'd take me a day off. And Lorraine's not been feeling too strong, I thought the fresh air would do her some good." She smiled a little painfully as she spoke. Lorraine looked amused.

"Yes, it will, nothing like God's fresh air to help the feeble."

At this description of herself as feeble Lorraine looked ready to fall into the Hudson and coughed nastily into her handkerchief. David, impelled by his own perverse demon, looked at Johnnie quickly and murmured, "That's the truth, deacon." The deacon looked at him and smiled and turned to Mrs. Jackson. "We been hoping that your son might join our church someday. Roy brings him out to service every Sunday. Do you like the services, son?" This last was addressed in a hearty voice to David; who, recovering from his amazement at hearing Roy mentioned as his especial pal (for he was Johnnie's friend, it was to be with Johnnie that he came to church!) smiled and said, "Yes sir, I like them alright," and looked at Roy, who considered his father with an expression at once contemptuous, ironic and resigned and at Johnnie, whose face was a mask of rage. He looked sharply at the deacon again; but he, with his arm around Roy, was still talking.

"This boy came to the Lord just about a month ago," he said proudly. "The Lord saved him just like that. Believe me, Sister Jackson, ain't no better fortress for nobody, young or old, than the arms of Jesus. My son'll tell you so, ain't it, Roy?"

They considered Roy with a stiff, cordial curiosity. He muttered murderously, "Yes sir."

"Johnnie tells me you're a preacher," Mrs. Jackson said at last. "I'll come out and hear you sometime with David."

"Don't come out to hear me," he said. "You come out and listen to the Word of God. We're all just vessels in His hand. Do you know the Lord, sister?"

"I try to do His will," Mrs. Jackson said.

He smiled kindly. "We must all grow in grace." He looked at Lorraine. "I'll be expecting to see you too, young lady."

"Yes, we'll be out," Lorraine said. They shook hands. "It's very nice to have met you," she said.

"Goodbye." He looked at David. "Now you be good. I want to see you saved soon." He released Roy and started to walk away. "You kids enjoy yourselves. Johnnie, don't you get into no mischief, you hear me?"

He affected not to have heard; he put his hands in his pants' pockets and pulled out some change and pretended to count it. His hand was clammy and it shook. When his father repeated his admonition, part of the change spilled to the deck and he bent to pick it up. He wanted at once to shout to his father the most dreadful curses that he knew and he wanted to weep. He was aware that they were all intrigued by the tableau presented by his father and himself, that they were all vaguely cognizant of an unnamed and deadly tension. From his knees on the deck he called back (putting into his voice as much asperity, as much fury and hatred as he dared):

"Don't worry about me, Daddy. Roy'll see to it that I behave."

There was a silence after he said this; and he rose to his feet and saw that they were all watching him. David looked pitying and shocked, Roy's head was bowed and he looked apologetic. His father called:

"Excuse yourself, Johnnie, and come here."

"Excuse me," he said, and walked over to his father. He looked up into his father's face with an anger which surprised and even frightened him. But he did not drop his eyes, knowing that his father saw there (and he wanted him to see it) how much he hated him.

"What did you say?" his father asked.

"I said you don't have to worry about me. I don't think I'll get into any mischief." And his voice surprised him, it was more deliberately cold and angry than he had intended and there was a sardonic stress on the word "mischief." He knew that his father would then and there have knocked him down if they had not been in the presence of saints and strangers.

"You be careful how you speak to me. Don't you get grown too fast. We get home, I'll pull down those long pants and we'll see who's the man, you hear me?"

Yes we will, he thought, and said nothing. He looked with a deliberate casualness about the deck. Then they felt the lurch of the boat as it began to move from the pier. There was an excited raising of voices and "I'll see you later," his father said, and turned away.

He stood still, trying to compose himself to return to Mrs. Jackson and Lorraine. But as he turned with his hands in his pants' pockets he saw that David and Roy were coming toward him and he stopped and waited for them.

"It's a bitch," Roy said.

David looked at him, shocked. "That's no language for a saved boy." He put his arm around Johnnie's shoulder. "We're off to Bear Mountain," he cried, "*up* the glorious Hudson"—and he made a brutal gesture with his thumb.

"Now suppose Sylvia saw you do that," said Roy, "what would you say, huh?"

"We needn't worry about her," Johnnie said. "She'll be sitting with the old folks all day long."

"Oh, we'll figure out a way to take care of *them*," said David. He turned to Roy. "Now you the saved one, why don't you talk to Sister Daniels and distract her attention while we talk to the girl? You the baby, anyhow, girl don't want to talk to you."

"I ain't got enough salvation to talk to that hag," Roy said. "I got a Daddy-made salvation. I'm saved when I'm with Daddy." They laughed and Roy added, "And I ain't no baby, either, I got everything my Daddy got."

"And a lot your Daddy don't dream of," David said.

Oh, thought Johnnie, with a sudden, vicious, chilling anger, *he doesn't have to dream about it!*

"Now let's act like we Christians," David said. "If we was real smart now, we'd go over to where she's sitting with all those people and act like we wanted to hear about God. Get on the good side of her mother."

"And suppose *he* comes back?" asked Johnnie.

Gabriel was sitting at the other end of the boat, talking with his wife. "Maybe he'll stay there," David said; there was a note of apology in his voice.

They approached the saints.

"Praise the Lord," they said sedately.

"Well, praise Him," Father James said. "How are you young men today?" He grabbed Roy by the shoulder. "Are you coming along in the Lord?"

"Yes, sir," Roy muttered, "I'm trying." He smiled into Father James's face.

"It's a wonderful thing," Brother Elisha said, "to give up to the Lord in your youth." He looked up at Johnnie and David.

"Why don't you boys surrender? Ain't nothing in the world for you, I'll tell you that. He says, 'Remember thy Creator in the days of thy youth when the evil days come not.'"

"Amen," said Sister Daniels. "We're living in the last days, children. Don't think because you're young you got plenty of time. God takes the young as well as the old. You got to hold yourself in readiness all the time lest when He comes He catch you unprepared. Yes sir. Now's the time."

"You boys going to come to service today, ain't you?" asked Sister McCandless. "We're going to have service on the ship, you know." She looked at Father James. "Reckon we'll start as soon as we get a little further up the river, won't we, Father?"

"Yes," Father James said, "we're going to praise God right in the middle of the majestic Hudson." He leaned back and released Roy as he spoke. "Want to see you children there. I want to hear you make a *noise* for the Lord."

"I ain't never seen none of these young men Shout," said Sister Daniels, regarding them with distrust. She looked at David and Johnnie. "Don't believe I've ever even heard you testify."

"We're not saved yet, sister," David told her gently.

"That's alright," Sister Daniels said. "You *could* get up and praise the Lord for your life, health and strength. Praise Him for what you got, He'll give you something more."

"That's the truth," said Brother Elisha. He smiled at Sylvia. "I'm a witness, bless the Lord."

"They going to make a noise yet," said Sister McCandless. "Lord's going to touch everyone of these young men one day and bring them on their knees to the altar. You mark my words, you'll see." And she smiled at them.

"You just stay around the house of God long enough," Father James said. "One of these days the Spirit'll jump on you. I won't never forget the day It jumped on me."

"That *is* the truth," Sister McCandless cried, "so glad It jumped on me one day, hallelujah!"

"Amen," Sister Daniels cried, "amen."

"Looks like we're having a little service right now," Brother Elisha said, smiling. Father James laughed heartily and cried, "Well, praise Him anyhow."

"I believe next week the church is going to start a series of revival meetings," Brother Elisha said. "I want to see you boys at every one of them, you hear?" He laughed as he spoke and added as David seemed about to protest, "No, no, brother, don't want no excuses. You *be* there. Get you boys to the altar, then maybe you'll pay more attention in Sunday School."

At this they all laughed and Sylvia said in her mild voice, looking mockingly at Roy, "Maybe we'll even see Brother Roy Shout." Roy grinned.

"Like to see you do some Shouting too," her mother grumbled. "You got to get closer to the Lord." Sylvia smiled and bit her lip; she cast a glance at David.

"Now everybody ain't got the same kind of spirit," Brother Elisha said, coming to Sylvia's aid. "Can't *all* make as much noise as you make," he said, laughing gently, "we all ain't got your energy."

Sister Daniels smiled and frowned at this reference to her size and passion and said, "Don't care, brother, when the Lord moves inside you, you bound to do something. I've seen that girl Shout all night and come back the next night and Shout some more. I don't believe in no dead religion, no sir. The saints of God need a revival."

"Well, we'll work on Sister Sylvia," said Brother Elisha.

Directly before and behind them stretched nothing but the river, they had long ago lost sight of the point of their departure. They steamed beside the Palisades, which rose rough and gigantic from the dirty, broad and blue-green Hudson. Johnnie and David and Roy wandered downstairs to the bottom deck, standing by the rail and leaning over to watch the white, writhing spray which followed the boat. From the river there floated up to their faces a soft, cool breeze. They were quiet for a long time, standing together, watching the river and the mountains and hearing vaguely the hum of activity behind them on the boat. The sky was high and blue, with here and there a spittle-like, changing cloud; the sun was orange and beat with anger on their uncovered heads.

And David muttered finally, "Be funny if they were right."

"If who was right?" asked Roy.

"Elisha and them—"

"There's only one way to find out," said Johnnie.

"Yes," said Roy, "and I ain't homesick for heaven yet."

"You always got to be so smart," David said.

"Oh," said Roy, "you just sore because Sylvia's still up there with Brother Elisha."

"You think they going to be married?" Johnnie asked.

"Don't talk like a fool," David said.

"Well it's a cinch you ain't never going to get to talk to her till you get saved," Johnnie said. He had meant to say "we." He looked at David and smiled.

"Might be worth it," David said.

"*What* might be worth it?" Roy asked, grinning.

"Now be nice," David said. He flushed, the dark blood rising beneath the dark skin. "How you expect me to get saved if you going to talk that way? You supposed to be an example."

"Don't look at me, boy," Roy said.

"I want you to talk to Johnnie," Gabriel said to his wife.

"What about?"

"That boy's pride is running away with him. Ask him to tell you what he said to me this morning soon as he got in front of his friends. He's your son, alright."

"What did he say?"

He looked darkly across the river. "You ask him to tell you about it tonight. I wanted to knock him down."

She had watched the scene and knew this. She looked at her husband briefly, feeling a sudden, outraged anger, barely conscious; sighed and turned to look at her youngest child where he sat involved in a complicated and strenuous and apparently joyless game which utilized a red ball, jacks, blocks and a broken shovel.

"I'll talk to him," she said at last. "He'll be alright." She wondered what on earth she would say to him; and what he would say to her. She looked covertly about the boat, but he was nowhere to be seen.

"That proud demon's just eating him up," he said bitterly.

He watched the river hurtle past. "Be the best thing in the world if the Lord would take his soul." He had meant to say "save" his soul.

Now it was noon and all over the boat there was the activity of lunch. Paper bags and huge baskets were opened. There was then revealed splendor: cold pork chops, cold chicken, bananas, apples, oranges, pears, and soda-pop, candy and cold lemonade. All over the boat the chosen of God relaxed; they sat in groups and talked and laughed; some of the more worldly gossiped and some of the more courageous young people dared to walk off together. Beneath them the strong, indifferent river raged within the channel and the screaming spray pursued them. In the engine room children watched the motion of the ship's gears as they rose and fell and chanted. The tremendous bolts of steel seemed almost human, imbued with a relentless force that was not human. There was something monstrous about this machine which bore such enormous weight and cargo.

Sister Daniels threw a paper bag over the side and wiped her mouth with her large handkerchief. "Sylvia, you be careful how you speak to these unsaved boys," she said.

"Yes, I am, Mama."

"Don't like the way that little Jackson boy looks at you. That child's got a demon. You be careful."

"Yes, Mama."

"You got plenty of time to be thinking about boys. Now's the time for you to be thinking about the Lord."

"Yes'm."

"You *mind* now," her mother said.

"Mama, I want to go home!" Lois cried. She crawled into her mother's arms, weeping.

"Why, what's the matter, honey?" She rocked her daughter gently. "Tell Mama what's the matter? Have you got a pain?"

"I want to go home, I want to go home." Lois sobbed.

"A very fine preacher, a man of God and a friend of mine will run the service for us," said Father James.

"Maybe you've heard about him—a Reverend Peters? A real man of God, amen."

"I thought," Gabriel said, smiling, "that perhaps I could bring the message some Sunday night. The Lord called me a long time ago. I used to have my own church down home."

"You don't want to run too fast, Deacon Grimes," Father James said. "You just take your time. You been coming along right well on Young Ministers' Nights." He paused and looked at Gabriel. "Yes, indeed."

"I just thought," Gabriel said humbly, "that I could be used to more advantage in the house of God."

Father James quoted the text which tells us how preferable it is to be a gate-keeper in the house of God than to dwell in the tent of the wicked; and started to add the dictum from Saint Paul about obedience to those above one in the Lord but decided (watching Gabriel's face) that it was not necessary yet.

"You just keep praying," he said kindly. "You get a little closer to God. He'll work wonders. You'll see." He bent closer to his deacon. "And try to get just a little closer to the *people*."

Roy wandered off with a gawky and dazzled girl named Elizabeth. Johnnie and David wandered restlessly up and down the boat alone. They mounted to the topmost deck and leaned over the railing in the deserted stern. Up here the air was sharp and clean. They faced the water, their arms around each other.

"Your old man was kind of rough this morning," David said carefully, watching the mountains pass.

"Yes," Johnnie said. He looked at David's face against the sky. He shivered suddenly in the sharp, cold air and buried his face in David's shoulder. David looked down at him and tightened his hold.

"Who do you love?" he whispered. "Who's your boy?"

"You," he muttered fiercely, "I love you."

"Roy!" Elizabeth giggled, "*Roy Grimes*. If you *ever* say a thing like that *again*."

Now the service was beginning. From all corners of the boat there was the movement of the saints of God. They gathered together their various possessions and moved their chairs from top and bottom decks to the large main hall. It was early afternoon, not quite two o'clock. The sun was high and fell everywhere with a copper light. In the city the heat would have been insupportable; and here, as the saints filed into the huge, high room, once used as a ballroom, to judge from the faded and antique appointments, the air slowly began to be oppressive. The room was the color of black mahogany and coming in from the bright deck, one groped suddenly in darkness; and took one's sense of direction from the elegant grand piano which stood in the front of the room on a little platform.

They sat in small rows with one wide aisle between them, forming, almost unconsciously, a hierarchy. Father James sat in the front next to Sister McCandless. Opposite them sat Gabriel and Deacon Jones and, immediately behind them, Sister Daniels and her daughter. Brother Elisha walked in swiftly, just as they were beginning to be settled. He strode to the piano and knelt down for a second before rising to take his place. There was a quiet stir, the saints adjusted themselves, waiting while Brother Elisha tentatively ran his fingers over the keys. Gabriel looked about impatiently for Roy and Johnnie, who, engaged no doubt in sinful conversation with David, were not yet in service. He looked back to where Mrs. Jackson sat with Lorraine, uncomfortable smiles on their faces, and glanced at his wife, who met his questioning regard quietly, the expression on her face not changing.

Brother Elisha struck the keys and the congregation joined in the song, *Nothing Shall Move Me from the Love of God*, with tambourine and heavy hands and stomping feet. The walls and the floor of the ancient hall trembled and the candelabra wavered in the high ceiling. Outside the river rushed past under the heavy shadow of the Palisades and the copper sun beat down. A few of the strangers who had come along on the outing appeared at the doors and stood watching with an uneasy amusement. The saints sang on, raising their strong voices in praises to Jehovah and seemed unaware of those unsaved who watched and who, some day, the power of the Lord might cause to tremble.

The song ended as Father James rose and faced the congregation, a broad smile on his face. They watched him expectantly, with love. He stood silent for a moment, smiling down upon them. Then he said, and his voice was loud and filled with triumph:

"Well, let us all say, Amen!"

And they cried out obediently, "Well, Amen!"

"Let us all say, praise Him!"

"Praise Him!"

"Let us all say, hallelujah!"

"Hallelujah!"

"Well, glory!" cried Father James. The Holy Ghost touched him and he cried again, "Well, bless Him! Bless His holy name!"

They laughed and shouted after him, their joy so great that they laughed as children and some of them cried as children do; in the fullness and assurance of salvation, in the knowledge that the Lord was in their midst and that each heart, swollen to anguish, yearned only to be filled with His glory. Then, in that moment, each of them might have mounted with wings like eagles far past the sordid persistence of the flesh, the depthless iniquity of the heart, the doom of hours and days and weeks; to be received by the Bridegroom where He waited on high in glory; where all tears were wiped away and death had no power; where the wicked ceased from troubling and the weary soul found rest.

"Saints, let's praise Him," Father James said. "Today, right in the middle of God's great river, under God's great roof, beloved, let us raise our voices in thanksgiving that God has seen fit to save us, Amen!"

"Amen! Hallelujah!"

"—and to keep us saved, Amen, to keep us, oh glory to God, from the snares of Satan, from the temptation and the lust and the evil of this world!"

"Talk about it!"

"*Preach!*"

"Ain't nothing strange, Amen, about worshiping God *wher-*

ever you might be, ain't that right? Church, when you get this mighty salvation you just can't keep it in, hallelujah! You got to talk about it—"

"Amen!"

"You got to live it, amen. When the Holy Ghost touches you, you *move*, bless God!"

"Well, it's so!"

"Want to hear some testimonies today, amen! I want to hear some *singing* today, bless God! Want to see some *Shouting*, bless God, hallelujah!"

"Talk about it!"

"And I don't want to see none of the saints hold back. If the Lord saved you, Amen, He give you a witness *every*where you go. Yes! My soul is a witness, bless our God!"

"Glory!"

"If you ain't saved, Amen, get up and praise Him anyhow. Give God the glory for sparing your sinful life, *praise* Him for the sunshine and the rain, *praise* Him for all the works of His hands. Saints, I want to hear some praises today, you hear me? I want you to make this old boat *rock*, hallelujah! I want to *feel* your salvation. Are you saved?"

"Amen!"

"Are you sanctified?"

"Glory?"

"Baptized in fire?"

"Yes! So glad!"

"*Testify!*"

Now the hall was filled with a rushing wind on which forever rides the Lord, death or healing indifferently in His hands. Under this fury the saints bowed low, crying out "holy!" and tears fell. On the open deck sinners stood and watched, beyond them the fiery sun and the deep river, the black-brown-green, unchanging cliffs. That sun, which covered earth and water now, would one day refuse to shine, the river would cease its rushing and its numberless dead would rise; the cliffs would shiver, crack, fall and where they had been would then be nothing but the unleashed wrath of God.

"Who'll be the first to tell it?" Father James cried. "Stand up and talk about it!"

Brother Elisha screamed, "Have mercy, Jesus!" and rose from the piano stool, his powerful frame possessed. And the Holy Ghost touched him and he cried again, bending nearly double, while his feet beat ageless, dreadful signals on the floor, while his arms moved in the air like wings and his face, distorted, no longer his own face nor the face of a young man, but timeless, anguished, grim with ecstasy, turned blindly toward heaven. *Yes, Lord*, they cried, *yes!*

"Dearly beloved . . ."

"Talk about it!"

"Tell it!"

"I want to thank and praise the Lord, amen . . ."

"Amen!"

". . . for being here, I want to thank Him for my life, health, and strength. . . ."

"Amen!"

"Well, glory!"

". . . I want to thank Him, hallelujah, for saving my soul one day. . . ."

"*Oh!*"

"Glory!"

". . . for causing the light, bless God, to shine in *my* heart one day when I was still a child, amen, I want to thank Him for bringing me to salvation in the days of my *youth*, hallelujah, when I have all my faculties, amen, before Satan had a chance to destroy my body in the world!"

"Talk about it!"

"He saved me, dear ones, from the world and the things of the world. Saved me, amen, from cardplaying . . ."

"Glory!"

". . . saved me from drinking, bless God, saved me from the streets, from the movies and all the filth that is in the world!"

"I *know* it's so!"

"He saved me, beloved, and sanctified me and filled me with the blessed Holy Ghost, *hallelujah!* Give me a new song, amen, which I didn't know before and set my feet on the King's highway. Pray for me beloved, that I will stand in these last and evil days."

"Bless your name, Jesus!"

During his testimony Johnnie and Roy and David had stood quietly beside the door, not daring to enter while he spoke. The moment he sat down they moved quickly, together, to the front of the high hall and knelt down beside their seats to pray. The aspect of each of them underwent always, in this company a striking, even an exciting change; as though their youth, barely begun, were already put away; and the animal, so vividly restless and undiscovered, so tense with power, ready to spring, had been already stalked and trapped and offered, a perpetual blood-sacrifice, on the altar of the Lord. Yet their bodies continued to change and grow, preparing them, mysteriously and with ferocious speed, for manhood. No matter how careful their movements, these movements suggested, with a distinctness dreadful for the redeemed to see, the pagan lusting beneath the blood-washed robes. In them was perpetually and perfectly poised the power of revelation against the power of nature; and the saints, considering them with a baleful kind of love, struggled to bring their souls to safety in order, as it were, to steal a march on the flesh while the flesh still slept. A kind of storm, infernal, blew over the congregation as they passed; someone cried, "Bless them, Lord!" and immediately, honey-colored Sister Russell, while they knelt in prayer, rose to her feet to testify.

From the moment that they closed their eyes and covered their faces they were isolated from the joy that moved everything beside them. Yet this same isolation served only to make the glory of the saints more real, the pulse of conviction, however faint, beat in and the glory of God then held an undertone of abject terror. Roy was the first to rise, sitting very straight in his seat and allowing his face to reveal nothing; just as Sister Russell ended her testimony and sat down, sobbing, her head thrown back and both hands raised to heaven. Immediately Sister Daniels raised her strong, harsh voice and hit her tambourine, singing. Brother Elisha turned on the piano stool and hit the keys. Johnnie and David rose from their knees and as they rose the congregation rose, clapping their hands singing. The three boys did not sing; they stood together, carefully ignoring one another, their feet steady on the slightly tilting floor but their bodies moving back and forth as the music grew more savage. And someone cried aloud, a timeless sound of wailing; fire splashed the open deck and filled the doors and bathed the sinners standing there; fire filled the great hall and splashed the faces of the saints and a wind, unearthly, moved about their heads. Their hands were arched before them, moving, and their eyes were raised to heaven. Sweat stained the deacon's collar and soaked the tight headbands of the women. Was it true then? and had there indeed been born one day in Bethlehem a Saviour who was Christ the Lord? who had died for them—for *them!*—the spat-upon and beaten with rods, who had worn a crown of thorns and seen His blood run down like rain; and who had lain in the grave three days and vanquished death and hell and risen again in glory—*was it for them?*

Lord, I want to go, show me the way!

For unto us a child is born, unto us a son is given—and His name shall be called Wonderful, the mighty God, the everlasting Father, the Prince of Peace. Yes, and He was coming back one day, the King of glory; He would crack the face of heaven and descend to judge the nations and gather up His people and take them to their rest.

Take me by my hand and lead me on!

Somewhere in the back a woman cried out and began the Shout. They looked carefully about, still not looking at one another, and saw, as from a great distance and through intolerable heat, such heat as might have been faced by the Hebrew children when cast bound into the fiery furnace, that one of the saints was dancing under the arm of the Lord. She danced out into the aisle, beautiful with a beauty unbearable, graceful with grace that poured from heaven. Her face was lifted up, her eyes were closed and the feet which moved so surely now were not her own. One by one the power of God moved others and—as it had been written—the Holy Ghost descended from heaven with a Shout. Sylvia raised her hands, the tears poured down her face, and in a moment, she too moved out into the aisle, Shouting. Is it true then? the saints rejoiced, Roy beat the tambourine. David, grave and shaken, clapped his hands and his body moved insistently in the rhythm of the dancers. Johnnie stood beside him, hot and faint and repeating yet again his struggle, summoning in panic all his forces, to save him from this frenzy. And yet daily he recognized that he was black with sin, that the secrets of his heart were a stench in God's nostrils. *Though your sins be as scarlet they shall be white as snow. Come, let us reason together, saith the Lord.*

Now there was a violent discord on the piano and Brother Elisha leapt to his feet, dancing. Johnnie watched the spinning body and listened, in terror and anguish, to the bestial sobs. Of the men it was only Elisha who danced and the women moved toward him and he moved toward the women. Johnnie felt blow over him an icy wind, all his muscles tightened, as though they furiously resisted some imminent bloody act, as the body of Isaac must have revolted when he saw his father's knife, and, sick and nearly sobbing, he closed his eyes. It was Satan, surely, who stood so foully at his shoulder; and what, but the blood of Jesus, should ever set him free? He thought of the many times he had stood in the congregation of the righteous—and yet he was not saved. He remained among the vast army of the doomed, whose lives—as he had been told, as he now, with such heart-sickness, began to discover for himself—were swamped with wretchedness and whose end was wrath and weeping. Then, for he felt himself falling, he opened his eyes and watched the rejoicing of the saints. His eyes found his father where he stood clapping his hands, glittering with sweat and overwhelming. Then Lois began to shout. For the first time he looked at Roy; their eyes met in brief, wry wonder and Roy imperceptibly shrugged. He watched his mother standing over Lois, her own face obscurely troubled. The light from the door was on her face, the entire room was filled with this strange light. There was no sound now except the sound of Roy's tambourine and the heavy rhythm of the saints; the sound of heavy feet and hands and the sound of weeping. Perhaps centuries past the children of Israel led by Miriam had made just such a noise as they came out of the wilderness. *For unto us is born this day a Saviour who is Christ the Lord.*

Yet, in the copper sunlight Johnnie felt suddenly not the presence of the Lord, but the presence of David; which seemed to reach out to him, hand reaching out to hand in the fury of flood-time, to drag him to the bottom of the water or to carry him safe to shore. From the corner of his eye he watched his friend, who held him with such power; and felt, for that moment, such a depth of love, such nameless and terrible joy and pain, that he might have fallen, in the face of that company, weeping at David's feet.

Once at Bear Mountain they faced the very great problem of carrying Sylvia sufficiently far from her mother's sight to present her with her birthday present. This problem, difficult enough, was made even more difficult by the continual presence of Brother Elisha; who, inspired by the afternoon's service and by Sylvia's renewal of her faith, remained by her side to bear witness to the goodness and power of the Lord. Sylvia listened with her habitual rapt and painful smile. Her mother on the one side and Brother Elisha on the other, seemed almost to be taking turns in advising her on her conduct as a saint of God. They began to despair, as the sun moved visibly westward, of ever giving her the gold-plated butterfly which rested uncomfortably in David's waistcoat pocket.

Of course, as Johnnie once suggested, there was really no reason they could not go up to her, surrounded as she was, and give her the jewel and get it over with—the more particularly as David evinced a desire to explore the wonders of Bear Mountain until this mission should have been fulfilled. Sister Daniels could scarcely object to an innocuous memento from three young men, all of whom attended church devoutly and one of whom professed salvation. But this was far from satisfactory for David, who did not wish to hear Sylvia's "thank-yous" in the constricting presence of the saints. Therefore they waited, wandering about the sloping park, lingering near the lake and the skating rink and watching Sylvia.

"God, why don't they go off somewhere and sleep? or pray?" cried David finally. He glared at the nearby rise where Sylvia and her mother sat talking with Brother Elisha. The sun was in their faces and struck from Sylvia's hair as she restlessly moved her head, small blue-black sparks.

Johnnie swallowed his jealousy at seeing how Sylvia filled his comrade's mind; he said, half-angrily, "I still don't see why we don't just go over and give it to her."

Roy looked at him. "Boy, you sound like you ain't got good sense," he said.

Johnnie, frowning, fell into silence. He glanced sidewise at David's puckered face (his eyes were still on Sylvia) and abruptly turned and started walking off.

"Where you going, boy?" David called.

"I'll be back," he said. And he prayed that David would follow him.

But David was determined to catch Sylvia alone and remained where he was with Roy. "Well, make it snappy," he said; and sprawled, full length, on the grass.

As soon as he was alone his pace slackened; he leaned his forehead against the bark of a tree, shaking and burning as in the teeth of a fever. The bark of the tree was rough and cold and though it offered no other comfort he stood there quietly for a long time, seeing beyond him—but it brought no peace—the high clear sky where the sun in fading glory traveled; and the deep earth covered with vivid banners, grass, flower, thorn and vine, thrusting upward forever the brutal trees. At his back he heard the voices of the children and the saints. He knew that he must return, that he must be on hand should David at last outwit Sister Daniels and present her daughter with the golden butterfly. But he did not want to go back, now he realized that he had no interest in the birthday present, no interest whatever in Sylvia—that he had had no interest all along. He shifted his stance, he turned from the tree as he turned his mind from the abyss which suddenly yawned, that abyss, depthless and terrifying, which he had encountered already in dreams. And he slowly began to walk, away from the saints and the voices of the children, his hands in his pockets, struggling to ignore the question which now screamed and screamed in his mind's bright haunted house.

It happened quite simply. Eventually Sister Daniels felt the need to visit the ladies' room, which was a long ways off. Brother Elisha remained where he was while Roy and David, like two beasts crouching in the underbrush, watched him and waited their opportunity. Then he also rose and wandered off to get cold lemonade for Sylvia. She sat quietly alone on the green rise, her hands clasped around her knees, dreaming.

They walked over to her, in terror that Sister Daniels would suddenly reappear. Sylvia smiled as she saw them coming and waved to them merrily. Roy grinned and threw himself on his belly on the ground beside her. David remained standing, fumbling in his waistcoat pocket.

"We got something for you," Roy said.

David produced the butterfly. "Happy birthday, Sylvia," he said. He stretched out his hand, the butterfly glinted oddly in the sun, and he realized with surprise that his hand was shaking. She grinned widely, in amazement and delight, and took the pin from him.

"It's from Johnnie, too," he said. "I—we—hope you like it—"

She held the small gold pin in her palm and stared down at it; her face was hidden. After a moment she murmured, "I'm so surprised." She looked up, her eyes shining, almost wet. "Oh, it's wonderful," she said. "I never expected anything. I don't know what to say. It's marvelous, it's wonderful." She pinned the butterfly carefully to her light blue dress. She coughed slightly. "Thank you," she said.

"Your mother won't mind, will she?" Roy asked. "I mean—" he stammered awkwardly under Sylvia's sudden gaze—"we didn't know, we didn't want to get you in any trouble—"

"No," David said. He had not moved; he stood watching Sylvia. Sylvia looked away from Roy and up at David, his eyes met hers and she smiled. He smiled back, suddenly robbed of speech. She looked away again over the path her mother had taken and frowned slightly. "No," she said, "no, she won't mind."

Then there was silence. David shifted uncomfortably from

one foot to the other. Roy lay contentedly face down on the grass. The breeze from the river, which lay below them and out of sight, grew subtly more insistent for they had passed the heat of the day; and the sun, moving always westward, fired and polished the tips of trees. Sylvia sighed and shifted on the ground.

"Why isn't Johnnie here?" she suddenly asked.

"He went off somewhere," Roy said. "He said he'd be right back." He looked at Sylvia and smiled. She was looking at David.

"You must want to grow real tall," she said mockingly. "Why don't you sit down?"

David grinned and sat down cross-legged next to Sylvia. "Well, the ladies like 'em tall." He lay on his back and stared up at the sky. "It's a fine day," he said.

She said, "Yes," and looked down at him; he had closed his eyes and was bathing his face in the slowly waning sun. Abruptly, she asked him:

"Why don't you get saved? You around the church all the time and you not saved yet? Why don't you?"

He opened his eyes in amazement. Never before had Sylvia mentioned salvation to him, except as a kind of joke. One of the things he most liked about her was the fact that she never preached to him. Now he smiled uncertainly and stared at her.

"I'm not joking," she said sharply. "I'm perfectly serious. Roy's saved—at least he *says* so—" and she smiled darkly, in the fashion of the old folks, at Roy—"and anyway, you ought to be thinking about your soul."

"Well, I don't know," David said. "I *think* about it. It's—well, I don't know if I can—well, live it—"

"All you got to do is make up your mind. If you really want to be saved, He'll save you. Yes, and He'll keep you too." She did not sound at all hysterical or transfigured. She spoke very quietly and with great earnestness and frowned as she spoke. David, taken off guard, said nothing. He looked embarrassed and pained and surprised. "Well, I don't know," he finally repeated.

"Do you ever pray?" she asked. "I mean, *really* pray?"

David laughed, beginning to recover himself. "It's not fair," he said, "you oughtn't to catch me all unprepared like that. Now I don't know what to say." But as he looked at her earnest face

he sobered. "Well, I try to be decent. I don't bother nobody."
He picked up a grass blade and stared at it. "I don't know," he
said at last. "I do my best."

"*Do* you?" she asked.

He laughed again, defeated. "Girl," he said, "you *are* a killer."

She laughed too. "You black-eyed demon," she said, "if I
don't see you at revival services I'll never speak to you again." He
looked up quickly, in some surprise, and she said, still smiling,
"Don't look at me like that. I mean it."

"All right, sister," he said. Then: "If I come out can I walk
you home?"

"I got my mother to walk me home—"

"Well, let your mother walk home with Brother Elisha," he
said, grinning. "Let the old folks stay together."

"Loose him, Satan!" she cried, laughing, "loose the boy!"

"The brother needs prayer," Roy said.

"Amen," said Sylvia. She looked down again at David. "I want
to see you at church. Don't you forget it."

"All right," he said. "I'll be there."

The boat whistles blew at six o'clock, punctuating their holiday;
blew, fretful and insistent, through the abruptly dispirited park
and skaters left the skating rink; boats were rowed in furiously
from the lake. Children were called from the swings and the
seesaw and the merry-go-round and forced to leave behind the
ball which had been lost in the forest and the torn kite which
dangled from the top of a tree. ("Hush now," said their parents,
"we'll get you another one—come along." "*Tomorrow?*"—
"Come along, honey, it's time to go!") The old folks rose from
the benches, from the grass, gathered together the empty lunch-
basket, the half-read newspaper, the Bible which was carried
everywhere; and they started down the hillside, an army in disor-
der. David walked with Sylvia and Sister Daniels and Brother
Elisha, listening to their conversation (good Lord, thought Johnnie, don't they ever mention anything but sin?) and carrying
Sylvia's lunch-basket. He seemed interested in what they were
saying; every now and then he looked at Sylvia and grinned and
she grinned back. Once, as Sylvia stumbled, he put his hand on

her elbow to steady her and held her arm perhaps a moment too long. Brother Elisha, on the far side of Sister Daniels, noticed this and a frown passed over his face. He kept talking, staring now and then hard at Sylvia and trying, with a certain almost humorous helplessness, to discover what was in her mind. Sister Daniels talked of nothing but the service on the boat and of the forthcoming revival. She scarcely seemed to notice David's presence, though once she spoke to him, making some remark about the need, on his part, of much prayer. Gabriel carried the sleeping baby in his arms, striding beside his wife and Lois—who stumbled perpetually and held tightly to her mother's hand. Roy was somewhere in the back, joking with Elizabeth. At a turn in the road the boat and the dock appeared below them, a dead gray-white in the sun.

Johnnie walked down the slope alone, watching David and Sylvia ahead of him. When he had come back, both Roy and David had disappeared and Sylvia sat again in the company of her mother and Brother Elisha; and if he had not seen the gold butterfly on her dress he would have been aware of no change. She thanked him for his share in it and told him that Roy and David were at the skating rink.

But when at last he found them they were far in the middle of the lake in a rowboat. He was afraid of water, he could not row. He stood on the bank and watched them. After a long while they saw him and waved and started to bring the boat in so that he could join them. But the day was ruined for him; by the time they brought the boat in, the hour, for which they had hired it, was over; David went in search of his mother for more money but when he came back it was time to leave. Then he walked with Sylvia.

All during the trip home David seemed preoccupied. When he finally sought out Johnnie he found him sitting by himself on the top deck, shivering a little in the night air. He sat down beside him. After a moment Johnnie moved and put his head on David's shoulder. David put his arms around him. But now where there had been peace there was only panic and where there had been safety, danger, like a flower, opened.

SHAWN STEWART RUFF

Meredith's Lie

Without opening her eyes she wrested her hand in between their bodies and led Cecil as though he were a
child. Even in the excited, blind silence, she could feel his eyes
burning through hers to the truth, that she was not a virgin,
she'd done this before. She told herself she did not care—sex
had nothing to do with truth, nor with love—and shielded her
mind from her thoughts as floods of pleasure sluiced through
her body. But the second she opened her eyes, even pleasure
could not press down the perverse feeling that on top of her was
innocence itself. She imagined Cecil's lips mouthing what he'd
confessed when he'd arrived: "I've never had sex before." Nothing had ever struck her as so stupidly funny, and she had
laughed hysterically. She had assumed all along that he, like
most athletes, was cautiously or carelessly sybaritic. He was captain and quarterback of the football team, one of the smartest
boys at school, going to UCLA on a full scholarship in the fall,
and although his eyes were slightly crossed, he was thick-jawed
and razor-bumpless, with a complexion like a Tootsie Roll. Rumor had it that he was screwing the team's lead cheerleader,
Heather—a white orchid in a garden of white girls stacked like

53

Playboy bunnies, with blinding blond hair. Could it be possible that he had saved his virginity for Meredith?—who was neither a bombshell cheerleader nor white, but a flat-chested cellist going to Juilliard in the fall, with a boyish Afro and an ass she knew would cause her embarrassment later in life. When he, in the same innocence in which he'd confessed, had asked if she too was a virgin, she nodded in slow humiliation yes, realizing, too, that she had the potential, and the desire, to hurt him. Surely no man had a right to expect purity, especially when so few could give it. But if he was foolish enough to desire it, or naive enough to believe that she could still be a virgin after dating Bruce since eighth grade, then she was outraged enough to give him an untouched, intact virginity to believe in, while clinging to her own instinct that he was lying. Indeed, if he had wanted her to believe in his innocence he would not have declared it so easily. In her shade-drawn bedroom, though, their bodies knotted, she realized she had erred in doubting him. His muscular shyness lent endearing veracity to his claim of virginity. He had removed his underwear while under the bedspread and had asked in the dumb-jock voice that made it hard to believe he'd be valedictorian of the class if she was sure her parents weren't coming home. Even more convincing, he perspired as though he'd just played two quarters of vigorous passing, drenching her sheets. And the event was over in disappointing, pounding minutes after it had begun.

"The coach always says that we shouldn't do it before a game because it saps so much energy," he said afterward, on his side, panting, a libidinous smirk on his face. "I see what he means. Jeez, I hope I don't lose the game for us tonight."

"Oh, Cecil," she said. "Really, you can't be that tired." His pillow talk amused and embarrassed her. Glimpsing her reflection in the mirror across the room, she pulled the sheet over her exposed breasts. Her lips were as red and dark as a desiccated rose. For a second she thought she might cry—but not now, not in front of him!

"No," he said. "Guess not. In fact, I could do it again." His eyebrows shimmied.

"Nasty boy! You've got to go." She diagrammed his dark,

muscled chest with her callused finger, paused at his nipple, which reminded her of a raisin. "I won't be responsible for any of your fumbles."

"I have never fumbled." He was indignant.

"There's a first time for everything."

He seemed not to have heard. "I don't know what Bruce did to make you dump him, Meredith, but I'm glad you did." he said. "When you asked me out, I thought you were teasing me. Cuckolding, that's what it's called—remember Chaucer?"

She wanted to tell him not to mention Bruce again, but instead she reached under the cover to touch his sheathed penis, now standing again at full attention. "I'm not married," she added, fluttering her eyelashes.

Between his rolling laughter and his overdue departure Meredith ceased to be aware of him. She found it next to impossible to concentrate. His eyes confused her. One seemed to stare at her, the other askance, and she could not determine on what either focused. His voice traveled directly over her head, missing her ears altogether, so that she constantly struggled to listen to him. His fickle eyes and dillydally dialogue bothered her less than the fact that his talents lay in violence—her opinion of football—and that her parents had chosen him alone, to the exclusion of Bruce, as worthy of her. Cecil's father was on the Cincinnati attorney general's staff; his mother was a gynecologist who worked with low-income women in downtown Cincinnati's Over the Rhine neighborhood. Bruce did not know his father; his mother was on welfare.

While Cecil showered in the bathroom, Meredith vaulted from the paisley sheets, then dressed quickly and carelessly, so that when he returned there'd be no question it was time for him to go. Returning from the bathroom, he went on and on about plays and diagrams for the football game tonight. He even babbled climbing into his underwear and jeans. With his backside facing her, Meredith roughly brushed her hair into order. Suddenly he asked, "You really think our folks wanted us to—"

"Fuck? Sure." She wondered if he found it odd that she could say such things and claim virginity. She was, after all, a proper child of proper parents. "Obviously, Cecil, my folks would die if they knew we were, but I think they'd die in peace knowing it was you who fucked me."

"You're so open, Meredith. I always admired that about you. I like the way you told your father, when he said you should play for my parents, that you weren't a CD to be popped in on command. If I'd talked to my dad like that, I'd've been grounded for the rest of the year. Maybe even DOA. My father thinks you're rude, my mother says you're a spoiled brat."

Meredith smiled; she liked to believe everyone thought that she was odious. "Did he think my Afro was a little too ethnic?"

"Come to think of it, he did say he liked you better with long hair," he volunteered enthusiastically.

Meredith was amused. "Thinks I'm a little tar baby, huh? The trouble with educated black folks that have money, Cecil, is that they become like white folks. They don't like anything that reminds them they're not white."

"Well, I like you like that—just as you are. But I have to admit I never thought we'd end up together, uh, you know. Doing it!" He laughed, embarrassed.

"Fucking, you mean."

He nodded.

"Say it."

"FUCKING," he repeated, shouting. He repeated it again, this time calmly, as though whispering, with a conspiratorial smirk on his face that revealed the silver of the retainer lurking behind his teeth in a mouth as pink as Pepto-Bismol. "You're really down, Meredith, you know that?"

"Right."

"Every game I ever play from now on, I'm gonna win for you."

She thanked him extravagantly, promised to be at the game tonight without admitting her loathing of football, and ushered him out the back door through which he had surreptitiously entered. She'd be late for rehearsal again. Emily would be pissed. But she couldn't leave the house a wreck. Her parents weren't due to return until Sunday, but they could get home any time between now and then. They had gone south to Louisiana for the twilight of her paternal grandmother's life. Meredith had been allowed to stay behind only because of the upcoming concert and midterms, on the condition that she spend the night at friends of her parents, where her mother called each evening for reassurance, at ten sharp. As it was, she would never make it to the Roundtrees' before her mother called, especially if she hung out with Cecil after the game. She yanked the sheets from her bed and fed them to the washer, straightened her room up, then showered Cecil's scent from her body. On her way from the bathroom she noticed the prophylactic floating in the toilet like an elongated jellyfish. One flush sent it wriggling away.

As glad as she was to have exacted a kind of revenge on everyone, she realized as she was driving to school that she might have made a mistake. Beyond the cherishable irony that she had slept with the chosen boy was the pain that drove her to him: Bruce's betrayal. Dating certainly would have made the point; by sleeping with Cecil she had possibly gone too far. Though for as long as she'd known Cecil he had been a constant reminder of how terrible puberty was, she liked him a lot. Ten years from now this giant of a man might be a star quarterback with millions in his bank accounts, endorsing products like Wheaties or Nikes, or be a spokesman for the United Negro College Fund, his face immortalized in *Ebony* for all black people to be proud of. It had only been five years ago, though, that he was an overweight black boy perpetually suffering from prickly heat, his smile held together by chains of aluminum braces. Through junior high school, insults from both white and black kids had ricocheted through the corridors, pointing out some or other oddity in his physiognomy. Cecil had born his suffering like Gandhi, aced every course, and spoken with an automated, indifferent clarity that had struck Meredith even then as slightly inhuman. Yet from the moment she first saw him, slouching into Honors English, she had liked him—because he was, besides herself, the only other black student in the class—and a week later she felt keenly sorry for him because he was cross-eyed, too big, too black, and too smart to fit into any of the picky Walnut Hills cliques. Sympathy did not extend it-self to dating then, however. One evening she came home and was told to prepare for dinner because the Ingrams were coming by. Seated in the living room was Cecil. Not knowing the Ingrams, she had been thoroughly mortified; in her wildest ideas Cecil Ingram would never sit across from her at a dinner table. They had never even spoken to each other. He, dressed as though he were going to church, seemed as shocked as Meredith and tipped over his glass. While Meredith's mother mopped up the mess, Cecil's called her son clumsy. In fact it was because he was cross-eyed, Meredith was convinced.

Her initial impression of Cecil did not improve with his blossoming. The image of the handsome hunk he'd turned into could never replace the memory of him cross-eyeballing her at the dining room table. In those days, even when out of sympathy she had spoken to him, he seemed rattled and confused, the opposite of his lifeless, textbook performance in class. As far as she was concerned, he was socially retarded. Weeks after that indelible dinner, he decided to risk confronting her, waiting after class just to say, as he explained, hello, to inquire after her parents, and to say how much he had enjoyed dinner. Meredith, nettled, told him she was in a hurry. The following day he waited for her again, only this time he succeeded in inviting her to a movie before she could flee. Of course she refused him, and to ensure that he never asked her again, she added that she had a boyfriend who went to the Performing Arts School; she even went so far as to name him—Bruce, who was then as unappealing to her as Cecil was. None the wiser, Cecil stopped pestering her. Or so she had thought.

One day later that same year, she noticed him following her to music class, then spying on her at rehearsal. This, Meredith thought, was going too far. The next day in class she waited for him. As they silently walked along the hall, she periodically checked his face. He was nervous; she liked this. When they cleared the herd of students passing classes, she, showing grave concern, said, "My boyfriend Bruce saw you at the rehearsal last night, and he wasn't too thrilled because he thinks you've got a crush on me. He's very jealous. Before he gets really pissed, I told him that I would have a talk with you." An eggplant hue glossed over Cecil's face. Stuttering, he blurted out that her parents had told his that she had no boyfriend. What? "They don't know shit about me!" Meredith snapped, as Cecil shrank in horror from her. That night she told her parents that she could choose her own boyfriends and didn't need their help. Cecil did not ask her out again until her junior year, when he'd already transmogrified handsomely. Even then she was suspicious of his motives. But then she could honestly claim that she was dating Bruce. "I'm in love," she said to him.

It amused Meredith that Cecil had been shocked when last Tuesday he spotted her on the track field and, away from the animal howls of his teammates, learned she was summoning him for a date. The expression on his sweat-soaked face made Meredith wonder if she had asked him just to see if he was still interested after three years of rejection. "What about Bruce?" he had inquired, both eyes focusing on her, which struck her as uneasily as when they did not. "It's over," she insisted. "I'm too young for a commitment. Besides, you're the one." Instinctive pessimism or a pervasive dullness checked his tongue. "I'm not joking," she insisted. Then he grinned as if uncertain of his good fortune and said, "I just never thought you'd go out with me, that's all."

In Cecil's new Subaru they had gone to see *Mo' Better Blues* at a theater downtown. Meredith stood aside while Cecil bought the tickets, apprehensive yet intrigued; without knowing it he was buying them from Bruce, who worked the ticket booth to pay for his piano lessons and keep the jalopy he had just bought running. Bruce might recognize Cecil, though: Meredith had pointed his mug out in their 1989 yearbook. Meredith could hardly see Bruce for the glare on the ticket-booth window. Apparently he didn't notice Cecil, and Meredith became more aggressive. Just before they went into the theater, she grabbed Cecil's hand and stopped in front of a poster, in view of the ticket booth, pretending to read. She heard her name called over a microphone and jerked with horror. It was as embarrassing as sitting in class and having her name broadcast on the PA system. Cecil nudged her, which made Meredith angrier. She looped her arm through his, explaining that it was somebody she didn't want to talk to and that it was best to ignore it, and they went inside. In the dark theater, she found her own behavior inscrutable. She had planned all along to make a point to Bruce with this date, so why was she burning with agitation? She scarcely watched the film, but the sexy images pierced her distraction. At some point Cecil reached for her hand. At another he leaned to her lips, kissed her; she opened her mouth to receive his enormous tongue. By the end of the movie he had succeeded in exciting her. She fantasized what it would be like to sleep with him—so much man!—but she thought of Bruce's tenderness and shuddered with sadness. When the lights came on, she hastily removed herself from Cecil's embrace and collected her things, conveying the impression that she only tolerated this date.

Outside the theater Bruce had waited, leaning against a parking meter. He was dressed like Humphrey Bogart in *Casablanca*—dark wool zoot suit with enormous shoulders and the Stetson Meredith had picked up at the Salvation Army in Norwood. In a lapse moment, on seeing him she smiled as if nothing were wrong; realizing her tactical error, she grabbed Cecil's arm. Bruce confronted them, scowling, his eyebrows a straight, thick black hedge dividing his face.

"Hey, Meredith. Cecil, how ya doing? I'm Bruce," he said, matter-of-factly.

"Bruce? Oh yeah, Bruce!" Cecil repeated, stupidly.

"Right. You bought a ticket from me. Excuse me, but I need to talk to Meredith for a second. In private."

Cecil started to move, but Meredith would not release his arm. Cecil was confused, as though in a game plan with crossed signals.

"Please—" Bruce playfully whined.

"No," Meredith snapped.

Anger trembled in his voice. "What about our rehearsal for the concert? Are we still doing it?" he demanded.

"We don't need to rehearse it. We've played it to death," she said with equal aggression.

Bruce violently folded his arms together, grinding his jaws. Then his anger suddenly became eclipsed by sadness. "What's wrong, Meredith?"

"I'll see you at the concert," she said, smiling weakly.

Driving home, Cecil had asked if she had known Bruce was going to be there at the theater. Yes, she said.

"Were you using me to get back at him?"

Meredith hesitated. "No," she had said, finally.

She had neither noticed nor cared if his eyes searched hers for truth, for she was invaded by misery and the desire to surrender to Bruce. When he said, "Good. He seems like a nice guy," Meredith had nodded in silent assent. When he dropped her off, she had told him to meet her after school because her parents were out of town. He had looked at her suspiciously, like someone used to being duped, but agreed anyway. An hour before he came, she sat in the quiet of the dark living room. Her cello stood erect in its stand. She wedged it between her legs and began to bow, gently, feeling the vibrations travel through her body. Twenty minutes later the phone rang. "Are you sure about this?" Cecil asked. She answered that she was.

The deed now done, though, she regretted it, the moment he confessed to being a virgin. True or not, he was too innocent, he didn't deserve to be hurt, she could never love him. On the other hand, men were not to be trusted.

The tears did not begin to fall until she was near school. They came in quick, tormented spasms that forced her head to the steering wheel. Hadn't she wanted to sleep with Cecil? No. "I hate you, Bruce! I hate you," she cried aloud, as car horns behind her screamed. Through misted eyes she guided her sputtering Volkswagen along the birch-lined streets. Strains of winter chilled the night, and even in the car, with the heat on, she wondered if she should have changed her skirt for jeans. Why on earth did she promise to go to Cecil's football game, anyway?

Walnut Hills High School was five miles away, clear across town in an impoverished area. The promising school had had the ill fortune to be directly in the path of a low-income, blue-collar insurgence forty or fifty years ago, though it desperately held on to its academic preeminence despite its environment. While her parents on the one hand applauded the advanced school, inasmuch as their only daughter was permitted attendance, on the other they turned blind eyes to the evidence that a black neighborhood would expose her to vastly more than they wished. From Meredith's perspective, nothing could be more perverse or dangerous than nuns, and she refused to go back to St. Mary's, where, she claimed, she'd done her time. "You'll just be switching prisons," her father joked. In the end, Meredith got her way. Walnut Hills was 85 percent white. But her triumph hinged on her acceptance of more parental meddling. According to her father's analysis, too many blacks in one place equal dangerous slum. He'd issue edicts for her to stay clear of this street and that movie theater, because the black kids hung out and that of course meant trouble. While it was understood that she could socialize with all the whites she could find—and in Hyde Park there was little else—white boyfriends were strictly forbidden. Clones of her family were the only types of blacks she knew firsthand, and if she was to fear any deviation from their middle-class example, then her parents had succeeded not only in implanting a fear in her of black boys living outside Hyde Park but in confusing her about why the lines beyond which one does not cross existed in the first place. She resented having her scalp burned so that her hair was acceptably straight, piling on mascara so her eyes looked light brown, listening to rock music when she preferred funk, all for the sake of fitting in and being attractive to white people she would at some point in her adult life, according to her parents, repudiate. "Whitey might be your boss, your doctor, your neighbor—but he is never your friend," was a platitudinous line her father was fond of fishing with during the deadening dinners they took to hosting. By dessert, "What's wrong with our people?" was the line toed. Except for Cecil's mother, who actually went out and did something with her convictions and knew firsthand problems the others had only read about, the guests were consistently mouthy hypocrites. Their alleged concern for the welfare of black people somehow never made it past cocktail chatter. Her father's dental practice, in a huge medical office building he and a partner owned, Monday through Thursday consisted of dorsal root decay, rampant periodontics, poor occlusions, reckless hygiene, all tended to and paid for by Medicaid. Friday and Saturday he fitted the bridges and installed the gold crowns of black school board members, doctors, lawyers—their class. Worse still, he owned property in the very neighborhoods forbidden to her—Avondale, Walnut Hills, Evanston. Meredith had no respect for these people, their ideas, those evenings—none!

And when her confusion did uncloud, in its place came a season of contempt. One clarifying incident changed her forever. With a gaggle of girls from school she had ridden to the King's Island Amusement Park. Hope, the girl driving, called the driver of a rusted Eldorado that had cut in front of her a nigger. From the backseat of the convertible they were riding in, Meredith observed her friends' straight hair flying through the air, their pointed noses, their eyes of every color except brown, and swallowed the bile welling up in her throat. None of the girls ever asked why she didn't hang out with them anymore, and it seemed tacitly agreed upon that their friendship, with the utterance of that one word, had been abrogated. As they had walked through the amusement park, Meredith saw herself in the context of racial history and realized that she was a modern-day casualty of it. She understood that she, the privileged, was equal to the unfortunate blacks—past and present—her parents despised. When she told her father what had happened, he said, "I wouldn't get bent out of shape over it, Meredith. Had I been in the situation, I might have called the man a nigger too. It's a kind of generic term of endearment these days." Her mother's response was the same. Meredith was ashamed, embarrassed, and livid all at once. Didn't they understand that, in the right situation, their BMW was no better than that ragged Eldorado, and they were nothing more than niggers—albeit from Hyde Park? Coming out of the mouth of a black person, the word was more than a self-flagellation, it was pathetic. How could they not see that?

Rather than attack her parents' alienating prestige, Meredith began to keep a silent vigil for her own independence. She began to see herself as a manifestation of their injustice, and became interested in her heritage. If it was necessary for her to be isolated from her race just to be liked, to be designated the exception, this meant that what she in essence was white people fundamentally despised. She felt both betrayed—she was not supposed to encounter such ugliness, given the privilege of her family's position—and violated. A fear of herself and the past, locked in the depths of her consciousness, had been exposed by that hateful word. Indeed, the emotional violence of her reaction to Hope's namecalling was perhaps as irrational and misguided as a skinhead's might have been on seeing Meredith riding in Hope's VW. Of course, if Meredith's opinions were razor-sharp, the measures she took to support them were cotton-wrapped: outside school and music she would not socialize with anyone not darker than or as dark as herself. Whenever possible she rode the bus into town, visited the public library, and buried herself in the black history section, reading everything black she could get her hands on. Once she'd even taken a cab through the projects in the area called Winton Terrace; she was so intensely uncomfortable, frightened even, by the disarray, the conspicuous violence of the place, that she knew she could never come there again. She knew nothing of such people; moreover, her family, Hyde Park, and her education would ensure forever that she never would know. By the time she was sixteen years old, she was broody, sour, friendless, and disillusioned with life.

One day she looked in the mirror at her permed hair and lopped it off until she was bald. Her mother went into hysterics, demanding that Meredith wear a wig. "You look like you've got cancer," she had shouted. Nothing could console her, not even when her father reminded her Meredith's hair would grow back. Only Bruce was pleased. He said she looked like a boy, except for her beautiful ass, and that she would have to wear lipstick now just to avoid confusion. She laughed and said she would braid his eyebrows if he didn't get them trimmed. And even as they laughed she comforted in his acceptance of her, her hairstyle, that his love had nothing do with "white" accessories. His joking in fact proved prophetic. One day two weeks before her father bought her the car, they had walked from Walnut Hills to Dana Avenue to catch the bus, holding hands. A group of boys driving by shouted "Faggots!" out of their car window. "See?" Bruce had said, nervously.

Before Bruce the only thing that consistently made her happy was music, perhaps all the more because there seemed nothing else. Art promised salvation and self-expression free of cultural abuse. Music gobbled her vulnerable emotions whole. It gave vent to a universal self-expression that race, politics, and philosophy had nothing to do with. And classical music was a way of succeeding in a white domain as a black woman—not permed to death and affected, but ethnic and brilliant. One either knew one's instrument or didn't, had intonation or didn't, knew the music or didn't, could make music or couldn't. Her parent's pretensions, exclusive Hyde Park, or the poor black people potted around the perimeter of the school—none bothered her anymore. Twice a week she took lessons with a Juilliard graduate, a cellist with the Cincinnati Symphony Orchestra. After school she came home to practice or remained at school to practice in the music room, or, when they performed together, she'd drive to Bruce's school to rehearse. Before she'd gotten her driver's license and her parents bought her the VW, on Saturdays, after her cello lesson, she'd bus over to the Cincinnati Conservatory of Music, alone or with Bruce, lock herself into a rehearsal cubicle, and play music all afternoon.

Unwittingly, and almost as an extension of her art, she fell in love with Bruce. She'd known him too long for love to have tiptoed by undetected, and it seemed that both feeling and desire for him had pounced upon her. Even so, she was perspicacious enough to accept that the very things about him that had initially turned her off—his poverty-ridden background and his appearance—later compelled her toward him. He'd always seemed timid and shy, though friendly. Gangly and, except for his beautiful hands, uncoordinated. And the satanic eyebrows annoyed her—they intersected at a point above the bridge of his long nose and reached outward like wings, with a span surpassing the length of his brow, narrowing to points on his temples. After three years of listening to each other play, criticizing, and rehearsing together, she'd felt nothing more for him than she had in the beginning when she met him after a concert, although his face had grown to meet his eyebrows, making him singularly and quirkily handsome.

The summer of her sophomore year, on July 1—she remembered because on August 1 she went to London with her parents—he was to have coached her for an audition with the Cincinnati Youth Orchestra. She had not seen him for a month; he'd been away at music camp. The rehearsal date had been prearranged, but Meredith could not recall whether she was to pick him up at his apartment or meet him at school. His mother's phone service had been temporarily disconnected. On the chance he'd be there, she went by the apartment. The summer sweltered, it seemed, much worse in front of his jaundiced building, where a clogged sewer added a nauseating stench. With the windows only cracked and the sunroof the only source of ventilation, Meredith was suffocating. She beeped the horn furiously. Still he didn't come. Finally she climbed out of the car and walked toward his building, aware, even in her impatience, of the grim surroundings. She'd been here before, yes, but never gotten out of the car. At a safe distance she could maintain a fantasy of life in this terrible neighborhood that her own neighborhood lacked, that it was in fact less horrible than her own. She had never asked Bruce about his life, quite simply because she did not want to know. It frightened her, and she wished to avoid it, perhaps for the same reasons her parents did, although of course she could not have appreciated that then. In the instant she walked into the building, the aristocratic black blood in her veins iced with revulsion. The hall was haunted by the odor of long-digested dinners, and the walls shone with grease and dirt. Her stomach flip-flopping, she climbed two flights and knocked on the door. A disheveled, toothless woman clutching a ragged dress over her sagging breasts answered, staring Meredith up and down. The smell of an overflowing litterbox leaked into the hall. No, Bruce was not home, no, she did not know where he was, try school.

At the conservatory, of course, she had found him, deeply engrossed in his piano, eyes closed, his face clenched in rapture. In the three weeks of living decently in a fresh, open place, he had become beautiful—his skin was burnished a deep rust, his lean and long body sensuous on the piano bench. An eerie, lonely plea poured from the piano, from him, from his soul, perhaps vivifying the utter serenity he'd left behind at music camp in upstate New York. Meredith thought she understood: it was the way she'd felt summers ago standing before the Grand Canyon—that she'd seen the most beautiful thing she'd ever seen in this life. So she sat down in a chair, closed her eyes, and remembered. Then she felt his hand on her shoulder. "Why are you crying?" he whispered, his eyes copper fires. Taking his hands into her own, she stood up, leaned into his body, watching all the while the unflinching, serious expression on his face as his arms bound her to him. Her mind became a Romantic canvas of all the beautiful places she'd been—Rome, Paris, Switzerland, Cairo, Nairobi—all the places privilege permitted. All the places poverty would deny him. The anagogy of each passed through her lips to his when they kissed. She had never kissed a boy before, much less loved one. In that moment, she felt understood for the first time in her life. Bruce knew.

And now it was all over. As if it never happened.

"You're late again," Emily Schumaker snapped when Meredith walked into the rehearsal room. She was doing scales up and down the keyboard, her face flushed with impatience.

"I got a flat," Meredith said, unpacking her cello.

"I don't have all day, Meredith. This is the third time you've been late."

"I said I'm sorry, Emily, what the hell do you want me to do?" she shouted.

"Try getting here on time," Emily shouted back.

"Look, it's been a shitty day. Please don't make it worse."

Meaning that she didn't have to do this concert at all. Well, that wasn't exactly true. The concert they were slotted to play the Schubert sonata for was the week before Thanksgiving vacation, and there was no getting out of it. Of course, she couldn't play it with Bruce after what had happened, and since she was committed to the performance and Emily was an excellent accompanist, there was no legitimate reason not to do the concert with her. When Meredith had asked Emily to accompany her, she seemed confused, reluctant, but then she had agreed. In fact, she had traveled to New York with Meredith, at Meredith's parents' expense, for the Juilliard audition, when Bruce suddenly had to take an audition at Curtis. She proved herself, and Meredith was accepted; Emily was not. Her talent, according to Bruce, would earn a position as a church pianist.

But Emily did not know the Schubert sonata and did not feel comfortable learning it in the little time they had, so they were playing the Brahms instead. Meredith liked the piece well enough, but because she sensed in Emily a hostility and was weighted down by despair over Bruce, her enthusiasm was gone. Still, they had been rehearsing for a week now and tonight played for over two hours, dissecting the first movement, extending and exaggerating notes, slowing the pizzicato until, musically high, Meredith was exhausted. At the end Meredith packed her cello up in silence. Just as she was about to leave, she asked Emily if she'd finished *Sister Carrie* yet. "I've got a hundred pages to read tonight or else I'm going to flunk the quiz tomorrow," she said.

Emily yanked her jacket from a chair and started to leave. Just beyond the door she stopped, her face a pyre of rage. "I just want to tell you that I'm really mad because you were so late. You think just because you're going to Juilliard that you're a prima donna. And I don't have anything important to do but wait for you! You black people and your stupid affirmative action," she cried. "It isn't fair." She ran out of the rehearsal room.

On a different day, in a different mood, and had the concert already been behind her, Meredith might have slapped her. But she was already stuffed with emotion, and there was no room for Emily. A wave of sadness washed over her. She sat down on the piano bench and fingered the keys, wondering what she should do. Should she back out of the concert altogether? Could Emily be counted on to follow through? Or should she just swallow her hurt and perform the Schubert with Bruce? Could she swallow her hurt? Their playing seemed inevitable. She'd gone so far as to call to have the program changed, only to be told it was too late, the program notes had gone to press, there was not time to find a replacement. Even as she rehearsed with Emily, in the back of her mind she knew she would perform with Bruce. It had nothing to do with her anger, which she knew she could not transcend, or with embarrassing them both in front of their families, friends, and teachers. It had to do with failure. She had a point to prove. Her parents wanted her to be a doctor, not a cellist. She was going to music school with the understanding that, if a life of performance proved unlikely, she would return to school so that she could teach music at the university or employ herself in a practical way, as a programmer for a radio station or critic for a newspaper—as long as she succeeded at something.

Too, the piano was Bruce's one-way ticket out of his world. Not performing with Bruce might exact a consequence greater than even failed love. Besides, everything had been planned. From their Schubert performance at Music Hall, to his solo performance of the Grieg piano concerto with the Youth Orchestra at the conservatory, to how they would live together in New York, how they would keep her parents from knowing about it. Even, after finishing Juilliard, when they would marry. June 1, 1996—for no other reason than that it was a date in the future of their long life together.

By her senior year even Meredith's parents had begun to accept Bruce, their fondness increasing in proportion to his success. Bruce had become somewhat of a local phenomenon, Cincinnati's prodigy. In celebration of Black History Month he'd given a Chopin and Schönberg recital at the Cincinnati Music Hall, which was written up favorably in the *Enquirer*. After that impressive feat, the acrimonious edge in her mother's voice rounded with a reserved affection. Her father, too, had been stunned by Bruce's achievement: it was unthinkable to both of them, indeed to the entire city, that a boy of such meager beginnings was capable of such brilliance. An act of charity or pity or respect or investment compelled them to offer to pay for his trip to New York for the Juilliard audition, and they were awed by his refusal to accept their gesture without bartering. In exchange for a bus ticket from Cincinnati to New York City and enough money for meals and a night's lodging at the YMCA, Bruce provided the ambience for two dinner parties and one cocktail party Meredith's parents gave. While Bruce humbly bused 700 miles, Meredith and Emily, chaperoned by her mother, would three weeks later jet to Manhattan, cab to her audition that afternoon, lunch at her father's expense at the Gotham Bar and

Grill, and return home by dinner, in tears. It seemed so unfair. Her whole life had been carte blanche, Bruce's, food stamps. His day would come, Meredith vowed.

"But I can't do it!" she cried, dropping onto the sofa in the music room.

"You've got all your life for love," was what her mother had said the first time she and her father met Bruce, after a concert junior year. The remark had irritated Meredith then. Now, devastated by betrayal and confused by priorities, she understood. Love complicated things. Her mother's words had stung, but youth obliged Meredith to resent the advice, to see it more as meddling; she could not plot how she and Bruce would live together and undermine it with doubt at the same time. The night Bruce had been introduced, Meredith found her mother sitting cross-legged on the sofa, hair in rollers, makeup stripped, pretending to be frightened when the door opened.

"I'm sure Bruce is nice, but you're too young to commit yourself to any more than college," she had said, gently; then, with near animosity, she added, "And don't you dare mention love to me!"

"Who said anything about a commitment or love?" Meredith had snapped. She looked at her mother incredulously, wanting to announce that she and Bruce had just fucked at Mt. Lookout Park. Then she realized, with strange shame, that she didn't know if Bruce had given to her what she had given to him. She had assumed she was his first. Why did that matter now?

"I could tell by the way you look at him that you are in love, Meredith. You think I've never been in love?"

"He's like me, Mom," she had said, once again uncertain. Could anyone raised in such an apartment be like her?

"I doubt it," her mother concluded, sanctimoniously.

"Because he's poor," Meredith had said angrily, "he's automatically worthless in your book. If he were Cecil, you wouldn't be so concerned, would you?"

"We've known Cecil for years, Meredith. We just met Bruce. There's a difference."

"You're right, there is. I don't like Cecil. I like Bruce. Why don't you give him a chance? Please, for me."

"Now you listen to me," her mother had said, with tenderness in her voice. "He'll break your heart, because that's what first loves do, and five years from now you'll regret all the mistakes you made."

"Mom, I'm not going to get knocked up, if that's what you mean," Meredith said dismissively.

"Oh, I know you won't. The regrets I'm talking about are the opportunities you passed up because of the promises some man made to you. Not everybody is entitled to love, Meredith. People who have nothing else to live for, and those who need someone to take care of or need to be taken care of. Build yourself a life. You may just find you're better off without love." Then she went to bed.

Afterward, Meredith had immediately phoned Bruce. "My mother thinks you're nice, which means your ghetto background bothers her but she won't admit it." As she spoke she remembered with contempt the introduction, and how her parents had marched away in a flurry of whispers. Bruce had cracked a pleased, ironic smile, hidden by his refined fingers, as Meredith snickered, quietly registering her parents disapproval. Whether because of their love or the musical intensity of their relationship, something about the way Bruce stood there struck her: his beautiful fingers poised on his soft lips, the delicate bones of his face, the smooth caramel-coated skin, the soft black hair that lay on his head like an infant's, and the copper eyes, two jewels under the thick, winged eyebrows. He was beautiful to her, but beautiful like a woman. It had amazed her that she'd never noticed this before, those facets of him. Right after the introduction, with the cello in the backseat and Bruce driving, they had immediately escaped to Mt. Lookout Park. There, they had spread an army blanket on the grass and made love, for the first time.

"Your mother's a charm," Bruce announced, laughing loudly into the receiver, so that he sounded strange to her. "So upright and uptight."

Meredith grew silly and pensive at once, hearing her mother's admonitions, overwhelmed by having fucked with Bruce, not sure why she was so suddenly concerned about his own virginity.

She had wanted to hang up and cry. No age would come when she was more mature, more sure that making love was the right thing to do, she thought as she had lain on the rich, soft earth, writhing under him and a blue blanket of darkness. Now she wasn't so sure. Tears irrigating her face, shaking as she held on to the receiver, Meredith had said to Bruce, "She also noticed that we're in love. She said that I would regret it. That first loves are always heartbreaks."

"How profound," Bruce had joked, guffawing into the receiver again. But there was irritation in his laughter, which had provoked her more. "If I graduated from Dartmouth like your old man did, your mother wouldn't like me."

His contempt was her own, of course, but all she heard was her own uncertainty.

"Will I, Bruce?"

"Will you what?"

"Regret it?"

"How the hell should I know, Meredith?" he had said, with a flippancy and anger that made Meredith age. After she had hung up that night, her virginal innocence already lost, a frightening truth planted itself in her mind: after all these years, she didn't really know him at all. But how well must you know someone to love them?

Cecil's football game!

She fled the music room, locking the door behind her, and ran down the long, poorly lit, cold halls, climbing up the four flights of stairs to the seniors' floor to her locker to get *Sister Carrie*. Faraway roars and cheers from the football game echoed through the corridors. Already it was quarter past nine, the game having been under way for nearly two hours. She retrieved the book and closed the locker door, and just as she was about to padlock it, she heard a door shut. Frightened, she turned to see Bruce approaching. She looped the padlock through and with rapid steps bolted off in the opposite direction. "Meredith," he called, in a low voice. But she didn't stop. She could hear hard-soled shoes against the tiled floor as they started into a dash after her, to intercept her, and only when he was directly behind her, standing on her shadow, did she stop, turning around to face him.

Swollen seconds went by before they spoke. His glasses clung to his shirt pocket. He stood only a hand taller than she, his soft mouth level with her eyes. His forehead shellacked with perspiration, and the long, bristly eyebrows glistening. In the dim hall light he seemed dark, glowing even. I don't know you, she thought, remembering the afternoon a week ago when she had fled a rehearsal room after seeing him kiss a man. The memory galvanized a part of her hurt into hatred, an indissoluble substance in her consciousness. They were to have celebrated her acceptance to Juilliard, and she had left school early to meet him at six-thirty. The auditorium door had been locked, so she quietly entered through the stage door. She could hear a beautiful tenor's voice singing Mahler in an embarrassing German. She waited in the shadows, able to see the back of Bruce and the profile of the tenor, who she realized was Derrick, a longtime friend of Bruce's who was going to Eastman in the fall. Derrick's corkscrew-permed hair shone in the stage light. Abruptly the singing ceased, replaced by sobbing. Bruce stood up, gently put his hand on Derrick's shoulder: "Don't worry about it, there's nothing you can do." Derrick buried himself in Bruce's arms, not in desperation, as it would have appeared, but sensuously. As she watched this display, the strangest feeling of disgust besieged Meredith. Then Derrick lifted his head from Bruce's chest and, looking at him intensely, kissed him. A brief passionate kiss, his face angled to Bruce's while his hands cupped Bruce's face. After a moment, Bruce pushed Derrick away. "Someone might see us," he said. Meredith did not hear any more; as quietly as she had come in she departed, devastated, in tears.

I hate you, she thought, looking at him now.

"I"—he swallowed hard—"I heard you rehearse. You sound great. Somebody needs to teach Emily not to pluck the keys." He smiled nervously, then slowly ran his tongue across his lips. He wiped his forehead with his hand.

"Thanks," she said weakly.

"Maybe we'll play—"

"Bruce, I'm in a hurry." She turned to go, but he called her name again. This time there were tears in his eyes, agony contorting his face. "Why won't you talk to me? What have I done? Tell me."

His destitution mocked her. "Please leave me alone. I don't want to hurt you. Don't you understand that we're finished. I'm dating Cecil. I don't want to talk to you again, ever. Now leave me alone."

"But why? You don't even like Cecil. What's the matter with you? You—"

Suddenly a great rage burned through her. "Me? Not me, you. You and Derrick—I saw—I saw you kissing him. You let him kiss you on the mouth. 'Somebody might see us,' I heard you, you shit, you fag."

His body tensed as though it had been shot. "It was a mistake, Meredith. It just happened. His father's on heroin, and his mother doesn't want him to go to Eastman, she's afraid of being by herself. I hugged him because he needed someone to hug him. He kissed me . . . he took advantage of my . . . he . . . he said he loved me. But I love you, Meredith. Only you."

"Liar! I bet you even fuck him," Meredith cried, confused, unable to remember how it was that Bruce was kissing Derrick, because she had not been watching Bruce, couldn't watch Bruce because it hurt too much, and had only seen Derrick's passion. Was Bruce enjoying it, were his arms around Derrick the way he put them around her, or was he loathing it? "You're a fag, face it! I have. That's why you hang around him. Only don't tell me that you love me!"

"It's not true, Meredith. Would I be here if I didn't love you? I'm not gay," he sobbed.

"Gay!" she repeated, calmly, as though letting it sink to depths. Then she ran down the hall, down the stairs and outside, away from the building, her breath coming in violent heaves. In the distance the crowd's roars surrounded her. Laughter, the razz of the cheerleaders, and the fans' rumbling voices, reverberated through the chilled night, promising victory or turbulent disappointment. The football field's lights burned brightly like a lighthouse on the edge of darkness. A desperate vessel lost in the unfathomable seas, Meredith drifted toward it, trembling, crying, exhausted. But she needed Cecil.

Thankfully the game was nearly over, with Walnut Hills leading by six points, twenty to fourteen. She climbed high into the bleachers, waving periodically at friends. Once college commenced, if she never saw these people, this school, this city, again, she would be grateful. She sat near a group of raucous girls ra-raing the inevitable victory and stared out at the vast field, on which the controlled clash was taking place. The announcer's words were meaningless and jumbled. Roger Bacon High, their opponent, scored a touchdown, then scored a goal. Number 1, quarterback, was Cecil Ingram, she knew from his varsity letter jacket. He passed and bulleted the ball perfectly, and with each play the team advanced down the field. The scoreboard flashed one minute and fifty-five seconds left to play. Cecil passed clear down to the goalpost, but the ball was intercepted by the other team, the interceptor running from one goalpost to the other for a touchdown. The field goal was good, giving Roger Bacon the lead by one point.

Forty seconds left. Roger Bacon kicked off. Walnut Hill's receiver was squashed moments after he'd caught the ball. Twenty seconds left. Cecil trotted onto the field. Huddled together with his teammates, he engaged his team members in his plans, and growling like lions, they burst asunder. Cecil seemed to stop playing football, though; his eyes searched the stands, then as though he'd found what he was looking for, he waved his hand, as he had done when he had spotted her on the practice field that afternoon she'd come to ask him for a date: his forearm moving back and forth like a windshield wiper. A strange chill went through Meredith: Cecil would love her for the rest of his life. She blushed with embarrassment that her duplicity had won his devotion, his love. She watched him move, curiously detached, as though seeing him for the first time. He hurled a long pass. The crowd went hysterical as the ball eagled over the field and landed in the nest of a team member. The man galloped with the ball the twenty yards to the goalpost and bucked and stomped when he arrived, slamming the ball to the ground.

The crowd's felicity flowed onto the field in riotous whooping and hollering. Most of the team miraculously vanished through the tunnels into the locker room before the rush overwhelmed them. After a time, the celebration subdued, the crowd dissipated, trickled out to the parking lot, and went home. Only then did Meredith walk down onto the field, near the tunnel through which the teams disappeared, where she expected Cecil would shortly reappear. Two white girls from French class waved as they passed on their way to the parking lot, and Meredith wondered if gossip had started about her and Cecil. The chilly air blew gently, and she wombed herself into her jacket as much as possible, then crossed her legs, making culottes of her miniskirt to keep the air out. Bored, she reached into her backpack and removed what she thought was Dreiser but was instead Toni Morrison's *Beloved*, which Bruce had given her for her seventeenth birthday. *To my beloved*, it had been inscribed. For two weeks she had carried the book around unopened; as she had complained when Bruce had asked if she'd read it yet, she couldn't read anything else about slavery, she was sick of it. Now she opened it and shortly was deeply immersed, connected to Bruce again, perhaps by the occasion for which he'd given it, or by a indelible past that intrigued and frightened her. Several pages later her attention veered from the page, and she looked to her right. Twenty yards away, leaning against the same wall she was propped up against, was Bruce. At first she turned away. Even then his image persisted in her mind, so she turned back, met his eyes, and felt his presence rush over her like a gentle warm breeze. "What should I do?" she cried to herself.

He inched toward her. Less than fifteen feet lay between them when Cecil trotted out of the locker room onto the field, paused briefly to scan the area for Meredith, allowed himself to be congratulated by the adulated fans, then headed toward her.

Charged with the voltage of victory, he gathered her up into his powerful arms. "Hot damn!" he shouted. "Did we play football or did we play football?" Crushed in his leather-sleeved arms, her head just clear of his shoulders, she saw Bruce turn and walk away.

"Way to go, Big C!" someone shouted.

She felt like a child squeezed in the affections of an adult. She squirmed just enough to let him know she wanted to be released.

"That was the best game of the year. Twenty-six to twenty-one. Hot damn," he brayed, exhilarated. She'd never seen him so animated. "When I saw you sitting in the bleachers, I knew we'd win. I knew it."

"You were waving at me?" she asked.

"Nobody else," he said.

"I didn't realize you play so well. But I guess if you didn't you wouldn't be going to UCLA on scholarship, would you?"

"Well," he said, "I had choices—athletic scholarships pay more." He laughed, with a certainty that reminded her of her father. "I think I played so well because I dedicated the game to you. Or, contrary to what the coach says, because of the exercise I got this afternoon," he said stupidly.

She cringed in embarrassment. "I should be getting home. My parents should be home by now."

"I thought you said they wouldn't return until Sunday night."

"My mistake. Tonight. They called right after you left."

As they walked in silence toward the parking lot, he reached for her hand and held it. A tingle went through her body, like electricity, and she shivered. "You don't like football, do you?" he asked suddenly.

"No," she said. Silence escorted them the rest of the way to the car. At one point in their walk, she turned to look at him, as though to remind herself of what he looked like. His eyes flew away like frightened birds. This intrigued her, but as she looked away she spotted Bruce, standing under a lamppost, leaning against a mailbox. He was waiting for her.

"Meredith," Cecil said, suddenly pulling her to him, his breath antiseptically sweet, sweat sprinkling his brow. He reached for her other hand, gently taking it into his own. He seemed to think better of this tête-à-tête, and they started walking again, toward Bruce. Suddenly Cecil said, "I lied to you about being a virgin. The fellahs all do it with virgins, you know, so the girls won't think we're studs. But I didn't want you to think that you were just another girl I was screwing around with.

Since that first time I came to dinner at your house, you've been very special to me. Making love with you was the best. I've never been with a black girl before."

Stepping beyond the eclipse of light into darkness, Bruce seemed to hesitate. Then he stopped, slowly turned around. Meredith gripped Cecil's arm tighter. Even with so many yards and so much misery between them, they could see each other clearly. She defiantly stared over him, around him, but inevitably at him, desperately. Just tell me now that it was all a mistake, that you don't like men, that you love only me, and I'll take you back, I love you. Her eyes pleaded. With an acknowledging nod, as though he'd heard her silent pleas, he vanished into the night.

"Meredith." Shame colored Cecil's voice. In front of her car they stopped, and he grasped her shoulders with his strong, muscled hands. Her face was shiny with tears. "Don't cry," he said, softly, "I'll never lie to you again. I swear I won't. I love you."

The words were like a splash of cold water on her face, reviving her from the revery of Bruce. For a second she didn't know him. Then she smiled wanly and climbed into her car. Both his eyes looked directly into hers, tremulous and vulnerable and purged. "Forgive me!" he begged.

Without having heard a word of his confession, but sensing the need for a response, she said yes. She kissed him briefly, finally. As she drove away, the words scissoring him out of her life shaped themselves. Friendship was all she could offer; ambition would carry them to opposite ends of the continent, "even though I carried it one step too far," as she would later write. When she approached her driveway, she saw Bruce's jalopy on the corner, then Bruce sitting on the steps of the house, his attention locked on her arrival as though he were willing it. She deadened the doubt in her heart and climbed out of the car. As she approached him, she realized that she would forgive him and trust him, that it was vain to fight it, for her love would not allow her to do otherwise.

Blood Is Thicker
Than Water

JACQUELINE WOODSON

◎◿◎

What Has Been
Done to Me

Mama is sitting across from me sipping her third vodka
tonic. She sips nervously, bringing the glass to her lips
for quick tastes before setting it down again—too far away from
her so that she has to reach across the table to retrieve it. I stare
at her dark fingers, nearly black at the knuckles, and the thin
gold bracelet steady on her wrist. Mama is not a slim woman,
though she says there was a time before us, me and my sister and
brothers, that she was as small as I am, maybe smaller. When
she is reminiscing she warns me that there will come a time
when I too will blow up like a balloon, too quick to stop the
pockets of fat from collecting at the back of my neck and around
my waist. It has not happened to me yet. But I watch for signs.

My seltzer goes flat in front of me now. In the quiet restaurant our conversation is filled with too much silence. We were,
and always have been, strangers.

"I'm ready to go home *now*," Mama says after a while and
picks up her drink again. "Everyone talked about how fun this
Mardi Gras thing would be. Just a bunch of noise and crowds. I
could get that at home."

Mama has brought me here to celebrate our birthdays. We

were born on the same day, twenty-five years apart. Fifty is harder on Mama than twenty-five is on me. I see the worry lines that have creased a path across her forehead, the strands of gray hair braided into her cornrows. I did not want to come.

"I bought the tickets already," Mama said into the phone, the Saturday before my birthday party. "I've never been anywhere."

"I had plans with friends, Mama," I reminded her, hoping the sound of my voice would also convey the fact that we had not sat down to dinner together in five years and would have absolutely nothing to talk about. It didn't.

"It'll be real nice," Mama continued as though I hadn't spoken. "We can have dinner in those Cajun restaurants. Maybe hear some jazz somewhere. I bought everything for you, the plane ticket, the hotel room. It's all paid for. Happy Birthday."

When Mama looks at me now, I shrug. I had not expected anything from this trip, so it is not a disappointing one. New Orleans isn't friendly to dark strangers.

"Maybe we could change our tickets," I offer. "See if we can leave tomorrow."

Behind me in New York, I have left a new lover. We have been in New Orleans two days now and I have refused to brush my teeth for fear that the taste of her might leave my mouth, the tips of my fingers. I have left a group of friends, whom I have grown close to in the three years since I have been out. I have left an apartment I share with my best friend, Dana, nights in the lamp-lit living room drinking rum in intimate groups, potluck dinners with too much tabouli, couples evenings and evenings out alone. Mama has left no one and nothing but the familiarity of a house she has lived in for twenty-two years, a bookshelf of best-seller novels that she reads lying in bed on her side, and a living room full of plants that cover one whole wall. And a memory of us the children, who, one by one, left her behind. Each taking as we went a different recollection of childhood.

"That man over there favors Joe, doesn't he?" Mama points and I turn in my chair to take in the man sitting alone at the bar. He is light-skinned with a beard. The man wears a jogging suit and sneakers. "You remember Joe, don't you?"

I nod. "You kicked William out because you were going to marry him."

Mama looks surprised for a moment then reaches for her drink again. "William shouldn't have been there in the first place," she mumbles.

"But he came back," I say, and Mama goes quiet, staring down into her glass.

Joe was going to buy Mama a house if she married him. A big house out on Long Island. With a pool if we wanted. There were five of us in three rooms then. Mama and William sleeping in the living room on a convertible sofa. Me and my sister, Pauline, in the middle room on a double bed. In the back room, my brothers Raymond and Tyrone and my Uncle Michell when he was home on furlough or out on probation. The apartment was a railroad with a small kitchen and bathroom falling off like the bottom of an "L."

Years later, Raymond, because he was the oldest, would be the first to leave, marrying the first woman he made love to and inheriting with her the five girls she had from a previous relationship. Then Pauline, moving at twenty-three to Hawaii where she hoped to grow her own pot because it was nearly impossible to buy the amount she consumed daily in New York on an office manager's income. I would follow behind her because I had fallen in love with someone Mama banned from the house, taking with me only the clothes I had bought working summer jobs between semesters at college and the books I had held on to through the years. Tyrone would be the last to go, following in the footsteps of my uncle, his favorite relative, ending up in Dannemora State Penitentiary with three years for possession and intent. I never learned what he possessed nor what he intended to do with it. Ours was not a family to process.

William and Mama had fought the day before Joe came over to make his promises. Then William packed a small suitcase and was gone. We waited. When Mama married Joe, Raymond was going to ask him for a Lionel train set. Pauline wanted a sewing machine. Tyrone wanted a box of toys. And I—sitting in the center of the circle of my brothers and sister—was going to be the first to tell my best friend, Clarise, that I had a father. A family. Like the Brady Bunch but smaller. Like the Partridge family but without any music except the saxophone Raymond played when the school let him bring it home and the love songs he wrote in secret. Years later, fighting the wars of adolescence with myself, I would steal his songs and write the lyrics on the sidewalk to amuse my friends, to embarrass my brother.

But Mama came home alone that night, pulling Milky Ways and Three Musketeers out of her bag. We huddled around her, expectant. Tyrone had started packing. Two pair of shorts and an undershirt were neatly folded in the bottom of a small blue leather-like suitcase.

"I can't marry him," Mama said, and I felt the chocolate and caramel go hard in my mouth. "He's not my type."

Later, as we lay in our beds, I heard the wall being peeled away in my brothers' room.

"Tyrone's eating plaster again," I whispered to Pauline.

"Mind your business and go to sleep," she whispered back, then sniffed.

On the bunk bed above Tyrone's, Raymond lay humming one of his made-up songs. In the cramped apartment, it was hard not to hear ourselves grieving.

William came in near dawn, leaving the smell of stale alcohol through our room as he passed.

That night Mama and William's bed moaned under the weight of them. That night I dreamed of swingsets and swimming pools and families.

At school the following Monday, I am yelled at for wetting my pants and sent home. The house is quiet and empty when I get there. There is no shower so I run lukewarm water into the bathtub and wash my skirt and panties while I bathe. William comes home at one o'clock. When I come out of the bathroom, he is sitting on my bed, stroking his crotch and smiling.

"I saw him again after he moved out the second time," I say to Mama now. She has ordered another vodka tonic and her eyes are growing distant behind the tall glass. Behind me, I hear the restaurant filling up. There is soft laughter coming from the table next to us and when I look over, I see that two women are sitting there. I smile, hoping to convey to them our common preference. My smile is not returned. Too often now I am realizing race gets seen first. It takes a longer look to see queerness. Many of the white women in New Orleans, like the ones I've seen in South Carolina, Puerto Rico, Amsterdam and Brooklyn, just don't have the time.

"Where'd you see him?"

"Once, when I was in high school, I saw him coming around the corner on Putnam. He wasn't drinking anymore, he said."

"You stopped and talked to him?" Mama folds her lips into her mouth. She is not mad, just curious.

"What else was I supposed to do?"

"But that was the whole reason I asked him to leave. Because of you and Pauline. People were warning me that he shouldn't be in the house with you two getting older . . ."

I look up at Mama and for the first time in three days, our eyes actually meet. Then my head begins to move on its own accord, slowly, from side to side.

"You never asked him to leave, Mama," I nearly whisper. "He left on his own."

"Is that what he told you?"

"No! That's what I remember. I was there, Mama. I heard you beg him not to go!"

They had been fighting for a long time when William left that fall. From the shelf above the closet he and Mama shared, he took the duffel he had ordered from a Spiegel catalog the month before and a small suitcase. There were at least a dozen suitcases and bags on that shelf, none of which had been used by any of us.

"I'm tired of being here living like a roach," William yelled. "And these kids not even mine!"

And Mama, sitting on the edge of her bed, shooed us out of the room, but not before the four of us, piled into the doorway, saw her there, tears smearing dark mascaraed trails down into her mouth.

"So what am I supposed to do here with this, William?

Where you going to go? Why don't you just stay here until you get yourself situated someplace? I'm not asking you for anything else . . ."

In the next room, I climbed beneath the thin sheet on my bed. I would never beg. If I lived to be a thousand, I would never beg for anything.

Pauline sat down beside me and began stroking the bottoms of my feet with her hand. The sensation was strange, new and soft.

"I hope he leaves," I whispered to her. "I hope he takes the express train the hell out of here."

"Don't curse," Pauline whispered back. Then after a moment, in a voice I could barely hear, she added, "Me too." We stared at each other. Our silence revealing our mutual connection to William.

"You're misremembering," Mama says to me now, pushing her glass across the table like an offering.

I tip the slithers of ice into my mouth and get up to leave.

"No I'm not, Mama. I wish I could remember it differently though. I can't. And neither can Pauline or Raymond or Tyrone. It's like a brick or something that somebody's tied around my neck . . ."

Mama shakes her head. "That's ridiculous. Nobody's carrying around any bricks. You were a lot younger then. You know how sometimes what happens gets mixed around a little over the years."

I reach into my back pocket, pull out the ten-dollar bill I have there and place it on the table beside my empty glass. "I'll pay for my stuff," I say softly.

"No. Don't be sil—"

"I don't mind. I'll meet you later at the hotel."

Walking out, I pass the man who looks like Joe. When our eyes meet, he smiles and beckons me toward the seat next to him. I give him the finger and keep walking.

Outside, I push through a crowd of college-looking boys guzzling beer, then look back through the plate glass window and see

Mama, staring off above her glass. I swallow hard and swear I will never let myself be broken.

I push through another crowd of tourists snapping pictures of a Commercial Street hotel and make my way toward the one queer bar I have found. There are no women inside, so I buy a beer and carry it across the street, to a dark alcove underneath an abandoned building. In the distance, I can hear laughter coming from both the bar and the other end of Commercial Street. There is a parade heading in my direction. Slowly, the bands grow louder. I guzzle my beer then run across to the bar for another one, walking back to the alcove slowly so as not to spill.

During Mardi Gras people go out and do all the things they've wanted to do all their lives but couldn't because others were around cautioning them against making fools of themselves. Some dress up in outrageous costumes, often of the opposite sex. Still others find comfort in exposing themselves to the crowds. Standing there, I wonder what I would do if I cared enough about the event. There is nothing. What I have done, and what has been done to me, is enough to make a hundred Mardi Gras.

I crush my cigarette against the cobbled street, light another one immediately, enjoying the sudden heat and light of the flame on my face. Across the street, the boys exit the bar in groups and pairs. I watch them for a long time, until the parade takes over the street between us.

You spend your life waiting for the moment when you are free of the history your life makes for you—the moment you can step outside of who you once were into the body of the person you have always been becoming. Then, from that point on, the things that have been done to you no longer matter. They become a part of a past . . . a past that you are no longer a part of . . . a past that never existed.

When I can stand the parade no longer, I fling my cigarette into the crowd, pop a breath mint and head back to the hotel. I know Mama will be waiting.

CHARLES W. HARVEY

To Taste Fire
Once More

I looked up and saw reflected in a distant mirror, this hefty soft-faced man between two old crippled women, walking away from me. When they got to the corner of the glass wall, my man and his two ladies suddenly disappeared. It was as if a huge mirrored blade had chopped them from my vision. I shifted my eyes to the left, and there they were again, coming toward me, gaining height with each slow step they took.

Seems like I had been sitting all morning in my yellow laminated chair in Sears's gray-walled waiting room, getting ripped off by the minute. My mama's little car was in their big shop. All I could do before my Savior and his Mary and Martha appeared to me in this vision was sit and watch the clock on the wall. Except it wasn't a real clock like nine o'clock, ten o'clock, et cetera, et cetera. It was a Sears dollar-sign clock, ticking off the dollars they were making off women and weak men like me. At first it started off slow, because there weren't too many customers there in the early morning. So it inched: one dollar . . . one dollar . . . one dollar . . . one dollar . . . Its speed quickened as an odd lot of souls filled up the waiting room. It ran so fast, I couldn't keep up with it. Like a jazz man's horn:

one one one one one . . . dollar!
one one one one one . . . dollar!
one one one one one . . . dollar!
one one one one one . . . dollar!

That noise beat on my ears. A mad saxophone player filling the room with his insanity. My eyes got all crossed trying to keep up with the digital readout running across the clock's face like a flow of red water. I couldn't stand it anymore.

That's when I noticed them.

My hefty man had on a pure purple lace shirt, brown flannel-like pants that flapped around his ankles, and brown-and-white wingtips ready to spread their wings and fly! He wore a vest and a cowboy hat too. He walked right between those two crippled women. The three of them plodded like old mules. One old lady was blue-black. She had on a white T-shirt with Mickey Mouse on the front (her jutting bosom made Mickey's ears elephantine), red stretch pants that stretched from Houston to Odessa. She leaned on a four-pronged walker and lumbered like an old hippo. The other ancient puss was the color of my beautiful orange-brown man. And bless her poor lame self, when she sat down her lime dress flew up, and her thighs went their separate ways. Her chintzy black wig was an unruly swatch of poodle hair, shining and fully blessed by the fluorescent lights. Old brown boy sits next to me. His rump hit the seat and stirred up a funny-smelling breeze that sneaked into my nose and down my throat.

"Man, I got me some trouble this morning. I got hands full of trouble," he said, half smiling and squinting his gray trout eyes at me all at the same time. Then his trouble started yapping at him.

"Bully! I say, Bully! You gone let your mama and your aunty die of thirst in this here steaming room? Get up off your behind, boy, and get us a Coke!" Her wig bounced up and down, and all them gray hairs underneath peeped out and waved at everybody. Bully got up like a man who carried his trouble in his rear end.

"I don't want no Coke. Ain't they got orange Nehi?" Bully's aunt asked.

"Lord, Gladys, I ain't seen a Nehi sodawater in years. Let Bully buy you a Coke or a Seven-Up."

"I want a cup of coffee!"

"Aunt Gladys, there ain't no coffee here," Bully half whined.

"There's coffee somewhere in Houston!"

"Gladys, I swear, you sure is contrary," said Bully's mother.

"Aw, go on and get me a Coke. Shoot!"

Bully grasped both sides of the red-and-white vending machine and leaned forward. He studied the selection buttons like a man reading names on a memorial. Bully dropped his coins into the slot, letting each one trip the machine's registers and make that electronic gargling sound before dropping the other. The Cokes crashed down the chute like clattering bowling pins.

"Oh, Bully! Do you have to make so much noise! If you didn't want to buy the things, why didn't you say so?"

"Mama, what you want me to do, reach my hand up in there and pull them out? That's a machine. I ain't got no kind of control over it."

"Inez, I told you a long time ago you ought to have put a strap across his naked ass when he was growing up. Look how he talks to you now."

"Hush up, Gladys. Just because you beat your child to a cripple—"

"She deserved every lick. Bully, this thing ain't cold!"

"Mine ain't either," Bully's mama said. "Neither is my heart."

"I doubt if you'll be invited to sit at any Saint's table soon," Bully's aunt retorted.

Bully sat down next to me again. His knee brushed mine because I was sitting wide-legged and mannish. I moved my leg away a little, and again his knee sought mine. I got mad. I wondered why this lace cowboy was trying to invade my space.

"Man, I got me a lot of trouble. You want some of my trouble?" He squeezed my arm with his soft hand and smiled. "Just look at them. Ain't they beautiful?"

I looked at the old women slurping their Cokes, their fish lips trembling, their legs gapped; Aunt Gladys's wig sitting cockeyed, and Inez's stretch pants about to explode cellulite. They were

Halloween and Mardi Gras sitting side by side. I looked at Bully. There was a thin mustache above boyish lips—thin and petulant, slightly upturned. Lips that I kissed when I was nineteen. Carl Anthony! Lord. Lord.

Jesus, make him go away now like you did then. You let the devil cut his body to ribbons in that filthy bookstore. The men, too busy to notice his dying, groped and danced in that boy's blood. I don't want to go back to those memories. Tell your imp to slay this memory. I don't want to grieve all over again. Grief, my constant lover. When I was a child, it chose me. Grief led the chorus at my father's funeral.

"Who killed Bully Red with that sweet sweet sweet potato pie?" Fingers pointed at my mama and Aunt Gladys. My father had sown his seed in both women and was going to leave them for a white woman.

Grief, secrets, and hate vised us. You look at me, and you see my father's smooth red-clay face. A face that Carl Anthony kissed. Carl, my moment of salvation and freedom. Lord, why can't a moment be forever? Me and Carl Anthony under the spell of the funk of piss-filled toilets and the faint rose of Lifebuoy soap in the steamed air. Carl Anthony's solid brown body trembling as if an electric current was trickling through him. Our tongues were tiny electric eels. Our fingers, the tentacles of jellyfish. I looked at Bully's mouth and felt my tongue push toward my lips to escape my mouth and seek sweet fruit. Suddenly a blast of cold rushed out of the air vent above me and hit me in the face. I was startled. My revulsion rose.

"Say, mister, I don't like your soft hand on my arm. And I don't like the feeling it's making me feel. So keep your trouble to yourself."

"Bully, I want a chocolate bar," his mama pleaded.

"Bully, is they got a toilet in here? I told you I been taking some medicine. I wish y'all hada left me at home."

Bully took his hand off my arm but kept his knee, which felt like a stone, next to mine. He looked at me with eyes old and cloudy like a long-dead trout. He sighed. As his foul breath left him, some invisible force pulled his mouth into a frown. His neck disappeared, and his whole head sank into his fat chest.

I roll my eyes, get up, brush my ass pocket off, and leave my ass of trouble behind me in that chair. I feel too glad to be free. The hot sun kisses my face when we meet on the other side of the glass door. Then in all of that warmth, I feel a thin, cold hand on my wrist. "Bully! Bully!" a voice calls me. I turn and look straight into Mama's quivering face.

Trapped. I am still sitting, hammered and vised between these two old women. There, outside, is some other sassy gum-smacking buck, tasting freedom. I watch him race across the street, daring the oncoming cars to strike him down. When he gets to the other side, he stuffs his hands in the front pockets of his blue jeans. He cocks his head to the side and takes on this slow I-own-the-world hip-swaying walk. I watch him for blocks until the heat vapors rise from the sidewalk and consume him. I catch myself feeling ashamed for watching him, wanting him, wishing he could move me backward through my years (fifty, forty, thirty . . .), ashamed for feeling that just a touch of his flesh would propel me back to the blood, sweat, and soap arms of Carl Anthony—to taste fire once more. I sit and shiver between these ancient women, waiting for the clock to stop.

BECKY BIRTHA

❧

Ice Castle

I

Gail. Gail Fairchild Jenner. The same Jenner as the city
councilman for the West Side. The same Fairchild that
the library up on the campus was named for. White Anglo-
Saxon Protestants. The Bourgeoisie. What the hell was she doing in love with somebody with a name like that?

Only Maurie didn't know those things at first. She met Gail
up on the campus, at the Women's Center, and thought she was
just anybody. Somebody going to school part-time at night,
somebody halfway poor—just anybody.

Maurie was not a student anymore. She'd been out of college
a year now. Before that, working the whole time, it had taken her
seven years from start to finish. She figured Gail's life might be
something like her own.

Gail wore big round glasses. Her large hands kept pushing the
short, light brown curls back away from her high forehead, and
the curls kept falling back to cover it anyway. Gail was tall and
long-limbed, in the standard blue jeans everyone wore but Maurie—who was always coming from work—and an Aran knit
sweater Maurie should have known was expensive, only she was

thinking Gail would have made it herself. So there was nothing, really, to give Gail Fairchild Jenner away.

"My name's Gail—Gay." Could she really be that obvious—or that naive? Gay—was she? Was that the point? Now she was laughing, and Maurie was confused. I won't call her that. I'll call her Gail.

And what else had Gail said? Maurie strained to recall every word. It was at the Women's Center's annual poetry reading, and Maurie had been the last to read.

She loved giving readings—that was the one time when she felt completely visible. For all her colorfulness, for all her beads and bangles and bright batik prints, most of the time she felt that other people didn't see all of her. They saw only what mattered most to them at the time—her race, or her gender, or perhaps her age—and then didn't bother to look any further. It was only when she was on stage, standing up among a room full of attentive listeners, that she felt all her colors leap into focus.

Here in this wintry city, surrounded by pale, restrained faces, her full-blown features and deep colors felt like a rich, tropical ripeness. Her tan skin, freshly oiled, held the faint smell of coconut and glowed beneath the sliding silver bracelets that rang against one another when she lifted her hands. She could feel the same glow in her face. The trade beads and cowrie shells that she had braided into her hair swung and clattered softly against one another. And the soft lamplight picked up all the colors in the woven fabric she wore around her shoulders—the saffron yellow, the green, the earth red and the black. At times like this she felt thoroughly visible and utterly sure of herself, high and happy and perfectly loveable.

She loved reading last because she felt like the spotlight stayed on her, a lingering aura, long after the program was over. Her words would be the ones that echoed in people's memories; she would be the one they came up to talk to over the wine and cheese. And maybe some night some new person would come, excited by her work, curious about her life . . .

She balanced her Wheat Thins and mozzarella cheese in a

napkin and turned around to find Gail standing before her, long-legged and spare in the loose, bone-colored sweater, a spill of tousled brown curls capping her face.

"You're good," was the first thing Gail said.

"Thanks," Maurie said, smiling, pleased. And Gail was smiling back, her gray-blue eyes keeping Maurie's with an intensity that held her connected, in spite of the chattering crowd. So that Maurie waited, knowing they had more to say to each other.

"Why do you write poetry?"

It was a question nobody had ever asked after a reading, and it took her so unexpectedly that Maurie told the truth without thinking. "Because I want people to love me."

Gail let out a gasp of surprised laughter. "Seriously? Does it work? Do they?"

"I don't know. . . ." Maurie was suddenly self-conscious. "They don't tell. . . ."

"No one has ever walked up to you after a reading and said, 'Hey.'" And for a moment everything stopped and hung, precarious. "'I've fallen in love with you.'"

Maurie stared, caught in the storm-colored eyes. Gail stood so close that Maurie could inhale the faint, warm scent of her skin, damp beneath the layers of jersey and wool. She was still smiling, but now the line of her smile was a question, waiting.

How did we start talking about this? Who *is* this woman, and why is she asking me this?

"I didn't mean I'd expect somebody to do that." She was losing ground, the performer's sureness and self-confidence ebbing away. She turned back to the refreshment table, and Gail was right beside her, filling Maurie's Dixie cup from the half-gallon jug of wine, and then filling her own.

"But you'd like it if someone did." Her voice was too low, too familiar, and Maurie backed up a step. What was going on? Was Gail coming on to her? Was this how women . . . got started? She was confused, nonplussed, yet at the same time still pleased.

"Well, everybody wants to be loved." But what she was thinking was that all the poems she had read that night had been about women. She had planned it that way as a matter of course, because this was the Women's Center. But all those women in the poems. So what must this Gail think? Maurie took a swallow, the purple liquor sharp in her throat.

"And you . . . fall in love with people very easily."

No one ever talked to her this way. Gail's words, the closeness of her seemed to demand an answer. Her expectant eyes were like a wide, wet winter sky. "Yes," Maurie admitted. "Yes, I fall in love with people all the time."

"Maurie, hi. I really like that one poem you read—about the old woman in the bandana, on the bus, and how she used to be the prettiest girl at all the dances. . . ." She was aware of the event again, the festivity. That whole business with Gail had scarcely taken a minute. No one had even left yet. But now Roberta was asking her, "Do you want a ride? I have to leave now, because I promised Gary I'd pick him up after his class."

"I don't think I'm ready to leave yet. But thanks, anyway." She said it with no idea how she would get back to the West Side. Of course, she could take the bus, but they ran so seldom after nine at night. She pictured the dark, deserted corner where she'd have to get off the Main Street bus and wait for the Twenty-six. There was nothing there—just the tall iron fence and wide gates of the cemetery behind her, and the flick of car lights cruising across her body, one after another. She knew it wasn't safe. She didn't care.

There was the rest of the social thing spinning out. She talked to the other readers, to women she remembered from her English classes. She drank Chianti in the Dixie cup and listened, asked questions and answered questions, and watched Gail across the room, drinking Chianti, too, but standing alone. It was plain Gail was watching her, was waiting, too, for this to be over.

The crowd gradually thinned, quieted, until the last women had their coats on, at the door, and one of them looked from Gail to Maurie and said, "You two got a way to get home?" *You two.* At the same time they both said yes, and the woman who'd asked them said, "O.K. I need to drop these evaluations off at American Studies, and then I'll be back to lock up. But if your ride comes before that, could you just make sure the door's shut tight?"

"*Do* we have a ride home?" Maurie asked, after the others were gone.

Gail nodded, added, "We might have to wait awhile. My sister's supposed to pick me up." Gail dropped down on the couch at the side of the room and stretched out. Maurie hesitated, then sat down crosslegged on the floor near the end of the couch. She leaned against the wall. The room that had been crowded too small a few minutes before was suddenly vast and silent. She couldn't take her eyes off Gail's curly head, lying on her sweater-clad arms. . . .

"Maurie." It was the first time Gail said her name. "Maurie, do you ever fall in love with women?"

"Oh, yeah. At least as often as I've fallen in love with men." That muddled everything. Why had she brought up men? She wasn't being clear. But it wasn't clear, anymore, even to her. She *had* fallen in love with men. And women, too. She would try to tell what was true. "I've fallen in love with women lots of times. But nothing's ever come of it. We never did anything about it. Or maybe they didn't feel the same way. . . ."

She'd often imagined it otherwise—the woman with whom things would go differently. A woman her age, or maybe a little older, with the same experiences behind her. Who'd already been through college, and communes, and consciousness-raising groups, and was through with all the double dealing and disappointments that went down with men. Who was just as ready, now, as she.

"Maurie, how old are you?"

"Twenty-five."

Gail sat up on the couch and drew her knees in suddenly to her chest. "How old do you think I am?"

"I don't know." She began to look at Gail closely, at the smooth unblemished complexion, the gangly, still awkward limbs.

"Younger than me," she said slowly. "Maybe twenty-one or . . . twenty."

"I just turned seventeen last week."

The sister who came didn't look anything like Gail. The dark fringe of bangs that edged straight across her brow gave her face a scowl. Or maybe that scowl was because of Maurie. . . . In the dark car, in their bulky winter clothing, the three of them sat squeezed together in the front seat while the radio played AM inanity. She could tell when Gail turned toward her, feel her eyes on her. It was too dangerous to turn and meet them; she kept her focus out through the windshield.

There had been no snowfall to speak of yet, this year. The dry, scant flickers that were falling now would not stay on the ground. Still, Gail's sister steered the big station wagon carefully through the deserted streets. In Gail's family, there were still another sister and three brother Jenners. Six altogether. They'd be all over the West Side!

Maurie tried to think of the things to say that the sister might expect from her. But she felt slow, flushed and heavy-headed, too stoned. She wished desperately that she and Gail could be alone. Gail's mittened hand lay against Maurie's corduroy covered thigh—loosely, casually, staying.

II

As much as Maurie hated the winter, hated going out in the cold, three times in three days she walked up toward Chapin Parkway. Her face burned in the assault of the wind; her toes froze after the first five minutes. She walked toward the block of the Parkway where Gail lived—only five blocks from Maurie's apartment—coming closer each time, and then going home. The third time she walked past the house. It was stone, set back in a deep lawn, with a drive curving around the side. It seemed to have hundreds of windows, all of them polished bright and shining like magnifying glasses.

She felt outrageously conspicuous. In her life, among people she didn't know, she often felt exotic. She liked that feeling, to be someone special who stood out from the crowd. But in this neighborhood, even though there was not another person on the block, she felt garish and outlandish. The color of her skin felt like a sunlamp burn—over-exposed and wrong. The beads she had braided into her hair seemed artless, and the colors in her skirt, the bright lacings in her knee-high boots, loud and gaudy. She kept her eyes focused straight ahead, and did not look to see who might be watching from those many windows.

Gail had given her a phone number, but she couldn't call her. Not at home. Among all those people, the odds that Gail would pick up the phone were only one in nine. Who could she tell them she was?

Evenings when she stayed in her apartment, she sat by the window, waiting, watching the sky darkening into that deep, luminous blue—a long half hour. Then indigo. Then night. Outside in the alley, the wind whipped and wheeled, rattling the glass, shrieking and whistling round the corners of the building. She was glad there was still no snow. But without it the winter seemed even more relentless.

Nobody would be out walking on nights like this. She could come. She could bundle up so well that no one would recognize her anyway. And no one would see her turn down the alley, slip in at the downstairs door. Come on Gail. You have to come here. Because I can never come to you. A white woman, a younger woman could maybe get away with it. Show up some Saturday afternoon in Nikes and a baggy sweatshirt, just "Tell your Mama and your Papa I'm a little schoolgirl, too." But not Maurie.

Saturday night she turned the radio to the blues show that came on every week. She was drinking *vin rose*. She might as well keep on, and get drunk by herself. It seemed appropriate. It was late, going on eleven, when the phone rang.

"I couldn't call you before. My brother Ted listens to everyone's phone calls. This family is like the headquarters of the FBI. My kid sister Wendy snoops in my drawers all the time. And my mother's just as bad—always finding excuses to poke around in my room. Daddy just 'checks up'—you know, finds out from neighbors and friends of his where you've been seen and in the company of whom. I hate living in this family!"

"Sounds familiar." Maurie grinned into the receiver. "I

couldn't wait to go away to school." She'd had to pay a high price for that privilege—waiting tables, typing, through the summers and the semesters, too.

"I wanted to live in the dorm, but they wouldn't let me. They think I'm too young. And anyway, they're not going to pay room and board for me to live at the other end of the same town. Not that they couldn't afford it."

"Listen," Maurie broke in. "Can we . . . did your brother go out tonight? The one who listens to your calls, I mean."

"Oh, I'm not at home."

"Where are you?" She pictured Gail standing in a telephone booth while the traffic passed and the wind stormed at the glass walls. There was a pay phone on the corner of Elmwood Avenue, half a block away. Maybe Gail had forgotten exactly where Maurie lived. . . .

"I'm babysitting tonight. The kids finally went to sleep."

"Oh. Babysitting."

"You have a regular job, don't you?" Gail's voice was wistful. "What do you do?"

"I teach. At a co-op pre-school." For a second she thought about the children in her class, their parents. . . . What would they think if they knew what she was up to? What *was* she up to? Trying to seduce a seventeen-year-old kid?

"What about you?" she asked. "What are you doing in school?"

"Failing." Laughing. Nervous, embarrassed.

"Why?"

"I'm not doing it on purpose. I just—don't care about it enough. It's not that important to me."

"What is important to you?" Wishing she would say, "You."

"I don't know," Gail said. "I'm trying to figure that out. I'm real depressed a lot of the time. I drink too much. Sometimes I think I'm suicidal."

"Maybe you don't belong in school right now. Christ, you only just *turned* seventeen. You must be precocious as hell."

"But I'm *failing*."

"That happens to a lot of people," Maurie said. "I failed courses my first year in college, too."

"But I'm supposed to be so spectacular. Everybody's holding their breath, waiting for me to distinguish myself. Since I refuse to be a social butterfly, I'm supposed to be a scholar."

"They *want* you to be a social butterfly?"

"You don't know my family," Gail said. "I mean, my mother sent me to etiquette school. And dancing lessons. Then, last year, I was supposed to be a debutante. We almost came to blows over that."

Maurie laughed. "You don't mean that, seriously?"

"Yeah, I do. Some etiquette, huh? She used to hit me all the time when I was little. Just over anything. Like if I left my stuff on the dining room table, or if I forgot to change my clothes when I came home from school. She was always hitting me. Now that I'm bigger than her, she doesn't dare. But she gets her way most of the time, anyway."

Her own anger flared up so fully and swiftly it surprised Maurie. She could see Gail as, maybe, a ten-year-old: an awkward, big-boned child who could never do anything right— blinking back tears from the red-faced sting of a full-handed slap. Those people. They had everything. Why did they have to hit a kid?

"My mother drinks even more than I do," Gail said. "I think she's an alcoholic."

"What about your father?" Maurie asked, finally.

"Dad's okay, I guess. He's pretty liberal, compared to a lot of kids' parents. He doesn't try to run my life too much. He just doesn't understand—about this college thing—that this just isn't what I want to be doing."

"And what is it," she asked again, "you'd rather be doing?"

Gail was thinking. "I really love track," she said, after a little while. "I guess I'd just spend all my time doing sports if I could. Hey," her voice suddenly came alive, "do you run?"

"No. . . ."

"Do you play tennis? Do you ski?"

Maurie sat holding the phone, wishing, for the first time in years, that she were somebody else.

After she hung up, Maurie thought over what more she knew of Gail now. Not much. Gail played the clarinet. Badly. But her mother didn't want her to quit. Gail had never held down a paying job in her life. Gail definitely did not belong in a ballroom. . . . But why hadn't Maurie asked the things she really wanted to know? Why hadn't she asked Gail if *she* ever fell in love with women? Or when she could see her again?

Gail called her once—twice again. From another sitting job, from the campus one night. No, her mother always expected her home for dinner. She'd want to know who the friend was, to meet her first. She was going on a skiing trip this weekend with her sister's youth group from church. She had exams to study for next week—final exams. It was a joke; she knew she would fail them all. But studying would look good, anyway. Her parents didn't have any idea—and the blow wouldn't fall until they got her grades in January.

"I didn't expect you to be home again on a Saturday night," she told Maurie. "Two weeks in a row. Don't you ever go out?"

"I guess I'm not much of a party-goer." But she had been asked to a party—over at Wendell's tonight. She'd forgotten, conveniently, wanting to stay home in case the phone rang.

"What were you doing?"

Drinking again. Wishing you'd call. Writing a poem about you. "Nothing."

The other nights—when Gail didn't call—would lag and creep. This was not the way she had expected this thing to go. She wasn't sure what exactly she had wanted, but knew this wasn't turning out to be it. Sometimes the tedium sent Maurie out of the house, hurled her into the early darkness to force her way against the wind, up Elmwood Avenue, toward the Parkway. The wind chill factor was often well below zero, but at least it hadn't snowed yet. The shops along the Avenue were open late, lit up for the holidays. Maybe Gail would have to do some Christmas shopping. . . .

Roberta and Gary lived on Elmwood Avenue. She hadn't called or stopped in to visit for a long time. She didn't do it now. What could she say when they asked what was going on in her life?

Wendell lived a few blocks down, on Lafayette. She could

imagine his response. He'd pretend that he was trying to take her seriously. "Now wait a minute. Lemme make sure I get this straight. She rich. She white. And she *how* old? And you in *what* with this chick?" She had always thought Wendell was fun, had always laughed at the way he spared no one, nothing with his jokes. Now she felt like she had to protect herself.

Once, when she got off work at three-thirty, instead of going home she took the bus in the other direction—up to the campus. She wandered around randomly, then bought coffee in the Rathskeller—where students who were failing usually hung out. Sitting alone, drinking her coffee, it occurred to her that the answer was to go away. She would go away for Christmas—back to Boston, to spend the holiday with her family. Maybe it would put this whole thing in a different perspective. Maybe she would forget all about Gail.

III

Then she came. Two days before Maurie was to leave for Boston, the phone rang—nine o'clock on Saturday morning—and she knew in an instant it was Gail. "Listen. I could come over this morning. My mother's out of town and Nancy and Ted are off in Williamsburg at my cousins'. I have to go to a music lesson this afternoon, but I have a couple of hours until then. . . ."

Gail seemed to take up all the space in Maurie's small, square living room. She sat on the couch—it was a day bed, really—and made the legs look spindly, rickety. She slouched down, and her long legs stretched most of the way across the floor. She had thrown the bright blue jacket on the only other chair, where it collapsed looking winded, with its arms flung out. Now Gail was rubbing the fog from her glasses in the folds of another expensive sweater—soft blue and green. In the daylight, her short curls looked more gold than brown.

"Are you hungry?" Maurie asked. "I mean, I was just going to fix myself some breakfast when you called. So I thought I'd wait to see if you wanted some too."

A wide smile. "What are you having?" An adolescent's insatiable appetite.

"Eggs and toast, and orange juice. I could make you eggs, however you like."

Gail was interested, had followed her into the narrow kitchen. "How are you having yours?"

"Poached."

"I'll have one, too."

She filled the saucepan and set it on the burner, began to slice the bread. "One poached egg on toast, coming up."

"No, just plain."

"Just plain? Just one egg? All by itself?" Maurie had never eaten a poached egg except on toast, in her whole life. "You don't want *any* toast?"

"Well, maybe one piece. On the side."

Her own eggs came out perfect, every morning. This morning she did everything the same way she always did, boiling the water and turning it down, then stirring to make a funnel in the center of the pot, slipping the egg from the saucer into the swirling center. But the white splayed out from the yolk and spread, in lumpy streamers, all through the water. She had forgotten to flip the timer, and as soon as she scooped the egg out, she knew it would be runny and underdone. It sat there, a pale and almost colorless blob, while the water ran off into a puddle around it, on the white china plate. She had forgotten the toast, and now it was scorched from her quirky, antiquated toaster, one side undone, the other crisp black. She forgot to put the salt on the table, too, didn't think of it until she sat down to eat her own egg—and Gail was already finished by then. There was no butter, because Maurie never bought anything but margarine. But Gail insisted that everything was fine.

Maurie had imagined this visit so many times. She had always thought it would be evening—the two of them surrounded by quiet jazz and soft lamplight. She had wanted Gail to be charmed by her tiny apartment, and the way she had decorated it—the brilliant African fabric that covered one wall in a sunburst of color, and the instruments: the big-bellied calabash with its shiny beads that hung from a strap on the wall above the chair, the tall conga drum in the corner. Sometimes when people came in they would start to play with the instruments. Almost no one could resist the kalimba, resist pressing a few notes from its flat metal prongs. And then, later, she'd thought that Gail might ask to see more of her poetry. . . .

But Gail was restless, moving quickly from the kitchen back to the other room, stretching her long legs out, drawing them in, taking off her glasses and cleaning them again, glancing from time to time out the window that faced on the empty alley. "Let's go out," she said.

"Out? But . . . it's freezing. It looks like it's going to snow."

Gail's eyes were excited, alive for the first time since she'd come. "Maybe it will!" And when Maurie joined her at the window, kneeling beside her on the couch, Gail said, "It was beautiful, walking over here. The clouds are so thick, and so low. . . . We can go over to the cemetery. There's never anybody there."

Never anybody there—to see what? Go to the cemetery—and do what? Go for a *walk*, in *Buffalo*, in *December*? Incredible as it seemed, she was pulling on her own sweater, her jacket, muffler, going out to walk in the cemetery, in the middle of winter, with Gail.

They walked side by side, following the wide road that led through the center of the grounds. Everything was frozen solid—the stiff colorless grass and the creek. It seemed as if their voices had frozen up inside them. There was no sound, except the crunch of the two pairs of boots in the gravel at the edge of the road, and now and then a bird calling.

They didn't touch. Yet Maurie could feel a kind of aura, like a magnetic field, surrounding Gail, as though there were electric in the blue of Gail's down jacket, a charged field that was tangibly alive, the closer Maurie's body shifted toward Gail's. She wondered if Gail could feel it, too.

Gail took long steps, her hands swinging at her sides, and stared straight ahead into the distance, at the bare lace of tree branches far off against the low gray sky. Maybe Maurie was wrong. Maybe Gail didn't feel anything. And nothing was going to happen—not today, not any other day. Maybe thinking that there was anything between them was just building castles in the air—fantastic creations spun from nothing—elaborate towers, tunnels and turrets, whimsical twists and turns. Elegant fragile architecture that simply wasn't there.

In the air—but what she pictured was a castle made of ice. High walls arched into vast doorways and cathedral roofs. Down long halls, footsteps rang like bells and echoed up the steep stairways, through the vaulted, empty rooms. Exquisitely beautiful—but not a place where anyone could live, not a place she could stay. The air inside—cold as crushed crystal, filling the lungs. The castle perfect, solid and sound, as shiny and smooth as glass. On the first day of summer it would be gone.

Gail's voice, disappointed, broke the silence. "It isn't going to snow. It's too cold." And then, a few steps further, "I have to head back. I've got to get to my lesson."

"Gail?" Maurie's own voice sounded as sharp, as penetrating as a bird's. A gulp of cold air slid down her throat. "Gail, are you a lesbian?"

There was a long, quiet stretch. They were going uphill, and she could hear herself breathing hard, the air coming forth in rhythmic puffs from her open lips. Finally Gail answered.

"I don't know. I've never been—involved with anyone. But I think it would be women—a woman—if I did."

Maurie didn't think before she said the next words—they just came. "Are you afraid of me?"

Gail turned to her, surprised. But there was something else—relief—in her face. "Yeah. You're right. Yeah, I guess I am."

"Of what? Why?" And when Gail didn't answer, just shook her head, she asked, "What do you think of me? I mean, who did you think I was? Why did you want to know me?"

Gail turned to her as if to explore Maurie's face for the answer. "I *did* want to know you. I mean I still do. But it was . . . you just seemed so different from me. I don't mean just . . ." she looked away, then back, "in the obvious ways. Well, maybe that's part of it, but it was more. There's a way you've got about you—standing up there reading those poems, you just seemed so sure of yourself, so absolutely you. All the while you were reading

I kept thinking—I saw something in you that I wanted, wanted to have, wanted to be. . . ."

Gail's stride was still long, determined, the heels of her boots biting into the frozen gravel. But the pace had slowed. "When we gave you a ride home, and I saw where you lived, on that alley over that garage, all by yourself, I just thought you must have your life all together, exactly the way you want it to be. And then I couldn't imagine what you were doing trying to let me into it. I thought—I must have been wrong about you. I thought you'd know better than that."

"You think that little of yourself?"

More long, silent steps, slower. Gail's head was down now, eyes on the toes of her boots, and she didn't answer.

"So is that what you think of me, now? That I'm not all that wonderful after all, since I want to be . . . friends with you?"

"I don't know what to think anymore." At the crest of the hill, as Gail raised her head, a draft of wind lifted the muffler at her neck, blew back the loose spray of curls around the edge of her face, and settled it back. They walked on. "I think, maybe," Gail said, "I'm not sure if I should see you again."

The words tumbled the world awry. Panic, fear flew flapping through Maurie like a wounded bird. "You don't want to see me again?"

"Oh, yeah. I'd like to. . . ."

The unspoken end of Gail's sentence hung in the air—the part that began with the word "but"—while the panic inside Maurie lurched and beat. She asked, "Because of your family?"

"No, not them." Gail flicked her head in a single, abrupt shake. "They can't run my life forever. I just don't want to—ruin it for you."

"Ruin how? Ruin what?"

"Anything—everything."

They kept walking, back the way they had come. Beside her, Gail's green woolen mittens swung at her sides, in the rhythm of her stride. Her face was downcast again.

The noise of traffic was audible once more—a long lean on a car horn, and now the loose, futile clanking of somebody's snow chains against the dry road surface. The Delaware Avenue gate loomed suddenly just a few yards away.

Maurie's face, her hands, even her toes were tingling with heat. "Look," she said, the words crowding out in a rush. "You don't have to protect me. Maybe you don't like yourself all that much, but *I* like you. . . ." In Gail's face she caught her response—the quick flash of irrepressible pleasure. ". . . And I want to see you again."

At the corner of Gail's block they stood lingering awkwardly by the curb. As if she could hear the question in Maurie's mind, Gail said, "I'm going to be out of town for a couple weeks. I have to go to my grandparents' in Philadelphia, and then down to St. Croix. . . ."

"St. Croix!"

But Gail was shaking her head. "It's no big deal. We go practically every year. My whole family's going to be there—and believe me, they could ruin Paradise!"

"When will you be back?"

"Saturday before New Year's."

Someone came out of one of the houses on Gail's block, and they both grew suddenly alert, moved another foot apart—then caught each other's eyes in a sheepish smile. "I'm going away, too," Maurie said. "Down to Boston, to spend Christmas with my folks."

Gail laughed. "God, I wish I didn't have to do that. And you're going five hundred miles out of your way so that you can? Incredible!"

Now a car pulled into a drive at the far end of the street, and Gail half turned to go, squinting down the block.

"Will you call me when you get back, Gail?"

"O.K."

"Is that a promise?"

"I don't know. . . ."

IV

The child in the picture wore a crimson dress and carried a lunch pail in one hand and a schoolbag that looked enormous in the other. A complicated pattern of elaborate cornrows framed her penny brown face. Her wide smile was toothless in the front.

"Kasinda. The first day of school."

"That's right."

"This is priceless. Would you ask Aunt Laverne to get a copy made for me?"

"You can ask her yourself, Maurie. They'll be over tomorrow night."

"For dinner? The kids and everyone?"

"Kids and all. Laverne said I'd better not let you sneak out of here this time without her getting a chance to see you. She says the last time she had a good talk with you was that summer we were all down on the Cape at Joe Franklin's place. That was two years ago, if it was a day. Laverne wasn't even expecting Zaki yet." Maurie's mother moved back to the stove and lifted the lid on the pot roast. The aroma of onions and hot, meaty juices steamed out into the kitchen.

Maurie watched her movements, feeling half at home, and half like a guest. She always expected things in this house to look exactly as they had all the while she was growing up—when there was no money for new appliances and floors. But Pop and Uncle Jerome had redone the kitchen three years ago. And now, here was this modern, avocado-colored, six-burner range—and then on top of it that old blue and white mottled pot with the chipped lid, the one that had been on the stove Sundays and holidays ever since Maurie could remember.

Her mother, too, was a study in contrasts. The gray knit pants and yellow jersey would have looked as fresh and modern as the new kitchen, except for the faded print apron, ruffled and rickracked, that completed her outfit. Maurie and Toby had given it to her for Mother's Day, some fifteen years ago.

"We ought to do that again. You could get down for a week or two in the summer, couldn't you?"

Yes, she could come back, year after year, and know exactly what to expect. But what if, one year, she didn't come? Or brought somebody with her?

"This ought to be done right on time. I just have to make up a pan of rolls and . . ."

"I'll do the rolls." She uncovered the bowl of dough, searched under the sink for the square tin her mother always used. She tried to imagine Gail in this kitchen. Gail wouldn't know which pan to use for the bread, or the melted butter. Would her hands know how to shape rolls? Would she seem to take up all the space in this kitchen the way she had in Maurie's apartment? Would everything here look too gaudy and new, or too shabby and old?

When she cleared the table, she looked again through the pictures. Most of them were of the children—Kasinda and Kalil and their baby brother. There was one of her aunt and uncle together, in wet bathing suits, with their arms around each other. Something that simple. Just a picture of the two of you, at the beach last summer, to send home to the folks. . . . She squared the edges of the stack of photos and dropped them back into their bright yellow envelope. She wiped across the oilcloth with the damp dishrag.

At Christmas dinner the following afternoon, they were all there in person—along with her maternal grandmother, a great-aunt and a second cousin. Her brother Toby had driven in from New Haven. Pop did almost all the talking, and still managed to eat most of the rolls. Mom ran in and out of the kitchen and never got around to taking off her apron. When the baby turned his bowl upside down and everyone laughed, Toby made a face at Maurie across the table and, down at the other end, Kasinda made practically the same face at Kalil. Everything going according to plan—everybody doing exactly what was expected.

And what would all the family do if she told them? Or somehow they found out? Looking around the table, she couldn't imagine a setting in which what she was contemplating could be more scandalous. Unless maybe it was *her* parents' house. What was Gail doing now? Were several generations of Jenners sitting down to a formal candlelit Christmas dinner in Philadelphia? Roast goose? Plum pudding? Champagne? Were they having a barbecue on a beach in St. Croix? Was Gail thinking about Maurie?

Finally, the next day, she got to sneak away with Toby. They drove into town and then over the bridge across the Charles, into Cambridge, parked the car and walked through the Common toward Harvard Square. Toby pulled his pipe from the wide pocket of his softly padded jacket. The bowl was already filled and ready to light. At home, he never smoked. She wasn't even sure if Mom and Pop knew he smoked a pipe. *She* had never told them.

He inhaled the first breath and blew it out in a blue puff. "God, it's good to get out of there. That place always makes me feel like I'm ten years old. It's like a time warp, every time I come back." She nodded and laughed along with him. "You'd hardly believe I was a fully functioning adult back in New Haven. Whatever Pop wants me to do, I end up going along with it. I can't say no to him any easier than I could when I was only four foot tall."

She remembered him like that—four foot tall—a skinny kid with a narrow chest who couldn't fight or even insult people properly, who got teased unmercifully for his sallow "yellow" complexion and his tight black curls, and who cried more easily than she did. Pop had always wanted Toby to learn to fight back. . . . She and Toby had never, either of them, fit in, but they managed to make it all right for each other.

In the summertime, when all the other kids were out playing, both of them carrying books home from the library together made it all right. When he started reading the *Daily Worker* every day and going to the Du Bois Club meetings after school, she acted like that was perfectly normal behavior for a fifteen-year-old boy. When she wore her beads and peasant skirt and sandals, and a huddle of girls on a porch giggled as she and Toby walked by, and then one of them called out, "Hey girl! Don't you know they ain't no such thing as black hippies?" Toby pretended he hadn't heard a thing.

He had still been that skinny-chested kid, all through high school, but now—she watched him while he talked. Now his hands were big and competent looking, one of them waving the pipe around to accent his words. Now his chest was broad as a barrel, and his skin had weathered to a richer tone, like fine leather. Now there was a short thick beard, which matched the curls. She hadn't paid much attention to his changing, but today here he was—a grown man.

"Did you see me up on the ladder? Gee, I thought the whole neighborhood was watching. I swear I thought I was gonna break my neck, perched up there with all those strings of lights draped around me. I felt like a blasted Christmas tree. You know where the steps are, at the front of the porch. Well, you can't set the ladder flat because of the steps. Pop's supposed to be holding the ladder steady; instead he's checking out all the extension cords, going, 'Wait a minute—this ain't the right one here—no —this one don't fit together. . . .' I thought any second he's gonna plug in the wrong one, and I'm gonna light up and go blinking off and on. They can just leave me up here, and forget about Christmas decorations."

"Remember that time they were going out, and Pop was instructing us about what to do in case the Christmas tree caught on fire?" she asked, laughing.

"Yeah." Toby mimicked Pop's most serious face, and they both said it, chanting out in unison, just as they had in answer to Pop's question that night long ago. "Crawl under the Christmas tree and pull out the cord."

"I woulda done it too," Toby said, shaking his head. "I probably would do it today, if Pop told me to."

"What gets me," she said, "is how I feel like I can't talk about what's really going on in my life. Like they don't really want to know that I *have* a life, outside of them. So I feel like I'm only half real."

"Yeah, I know. Same here." He looked across at her, from under the Greek fisherman's cap that was pulled down low on one side, his familiar black eyes twinkling, set deep in the tan face. When they were kids, he used to claim he could read her mind. "So what really is going on in your life? You writing much?"

"Some." She hoped he wouldn't ask if she'd brought any of her new poems with her this trip. Lately, they were all love poems about Gail. She added, "Nothing terribly profound."

When she didn't elaborate, he went on. "How's your love life? You know—the big 'S'?"

She shook her head. "Nonexistent." But her face was suddenly hot. Nobody but Toby would have seen the subtle color change.

He looked at her closer, a smile widening his face. "You fell for somebody, huh? Or somebody fell for you."

"Cut it out, Toby. I'm entitled to a private life." Yet she really wanted to tell him. The way she'd been able to tell no one but him when she was twelve and that man in the car had stopped her to ask for directions, and she'd gone up to the window—how frightened she'd been when she saw he had his pants down all the way around his ankles. . . . She wanted to tell the way she'd been able to, years later, when she first had sex with a man, and Toby had reassured her that it was all right, that she didn't have to feel guilty, that passion was a perfectly healthy, moral thing to feel. The way he'd been able to tell her, when he was going out with a white girl—Rochelle Herman—when Maurie and Toby were both still in high school, and he trusted Maurie not to tell their parents, and she never did. And then, in New Haven, when he was living with Aileen. Maurie had gone and stayed with them, and thought of Aileen as a sister-in-law, those two years. But she never told.

"Who's the lucky guy?" he teased.

"It's nothing like that. It's . . . just a crush. A bad crush— that won't amount to anything." She could hear Stevie Wonder's voice singing accusingly. "You got it bad girl. . . ."

"You can tell," he said again. "We're all adults here."

I wish we were. Instead she said, "Isn't that strange, Toby? Isn't it? We *are* adults, finally—you and me. When I was a kid I used to look at Mom and Uncle Jerome sometimes, and think about how they were sister and brother, Toby, like you and me. And that now they were two grownups—but they were *still* sister and brother. And I couldn't get over that fact. It just used to amaze me. I always wondered what it would feel like, if it ever happened to us. And now here we are—a grown-up sister and brother. . . ."

"Crossing the Common in the chill December air," he struck a pose, pipe in hand, "trudging through the dry, decaying leaves, reminiscing about our lost youth. . . ."

"Yeah." She giggled. "Walking and talking—just a couple of boring grownups."

At the end of the day, after another company dinner, after a long evening of her father's stories and his interminable advice, she sat on the bed in the little room at the back of the second floor. Yellow print curtains she had chosen when she was fourteen still hung at the window. The desk, unbelievably small and impractical, stood in the corner, and on the shelves above it were the few children's books that she had managed to get secondhand, after falling in love with copies borrowed from the public library: Laura Ingalls Wilder, Edith Nesbitt, Marguerite Di Angeli. What a strange child she must have been growing up black in Boston, in the 1960s, and reading all the time of prairies and gardens and moors, about children from Sweden and England, writing poems about places she had never seen, and wishing she came from some exotic, faraway land, too—not being able to see who she was.

She remembered, she used to light the room with candles when her parents were not at home. The flickering flames made the colors dance in the psychedelic posters she had taped on the wall. That part had come later. But now it was all mixed up together with the little girl stuff. *Siddhartha* and *The Prophet* sat on the shelf right next to A *Little Princess*. A box of incense lay on the windowsill beside a cluster of china horses—God, her mother must come in here and dust this stuff every week.

She took a stick of incense from the package and lit a match to its end. In a curl of pungent sandalwood smoke, those last years came rushing back. How trapped she had felt in this room, burning incense and candles, how powerless to change anything about her life. It was easy, when she was here, to slide into feeling powerless again. Just like Toby had said. . . . But she hadn't really been powerless, even then. She had left home. . . .

She stood up and faced herself in the mirror that hung over

the dresser. It was such a small mirror only her face showed. She hadn't wanted any mirror, in those days. It had taken her so long to learn to love herself, as she was.

But she did now. She studied the face framed in the square of dark wood, and she liked everything she saw—the thick eyebrows that she was glad she had never plucked, the wingspread nose and ripe, melon lips, and her coloring, sand tan like everyone else in the family. She didn't care anymore that her hair wasn't as "good" as Toby's. She had her mother's chin, long and proud. The neck of the robe opened to the beginning of the swelling of her full breasts. That was as far as the mirror would let her see. But she knew the rest, loved it all. Somebody else could love her too, if she'd let herself. . . .

She turned away from the mirror and back to the bookshelf, looking for something she could use to read herself to sleep. She pulled out a slim paperback volume of poems—Federico García Lorca. Later, when she had washed up and snuggled down under the covers to read, the book fell open of its own accord and a paper marker fell out. The place it had marked was the end of the introduction, written by an editor or translator, but quoting the poet's own words about himself: "I write poetry because I want people to love me."

It was the last night Maurie was there that it came up, completely casually, after dinner, while everyone was still at the table. Luckily, there were only the four of them that night, no guests.

"Guess who I saw in town this morning," Maurie's mother announced to the table at large. "Francine Albertson."

Maurie remembered the Albertsons—neighbors who had once been her parents' best friends, but had moved years ago. She remembered the children—Franny, with the stuffed panda bear she carried everywhere, and the ribbon always untied on her top plait, hanging down in front of her face. Jerry, in a too-big police cap, flinging out his arms to block the sidewalk, shouting, "Red light!" "What are Franny and Jerry doing now?" she asked.

Before her mother could answer, her father made a noise—

somewhere between a harrumph and a sigh—shaking his head. "It's a shame about that boy. A real shame. He was such a goodlooking kid, too."

"Jerry? What happened to him?" She imagined a car accident, or his face slashed up by a gang of muggers.

But now Pop had apparently said all he wanted to on the subject. "Just fell in with the wrong crowd, I guess." That old adult/kid routine—covering up. And then just to their mother, exactly as if Maurie and Toby were a couple of pre-schoolers and simply wouldn't hear him, "I felt so bad for Al, when he told me. I didn't know what to say. I don't even know why he told me. What a thing to have happen to a man."

After he left the room, she turned to her mother, to find her suddenly busy clearing the plates from the table, her lips pressed together into a flat, tight line. She disappeared into the kitchen with her hands full, and almost immediately her voice rose in song.

> *"Jesus paid it all*
> *All to him I owe*
> *Sin had left a crimson stain. . . ."*

Maurie turned to Toby. "What was that all about?"

He met the question with that innocent smile of complicity they'd always shared. "He's gay," Toby said. "Jerry Albertson. I used to run into him on the campus sometimes, when I had that summer job at the bookstore." He glanced out toward the living room, where their father had turned on the TV, then back at her. "I guess he came out to his old man."

She was stunned. She could not, for anything, think what would be the totally natural thing to say. Words stammered out. "Pop thinks it's that bad?"

"Yeah. All he can see is a blot on the old man's character. A failed father somewhere in the background. Fathers are responsible for everything, you know." He chuckled. Dropped his voice. "Mom has a much less Freudian outlook: It's a sin. Whatever the question was—Jesus is the answer."

She ought to be able to laugh along with him, joke about this.

She hadn't seen the Albertsons in ten years. None of them should matter to her, at all. There was a tremor in her voice, asking, "What do *you* think?"

"Me?" He shrugged. "I think it's the twentieth century. I've been to Greenwich Village."

She tried to steal a glance at him, and met his eyes. They were no longer laughing, but steady and thoughtful. She couldn't go on with this conversation, couldn't let him watch her face for another minute. He was too sharp, knew her too intimately. She got up and began to gather the serving dishes, following her mother into the kitchen.

So now she knew what it would be like. Mom would think she was a sinner. Dad would think he was a failure. Only Toby . . . but she could never tell, not even Toby. She'd have to lie to them for the rest of her life. It felt like lying already, like she'd been lying ever since she got here.

"You put the food away. I'll wash," she told her mother. And ran the water hard so she wouldn't have to talk just now.

V

Twelve long hours on the bus, to ask herself questions. Framingham, Worcester . . . not sleeping, watching the shopping malls and parking lots, and then the silent dark fields slip by. Springfield, Albany, Schenectady . . . unlit farmhouses, lighted cloverleafs, on and off the throughway . . . Amsterdam, Johnstown, Utica.

Of course, Mom had wanted her to stay. "I don't understand why you have to leave today, Maureen. It's only *Friday*! We've hardly even had a chance to see you. What do you have to go back so soon for?"

"I just need to be able to spend the weekend at home." She watched her mother's face draw in at the word "home," and she hurried on. "I've got to have my lesson plans done by the time school starts Monday. The kids'll be really high, and I want to have my act together." Another lie.

Oneida. Syracuse. A couple of sleepy-eyed college students—a boy and a girl—gathered together their hats, backpacks, book bags, a stray glove, a guitar. Just the way they collected their belongings, either of them grabbing whatever was closest, made her think that probably they lived together. Stumbling groggily down the aisle, they looked too young to be sexually active, "living in sin," her mother would say. . . . A new thought pulled her fully awake. It was all right if both of you were kids. But if one was an adult, and the other—seventeen? There were laws, of course.

Did it matter? Being a lesbian was against the law, too.

She stared out through the glass at the sleeping streets. Somewhere along the way it had begun to snow. The windshield wipers slogged back and forth in a dull, blunt rhythm, and the questions licked and nudged at the edges of her mind. Was it taking advantage of Gail? Was it Gail, after all, that drew her? Or had she just needed a Gail, a someone . . . female . . . ? What if nothing more happened between them? Would Maurie still end up a lesbian? Was she one already? Geneva, Canandaigua, all around the Finger Lakes, the long way home.

The woman next to her had fallen asleep and sagged over to take up three-quarters of the seat. Maurie's knees and her back ached and there was a splintery knot in her neck. Rochester, finally. Only another hour now, along the canal.

Twelve hours in all, and no answers—only the long yearning to be home, the absolute certainty that the only place she wanted to be was in that gray city on Lake Erie that Gail would be coming home to, this same morning.

Letting herself into the apartment in the gray dawn light, she piled her bags in the kitchen just inside the door, slung her jacket over a chair. She'd meant to go right to sleep and sleep far into the afternoon, but her head was whizzing, whirring. She would put something mellow on the turntable, then brew a pot of chamomile tea, and drink it while she read her mail, winding down.

After two cups, after opening all the Christmas cards, she was still on a zingy high. She felt as if she were still in motion, traveling toward some destination just a little beyond her. On her feet now, she moved from one end of the small space to the other, then back again, and finally to the window.

The sky was white, clearing. The snow was finished. Several inches deep, it clung in a curve to the window frame and hooded the fences and ash cans beyond. The alley was a canyon, filled with a river of snow, that would open to other snowlogged streets, flow past banks of bulgy white cars and bushes—everything soft and anonymous, the city taken by storm.

All of a sudden, she was flinging on her things again, pulling tight at her boot laces, drawing them criss-cross over each other, and then throwing open the suitcase, burrowing haphazardly through the Christmas gifts and toilet articles to find her warmest sweater. As she stepped outside, a gust of wind shoved against her back, and she lurched forward a few awkward staggers, then laughed and ran with it, letting it push her in a clumsy run through the drifts up the alley, and onto the Avenue.

Fifteen minutes later, her heart pounding, Maurie stood in the middle of the unploughed street and faced the stone house on Chapin Parkway. There was no one else on the block, no movement about the house. Huge icicles that sparkled like cut crystal hung from the rainpipes and eaves. In the pearl bright morning light, the many windows glistened like ice. There was no trace of the elegant curving drive that swept around the side, or the steps that led up to the main door, between the two tall columns. There was only snow—deep and unruffled, the yard one with the yard next door, the sidewalk and the street: an open sea of snow.

A moment ago, she had thought this her destination, where she was headed this morning once and for all. But her fingers and feet were tingling; she felt full and vibrantly alive, not yet at the end of this venture. She squinted a moment longer at the house, then took a deep breath. The air was as fresh as cold springwater. Her breath rushed out, and she couldn't stop the smile that took over her face. She turned from the house and pushed on, past it.

At Delaware Avenue, Maurie crossed the deserted street against the light, and slogged in through the wide-standing gate to the cemetery. Alone in the open space, she waded deep into the drifts, leaving her mark—trails and twists and figure eights, crazy spirals and mazes no one would ever understand. She sank knee deep in soft banks and slid on the frozen creek. At the top of the hill, where the wind had blown the road almost bare, she spun in dizzy laughing circles under the bright sky. She filled her lungs with the icy air, and called and shouted aloud, stuck her two fingers in her mouth and spurted out a whistle that frightened all the birds from a snow-laden evergreen. And then she sang—in a loud voice that cracked from the long night of silence—the first song that came to her, dancing in the snow.

With a stick broken from a fallen branch, she began to write, in huge letters through the fresh snow. First she wrote "I love you." It didn't matter if it didn't keep, if the wind or the sun erased it, or more snow fell to cover it up. Right now, this day, this hour, it was real, it was true—and wonderful. "I love you," she wrote again and again, leaving the message, a loud tell-tale secret, all over Forest Lawn. She drew hearts with arrows through them, crooked stars and crescent moons with sleepy smiling faces, wrote her name and wrote the words again.

It was fully daylight now; the sun had broken through. On a last clear patch of snow, by the fence on the expressway side, there was space for one more message. She drew a circle, and added the two more lines that turned it into a woman's symbol. And then another woman's symbol right beside it, overlapping, intertwined. She had seen that design displayed again and again at the women's center—on posters for upcoming events, in the newsletter, on buttons some of the women wore pinned to their clothing. . . . Now she understood that need to display it, to say it somehow.

Her toes were wet, even through her leather boots, her fingers and face numb. Bits of ice clung to her wet mittens, with the dank smell of damp wool. Heading back down the hill, she smiled at the message that greeted her everywhere. It suddenly struck her who the words were really meant for—how right it was that she should be the one to read them, over and over again.

She had made her own trail, and she followed it, the way she'd come—all the way to the Delaware Avenue gate. At the gate she turned back to gather in one last view of this new place, this playland of sunshine and snow. But the city this Saturday morning seemed a new place too, shimmering and alight, friendly and full of promise, and still soft-edged and vulnerable under its coverlet of snow. A huge yawn pushed her jaws apart, and then another; a long sigh. She crossed the street and ploughed on toward Elmwood Avenue, toward the alley—coming home.

BRUCE MORROW

Near the End of
the World

Sometimes I have visions. Mostly they're about me jumping off a roof, or something. Sometimes they're about me and other people taking the big leap—off a cliff, a diving board. Off the curb, into the gutter. I call them visions because they're not dreams, you know, they're not at night while I'm in bed, trying to sleep. I don't dream—or at least I don't remember my dreams. Each morning when I wake it's like someone presses a button and my eyes just pop open.

But since I've been out here in California (I've decided not to go back to college) and got these tattoos, the visions, the things I envisioned happening to me, don't bother me anymore.

It had gotten worse. Before I came out West I was imagining not only that I was falling but that someone, my father as a little boy, was pushing me. He'd run up behind me, scream, and knock me over; over and over again; his fist, hard as stone, would jab into my diaphragm and force the air out of my lungs, like a hard hiccup. And even though each successive push would be as unexpected as the first, I never fell. These vines would leap out of the ground, grab hold of my ankles and wrist, and twist, binding me till I couldn't move. Scary. I could smell them, too, bitter, pungent green leaves, sweet sickening flowers I couldn't name—but their identities would be so clear to me, stuffed up my nose, sliming my tongue, smothering me.

Although I remember these visions happening in Venice Beach, on an old boardwalk like the one at Coney Island, I know this can't be true. There's no boardwalk in Venice. Only blacktop and sand. But I remember walking on weather-worn wood planks in Venice and carrying my big blue backpack, which contained everything that was important to me. I was checking it all out. The muscle men, the surfers, the tangerine-orange and lime-green bikinis. Bodies. Bodies laid out all in the same direction, neatly in groups of twos and threes, as if a caretaker had placed them there to rest—for good. I was looking at everything: the bikinis and the bodies; the water rocking, slamming itself into white foam, softly sliding onto the sand, then slowly slipping back; the zigzag pattern of the boardwalk (that's the way I remember it) under my feet; the little stores and booths, tucked under the shade of their own roofs. I felt all right, fine, because all I had to do was follow the boardwalk and not think about which direction to go in. No forks. No exit ramps. Then the vines crept up and grabbed my ankles, wrapped around them. I almost tripped, but the strength of the vines held me up as they stretched and took hold of my neck. I felt like I was being pulled down, straight down into the boardwalk, into the zigs of the zags. They wouldn't let me go, wouldn't go away. Some Rollerblade kids streaked by and I heard them call me something I've never heard before or never heard used that way. (What was it? I can't remember.) And more Rollerbladers. And skateboarders. I thought they were trying to run me over—I'm the pin and they're the bowling balls—but they flew past me, shrinking into neon-colored flames, down the boardwalk.

This woman, dressed all in white, must have seen the whole thing. Her eyes, golden in the brilliant sunlight, focused on me and me only as she ran toward me, shouting, waving her hands and yelling, "Move. The lane, the lane. Get out the lane." Then she touched me, and the vines were gone and I could breathe. She yanked me over. "The lane, that's the skating lane and these kids are likely to run you over nowadays." I rubbed my wrist, and

I could see red welts around it. She kept talking, a lot, real fast, like she was on speed or something; but she pronounced each word with the utmost care. "They glow in the night, you know. Scares the hell out of me, too." Long strands of brown hair clung to her pale, sweat-dampened face, and her nostrils flared as she spoke. She looked fit but not slender, middle-aged—forty-five, fifty—but not old, beautiful but not pretty.

I offered thanks for the rescue, but she seemed to not hear me, telling me about how all these fluorescent colors everybody wears out here in California are signaling UFOs, and I better get myself some protection before I get picked up for extermination. Insects get exterminated, I tried to tell her, but that was the wrong thing to say. She went off on how the Nazis exterminated tons of Jews: "They measured them by weight, not as individuals." How all kinds of exterminations had occurred. In the Soviet Union. In Cambodia. In America. "Don't see no Aztecs running around, do you?" She went on. And on.

She told me that these skateboard and Rollerblade kids knew something, and that's why they all had at least one neon-colored article on at all times. "Keeps their skates safe, too, with fluorescent wheels," she explained. I noticed she had on those Day-Glo cords around her neck, her wrist, and her ankles, the ones they sell at baseball games and afterward you have to keep in the refrigerator to recharge.

I don't know what made me tell her this, what made me talk to her, but I told her I was having all these visions about being bound and strangled by vines. I had to make myself stop. I didn't tell her then why I'd come out here from New York, why I was trying not to think; but thinking about it was all I could do. My father had been sick for two years with AIDS when he died (I dropped out of my first year at Swarthmore to care for him), and some days, close to the end, he couldn't recognize me, or he'd think I was him and he was all young again and have conversations with himself my whole visit: "You've got to set an example for your race. Get married. Get affirmative-actioned, Mel. And stop having that part cut into your hair. You're a respectable accountant, a family man. Not Shaft."

Since we shared the name Melvin, it could get confusing. But

I knew he wasn't talking to me; he was talking to his younger self, twenty years old, in college, married, and miserable.

Sometimes he wouldn't talk to me at all. Sometimes he'd ask me to leave his semiprivate hospital room. He'd say I smelled like the rotting earth; or he'd say the smell of my shampoo offended him: "You're no Breck girl; you're a black boy. And ain't no Breck girls black, and no black boys use Breck. We use Prell." Sometimes he'd call the nurse and have the flowers I'd just bought for him removed from his room: "Poinsettias in Puerto Rico can be beautiful and grow as tall as cherry trees. Poinsettias at Christmastime in New York—or Oklahoma—are awful. Nothing could be tackier."

The virus had gotten inside his brain, the doctor told me. His mind had been completely taken over, and he needed constant care. (There was never any time for me to register at City College. Or Hunter. Every time he got a little better I took him home and waited on him until the hospital had to take him back. That's how the insurance worked.)

"Get yourself some fluorescents," said the woman on the beach still talking a mile a minute. "That's what I'd do." And I imagined the many alien particles that had taken over my father's body retreating, shrinking away from fluorescent colors. Running. "Sounds strange," she continued, "but you can die from a trick of the mind. If that is what it is."

I believed her. It made lots of sense to me—at the time.

Turned out she'd just invented this neon tattoo dye that gave permanent protection. She said she was a tattoo artist. Before I met her, I definitely wasn't into tattoos. But then she showed me her book, a black leatherbound notebook filled with color photographs, examples of her work—intricate miniature designs made with needle and dye.

"I would show you mine," she said, pointing to her white linen sarong, "but I don't know you well enough. That is, if you wanted to see the real thing and not reproductions."

I took her at her word. The photos didn't look like they'd been retouched or anything. She asked if she could just paint some colors on my skin. My skin, she kept saying, was such a beautiful color to go with her neons. "Must be a lot of cultures mixed in there. Powerful. Ancient. Thick blood. Like maple syrup. Makes your skin shine. But you don't have much meat on your bones. Put your backpack down."

"I'll forget it," I said in a panic. That bag had everything in it—all I owned, all that was truly mine.

She started painting on my wrist with a thin brush, about five squirrel hairs thick, in small dabs and strokes. It tickled, so I turned and looked out to the bright sky, the domed ceiling of a god's castle. Not that I'm religious or anything—or into crystals—but out here in California, it seems like the sky is the inside of a god's head, the clouds fissures on the brain where thoughts roll by. Or: the sky is the screen of a TV set seen from the inside. But who's watching on the outside? Gods? Aliens? Or viruses? Everything looked so washed out in the sunlight, even brightly colored bikinis looked pastel in the glare. The ocean appeared to be covered in white feathers that floated on the crests of waves. The whole sea ready to fly away. But where?

"You can look now. Hello. My friend, you can look now," she said. "Isn't it beautiful? It's a little rough sketch. I don't know why I painted that design, I'm usually not into flowers. I'll have better control with the needle. Do you like it?"

I didn't know what to say. They didn't look exactly like the ones in my visions, but they were close enough, close enough that I thought they *were* the vines that were always trying to pull me down.

"How'd you know?" I asked.

"I just started."

"But these are like the flowers in my visions. How'd you know? What are they?" I couldn't believe how detailed they were.

"Don't touch them yet. Let them dry. Well, let me see. These are wild daisies, and these chicory with miniature ivy leaves. Twinflowers, grass-of-parnassus, wild oats and hepatica and sea lavender." Seven different miniature florets in all. "I'm going to break for lunch," she continued. "Would you like to join me? Then I can get started afterward. At least on the wrist. I have to think about the rest."

She stood up and started putting things away. I didn't pay

much attention to what was going on, except the way the flowers twisted around my wrist and tied in a loose knot on the inside of my arm. It was a rough sketch, but it had the potential of being as intricate as an engraving.

"Are you coming?" she continued. "You can rest here if you want. Leave your bag here and I'll lock up. I know you've had an unsettling morning. My name's Tasha, by the way. Could you help me with some of this?"

"Melvin. Mel. Where are we going?" I asked. And in my first moment of relative calm in a long time, I set my backpack on the floor, lifted a large lunch basket, and followed Tasha down the boardwalk.

We walked to a less crowded part of the beach, where she set out a big white umbrella and white blanket. She didn't stop talking the whole time, asking for assistance, describing the lunch she'd prepared—a redleaf lettuce, tomato, and garbanzo bean salad with tahini vinaigrette dressing, cold brown rice with almonds and raisins, and whole-grain pita bread. She told me not to feel obligated to get a tattoo even though she had just saved my life and was sharing her lunch. Good sense of humor. Her yellow eyes flashed in the sun when she laughed, and she flicked her light chestnut hair out of her face at the end of each good chuckle.

She told me about her life. She was a native Californian but had gone to school back East, at Smith, and she hadn't been back in twenty-five years. She had learned how to tattoo in New York, back when New York was the capital of tattooing.

"After college," she said, "like everyone else, I guess, I moved to New York to seek my fame and fortune. Instead I worked as a secretary at a few law firms. All my girlfriends said I was lucky. 'How to Marry a Millionaire.' What better way is there to meet one than to work for one? But I didn't make a good cup of coffee, and I didn't take shorthand. I had a small flat on the Lower East Side, but when I got fired—no lawyer lover/husband for me—I moved out to a cheaper place in Brooklyn. A boarding-house for twenty-five dollars a month, I think. And I started hanging out there, going out to the beach, the rides, the freak show at Coney Island. Do you have enough salad dressing? It's in that dish. I just made it this morning, so tomorrow it'll really be great. You know, the spices start coming out.

"Anyway, I met this guy Tony, Tony the Pirate, they called him, and he taught me everything I know. He was the best. The best on the boardwalk. The Pirate," she repeated as if she were trying to conjure him up, "but he didn't have any fake appendages. What part of New York are you from?"

"Harlem," I said with difficulty. My mouth was full, and everything was so good, I couldn't stop stuffing myself long enough to talk. I hadn't eaten all morning; I hadn't eaten anything good for me in months. Saving money: the less I spent on food and stuff, the longer I could stay. I think Tasha could tell I didn't want to talk about myself, because she didn't wait for me to elaborate.

"Tony, Tony the Pirate? I don't know where he is now. See, they destroyed the tattoo business in New York in the sixties, said it contributed to the spread of disease—hepatitis, I think it was. They said that all the *crazies* were spreading hepatitis." She wiggled her fingers in the air when she said "crazies." "If they got rid of tattooing, then they'd get rid of all these undesirables, you know. Just like that. Poof.

"Back then New York was the center of everything, tattoos and crazies. We were professionals—not professional crazies; professional artists—working in the art capital of the world, and now we're illegal there. Everything went underground. Or disappeared. Everything went down except for you-know-what. So I made my way back home, to the beach, to a place where you can't go any farther. You know what I mean?"

She finished chewing the last of her salad and placed her dishes to the side. Her skin was warmly tanned, dark in contrast to the fluorescent jewelry she wore, dark against the white umbrella behind her, but light compared to mine. I noticed her fingers resting now in her lap, wrinkled at the knuckles—unadorned, practical fingers with closely trimmed nails and permanently stained cuticles. The pattern of veins on the back of her hands. She held her hands just so, poised, with the tips of index finger and thumb touching, as if they were kissing.

She started talking faster, and her story changed from New

York to the West as frontier to outer space. She said that the space and aeronautics industries were concentrated in the West because there were no other places on earth to explore. "I think it was Horace Greeley who told all those young ambitious men, 'Go West!' (It didn't make him president, but unlike all the other losers, he's remembered for something other than losing.) At the same time, I think, mid-nineteenth century, good old Ralph Waldo Emerson told those same robust young men—it's always young men, you see—'Hitch your wagon to a star.' Now he was always so prophetic. Really. You see, the question to ask," she said, laughing at what she'd just said, "is how close is California to the heavens? You could probably just hitch a couple of horses to space shuttle and go. And the aliens must know the answer to that one. That's why they're always coming here: they've run out of frontiers on their own planets. You must think I'm crazy."

I didn't know what to say; I was following the path of ideas she'd made, and I couldn't believe I was right there beside her. "It's funny," I said after a long pause, "we think alike, you know?" even though I didn't think this was true at all. But I couldn't find any more words. I'm not used to talking. Dad never used to let me get a word in edgewise. He always talked to me as if he was holding court—very royal, indeed. Taking care of him was like taking care of a prince—not a queen—a little prince lost at some edge of the world where his royal lineage wasn't apparent anymore: he lost his crown of silver hair before he lost his scepter of wit and intelligence. He lost a few teeth. His fingernails turned black.

"I want you to know," he said to me, "that I'm leaving you everything, all I have. Take my letters, my journals, all my books, my albums, and remember me. Remember me. I give you all these, my estate, my jewels, my leather chaps, my braided whip. Take it and use it wisely, sparingly. They won't know who you are until you pull out that mighty strap. It takes a masochist to create a sadist. Don't let them cut you to pieces. And don't be afraid to use commas. And exclamation points—I know they're so out of fashion." His hands, with their blackened nails, fluttered around his mouth, an open wound I could peer inside and see, past his swollen tongue, down his throat, to the sickness in his stomach, lungs, intestines, right through to the sphincter muscle he couldn't control anymore.

When Dad stopped talking altogether, I still didn't speak up. I didn't know what to say except, *How could you do this to me? I can't do this by myself, you crazy old man. I still need you. You would've died all alone without me. Crazy old man. There's no one left. Can't you see? There's nothing but your blackened nails, your stinking body, an open wound, your melting body, hot as wax. You fool. You damn fool, stop holding on.* But I didn't say that. Instead I started reading everything he gave me, his journals and books, his bills and business plans. My inheritance.

"You know," I said to Tasha, stumbling on my words, trying to fill in the blanks with anything that came to mind. "You know, that's why I came here. That's why Hollywood's here. The apparatus. You know what I mean? It's like a frontier, new technologies. The apparatus of film. And now there's Silicon Valley."

"Are you into computers?" she asked when I didn't say anything else. "I don't like them. I don't trust them. I did some designs on one once and then they disappeared. I couldn't find them, and I had spent hours on it."

She looked to the ocean and became very quiet. I could see her pulse beating at her temples and the speediness and slowness of her life. She was alone, like me, aware of the effects of atmospheric pressures and gravity weighing her down. I could tell that hers was a life of wishing to be more, daydreaming but never making it, getting distracted by the details of cutting vegetables and tearing green leaves; hers was a life of trusting others because the real enemy, aliens and viruses, could only come from another place. Like out there in the heavens.

I'm saying this now, but I wished I'd known it then. See, the thing is, Dad became more and more innocent as he got sicker, weaker. He smiled a lot. He stopped getting embarrassed when he burped loudly or drooled. He didn't cry out anymore when his diaper leaked and he had to lie there for hours in the mess, in the smell and everything. I know he stopped talking to me before he wasn't able to speak. He stopped looking at me before he went blind. I don't know why. I blamed him. Now I know it makes just as much sense to blame it all on aliens as it does to blame it on him, on his life after he left me and my mother and my sister. But I did. I held him responsible for his own death. Until I read his journals and diaries and letters and little poems he wrote in the margins of books. (I took them with me and read them on the bus ride out here; but before that all I knew was I was going to spread my father's ashes over the Pacific Ocean.)

When I was twelve Dad moved down to the Village while my mother, my sister, and I remained on 147th Street. He became a black queen—no, a prince—happy with his life and his lover, who died four years before him. I got scared when Walter died. I was sixteen, and these visions, which I now know were only panic attacks, would start and the anxiety would take control of my body, seizing me and squeezing me senseless. Like a carnival ride spinning out of control.

It was up to me to take care of everything when Dad got too sick to handle it himself. I paid the bills, closed all the accounts, cleaned up after him, washed him, made sure the hospital kept him there as long as possible. We couldn't afford a private nurse. We couldn't afford the hospital. The insurance kept trying to drop him, but I kept paying for the coverage. I also had my mother's lawyer give them a call. She helped when she could, but it was too hard for her. "I can only do so much," she said. "You might not understand, and I don't expect you to, but I can only do so much." She bought groceries for us once a week. After the second year I couldn't pay the maintenance on Dad's apartment anymore, so I turned it over to the management company, put all his stuff in storage, and moved in with friends. It was his fault, dammit, all of it, I thought when it was happening.

But now I know the reason Dad's fingernails were black and rotting. It was a black fungus, growing out of control. He hadn't painted them that way.

Tasha started gathering our picnic leftovers, and I tried to help, but she insisted on doing it herself. She said I looked emaciated. But finally she gave in and let me carry the basket back to her shop. Her Day-Glo necklace looked like a broken halo come to rest around her neck, her white sarong an apostle's robe. I wanted to be in love with her at that moment, and I could feel the blood rush to my face when she handed me the basket. I realized I didn't have my backpack with me. I thought I'd lost it. His ashes were in there. In a plastic bag. In a cardboard box. Lumpy, grey cinders, smooth to the touch. Unburned shards of teeth and bone. I could feel the thump, thump in my ears, pounding out the sound of the crashing waves, consuming me. I was on a roller-coaster, in the first car, holding my hands up, screaming and laughing. But I wasn't. I was holding it all in, and I had to tell myself to breathe, let it out, breathe.

They started again. Sea lavender and wild oats, goldenrod and witch hazel, grass-of-parnassus and strong green vines. I knew their names now. Pollen in my eyes and nose, a catch in the back of my throat. So, I kept thinking: I'm like him, every day I'm more and more like him, I want to be like him, I have no other choice. Soft petals. Fibrous, tough stems. If there is such a thing as a gay gene, then I think it was passed on to me. But not the virus. I tried to get that all by myself. Not exactly by myself, but in a selfish, half-crazed, half-I-don't-know-what moment. A one-night stand of unsafe sex back at school, when I hated myself and hated my father. Hated everything gay. They won't go away. Aromatic leaves. Thin prickly thorns. Trickles of blood on my arms, legs, dripping from my eyes, connecting me to him and him to us all.

All I did, all I could do, was wipe the tears away, and catch my breath, and wipe the tears away.

"I know, you don't have to tell me," Tasha said in a very low voice. "Just let it take its time to get out of your stomach and into your bloodstream. You shouldn't go so long without eating. It ain't good," she said, and the panic retreated.

We walked in silence back down the beach, and I thought how I couldn't get enough of California, couldn't take it all in. The endless sky. The sun setting over the ocean. Everything has a reason out here in California. Earthquakes happen because . . . UFOs are seen more often because . . . You have to have dreams because . . . I met Tasha just in time because, because, because I came to L.A. after my father died. Because there was no place else to go. Because I couldn't go any farther. I came out here to get rid of his ashes, spread them out in the desert or sprinkle them in the ocean. But now I think I'm going to keep them. They keep me anchored, keep me from floating off the edge, away, somewhere.

We walked back to Tasha's booth, and she checked the painting on my wrist. She asked if I was ready, and I said yes. I didn't want to rationalize, give myself time to figure it all out. I sat, and she sat holding my hand and arm so I couldn't move around, get away from the pain. I didn't look at what she was doing, and after a while the stinging went away. I missed the hurting. I wanted to know the pain—just like when I was a kid and the dentist did four, five fillings a visit without Novocain, and the only thing that was unpleasant was the smell of burning enamel and the stiff neck afterward from holding my head in one place for so long. That was the first time Dad said I was like him, taking all the pain and holding it all in.

Bad Blood

AMIRI BARAKA

The Alternative

This may not seem like much, but it makes a difference. And then there are those who prefer to look their fate in the eyes.

—ALBERT CAMUS,
BETWEEN YES AND NO

The leader sits straddling the bed, and the night, tho innocent, blinds him. (Who is our flesh. Our lover, marched here from where we sit now sweating and remembering. Old man. Old man, find me, who am your only blood.)

Sits straddling the bed under a heavy velvet canopy. Homemade. The door opened for a breeze, which will not come through the other heavy velvet hung at the opening. (Each thread a face, or smell, rubbed against himself with yellow glasses and fear at their exposure. Death. Death. They (the younger students) run by screaming. Tho impromptu. Tho dead, themselves.

The leader, at his bed, stuck with 130 lbs. black meat sewed to failing bone. A head with big red eyes turning senselessly. Five toes on each foot. Each foot needing washing. And hands that dangle to the floor, tho the boy himself is thin small washed out, he needs huge bleak hands that drag the floor. And a head full of walls and flowers. Blinking lights. He is speaking.

"Yeh?"

The walls are empty, heat at the ceiling. Tho one wall is painted

with a lady. (Her name now. In large relief, a faked rag stuck
between the chalk marks of her sex. Finley. Teddy's Doris. There
sprawled where the wind fiddled with the drying cloth. Leon
came in and laughed. Carl came in and hid his mouth, but he
laughed. Teddy said, "Aw, Man."

"Come on, Hollywood. You can't beat that. Not
with your years. Man, you're a schoolteacher 10 years after weeping for this old stinking bitch. And hit with a aspirin bottle
(myth says)."

The leader is sprawled, dying.
His retinue walks into their comfortable cells. "I have durawings," says Leon, whimpering now in the buses from Chicago.
Dead in a bottle. Floats out of sight, until the Africans arrive
with love and prestige. "Niggers." They say. "Niggers." Be happy
your ancestors are recognized in this burg. Martyrs. Dead in an
automat, because the boys had left. Lost in New York, frightened
of the burned lady, they fled into those streets and sang their
homage to the Radio City.

The leader sits watching the window. The dried
orange glass etched with the fading wind. (How many there
then? 13 Rue Madeleine. The Boys Club. They give, what he has
given them. Names. And the black cloth hung on the door
swings back and forth. One pork chop on the hot plate. And how
many there. Here, now. Just the shadow, waving its arms. The
eyes tearing or staring blindly at the dead street. These same
who loved me all my life. These same I find my senses in. Their
flesh a wagon of dust, a mind conceived from all minds. A country, of thought. Where I am, will go, have never left. A love, of
love. And the silence the question posed each second. "Is this
my mind, my feeling. Is this voice something heavy in the locked
streets of the universe. Dead ends. Where their talk (these
nouns) is bitter vegetable." That is, the suitable question rings
against the walls. Higher learning. That is, the moon through
the window clearly visible. The leader in seersucker, reading his
books. An astronomer of sorts. "Will you look at that? I mean,
really, now, fellows. Cats!" (Which was Smitty from the City's
entree. And him the smoothest of you American types. Said,
"Cats. Cats. What's goin' on?" The debate.

The leader's job (he keeps it still, above the streets, summers of low smoke, early evening drunk and wobbling thru the world. He keeps it, baby. You dig?) was absolute. "I have the abstract position of watching these halls. Walking up the stairs giggling. Hurt under the cement steps, weeping . . . is my only task. Tho I play hockey with the broom & wine bottles. And am the sole martyr of this cause. A.B., Young Rick, T.P., Carl, Hambrick, Li'l' Cholley, Phil. O.K. All their knowledge "Flait! More! Way!" The leader's job . . . to make attention for the place. Sit along the sides of the water or lay quietly back under his own shooting vomit, happy to die in a new grey suit. Yes. "And what not."

How many here now? Danny. (brilliant dirty curly Dan, the m.d.) Later, now, where you off to, my man. The tall skinny farmers, lucky to find sales and shiny white shoes. Now made it socially against the temples. This "hotspot" Darien drunk teacher blues . . . "and she tried to come on like she didn't even like to fuck. I mean, you know the kind. . . ." The hand extended, palm upward. I place my own in yours. That cross, of feeling. Willie, in his grinning grave, has it all. The place, of all souls, in their greasy significance. An armour, like the smells drifting slowly up Georgia. The bridge players change clothes, and descend. Carrying home the rolls.

Jimmy Lassiter, first looie. A vector. What is the angle made if a straight line is drawn from the chapel, across to Jimmy, and connected there, to me, and back up the hill again? The angle of progress. "I was talkin' to ol' Mordecai yesterday in a dream, and it's me sayin' 'dig baby, why don't you come off it?' You know."

The line, for Jimmy's sad and useless horn. And they tell me (via phone, letter, accidental meetings in the Village. "Oh he's in med school and married and lost to you, hombre." Ha. They don't dig completely where I'm at. I have him now, complete. Though it is a vicious sadness cripples my fingers. Those blue and empty afternoons I saw him walking at my side. Criminals in that world. Complete heroes of our time. (Add Allen to complete an early splinter group. Muslim heroes with flapping pants. Raincoats. Trolley car romances.)

And it's me making a portrait of them all. That was the leader's job. Alone with them. (Without them. Except beautiful faces shoved out the window, sunny days, I ran to meet my darkest girl. Ol' Doll. "Man, that bitch got a goddamn new car." And what not. And it's me sayin' to her, Baby, knock me a kiss.

Tonight the leader is faced with decision. Brown had found him drunk and weeping among the dirty clothes. Some guy with a crippled arm had reported to the farmers (a boppin' gang gone social. Sociologists, artistic arbiters of our times). This one an athlete of mouselike proportions. "You know," he said, his withered arm hung stupidly in the rayon suit, "That cat's nuts. He was sittin' up in that room last night with dark glasses on . . . with a yellow bulb . . . pretendin' to read some abstract shit." (Damn, even the color wrong. Where are you now, hippy, under this abstract shit. Not even defense. That you remain forever in that world. No light. Under my fingers. That you exist alone, as I make you. Your sin, a final ugliness to you. For the leopards, all thumbs jerked toward the sand.) "Man, we do not need cats like that in the frat." (Agreed.)

Tom comes in with two big bottles of wine. For the contest. An outing. "Hugh Herbert and W. C. Fields will now indian wrestle for ownership of this here country!" (Agreed.) The leader loses . . . but is still the leader because he said some words no one had heard of before. (That was after the loss.)

Yng Rick has fucked someone else. Let's listen. "Oh, man, you cats don't know what's happenin'." (You're too much, Rick. Much too much. Like Larry Darnell in them ol' italian schools. Much too much.) "Babes" he called them (a poor project across from the convents. Baxter Terrace. Home of the enemy. We stood them off. We Cavaliers. And then, even tho Johnny Boy was his hero. Another midget placed on the purple. Early leader, like myself. The fight of gigantic proportions to settle all those ancient property disputes would have been between us. Both weighing close to 125. But I avoided that like the plague, and managed three times to drive past him with good hooks without incident. Whew, I said to Love, Whew. And Rick, had gone away from them, to school. Like myself. And now, strangely, for the Gods are white our teachers said, he found himself with me. And all the gold and diamonds of the crown I wore he hated. Though, the new wine settled, and his social graces kept him far enough away to ease the hurt of serving a hated master. Hence "babes," and the constant reference to his wiggling flesh. Listen.

"Yeh. Me and Chris had these D.C. babes at their cribs." (Does a dance step with the suggestive flair.) "Oooooo, that was some good box."

Tom knew immediately where that bit was at. And he pulled Rick into virtual madness . . . lies at least. "Yeh, Rick. Yeh? You mean you got a little Jones, huh? Was it good?" (Tom pulls on Rick's sleeve like Laurel and Rick swings.)

"Man, Tom, you don't have to believe it, baby. It's in here now!" (points to his stomach.)

The leader stirs. "Hmm, that's a funny way to fuck." Rick will give a boxing demonstration in a second.

Dick Smith smiles, "Wow, Rick you're way," extending his hand, palm upward. "And what not," Dick adds, for us to laugh. "O.K., you're bad." (At R's crooked jab.) "Huh, this cat always wants to bust somebody up, and what not. Hey, baby, you must be frustrated or something. How come you don't use up all that energy on your babes . . . and what not?"

The rest there, floating empty nouns. Under the sheets. The same death as the crippled fag. Lost with no defense. Except they sit now, for this portrait . . . in which they will be portrayed as losers. Only the leader wins. Tell him that.

Some guys playing cards. Some talking about culture, i.e., the leader had a new side. (Modesty denies. They sit around, in real light. The leader in his green glasses, fidgeting with his joint. Carl, in a brown fedora, trims his toes and nails. Spars with Rick.

Smells his foot and smiles. Brady reads, in his silence, a crumpled black dispatch. Shorter's liver smells the hall and Leon slams the door, waiting for the single chop, the leader might have to share. The door opens, two farmers come in, sharp in orange suits. The hippies laugh, and hide their youthful lies. "Man, I was always hip. I mean, I knew about Brooks Brothers when I was 10." (So sad we never know the truth. About that world, until the bones dry in our heads. Young blond governors with their "dads" hip at the age of 2. That way. Which, now, I sit in judgment of. What I wanted those days with the covers of books turned toward the audience. The first nighters. Or dragging my two forwards to the Music Box to see Elliot Nugent. They would say, these dead men, laughing at us, "The natives are restless," stroking their gouty feet. Gimme culture, culture, culture, and Romeo and Juliet over the emerson.

How many there now? Make it 9. Phil's cracking the books. Jimmy Jones and Pud, two D.C. boys, famous and funny, study "zo" at the top of their voices. "Hemiptera," says Pud. "Homoptera," says Jimmy. "Weak as a bitch," says Phil, "Both your knowledges are flait."

More than 9. Mazique, Enty, operating now in silence. Right hands flashing down the cards. "Uhh!" In love with someone, and money from home. Both perfect, with curly hair. "Uhh! Shit, Enty, hearts is trumps."

"What? Ohh, shit!"

"Uhh!", their beautiful hands flashing under the single bulb.

Hambrick comes with liquor. (A box of fifths, purchased with the fantastic wealth of his father's six shrimp shops.) "You cats caint have all this goddam booze. Brown and I got dates, that's why and we need some for the babes."

Brown has hot dogs for five. Franks, he says. "Damn, Cholley, you only get a half of frank . . . and you take the whole motherfucking thing."

"Aww, man, I'll pay you back." And the room, each inch, is packed with lives. Make it 12 . . . all heroes, or dead. Indian chiefs, the ones not waging their wars, like Clark, in the legal mist of Baltimore. A judge. Old Clark. You remember when we got drunk together and you fell down the stairs. Or that time you fell in the punch bowl puking, and let that sweet yellow ass get away? Boy, I'll never forget that, as long as I live. (Having died seconds later, he talks thru his rot.) Yeh, boy, you were always a card. (White man talk. A card. Who the hell says that, except that branch office with no culture. Piles of bullion, and casual violence. To the mind. Nights they kick you against the buildings. Communist homosexual nigger. "Aw man, I'm married and got two kids."

What could be happening? Some uproar. "FUCK YOU, YOU FUNNY LOOKING SUNAFABITCH."

"Me? Funnylooking? Oh, wow. Will you listen to this little pointy head bastard calling *me* funny looking. Hey, Everett. Hey Everett! Who's the funniest looking . . . me or Keyes?"

"Aww, both you cats need some work. Man, I'm trying to read."

"Read? What? You gettin' into them books, huh? Barnes is whippin' your ass, huh? I told you not to take Organic . . . as light as you are."

"Shit. I'm not even thinking about Barnes. Barnes can kiss my ass."

"Shit. You better start thinking about him, or you'll punch right out. They don't need lightweights down in the valley. Ask Ugly Wilson."

"Look, Tom, I wasn't bothering you."

"Bothering me? Wha's the matter with you ol' Jimmy. Commere boy, lemme rub your head."

"Man, you better get the hell outta here."

"What? . . . Why? What you gonna do? You can't fight, you little funny looking buzzard."

"Hey, Tom, why you always bothering ol' Jimmy Wilson. He's a good man."

"Oh, oh, here's that little light ass Dan sticking up for Ugly again. Why you like him, huh? Cause he's the only cat uglier than you? Huh?"

"Tom's the worst looking cat on campus calling me ugly."

"Well, you are. Wait, lemme bring you this mirror so you can see yourself. Now, what you think. You can't think anything else."

"Aww, man, blow, will you?"

The pork chop is cooked and little charlie is trying to cut a piece off before the leader can stop him. "Ow, goddam."

"Well, who told you to try to steal it, jive ass."

"Hey, man, I gotta get somea that chop."

"Gimme some, Ray."

"Why don't you cats go buy something to eat. I didn't ask anybody for any of those hot dogs. So get away from my grease. Hungry ass spooks."

"Wait a minute, fella. I know you don't mean Young Rick."

"Go ask one of those D.C. babes for something to eat. I know they must have something you could sink your teeth into."

Pud and Jimmy Jones are wrestling under Phil's desk.

A.B. is playin' the dozen with Leon and Teddy. "Teddy are your momma's legs as crooked as yours?"

"This cat always wants to talk about people's mothers! Country bastard."

Tom is pinching Jimmy Wilson. Dan is laughing at them.

Enty and Mazique are playing bridge with the farmers. "Uhh! Beat that, jew boy!"

"What the fuck is trumps?"

The leader is defending his pork chop from Cholley, Rick, Brady, Brown, Hambrick, Carl, Dick Smith, (S from the City has gone out catting.

"Who is it?"

A muffled voice, under the uproar, "It's Mister Bush."

"Bush? Hey, Ray . . . Ray."

"Who is it?"

Plainer. "Mister Bush." (Each syllable pronounced and correct as a soft southern american can.) Innocent VIII in his bedroom shoes. Gregory at Canossa, raging softly in his dignity and power. "Mister Bush."

"Ohh, shit. Get that liquor somewhere. O.K., Mr. Bush, just a second. . . . Not there, asshole, in the drawer."

"Mr. McGhee, will you kindly open the door."

"Ohh, shit, the hot plate. I got it." The leader turns a wastepaper basket upside-down on top of the chop. Swings open the door. "Oh, Hello Mister Bush. How are you this evening?" About 15 boots sit smiling toward the door. Come in, Boniface. What news of Luther? In unison, now.

"Hi . . . Hello . . . How are you, Mister Bush?"

"Uh, huh."

He stares around the room, grinding his eyes into their various hearts. An unhealthy atmosphere, this America. "Mr. McGhee, why is it if there's noise in this dormitory it always comes from this room?" Aww, he knows. He wrote me years later in the air force that he knew, even then.

"What are you running here, a boys' club?" (That's it.) He could narrow his eyes even in that affluence. Put his hands on his hips. Shove that stomach at you as proof he was an authority of the social grace . . . a western man, no matter the color of his skin. How To? He was saying, this is not the way. Don't act like that word. Don't fail us. We've waited for all you handsome boys too long. Erect a new world, of lies and stocking caps. Silence, and a reluctance of memory. Forget the slow grasses, and flame, flame in the valley. Feet bound, dumb eyes begging for darkness. The bodies moved with the secret movement of the air. Swinging. My beautiful grandmother kneels in the shadow weeping. Flame, flame in the valley. Where is it there is light? Where, this music rakes my talk?

"Why is it, Mr. McGhee, when there's some disturbance in this building, it always comes from here?" (Aww, you said that . . .)

"And what are all you other gentlemen doing in here? Good night, there must be twenty of you here! Really, gentlemen, don't any of you have anything to do?" He made to smile, Ha, I know some of you who'd better be in your rooms right now hitting those books . . . or you might not be with us next semester. Ha.

"O.K., who is that under that sheet?" (It was Enty, a student dormitory director, hiding under the sheets, flat on the leader's bed.) "You, sir, whoever you are, come out of there, hiding won't do you any good. Come out!" (We watched the sheet, and it quivered. Innocent raised his finger.) "Come out, sir!" (The sheet pushed slowly back. Enty's head appeared. And Bush more embarrassed than he.) "Mr. Enty! My assistant dormitory director, good night. A man of responsibility. Go-od night! Are there any more hiding in here, Mr. McGhee?"

"Not that I know of."

"Alright, Mr. Enty, you come with me. And the rest of you had better go to your rooms and try to make some better grades. Mr. McGhee, I'll talk to you tomorrow morning in my office."

The leader smiles, "Yes." (Jive ass.)

Bush turns to go, Enty following sadly. "My God, what's that terrible odor . . . something burning." (The leader's chop, and the wastepaper, under the basket, starting to smoke.) "Mr. McGhee, what's that smell?"

"Uhhh," (come-on, baby) "Oh, it's Strothers' kneepads on the radiator! (Yass) They're drying."

"Well, Jesus, I hope they dry soon. Whew! And don't forget, tomorrow morning, Mr. McGhee, and you other gentlemen had better retire, it's 2 in the morning!" The door slams. Charlie sits where Enty was. The bottles come out. The basket is turned right-side up. Chop and most of the papers smoking. The leader pours water onto the mess and sinks to his bed.

"Damn. Now I have to go hungry. Shit."

"That was pretty slick, ugly, the kneepads! Why don't you eat them they look pretty done."

The talk is to that. That elegance of performance. The rite of lust, or self-extinction. Preservation. Some leave, and a softer uproar descends. Jimmy Jones and Pud wrestle quietly on the bed. Phil quotes the *Post*'s sport section on Willie Mays. Hambrick and

Brown go for franks. Charlie scrapes the "burn" off the chop and eats it alone. Tom, Dan, Ted and the leader drink and manufacture lives for each person they know. We know. Even you. Tom, the lawyer. Dan, the lawyer. Ted, the high-school teacher. All their proper ways. And the leader, without cause or place. Except talk, feeling, guilt. Again, only those areas of the world make sense. Talk. We are doing that now. Feeling: that too. Guilt. That inch of wisdom, forever. Except he sits reading in green glasses. As, "No, no, the utmost share/Of my desire shall be/Only to kiss that air/That lately kissèd thee."

"Uhh! What's trumps, dammit!"

As, "Tell me not, Sweet, I am unkind/That from the nunnery/Of thy chaste breast and quiet mind/To war and arms I fly."

"You talking about a lightweight mammy-tapper, boy, you really king."

Oh, Lucasta, find me here on the bed, with hard pecker and dirty feet. Oh, I suffer, in my green glasses, under the canopy of my loves. Oh, I am drunk and vomity in my room, with only Charley Ventura to understand my grace. As, "Hardly are those words out when a vast image out of *Spiritus Mundi*/Troubles my sight: somewhere in sands of the desert/A shape with lion body and the head of a man/A gaze blank and pitiless as the sun/Is moving its slow thighs, while all about it/Reel shadows of the indignant desert birds."

Primers for dogs who are learning to read. Tinkle of European teacups. All longing, speed, suffering. All adventure, sadness, stink and wisdom. All feeling, silence, light. As, "Crush, O sea the cities with their catacomb-like corridors/And crush eternally the vile people/The idiots, and the abstemious, and mow down, mow down/With a single stroke the bent backs of the shrunken harvest!"

"Damn, Charlie, We brought back a frank for everybody . . . now you want two. Wrong sunafabitch!"

"Verde que te quiero verde./Verde viento. Verdes ramas./El barco sobre la mar/y el caballo en la montaña."

"Hey, man, I saw that ol' fagit Bobby Hutchens down in the lobby with a real D.C. queer. I mean a real way-type sissy."

"Huh, man he's just another *actor* . . . hooo."

"That cat still wearing them funny lookin' pants?"

"Yeh, and orange glasses. Plus, the cat always needs a haircut, and what not."

"Hey, man you cats better cool it . . . you talkin' about Ray's main man. You dig?"

"Yeh. I see this cat easin' around corners with the cat all the time. I mean, talkin' some off the wall shit, too, baby."

"Yeh. Yeh. Why don't you cats go fuck yourselves or something hip like that, huh?"

"O.K., ugly Tom, you better quit inferring that shit about Ray. What you trying to say, ol' pointy head is funny or something?"

"*Funny . . . how the sound of your voice . . . thri-ills me. Strange . . .*" (the last à la King Cole.)

"Fuck you cats and your funny looking families too."

A wall. With light at the top, perhaps. No, there is light. Seen from both sides, a gesture of life. But always more than is given. An abstract infinitive. To love. To lie. To want. And that always . . . to want. Always, more than is given. The dead scramble up each side . . . words or drunkenness. Praise, to the flesh. Rousseau, Hobbes, and their betters. All move, from flesh to love. From love to flesh. At that point under the static light. It could be Shostakovich in Charleston, South Carolina. Or in the dull windows of Chicago, an unread volume of Joyce. Some black woman who will never hear the word *Negress* or remember your name. Or a thin preacher who thinks your name is Stephen. A wall. Oh, Lucasta.

"Man, you cats don't know anything about Hutchens. I don't see why you talk about the cat and don't know the first thing about him."

"Shit. If he ain't funny . . . Skippy's a punk."

"How come you don't say that to Skippy?"

"Our Own Boy, Skippy Weatherson. All-coon fullback for 12 years."

"You tell him that!"

"Man, don't try to change the subject. This cat's trying to keep us from talking about his boy, Hutchens."

"Yeh, mammy-rammer. What's happenin' McGhee, ol' man?"

"Hooo. Yeh. They call this cat Dick Brown. Hoooo!"

Rick moves to the offensive. The leader in his book, or laughs, "Aww, man, that cat ain't my boy. I just don't think you cats ought to talk about people you don't know anything about! Plus, that cat probably gets more ass than any of you silly-ass mother fuckers."

"Hee. That Ray sure can pronounce that word. I mean he don't say mutha' like most folks . . . he always pronounces the mother *and* the fucker, so proper. And it sure makes it sound nasty." (A texas millionaire talking.)

"Hutchens teachin' the cat how to talk . . . that's what's happening. Ha. In exchange for services rendered!"

"Wait, Tom. Is it you saying that Hutchens and my man here are into some funny shit?"

"No, man. It's you saying that. It was me just inferring, you dig?"

"Hey, why don't you cats just get drunk in silence, huh?"

"Hey, Bricks, what was Hutchens doin' downstairs with that cat?"

"Well, they were just coming in the dormitory, I guess. Hutchens was signing in that's all."

"Hey, you dig . . . I bet he's takin' that cat up to his crib."

"Yeh, I wonder what they into by now. Huh! Probably suckin' the shit out of each other."

"Aww, man, cool it, willya . . . Damn!"

"What's the matter, Ray, you don't dig love?"

"Hey, it's young Rick saying, that we oughta go up and dig what's happenin' up there?"

"Square mother fucker!"

"Votre mere!"

"Votre mere noir!"

"Boy, these cats in French One think they hip!"

"Yeh, let's go up and see what those cats are doing."

"Tecch, aww, shit. Damn, you some square cats, wow! Cats got nothing better to do than fuck with people. Damn!"

Wall. Even to move, impossible. I sit, now, forever where I am. No further. No farther. Father, who am I to hide myself? And brew a world of soft lies.

Again. "Verde que te quiero verde." Green. Read it again Il Duce. Make it build some light here . . . where there is only darkness. Tell them "Verde, que te quiero verde." I want you Green. Leader, the paratroopers will come for you at noon. A helicopter low over the monastery. To get you out.

But my country. My people. These dead souls, I call my people. Flesh of my flesh.

At noon, Il Duce. Make them all etceteras. Extras. The soft strings behind the final horns.

"Hey, Ray, you comin' with us?"

"Fuck you cats. I got other things to do."

"Damn, now the cat's trying to pretend he can read Spanish."

"Yeh . . . well let's go see what's happening cats."

"Cats, Cats, Cats . . . What's happenin'?"

"Hey, Smitty! We going upstairs to peep that ol' sissy Hutchens. He's got some big time D.C. faggot in there with him. You know, we figured it'd be better than 3-D."

"Yeh? That's pretty hip. You not coming, Ray?"

"No, man . . . I'm sure you cats can peep in a keyhole without me."

"Bobby's his main man, that's all."

"Yeh, mine and your daddy's."

Noise. Shouts, and Rick begs them to be softer. For the circus. Up the creaking stairs, except Carl and Leon who go to the freshman dorm to play ping-pong . . . and Ted who is behind in his math.

The 3rd floor of Park Hall, an old 19th-century philanthropy, gone to seed. The missionaries' words dead & hung useless in the air. "Be clean, thrifty, and

responsible. Show the anti-Christs you're ready for freedom and God's true word." Peasants among the mulattoes, and the postman's son squats in his glasses shivering at his crimes.
"Hey, which room is his?"
"Three Oh Five."
"Hey, Tom, how you know the cat's room so good? This cat must be sneaking too."
"Huhh, yeh!"
"O.K. Rick, just keep walking."
"Here it is."
"Be cool, bastard. Shut up."
They stood and grinned. And punched each other. Two bulbs in the hall. A window at each end. One facing the reservoir, the other, the fine-arts building where Professor Gorsun sits angry at jazz. "Goddamnit none of that nigger music in my new building. Culture. Goddamnit, ladies and gentlemen, line up and be baptized. This pose will take the hurt away. We are white and featureless under this roof. Praise God, from whom all blessings flow!"
"Bobby. Bobby, baby."

"Huh?"
"Don't go blank on me like that, baby. I was saying something."
"Oh, I'm sorry . . . I guess I'm just tired or something."
"I was saying, how can you live in a place like this. I mean, really, baby, this place is nowhere. Whew. It's like a jail or something eviler."
"Yes, I know."
"Well, why don't you leave it then. You're much too sensitive for a place like this. I don't see why you stay in this damn school. You know, you're really talented."
"Yeh, well, I figured I have to get a degree, you know. Teach or something, I suppose. There's not really much work around for spliv actors."
"Oh, Bobby,

you ought to stop being so conscious of being coloured. It really is not fashionable. Ummm. You know you have beautiful eyes."

"You want another drink, Lyle?"

"Ugg. Oh, that cheap bourbon. You know I have some beautiful wines at home. You should try drinking some good stuff for a change. Damn, Bob, why don't you just leave this dump and move into my place? There's certainly enough room. And we certainly get along. Ummm. Such beautiful eyes and hair too."

"Hah. How much rent would I have to pay out there. I don't have penny the first!"

"Rent? No, no . . . you don't have to worry about that. I'll take care of all that. I've got one of those gooood jobs, honey. U.S. guvment."

"Oh? Where do you work?"

"The P.O. with the rest of the fellas. But it's enough for what I want to do. And you wouldn't be an expense. Hmmp. Or would you? You know you have the kind of strong masculine hands I love. Like you could crush anything you wanted. Lucky I'm on your good side. Hmmp."

"Well, maybe at the end of this semester I could leave. If the offer still holds then."

"Still holds? Well why not? We'll still be friends then, I'm certain. Ummm. Say, why don't we shut off that light."

"Umm. Let me do it. There. . . . You know I loved you in Jimmy's play, but the rest of those people are really just kids. You were the only person who really understood what was going on. You have a strong maturity that comes through right away. How old are you, Bobby?"

"Nineteen."

"O baby . . .

that's why your skin is so soft. Yes. Say, why wait until the end of the semester . . . that's two months away. I might be dead before that, you know. Umm."

The wind moves thru the leader's room, and he sits alone, under the drooping velvet, repeating words he does not understand. The yellow light burns. He turns it off. Smokes. Masturbates. Turns it on. Verde, verde. Te quiero. Smokes. And then to his other source. "Yma's brother," Tom said when he saw it. "Yma Sumac, Albert Camus. Man, nobody wants to go by their right names no more. And a cat told me that chick ain't really from Peru. She was born in Brooklyn man, and her name's Camus too. Amy Camus. This cat's name is probably Trebla Sumac, and he ain't French he's from Brooklyn too. Yeh. Ha!"

In the dark the words are anything. "If it is true that the only paradise is that which one has lost, I know what name to give that something tender and inhuman which dwells within me today."

"Oh, shit, fuck it. Fuck it." He slams the book against the wall, and empties Hambrick's bottle. "I mean, why?" Empties bottle. "Shiiit."

When he swings the door open the hall above is screams. Screams. All their voices, even now right here. The yellow glasses falling on the stairs, and broken. In his bare feet. "Shiit. Dumb ass cats!"

"Rick, Rick, what's the cat doing now?"

"Man, be cool. Ha, the cat's kissin' Hutchens on the face, man. Um-uh-mm. Yeh, baby. Damn, he's puttin' his hands all over the cat. Aww, rotten motherfuckers!"

"What's happening?"

"Bastards shut out the lights!"

"Damn."

"Gaw-uhd damn!"

"Hey, let's break open the door."

"Yeh, HEY, YOU CATS, WHAT'S HAPPENING IN THERE, HUH?"

"Yeh. Hee, hee. OPEN UP, FAGGOTS!"

"Wheee! HEY LET US IN, GIRLS!"

Ricky and Jimmy run against the door, the others screaming and jumping, doors opening all along the hall. They all come out, screaming as well. "LET US IN. HEY, WHAT'S HAPPENIN', BABY!" Rick and Jimmy run against the door, and the door is breaking.

"Who is it? What do you want?" Bobby turns the light on, and his friend, a balding queer of 40 is hugged against the sink.

"Who are they, Bobby? What do they want?"

"Bastards. Damn if I know. GET OUTTA HERE, AND MIND YOUR OWN DAMN BUSINESS, YOU CREEPS. Creeps. Damn. Put on your clothes, Lyle!"

"God, they're trying to break the door down, Bobby. What they want? Why are they screaming like that?"

"GET THE HELL AWAY FROM THIS DOOR, GODDAMNIT!"

"YEH, YEH. WE SAW WHAT YOU WAS DOIN' HUTCHENS. OPEN THE DOOR AND LET US GET IN ON IT."

"WHEEEEEE! HIT THE FUCKING DOOR, RICK! HIT IT!"

And at the top of the stairs the leader stops, the whole hall full of citizens. Doctors, judges, first negro directors of welfare chain, morticians, chemists, ad men, fighters for civil rights, all admirable, useful men. "BREAK THE FUCKIN' DOOR OPEN, RICK! YEH!"

A wall. Against

it, from where you stand, the sea stretches smooth for miles out. Their voices distant thuds of meat against the sand. Murmurs of insects. Hideous singers against your pillow every night of your life. They are there now, screaming at you.

"Ray, Ray, comeon man help us break this faggot's door!"

"Yeh, Ray, comeon!"

"Man, you cats are fools. Evil stupid fools!"

"What? Man, will you listen to this cat."

"Listen, hell, let's get this door. One more smash and it's in. Comeon, Brady, lets break the fuckin' thing."

"Yeh, comeon you cats, don't stand there listenin' to that pointy head clown, he just don't want us to pop his ol' lady!"

"YEH, YEH. LET'S GET IN THERE. HIT IT HIT IT!"

"Goddamnit. Goddamnit, get the fuck out of here. Get outta here. Damnit Rick, you sunafabitch, get the hell outtahere. Leave the cat alone!"

"Man, don't push me like that, you lil' skinny ass. I'll bust your jaw for you."

"Yeh? Yeh? Yeh? Well you come on, you lyin' ass. This cat's always talking about all his 'babes' and all he's got to do is sneak around peeping in keyholes. You big lying asshole . . . all you know how to do is bullshit and jerk off!"

"Fuck you, Ray."

"Your ugly ass mama."

"Shiit. You wanna go round with me, baby?"

"Comeon. Comeon, big time cocksman, comeon!"

Rick hits the leader full in the face, and he falls backwards across the hall. The crowd follows screaming at this new feature.

"Aww, man, somebody stop this shit. Rick'll kill Ray!"

"Well, you stop it, man."

"O.K., O.K., cut it out. Cut it out, Rick. You win man. Leave the cat alone. Leave him alone."

"Bad Rick . . . Bad Rick, Bad ass Rick!"

"Well, man, you saw the cat fuckin' with me. He started the shit!"

"Yeh . . . tough cat!"

"Get up Ray."

And then the door does open and Bobby Hutchens stands in the half light in his shower shoes, a broom in his hands. The boys scream and turn their attention back to Love. Bald Lyle is in the closet. More noise. More lies. More prints in the sand, away, or toward some name. I am a poet. I am a rich famous butcher. I am the man who paints the gold balls on the tops of flagpoles. I am, no matter, more beautiful than anyone else. And I have come a long way to say this. Here. In the long hall, shadows across my hands. My face pushed hard against the floor. And the wood, old, and protestant. And their voices, all these other selves screaming for blood. For blood, or whatever it is fills their noble lives.

BENNETT CAPERS

The Truth of
the Matter

E ven now, as I drove out to John's Island, I wondered what I
had gotten myself into. I glanced over at my brand-new,
unopened notebook and reminded myself that somehow I'd
have to come back with a story. That is, if I wanted to keep my
job with the News & Courier.

I had been hired a week earlier and had spent most of my
time since then apprenticing myself to other staff reporters,
checking spelling mistakes that weren't caught by the word
processors. Then today the editor had called me into his office,
looked me up and down, and told me he wanted me to drive out
to John's Island and look into a shooting that had happened a
year ago.

A year-old shooting. I wanted to ask him if he considered that
news.

"We want to do a sort of year-ago-today story on this shooting," he told me. "It wasn't just any old shooting either. What
happened is this: A minister's son wrecks his dad's car, completely destroys this beautiful Cadillac. The son's okay, but
when he gets home that night he and his minister father start
fighting. Next thing you know a gun goes off and everyone says

the minister shot himself, and that's how the police report it. Now it's a year later, and the wife's in an insane asylum. Furthermore, the son's not speaking to anybody. It's like he's in a trance. Sounds like something's there, doesn't it?"

"Yes, sir," I said, although it didn't sound like much to me.

"Anyway, for a place like Charleston that's an interesting story. We want you to look into it. Find out what really happened. Like a human interest story. The kind you get in New York."

I considered reminding him that I'd gone to college in New Haven, not New York. Instead, I mumbled another, "Yes, sir." *You'll say Yes, sir and Yes, ma'am to everything, even if you disagree and your heart tells you differently*, the girl I'd been living with in New Haven had said the week before I'd left. By then Moira and I were at the stage where we were deciding which things were mine and which were hers, and the words she threw at me were few and bitter and usually contained hidden meanings to decipher. *You'll say Yes, sir.* I'd wanted to tell her that the South wasn't like that anymore. But I had said nothing.

"You're from Charleston originally, right?" the editor asked, bringing me back to the newsroom and the present. He narrowed his eyes. "You sure don't sound like it. Picked up one of those northern accents, huh? Don't look like it either." I wondered what I must look like to him, notebook firmly in hand, pencil behind my left ear, dressed like a southern reporter in khakis and an oxford shirt. Did I look eager? Did I even look like a reporter? I imagined him wondering why I'd come back. Or why I went away in the first place. "Anyway, I guess you know how it is on John's Island. The people there are illiterate for the most part and still speak some kind of Gullah dialect, but I'm sure you'll be able to understand them. The thing is they're a real quiet kind of people. That's why I'm thinking you'll be good for this story. Those people don't like to speak around us. They'll nod and smile, but they won't answer our questions. That's why we're sending you in there. They'll talk to you."

By *those people*, he meant poor blacks. By *us*, he didn't mean me. I imagined Moira's cynical voice. *Send him to do the black*

stories, he has that special edge. And if he fucks up, let him cover
sports. His people know sports inside out.

"So where do I start?"

For a second or two he rearranged papers on his desk, and I
wondered if he'd forgotten I was still standing there. He took off
his glasses and wiped them, then put them back on. He
scratched at some dandruff in his hair. "Well, the wife wouldn't
be much help. She's in an asylum now. And from what I've
heard, the reverend's son isn't speaking to anybody. I don't mean
just reporters. He's not speaking to *anyone* anyone. If I were you
I'd see what I could get out of the son's old girlfriend. Avey
Toomer. Works at a little store her father owns. Can't miss it.
It's called the Convenience Store."

I nodded and said, "Yes, sir."

I'd never been to John's Island, even though it was only twenty
or so miles outside Charleston. I'd read somewhere that during
slavery there had been several large sugar plantations on the
island.

Black faces smiled at me as I drove along a barely paved road.
Dogs sat lazily in the middle of the road, scratching at fleas and
empty patches of skin, and I often had to honk my horn to get
them to move. The one-story shacks lining the road looked as if
they'd never been painted. Many had plastic sheets where glass
windows should have been.

I drove until I reached a clearing and saw a group of men
sitting on a porch, smoking cigars and staring at me as I parked
my car. I grabbed my notebook, opened the door, and was immediately hit by a wave of heat and a salty smell so strong I
almost gagged. I remembered that John's Island was surrounded
by a marsh. I started to lock my car, and then remembered that
out here I didn't have to. These people would no more steal than
they would eat their own flesh. Or at least that's what I'd heard.

"I'm looking for something called the Convenience Store," I
said as I approached the men.

One of the younger men started laughing. He pointed to a
sign. "You looking at it, mister."

A hand-painted wooden sign had been propped against the edge of the porch: THE CONVEYANCE STORE.

"Air-conditioning, huh?" a grey-haired man with one dangling grey tooth asked, jutting his chin in the direction of the car.

I nodded.

"What kinda make would that be?"

Would that be? I ignored the question. "Where can I find Avey Toomer?"

"Just inside. Figured you was here to see her. Hot piece of ass on her."

"You ain't around from here, is you?" another asked as I stepped inside the store.

"Better not let her daddy catch you," I heard one of the men call behind me.

The store looked much as I'd imagined it would. Canned goods. Shelves lined with jars of pigs' feet. A young girl stood behind the counter, resting her elbows on the cash register. I got the impression she was daydreaming. She couldn't have been more than seventeen. The book *Mules and Men* lay open on the counter. I cleared my throat. "Avey Toomer?"

She smiled. "I'm Avey. How can I help you?"

She spoke differently from the men, not as much a quick-speak about her. I introduced myself and told her I was a re-porter from the *News & Courier*, researching the Reverend McCoy's death. I flipped open my notebook and immediately felt foolish, like someone pretending to be a reporter. For the second time that day I wondered what I must look like. I pressed on. "Is there anything you can tell me about how he died?"

"I don't know what I can tell you that's not already public knowledge." Here she looked past my shoulder to where the group of men were sitting on the store porch. "Each one of them can tell you stories about what happened."

"I'm asking you."

Avey looked at me with the weariness of one who's told the same story too many times, only to be asked to repeat it yet again. That was how she spoke now, as if she were repeating something she'd long ago committed to memory. "Well, as you probably already know, the Reverend McCoy killed himself. He shot himself in the face. A lot of people around here don't believe that, but it's true. He was depressed—manic depression, I think they call it—and that night especially so. People were saying he'd been pocketing church funds. His wife seemed to be losing her mind. And Graham had just come home from the prom without his father's Cadillac. I imagine finding out about the car is what pushed him over. Graham wrecked it, you see."

Here I must have given her a look of incredulity.

"You may think that's silly, but if you look around you, you'll notice that not many people on John's Island have cars. And certainly no one has a Cadillac. Rev. McCoy's Cadillac separated him from the rest of the people here. He took his car very seriously."

"And his son Graham wrecked it?"

"Totaled it is more like it. An accident. I feel partly to blame. You see, Graham and I had gone to the high school prom together that night, and we had a fight. Over something silly, really. I truly don't remember over what. And Graham stormed off the dance floor and drove off in a huff. Plus he'd been drinking that night. Everybody drinks at the prom. You know how kids are." She said this without a trace of irony, as if her own teenage years were long past.

"About an hour later I heard the sirens, but it didn't occur to me that they might be for Graham. And then later that night I heard sirens again. It wasn't until the next morning that I learned Graham had been in an accident but was okay. Drove straight into a tree but was okay. And that Graham's father had shot himself. You can't imagine the thoughts that went through my mind. The shock. Everybody was shocked by the whole thing. Especially Graham."

"From what I hear, he doesn't talk to anyone."

"He's still mourning. That's all. Each person has his own way of grieving. And think about it. If you were only eighteen and your father committed suicide and your mother had to be taken to an asylum, you might react the same way. I mean, not speak to anyone for a while. It's not that strange."

"Where can I find him?"

"Just up the road a bit. You can't miss his house. These shanties continue about half a mile or so. Then you reach a paved road with streetlights. The only streetlights on the island. You'll see six two-story houses with paint. Graham lives in the largest of the six houses. There's three hanging baskets in front." Here she smiled at me. "He won't speak to you, though."

"I'll take my chances."

I was halfway out the store when Avey called me. I turned to face her. "I didn't paint that sign outside," she said. "I just wanted you to know that. I'm going to Spelman College in September." I nodded.

I stepped onto the porch and was struck again by the salty, marshlike smell. I felt a wave of nausea and rested my hand on the banister. The men were gathered around my car, peering though the windows. Somebody nudged somebody who nudged somebody else, and they all looked up at me. "Nice car," one of the men said. They made a space so I could get through them and open the car door. I rolled down the window, thinking that maybe it looked silly using an air conditioner in front of people who probably didn't even have electric fans.

"She's a babe, ain't she?" one of them said as I put my key in the ignition.

"It's a nice car," I said. Then it occurred to me they were talking about the girl, Avey.

"Yeah, I'm gonna give it to her good one of these days," another man said. He scratched his goatee.

A third man, this one in overalls and a plaid shirt, snorted. "Just don't let her daddy catch you."

"I'd whip his ass and make him watch."

"Hot ass on her. And the way she shakes that stuff. She'll get what's coming to her one of these days."

I backed the car up a few feet. Just as I was about to shift into drive, one of the younger guys came running up to the car. He grinned sheepishly and wiped the sweat off his forehead with the back of his hand. His Jheri curls glistened in the sun. "What'd she tell you in there?" His breath smelled like stale beer.

"Rev. McCoy killed himself. But I'm sure you already knew that."

"Kill hisself? That's what she told you. Well, if you believe that you a bigger fool than we took you for."

"What?"

"Just that there weren't no suicide. When you ever know a black fellow to kill hisself? You think on that."

"What do you mean?"

But already he had disappeared into the crowd of men talking about Avey as if she were a wishbone. I wanted to stay and ask him more questions, but the queasiness in my stomach was getting worse. I figured anything he wanted to tell me could wait until tomorrow.

The next day I drove back to John's Island, hoping to see the guy who'd spoken to me and then maybe speak to Graham. I parked my car just outside the Conveyance Store, and again the men sitting on the porch looked up from their checker games and boasting tales. However, when I approached them and asked about the young man with Jheri curls, none of them seemed to know whom I was talking about. Instead, they kept asking me where I was from. They said I didn't talk like a Charleston fellow.

Since the marshy air didn't seem as heavy as it had the day before, I decided to walk to Graham's house. I followed the road Avey had suggested. More shacklike houses lined the road. In many of the grassless yards sat old women, who stared at me with unabashed curiosity. Were they trying to place me as somebody's boy, or somebody else's cousin? Other yards were filled with barely dressed children. They all had big bellies and big navels. Some of them pointed at me and smiled before resuming their games of Miss Mary Mack, Double Dutch, and others I didn't recognize. Occasionally their mothers, some pregnant again, all with their hair hot-combed straight and wearing dullish white dresses, would stick their heads out. Some of the women's hands were covered with flour. Others came out carrying old-fashioned skillets.

I figured that while I was passing through I may as well see what I could find out from these people about the Reverend McCoy. The women I approached, however, each gave me the same answer: "Don't know. Up the shreet."

About half a mile along the road, I reached "up the shreet." A paved road, streetlights without sidewalks, and six houses that had seen paint recently. Just looking at the area, I could tell this was the island's equivalent to Charleston's Battery, with its antebellum mansions. I went to the largest house, a white house with three hanging baskets on the porch. Graham's house. I rang the doorbell. No one answered.

I decided to knock on the doors of the other five houses. Here the women were friendlier, actually inviting me into their "parlors." Still, I sensed that they were avoiding a lot of my questions. Even though they chatted easily about the weather and Charleston and offered me "lem'nade" or "ice tea," they grew reticent when I began asking about the Reverend McCoy.

This much, though, I did gather:

From Mrs. Walker, the woman who lived in the house across from the McCoys, I found out that an hour before the ambulance came for the reverend, he was pacing back and forth on his front porch. "He was worried about the rumors concerning his appropriating church assets?" I asked her.

"What?"

"Worried about gossip he was robbing the church blind."

"Naw. This was prom night. Judging by the length of his steps when he was pacing back and forth, I'd say he was fretting over his Cadillac." She suggested I see Mrs. Hurston if I wanted to hear the whole story.

From Mrs. Morrison, or more precisely from her younger brother, who had passed the McCoy house on his way home from a crap game, that the Reverend McCoy was standing on the porch at 1:30 A.M. that same night, no longer pacing but just standing there looking out into the street. That if I wanted to know "everything that went down," I should see the local gossip, Mrs. Hurston.

From Gloria, Mrs. Walker's thirty-one-year-old daughter, that the sound of sirens woke her up at approximately 1:45 A.M., and she looked out her window to see what all the commotion was. "Looking back on it, I guess these sirens were going to the scene of the car accident." That just as she was looking out her window, the Reverend McCoy was inside *his* house looking outside *his* living room window. She waved, but the reverend might not have seen her, because he didn't wave back. Behind him could be seen the silhouette ("shadow" was her exact word) of Mrs. McCoy, standing in the doorway in a nightgown, sucking on a butterscotch. Gloria went back to sleep and woke again to the sound of a shot ("at first I thought it might be firecrackers") at approximately 4:30 A.M. A few minutes later she heard sirens again, which stopped right outside her window. She got dressed and went outside, and that's when she found out that the Reverend McCoy was shot in the face, straight through the eyes.

And from Terry, Gloria's friend, that the sirens didn't have to wake Gloria either the first or the second time because Gloria was up entertaining a certain married male friend, and that it was doubtful that Gloria could tell from across the street and through two windows that Mrs. McCoy was sucking on a butterscotch candy. And that no matter what I did, if it's the "truth and nothing but" I was after, I should stay away from that old hag, Mrs. Hurston.

I decided to pay Mrs. Hurston a visit.

"Yeah?"

"Are you Mrs. Hurston?" I asked.

"That depends. What you looking for her for? You ain't from around here, are you?"

I shook my head and opened the gate to the walkway. In the middle of the yard stood a small cross made out of safety reflectors. The woman kept rocking back and forth, her suspicious eyes never leaving me.

"Did you ask if you could open that gate? Did I ask you to come in?"

I stopped in midstep.

"That's better. Now state your name and business."

I told her that I was a reporter and wanted to ask some questions about Reverend McCoy.

"Too late. He's dead already."

I explained to her that I wanted to find out the circumstances of his death.

"You from the *Chronicle*? Got any free copies with you?" I shook my head no. The *Chronicle* was Charleston's black newspaper.

I was still standing on the walkway of her front yard, banana-leaf plants and four-foot sunflowers on either side of me. "Can I come up now?"

"*May* I," she said. "Yes, you may."

I started climbing the porch steps, and that's when I saw how old Mrs. Hurston really was. Her face was sunken in and shiny, but like many old black women she had no wrinkles. A jet-black wig barely covered her head—I could see her own coarse, gray strands underneath. She had a patchwork quilt wrapped around her, though it must have been at least 95 degrees. From the open front door came the smell of cabbage and bacon drippings. I shook her hand, and she gave me a look that told me she'd never had a man shake her hand before, and I leaned against the porch banister. A black cat was sleeping peacefully underneath the shade of Mrs. Hurston's porch swing. I turned to a fresh sheet in my notepad. "I'm hoping you can tell me what you know about the Reverend McCoy's death."

She closed her eyes, and for a second I thought she had nodded off to sleep. Then she started speaking, her eyes still closed, as if this were a seance and she was a medium. "Well, he's dead. You know that much. Do you know about the funeral?" She didn't wait for me to answer. "It was a beautiful funeral. Two hours late, but that's C.P. time for you. A good turnout, though. So many people that everybody couldn't fit in the church. Had to put speakers outside so people who couldn't fit in could hear what was going on. Although I suspect most of what they heard over the speakers was the reverend's wife unwrapping her butterscotch candies. You know how loud plastic can be.

"The reverend's wife was her old self at the funeral. Nose so high in the air you'd think her neck would break. Sitting on the front pew and sucking on her butterscotch candies. She had on the same black hat and the same black veil she had on when our deacon Mr. Gaines died. But her dress was new. Got it from Condon's in the city. She always was one for appearances, if you know what I mean. The reverend himself was the same way. Graham sat beside her on the front pew. The first time I lay eyes on him I knew there was trouble around the corner. And next to him there were some white men from Charleston. They always send representatives out when a preacher or somebody dies," Mrs. Hurston said, lingering on the word "representatives." "It was a lovely funeral."

"Actually, I'm more interested in how he died than how he was buried."

Mrs. Hurston continued as if she hadn't heard me. "Of course, Mrs. McCoy's on Bull Street now. Hardly even remembers her own name, or so folks say. Most people think it's the secret she kept that drove her crazy. Others say, naw, it was her son drove her crazy. And then other folks 'round here say it's the wrath of God come down on her for lying through her teeth that the reverend shot himself."

"He didn't shoot himself?"

Mrs. Hurston opened her eyes and glared at me. "Did I say he didn't shoot himself?"

"You said—"

"What do the police records say?"

I told her what my editor had told me, that his death was listed as a suicide.

"I mean about the car accident his boy was in that same night. What do those police records say?"

I shrugged.

Mrs. Hurston sucked her teeth with satisfaction, as if I'd proved her point. Just then she sat up in her porch swing. "Look. By the sea muckle. He's leaving his house now."

I looked to where she was pointing. A young man wearing white pants and a white tank top was passing by.

"That's Graham," Mrs. Hurston said.

I excused myself and ran after him. "He won't speak to you," Mrs. Hurston called after me.

I called out his name, but he ignored me. I followed him. I had to walk quickly to keep up. I followed him for what would have been a few blocks if we were in a city but out here on the island was just a stretch of road. I kept a safe distance behind him. On either side of us were shacklike houses again, but these were a lot closer together, with narrow pathways between them. I wanted to see where he was going, but he ducked away somewhere, and I lost him.

When I got back to Charleston I followed up on the first of two leads Mrs. Hurston had given me. I called up an old friend from high school who was now working for the police department, asking him to see what he could find under the police files on a car accident involving Graham McCoy.

"McCoy," he said. "Any relation to the Reverend McCoy who killed himself out there?"

"The son."

"Hmm. Okay, I'll give you a call if I find something."

"Can't you just call it up on the computer and tell me now?"

"Computer? You in Charleston, not New York."

"New Haven."

"New what? Listen, you want me to call you or what?"

I gave him my phone number.

"Hey," he said just as I was about to hang up.

"What?"

"What are the girls like in New York or New Heaven or whatever you call it? They as easy as everybody says?"

I thought of Moira. It had been she who'd led me to her bed the night of our first date. She who'd kissed a trail across my body. And she who, after a year and a half of us living together, had cried when I finally left. Easy? "Yeah," I said, thinking it was too complicated to explain. "Easy as pie."

In fact, it'd been Moira who'd asked me to leave. She told me to get out and then cried when I finally left. Those last two weeks were filled with silence for the most part, the two of us exchanging words only to confirm what was hers and what was mine, and to discuss arrangements for her to ship my furniture to me, the two of us knowing that she'd simply sell it as soon as I left. Only once during those last two weeks did she venture to the topic that was really on her mind. While she was fingering the boxes of books I'd packed, she asked me if I loved her. I had tried to make a joke of it. "Not with the way you're treating me. Kicking me out and all."

Moira shook her head. "Tell me the truth. Did you ever love me? I mean, have you ever loved anyone?" The earnestness in her voice took me by surprise. When she'd asked me this question before, I'd always answered with a perfunctory yes, all the while knowing that whatever I felt for her, it wasn't love. But was it possible that I'd never loved anyone? I thought of the women that had come before Moira. No, I hadn't loved any of them.

"Well," Moira said, her voice vulnerable. "Did you ever love me?"

I lied as I had before. "Yes," I said. "Of course," I said. "I still do."

Moira narrowed her eyes. A week later, when I left, she didn't try to stop me.

The next day I called my editor to let him know how my research was going and to tell him about my second lead. He told me to keep on the story, but that the paper couldn't pay for my traveling expenses to the state capital. I went to an ATM, took out forty dollars of my own money for gas and food, and drove to Columbia. I knew then that I wasn't doing this just for the *News & Courier*. I still had the detachment required for an investigative journalist, and yet at the same time I felt that I was unraveling mysteries too personal for detachment. I was beginning to feel that I knew the Reverend McCoy. That I knew Graham.

Once in Columbia, it didn't take me long to find Bull Street. It's funny, as a child I used to hear grown-ups joking about how if so and so didn't do such and such she was going to end up on Bull Street. It was always a she, the way people told it. And everyone knew that Bull Street was the location of the state-funded asylum.

I told the nurse at the front desk that I was the son of Mrs.

Carrie Mae McCoy, figuring if I told them I was a reporter they wouldn't let me in. The nurse, a short, middle-aged woman with white hair and big glasses, led me down a wide corridor with shiny white floors and walls. I had expected the asylum to be noisy, with attendants everywhere physically constraining problem patients and injecting them with sedatives. But it was deathly quiet, as if no one really lived there.

The nurse opened a door marked N15, and I followed her into a small room the size of my kitchen. Both the floor and the walls were shiny white. One window was at the far end of the room, and there were bars outside the window. In the middle of the room was an army-cot-size bed with a very thin mattress covered by bleached white sheets. Next to the bed, in a white chair, sat a medium-complexioned woman, rather thin, staring at nothing.

"Your son's here, Mrs. McCoy," the nurse said loudly. Then she said to me, as if my "mother" weren't in the same room, "She's not too talkative these days."

The nurse left and I stood in front of Mrs. McCoy. She continued to stare straight ahead, her eyes landing on my crotch area. I moved to the side. "Mrs. McCoy," I said.

She didn't move.

"Mrs. McCoy."

Still she sat, seemingly oblivious to my presence.

"Mrs. McCoy." I touched her shoulder. No sooner had I done this than she twisted her head around and bit my hand. It was lizardlike, the way she did it, and I was almost too shocked to pull my hand away when she twisted again for a second bite.

"Butterscotch," she said.

I backed away a safe distance. "Mrs. McCoy," I said, "I want to ask you about your husband and the events that took place on May twenty-first last year. I need to know what happened. What really happened."

For a second Mrs. McCoy looked at me as if she recognized me, or at least as if she knew who she was and what was going on. Then she spoke. "Butterscotch butterscotch butterscotch butterscotch butterscotch butterscotch butterscotch butterscotch butterscotch butterscotch butterscotch butterscotch."

I stayed there for fifteen minutes, hoping she'd say something else. She didn't.

When I got home, there was a message on my answering machine from my friend at the police station. It said, "In reference to Graham McCoy's car accident. Didn't find much except basic information. Accident occurred on May twenty-first of last year at approximately one-twenty A.M. on Main Road. Car was a late-model white Cadillac, license number GHE one-nine-two. Driver was Graham McCoy, as you already know. Driver was slightly intoxicated and drove into a tree. According to the officer present, based on the damage to the car, the driver was most likely going twenty to thirty miles in excess of the speed limit. Driver was unscarred. Unidentified white male passenger was dead upon arrival. No charges brought."

The next morning I got up early and headed out to John's Island to speak to Mrs. Hurston again. The person I ran into first, however, was Graham. I was parking my car across the street from Mrs. Hurston's house when I saw him, still wearing his white pants and white tank top, this time heading toward his house. I hurried out of the car. I called out his name. He didn't turn around, so I called it again. I quickened my step to catch up with him. He turned into the walk of his house and had already climbed the porch steps by the time I was close to him. He didn't turn to look at me. I started to touch his shoulder, but for some reason I didn't. We were standing on the porch—and here everything plays back as if it's in slow motion, though it couldn't have been. We were on the porch, and he was opening his front door, fumbling with his key, when I said his name again. He opened the door, and just before going in he turned and looked at me. All of a sudden I remembered the dream I had had the night before, in which I was in the backseat of a white Cadillac, and Graham and a white boy his age were in front. Graham was driving, and the two of them were whispering to each other, and I couldn't hear what they were saying. I woke up shaking, bathed in sweat. Now, Graham and I were staring at each other face to

face. For a second or a minute or a lifetime we stood like that.
Then he opened the door wider and went inside, locking the
door behind him. For a while longer I stood on his porch, wondering what had just happened.

"Didn't speak to you, huh?" Mrs. Hurston said when I
climbed her front porch steps. I realized then that she'd been
sitting there watching the entire incident.

I shook my head.

"And I see now you're taking the liberty to climb up my steps
and sit on my porch without even so much as a 'May I' or 'Good
morning.'" She smiled at me and pushed a small brown paper
bag my way. Boiled peanuts were in the bag, and for a while we
sat like that, not saying anything, but just passing a bag of boiled
peanuts between us and eating slowly. Neither one of us cared
that it was only ten o'clock in the morning and we were eating
boiled peanuts.

"So there was an unidentified white male passenger," I said
after a while.

Mrs. Hurston nodded her head. "So you've done your homework this time."

"You know what really happened, don't you?"

"I know only what people tell me."

"Which is?"

She chewed softly on a boiled peanut, sucking the salt juices
out of the shell. "What people say is that after Graham left the
prom he went and picked up a white friend of his, and that the
two of them parked on the side of the road. Nobody would've
known 'cept a white policeman came and thought it was suspicious, a Cadillac sitting in the middle of nowhere like that. He
pointed his bright lights at the car and called, 'What y'all boys
up to? Y'all drinking?' Of course, some folks like to say he said
'colored boys' or 'nigger boys' when he called to them. Folks will
be folks and make a story something it never was. Anyway, before the policeman could even finish his words, Graham had
started up his daddy's Cadillac and near ran the policeman over
driving out of there so fast.

"Of course, some say it's that buckra policeman's fault for
chasing them. Others say those two were doing wrong and got

their just punishment. All we know for true is that there were sirens and flashing lights near to wake this whole island. And that Graham crashed in the old magnolia tree where they hanged Denmark Vesey. Hardly a scratch on his naked body. And the white policeman, as soon as he found out that Graham's daddy was the Reverend McCoy, all he did was give Graham a speeding ticket. A speeding ticket. Didn't ask what a black boy and a white boy was doing naked in a car together. The white boy, they say they had to scrape his body up from the windshield, from the metal, from the tree. Nobody could identify him. More likely no one wanted to. They say the Spanish moss stopped growing on that tree after that.

"After the ambulance came and everything was cleared up, the policeman drove Graham home and told the Reverend McCoy what had happened. Then the policeman left. You can imagine what happened after that."

"Graham and his daddy fought."

Mrs. Hurston nodded. "Graham's the only one left now. We don't like that kind of perversion around here." Her mouth twisted into a smile. "Sometimes the younger children throw pebbles and stones at him."

I winced.

"Ain't I tell you he'd come back for seconds," one of the porch-front men said as I approached the Conveyance Store.

"Can't stay away from her once you seen that ass," another joked.

"Best piece of ass in the Carolinas."

"You'll never find out."

"This boy will. Won't you?" another said as everyone turned toward me. I shrugged, and just then something in the way these men looked at me changed. They went back to their checker games and to their quiet joking, and it was as if they had seen something in my shrug they hadn't wanted to see.

I opened the screen door to the store, setting off the little bell. Avey was standing in the same place, behind the same cash register. *Mules and Men* still lay open on the counter. Avey looked up.

"You didn't tell me everything," I said.

"I beg your pardon."

"You didn't tell me that there was somebody else in the car when the accident happened."

"There was somebody else in the car when the accident happened," she said dryly. "So what? Is that supposed to change something?"

"There was someone else in the car. A boy who was never identified. Didn't you think that mattered?"

"It matters that Graham picked up a hitchhiker while he was driving home? Whatever you say."

"Is it true that the two of them were naked when the police car arrived?"

"I wasn't there, was I? Neither were you. Only that policeman knows the answer to that."

"Reverend McCoy didn't shoot himself. Graham shot him. Reverend McCoy found out Graham was of a certain persuasion and confronted him with the truth. The two of them started arguing. Graham found his father's gun and shot him. Isn't that what happened? The mother tried to cover it up to look like a suicide, but it wasn't. Isn't that right? Isn't that the truth?"

She smiled at me. "What do you think? Maybe Graham did shoot his father. Or maybe the Reverend McCoy, incensed by the knowledge of his son's sexual persuasion, killed himself. Or maybe Graham's mother pulled the trigger. Did you forget about that possibility?"

"Don't you care about the truth?"

"No, I don't. I was his girlfriend and I don't give a damn about what really happened. And you wanna know why? Because it doesn't matter. Any one of those versions could be true, or maybe we're wrong about all of them. But in the end it doesn't matter. No matter how you look at it, the reverend is dead, his wife's in an insane asylum, and Graham's not speaking to anyone. The truth? No, I don't care. But you seem to. And you didn't even know him. Why do you think that is? That you care so much?"

I stood there for a second unable to answer. Why did I care? I backed out of the store, nearly knocking over a stack of newspapers by the door.

That night, I sat in my apartment on King Street, the window open, the ceiling fan turning, the Neville Brothers playing in the background, and just wrote. Occasionally I got up and made myself some coffee. Once or twice I even stood by the window drinking it, looking out at Condon's Department Store across the street, wondering why they had painted the department store pink. I thought of Moira. *Tell me the truth,* she had said. And I had wondered why the truth mattered.

At six A.M., I printed up my final draft on the dot matrix printer attached to my Macintosh. I drove the few blocks to the newsroom, pushed open the door to the editor's office.

"Done?" he asked. I handed him the story. He sat back in his swivel chair and began reading rapidly, thumbing the pages, then grunting and starting over at the beginning. I coughed, and he held up one finger, just a minute longer. Finally, he turned to me.

"So," he said.

For a moment we were both silent. I said, "Well?"

"It's good, really good. You can write. You have a certain style. We just have to straighten out a few things." He pulled out a cigarette and lit it. "Nothing major stylistically. As far as content, though—" He paused.

"Content," I prompted him.

"Well, a few things we'll have to take out. We sort of have a broad-based audience. The stuff about Graham McCoy and that other boy being naked in a car together."

"It's what happened." *The truth,* I almost said.

"I think the story reads the same if the McCoy boy was just in the car by himself, listening to the radio or something."

"Yes, sir."

The editor narrowed his eyes. "You agree, don't you?"

"Yes, sir."

You'll say Yes, sir and Yes, ma'am to everything, even if you disagree and your heart tells you differently. At the time, I'd thought Moira was talking about the South. Only now did I realize she was talking about us. About me.

"Ready for your next assignment?"

I didn't answer. I walked out of his office, out of the building. When I got to my car, I stood there, looking at my reflection in the car window. Looking to see what I looked like. As if the truth were written on my face.

RANDALL KENAN

Run, Mourner, Run

. . . for there is no place that does not see you.
You must change your life.

—Rilke

Dean Williams sits in the tire. The tire hangs from a high and fat sycamore branch. He swings back and forth, back and forth, so that the air tickles his ears. His legs, now lanky and mannish, drag the ground. Not like the day his father first hung the tire and hoisted a five-year-old Dean up by the waist and pushed him and pushed him and pushed him, higher and higher—"Daddy, don't push so hard!"—until Dean, a little scared, could see beyond the old truck and out over the field, his heart pounding, his eyes wide; and his daddy walked off that day and left Dean swinging and went back to the red truck and continued to tinker under the hood, fixing . . . Dean never knew what.

Eighteen years later Dean sits in the tire. Swinging. Watching the last fingers of the late October sun scratch at the horizon. Waiting. Looking at an early migration of geese heading south. Swinging. Waiting for his mama to call him to supper—canned peas, rice, Salisbury steak, maybe. His daddy always used to say Ernestine wont no good cook, but ah, she's got.

Dean Williams stares off at the wood in the distance, over the soybean fields to the pines' green-bright, the oaks and the sycamores and the maples all burnt and brittle-colored. Looking at the sky, he remembers a rhyme:

A *red sky at night is a shepherd's delight*
A *red sky in the morning is a shepherd's warning.*

Once upon a time—what now seems decades ago rather than ten or fifteen years—Dean had real dreams. In first grade he wanted to be a doctor; in second, a lawyer; in third, an Indian chief. He read the fairy stories and nursery rhymes, those slick shiny oversized books, over and over, and Mother Goose became a Bible of sorts. If pigs could fly and foxes could talk and dragons were for real, then surely he could be anything he wanted to be. Not many years after that he dropped out and learned to dream more mundane dreams. Yet those nuggets from grade school stayed with him.

Dean Williams sits in the tire his daddy made for him. Thinking: For what?

See, there's somebody I want you to . . . to . . . Well, I want you to get him for me. So to speak.

Percy Terrell had picked him up that day, back in March. Percy Terrell, driving his big Dodge truck, his Deere cap perched on his head, his grey hair peeking out, his eyes full of mischief and lies and greed and hate and.

Son, I think I got a job for you.

Sitting in the cab of that truck, groceries in his lap (his Ford Torino had been in need of a carburetor that day), he wondered what Percy was up to.

Now of course this is something strictly between me and you.

On that cemetery-calm day in March, staring into the soybean field and his mama's house, the truck stopped on the dirt road between the highway, he wondered whether Percy wanted to make a sexual proposition. It wouldn't have been the first time a grey-haired granddaddy had stopped his truck and invited Dean in. Dean had something of a reputation. Maybe Percy had found out that Dean had been sleeping with burly Joe Johnson, the trucker. Maybe somebody had seen him coming out of a bar in Raleigh or in Wilmington or in.

. . . if you dare tell a soul, it'll be your word against mine, boy. And well . . . you'd just be fucking yourself up then.

How could he have known what he'd be getting himself into? If some fortune-teller had sat him down and explained it to him, detail by detail; if he'd had some warning from a crow or a woodchuck; if he'd had a bad dream the night before that would.

Land.

Land?

They own a parcel of land I want. Over by Chitaqua Pond. In fact they own the land under Chitaqua Pond. I got them surrounded a hundred acres on one side, two hundred acres on one side, one fifty on the other.

How much land is it?

It ain't how much that matters, son. They're blocking me. See? I want—I need that land. Niggers shouldn't own something as pretty as Chitaqua Pond. Got a house on it they call their homeplace. Don't nobody live in it. Say they ain't got no price. We'll see.

When he was only a tow-headed twenty-four-year-old with a taste for hunting deer and redheads, Percy Terrell had inherited from his daddy, Malcolm Terrell, about three thousand acres and a general store to which damn-near everyone in Tims Creek was indebted. Yet somehow fun-loving Percy became Percy the determined; hell-raising Percy became Percy the cunning, Percy the sly, Percy the conniving, and had manipulated and multiplied his inheritance into a thousand acres more land, two textile mills, a chicken plant, part ownership in a Kentucky Fried Chicken franchise in Crosstown, and God only knew what else. The day he picked Dean up he had been in the middle of negotiating with a big corporation for his third textile mill. Before that day Percy had never said so much as "piss" to Dean. In Percy's eyes Dean was nothing more than poor white trash: a sweet-faced, dark-haired faggot with a broken-down Ford Torino, living with his chain-smoking mama in a damn-near condemned house they didn't even own. So it was like an audience with the king for Dean to be picked up by ole Percy on the side of the road, for him to stop the car, to turn to Dean and say: I want you to get to know him. Real good. You get my meaning?

Sir?

You know what I mean. He likes white boys. He'll just drool all over you. Who knows. He probably already does.

That day in March Dean hardly knew who Raymond Brown was. Only that he was the one colored undertaker in town. How could he have known he was something of a prince, something of a child, something of a little brown boy in a man's grey worsted-wool suit, with skin underneath smooth like silk? So he sat there thinking: This one of them dreams like on TV? Surely, he wasn't actually sitting in a truck with the richest white man in Tims Creek being asked to betray the richest black man in Tims Creek . . . Shoot! Sure as hell must be a dream.

Sex with a black man. His first one—his only one till Ray—had been Marshall Hinton in the ninth grade just before Dean dropped out of high school. It had been nothing much: nasty, sweaty, heartbeat-quick—but Dean still remembered the touch of that boy's skin, petal-soft and hard at the same time—and the sensation lingered on his fingertips. With that on his mind, part of the same evil dream, with the shadow of Percy Terrell sitting there next to him in his shadow-truck, Dean had asked: Let's say I decide to go along with this. Let's just say. What do I get out of it?

What do I get?

Had he actually said that? He could easily have said at that point: No thank you, Mr. Imaginary Percy Terrell. I know this is a test from the Lord and I ain't fool enough to go through with it. I ain't stupid enough. I ain't drunk enough. I ain't.

What do I get?

You know that factory I'm trying to buy from International Spinning Corporation? You work at that plant, don't you?

Yeah.

Well, how would you like a promotion to foreman? And a six-thousand-dollar raise?

More a dream or less a dream? Dean couldn't tell. But the idea—six thousand dollars—how much is that a month?—a promotion. How long does it take most people to get to foreman?

John Hyde? Fred Lanier? Rick Batts? Ten, fifteen, seventeen years. And they're still on line. Foremen come in as foremen. That simple. People like Dean never get to be foremen . . . and six thousand dollars.

I don't understand, Mr. Terrell, how—?

You just get him in bed. That's all. I'll worry about the rest.

But how do I—?

Ever heard of a bar called The Jack Rabbit in Raleigh?

Yeah. A colored bar.

He goes there every second Saturday of every month, I'm told.

Dean stared at the dashboard. He admired the electronic displays and the tape deck with a Willie Nelson tape sticking out—

What kind of guarantee I get?

Percy chuckled. A flat, good-ole-boy chuckle, with a snort and a wheeze. For the first time Dean was a little scared. Son, you do my bidding you don't need no guarantee. This—he stuck out his hand—this is your guarantee.

Dean had walked into the kitchen that day and looked down at his mama, who sat at the kitchen table reading the *National Enquirer*, a cigarette hanging out of her mouth, ashes on her tangerine knit blouse, ashes on the table. Water boiling on the stove. The faucet they could never fix, dripping. Dripping. The linoleum floor needing mopping—it all seemed like a dream. Terrell.

Just get him in bed.

What Percy Terrell want with you?—She watched him closely as he put the grocery bags on the counter.

Nothing.

She harrumphed as she got up to take the cans out of the brown paper bag and finish supper. He stopped and took a good long look at her; he noticed how thin his mama was getting. How her hair and her skin seemed washed out, all a pale, whitish-yellow color. Is that when he decided to do it? When he took in how the worry about money, worry about her doctor bills, the worry about her job—when she had a job—worry about her health, worry about Dean, had fretted away at her? Piece by piece, gnawing at her, so manless, so perpetually sad.

He remembered how she had been when his daddy was alive. Her hair black. Her eyes child-like and playful. Her body full and supple and eager to please a man. She did her nails a bright red then. Went to the beauty parlor. Now she bit her nails, and her head was a mess of split ends.

Dean sits in a tire. A tire hung off the great limb of a syca-more tree. Swinging. Watching smoke rising off in the distance a ways. Someone burning a field maybe. But it's the wrong time of year. People are still harvesting corn.

No, it wasn't for his mama that he did it. He hated the line. Hated the noise and the dust and the smell. But he hated the monotony and the din even more, those millions of damn mil-lions of fucking strands of thread churning and turning and go-ing on and on and on. What did he have to lose? What else did he have to trade on but his looks? A man once told him: Boy, you got eyes that could give a bull a hard-on. Why not use them?

> *Oh, Mother, I shall be married to*
> *Mr. Punchinello*
> *Mr. Punch*
> *Mr. Joe*
> *Mr. Nell*
> *Mr. Lo*
> *To Mr. Punch. Mr. Joe.*
> *To Mr. Punchinello.*

That very next day in March at McTarr's Grocery Store he saw him. Dean's mama had asked him to stop on the way back home and pick up a jar of mayonnaise. Phil Jones gave him a lift from the plant, and as he got out and was walking into the store Raymond Brown drove up in his big beige Cadillac.

He'd seen Ray Brown all his life, known who he was by sight and such, but he had never really paid him any mind. Over six foot and in a dark-navy suit. A fire-red tie. A mustache like a pencil line. Skin the color of something whipped, blended, and rich. A deep color. Ray walked with a minister's majesty.

Upright. Solemn. His head held up. Almost looking down on folk.

Scuse me, Mr. Brown.

Had he ever really looked into a black man's eyes before then? Dean stood there, fully intending to find some way to seduce this man, and yet the odd mixture of things he sensed coming out of him—a rock solidness, an animal tenderness, a cool wariness—made Dean step back.

Yeah? What can I do for you?—Ray spoke in a slow, round baritone. Very proper. (Does he like me?) He kept his too-small-for-a-black-man's nose in the air. (Does he know I'm interested?) Raised an eyebrow. (He just thinks I'm white trash.)— Can I help you, young man?—Ray started to step away.

W . . . what year is your car?

My? Oh, an '88.

Fleetwood?

No, Eldorado.

Drive good?

Exceedingly.

Huh?

Very.

Dean tried to think of something more to say without being too obvious to the folk going into the store. (What if Percy was tricking me? What if Ray Brown don't go in for men? What if—?)

That it?

Ah . . . yeah, I—

Well, please excuse me. I'm in something of a hurry. Ray nodded and started to walk off.

Mr. Ray—

When Raymond Brown turned around, the puzzled look on his face softened its sternness: Dean saw a boy wanting to play. Ray smiled faintly, as if taking Dean in for the first time. His eyes drifted.—Well, what is it?

Nothing. See you later.—Dean smiled and looked down a bit, feigning shyness.

A grin of recognition passed over Ray's face. His eyes narrowed. At once he was all business again; he turned without a word or a gesture and walked into the store.

Lavender blue and rosemary green,
When I am king you shall be queen;
Call up my maids at four o'clock,
Some to the wheel and some to the rock;
Some to make hay and some to shear corn,
And you and I will keep the bed warm.

Dean Williams gazes down now at the trough in the earth in which his feet have been sliding. For eighteen years. Sliding. The red clay hard and baked after years of sun and rain and little-boy feet. Exposed. His blue canvas hightops beaten and dirty and frayed but comfortable. His mother says time and again he should get rid of them. A crow *caw-caw-ca-caws* as it glides over his head, as he swings in the old tire. As he thinks. As he wonders what Raymond Brown is doing. Thinking. At this moment.

Some things you just let happen, Ray had said that night. Dean never quite understood what he meant by that. Ray gestured grandly with his hands as he went on and on. He was a little pompous—is that the word? A little stuck-up. A little big on himself and his education. With his poetry and his books and his reading and his plays. But he had such large hands. Well-manicured. So clean. And a gold ring with a shiny black stone he called onyx. He said his great-granddaddy took it off the hand of his slavemaster after killing him. Dean had thought an undertaker's hands would be cold as ice; Ray's hands were always warm.

A few days after McTarr's, Dean finally made his play at The Jack Rabbit. A rusty, run-down, dank, dark, sleazy, sticky-floored sort of place, with a smudged, wall-length mirror behind the bar, a small dance floor crowded with men and boys, mostly black, jerking or gyrating to this guitar riff, to that satiny saxophone, to this syrupy siren's voice, gritty, nasty, hips, heads, eyes, grinding. Dean found Ray right off, standing at the edge of the bar, slurping a scotch and soda, jabbering to some straggly-looking, candy-assed blond boy with frog-big blue eyes, who looked on as if Ray were speaking in Japanese or in some number-filled computer language.

Scuse me, Mr. Ray.

Ray Brown's eyes narrowed again the way they had in front of McTarr's. This time Dean did not have to wonder if Ray was interested. The straggly-looking boy drifted away.

You're that Williams boy, aren't you?

Yeah.

Buy you a drink?

Some smoky voice began to sing, some bitter crooning, some heart-tugging melody, some lonely piano. They were playing the game now, old and familiar to Dean, like checkers, like Old Maid; they were dancing cheek to cheek, hip to thigh. Dean knew he could win. Would win.

Ray talked. Ray talked about things Dean had no notion or knowledge of. Ray talked of school (Morehouse—the best years of my life. I should have become an academic. I did a year in Comp Lit at BU. Then my father died and my Aunt Helen insisted I go to mortuary school); Ray talked of his family (You know, my mother actually forbade me to marry Gloria. Said she was too poor, backward, and good-for-nothing. Wanted me to marry a Hampton or a Spelman girl); Ray talked of the funeral business (It was actually founded by my great-grandfather, Frederick Brown. What a man. Built it out of nothing. What a man. Loved to hunt. He did); Ray talked of undertaking (I despise formaldehyde; I loathe dead people; I abhor funerals); Ray talked on the President and the Governor and the General Assembly (Crooks! Liars! Godless men!); Ray talked. In soft tones. In icy tones. In preacher-like tones. This moment loud and thundering, his baritone making heads turn; the next moment quiet, head tilted, a little boy in need of a shoulder to lean on. Dean had never heard, except maybe on the radio and on TV, someone who knew so damn much, who carried himself just so, who.

But my wife—Ray would somehow smile and look despairing at the same time—I love her, you know. She could have figured it out by now. She's not a dumb woman, really.

Why hasn't she?

Blinded. Blinded by the Holy Ghost. She's full of the Holy Ghost, see.—Ray went off on a mocking rendition of a sermon, pounding his fists on the bar for emphasis (cause we're all food for worms, we know not the way to salvation, we must seek—yes, seek—*Him*). He broke off.—Of course there's the money too.

The money?

Yeah, my money.

Oh.

Ray became silent. He stared at Dean. The bartender stood at the opposite end of the bar wiping glasses with a towel; the smoky air had cleared somewhat but still appeared blue-grey, alight with neon; one lone couple ground their bodies into each other on the dance floor to a smoldering Tina Turner number.

How about you?

What about me?

Whom do you love?

Dean laughed.—Who loves me is the real question. Don't nobody give a shit about me. My mama, maybe.

Ray put his large hand over Dean's: Ray's full and strong, Dean's dry and brittle and rough and small.—Well, I wouldn't put it exactly like that. He kissed Dean's hand as though it were a small and frightened bird.

As simple as breaking bones. Had he thought of Percy and how he was to betray this mesmerizing man? Did he believe he could? Would?

I want to show you something.

Yeah, I'll bet.—Dean smirked.

No, really. A place. Tonight. Come on.

They drove back to Tims Creek, down narrow back roads, through winding paths, alongside fields, into woods, into a meadow Dean had never seen before, near Chitaqua Pond. They arrived at the homeplace around midnight.

Is this where you take your boys?

Where did you think? To the mortuary?

So the house actually exists, Dean thought. This is for real. Part of him genuinely wanted to warn Ray, to protect him. But as Ray gave him a brief tour of the house where he had grown up (Can you believe this place is nearly ninety years old?): the kitchen with the deep enamel sink and the wood stove, the pantry with the neat rows of God-only-knows-how-old preserves and cans and boxes, the living room with the gaping fireplace where Christmas stockings had hung, the surprisingly functional bathroom; as they entered the bedroom where measles had been tended and babies created; as Ray rambled on absently about his Aunt Helen and Uncle Max (Aunt Helen is my great-grand-daddy's youngest sister. She insists nothing change about this house. Nothing. If we sold it, it'd kill her); as he undressed Dean (No, please, allow me); as Dean, naked, stood with his back to Ray, those tender fingers exploring the joints and the hinges of his body; as a wet, warm tongue outlined, ever so lightly, the shape of his gooseflesh-cold body, Ray mumbling trance-like (All flesh is grass, my love, sweet, sweet grass) between bites, between pinches; as they slid into the plump feather bed that *scree-eee-creeked* as they lay there, underneath a quilt made by Ray's great-grandmother, multicolored, heavy; as they joined at the mouth; as Dean trembled and tingled and clutched—all the while in his ears he heard a noise: faint at first, then loud, louder, then deafening: and he was not sure if the quickening *thu-thump-thump, thu-thump-thump* of his heartbeat came from Ray's bites on his nipples or from fear. Dean felt certain he heard the voices of old black men and old black women screaming for his death, his blood, for him to be strung up on a Judas tree, to die and breathe no more.

> *Far from home across the sea*
> *To foreign parts I go;*
> *When I am gone, O think of me*
> *And I'll remember you.*
> *Remember me when far away,*
> *Whether asleep or awake.*
> *Remember me on your wedding day*
> *And send me a piece of your cake.*

Dean!—His mother calls to him from the door to the house where she stands.—Dean! Did you get me some Bisquick?

Noum, he yells back, not stopping his back-and-forth, the

rope on the limb creaking like the door to a coffin opening and closing.

How could you forget? I asked you this morning.

I just did.

You "just did." Shit. Well, we ain't got no bread neither so you'll just eat with no bread. Boy, where is your mind these days? Dean says nothing. He just rocks. Remembering. Noting the sky richening and deepening in color. Remembering. Seeing what he thinks might be a deer, way, way out. Remembering.

Remembering how it went on for a month, the meetings at the homeplace. Remembering how good being with Ray felt as spring crept closer and closer. Remembering the daffodils and the crocuses and the blessed jonquils and eating chocolate ice cream from the carton in bed afterward and mockingly calling each other honey and listening to the radio and singing, and Ray quoting some damn poet ("There we are two, content, happy in beauty together, speaking little,/perhaps not a word," as Mr. Whitman would say), and would nibble at his neck and breathe deeply and let out a little sigh and say: I've got to get home. Gloria—yeah, yeah, I know. I know—remembering how he would tell himself: I ain't jealous of no black woman and of no black man. I don't care how much money he got. Remembering how he would drive home and climb into his cold and empty bed with the bad mattress and reach up and pull the metal chain on the light bulb that swung in the middle of the room. Remembering how he would huddle underneath the stiff sheets, thinking of Ray's voice, the feel of his skin, the smell of his aftershave, imagining Ray pulling into the driveway of his ranch-style brick house, dashing through rooms filled with nice things, wall-to-wall-carpeted floors, into the shower, complaining of the dealers and their boring conversations (I'm really sorry, honey, John Simon insisted we go to this barbecue joint in Goldsboro after the meeting and told me all this tedious foolishness about his mother-in-law and)—how he would probably kiss her while drying himself with a thick white towel as she sat reading a Bible commentary, and she would smile and say, Oh, I understand, Ray, and he would ooze his large mahogany body into a king-sized bed with her under soft damask sheets, fresh and clean and warm, and say, Night, honey, and melt away into dreams, perhaps not even of Dean.—Hell, I don't give a shit, Dean would think, staring into his bare, night-filled room. So what if he doesn't. So what if he does. Don't make no nevermind to me, do it? I'm in it for the money. Right?

Yet Dean had no earthly idea what Percy had in mind for Ray and, after a few weeks, thought it might have already happened or maybe never would.

But one morning, one Sunday morning in April, when Gloria and the girls had gone to Philadelphia for a weekend to see a sick sister and Ray had decided to spend the night with Dean at the homeplace, the first and only time Dean was to see morning there (through the window that sunrise he could see a mist about the meadow and the pond), while they lolled, intertwined in dreams and limbs, he heard the barking of dogs. Almost imperceptible at first. They came closer. Louder. He heard men's voices. As he turned to jog Ray awake he heard someone kick in the front door. The sound of heavy feet trampling. Hooting. Jeering.

Where is they? Where they at? I know they're here.

The order and the rhyme of what happened next ricocheted in a cacophony in Dean's head even now: Ray blinks awake: Percy: his three sons: the sound *snap-click-whurrr, snap-click-whurrr, snap-click-whurrr*: dogs yapping: tugging at their leashes: Well, well, well, look-a-here, boys, salt-n-pepper: a dog growls: the boys grin and grimace: Dean jumping up, naked, to run: Get back in that bed, boy: No I—: I said, get back in that bed: *snap-click-whurrr, snap-click-whurrr*: a Polaroid camera, the prints sliding out like playing cards from a deck: the sound of dogs panting: claws on wooden floors: the boys mumbling under their breath: fucking queers, fucking faggots: damn, out of film.

Like a voice out of the chaos Ray spoke, steely, calm, almost amused.—You know, you *are* trespassing, Terrell.

Land as good as mine now, son. I done caught you in what them college boys call *flagrante delicto*, ain't that what you'd call it, Ray? You one of them college boys. In the goddamn flesh. You got to damn-near give me this here piece of property now, boy.

How do you figure that, Percy?

You a smart boy, Ray. I expect you can figure it.

Ray reached toward the nightstand. (A gun?)

A Terrell boy slammed a big stick down on the table in warning. A dog snapped.

Ray shrugged sarcastically.—A cigarette, maybe?

Bewildered, the boy glanced to his father, who warily nodded okay. Ray pulled out a pack of Lucky Strikes—though Dean had never known him to smoke—and deftly thumped out a single one, popped it into his mouth, reached for his matches, lit it, inhaled deeply, and blew smoke into the dog's face. The hound whined.

You got to be kidding, Terrell. You come in here with your boys and your dogs and pull this bullshit TV-movie camera stunt and expect me to whimper like some snot-nosed pickaninny, "Yassuh, Mr. Terrell, suh, I'll give you anything, suh. Take my house. Take my land. Take my wife. I sho is scared of you, suh." Come off it.—He drew on his cigarette.

Percy's face turned a strawberry color. He stood motionless. Dean expected him to go berserk. Slowly he began to nod his head up and down, and to smile. He put his hands on his hips and took two steps back.—Now, boys, I want you to look-a-here. I respect this man. I do. I really do. How many men do you know, black or white, could bluff, cool as a cucumber, caught butt-naked in bed with a damn whore? A white boy whore at that. Wheee-hooo, boy! you almost had me fooled. Shonuff did.—Percy curled his lip like one of his dogs.—But you fucked up, boy. May as well admit it.

Ray narrowed his eyes and puffed.

You a big man in this county, Ray. You know it and I know it. Think about it. Think about your ole Aunt Helen. Think about what that ole Reverend Barden'll say. A deacon and a trustee of his church. Can't have that. Think of your business. Who'll want you to handle their loved ones, Ray? Think of your *wife*. *Your girls*. I got me some eyewitnesses here, boy. Let somebody get one whiff of this . . . He turned with self-congratulatory delight to his boys. They all guffawed in unison, a sawing, inhuman sound.

Think on it, Ray. Think on it hard. Like I said, you're a smart boy. I'll enjoy finally doing some business with you. And it won't be on a cool slab, I guarantee.

Percy walked, head down, feet clomping, over to Dean. He reached over and mussed Dean's hair as though he were some obedient animal.—You did a fine job, son. A mighty fine job. I'll take real good care of you. Just like I promised.

Dean had never seen Ray's face in such a configuration of anger, loathing, coldness, disdain, recognition, as though he suddenly realized he had been in bed with a cottonmouth moccasin or a stinking dog. It made the very air in the room change color. He stubbed out his cigarette and stared out the window.—Get out of my house, Terrell.—He said it quietly but firmly.

Oh, come on, Ray. Don't be sore. How else did you think you could get your hands on such a *fine* piece of white ass? I'm your pimp, boy. I'll send the bill directly.

Get out.

Percy patted Dean's head again.—I'll settle up with you later. Come on, boys. We's done here.—He tipped his hat to Ray, turned, and was gone, out the door, the boys and the dogs and the smell of mud and canine breath and yelping and stomping trailing out behind him like the cloak of some wicked king of darkness. Dean sat numb and naked, curled up in a tight ball like a cat. As if someone had snatched the covers from him and said: Wake up. Stop dreaming.

You get the hell out too.—Ray sat up, swinging his feet to the floor. He reached for another cigarette.

Dean began to shiver; more than anything else he could imagine at that moment, he wanted Ray to hold him, more than six thousand dollars, more than a new car. He felt like crying. He reached out and saw his pale hand against the broad bronze back and sensed the enormity of what he had done, that his hand could never again touch that back, never glide over its ridges and bends and curves, never linger over that mole, pause at this patch of hair, that scar. He looked about the room for some sign of change; but it remained the same: the oil lamp: the warped mirror: the walnut bureau: the cracked windowsill. But it would soon be gone. Percy would see to that.

Ray, I'm s—

I don't want to hear you. Okay? I don't want to see you. I don't want to know you. Or that you even existed. Ever. Get out. Now.

As Dean stood and pulled his clothes on, he wanted desperately to hate Ray, to dredge up every nigger, junglebunny, cocksucking, motherfucking, sambo insult he could muster; he wanted to relearn hate, fiery, blunt, brutal; he wanted to unlearn what he had learned in the very bed on which he was turning his back, to erase it from his memory, to blot it out, scratch over it. Forget. Walking out the door he paused, listening for the voices of those dark ancestors who had accosted him upon his first entering. They were still. Perhaps appeased.

> *Little Miss Tuckett*
> *Sat on a bucket,*
> *Eating some peaches and cream.*
> *There came a grasshopper*
> *And tried hard to stop her,*
> *But she said, "Go away, or I'll scream."*

Dean looks over at his Ford Torino and worries that it may never run again. It has been in need of so many things, a distributor cap, spark plugs. The wiring about shot. Radiator leaks. He just doesn't have the money. Will he ever? He stands up with the tire around him and walks back, back, back, and jumps up in the air, the limb popping but holding. He swings high. He pushes a little with his legs on the way back. He goes higher. Higher.

Who said money is the root of all evil? Or was it the love of money? Love.

Six thousand dollars. This is my guarantee.

Dean waited six months. Twenty-four weeks. April. May. June. July. August. September. He watched the spring mature into summer and summer begin to ripen into autumn. He waited as his mother went into the hospital twice. First for an ovarian cyst. Next for a hysterectomy. He waited as the bills the insurance company would not take care of piled high. He waited as his mother was laid off again. He waited as the news blared across the York County *Cryer* and the Crosstown papers and the Raleigh papers: TERRELL FAMILY BUYS TEXTILE MILL, INTERNATIONAL SPINNING SOLD TO TERRELL INTERESTS, INTERNATIONAL SPINNING TO BECOME YORK EAST MILL. He waited through work, through the noise and the dust, through the gossip about daughters who ran off with young boys wanting to be country music stars, grandmothers going to the old folks' home, adulterous husbands and unwed mothers. He waited through some one-night stands with nameless truckers in nameless truckstops and bored workers at boring shopping malls. He waited. He waited through the times he ran into Ray, who ignored him. He waited through the times he had only a nickel and a dime in his pocket and had to borrow for a third time from his cousin Jimmy or his uncle Fred, and his mama would have to search and search in the cabinets for something to scare up supper with. He waited. He waited through news of Terrell making a deal with the Brown family for a tiny piece of property over by Chitaqua Pond, and of Raymond Frederick Brown's great-aunt Helen making a big stink, and taking to her bed ill. They said she was close to dead. But Dean waited. And waited. One hundred sixty and eight days. Waiting.

I'm going to Terrell, he finally decided on the last day of September. A late-summer thundercloud lasted all that day. Terrell still worked out of the general store his father had built, in an office at the back of the huge, warehouse-like structure. His boys ran the store. What if he says he ain't gone do nothing? What do I do then? Dean stood outside the store peering inside, wind and rain pelting his face.

Terrell kept the store old-fashioned: a potbellied stove that blazed red-hot in winter: a glass counter filled with bright candies: a clanging granddaddy National Cash Register. The cabinets and the benches and the dirt all old and dark. Deer heads looked down from the walls. Spiderwebs formed an eerie tent under the ceiling. As Dean entered, he looked back to the antique office door with TERRELL painted on the glass; it seemed a mile from the front door.

What you want? The oldest Terrell boy held a broom.

Come to see your daddy.

What for?

Business.

What kind of business?

Between him and me.

The youngest Terrell walked up to Dean.—Like hell.

Dean saw Percy through the glass, preparing to leave. He jumped between the boys and ran.

Hey, where the hell you going?

Dean's feet pumped against the pine floor. He could hear six feet in pursuit. Terrell tapped on his hat as Dean slid into the wall like a runner into home plate, out of breath.—Mr. Terrell, Mr. Terrell, I got to talk to you. I got—

What you want, son?

Panting, Dean began to speak, the multitude of days piling up in the back of his throat crowding to get out all at once.—You promised. My mama been in the hospital twice since March. My car's broke down. I just need to know when. When I—

When what, son?

All he had wished to tell Percy seemed to dry up in his head like spit on a hot July sidewalk. His mouth hung open. No words fell out.—You . . . you guaranteed . . .

"Guaranteed"? Boy, what *are* you talking about?—Terrell turned the key in the office door.

Ray Brown. Ray. You know. You promised. You . . .

Son—Terrell picked up his briefcase and turned to go—I don't know what in the Sam Hill you talking about.

Dean grabbed Percy's sleeve. The boys tensed.—Please, Mr. Terrell. Please. I did everything you asked. I . . .

Percy stared at Dean's hand on his sleeve for an uncomfortably long period. He reached down with his free hand and knocked Dean's away as though it were a dead fly.—Don't you ever lay a hand on me again, faggot.

He began to walk away, calling behind him: Don't be too long closing up, boys. You know how your mama gets when you're late.

Dean stood in the shadows watching Percy walk away.—I'll

tell, goddamn it. I'll tell.—Dean growled, not recognizing his own voice.

Percy stopped stock-still. With his back to them all, he raised his chin a slight bit.—Tell? Who, pray tell, will you tell?—He pivoted around, a look of disgust smearing his face.—And who the *fuck* would believe you?

Dean felt his breathing come more labored, heavy. He could not keep his mouth closed, though he could force out no words. He felt saliva drooling down his chin.

Look at you—Percy's head jerked back—Look-at-you! A pathetic white-trash faggot whore. Who would think any accusation you brought against me, specially one as far-fetched as what you got in mind to tell, would have nary one bit of truth to it. Shit.—Percy said under his breath. He walked to the door.—Show him the way out, boys. And don't be late now, you hear?—The wind *wa-banged* the door shut.

They beat him. They taunted him with limp wrists and effeminate whimpers and lisps. They kicked him. Finally they threw him out into the rain and mud. Through it all he said not a mumbling word. He did not weep. He sat in a puddle. In the rain. One eye closed. His bruises stinging. The taste of blood in his mouth. He sat in some strange limbo, some odd place of ghosts and shadows, knowing he must rise, knowing he had been badly beaten, knowing that the boys had stopped on their way out and, snickering, dropped a twenty-dollar bill in front of him (We decided we felt sorry for you. Here's a little something for you. Price of a blowjob), knowing he could use the money, knowing he would be late for supper, knowing he could never really explain, never really tell anyone what had happened, knowing he would surely die one day, hoping it would be now. He could not move.

After a while, though he had no idea how long a while, something stopped the rain from falling on him. An old man's voice spoke to him: You all right, son? You lose something?

Is that you, Lord? he thought. Have you come to take me? With all the energy he could gather he lifted his head and looked through his one good eye.

An umbrella. An old grey-haired, trampy-looking man Dean

did not know. Not the Lord. Dean opened his mouth and the cut in his lip spurted fresh blood into his mouth. He moaned. No I'll be all right yes yes yes I will be all right yes.

Yes, sir. I did lose something. Something right fine.

> Moses supposes his toeses are roses,
> But Moses supposes erroneously;
> For nobody's toeses are posies of roses
> As Moses supposes his toeses to be.

Dean!—His mother calls to him.—Dean! Supper's ready. Better come on.

Dark has gobbled up the world. He can see the light from a house here and there. People are sitting down to suppers of peas and chicken. A bat's *ratta-tatta-tatta* wings dip by. He continues to swing. He continues to wait. He continues to wonder.

Wondering about how two weeks after going to Terrell's office—two weeks after, the wounds and bruises had mostly healed—two weeks after knowing he would not get a raise or a promotion, two weeks of wondering if he should tell someone something, how he was walking down the road toward home with two bags of groceries. How the bag split and how rice, beans, canned tuna, garbage bags, white bread, and all came tumbling to the ground (though the milk carton didn't burst, he was happy to see), and how as he knelt down to pick everything up a beige Cadillac drove up, and how he heard the electric *whur* of the power windows going down, and how he heard a soft female voice say—Can I help you out?

He had never actually met Gloria Brown. She sat behind the wheel, her honey skin lightly powdered and smooth, her lips covered in some muted red like pink but not pink, her eyes intelligent and brown. In the backseat perched her two daughters, Ray's two daughters, their hair as shiny black as their patent-leather shoes. Their dresses white and green and neat.

It's all right, ma'am. I'm just down the road a piece.

But it's on my way. And you do seem to be having a little trouble. Hop on in. No trouble.

Dean collected the food and got into the front seat. I've never been in this car, he thought, feeling somehow entitled while knowing he had no right.

An a cappella gospel song in six-part harmony rang out from the stereo. Awful fine car, Dean wanted to say. But didn't.

We're heading to a revival meeting over at the Holiness Church.—She held the wheel gingerly, as if intimidated by the big purring machine. Her fingernails flashed an earthy orange color. Dean could smell her sweet and subtle perfume.

What church do you belong to?

Me? I don't, ma'am.

That's a shame. Well, you know Jesus loves you anyway. Are you saved?

Saved? From what?

Why, from Hell and Damnation, of course.

I guess not.

Well, keep your heart open. He'll speak to you. "For all have sinned and fallen short of the will of God."

Dean felt slightly offended but could think of nothing to say. He groped for words. Finally he said: Some things you just let happen.

Gloria turned to him the way one would turn upon hearing the voice of someone long dead; at first puzzled, then intrigued.—My husband always says that. Now ain't that funny.

Dean forced a chuckle.—Yes, ma'am. I reckon it is.

Gloria dropped him off at his house, her voice lilting after him with concern (Can you get to the house all right? Want the girls to help you?). He thanked her, no, he could manage. The Cadillac drove off into the early evening. This a road of ghosts, he thought. Spooks just don't like for a soul to know peace. Keep on coming to haunt.

> *If all the world was apple pie*
> *And all the sea was ink,*
> *And all the trees were bread and cheese,*
> *What would we have to drink?*

Dean! Boy, you better bring your butt on in here, now. Food's getting cold.

He doesn't feel hungry. He doesn't feel like sitting at the table with his mama. He doesn't feel like listening to her talk and complain or to the TV or to the radio. He doesn't feel like telling her that he was notified today that as of next Friday he will be laid off "indefinitely." He feels like sitting in the tire. Like swinging. Like waiting.

Waiting for the world to come to an end. Waiting for this cruel dream world to pass away. Waiting for the leopard to lie down with the kid and the goats with the sheep. Waiting for everything to be made all right—cause I know it will be all right, it has to be all right—and he will sit like Little Jack Horner in a corner with his Christmas pie and put in a thumb and pull out a plum and say: What a good, what a good, O what a good boy am I.

Behind Closed Doors

SAPPHIRE

There's a Window

"**I**s this just something to do till you get out? Till you get back to your old man?" she sneered.

I didn't answer her. I just kept pushing her blue denim smock further up her hips. The dress was up to her waist now. I wanted to get one of her watermelon-sized breasts in my mouth. I was having trouble with her bra.

"Take off your bra."

"Oh, you givin' orders now," she said, amused. Her short spiked crew cut and pug nose made her look like a bulldog. Her breath smelled like cigarettes, millions of 'em.

"Yeah," I asserted, "I'm giving orders. Take that mutherfuckin' harness off."

She laughed tough but brittle. The tough didn't scare me, the brittleness did. She nuzzled my ear with her nose, her hot, moist lips on my neck. "Call me Daddy," she whispered.

Oh no, I groaned. She stuck her tongue under my chin. It was like a snake on fire. Fuck it, I'd call her anything.

"O.K., Daddy," I sneered. "Take off your bra." Something went out of her. I felt ashamed. "I'm sorry," I whispered trying to put it back. I had the dress up over her waist now.

"Take it off," I whispered.

"My blues!" she protested, referring to the denim prison smock.

"Yeah, I don't wanna fuck no piece of denim. Take off that ugly ass dress." I was eating up her ear now. My tongue carousing behind her ear and down her neck that smelled like Ivory Soap and cigarette smoke. I was sitting on top of her belly pumping my thighs together sending blood to my clitoris as I pulled the dress over the top of her head. I was riding, like the Lone Ranger on top of Silver. No, take that back. Annie Oakley, I was riding like Annie Oakley. Actually, I should take that back, too, but I can't think of any black cowgirls right off hand. Looking down at her face I wanted to turn away from it, keep my eyes focused on the treasure behind the white cotton harness. Hawk-eyed, crew cut butch, she was old compared to me. How the fuck did she keep her underwear so clean in this dingy hole, I marveled. They acted like showers and changes of clothes were privileges. I leaned down stuck my tongue in her mouth realized in a flash the Ivory Soap clean bra and perspiration breaking out on her forehead was all for me.

She was trying. Trying hard. Probably being flat on her back with me on top of her was one of the hardest things she'd ever done. I admired her for a moment. Shit, she was beautiful! Laying up under me fifty years old, crew cut silver. I'd told her in the day room when she slammed on me, "Hey, baby, I don't want no one putting no bag over my head pulling no train on me. Shit, baby, if we get together it's got to be me doing the wild thing, too!"

She'd said, "Anything you want, Momi."

I slid down in the brown country of her body following blue veins like rivers; my tongue, a snake crawling through dark canyons, over strange hills, slowing down at weird markings and moles. I was lost in a world, brown, round, smelling like cigarette smoke, pussy and Ivory Soap. My hands were on her ass pulling her cunt closer to my mouth.

"Here," she said pushing something thin slippery and cool into my hand. I recognized the feel of latex.

"Just to be on the safe side," she said.

My heart swelled up big-time inside my chest. Here we was in death's asshole, two bitches behind bars, hard as nails and twice as ugly—caring. She *cared* about me, she cared about herself. I stretched the latex carefully over her wet opening. "Hold it," I instructed while I pulled her ass down to my mouth. I started to suck; that latex might keep me from tasting but it couldn't keep me from feeling. And I was a river now, overflowing its banks, rushing all over the brown mountains. I was a black cowgirl, my tongue was a six shooter and my fingers were guns. I was headed for the canyon, nobody could catch me. I was wild. I was bad.

"Oh, Momi," she screamed.

Um huh, that's me, keep calling my name. I felt like lightning cutting through the sky. She pulled me up beside her. I stuck my thigh between her legs and we rode till the cold cement walls turned to the midnight sky and stars glowing like the eyes of Isis. The hooves of our horses sped across the desert sand, rattlesnakes took wings and flew by our side. The moon bent down and whispered, "Call me Magdelina, Momi. Magdelina is my name."

Our tongues locked up inside themselves like bitches who were doin' life. No one existed but us. But the whispering moon was a memory that threatened to kill me. She slid down grabbing my thighs with her big callused hands.

"Yeah, yeah, yeah," the words jumped out my throat like little rabbits. "Go down on me go down on me." Her tongue was in my navel. "Use dat latex shit," I told her.

"Do I have to, mamasita?"

"Yeah," I said, "I like the feel of it." I lied. My heart got big size again. They didn't give nothin' away in this mutherfucker. How many candy bars or cigarettes had she traded for those little sheets of plastic?

"Ow!" Shit, it felt good her tongue jamming against my clitoris. Oh please woman don't stop I begged but at the same time in the middle of my crazy good feeling something was creeping. I tried to ignore it and concentrate on the rivers of pleasure she was sending through my body and the pain good feel of her fingers in latex gloves up my asshole. But the feeling was creeping in my throat threatening to choke me. Nasty and ugly it moved up to my eyes and I started to cry. She looked at me concerned and amazed, "Mira Momi, did I do something wrong?" She glanced around, then at herself as if to assess where evil could have come from. "Not this damn thing?" she says incredulously. Her eyes gleam with the hope of alleviating my pain as she hastily unhooks her bra. I shake my head no no but she has her head down, her hands behind her back pulling the white whale off her brown body.

"I . . . I don' know, you know I have this *thing* about being totally naked—*here* you know. I ain't been naked in front of nobody since I been here, 'cept, you know, doctors and showers and shit," she laughed in her glass voice. "It jus' ain't that kind of place, mamasita. You know you snatch a piece here, there; push somebody's panties to the side in the john so you can finger fuck five minutes before a big voice comes shouting, 'What's takin' you so long in there!' Least that's what it's been like for me. Seven years," she said. The glass broke in her throat. "Seven years."

Her words overwhelmed me. I felt small and ashamed with my pain. But this thing in my throat had snatched my wings. I knew I had to speak my heart even though it felt juvenile and weak. Speak or forever be tied up to the ground.

"I ain't seen the moon or the stars in six months." I felt ashamed—six months next to seven years on the edge of nothing. Silly shit to be tear-jerking about. I started to cry. I had seven years to do yet. She'd be gone by the time I turned around twice. She looked at me thoughtfully, her gray crew cut seemed like a luminous crown on top her forehead creased with lines. "Listen," she said quietly. "In six months or so you'll go from days in the laundry to the midnight to 8 A.M. kitchen shift if your behavior is good. Volunteer to peel the potatoes. There's a window over where they peel the vegetables. You can see the moon from that window."

I felt the nipples of her huge breasts hardening in my fingers. We retrieved two more precious pieces of latex, fitted ourselves in a mean sixty-nine and sucked each other back to the beginning of time. I was a cave girl riding a dinosaur across the steamy paleolithic terrain snatching trees with my teeth, shaking down the moon with my tongue.

RICHARD BRUCE NUGENT

Smoke, Lilies and Jade

*H*e wanted to do something . . . to write or draw . . . or
something . . . but it was so comfortable just to lay
there on the bed . . . his shoes off . . . and think . . . think
of everything . . . short disconnected thoughts—to wonder
. . . to remember . . . to think and smoke . . . why wasn't he
worried that he had no money . . . he *had* had five cents . . .
but he had been hungry . . . he *was* hungry and still . . . all
he wanted to do was . . . lay there comfortably smoking . . .
think . . . wishing he were writing . . . or drawing . . . or
something . . . something about the things he felt and thought
. . . but what did he think . . . he remembered how his
mother had awakened him one night . . . ages ago . . . six
years ago . . . Alex . . . he had always wondered at the
strangeness of it . . . she had seemed so . . . so . . . so just
the same . . . Alex . . . I think your father is dead . . . and
it hadn't seemed so strange . . . yet . . . one's mother didn't
say that . . . didn't wake one at midnight every night to say
. . . feel him . . . put your hand on his head . . . then
whisper with a catch in her voice . . . I'm afraid . . . sh don't
wake Lam . . . yet it hadn't seemed as it should have seemed

. . . even when he had felt his father's cool wet forehead . . .
it hadn't been tragic . . . the light had been turned very low
. . . and flickered . . . yet it hadn't been tragic . . . or weird
. . . not at all as one should feel when one's father died . . .
even his reply of . . . yes he is dead . . . had been common-
place . . . hadn't been dramatic . . . there had been no tears
. . . no sobs . . . not even a sorrow . . . and yet he must have
realized that one's father couldn't smile . . . or sing any more
. . . after he had died . . . every one remembered his father's
voice . . . it had been a lush voice . . . a promise . . . then
that dressing together . . . his mother and himself . . . in the
bathroom . . . why was the bathroom always the warmest room
in the winter . . . as they had put on their clothes . . . his
mother had been telling him what he must do . . . and cried
softly . . . and that had made him cry too but you mustn't cry
Alex . . . remember you have to be a little man now . . . and
that was all . . . didn't other wives and sons cry more for their
dead than that . . . anyway people never cried for beautiful
sunsets . . . or music . . . and those were the things that hurt
. . . the things to sympathize with . . . then out into the snow
and dark of the morning . . . first to the undertaker's . . . no
first to Uncle Frank's . . . why did Aunt Lula have to act like
that . . . to ask again and again . . . but when did he die . . .
when did he die . . . I just can't believe it . . . poor Minerva
. . . then out into the snow and dark again . . . how had his
mother expected him to know where to find the night bell at the
undertaker's . . . he was the most sensible of them all tho . . .
all he had said was . . . what . . . Harry Francis . . . too bad
. . . tell mamma I'll be there first thing in the morning . . .
then down the deserted streets again . . . to grandmother's
. . . it was growing light now . . . it must be terrible to die in
daylight . . . grandpa had been sweeping the snow off the yard
. . . he had been glad of that because . . . well he could tell
him better than grandma . . . grandpa . . . father's dead . . .
and he hadn't acted strange either . . . books lied . . . he had
just looked at Alex a moment then continued sweeping . . . all
he said was . . . what time did he die . . . she'll want to know
. . . then passing thru the lonesome street toward home . . .

Mrs. Mamie Grant was closing a window and spied him . . .
hallow Alex . . . an' how's your father this mornin' . . . dead
. . . get out . . . tch tch tch an' I was just around there with a
cup a' custard yesterday . . . Alex puffed contentedly on his
cigarette . . . he was hungry and comfortable . . . and he had
an ivory holder inlaid with red jade and green . . . funny how
the smoke seemed to climb up that ray of sunlight . . . went up
the slant just like imagination . . . was imagination blue . . .
or was it because he had spent his last five cents and couldn't
worry . . . anyway it was nice to lay there and wonder . . . and
remember . . . why was he so different from other people . . .
the only things he remembered of his father's funeral were the
crowded church and the ride in the hack . . . so many people
there in the church . . . and ladies with tears in their eyes . . .
and on their cheeks . . . and some men too . . . why did
people cry . . . vanity that was all . . . yet they weren't exactly
hypocrites . . . but why . . . it had made him furious . . . all
these people crying . . . it wasn't *their* father . . . and he
wasn't crying . . . couldn't cry for sorrow altho he had loved his
father more than . . . than . . . it had made him so angry that
tears had come to his eyes . . . and he had been ashamed of his
mother . . . crying into a handkerchief . . . so ashamed that
tears had run down his cheeks and he had frowned . . . and
some one . . . a woman . . . had said . . . look at that poor
little dear . . . Alex is just like his father . . . and the tears
had run fast . . . because he *wasn't* like his father . . . he
couldn't sing . . . he didn't want to sing . . . he didn't want
to sing . . . Alex blew a cloud of smoke . . . blue smoke . . .
when they had taken his father from the vault three weeks later
. . . he had grown beautiful . . . his nose had become perfect
and clear . . . his hair had turned jet black and glossy and silky
. . . and his skin was a transparent green . . . like the sea only
not so deep . . . and where it was drawn over the cheek bones a
pale beautiful red appeared . . . like a blush . . . why hadn't
his father looked like that always . . . but no . . . to have sung
would have broken the wondrous repose of his lips and maybe
that was his beauty . . . maybe it was wrong to think thoughts
like these . . . but they were nice and pleasant and comfortable

. . . when one was smoking a cigarette thru an ivory holder
. . . inlaid with red jade and green . . . .

  he wondered why he couldn't find work . . . a job . . .
when he had first come to New York he had . . . and he had
only been fourteen then was it because he was nineteen now
that he felt so idle . . . and contented . . . or because he was
an artist . . . but was he an artist . . . was one an artist until
one became known . . . of course he was an artist . . . and
strangely enough so were all his friends . . . he should be
ashamed that he didn't work . . . but . . . was it five years in
New York . . . or the fact that he was an artist . . . when his
mother said she couldn't understand him . . . why did he
vaguely pity her instead of being ashamed . . . he should be
. . . his mother and all his relatives said so . . . his brother
was three years younger than he and yet he had already been
away from home a year . . . on the stage . . . making thirty-
five dollars a week . . . had three suits and many clothes and
was going to help mother . . . while he . . . Alex . . . was
content to lay and smoke and meet friends at night . . . to
argue and read Wilde . . . Freud . . . Boccacio and Schnitzler
. . . to attend Gurdjieff meetings and know things . . . Why
did they scoff at him for knowing such people as Carl . . .
Mencken . . . Toomer . . . Hughes . . . Cullen . . . Wood
. . . Cabell . . . oh the whole lot of them . . . was it because
it seemed incongruous that he . . . who was so little known
. . . should call by first names people they would like to know
. . . were they jealous . . . no mothers aren't jealous of their
sons . . . they are proud of them . . . why then . . . when
these friends accepted and liked him . . . no matter how he
dressed . . . why did mother ask . . . and you went looking
like that . . . Langston was a fine fellow . . . he knew there
was something in Alex . . . and so did Rene and Borgia . . .
and Zora and Clement and Miguel . . . and . . . and . . .
and all of them . . . if he went to see mother she would ask
. . . how do you feel Alex with nothing in your pockets . . . I
don't see how you can be satisfied . . . Really you're a mystery
to me . . . and who you take after . . . I'm sure I don't know
. . . none of my brothers were lazy and shiftless . . . I can

never remember the time when they weren't sending money
home and when your father was your age he was supporting a
family . . . where you get your nerve I don't know . . . just
because you've tried to write one or two little poems and stories
that no one understands . . . you seem to think the world owes
you a living . . . you should see by now how much is thought
of them . . . you can't sell anything . . . and you won't do
anything to make money . . . wake up Alex . . . I don't know
what will become of you . . . .

it was hard to believe in one's self after that . . . did Wilde's
parents or Shelley's or Goya's talk to them like that . . . but it
was depressing to think in that vein . . . Alex stretched and
yawned . . . Max had died . . . Margaret had died . . . so
had Sonia . . . Cynthia . . . Juan-Jose and Harry . . . all
people he had loved . . . loved one by one and together . . .
and all had died . . . he never loved a person long before they
died . . . in truth he was tragic . . . that was a lovely appella-
tion . . . The Tragic Genius . . . think . . . to go thru life
known as The Tragic Genius . . . romantic . . . but it was
more or less true . . . Alex turned over and blew another cloud
of smoke . . . was all life like that . . . smoke . . . blue
smoke from an ivory holder . . . he wished he were in New
Bedford . . . New Bedford was a nice place . . . snug little
houses set complacently behind protecting lawns . . . half
open windows showing prim interiors from behind waving cool
curtains . . . inviting . . . like precise courtesans winking
from behind lace fans . . . and trees . . . many trees . . .
casting lacy patterns of shade on the sun dipped sidewalks . . .
small stores . . . naively proud of their pseudo grandeur . . .
banks . . . called institutions for saving . . . all naive . . .
that was it . . . New Bedford was naive . . . after the sophistication of New York it would fan one like a refreshing breeze . . .
and yet he had returned to New York . . . and sophistication
. . . was he sophisticated . . . no because he was seldom
bored . . . seldom bored by anything . . . and weren't the sophisticated continually suffering from ennui . . . on the contrary . . . he was amused . . . amused by the artificiality of
naivety and sophistication alike . . . but may be that in itself

was the essence of sophistication or . . . was it cynicism . . .
or were the two identical . . . he blew a cloud of smoke . . . it
was growing dark now . . . and the smoke no longer had a ladder to climb . . . but soon the moon would rise and then he
would clothe the silver moon in blue smoke garments . . . truly
smoke was like imagination . . . .

Alex sat up . . . pulled on his shoes and went out . . . it
was a beautiful night . . . and so large . . . the dusky blue
hung like a curtain in an immense arched doorway . . . fastened with silver tacks . . . to wander in the night was wonderful . . . myriads of inquisitive lights . . . curiously prying into
the dark . . . and fading unsatisfied . . . he passed a woman
. . . she was not beautiful . . . and he was sad because she did
not weep that she would never be beautiful . . . was it Wilde
who had said . . . a cigarette is the most perfect pleasure because it leaves one unsatisfied . . . the breeze gave to him a
perfume stolen from some wandering lady of the evening . . .
it pleased him . . . why was it that men wouldn't use perfumes
. . . they should . . . each and every one of them liked perfumes . . . the man who denied that was a liar . . . or a cow-
ard . . . but if ever he were to voice that thought . . . express
it . . . he would be misunderstood . . . a fine feeling that
. . . to be misunderstood . . . it made him feel tragic and
great . . . but maybe it would be nicer to be understood . . .
but no . . . no great artist is . . . then again neither were fools
. . . they were strangely akin these two . . . Alex thought of a
sketch he would make . . . a personality sketch of Fania . . .
straight classic features tinted proud purple . . . sensuous fine
lips . . . gilded for truth . . . eyes . . . half opened and lids
colored mysterious green . . . hair black and straight . . .
drawn sternly mocking back from the false puritanical forehead
. . . maybe he would made Edith too . . . skin a blue . . .
infinite like night . . . and eyes . . . slant and grey . . . very
complacent like a cat's . . . Mona Lisa lips . . . red and seductive as . . . as pomegranate juice . . . in truth it was fine
to be young and hungry and an artist . . . to blow blue smoke
from an ivory holder . . . .

here was the cafeteria . . . it was almost as tho it had jour-

neyed to meet him . . . the night was so blue . . . how does
blue feel . . . or red or gold or any other color . . . if colors
could be heard he could paint most wondrous tunes . . . sym-
phonious . . . think . . . the dulcet clear tone of a blue like
night . . . of a red like pomegranate juice . . . like Edith's lips
. . . of the fairy tones to be heard in a sunset . . . like rubies
shaken in a crystal cup . . . of the symphony of Fania . . .
and silver . . . and gold . . . he had heard the sound of gold
. . . but they weren't the sounds he wanted to catch . . . no
. . . they must be liquid . . . not so staccato but flowing varia-
tions of the same caliber . . . there was no one in the cafe as
yet . . . he sat and waited . . . that was a clever idea he had
had about color music . . . but after all he was a monstrous
clever fellow . . . Jurgen had said that . . . funny how characters in books said the things one wanted to say . . . he would
like to know Jurgen . . . how does one go about getting an
introduction to a fiction character . . . go up to the brown
cover of the book and knock gently . . . and say hello . . .
then timidly . . . is Duke Jurgen there . . . or . . . no because if one entered the book in the beginning Jurgen would
only be a pawn broker . . . and one didn't enter a book in the
center . . . but what foolishness . . . Alex lit a cigarette . . .
but Cabell was a master to have written Jurgen . . . and an
artist . . . and a poet . . . Alex blew a cloud of smoke . . . a
few lines of one of Langston's poems came to describe
Jurgen. . . .

> *Somewhat like Ariel*
> *Somewhat like Puck*
> *Somewhat like a gutter boy*
> *Who loves to play in muck.*
> *Somewhat like Bacchus*
> *Somewhat like Pan*
> *And a way with women*
> *Like a sailor man . . .*

Langston must have known Jurgen . . . suppose Jurgen had
met Tonio Kroeger . . . what a vagrant thought . . . Kroeger

. . . Kroeger . . . Kroeger . . . why here was Rene . . . Alex had almost gone to sleep . . . Alex blew a cone of smoke as he took Rene's hand . . . it was nice to have friends like Rene . . . so comfortable . . . Rene was speaking . . . Borgia joined them . . . and de Diego Padro . . . their talk veered to . . . James Branch Cabell . . . beautiful . . . marvelous . . . Rene had an enchanting accent . . . said sank for thank and souse for south . . . but they couldn't know Cabell's greatness . . . Alex searched the smoke for expression . . . he . . . he . . . well he has created a phantasy mire . . . that's it . . . from clear rich imagery . . . life and silver sands . . . that's nice . . . and silver sands . . . imagine lilies growing in such a mire . . . when they close at night their gilded underside would protect . . . but that's not it at all . . . his thoughts just carried and mingled like . . . like odors . . . suggested but never definite . . . Rene was leaving . . . they all were leaving . . . Alex sauntered slowly back . . . the houses all looked sleepy . . . funny . . . made him feel like writing poetry . . . and about death too . . . an elevated crashed by overhead scattering all his thoughts with its noise . . . making them spread . . . in circles . . . then larger circles . . . just like a splash in a calm pool . . . what had he been thinking . . . of . . . a poem about death . . . but he no longer felt that urge . . . just walk and think and wonder . . . think and remember and smoke . . . blow smoke that mixed with his thoughts and the night . . . he would like to live in a large white palace . . . to wear a long black cape . . . very full and lined with vermillion . . . to have many cushions and to lie there among them . . . talking to his friends . . . lie there in a yellow silk shirt and black velvet trousers . . . like music-review artists talking and pouring strange liquors from curiously beautiful bottles . . . bottles with long slender necks . . . he climbed the noisy stair of the odorous tenement . . . smelled of fish . . . of stale fried fish and dirty milk bottles . . . he rather liked it . . . he liked the acrid smell of horse manure too . . . strong . . . thoughts . . . yes to lie back among strangely fashioned cushions and sip eastern wines and talk . . . Alex threw himself on the bed . . . removed his shoes . . . stretched and relaxed

. . . yes and have music waft softly into the darkened and incensed room . . . he blew a cloud of smoke . . . oh the joy of
being an artist and of blowing blue smoke thru an ivory holder
inlaid with red jade and green . . .

the street was so long and narrow . . . so long and narrow . . .
and blue . . . in the distance it reached the stars . . . and if
he walked long enough . . . far enough . . . he could reach
the stars too . . . the narrow blue was so empty . . . quiet
. . . Alex walked music . . . it was nice to walk in the blue
after a party . . . Zora had shone again . . . her stories . . .
she always shone . . . and Monty was glad . . . every one was
glad when Zora shone . . . he was glad he had gone to Monty's
party . . . Monty had a nice place in the village . . . nice
lights . . . and friends and wine . . . mother would be scan-
dalized that he could think of going to a party . . . without a
copper to his name . . . but then mother had never been to
Monty's . . . and mother had never seen the street seem long
and narrow and blue . . . Alex walked music . . . the click of
his heels kept time with a tune in his mind . . . he glanced into
a lighted cafe window . . . inside were people sipping coffee
. . . men . . . why did they sit there in the loud light . . .
didn't they know that outside the street . . . the narrow blue
street met the stars . . . that if they walked long enough . . .
far enough . . . Alex walked and the click of his heels sounded
. . . and had an echo . . . sound being tossed back and forth
. . . back and forth . . . some one was approaching . . . and
their echoes mingled . . . and gave the sound of castenets . . .
Alex liked the sound of the approaching man's footsteps . . .
he walked music also . . . he knew the beauty of the narrow
blue . . . Alex knew that by the way their echoes mingled . . .
he wished he would speak . . . but strangers don't speak at four
o'clock in the morning . . . at least if they did he couldn't
imagine what would be said . . . maybe . . . pardon me but
are you walking toward the stars . . . yes, sir, and if you walk
long enough . . . then may I walk with you I want to reach the
stars too . . . perdone me senor tiene vd. fosforo . . . Alex
was glad he had been addressed in Spanish . . . to have been

asked for a match in English . . . or to have been addressed in
English at all . . . would have been blasphemy just then . . .
Alex handed him a match . . . he glanced at his companion
apprehensively in the match glow . . . he was afraid that his
appearance would shatter the blue thoughts . . . and stars
. . . ah . . . his face was a perfect complement to his voice
. . . and the echo of their steps mingled . . . they walked in
silence . . . the castanets of their heels clicking accompani-
ment . . . the stranger inhaled deeply and with a nod of content and a smile . . . blew a cloud of smoke . . . Alex felt like
singing . . . the stranger knew the magic of blue smoke also
. . . they continued in silence . . . the castanets of their heels
clicking rythmically . . . Alex turned in his doorway . . . up
the stairs and the stranger waited for him to light the room . . .
no need for words . . . they had always known each other . . .
as they undressed by the blue dawn . . . Alex knew he had
never seen a more perfect being . . . his body was all symmetry
and music . . . and Alex called him Beauty . . . long they lay
. . . blowing smoke and exchanging thoughts . . . and Alex
swallowed with difficulty . . . he felt a glow of tremor . . .
and they talked and . . . slept . . .

Alex wondered more and more why he liked Adrian so . . .
he liked many people . . . Wallie . . . Zora . . . Clement
. . . Gloria . . . Langston . . . John . . . Gwenny . . . oh
many people . . . and they were friends . . . but Beauty . . .
it was different . . . once Alex had admired Beauty's strength
. . . and Beauty's eyes had grown soft and he had said . . . I
like you more than any one Dulce . . . Adrian always called
him Dulce . . . and Alex had become confused . . . was it
that he was so susceptible to beauty that Alex liked Adrian so
much . . . but no . . . he knew other people who were beautiful . . . Fania and Gloria . . . Monty and Bunny . . . but he
was never confused before them . . . while Beauty . . .
Beauty could make him believe in Buddha . . . or imps . . .
and no one else could do that . . . that is no one but Melva
. . . but then he was in love with Melva . . . and that explained that . . . he would like Beauty to know Melva . . .
they were both so perfect . . . such complements . . . yes he

would like Beauty to know Melva because he loved them both
. . . there . . . he had thought it . . . actually dared to think
it . . . but Beauty must never know . . . Beauty couldn't understand . . . indeed Alex couldn't understand . . . and it
pained him . . . almost physically . . . and tired his mind
. . . Beauty . . . Beauty was in the air . . . the smoke . . .
Beauty . . . Melva . . . Beauty . . . Melva . . . Alex   slept
. . . and dreamed

he was in a field . . . a field of blue smoke and black poppies
and red calla lilies . . . he was searching . . . on his hands and
knees . . . searching . . . among black poppies and red calla
lilies . . . he was searching and pushed aside poppy stems . . .
and saw two strong white legs . . . dancer's legs . . . the contours pleased him . . . his eyes wandered . . . on past the
muscular hocks to the firm white thighs . . . the rounded buttocks . . . then the lithe narrow waist . . . strong torso and
broad deep chest . . . the heavy shoulders . . . the graceful
muscled neck . . . squared chin and quizzical lips . . . grecian
nose with its temperamental nostrils . . . the brown eyes looking at him . . . like . . . Monty looked at Zora . . . his hair
curly and black and all tousled . . . and it was Beauty . . .
and Beauty smiled and looked at him and smiled . . . said . . .
I'll wait Alex . . . and Alex became confused and continued his
search . . . on his hands and knees . . . pushing aside poppy
stems and lily stems . . . a poppy . . . a black poppy . . . a
lily . . . a red lily . . . and when he looked back he could no
longer see Beauty . . . Alex continued his search . . . thru
poppies . . . lilies . . . poppies and red calla lilies . . . and
suddenly he saw . . . two small feet olive-ivory . . . two well
turned legs curving gracefully from slender ankles . . . and the
contours soothed him . . . he followed them . . . past the
narrow rounded hips to the tiny waist . . . the fragile firm
breasts . . . the graceful slender throat . . . the soft rounded
chin . . . slightly parting lips and straight little nose with its
slightly flaring nostrils . . . the black eyes with lights in them
. . . looking at him . . . the forehead and straight cut black
hair . . . and it was Melva . . . and she looked at him and
smiled and said . . . I'll wait Alex . . . and Alex became con-

fused and kissed her . . . became confused and continued his
search . . . on his hands and knees . . . pushed aside a poppy
stem . . . a black-poppy stem . . . pushed aside a lily stem
. . . a red-lily stem . . . a poppy . . . a poppy . . . a lily
. . . and suddenly he stood erect . . . exultant . . . and in his
hand he held . . . an ivory holder . . . inlaid with red jade
. . . and green . . . .

and Alex awoke . . . Beauty's hair tickled his nose . . .
Beauty was smiling in his sleep . . . half his face stained flush
color by the sun . . . the other half in shadow . . . blue
shadow . . . his eye lashes casting cobwebby blue shadows on
his cheek . . . his lips were so beautiful . . . quizzical . . .
Alex wondered why he always thought of that passage from
Wilde's *Salome* . . . when he looked at Beauty's lips . . . I
would kiss your lips . . . he *would* like to kiss Beauty's lips . . .
Alex flushed warm . . . with shame . . . or was it shame . . .
he reached across Beauty for a cigarette . . . Beauty's cheek felt
cool to his arm . . . his hair felt soft . . . Alex lay smoking
. . . such a dream . . . red calla lilies . . . red calla lilies . . .
and . . . what could it all mean . . . did dreams have meanings . . . Fania said . . . and black poppies . . . thousands
. . . millions . . . Beauty stirred . . . Alex put out his cigarette . . . closed his eyes . . . he mustn't see Beauty yet . . .
speak to him . . . his lips were too hot . . . dry . . . the
palms of his hands too cool and moist . . . thru his half closed
eyes he could see Beauty . . . propped . . . cheek in hand
. . . on one elbow . . . looking at him . . . lips smiling quiz-
zically . . . he wished Beauty wouldn't look so hard . . . Alex
was finding it difficult to breathe . . . breathe normally . . .
why *must* Beauty look so long . . . and smile *that* way . . . his
face seemed nearer . . . it was . . . Alex could feel Beauty's
hair on his forehead . . . breathe normally . . . breathe normally . . . could feel Beauty's breath on his nostrils and lips
. . . and it was clean and faintly colored with tobacco . . .
breathe normally Alex . . . Beauty's lips were nearer . . . Alex
closed his eyes . . . how did one act . . . his pulse was hammering . . . from wrists to finger tip . . . wrist to finger tip
. . . Beauty's lips touched his . . . his temples throbbed . . .

throbbed . . . his pulse hammered from wrist to finger tip . . . Beauty's breath came short now . . . softly staccato . . . breathe normally Alex . . . you are asleep . . . Beauty's lips touched his . . . breathe normally . . . and pressed . . . pressed hard . . . cool . . . his body trembled . . . breathe normally Alex . . . Beauty's lips pressed cool . . . cool and hard . . . how much pressure does it take to waken one . . . Alex sighed . . . moved softly . . . how does one act . . . Beauty's hair barely touched him now . . . his breath was faint on . . . Alex's nostrils . . . and lips . . . Alex stretched and opened his eyes . . . Beauty was looking at him . . . propped on one elbow . . . cheek in his palm . . . Beauty spoke . . . scratch my head please Dulce . . . Alex was breathing normally now . . . propped against the bed head . . . Beauty's head in his lap . . . Beauty spoke . . . I wonder why I like to look at some things Dulce . . . things like smoke and cats . . . and you . . . Alex's pulse no longer hammered from . . . wrist to finger tip . . . wrist to finger tip . . . the rose dusk had become blue night . . . and soon . . . soon they would go out into the blue . . . .

the little church was crowded . . . warm . . . the rows of benches were brown and sticky . . . Harold was there . . . and Constance and Langston and Bruce and John . . . there was Mr. Robeson . . . how are you Paul . . . a young man was singing . . . Caver . . . Caver was a very self assured young man . . . such a dream . . . poppies . . . black poppies . . . they were applauding . . . Constance and John were exchanging notes . . . the benches were sticky . . . a young lady was playing the piano . . . fair . . . and red calla lilies . . . who had ever heard of red calla lilies . . . they were applauding . . . a young man was playing the viola . . . what could it all mean . . . so many poppies . . . and Beauty looking at him like . . . like Monty looked at Zora . . . another young man was playing a violin . . . he was the first real artist to perform . . . he had a touch of soul . . . or was it only feeling . . . they were hard to differentiate on the violin . . . and Melva standing in the poppies and lilies . . . Mr. Phillips was singing . . . Mr. Phillips was billed as a basso . . . and he had kissed her . . . they were applauding . . . the first young man was singing again . . . Langston's spiritual . . . Fy-ah-fy-ah-Lawd . . . fy-ah's gonna burn ma soul . . . Beauty's hair was so black and curly . . . they were applauding . . . encore . . . Fy-ah Lawd had been a success . . . Langston bowed . . . Langston had written the words . . . Hall bowed . . . Hall had written the music . . . the young man was singing it again . . . Beauty's lips had pressed hard . . . cool . . . cool . . . fy-ah Lawd . . . his breath had trembled . . . fy-ah's gonna burn ma soul . . . they were all leaving . . . first to the roof dance . . . fy-ah Lawd . . . there was Catherine . . . she was beautiful tonight . . . she always was at night . . . Beauty's lips . . . fy-ah Lawd . . . hello Dot . . . why don't you take a boat that sails . . . when are you leaving again . . . and there's Estelle . . . every one was there . . . fy-ah Lawd . . . Beauty's body had pressed close . . . close . . . fy-ah's gonna burn my soul . . . let's leave . . . have to meet some people at the New World . . . then to Augusta's party . . . Harold . . . John . . . Bruce . . . Connie . . . Langston . . . ready . . . down one hundred thirty-fifth street . . . fy-ah . . . meet these people and leave . . . fy-ah Lawd . . . now to Augusta's party . . . fy-ahs gonna burn ma soul . . . they were at Augusta's . . . Alex half lay . . . half sat on the floor . . . sipping a cocktail . . . such a dream . . . red calla lilies . . . Alex left . . . down the narrow streets . . . fy-ah . . . up the long noisy stairs . . . fy-ahs gonna bu'n ma soul . . . his head felt swollen . . . expanding . . . contracting . . . expanding . . . contracting . . . he had never been like this before . . . expanding . . . contracting . . . it was that . . . fy-ah . . . fy-ah Lawd . . . and the cocktails . . . and Beauty . . . he felt two cool strong hands on his shoulders . . . it was Beauty . . . lie down Dulce . . . Alex lay down . . . Beauty . . . Alex stopped . . . no no . . . don't say it . . . Beauty mustn't know . . . Beauty couldn't understand . . . are you going to lie down too Beauty . . . the light went out expanding . . . contracting . . . he felt the bed sink as Beauty lay beside him . . . his lips were dry . . . hot . . . the palms of his hands so

moist and cool . . . Alex partly closed his eyes . . . from beneath his lashes he could see Beauty's face over his . . . nearer
. . . nearer . . . Beauty's hair touched his forehead now . . .
he could feel his breath on his nostrils and lips . . . Beauty's
breath came short . . . breathe normally Beauty . . . breathe
normally . . . Beauty's lips touched his . . . pressed hard . . .
cool . . . opened slightly . . . Alex opened his eyes . . . into
Beauty's . . . parted his lips . . . Dulce . . . Beauty's breath
was hot and short . . . Alex ran his hand through Beauty's hair
. . . Beauty's lips pressed hard against his teeth . . . Alex
trembled . . . could feel Beauty's body . . . close against his
. . . hot . . . tense . . . white . . . and soft . . . soft . . .
soft . . . .

they were at Forno's . . . every one came to Forno's once maybe
only once . . . but they came . . . see that big fat woman
Beauty . . . Alex pointed to an overly stout and bejeweled lady
making her way thru the maze of chairs . . . that's Maria Guer-
rero . . . Beauty looked to see a lady guiding almost the whole
opera company to an immense table . . . really Dulce . . . for
one who appreciates beauty you do use the most abominable
English . . . Alex lit a cigarette . . . and that florid man with
white hair . . . that's Carl . . . Beauty smiled . . . The Blind
Bow Boy . . . he asked . . . Alex wondered . . . everything
seemed so . . . so just the same . . . here they were laughing
and joking about people . . . there's Rene . . . Rene this is my
friend Adrian . . . after that night . . . and he felt so unem-
barrassed . . . Rene and Adrian were talking . . . there was
Lucricia Bori . . . she was bowing at their table . . . oh her
cousin was with them . . . and Peggy Joyce . . . every one
came to Forno's . . . Alex looked toward the door . . . there
was Melva . . . Alex beckoned . . . Melva this is Adrian . . .
Beauty held her hand . . . they talked . . . smoked . . . Alex
loved Melva . . . in Forno's . . . every one came there sooner
or later . . . maybe once . . . but . . . .

up . . . up . . . slow . . . jerk up . . . up . . . not fast
. . . not glorious . . . but slow . . . up . . . up into the sun

. . . slow . . . sure like fate . . . poise on the brim . . . the brim of life . . . two shining rails straight down . . . Melva's head was on his shoulder . . . his arm was around her . . . poise . . . the down . . . gasping . . . straight down . . . straight like sin . . . down . . . the curving shiny rail rushed up to meet them . . . hit the bottom then . . . shoot up . . . fast . . . glorious . . . up into the sun . . . Melva gasped . . . Alex's arm tightened . . . all goes up . . . then down . . . straight like hell . . . all breath squeezed out of them . . . Melva's head on his shoulder . . . up . . . up . . . Alex kissed her . . . down . . . they stepped out of the car . . . walking music . . . now over to the Ferris Wheel . . . out and up . . . Melva's hand was soft in his . . . out and up . . . over mortals . . . mortals drinking nectar . . . five cents a glass . . . her cheek was soft on his . . . up . . . up . . . till the world seemed small . . . tiny . . . the ocean seemed tiny and blue . . . up . . . up and out . . . over the sun . . . the tiny red sun . . . Alex kissed her . . . up . . . up . . . their tongues touched . . . up . . . seventh heaven . . . the sea had swallowed the sun . . . up and out . . . her breath was perfumed . . . Alex kissed her . . . drift down . . . soft . . . soft . . . the sun had left the sky flushed . . . drift down . . . soft down . . . back to earth . . . visit the mortals sipping nectar at five cents a glass . . . Melva's lips brushed his . . . then out among the mortals . . . and the sun had left a flush on Melva's cheeks . . . they walked hand in hand . . . and the moon came out . . . they walked in silence on the silver strip . . . and the sea sang for them . . . they walked toward the moon . . . we'll hang our hats on the crook of the moon Melva . . . softly on the silver strip . . . his hands molded her features and her cheeks were soft and warm to his touch . . . where is Adrian . . . Alex . . . Melva trod silver . . . Alex trod sand . . . Alex trod sand . . . the sea *sang* for her . . . Beauty . . . her hand felt cold in his . . . Beauty . . . the sea *dinned* . . . Beauty . . . he led the way to the train . . . and the train dinned . . . Beauty . . . dinned . . . dinned . . . her cheek *had* been soft . . . Beauty . . . Beauty . . . her breath *had* been perfumed . . . Beauty . . . Beauty . . . the sands *had* been silver . . . Beauty . . . Beauty . . . they left the train . . . Melva walked music . . . Melva said . . . don't make me blush again . . . and kissed him . . . Alex stood on the steps after she left him and the night was black . . . down long streets to . . . Alex lit a cigarette . . . and his heels clicked . . . Beauty . . . Melva . . . Beauty . . . Melva . . . and the smoke made the night blue . . .

Melva had said . . . don't make me blush again . . . and kissed him . . . and the street had been blue . . . one *can* love two at the same time . . . Melva had kissed him . . . one *can* . . . and the street had been blue . . . one *can* . . . and the room was clouded with blue smoke . . . drifting vapors of smoke and thoughts . . . Beauty's hair was so black . . . and soft . . . blue smoke from an ivory holder . . . was that why he loved Beauty . . . one *can* . . . or because his body was beautiful . . . and white and warm . . . or because his eyes . . . one *can* love . . . .

JOHN EDGAR WIDEMAN

The Statue of Liberty

One of the pleasures of jogging in the country is seeing those houses your route takes you past each day and wondering who lives in them. Some sit a good distance from the road, small, secluded by trees, tucked in a fold of land where they've been sheltered thousands of years from the worst things that happen to people. A little old couple lives in this kind. They've raised many children and lost some to the city but the family name's on mailboxes scattered up and down the road, kids and grandkids in houses like their folks', farmers like them, like more generations than you'd care to count back to England and cottages that probably resemble these, Capes, with roofs pulled down almost to the ground the way the old man stuffs on a wool cap bitter February days to haul in firewood from the shed. There are majestic hilltop-sitters with immaculate outbuildings and leaded glass and fine combed lawns sloping in every direction, landmarks you can measure your progress by as you reel in the countryside step by step jogging. I like best those ramshackle outfits—you can tell it's an old farm two young people from the city have taken over with their city dreams and city habits because it's not a real farm anymore, more some-

222

body's idea of what living in the country should be at this day and time. A patched-together look, a corniness and coziness like pictures in a child's book, these city people have a little bit of everything growing on their few acres, and they keep goats, chickens, turkeys, ducks, geese, one cow—a pet zoo, really, and a German shepherd on a chain outside the trailer they've converted to a permanent dwelling. You know they smoke dope and let their kids run around naked as the livestock. They still blast loud city music on a stereo too big for the trailer and watch the stars through a kind of skylight contraption rigged in the tin roof and you envy them the time they first came out from the city, all those stars and nobody around but the two of them, starting out fresh in a different place and nothing better to do than moon up at the night sky and listen to the crickets and make each other feel nice in bed. Those kinds of houses must have been on your jogging route once. You look for them now beneath overloaded clotheslines, beyond rusted-out car stumps, in junk and mess and weeds, you can't tell what all's accumulated in the front yard from where you pass on the road.

A few houses close to the road. Fresh paint and shutters and shrubs, a clean-cut appearance and you think of suburbs, of neat house after house exactly alike, exactly like this one sitting solitary where it doesn't fit into the countryside. Retired people. Two frail old maids on canvas folding chairs in the attached garage with its wizard door rolled up and a puffy, ginger-colored cat crossing from one lady's stockinged feet to the other lady's stockinged feet like a conversation you can't hear from the road. Taking the air in their gazebo is what they're thinking in that suburban garage with its wide door open.

In the window of another one only a few yards from the road you can't tell if there's a person in the dark looking out because the panes haven't been washed in years. A house wearing sunglasses. You have a feeling someone very very old is still alive inside watching you, watching everything that passes, a face planted there in the dark so long, so patient and silent it scares you for no good reason. A gray, sprawled sooty clapboard swaybacked place a good wind could knock over but that wind hasn't blown through yet, not in all the time it's taken the man and woman who live here to shrivel up and crack and curl like the shingles on their steep roof that looks like a bad job of trying to paint a picture of the ocean, brushstrokes that don't become stormy ocean waves but stay brushstrokes, separate, unconnected, slapped on one after another in a hurry-up, hopeless manner that doesn't fool anyone.

A dim-shouldered, stout woman in a blue housedress with a lacy dirty white collar is who I imagine staring at me when I clomp-clomp-clomp by, straining on the slight grade that carries me beyond this house and barn people stopped painting fifty years ago, where people stopped living at least that long ago but they're too old now to die.

Once I thought of an eye large enough to fill the space inside those weather-beaten walls, under that slapdash roof. Just an eye. Self-sufficient. Enormous. White and veiny. Hidden in there with nothing else to do but watch.

Another way jogging pleasures me is how it lets me turn myself into another person in another place. The city, for instance. I'm small and pale running at night in a section of town I've been warned never to enter alone even in daylight. I run burning with the secret of who I am, what I'm carrying, what I can do, secrets no one would guess just watching me jog past, a smallish, solitary white woman nearly naked on dangerous streets where she has no business being. She's crazy, they think. Or asking for it. But no one knows I can kill instantly, efficiently, with my fingers, toes and teeth. No one can see the tiny deadly weapons I've concealed on my person. In a wristband pouch. Under a Velcro flap in my running shorts. Nor would anyone believe the speed in my legs. No one can catch me unless I want to be caught.

When the huge black man springs from the shadows I let him grapple me to the ground. I tame him with my eyes. Instantly he understands. Nothing he could steal from me, throwing me down on the hard cement, hurting me, stripping me, mounting me with threats and his sweaty hand in my mouth so I won't scream, none of his violence, his rage, his hurry to split me and pound himself into me would bring the pleasure I'm ready to give of my own free will. I tell him with my eyes that I've been running to meet him. I jog along his dangerous streets because

I'm prepared for him. He lets me undress him. I'm afraid for a moment his skin will be too black and I'll lose him in this dark alley. But my hands swim in the warmth of him. His smell, the damp sheen tells me he's been jogging too. It's peaceful where we are. We understand each other perfectly. Understand how we've been mistaken about each other for longer than we care to admit. Instead of destroying you, I whisper to him, I choose to win you with the gentleness in my eyes. Convert you. Release you. Then we can invent each other this quiet way, breath by breath, limb by limb, as if we have all the time in the world and our bodies are a route we learn jogging leisurely till the route's inside us, imagining us, our bodies carried along by it effortlessly. We stand and trot off shoulder to shoulder. He has Doberman legs. They twirl as if on a spit.

For weeks now they've been going by each morning. Crooker hears them first. Yapping and thrashing, running the length of her chain till it yanks her back to reality. A loud, stupid dog. I think she believes she's going to escape each time she takes a dash at her chain. She barks and snarls at them and I'd like to rubber-band her big mouth shut.

Quiet, Crooker. Hush.

Leave her be, Orland grumps to me. Barking's her job. She gets fed to bark.

We both know Crooker's useless as a watchdog. She growls at her reflection in the French doors. She howls at birds a mile away. A bug can start her yelping. Now she's carrying on as if the Beast from Babylon's slouching down the road to eat us all for breakfast and it's nobody but the joggers she's seen just like I've seen them every morning for a week. Passing by, shading to the other edge of the road because they don't want to aggravate a strange, large country dog into getting so frantic it just might snap its chain.

Nothing but those joggers she's barking at. Shut up, Crooker.

How do you know those people ain't the kind to come back snooping around here at night? Pacify the dog and them or others like them be right up on top of us before we know it.

Orland, please. What in the world are you grumbling about? You're as bad as she is.

I pay her to bark. Let her bark.

She's Crooker because at birth her tail didn't come out right. An accident in the womb. Her tail snagged on something and it's been crook-ended since. Poor creature couldn't even walk through the door of life right. But she was lucky too. Molly must have been spooked by the queerness of that tail. Must have been the humped tail because Molly ate every other pup in that litter. Ate them before we caught on and rescued this crook-tailed one.

When they pass by the window Orland doesn't even glance up. He doesn't know what he's missing. Usually he's gone long before they jog past. I forget what kept him late the morning I'm recalling. It's not that he's a hard worker or busy or conscientious. For years now the point's been to rise early and be gone. Gone the important part. Once he's gone he can figure out some excuse for going, some excuse to keep himself away. I think he may have another place where he sleeps. Tucks himself in again after he leaves my bed and dreams half the day away like a baby. Orland misses them. Might as well be a squirrel or moth riling Crooker. If he knew the woman looked as good as she does in her silky running shorts, he'd sure pay attention. If he knew the man was a big black man his stare would follow mine out the window and pay even more attention.

They seem to be about my age more or less. Woman rather short but firm and strong with tight tanned legs from jogging. She packs a bit more weight in the thighs than I do, but I haven't gained an inch anywhere nor a pound since I was a teenager. My face betrays me, but I was blessed with a trim, athletic high school beauty queen's figure. Even after the first two children Orland swore at me once when he pulled off my nightie, Damned Jailbait.

The man's legs from ankle to the fist of muscle before the knee are straight and hard as pipes, bony as dog's legs then flare into wedges of black thigh, round black man's butt. First morning I was with the kids in the front yard he waved. A big hello-how-are-you smiling-celebrity wave the way black men make you think they're movie stars or professional athletes with a big, wide wave, like you should know them if you don't and that momentary toothy spotlight they cast on you is something special from that big world where they're famous. He's waved every morning since. When I've let him see me. I know he looks for me. I wasn't wearing much more than the kids when he saw me in the yard. I know he wonders if I stroll around the house naked or sunbathe in the nude on a recliner behind the house in the fenced yard you can't see from the road. I've waited with my back close enough to the bedroom window so he'd see me if he was trying, a bare white back he could spot even though it's hard to see inside this gloomy house that hour in the morning. A little reward, if he's alert. I shushed Crooker and smiled back at him, up at him the first time, kneeling beside Billy, tying my Billyboy's shoe. We're complete smiling buddies now and the woman greets me too.

No doubt about it he liked what he saw. Three weeks now and they'd missed only two Sundays and an odd Thursday. Three times it had rained. I didn't count those days. Never do. Cooped up in the house with four children under nine you wouldn't waste your time or energy either, counting rainy, locked-in days like that because you need every ounce of patience, every speck of will, just to last to bedtime. Theirs. Which on rainy cooped-up days is followed immediately by yours because you're whipped, fatigued, bone and brain tired living in a child's world of days with no middle, end or beginning, just time like some Silly Putty you're stuck in the belly of. You can't shape it; it shapes you, but the shape is no real shape at all, it's the form-lessness of no memory, no sleep that won't let you get a handle on anything, let you be anything but whatever it is twisted, pulled, worried. Three weeks minus three minus days that never count anyway minus one Thursday minus twice they perhaps went to church and that equals what? Equals the days required for us to become acquainted. To get past curiosity into *Hi there*. To follow up his presidential candidate's grin and high-five sa-lute with my cheeriness, my punch-clock punctuality, springing tick-tock from my gingerbread house so I'm in sight, available, when they jog by. Most of the time, apparently. Always, if he takes the trouble to seek me out. As if the two of them, the tall black man and his shortish, tanned white lady companion, were yoked together, pulling the sun around the world and the two of them had been circling the globe forever, in step, in time with each other, round and round like the tiger soup in a Little Black Sambo book I read to my children, achieving a rhythm, a high-stepping pace unbroken and sufficient unto itself but I managed to blend in, to jog beside them invisible till I learned their pace and rhythm, flowing, unobtrusive, even when they both discovered me there, braced with them, running with them, undeniably part of whatever they think they are doing every morning when they pass my house and wave.

He liked what he saw because when they finally did stop and come in for the cool drinks I'd proposed first as a kind of joke, then a standing offer, seriously, no trouble, whenever, if ever, they choose to stop, then on a tray, two actual frosty tumblers of ice water they couldn't refuse without hurting my feelings, he took his and brushed my fingertips in a gesture that wasn't accidental, he wasn't a clumsy man, he took a glass and half my finger with it because he'd truly liked what he saw and admired it more close up.

Sweat sheen gleamed on him like a fresh coat of paint. He was pungent as tar. I could smell her mixed in with him. They'd made love before they jogged. Hadn't bothered to bathe before starting off on their route. She didn't see me remove my halter. He did. I sat him where he'd have to force himself to look away in order not to see me slip the halter over my head. I couldn't help standing, my arms raised like a prisoner of war, letting him take his own good time observing the plump breasts that are the only part of my anatomy below my neck not belonging to a fourteen-year-old girl. She did not see what I'd done till I turned the corner, but she seemed not to notice or not to care. I didn't need to use the line I'd rehearsed in front of the mirror, the line that went with my stripper's curtsy, with my arm stretched like Miss Liberty over my head and my wrist daintily cocked, dangling in my fingers the wisp of halter: We're very casual around here.

Instead, as we sit sipping our ice waters I laugh and say, This weather's too hot for clothes. I tease my lips with the tip of my tongue. I roll the frosted glass on my breasts. This feels so nice.

Let me do you. I push up her tank top. Roll the glass on her flat stomach.

You're both so wet. Why don't you get off those damp things and sit out back? Cool off awhile. It's perfectly private.

I'll fetch us more drinks. Not too early for something stronger than water, is it?

They exchange easily deciphered looks. For my benefit, speaking to me as much as to each other. Who is this woman? What the hell have we gotten ourselves into?

I guide her up from the rattan chair. It's printed ruts across the backs of her thighs. My fingers are on her elbow. I slide open the screen door and we step onto the unfinished mess of flagstone, mismatched tile and brick Orland calls a patio. The man lags behind us. He'll see me from the rear as I balance on one leg then the other, stepping out of my shorts.

I point her to one of the lawn chairs.

Make yourself comfortable. Orland and the kids are gone for the day. Just the three of us. No one else for miles. It's glorious. Pull off your clothes, stretch out and relax.

I turn quickly and catch him liking what he sees, all of me naked, but he's wary. A little shocked. All of this too good to be true. I don't allow him time to think overly long about it.

You're joining us, aren't you? No clothes allowed.

After I plop down I watch out of the corner of my eye how she wiggles and kicks out of her shorts, her bikini underwear. Her elasticized top comes off over her head. Arms raised in that gesture of surrender every woman performs shrugging off what's been hiding her body. She's my sister then. I remember myself in the mirror of her. Undressing just a few minutes before, submitting, taking charge.

Crooker howls from the pen where I've stuffed her every morning since the first week. She'd been quiet till his long foot in his fancy striped running shoe touched down on the patio. Her challenge scares him. He freezes, framed a moment in the French doors.

It's OK. She's locked in her pen. All she'd do if she were here is try to lick you to death. C'mon out.

I smile over at the woman. Aren't men silly most of the time?
Under that silence, those hard stares, that playacting that's supposed to be a personality, aren't they just chickenhearted little
boys most of the time? She knows exactly what I'm thinking
without me saying a word. Men. Her black man no different
from the rest.

He slams the screen door three times before it catches in the
glides that haven't been right since Orland set them. The man
can't wait to see the two of us, sisters again because I've assumed the same stiff posture in my lawn chair as she has in hers,
back upright, legs extended straight ahead, ankles crossed. We
are as demure as two white ladies can be in broad daylight displayed naked for the eyes of a black man. Her breasts are girlish,
thumb nippled. Her bush a fuzzy creature in her lap. I'm as I
promised. He'll like what he'll see, can't wait to see, but he's
pretending to be in no hurry, undoing his bulky shoes lace by
lace instead of kicking them off his long feet. The three chairs
are arranged in a **Y**, foot ends converging. I steered her where I
wanted her and took my seat so he'll be in the middle, facing us
both, her bare flesh or mine everywhere he turns. With all his
heart, every hidden fiber he wants to occupy the spot I've allot-
ted for him, but he believes if he seems in too much of a rush,
shows undue haste, he'll embarrass himself, reveal himself for
what he is, what he was when Crooker's bark stopped him short.

He manages a gangly nonchalance, settling down, shooting
out his legs so the soles of three pairs of feet would kiss if we
inched just a wee bit closer to the bull's-eye. His shins gleam like
black marble. When he's jogging he flows. Up close I'm aware of
joints, angles, hinges, the struts and wires of sinew assembling
him, the patchwork of his dark skin, many colors, like hers, like
mine, instead of the tar-baby sleekness that trots past my window. His palms, the pale underpads of his feet have no business
being the blank, clownish color they are. She could wear that
color on her hands and feet and he could wear hers and the
switch would barely be noticeable.

We're in place now and she closes her eyes, leans back her
head and sighs. It is quiet and nice here. So peaceful, she says.
This is a wonderful idea, she says, and teaches herself how to

recline, levers into prone position and lays back so we're no longer three wooden Indians.

My adjustment is more subtle. I drop one foot on either side of my chair so I'm straddling it, then scoot the chair with me on it a few inches to change the angle the sun strikes my face. An awkward way to move, a lazy, stuttering adjustment useful only because it saves me standing up. And it's less than modest. My knees are spread the width of the lawn chair as I ride it to a new position. If the man has liked what he's seen so far, and I know he has, every morsel, every crumb, then he must certainly be pleased by this view. I let him sink deeper. Raise my feet back to the vinyl strips of the leg rest, but keep my knees open, yawning, draw them towards my chest, hug them, snuggle them. Her tan is browner than mine. Caramel then cream where a bikini shape is saved on her skin. I show him the bottom of me is paler, but not much paler than my thighs, my knees I peer over, knees like two big scoops of coffee ice cream I taste with the tip of my tongue.

I'm daydreaming some of the things I'll let them do to me. Tie my limbs to the bed's four corners. Kneel me, spread the cheeks of my ass. I'll suck him while her fingers ply me. When it's the black man's turn to be bondaged and he's trussed up too tight to grin, Orland bursts through the bedroom door, chain saw cradled across his chest. No reason not to let everything happen. They are clean. In good health. My body's still limber and light as a girl's. They like what they see. She's pretending to nap but I know she can sense his eyes shining, the veins thickening in his rubbery penis as it stirs and arches between his thighs he presses together so it doesn't rear up and stab at me, single me out impolitely when there are two of us, two women he must take his time with and please. We play our exchange of smiles, him on the road, me with Billy and Sarah and Carl and Augie at the edge of our corn patch. I snare his eyes, lead them down slowly to my pearly bottom, observe myself there, finger myself, study what I'm showing him so when I raise my eyes and bring his up with me again, we'll both know beyond a doubt what I've been telling him every morning when he passes is true.

No secrets now. What do you see, you black bastard? My

pubic hair is always cropped close and neat, a perfect triangle decorates the fork of the Y, a Y like the one I formed with our lawn chairs. I unclasp my knees, let them droop languorously apart, curl my toes on the tubing that frames my chair. She may be watching too. But it's now or never. We must move past certain kinds of resistance, habits that are nothing more than habits. Get past or be locked like stupid baying animals in a closet forever. My eyes challenge his. Yes those are the leaves of my vagina opening. Different colors inside than outside. Part of what's inside me unfolding, exposed, like the lips of your pouty mouth.

The petals of my vagina are two knuckles spreading of a fist stuck in your face. They are the texture of the softest things you've ever touched. Softer. Better. Fleece bedding them turns subtly damp. A musk rises, gently, magically, like the mist off the oval pond that must be included in your route if you jog very far beyond my window. But you may arrive too late or too early to have noticed. About a half mile from here the road climbs as steeply as it does in this rolling countryside. Ruins of a stone wall, an open field on the right, a ragged screen of pine trees borders the other side and if you peer through them, green of meadow is broken just at the foot of a hill by a black shape difficult to distinguish from dark tree trunks and their shadows, but search hard, it rests like a mirror into which a universe has collapsed. At dawn, at dusk the pond breathes. You can see when the light and air are right, something rare squeezed up from the earth's center, hanging over this pond. I believe a ghost with long, trailing hair is marooned there and if I ever get my courage up, I've promised myself I'll go jogging past at night and listen to her sing.

SAMUEL R. DELANY

The Place
of Excrement

The remainder of this tale is a love story.

When they're happening to you, not when you're hearing them, love stories are funny and scary and kind of unbelievable and turn your head around because they make you do and think and say things you'd never otherwise do or say. This one was, in that sense, classic. Just like I'll never forget the day I decided I had AIDS (that April 25, with Tony), I'll never forget the day *this* part of the story started: it was about three weeks after having my cellar session on Tony's return, with Jimmy getting all upset. We'd gone through a loud, sweaty July Fourth, on which Pheldon turned up with barbecued ribs and chicken and potato salad and champagne, half a dozen friends and a van (driven by Lewey, the redheaded sanitation worker), and we all went on this picnic up at Bear Mountain, which was only moderately crazily crowded that year.

The day I'm talking about was, however, Tuesday, July 18; I remember because it was also the day I decided to do something about Almira Adler's request.

At work (back in suit and tie, in that blue-walled, anonymous office with three names, the last one joined to the first two by an ampersand), I wondered whether, if I wanted to go to the Pit and ask about what had happened on September 23, 1973, I'd do better with lots of people there (maybe some who even went back that far) or with only a few (that is, when somebody might have time to talk to me). Tuesday is the deadest night in any bar. But I decided to go that night.

The office chat was of rain that evening. I didn't have an umbrella. Go home first then, I decided, change, and come back downtown. When I got out at my subway stop and, minutes later, turned from Broadway's crush up Eighty-second, it was a warm quarter to seven. The light had a bronzy gloom, that might, yes, have meant rain.

A quarter of the way down the block, he stood—fists in his sweatshirt's pouches, looking across at the church. (You remember him: the big guy on the Broadway island who'd fished the hamburger from the refuse can . . .) I neared: he was standing before the small gateway blocking the alley between the two apartment buildings—the one the wag had wired a piece of plywood over and spray-painted across it I AM THE DOOR!

Weighted down by his fists, his sweatshirt was open over his chest's forest, his gut's rug. As I got closer and closer to him, things kept striking me:

The front was torn almost free from one of his running shoes, so that, with the upper flopped over to the side, I saw a big, naked foot, in the rubber rim, the broad nails picked back about as far—I suddenly remembered—as his fingernails had been. Now he took one fist from his sweatshirt, raised it to his mouth, and began to chip at his nails with his lower teeth, while he watched me over his knuckles. Thirty-three? Thirty-five? For some reason, with his beard and his rumpled hair, behind his fist he smiled—at me; or maybe he was just a bear who smiled a lot.

I smiled back.

He nodded, still gnawing, still smiling.

Within his wool pants, his other hand moved around toward his groin. For a moment, I glimpsed in outline what hung there—which was considerable. Inside his pants he scratched himself; and watched me. And smiled.

Walking on to the corner, I wondered if that had been some sort of a come-on. The light lifted behind the dark grille to WALK, and I crossed the street.

Up in the apartment, I changed my clothes. While I was in the bedroom, tugging off slacks and pulling on jeans, I thought: Here's the whole country, busy replacing vinyl with tape and worrying if it's going to have to go through the whole process again a year or so from now with the new, silver CDs; since the Berlin Wall tumbled last November, millions are paused for the leap into cyberspace, where everything glitters and soars, but nothing dribbles or squishes; the summer is getting into Spandex and roller blades; the number of AIDS cases is now within a stone's throw, one way or the other, of 100,000; a while ago, the Variety had been closed down because, said an article in the *Daily News*, "158 acts of unsafe sex" had been observed there by a plainclothes inspector over—what? Twenty minutes? I'd seen workers just last week, gutting the building and starting in on its refurbishment. (Even the Grotto had suffered a brief attempt to heterosexualize its operations, instituted and advertised by the management, called "lap dancing"; fortunately, it failed miserably, and things were now back to normal.) And only last week Phel called me to tell me that, as a black intellectual, I must pay more serious attention to rap, because, if nothing else, it's a black art that's *verbal*; but what does all this mean to a homeless white guy, not to mention all the other black ones down by law and out on the street in one torn sneaker, who may never have had occasion to call anything "marvelous," "excellent" or "awesome" in their lives? At the same time, I was rehearsing what I was going to be saying in half an hour down at the Pit: "Excuse me, but do you remember anybody who might have been working here in the early seventies . . . ? When that murder happened . . . ?"

With my umbrella, I came down again. When I stepped out on the stoop, it had started to rain—not hard, but steadily. The umbrella was a collapsible black Taiwanese thing. But because the evening was warm, I didn't put it up.

At the corner I crossed Amsterdam.

No longer standing, he sat, leaning forward on his knees, on a stoop at a building beside the gate. As I came down the block, he looked around at me. Again, this smile broke out on his bearded face. He looked right at me, too.

Water gemmed his hair. It was hard to tell what was glister and what was just the gray that brushed his head and beard as though a house painter's hand smeared with white paint had swiped him.

Again, I smiled back—and slowed.

I noticed one hand was back between his legs. Some of his hair was wetted to his forehead in little blades. Under his arms, a patch of his sweatshirt was still dry. But water glittered in his beard, over his mustache, on his eyelashes. I'd already decided, running into him this second time, I would speak: Hello . . . ? How're you doing . . . ? (Can I suck your dick? No, I'd leave that to our next encounter.) Kind of wet to be sitting out here? But the hand back in the shadow between his legs was moving, moving . . . moving, a rhythmic moving. On his thick forearm, hair lay down on the blocky muscles. The rolled-up sweatshirt was a tight band. Hanging over one knee in front, the hock of his wrist was thicker than both of mine.

I said, inanely: "What're you doing sitting out here in the rain?"

His hand kept working back in the shadow of his belly and lap. He kept on smiling. And, in a rough and slow voice, he said, "Sitting, here, getting, wet, and playing, with myself." The smile didn't break.

I swallowed. Because I was surprised.

As I stood there, my mouth went kind of dry and droplets ran down my forehead. "Bet it feels good."

"Sure do." He moved his shoulders up. "Wanna see?"

"Okay," I said, "Sure."

Sitting back, he let his knees fall wide: loose from his fly was a cock as thick as Tony's and more than a couple of inches longer. An inch wide and two-and-a-half inches long, a leathery cuff dangled off the end—and, while it wasn't the freakish five-and-a-half-inch skin the Piece o' Shit had had hanging from his meat, it was enough to send me back six years to that sunny Saturday in the park.

In the rain, he pulled his dick forward, first overhand, then underhand. I looked at it; the cuff waggled.

"Jesus," I said, "what have you been doing? Wearing yoni rings in that thing?"

His smile got sort of lopsided; he let his head drop to the side. "Now what you know about yoni rings?"

"Nothing," I said. "Really. I just knew somebody once who was into them. How *else* are you going to get a skin that long?"

"I used to wear 'em," he said. "Back when I was in a yoni club. You ever in one of them?"

"No. Like I said, just somebody I knew. Was your club in"—I tried to dredge up what little I remembered about the business—"in Montana?"

"Naw," he said. "We was in Florida, when I had me a job down there—shape-up; but I was workin' pretty regular then. I only wore 'em for about a year. Well, a year and a half—but only a year regular. I was up to where I could hold two in by themselves—three, if I used some adhesive tape around the edge. Then, when I went back on the bum, it got too much trouble. I think the fucker's shrunk back half an inch."

But some of them guys had skins on 'em eight, twelve, sixteen inches long. "Yeah, I've heard."

"They was wearin' *their* rings for years. Once I went on the bum again, I got lazy. You're the first person who wasn't in a club who just seen my dick and knowed right away how I got my skin like that." He sat up real tall now, to look up and down the street.

Probably because of the rain, though, no one was coming.

I can be disarmingly straightforward about sex; but when someone comes on that forward to me, myself I disarm pretty quick. "Um, eh—" I said, trying to think of something to say. "You looking to get that sucked on?"

"Sure." His big fingers urged *all* that skin back enough for me to glimpse the finger-width slit up the broad mushroom of its head; he slid it forward again. "You wanna suck it, that'd be nice." He leaned again on his knees, so that his working fist and the cock thrust out of it retreated in the shadow of his darkly furred gut. "What I'm really lookin' for, though"—as he leaned

forward, his smile broke apart; under it were all sorts of expectations and don't-give-a-fuck belligerence and even some fear, at
the same time as all of a big man's vulnerability—"is to find me
a nigger to piss on . . ."

I swallowed. The thud, thud, thud inside my chest got so
heavy that I staggered a little—I don't know whether he saw me.

His free hand left his knee and reached out; and I could see
his fingers were very rough, for all the rainwater. "Man, I need to
piss on a nigger so bad I could just about cry."

So I blinked and said: "Go ahead."

Now he patted the wet step next to him; I wasn't sure if he'd
heard.

Frowning a moment, I stepped up on the stoop and sat beside
him on the stone—and felt my jeans' seat soak.

"See across there"—he gestured with the hand not working in
the darkness of him—"that church?"

Above the visual stutter of its concrete steps, Holy Trinity had
recently polished its eight bronze doors (the two single ones on
the ends, the three pairs in the middle, under their half-waffle
irons of concrete tracery), three still open for summer.

"I could take you over there." His hand came back to fall on
my knee, beside his. He rubbed my leg a couple of times, tightened his grip on my jeans. "We could go inside. Down by the
altar—ain't nobody in there, now. Pissing on a nigger in church,
that'd really be something, wouldn't it? Or we could go down
into the subway. You go up to the far end of the station, where
nobody would see us—except if a train was coming in. Then it
would only be whoever was lookin' out the window. And they'd
whip all down to the other end of the station, so they couldn't
do anything anyway." He rubbed his immense hand on my leg
again. " 'Course, if you don't mind people seein', we could do it
right down on Broadway in the fuckin' Burger King. You go in
there, get some french fries and a hamburger, and just be sitting
there, eating—then this big, hairy, stupid motherfucker—me, I
mean—comes in like somebody you ain't never seen before, and
walks up to the table you're eating at, pulls out his dick, and
pisses right in your fucking *face*, nigger—all over your fuckin'

hamburger! All over the table—right in your fuckin' french fries—and when you look up, surprised, this guy aims his piss right *in* your fuckin' mouth. You ever had something like that happen to you? What'd you think you'd do if somebody like me did that to you?"

"I don't know." I took a breath. "Probably I'd say, 'Hey, thanks, fella!' Then, if the bread wasn't too wet, I'd go on eating my hamburger. I mean, I don't like a soggy bun on my hamburger—"

"Jesus, nigger—!" He barked a laugh. "You're too much!"

"What would *you* do, once you did it?"

He leaned forward again, still pulling on himself. "I don't know. I never had quite the nerve to do *that*, I mean. Yet. Or the black fella who wanted me to do it. I mean, not at the same time." He leaned closer to me. "But if I got me a nigger like that, I probably wouldn't want to turn him loose for a long time, man. A long time." He sat back again and frowned up at the sky. "God's pissin' on both of us now," he said. "The two of us. Right here."

"No, he isn't," I said. "Piss is warm. At least when it hits you. This isn't cold—it's a nice rain. But it's not warm."

He looked up and kind of chuckled. Then he said, "Yeah. I guess you're right."

I put the folded-up umbrella beside me on the step. "Come on, get up," I told him. "Turn around here."

He pushed himself upright—he was easily 6'4", if not taller. And thick, from his hips and gut to his chest and shoulders. He turned to face me. I leaned forward and forward, from the step and into a crouch—and when I took his dick in my mouth, he went, "Oh, *fuck*, man . . . !" I took hold of his legs. And began to suck him. Once I squeezed his head with my tongue: the cheese slid out into his leathery ruffle. "Shit, man . . . !" The rain peppered the back of my neck; it tickled my forehead. "Hey, if somebody walks by—"

I came off his thick, rod long enough to say, "Fuck them—unless it's a cop. You're too big, fella—nobody's gonna mess with you!"

He chuckled again—and slid his heavily skinned cock, thick as some flashlight handle, back into my face. "Yeah. That's true."

About three-quarters of a minute later, somebody *did* walk by, head down and hurrying in the rain—but I don't think realized what we were doing.

Baseball players.

I lifted my hand to the broad back of his. His turned, took hold of mine in his huge fingers; clearly more comfortable, he settled his feet wider apart. "You suck that good, little guy."

I raised my hand to his fly, got in under his heavy, hairy nuts, while I troweled my tongue once more beneath the broad shelf of his glans, deep within his thick and cheesy skin.

"You like to clean out all that shit, huh? Glad I kept it in there for you."

His big nuts were warm and heavy in my hand, and, when I pulled them out, hung down a good eight inches in their furry sack.

"You can swing on those fuckers a little—if you want." His other hand settled like a great cap on my head, moving with my pumping motion, speeding me up a few moments, then slowing me. I gathered the length of his sack in my hand and let my arm depend from it with its own weight, hair out the top tickling my fist, his nuts' bulge smooth around the bottom. "Yeah, put some weight on 'em. That's good."

I kept sucking.

A few minutes later, he said, "Yeah . . ." again; then, "I'm gonna piss in your face, little guy. You ready for me to pee in your mouth, you cocksuckin' nigger scumbag?"

Sucking, I nodded.

"Nigger, you're a low-down fuckin' jigaboo bastard." He gave my head a little push with his hand, without its coming away. "*Drink* my fuckin' piss!" And from the hard shaft I felt a trickle, then a flow, then a flood of hot salts.

I swallowed. It was incredibly hot—without burning.

"That's it, you fuckin' scumbag! *Suck* my dick while I piss in you, nigger."

At which point, somebody else passing said, "Hey—" Multiple steps sounded on the wet concrete. "Jesus—it's some homeless guy gettin' a blowjob from another one—right out on the street! Just like that! Man, in this fucking city, I guess you see *everything*, now . . . !"

I pulled back and off his dick—his hand came down from my head to grasp his outthrust penis and spray me, lap, chest, and face; I turned away enough to see the couple passing; the woman looked back.

His urine hit my face again—and she kind of jumped, turning quickly, to hurry off beneath her boyfriend's umbrella. And because that thing feels so good plugged into your head, I threw myself back on his cock again. He grunted, receiving the heat of me around him, in the rain. Still holding his cock, his fingers pushed against my mouth as I went down. Then they opened against my face, to move, rough as wood or stone, up my cheek, back to my head, over my hair. Forceful waters pressed within. "You suck a good dick, nigger—and drink that stuff like it's yours. Here—" He leaned back once more, to come out of my mouth, cockhead falling an inch. Piss hit my chin with its heat. His stream struck my chest. Inside my shirt, piss dribbled to my belly.

I took a couple of deep breaths.

"Drink some more, nigger . . . !"

So I caught him in my mouth again, and drank. And the last of his waters ran out. He moved his legs again, and I fell to pistoning rhythmically on his cock, seeking for his pressure, his pace, the speed that would loose his semen.

"Hold on, cocksucker . . . !" He came out of my mouth, and turned quickly to sit again on the stoop beside me. (I sat back down myself.) Again he leaned forward, to gesture with his head up the street, and growled, "Fuckin' cops . . ."

Though only one policeman came—quickly—down the street in a graphite gray rain-cloak, cap visor sticking out from under his hood. A moment later, a very thin man walking a nervous, wet Weimaraner turned up the steps we were sitting on, to climb the stoop and push inside through the door. Then two women walked by with umbrellas. The rain fell from the July evening, still wedged here and there with the last, brassy light.

"You want me to finish you off?" I said, up to the big guy's shoulder.

He grinned. "It felt pretty good . . . but I just take too long to cum." Then he added: "I'm just not too smart . . ." which seemed a non sequitur.

I was going to say something about what did brains have to do with coming. But there was something about the way he said it that made me look at him.

He said: "When I was in school, in the second grade, they said I was a slow learner—borderline retard. Even niggers can call *me* dumb." He looked pleased, even proud.

"Yeah?" I smiled. "You must be pretty dumb, then."

On his bearded face, the smile came on again like a street-light. "Yeah!" From the movement of his sweatshirt's shoulder, I could tell his hand was working back down between his legs.

I said: "You're probably too dumb to pour piss out of a boot."

While his big smile broke apart into a pure grin, he sat back and opened his legs again. His cock was still up. His fist was a blur on it.

"Man," I said, "you're so fuckin' stupid, you don't even know enough to come in out of the rain. You're probably the stupidest whitey running around homeless in this fucking neighborhood. You're so fucking stupid you'd piss on a nigger in the middle of the street then let him suck your fucking dick. You fucking re-tard—they don't make 'em any stupider than you, do they?"

He grunted—grunted again.

"You're one dumb sonofabitch, aren't you—you fucking dummy!"

He grunted a third time. "Yeah . . . take it, if you want it . . . !"

So I leaned over his leg, got half a dozen fists in my face, before his other hand clamped the back of my head and he pushed me down on him. Within my mouth, he erupted his thick and copious juice. Rocking forward over me, he held me to him with both hands, both arms. (And, of course, somebody else came by—but I don't know what they thought, seeing me with my head in his crotch and him leaning over me like that.) His great breaths got further apart—and quieter. Finally, he let me up.

With one hand on his big shoulder, I said: "It didn't take you all *that* long."

He was still breathing hard, though. "It don't, when somebody gets ahold of my thing like that. You picked up on that pretty fast."

I shrugged. "You don't really seem like you're that retarded, either."

"I'm pretty okay, I guess," he said. "I can't read and write—but I'm not stupid." He ran both his hands out to his knees, and back. "I sure ain't as stupid as they told me I was in the second grade. If I was *that* fuckin' stupid, I'd be dead! I was just raised different, is all. Me, I think I'm pretty smart, for what I gotta do with it. I get over, man—like you black fellas say. Hey, you know this little guy who hangs out in the park—got a beard like mine, only it's red—and more curly? Name's Tony?"

"Yeah," I said. "Sure!"

"Well, he said if I was to get my nut off with you tonight, I was to tell you that you owed him a penny."

Now I was the one who grinned. "You mean *Tony* sent you over here—for me? How'd you know who I was?"

"You're the guy Tony calls the professor." He leaned forward again, and pointed up the street. "Right? You live right across Amsterdam Avenue—in the first house there?"

"Yeah. But how—?"

"Tony said to look out for a black guy, about thirty—he said a good-looking black guy, too." He gave me another grin. "He said you would probably come on to me, if I looked like I was halfway interested. Tony said you were into some of the same things I was—piss and stuff."

"Well," I said. "I guess he knows if anyone does."

"It's nice," he said, "to meet somebody new, and get each other off like that—" Then he frowned. "Did you get off?"

"Naw," I said. "But that's okay."

"Aw, man! I thought you got your nut, back when you were drinking my piss."

"Don't worry," I said. "It'll be something nice to think about later—"

"Naw, man. I want you to get yours, too. I mean, you pulled a nice load out of me. It'd only be fair. You can do pretty much anything you want with me, man. I'm easy. I like to get mine—and I like the person I'm with to get his too. I could go another round—a couple of cans of beer, and I'll piss all over you some more. Pissing on black guys is a real thing with me—that's why Tony said I should come look for you. I already almost got in trouble about it, over in the park. I mean, *I* thought the nigger would like it. I could—"

I stopped him with a hand on his tree trunk of a leg. "Look, that's nice of you—what's your name?"

"Leaky. But some guys I make it with, they call me Dummy." He smiled at me. "I guess you figured it out—I kind of like that one. Not that I mind the other one either."

I grinned back. "Look, Dummy," I said. "I'm supposed to be going somewhere tonight—I probably won't be back for a couple of hours. It would be really nice if we could get together some other time so that—" Then I frowned. "Leaky's got to be a nickname, too, doesn't it? Just for curiosity, I was wondering what your real name was, unless it's none of my business—"

"Leaky," he repeated; then he chuckled. "That's what my old man named me. Leaky. A lot of the time, I don't even tell people that. For a while I used to tell them my name was 'Larry'—but then I'd go through the same thing, with social workers and stuff, 'cause they'd always want to write it down 'Lawrence.' So finally, I decided, what the fuck. My name *was* Leaky, so that's what I'd tell anybody who asked me. It sure ain't 'Lawrence'! Look: I shot my load. You didn't. If we get together again, I can make it up to you. How about that?"

"Fine," I said. "I'd like that."

But he was frowning now. "You're going someplace . . . like *that?*"

"I'm pretty well soaked through—but it's just a bar." I wondered if I should go home, get some dry clothes, and start again. Or maybe even put it off to another night. "I'll be all right." The rain, I figured, would dilute the pee; it was still in the high seventies, low eighties—and there was something kind of fun, I confess, about going into a place like the Pit right after I'd had a workout like this. "I just have to ask some people a few questions."

He sighed. "Okay—it's nice to meet you, professor . . . little guy"—he turned to me, stuck out his big grubby hand—"nigger." We shook.

"Good to meet you too, Leaky . . . Dummy." My hand, which is not small, was lost in his.

Then his other arm went around me, and he pulled me against him, my face against his wide, hairy chest, beside the brass teeth in his sweatshirt. I hugged him back. With one hand now, he rubbed the top of my head. In a kind of rough voice, he said, "I'll see you around, piss face . . ."

I dropped one hand between his legs. "Leaky . . . ?" I felt him move inside the wet wool of his pants.

He chuckled. As we turned loose, he said, "I ain't even kissed you—and I love to neck and kiss and swap spit and stuff. Well, I guess we got to save something for next time."

I grinned. "Yeah . . ."

I left him sitting on the stoop. Rain sluiced the sidewalk, like molten glass, into the gutter. In the drizzle, I started down toward Broadway.

Sopping as I was, I decided the air conditioning on the subway (if I got a car where it was working) might be a bit much. So, at Broadway, on the downtown side of Seventy-ninth Street, across from the First Baptist, I waited for a bus (fingering a token out of the folds of a wet jeans pocket is a chore!); when it pulled up, I got on—to realize, as I sat beside the droplet-sequined window, that I'd left my umbrella, rolled up, on the stoop where Leaky and I'd been sitting.

Sometimes you're just lucky. The bus was cool enough to take the damp out of the air, so that my clothes actually got noticeably drier on the trip down. Though, when I stood up to get off, in the blue plastic hollow of the seat where I'd been sitting a puddled surface shivered to the engine. I turned for the door. As I stepped outside at the corner of Fifty-first, the air was warmer than on the bus—and the rain, down to a warm mist, cut to nothing by the time I reached the middle of the next block. I walked over to Ninth Avenue and down.

Yes, my clothes were damp. But they weren't dripping wet, when I reached the Pit. Nor was I.

Outside the place, wearing a sleeveless undershirt, a pair of baggy camouflage fatigues and high-topped combat boots, a blond kid leaned against the brick wall beside the door, arms folded, head down. He could have been anywhere between nineteen and twenty-two.

It was easy to assume that he was waiting for the two guys talking over near the curb by the garbage can: one was tall, curly-headed, and Hispanic, in a sweatshirt unzipped over a bald chest. His hand was on the shoulder of a shorter, dark-haired white kid, with a muscular build and one of those athletic shirts, white and red down to his rib cage, fishnet hanging below that and out of his jeans. The two of them, bending together, whispered of exchanges of dope, of women, of fabulous formulas that controlled the neighborhood's glittering dreams of power.

I stepped down to the entrance, pushed open the black door with its dark glass panes, and walked into the black interior, with its mirrors, its orange lights across the ceiling. The entrance was crowded with a trio of archaic phone booths on the left, a cigarette machine on the right. Above that hung one of the monitors for the jukebox video—where, as I looked up, the camera swooped through a burned-out neighborhood, in which, now in this rotted-out window and again against that broken wall, long-haired musicians twonged and boinged at heavy-metal intensity.

The counter and its customers stretched away on the right. On the left a row of stools sat along the wall, till the place opened up in the back for a pool table under a low-hanging ceiling lamp, another mini-bar, and doors here and there, to the bathroom, to the kitchen; and—presumably—to the parking lot out back.

If you go to the Pit three times, and somebody asks you to describe it, you'll probably say something like the following: "The johns—the middle-aged and older men—sit at the bar, some of them in suits and ties, some dressed more sportily. The younger hustlers—the working men—sit along the wall, while the johns check them out either directly or by means of the mirror behind the bottles stacked at the bar's back. Now and again some hustler will join a john he already knows at the bar in conversation; or johns and hustlers will both go off into the back area to start conversations around the pool table, making their contacts there." Only then, when you come in the *fourth* time, looking for that pattern you just so carefully articulated, you notice a twenty-year-old muscle builder at the bar, clearly a hustler, nursing a rum and Coke between two older men who are paying him no mind whatsoever. Over by the wall, two tall, white-haired gentlemen, one in a tie, one in a sheepskin jacket, sit on stools either side of a voluble Puerto Rican kid, who's keeping them entertained with a cascade of loud stories about his cousin Luis. Another kid has been invited to the bar, where he and a john are talking intently. Still another, with a baseball cap turned backward and baggy jeans, wanders from the back to the front, and leaves—while in the back, shooting pool, is some guy, who, though he's wearing what looks like a high-school jacket and is pretty slender, with just a black T-shirt under it, is nevertheless—you see each time he turns to face you—in his late forties, if not early fifties. Certainly *he's* too old to be working—isn't he? But why is he dressed like that, acting like one of the working men, rather than a customer? (Though, to me, he was probably the sexiest-looking guy in the place, which makes you wonder . . .) Finally, sitting toward the back of the bar, a brown-skinned figure dressed in black lace and sable sequins flips a cigarette ash into an ashtray with the tap of a red-nailed finger—throwing *all* the systems of the world into question. Indeed, you realize now, the pattern you first intuited is only a reduction of a vast number of exceptions to itself that, at any moment, make up the customer configuration.

And, from half a dozen years before, I remembered Dave, back when the Fiesta was open, asking, "You mean all these guys are really *hustling?*"

I found a spot at the bar. I asked an Irish-looking bartender, who had a kind of youthful face in the half-light, but, up nearer, I saw was in his late forties: "Excuse me . . . ?"

With a smile, he leaned both hands, far apart, on the bar. "What can I get you?"

"Is there anyone here who'd have information about some things that might have gone on here, oh, seventeen or eighteen years ago?"

"Sure," he said. "The owner. You want to talk to her?"

"If I could."

"She was just about to leave, I think." Now he stood up and looked toward the back. "Hey! Is Aline back there?"

A brassy voice came out of the bar's shadowed and mirrored depths: "She's in the goddamned shitter, honey—what do you want her for?"

This was apparently some sort of joke that set everybody laughing. The bartender turned back to me. "Maybe in a couple of minutes. What would you like to drink?"

"Eh," I said, "vodka and tonic."

"You got it." A glass with ice emerged from below the counter. The bartender turned to swing a bottle of vodka from its place before the back mirror, to start pouring mid-swing. The bottle was back in place by the end of his circuit. Now he picked up a siphon attached to a gooseneck, and pressed a clear plastic button, the light within momentarily aglow on the underside of his thumb.

"Lime?" he asked. "Lemon?"

"Lime," I said.

He scooped up a green and gray tetrahedron from a white plastic tray, squeezed it, dashed it down with a splash, and slid it to me on a square napkin. "Two ninety-five—or do you want to start a tab?"

"That's okay," I said, and went digging in my damp jeans for my wallet.

He took my damp and rumpled bills; as he returned to clack my nickel on the bar, a hand landed on my shoulder: "Now, honey"—it was the same brassy voice that had shouted out a moment before, and so I understood the joke—"what can I do for you?"

"Hello!" I turned to her.

Towering, blonde, and massive, she wore a blouse as loose and large as something from Erda's maternity wardrobe, from prehistoric Willendorf. Through some trick of gestalt shift, she looked the same age as she had the first time I'd come here, just back from school and living in Manhattan for the first time. Below, she wore shiny patent-leather shoes and dark pants—that must have had at least a forty-eight or fifty waist.

"You're Aline, the owner?" In the other bars throughout the neighborhood, people were always mentioning her, telling which working man she'd just eighty-sixed, what acid comeback she'd made to whichever caustic queen who'd decided to trade repartee. How old, I wondered, had she been seventeen years ago: twenty-five? thirty? thirty-five?

"Me and Johnny—but we don't want *him* to know. So we *call* it mine." She smiled, and we shook hands.

Her hand small, her palm dry, like a woman's who did a lot of housework. "You wanted to ask me something?"

"Yes," I said. "I wanted to get some information—any information you had, about something that happened here, seventeen or eighteen years back. A young man was killed, stabbed to death—either in here, or in the parking lot just outside. He was twenty-nine years old—and a Korean. Korean-American. His name was Timothy Hasler, and he was a fairly well-known philosopher, even then. But he's become even more well-known since his death. No one was ever tried for his murder. But people are more and more interested in Hasler today, and we're trying to . . . well, collect as much information about how he died as we can."

For the beat of five, she looked at me, perfectly blank. Then she said, "Are you sure that was here? A lot of stuff goes on in this neighborhood. Seventeen or eighteen years ago? There were a lot of bars back then that are closed now—a lot rougher than this place ever was. The Haymarket. O'Neill's. That's the kind of thing that was more likely to have happened over there than here."

I frowned.

"Eighteen years ago—"

"Seventeen, actually," I corrected.

"Whatever." She went on: "That's a long time—I don't even know if I was around here then."

"When did you become owner of the Pit?" I asked.

"Late sixties, early seventies," she said.

"This happened," I said, "on September 23rd, 1973—it was somewhere after one in the morning. So it was really a continuation of September 22nd—"

"Well, then"—she nodded—"I would have been here. But I don't remember anything like that. That really sounds like something that would have happened in another place. Probably the Haymarket—they were always having set-tos over there. Or maybe it was one of the places that used to be over on Tenth Avenue. Some of them were pretty savage—you know, the closer you go to the river, the wilder it gets. They had some pretty rough spots over there. But we always tried to keep it cool in here—that's why we're still around." Then she frowned. "How old did you say this kid was?"

"He wasn't a kid," I said. "He was twenty-nine."

"Now," she said, "you see? We never had a lot of people that age hanging out around here. We have a lot of people over thirty-five—over forty, actually. We get a lot of kids under twenty-five. Just look around—you'll see what I mean. The kind of place this is hasn't really changed all that much since we got started. But we just don't have many customers your age—in that twenty-six- to thirty-six-year-old range. You should ask around and try to find out about some of them other places— that are closed down now. And didn't you say it was out in the parking lot? You know, ever since we been here, there've been people getting ripped off in that lot, getting roughed up, getting stabbed, getting shot—I mean two or three times a month. I don't even pay any attention to it anymore. But that doesn't have nothing to do with us, honey." She shook her head with a firm frown. "I'm afraid I don't know anything about what you're talkin'. That was a long time ago—and it probably didn't have nothing to do with us, anyway."

I said, "I'm pretty sure it was here."

"Naw." She shook her head with a small, definite shake.

"That wasn't here. Look, the next drink's on the house—hey, Donny?" With her elbow on the bar, she leaned across it. "This guy's next drink is on me!" Now she pulled back. "But you're not going to learn anything about stuff like that. It's too long ago. Nobody remembers that kind of shit. *Ehhh!*" She gave a little shiver that moved all through her bulk. "Who'd want to! I gotta go. I like to get out of here before the animals arrive." She started away, then turned back again, to lift a hand in which I saw a bunch of car keys, one between her rather girlish fingers: this smile was actually a nice one: "Down here we don't have too long a memory. It's probably better that way." She turned, like a silken tank, to move majestically toward the door—while Donny (I assume that was the bartender's name) came over and put a tumbler upside down in front of me on the counter.

"For your next drink," he said; and moved off.

The other bartender was only about three feet away—an older guy, well knit, in a blue sweater with a V neck showing a snarl of white hair on his chest; around his beret the hair was a darker and richer brown than Leaky's, who was at least fifteen years his junior—which, only after another minute of sipping, did I realize meant it was dyed. He moved away to do some work. I looked around, feeling a little lost. When my eyes swept past his—he was back, looking at me—he gave me a mellow smile. He picked up a rag—and did not wipe the bar around the three-quarters-empty basket of popcorn in front of me. "Aline sure gave *you* the brush-off. What were you asking her about, anyway?"

"Something that happened here. I guess she just didn't want to tell me about it."

"Management . . . !" he said, with a moue and a hand flipped at me on a wrist that broke dramatically. "She has to be like that. But she likes you—I don't know why."

"How long have you worked here?" I asked.

"Not steadily," he said. "But I'll tell you, I was a porter here the day Aline opened this place, Monday, October 13th, 1969—we started out as a pure exploitation of Stonewall. Nothing more, and nothing less. And by the first of the year, I was tending bar pretty regularly. Sometimes I've been away, but I always seem to come back."

"Well," I said, "there was a murder here—"

"There've been several!"

"A guy named Timothy Hasler—a Korean-American, twenty-nine years old. He was stabbed—"

"Oh, my God—" The bartender looked askance at me. "You're not really trying to find out about *that* one, are you? Our first murder was three weeks after we opened. A black kid named Willie, who started beating on a john named Edward Sloan, who had a heart attack—right *there*, not three feet away from where you're standing. Willie did three years for manslaughter. Now wouldn't you prefer to hear about that? Aline thought she was going to get closed down for sure, with something like that so soon after we opened up. But the parking-lot trick worked—since, I guess, it was the first time we tried it."

"Parking-lot trick?"

"If something happens to somebody, you do *not* leave 'em lying on the floor in here. You take them outside into the parking lot out back—*then* you call the police. Then you get some kid to say they were out back there and saw the body—and came in here shouting to call the cops. It's humane—I mean, we don't just *leave* them there. Are you sure you wouldn't rather hear about the June '80 robbery—that's the one that everybody gets such a kick out of! And I was working here the day *that* one happened. So were two phone repairmen, the same afternoon. About four o'clock these guys came in here with—my dear—a double-barreled *shot*gun! They made all the customers lie down on the floor. Then they made me go through and collect all the money and the wallets. And I'm cooperating, too—I'm being just as nice, and moving them toward the door, see, while I do it. I just wanted them out of here in the *worst* way, you know what I mean? Well, I've got them about halfway toward the door, and wouldn't you know, this crazy queen, lying down on the floor in the back, suddenly shouts out, 'Oh, I got another twenty, in my pocket here!' Like they were gonna go back and check?" He lowered his face, raised his eyebrows. "Well, of course they *did* go back—and got that poor shit's last twenty. Then they said I should lay down on the floor, too. And I said, 'Well, I don't think there's any *room*.' It was crowded in here that afternoon. But he hits me on the shoulder with the gun barrel—hard, too." He raised both hands like a kid gesturing "I give up." "Well, one of the phone repairmen was down on the floor right where I was standing—you talk about a cute pair of buns? So I lay down *right* on top of them, my dear. And they left." Laughing, he slapped the bar. "Then I called up Aline and told her, 'Honey, we been robbed at gunpoint. And I'm going to have a drink, shut the place down—and go *home!*'" He laughed again. "Oh, I'll tell you anything you want to know about this place. But I can't imagine you really want to hear about that Hasler business, now . . ."

"Yes, I do. Very much."

He leaned forward, put his hand on my forearm. "You're not some kind of cop—or a detective, or a newspaper reporter? Are you?"

"No." I shook my head. Then I thought, why not? "I'm a graduate student, doing a Ph.D. thesis in philosophy. Hasler was a philosopher—and I want to find out how he died."

He looked at me for a few moments—and I recalled the blank look Aline had given me. "Well, you don't *look* like a city father trying to shut us down."

The tall gray-haired man sitting beside me, who (I'd thought) wasn't even vaguely listening, said, "They don't make those in black, dear."

The bartender pulled back sharply. "Oh, yes they do. They certainly *do!* Tell me." He leaned toward me again. "When did you suck your last dick?"

I laughed. "You really want to know?"

"I would not have asked if I didn't."

"Actually," I said, "about forty minutes ago. This homeless guy—uptown. In the rain."

"Oh, my *dear*—!" His hand went to his throat, to fiddle there for a surprised moment. "I think I'll buy you a drink myself! Look, I don't know how much you know about this place. But you really have asked about a strange one—"

"You were here when it happened?"

"I was here that evening. A little after midnight, I went over to Tenth Avenue with some friends. And about one-thirty Philly Dan came running into the bar I was in, to tell me that this

Chinese fellow had just gotten stabbed here in the Pit. Korean—
I know! But nobody knew it at the time. So I came back. The
police were here by then, and I helped close up the place. And of
course nobody had anything else to talk about for the next three
weeks. So—no, I *wasn't* here when it actually *happened*. But I
was here just before—and just after."

"Do you know who did it? Or what it was about?"

He gave me the blank look again that brought back Aline's
first stare.

"What did people *say* happened?"

"Well, I was also there when the Chinese—Korean—fellow
came in: I noticed him right away. Like Aline said, we don't get
many guys that age. Nor do we get that many Orientals—at
least we didn't back in 1973—though only two weeks ago, we
were thinking of starting a Japanese businessman's night here.
We don't see any for a month. Then, suddenly, we get twelve at
a time—and, sometimes, they can become very"—he snapped
his fingers above his head like a Spanish dancer—"gay! The
problem, of course, wasn't him—your Korean friend. It was the
guy he brought in with him. I realized there was going to be
trouble as soon as I saw him."

"There was someone with him that night?"

"Oh, yes. This tall fellow—blond, I believe. Well built.
And . . ." Here he stopped.

"Then what happened?"

"Well, how much *do* you know about places like this? Not
much, I'd gather, from the way you came on with Aline. Or me."

"I used to go to the Fiesta fairly frequently, before it
closed—"

"And now sometimes you hang out at Cats," he finished.
"That's what I would have figured. But the Pit, see, is a hard-
core hustling bar. That's all it's here for. That's all the people
here are here for. Oh, like anyplace else, it's got a few guys who
just hang out and watch the action. But this isn't Cats. And it
sure isn't the Fiesta!"

I looked around. "It doesn't look too busy right now."

"Yeah? You hang around for another hour, hour and a half.
Even on Tuesday night, once you get past nine o'clock, nine-

thirty, this place makes the New York Stock Exchange look like a Sunday-school picnic. You talk about philosophy—really it's a matter of the philosophy of a place like this. If philosophy's what you'd call it."

"I'm kind of lost."

"You see," he said, "this place is a lot of older men who think the only way they can get anything worth having sexually is to pay for it. And the kids who come here are all kids who want to get paid—need to get paid. Some of them are supporting a habit, yeah. But it's astonishing how many of them have a wife and a kid that they're taking care of by coming in here on Thursday, Friday, Saturday night and going home with somebody a couple or three times in an evening. I know more than one kid who put himself though school this way—though, the truth is, most of them are just out to prove how big and bad they are. They *can* do it—so they *do* do it. But the thing that makes this whole place possible is a belief that sex—the kind of sex that gets sold here—is scarce. Because it's scarce, it's valuable. And because it's valuable, it goes for good prices. Now suppose, one day, you had some guy come in here—twenty, twenty-one, twenty-two: young, good body, nice-looking. But the thing about him was he didn't think sex was scarce at all. He thought it was all over the place. He didn't mind older guys—'cause he liked all sorts of guys, young, old, and everybody in between. As far as sex, he's one of these guys who lives his life with his hand in his pocket, playing with himself. And whipping it out and giving it to one of these"—he looked left and right, then leaned forward again to whisper, under his breath—"old cocksuckers here, well he just thinks that's the most fun you could possibly have in an evening. Money? He'd pay *them* to suck on it, if he thought they wanted it! So what happens if one of these guys comes in, starts hanging out here, huh?"

"I guess it kind of upsets the system—at least the one this place operates on."

"You better *believe* it does!" He pulled back. "Something like that happens, it generates a lot of hostility. Especially from the kids working here. Fast, too. I mean you could even say it was the principle of the thing—you ready for your next drink?"

Looking down, I was a little surprised I was. But I guess it's all the ice they put in the glass that makes the drink go so quickly.

He hailed Donny, and pointed down at my glass—and while Donny came to fill it, he went down to take care of some customers on his half of the bar. Then he was back: "It's funny that we don't get more of them, I suppose. As long as I been here, it seems to me to average out about three of these guys walking in here over any four-year period. By this time, I know enough not to even let 'em hang around for five minutes. A lot of times, they're pretty beat up—but we always have our share of those, too. Usually though, it's drugs, not sex. And to most of the fellas sitting at the bar, anyone under twenty-five looks good. Half of them are right out of some mental hospital. I actually *knew* one, once—when I was younger and a lot more naïve. Let him stay at my place for about two weeks—he didn't have any place else to be. *Child* abuse? The stories that kid told me about the things that had happened to him when he was a child—well, you tell me about how you got your little pink asshole—or your black ass"—he leaned forward, with a conspiratorial wink—"diddled half a dozen times by the priest after choir practice and a lollipop for your pains, and I'll tell you, it happened to me too, honey: and I loved every saintly centimeter he shoved into me— I just wished it was a little longer. But I have neither time nor sympathy for bullshit like that."

I smiled, feeling uncomfortable with his pronouncement. "It never happened to me," I said. "I'm not Catholic."

"Well, you know what I mean. But you have to keep a sense of proportion about these things, don't you think? How can you get seriously twisted out of shape by things like that, when you know what's really going on out here to some of these children— I feel sorry for them. I really do. But one of them comes in here, after he's gotten roughed up by the cops for beating off on the street corner at three in the afternoon—that was the last one, about a year back—and they think that finally *this* is someplace they can make out. Well, I go straight up to them and tell them they have to leave—no, baby! Not in five minutes. You're out of here. Now! It's for their own protection."

"Really."

"If one comes in when it's crowded, sometimes I can miss him for a half an hour or so. But, in twenty minutes, one of those guys in here throws off the whole chemistry of this place."

"How can you tell if somebody just walking in is one of them?"

He gave me a withering look. "I'm talking about the guys that everybody else in the world thinks of as perverts. I mean, if some kid walks in here and can't keep his hands off his crotch, and has a stupid shit-eating grin, and the next the thing you know he's got some old white-haired guy in the corner, and you know no money is going to change hands—I mean, ten times a night, some kid, sitting at the bar, is going to pull his pecker out and show it off to the old man sitting next to him, just to let him know what he's got. You can't do anything about that in a place like this. But if some kid's sitting at the bar, looking stupid and his arm is moving below the bar, real steady, and half a dozen guys are trying to get a look at him, without me or Aline or the waiter or somebody who works here seeing them—well, *then* you got a problem!"

I laughed. The bartender nodded at me knowingly.

"But that's who your friend Hasler brought in with him that night. There *was* hostility—there *were* problems. *Christ*, there were problems! And the Korean fellow just got in the way of them—maybe because he brought the kid in, that's why he ended up buying it. Now, I wasn't here. So the precise mechanics, I'm not real clear on. Say"—and he drew the word out, lengthily and thoughtfully—"you know who you ought to talk to? Apple Blossom—Ronnie Apple. He was here the night it happened. I mean, we must have talked about it nonstop over the whole next three weeks! He doesn't come in a lot anymore. But he drops in from time to time. You say this is going to get you your Ph.D?"

"Well, it'll make my getting it a little easier."

"Okay. I'm going to do my bit for affirmative action. Look, write your phone number down here." He handed me a card. "Next time Blossom comes in, I'll ask him if he wants to talk to you about it. And if he says okay, I'll give you a call, and you can set up a time to talk."

"He was in the bar? When it happened."

"He said he saw the whole thing. And though she is a character—and some of these queens want to be in the center of everything—still, I don't think she's a hopeless liar." He handed me a
pencil. As I wrote, he said with a leer: "Now they're all going to
think you're my new trick for the month!"

I looked up and smiled. "Say, thanks a lot. Really!"

"I haven't done anything for you yet, dear. And paper's cheap.
Right back behind the pool table, that's where your friend was
stabbed. As soon as it happened, a bunch of guys dragged him
out in the parking lot out back, and dropped him on the ground.
I told you: Aline has got this thing—as soon as anyone is really
hurt, out they go! Unless it's *real* cold. Anyway, that's when they
called the police. Of course, after all these years, the police
pretty well know: if it happens anywhere within fifty feet of this
place, they assume it *did* happen right here—even if it didn't,
sometimes. Aline's seen this place through some rough times.
But she and Jimmy have some very good connections. And, in
some ways, the coppers figure the Pit's a kind of calming influ-
ence on the neighborhood."

"Then she really knew what I was talking about?"

"She wasn't here at all the night it happened." He shrugged.
"I can vouch for that. It was a Saturday—and she stays away
from this place like the plague on weekends. She *might* have
forgotten. A lot's gone on here."

"What happened to the fellow who Hasler brought with
him?"

"Oh, he was cut!" He nodded again. "But he was scared too, I
guess; and he made it out the back. As did the person who did
the stabbing."

"It's funny," I said. "This is something I've been interested in
for years. But I've learned more about it this evening than I have
since I first got interested in Hasler." I took a breath. "Now I
have to figure out how to explain the details to somebody else.
I'm really anxious to talk with your friend—Apple Blossom?"

"Ronnie! Apple Blossom is just between you and me—you
know what I mean. But you just let me get you together with
him. He'll tell you the details of the whole thing. We're all

getting to that age where we like the idea of young people getting interested in what happened to us. Most of the kids in this place couldn't care less. They're the one's who're selling—not us."

"I'm going to go in the back," I said, "and walk around the pool table—maybe step out into the parking lot outside. Just to see where it happened."

"The door to the parking lot's locked. Aline's kept it that way for over ten years—except on those sultry summer nights, all too common I'm afraid, when our air conditioning is on the fritz. Then it's the only way to get a breeze through here. Or, of course, when we have to open it all of a sudden to get someone out."

"Oh." I got up from the bar chair.

"I wouldn't be surprised if it was because of the Hasler killing that she started locking it."

I left the counter, went into the back, and walked around the pool table, anyway. Behind it was a black door from which the brazen eye of a lock barrel stared at my chest: the door had no handle—I assumed it went to the lot.

Between the pool table and the door, I looked at the black floorboards, wondering if there were eighteen-year-old bloodstains under the paint. Then I went and left the talkative bartender a three-dollar tip.

"Why, thank you! You're not going to let me buy you that drink? Stick around for it. You give the place some class"—again he leaned forward—"which is what we say to all the cute numbers who come in here. Really, though. We like for our new customers to have a good time—at least on the first night. We want you to come back. On me—really. That was a vodka and tonic—?"

"Maybe next time," I said.

He said, smiling: "Maybe next time I won't feel like buying you one."

I couldn't think of anything to say. So I just laughed. And left.

Blood, Sweat, and Tears

MAUDE IRWIN OWENS

Bathesda
of Sinners Run

I t was like reading the Books of Chronicles, to read in the
Thornton family history of the attending succession of slave
women that formed the single line of Bathesda's ancestry. The
Thorntons had always boasted of their seven generations of slave
housekeepers who had directly descended from the housekeeper
of the first American Thornton. They would proudly point out
the precious, faded entries, so faithfully recorded in the old genealogy. The paternal side of the issue was always politely ignored in strict accordance with the manners and customs of the
South.

The scapegrace of the younger son of an English baron, Richard Thornton, was founder of the family. When gambling debts
and foul dueling forced him to flee his native land, he decided
upon the colony of George II under Governor Oglethorpe. His
first slave purchase was written in two sentences that seemed to
wink and laugh up at the reader with its tan ink and old fashioned lettering. It read:

"On this day did I barter my gold hilted sword, some lace and
several shillings to that villain from the Virginia colony whom I
do sorely despise—for a black wench to cook my porridge, brew

my tea and wash my linen. She is comely withal and methinks, the temper of a noble blooded colt; so I have named the vixen, Jezebel."

From this Jezebel on the issue became mulatto and less mulatto: for it was written that Jezebel foaled a likely mustard-colored filly whose father and master, with malicious humor, named her for his King and the colony.

So Jezebel became the mother of Georgie; who begat Abigail; whose brat was Callie; whose offspring was Ruth; whose child was Viney; whose daughter was Anne; and twenty years after slavery, came Bathesda.

To the utter amazement and chagrin of her erstwhile master and mistress, when the bell of freedom tolled for those in bondage, Anne betook herself from under the Thornton roof, in spite of all the inducements and cajoleries the Thorntons offered.

She married Enoch Creek, a fusion of Creek Indian, Negro and white who chose to select his surname from the Indian blood which dominated his being. He was a bitter man, having no faith or belief in mankind or the institutions and principles of mankind; a religion of hatred that banned all but Anne and much later, little Bathesda.

They founded a tiny home at Sinners Run, the Negro suburb of Thorntonville, Georgia, that had been called after a famous campmeeting revival sermon preached there, years back. Their cabin was a little apart and elevated from other huts and shacks of the Sinners Run people, so that they could look down upon the road which was alternatingly red clay or yellow mud and note the comings and goings of those who lived upon it.

Anne attended the Sinners Run Baptist Church regularly and prayed that her husband find salvation. Enoch traded at the store because it was necessary—but after that, all socializing with their neighbors ceased; unless in the case of illness, when Anne was a ministering angel and healer of the small community. Within her lean yellow hands was the strange, soothing power to allay pain, and from her husband, she learned much of the Indian mysteries of roots and herbs for medicinal use.

They were thrifty and got along. For twenty years they

worked, saved, improved their little two room home, and the acre upon which it stood. Anne was an expert needlewoman as Viney, Ruth and Callie had been before her; and she was in great demand in all the big houses down in Thorntonville. Enoch hired himself out as a plantation farmer, and in spite of his scowling silence, was known as a good hand.

Then, at the age of forty—when all hope of bearing the traditional girl-child had flown from the heart of Anne, it happened; and Bathesda made her advent into the life of Sinners Run.

Enoch smiled for the first time—his squinting Indian eyes snapping with delight at the yellow gypsy-like Anne in the role of Madonna, with the robust little papoose that was his. Of course the Thorntons got wind of it, investigated and greedily annexed one more generation to old Jezebel's descendants, although the essence of reflected glory had lost its flavor since the inconvenient Emancipation. The distinction of being the first of her line born out of slavery was the most disgraceful thing that could have been written about Bathesda, into the sacred Annals, according to Thornton opinion.

Two weeks later, Enoch stepped on a rusty spike. Blood-poisoning set in and, in spite of their combined knowledge of medicine and healing—his time had come to leave Anne and Bathesda, before Anne had convinced him there was a God.

Anne turned from the unmarked grave, and faced the world alone with her baby, unflinchingly—with that calm independence that asked no pity. She went about her sewing at the houses of her patrons, for a while, carrying her infant with her.

But as Bathesda began to toddle about, Anne realized her child should have home life, and be allowed to play in the vegetable patch and flower garden which Enoch had so painstakingly planted. So Anne took only work such as she could do at home, and her little daughter grew to be the marvel of the country side—a healthy, lovely child.

She attended the broken down school-house to be taught by a wizened old maid from Connecticut a few months a year, and she sat at her mother's knee during the school period . . . both struggling eagerly to master a clear fluent English. Anne, being ardently religious, insisted that the little girl read her Bible and attend church regularly, in which she was reluctantly obeyed.

Thus Bathesda grew up to womanhood. Beautiful—of deep-rooted intelligence handicapped by inadequate schooling, a pagan love for the gorgeous wonders of Nature and a passion for all things artistic. She became adept at the fine French seams and hemming; learned to feather-stitch the picturesque quilts on the huge frame, to weave highly imaginative Indian designs out of the bright silken rags into rugs and mats, to make the difficult Yankee hook rug, the knowledge of which had been introduced South by a Yankee Thornton bride; and best of all, she became an expert copier of the old antebellum samplers. Anne's sampler embroidering frame looked worm-eaten—it was so old; and Bathesda considered it with great reverence.

They made a picture to be remembered, sitting together at their artistic labors—the older woman and her daughter. Anne invariably talked religion to Bathesda having sensed a silent indifference which bespoke much of Enoch's atheism. When at the stuffy little church, the sermon had become highly exhortive, and the worshipers' downtrodden souls burst forth in howling primitive devotion to a God they desperately believed in—even when great tears spilled down her quiet mother's cheeks, Bathesda's sole reaction was a disdainfully cold squinting of her pretty black eyes.

"It's Enoch! It's Enoch!" mourned old Anne, as she watched the child of her old age flower into radiant womanhood with no change of heart.

"But Mother," Bathesda would say, "you take on so 'bout nothin'. Ain't we happy? We have always been different from them in our way of livin' and doin' things and so how can you expect me to be like them in their church doin's? You are not like them when you feel the spirit, Mother. You cry a little bit, but I have never seen you rear and tear and stomp and scream 'halleluliah' like someone crazy . . . I hate it! My church is the purple mist stealin' ahead of the red dawn—the chirpin' wood-chucks; wild wood blossoms! If I ever 'get religion,' Mother, 'twill be in that kind of church, and not among the sweaty, hysterical hypocrites of your church. Why! I believe to my soul,

Mother, you are the only real Christian among them, and do the least testifyin'!"

"Child—you don't understand. It is as real with them as life itself! It is given to each to work out his own destiny in the Lord, in his own way. It is the feelin' that they are weak and sinful that overpowers them so—in their strivin' to follow the Good Book."

"I don't care 'bout them anyways, Mother. We are better colored folks . . . that's all. It just ain't in them to be better. Look at their homes. Bare plank floors that all their scrubbin' and scourin' don't improve; walls plastered with newspapers full of pictures that they think are pretty; gunny-sacks tacked up to the windows . . . ugh! Give them their winter supply of potatoes, rice and hog meat . . . let them go to church and give chitterlin' suppers . . . plenty of shoutin' and back-bitin' and they are happy all winter long, Mother. But—look at our home!"

She waved her pale brown hand proudly around the room in which they sat. The walls were whitewashed. The floor was covered with a huge rag rug rich with colorful stripes and the single square window was draped with deep rose curtains that fluttered happily in the breeze. They had been made from flour bags soaked in kerosene to remove the printing, and dyed with berry juice. There were two fine old pieces of colonial mahogany in this outer room—a gigantic highboy and a marble-topped medicine chest. The other articles of furniture were three rush-bottomed chairs and a table that Enoch had made, and carved all over with the weirdly grotesque totem-pole gargoyles. Upon the mantel over the fireplace were a brilliant basket and two odd potteries, also relics of the Creek strain in the father of Bathesda. Small painted tubs and cans were in interesting groups about the room, filled with plants of various sorts.

"I don't suppose I should say I hate them, Mother dear," Bathesda continued, "but I can get along without them. I shall do as you have always done . . . when they're sick, I'll make them well if they call upon me—but I don't . . . I can't be one of them in religion or otherwise."

"Ah, my child," sadly smiled Anne, "you may have inherited the sense of medicine from Enoch, your father, but the Divine gift of healing can never descend upon a disbeliever . . . and you are the first of us women who has not been born with the gift since Mother Jezebel. She, even in her early day, was a Christian convert."

At this, Bathesda would shake her head impatiently as if flinging aside the admonitions of her mother, and the two long black braids would flare about her arms and shoulders. Then, bowing earnestly over her work, she would concentrate upon the exact copying of probably old Viney's intricately designed sampler with the words—"Little flakes make the biggest snow," ordered by an antique dealer from Savannah.

Bathesda's mother died in her sixtieth year, and never had there been such a funeral in the history of Sinners Run. Unlike her husband who had only a faithful wife and new born babe to follow him to his grave—the entire countryside turned out to do honor to Anne Creek. All of the present generation of Thorntons came from their town house in Savannah, in full force, much to the awe of the Sinners Run folk. They even hinted about how appropriate and fitting it would be if Anne were buried beside Viney, in Thorntonville; but Bathesda was obdurate.

"Thank you, Mr. and Mrs. Thornton, but my mother's place is beside her husband. My father has been alone out there, long enough."

So the Thorntons had a second lesson in Negro independence.

"Promise me, my daughter, that you will seek Jesus!" gasped Anne in her last consciousness. "Go to the church—seek Him until you find Him . . . and He will give you your birthright like he has given it to all the rest of us. Promise your poor old Mammy, Bathesda . . . baby!"

And so she had promised to seek religion and the power to heal the sick.

Bathesda lived on, as the years rolled by, much as when Anne lived. She made beautiful things with her graceful slender hands, and more money than she needed in her simple mode of living. She lived alone with the spirit presences of her parents, except for the loyal protection of a watch dog. She cared for the gay little flower garden tenderly and kept her graves freshly decorated in flower season. She grew her vegetables, also the roots and herbs with which she concocted her famous medicinal recipes. She attended the Sinners Run Baptist Church and contributed to its support; but the Indian in her worshiped only the wonders of Nature and she put no other gods before the beauty of the earth.

The colored people of Sinners Run envied and hated her, yet maintained a deceitful courtesy that permitted them to call upon her when in need of intervention with white people, money or in sickness. Her ability to always smooth the way for them, in any form of distress, was known with a certainty that was uncanny to their superstitious minds. She could do all except smooth out actual pain like her mother had done. However, she did her all, in the name of Anne . . . she herself caring little for these crude mean-hearted and petty people, who grinned in her face for favors, and hissed "half white bastard" behind her back. This last amused her, however, since her intelligence allowed her to see no difference between the black and yellow progeny of the illicit unions of slavery.

"What queer religion these folks have," laughed the woman, "it breaks forth in a certain place, and at a certain fixed time, then they lose it 'til the next time."

The women were especially incensed against her, because if they married at all, they invariably married men who Bathesda had rejected. She allowed each suitor in his time to visit her, sit as long as he pleased admiring her at the embroidering rack, while she, with serene indifference, hoped he would make his departure in time for her to take her dog and go to the crest for the sunset, or some such solitary jaunt. She could say "no" with a cool pleasantness that retained their goodwill; but the wives to whom she gave the men up hated her venomously for so doing. Hated her for wrapping her long glossy braids around and around her head in a coronet which made her a queen among them. Hated her for appearing so youthful despite her forty-seven years. Hated her for not shouting at church, and for failing to testify or profess. Hated her for having the prettiest house and garden in the community—for making the medicine that cured them. Hated her for weaving and embroidering while they took in washing, or labored beside their men in the cotton and corn fields. Hated her for her chaste aloofness of man, while they bore large families in the morass of poverty and misery. Hated her for showing contempt for the edicts of fashions and mail order houses up North or the cheap stores in Thorntonville and Savannah and for wearing the simply made, richly embroidered garments which none could duplicate. For all these reasons, the women of Sinners Run despised Bathesda.

Among them, she had one sincere friend in the person of young Becky Johnson. The dark-skinned girl had sought Bathesda in a frenzy one stormy midnight. Bathesda had donned her cape and accompanied the wild young mother to the bedside of her baby who was strangling with dyptheria. It was a simple deed; the swabbing of the little throat with boiled vinegar and salt, with a few directions, but the brown girl had hugged Bathesda's knees and kissed her comfortably shod feet in feverish adoration. The father, too, had looked dumb gratitude with brimming eyes. After this incident, Becky took Li'l Jim up to see Bathesda regularly, and Bathesda became greatly attached to the small family, such devotion from Becky having awakened within her cold nature, something akin to affection.

Becky's sister, mother, and grandmother strongly disapproved of this friendship. The sister, whose name was Cisseretta, was somewhat of a belle, and when rigged up in the cast-off clothes of the white people for whom she worked, was, for Sinners Run, quite elegant. She was light brown, with hazel eyes that were sly and coquettish. Her hair was of that yellowish cotton-batten sort, known as riney. She meant to marry better than had her older sister, and scorned the field hands as prospective husbands, although she was not averse to keeping them from dancing attendance on the less discriminating girls of her set.

The mother, Eliza Lambert, was about Bathesda's age and a malicious "yes" woman to gossip and trouble making, although too stupid herself to even instigate a healthy lie.

The grandmother, Granny Lou, was an ancient crone, black as pitch, who had lost track of her age, but knew everything pertaining to a scandalous nature concerning the families of both races for miles around. She sat in one corner year in and year out, wrapped in filthy shawls and hoods summer and winter, smoking her foul clay pipe, and spitting snuff into the maw of the tumble-down stove, or gumming her vicious old tales. She was reputed to be the oldest woman in that section of Georgia, and to have borne more children than she herself knew; Eliza, being her youngest, to whom she had hitched herself. Just as most of the trouble making and undercurrent of evilness in the neighborhood could usually be traced to the chair of Granny Lou and Lambert household, so was she guilty of inciting most of the fierce antipathy among the women against Bathesda.

One particular early autumn morning, she pursed and screwed her shrunken lips around to settle the snuff and saliva making a "Mpwhumn-mpwhumn" noise, and began lisping to Eliza who was washing:

"Heh, heh! Ah sees whar dat-ar new ministah done gine sottin' up to Thesdy's already—heh, heh! 'Pears lak to me dat you 'omans ain't slaves no moah an' oughten't go fer to put up wid sich cayin' on. Lize . . . Yo' Cissy tryin' to sot huh cap foah him, but 'pears lak to me, effen she gits him, won't be twell dat Thesdy's chawed 'im up an' spat him back at huh! Heh, heh!" and as if to suit the word with the action, she spat into the pink wood ashes which were falling out of the stove pit.

"Tain't nothin' to them Jezebel 'omans, noways. De white folks make me sick cayin' on so high 'bout dem. Day all sold dere souls to de debbil. Don't dey fool 'round wid roots 'n things? . . . mind how dey nebber show dere natchul age lak we'uns does?"

The silence that followed was broken by the sudsy slapping of wet clothes with home made lye soap. Eliza was too busy to bother about her old mother's chatter this morning, but Granny Lou was nothing loath to amusing herself.

"Becky, lak a li'l fool . . . she run up dere case day yaller 'oman do foah dat brat ahern, jis what any of ussen coulda did. Ah knows, chal! Yo Granny Lou knowed dem f'om way back to Callie!"

"Kyah, kyah, kyah! Granny Lou—hush you mouf," laughingly yelled Eliza above the suds, steam and slop, with perspiration dripping from her corn-rowed head into the tub.

Cisseretta, who had entered the room unnoticed, flared up angrily at the old hag's challenge—

"I wants Brother Parson Brown, and I's shore goin' to git him. 'Tain't goin' to be after Thesdy done chawed him, either, Granny!" So saying, she jammed her hands down upon her hips with her legs astride and frowned belligerently from her mother to her grinning grandmother.

The pine door swung open admitting Becky, resplendent in a soft white dress carrying Li'l Jim who was sportive in a blue smock and cap. The three women were aghast at the sudden picture. Poor Becky who was content to drudge in a one room cabin with her baby, for a husband who scarcely could pay for his fat back and meal down at the store—what right had she to look nicer than Cisseretta, the acknowledged social leader of Sinners Run!

"Whar'd je git dem cloes?" darkly inquired Eliza of her daughter.

"Oh Mammy! Ain't dey jist swell? Miss Thesdy done made dis up special foh me out o' brand new goods case. Ah told huh 'twas my second year married, today! See Li'l Jim? Ain't he grand? I has a big suppah foh Big Jim when he gits home and thought I would run in an' let you folks see us."

"Humph! 'Miss' Thesdy! Since whin did we start 'Missin' yaller niggers? Was Parson Brown anywhere bouts up there?" this from Cisseretta.

"Seems to me dat dose clo'es would scorch yo' skin, chal. Dat Thesdy is a woman wid no religion whatsomever," exasperatingly sighed Eliza.

"Jes' gib yo' all dose cloes fuh to git yo' wrapped up in huh, fudder—dan she gine conjuh yo' . . . heah me, now, heah me!" snapped old Granny Lou with a portentious shaking of her beshawled head.

Poor Becky! All her joyous happiness so quickly transformed to bitter antagonism.

"How come yo'all hates that pore woman so? What she done

done aginst you? All I seed she done was good! She's up dere in huh own pretty li'l house, amindin' huh business, and you folks down heah hatin' huh! Cisseretta? You won't make no hit wid Parson Brown . . . hatin' Miss Thesdy, 'cause he thinks she is jest grand! As for me and Big Jim, she saved our boy's life which is moah dan you what's his own kin-folks done, and we loves huh, even ef she ain't done professed 'ligion. From what I seed of huh and knowed of younes, she's a heap sight nigh to God dan you folks who eat out yo' hearts wid hatin' huh!"

She gathered the bewildered Li'l Jim up and left the scene of unsympathetic relatives, muttering to herself—"Gawd! Effen I stayed widdem any longer I would lose my own 'ligion. They's my own folks, but dey simply breed evilness, and I doesn't blame sweet Miss Thesdy from not minglin' wid 'em 'ceptin' when she has to."

In the Lambert cabin, Granny Lou was grunting—"See dat? She done got dat chal tu'ned agin huh own folks already . . . an' de preachuh eatin' out ob huh hand,"—with a cunning glance at Cisseretta.

"For two cents, Granny—" whined Cisseretta, petulantly, "I'd git the women together and go up to her ol' house and beat her up!"

"Kyah kyah! Lawsy me! Hush yo' mouf, chal!" elaborately guffawed her mother.

"Go hade, den . . . go hade! Do moah—an' talk less, honey!" huskily whimpered the old woman to her infuriated grandchild.

The day had been a busy one for Bathesda. She had contracted to make reproductions of the old samplers for an important Jewish antique dealer of Atlanta. Little Alice Thornton, quite grown up, and home from college, had motored out to see her, bringing with her her fiancé from Boston, an artist. He had begged for the privilege of painting Bathesda in all the glory of her little cottage and embroidering frames. To please Alice, she consented, on condition that it wouldn't interfere with her work.

"Like one of Millet's peasant women," he had said—"and that interior! Worthy of the old Dutch masters."

The young minister had sat awhile, explaining his well meant plan of progress for his congregation, which she knew would never be accepted by the deluded Sinners Run folks, the present pastor being their first seminary man. They understood only the old fashioned untrained "called-but-not-sent" type of ministering.

Becky and Li'l Jim dropped in with the new things she had made for them and the sight of the mother and child transformed by her handiwork thrilled her deeply.

She bent her queenly head over the crimson, green and purple threads she was interweaving so intricately into the words— "Heart within, God without" on the square of yellow, and smiled the smile of the middle-aged who had all they wanted in life—peace, pleasant labor, and contentment. Why should she be sad because of a God who withheld Himself, or the doubtful power of healing a people who despised her?

She decided to pick a fresh cabbage for her supper, and going to the door, was surprised to see Cisseretta Lambert approaching. With shifting eyes, and lowered brow, she informed Bathesda they had come to fetch her for a friend. At the little picket gate stood an old rickety home made cart with ill matched wheels, drawn by a sorry nag whose hips punctured his skin in miss-meal significance. Eliza was driving and perched beside her for all the world like a bundled up mummy sat Granny Lou.

"We kin fotch you there and back in no time, Thesdy. New folks jest come to Sinners Run, and powerful sick."

Bathesda hurriedly threw a light shawl around her shoulders with a strong sense of foreboding which she forcibly thrust out of her mind and joined the trio at the cart.

She and Cisseretta rode backwards with their feet swinging, and nothing was said by the four women as the half dead animal faltered along the lonely road pulling the unbalanced, lurching, wabbling vehicle behind them.

Then Eliza . . .

"Kyah kyah! Heah we all is, folksies! Kyah kyah! Lawdy, Lawdy, Lawd!"

Bathesda turned from the back end of the wagon and saw glaring malevolently at her the dark faces of ten or twelve women. They were as a pack of hungry hounds eager to be off on the chase. Cisseretta leaped from her seat on the wagon and rudely grabbed Bathesda, causing her to stumble to the ground on her knees. As if waiting for the initiative action from their leader, they pounced upon her, dragging her by the arms up the sloping hill side. The decrepit conveyance with the beswaddled old woman was left standing on the road.

The maddened women yelled violent invectives—brandished whips, twigs and sticks aloft, dragging her roughly uphill, not allowing her to regain her foothold or the freedom of her arms.

"Thought you'd git yo' claws on Revern Bro Brown, didn't you? We see 'bout dat, won't we? Cain't feed him none o' yo' hoodoo vittles . . . nuh-uh!"

"Yes indeedy. We is gwine to see 'bout all dis heah monkey business yo' been cayin' on all dese yeahs wid de men folks. . . ."

"Think you better dan ussens, doesn't you? Humph! Old half white niggers make me sick . . . cain't be white an' cain't be black!"

"Naw! We niggers don't want you and de white folks won't hab you!"

"Lawdy, Lawdy, Lawd today! Yeowh!"

"Pull huh ol' plaits down! Make me tiahd wid huh ol' dawg har! Wouldn't have straight har, mahself—Revelations say as plain as day—'har lak lambs wool' like ussen got. . . ."

"Sis Grenn? Dis is shoah a holy deed Cisseretta done called on us to do . . . to protect ouah poah pastor from de wiles ob dis sinner woman. . . ."

"Kyah kyah! Lawd today!"

They reached the summit of the hill which was capped with a small patch of woods. A few of the trees had recently been chopped down, judging by the fresh stumps. The several women in whose clutches Bathesda had fallen suddenly released their hold on her and jumped back out of her reach. But Bathesda merely stomped the caked dirt from her shoes and torn skirt, threw a quiet searching glance around the semicircle of women, and made to swing her loosened braids around her head.

This action galled Cisseretta, who saw in it a self assurance, a composure that was shaking the courage of her vigilance committee. She sprang at Bathesda heavily with an angry snarl, pushing her back into a tree which instantaneously crashed to the earth, sideways, sending Cisseretta and all the women scrambling and yelping down the hill.

"Conjuh woman! conjuh . . . Lawd Ah's feared!"

"Hoodoo stuff! Told yo'all we oughten to bother wid huh!"

"Lawd! Jist 'low me to git home once moah . . . please!"

"Cisseretta done got ussen into dis mess . . . !"

From the opposite direction came two white men, hurrying toward Bathesda who stood arranging her hair beside the fallen tree.

"Anybody hurt, Auntie? We are clearing these here woods for Ben Lovett who has bought the strip, and my buddy here—he sprained his joint while chopping down that 'un a few minutes ago. We went up to my shack after some liniment and we didn't 'reckon anyone would come along before we got back. The tree was nearly cut through and I 'spec a slight jostle knocked her over."

"No one was hurt. It fell to the side," murmured the yellow woman absently—eyes searching into the distance.

A delicate tenderness played over her face, and kindly wrinkles appeared about her mouth and forehead. Like Haggard's "She," Bathesda unexpectedly looked her age, all at once. She had dropped the cloak of a hardened, held-over youth, and taken on the ethereal robe of an inner beauty—a soul transformation had taken place.

She, for the first time, turned directly to the lumberjacks, and asked of the one with the bandaged arm—

"Is it bad?"

"Hurts mightily and swellin' every second."

She unwrapped the crude bandage, wiped away the stench of liniment, cupped her two hands about the swollen arm and gazed upward—her thin lips moving almost imperceptibly while the men stood transfixed.

She finally withdrew her hands, clenched them into tight fists and then shook them open and away from her, as if throwing off the contamination of alien flesh.

"Now . . . it is well!"

"Bill! Honest to John! She's right! The dad burned misery had gone completely, and look! The swellin' is goin' down right before my very eyes!"

"Good God! It is a miracle we've just witnessed! The woman's a saint." And he hastily crossed himself while the other man tested his healed arm by swinging an ax.

Bathesda went down the hill with wide masculine strides—the light winds causing her snagged skirt and white apron to billow and flurry. Her eyes were two muddy pools of tears. She was testifying.

"Up Calvary's rugged brow did I go, this day with Thee, dear Lord . . . To the very foot of the Cross . . . and I saw the bloody nails in Thy precious feet . . . the cruel thorns . . . and the bitter cup was spared me . . . me, a worthless worm . . . but Thou didst drink it to the dregs!"

And she went home with a new power—with understanding, tolerance and forgiveness; to be one of her people; to take care of Becky with her Li'l Jim and Big Jim; and the fragrant drops of rain pelted her in gentle benediction.

RICHARD WRIGHT

Man of All Work

—Carl! Carl!

—Hunh.

—Carl, the baby's awake.

—Yeah? Hummnn . . .

—Carl, the baby's crying.

—Oh, all right. I'll get up. It's time for her bottle.

—Be sure and heat it to the right temperature, Carl.

—Of course. Put on the light.

—How is she?

—Fine. Ha, ha! What a pair of lungs! She's really bawling us out. O.K., Tina. I'm getting your bottle right now. Oooowaaa . . . Lucy, you kind of scared me when you called me.

—I know, Carl. You haven't had much sleep lately. You're jumpy. Both of us are. You want me to feed her?

—No, no. It's nothing. I'll heat the bottle now.

—I hear Henry coming.

—Papa, Papa!

—Henry, go back to bed.

—Papa, can't I see Tina? I heard her crying.

278

—Come in, Henry. Carl, let Henry see the baby.

—Oh, sure.

—Henry, while Papa is heating the bottle, you can look at Tina.

—But, Mama, she's still so little.

—She's as big as you were when you were a week old.

—I never looked like *that*.

—Yes, you did. Not a bit different.

—But I don't remember when I—

—Of course, you don't. And Tina won't remember either when she grows up.

—All she knows is how to eat.

—We're born with that know-how, Henry. Oh, Henry, you didn't put on your house shoes and robe. How many times must I tell you that. You'll catch cold on that bare floor.

—O.K., Mama. But why does she cry so loud?

—That's the way babies are supposed to cry. She's healthy. Now, put your shoes and robe on if you want to watch Papa.

—Yessum.

—Lucy, here's the bottle. Feel it and see if it's warm enough.

—Seems just right to me, Carl.

—Papa, don't give her the bottle. I want to see you feed her.

—Then hurry up, Henry.

—Carl, let me feed her. Hand her to me.

—No. You lie still, Lucy. You're tired. The doctor said for you to rest. I can give the baby the bottle.

—I'm coming, Papa. Lemme see you feed her.

—O.K., son. Now, watch. I lift her head up a bit, then put the nipple in her mouth. See? She's stopped crying.

—Mama, Tina's eating!

—Ha, ha! Of course, Henry. Now, go to bed.

—O.K. Good night, Mama. Good night, Papa. Good night, Tina.

—Good night, Henry.

—Good night, son.

—He sure loves his little sister.

—Yes, he does. To him she's a toy.

—How do you feel, Lucy?

—Oh, all right. You know . . . Sometimes I'm quite normal, then I feel faint, weak . . .

—Darling, don't worry. You're upset. Just let me take care of everything. Ha, ha! Good thing you married a professional cook, eh?

—Carl, I wouldn't be so worried if I knew that we weren't going to lose the house.

—Sh. Don't talk so loud. Henry'll hear you.

—I'm sorry. We mustn't let him know that we've got trouble.

—Children have a way of sensing what's going on.

—Is she taking her milk all right?

—Gulping it down a mile a minute. Greedy thing.

—Oh, Carl, what're we going to do?

—Lucy, stop worrying. The doctor said—

—I can't help but worry, Carl.

—But that's what's making you sick. After you had Henry, you weren't ill.

—I know. But everything was all right then. Now, all of our money's tied up in this house and we can't make the last two payments. Oh, Carl, we mustn't lose our house.

—Honey, don't worry. Something'll turn up.

—Carl, did you sleep some?

—No. I just dozed a bit. Did you?

—No.

—Lucy, the doctor said—

—I know, Carl. But I can't help but worry.

—I'll think of something. You'll see.

—If we both hadn't lost our jobs at the same time. Giving birth knocked me out of my job. And your boss had to close his restaurant. Hard luck comes all at once.

—Lucy, look . . . She's finished her bottle.

—All of it?

—Every drop.

—Can you burp her?

—Sure.

—No. Hand her to me, Carl.

—No. Look. I'll just lift her gently and lay her across my shoulder. Like that . . . Then I'll pat her back. Easy does it. There! Did you hear it?

—Ha, ha! You did it as well as I could.

—Why not? Burping a baby's no mystery. Ha, ha. She's gone to sleep again.

—That warm milk always knocks her out.

—Okay, Tina. To bed you go now.

—Let me take a peek at her, Carl.

—Don't get up, Lucy. I'll bring her to you. Just lift yourself upon your elbow . . . There.

—Aw, she's a doll. Is she dry?

—I felt her diaper. It's dry. But it won't be for long.

—It never is. She looks like you, Carl.

—No. She looks like you, Lucy.

—Oh, come on. She looks like both of us.

—That's natural. She'd better not look like anybody else.

—Ha, ha. Are you jealous?

—I'll tuck her in. I think she'll be all right till morning.

—Carl, come back to bed. You've been up twice tonight.

—It's nothing. What time is it?

—It's five o'clock.

—What's that?

—That's the morning paper hitting the front door. I'll get it.

—Oh, come to bed, Carl. Get the paper later.

—No. I want to take a look at the want ads.

—Carl, don't be so nervous. Later . . .

—Lucy, I've got to smell out a job somehow. We've got only two fifty-dollar payments to make on this house. And, if I live, we're not going to lose this house. You go to sleep.

—Poor Carl. He does all he can. This shouldn't've happened to him.

—Darling, you won't mind if I keep the light on, will you? I want to study these ads.

—No, Carl. I'll try to sleep.

—Turn away from the light, hunh? Aw, let's see here . . . Yeah. MALE HELP WANTED: Machinists. Bricklayers. Pipe fitters.

Masons. Bookkeepers. Salesmen. Hunh. Not a single ad for a
cook.

—Carl, stop fretting and get some sleep.

—Aw, Lucy, I've *got* to get a job.

—Don't talk so loud. You'll wake the baby.

—I'm sorry, honey.

—Carl, we must try to be calm.

—Yeah. I know. No jobs for men in this paper . . . But
there're plenty of ads for domestic workers. It's always like that.

—Oh, Carl. If I were well, I'd get a cooking job.

—Hush, Lucy.

—Well, you mentioned jobs for women and—

—I wasn't hinting that you ought to go to work. You're ill.
Now, don't talk rot.

—Carl, I—

—Lucy, don't cry! Everything's going to be all right.

—I wish I could do something.

—Lucy, I'll find a job. You'll see. Aw, here's a wonderful ad.
Listen:

Cook and housekeeper wanted. Take care of one child and
small modern household. All late appliances. Colored cook
preferred. Salary: fifty dollars a week. References required.
608 South Ridgeway Boulevard. Mrs. David Fairchild.

—Oh, Carl! That job would solve our problem.

—Yeah, but they want a woman, Lucy. Ha, ha. I'm an A-1
cook. I wish to God I could sneak in and get that job.

—Aw, Carl, stop getting so worked up. I'm turning out the
light.

—Oh, O.K. Try to get some sleep, darling.

—Lucy.

—Humnnnn . . . Hunh?

—Look, Lucy.

—Yeah, Carl. W-what is it?

—Turn on the light, honey.

—All right. Just a sec, Carl. OHHHHHH! Who are you?

—Take it easy, Lucy. Don't yell.

—Who is that? Carl? Is that you, Carl?

—Yes, Lucy. Now, look, darling. Be calm.

—Oh, God! I thought you were somebody else. Oh, Carl, what are you doing? Those are my clothes you got on. You almost scared me to death.

—Listen, Lucy. Now, I'm—

—Carl, what's the matter?

—Sh. Don't wake up the children. Darling, now I'm—

—Oh, Carl. No. Don't do that. Is this a joke? Pull off my dress!

—Lucy, listen to me. I'm—

—Carl, have you gone crazy?

—Hush and listen to me. I know how to handle children. I can cook. Don't stop me. I've found a solution to our problem. I'm an army trained cook. I can clean a house as good as anybody. Get my point? I put on your dress. I looked in the mirror. I can pass. I want that job—

—Carl! Go 'way! TAKE OFF MY DRESS! No, no!

—Lucy, I'm going for that job advertised in the paper. Nobody'll see me leave. Don't worry. I'm going out the back way across the vacant lot, see? I'll take the bus behind the church. I've got it all figured out. Trust me. I'm going to work as a maid for two months in that white family. That means two hundred dollars. Half of that money'll pay off the house. The other half will keep us eating. You just stay home. Have Henry help you a bit while I'm gone and—

—Oh, God, no! You're wild, Carl!

—Be quiet, Lucy, and listen.

—God, I'm trembling . . . C-c-can't you see that—Oh, no!

—Lucy, don't cry.

—Carl, you're foolish.

—I'm not. I'll get that job.

—No. They'll find out.

—How?

—Carl, people can l-look at you and s-see that you're a man.

—Ha, ha. No, Lucy. I just looked at myself in the bathroom mirror. I've got on a dress and I look just like a million black women cooks. Who looks that close at us colored people anyhow? We all look alike to white people. Suppose you'd never seen me before? You'd take one look at me and take me for a woman because I'm wearing a dress. And the others'll do that too. Lucy, colored men are now wearing their hair long, like mine. Isn't that true? Look at Sugar Ray Robinson's hair. Look at Nat King Cole's hair. Look at all the colored men in the Black Belt. They straighten their hair. It's the style.

—Y-yes, but—

—All right. I'm just about your size. Your dresses fit me. I'll take your purse. I'll wear low-heeled shoes. What's more I don't need any make-up. A cook isn't supposed to be powdered and rouged. I've shaved very, very closely. I'm taking my razor with me; if my beard starts to grow, I'll sneak a quick shave, see? All I have to do is say 'Yessum, No'm,' and keep my mouth shut. Do my work. My voice is tenor; nobody'll notice it. I'll get the money we need and we're saved.

—Oh, Carl! Have you been drinking?

—I'm not drunk. I'm going for that job.

—Oh, Carl, if they catch you, they'll put you in jail.

—They won't suspect anything.

—They will. You'll see.

—They won't.

—Suppose they get suspicious of how you walk?

—They won't. There isn't much difference between a man's walk and a woman's. Look. I'm leaving my suit in the coal house; when I come back, I'll change this dress for my suit before coming into the house, see? Nobody'll know but you. When you're cooking for a family like that, you usually stay until after dinner—to do the dishes. It's fall now; the days are getting shorter. When I leave their house, it'll be night. Nobody among our folks'll see me. Like I told you, I'll change my clothes in the coal house and come in through the kitchen . . . You keep Henry near you, see? He'll know nothing.

—Carl, you'll make me scream! This is crazy!

—Darling, don't shout.

—Carl, if you go out of that door like that, I'll scream.

—Lucy, let me try this.

—No, no. Of all the damnfool ideas!

—Lucy, when I was in high school, I acted in plays. When I was in the army, I was in company plays. I can act good enough to fool white folks. And it's just for two months. Then we're fixed. Think. After two months, the house is safe, is ours.

—Carl, I don't want to talk to you. Leave me alone. AND GET OUT OF MY DRESS! *Now!* You hear! *Please . . .*

—Lucy, listen . . .

—CARL, PULL OFF MY DRESS!

—Lucy, look at me. Take your face out of the pillow. Be sensible. I'm taking a chance, but it'll come out all right.

—I don't want to look at you.

—Come on. Be a sport.

—The police'll catch you walking around in a dress and will put you in jail for impersonating a woman. And, if that happens, I'll leave you and the children! I'll just walk out, I swear to you. If you go out of that door in that dress, I'M THROUGH!

—How will anybody know? Lift up my dress? Ha, ha. Lucy. Don't be silly. It's easy to fool 'em.

—Carl, stop it! Stop it or I'll scream! I'll get up and scratch you! PULL OFF MY DRESS!

—Oh, O.K. O.K. I give up. I'll pull off your dress. I was only joking. Now, be calm, stop crying. Turn off the light and go to sleep.

—All right, Carl. But don't ever do that again, please. Oh, God, you scared me.

—O.K.

—You're really going to pull that dress off, aren't you?

—Sure, darling. I'll be back in a sec.

—And, Carl, don't worry so much. We'll solve things somehow, hunh? Oh, God, poor Carl. What's got into him? What can I do? He's worried sick. I thought I was having a nightmare when I saw him in my dress. I almost passed out. It's a wonder I didn't scream.

❧

—Hummnnn . . . Carl. Carl. *Carl!* Oh, God, where is he? He must be in the kitchen. It's almost eight o'clock. The baby needs feeding. CARL! CARL! Where's my robe? He didn't leave here. No, he wouldn't do that. But he's not in the kitchen. And he's not in the bathroom. CARL! *Oh, God, he's not in the house!* I've awakened the baby. Aw, my dress is gone. And my purse. AND MY SHOES! *Did he do that?* No, he wouldn't dare go out into the streets like that! Then where could he be? He's gone to that job, that crazy fool . . . He'll get into trouble. I know it. I know it.

—Mama.

—Yes, Henry.

—The baby's crying.

—Yes, I know, darling. Get back to bed. I'm fixing the baby's bottle.

—I'm hungry.

—I'll get you your breakfast in a minute. Just wait now.

—Where's Papa?

—He's gone out. He'll be back soon.

—Come in.

—Thank you, sir.

—My wife'll talk to you in a moment. What's your name?

—Lucy Owens, sir.

—How old are you?

—Thirty, sir.

—You live here in town?

—Yes, sir. Just a twenty-minute bus ride from here.

—You've done domestic work before? You can handle children?

—Oh, yes, sir. I've two children of my own.

—What ages?

—One's a year old and the other's six.

—Who looks after the young one when you work?

—My husband, sir. You see, he works at night in a lumbermill and is at home during the day.

—Have you references?

—Oh, yes, sir.

—Well, Lucy, my wife'll speak to you in a moment. This is her department. Sit down and wait a bit.

—Yes, sir. Thank you, sir.

—Anne, you'd better talk to her. She doesn't live far from here. Seems clean, strong. Knows her place. Name's Lucy Owens. Got two children.

—I'll talk to her and check her references. Dave, if she drinks, I'll not hire her.

—Use your judgment, Anne.

—How does she look? How old is she?

—Didn't ask her. Didn't notice her.

—If you didn't, it would be the first time.

—Aw, Anne, cut it out. Hire the woman if you want her.

—I'll talk to her.

—I'll shave now. If you decide to take her, you might let her try to rustle up some breakfast.

—We'll see.

—Good morning, ma'am.

—You're Lucy Owens?

—Yessum.

—Now, Lucy, do you think you can handle a child of six and do the work in the house?

—Oh, that's nothing, ma'am. Give me a try. I love kiddies.

—Here's my little daughter, Lily, now. Lily, come here. This is Lucy. She wants to work for us.

—Hello, Lucy.

—Hello, Miss Lily. My, you're pretty. How are you?

—Fine. Lucy, can you cook cakes?

—Ha, ha! Lucy, you'd better answer Lily. She's the boss at the table.

—Miss Lily, I can cook the best food you ever tasted. I make fudge, cakes, ice cream—everything. I'll put some flesh on you.

—Now, run along, Lily. Lucy, what about your references?

—Well, ma'am, I have a good reference. But the trouble is
that the folks I used to work for have gone to Europe and won't
be back for two months. You won't be able to check on me with
them. But there's Reverend Burke of the Pearl Street Baptist
Church. You can phone him any time you want and ask about
Sister Lucy Owens.

—I see. How long were you with your last family?

—Five years, ma'am.

—Lucy, I want to talk frankly to you. We had a girl here. But
she was a disappointment to me. She seemed so nice. But she
drank. And when she did, her conduct was awful. Guess you
know what I mean?

—Yessum. I think I know what you mean. But, ma'am, I don't
drink. I'm a straight, God-fearing woman. I just want to give you
an honest day's work. You see, ma'am, me and my husband's
buying our own place. We're responsible people.

—I like that. One should own one's own place. Well, you
seem clean, strong, quick.

—Oh, ma'am, you won't have any trouble from me.

—Well, Lucy, we said fifty dollars a week. You'll have to be
here at seven in the morning; we're generally asleep. But by the
time you get breakfast on the table, we'll be up and ready to eat.
When we've gone, you take care of Lily, do the housework, do
the wash when necessary, and prepare lunch and dinner. Generally, my husband's in every day for lunch. When I'm in the
neighborhood, I drop in for lunch. Understand?

—Yessum. That's quite all right. You just keep to your sched-
ule and tell me what you want done and I'll do it.

—That sounds good. Well, Lucy, I'm going to take a chance
on you. You're hired. I just look at a person and something tells
me that they ought to be all right.

—Thank you, ma'am.

—Now, Lucy, I'll show you around the house. This is the sun
porch. As you see, this is the entry. There's the living room.
Here's our bedroom. There's the bath. And here's Lily's room.
And that's a guest room. Here's the dining room. And here's the
kitchen.

—Oh, it's big, ma'am.

—To save trouble, we eat breakfast in the kitchen.

—I understand. Oh, what a pretty refrigerator.

—It's the latest. And there's the washing machine.

—I can handle 'em all, ma'am.

—The food's here in this pantry. Knives and forks and dishes are here. Soap powder. Mops. Brooms. There's the backyard where you hang up clothes to dry. But your main job's looking after Lily.

—Mama, does Lucy know about Little Red Riding Hood?

—Miss Lily, I know all about her.

—O.K., Lucy. Now, do you think you can rustle up some breakfast for us?

—I'll try, ma'am. What would you all want?

—What do you specialize in for breakfast, Lucy?

—Reckon you all would love some pancakes? I cook 'em light as a feather. You can digest 'em in your sleep.

—Just a moment, Lucy. Dave!

—Yeah, Anne.

—Lucy wants to try her hand at some pancakes. She says she's good at 'em.

—Well, tell her to rustle some up. I haven't had any good pancakes since Heck was a pup.

—You've got your orders, Lucy.

—Ha, ha! Yessum. Pancakes coming up. Hot and with maple syrup and butter. Ha, ha!

—Breakfast is ready, everybody!

—O.K., Lucy. Come on, Lily. Lucy, Lily and I always eat breakfast together. Mrs. Fairchild's still in the bath and will eat later. She's on a strict diet and will only want a slice of toast and black coffee. She won't leave for work until a bit later.

—I understand, sir.

—Lucy, these pancakes are wonderful. Anne, you ought to try one, really. Lily, tell Mama how good they are.

—Mama, they're like cake.

—Hummmnnn . . . I want a stack of five of 'em.

—Dave, watch your waistline.

—Lucy, I haven't had pancakes like this in years. Hummnnn . . .

—Better eat your fill of 'em, Mister Dave.

—Lily, take some more.

—Sure, Papa. They're so good.

—Mister Dave, you want me to make another batch for you?

—Yeah. You'd better cook me another batch, Lucy.

—O.K. Another batch of pancakes coming up!

—Oh, Papa, she cooks real good.

—Sh. Don't talk so loud. We don't want to spoil her. That gal knows her onions. Don't know what she put in these cakes, but I'm taking a third stack of 'em. Anne!

—Yes, Dave.

—I'm downing these cakes. God, they're good.

—All right, Dave. Glad you like 'em. See you at lunch, maybe. And, Lily, I want you to be nice to Lucy, hear? You obey her. No screaming, no tantrums.

—Yes, Mama. I like Lucy. She's big and strong. Papa, may I have another pancake?

—Anne, Lily's already eating better.

—I'm sure happy about that.

—And, Anne, this coffee's good. Hummmnnn . . . It's good to have a solid breakfast before hitting those streets in the morning.

—Well, Anne, I'm off. Will I see you for lunch?

—If I can make it, Dave. Good-by.

—Good-by, Papa.

—Good-by, Lily. Run on back into the kitchen and stay with Lucy while Mama takes her bath.

—Yes, Papa.

—Hello, Lucy. What're you doing?

—Come in, Lily. I'm washing the dishes. Be through in a sec.

—Lucy, can you sing?

—Oh, yes. Why?

—Then sing something for me. Bertha used to sing all the time.

—Well, what do you want me to sing?

—Songs like your people sing.

—Ha, ha. I know. Oh, all right. Let's see.

> *Swing low, sweet chariot*
> *Coming for to carry me home . . .*
> *Looked over Jordan and what did I see?*
> *A band of angels coming after me,*
> *Coming for to carry me home . . .*

—That's pretty. Wish I could sing like that.

—You can. When you're a bit older.

—How'd you learn to sing that song?

—It was so long ago, I've forgotten, Lily.

—Lucy, your arms are so big.

—Hunh?

—And there's so much hair on them.

—Oh, that's nothing.

—And you've got so many big muscles.

—Oh, that comes from washing and cleaning and cooking. Lifting heavy pots and pans.

—And your voice is not at all like Bertha's.

—What do you mean?

—Your voice is heavy, like a man's.

—Oh, that's from singing so much, child.

—And you hold your cigarette in your mouth like Papa holds his, with one end dropping down.

—Hunh? Oh, that's because my hands are busy, child.

—That's just what Papa said when I asked him about it.

—You notice everything, don't you, Lily?

—Sure. I like to look at people. Gee, Lucy, you move so quick and rough in the kitchen. You can lift that whole pile of dishes with one hand. Bertha couldn't do that.

—Just a lot of experience, Lily. Say, why don't you play with your dolls?

—I just like to watch you.

—Oh, Lucy!

—Mama's calling you, Lucy.

—Yessum, Mrs. Fairchild.

—Did you find that bundle of wash there in the hallway?

—Yessum. I see it.

—That's today's wash, Lucy.

—Yessum. I understand. Lily, suppose you come with me on the porch while I put this washing in the machine, hunh? Now, we'll put this soap powder in. Then we'll run in the hot water . . . Now, I'll dump all the white clothes in. There. Wasn't that quick? Now, I'll throw the switch. There. The clothes are being washed.

—Gee, Lucy, you work like a machine.

—God, child, you do notice everything, don't you? But don't look too much or you might see things you won't understand.

—What do you mean? How? Why?

—Ha, ha. Nothing. Now, Lily, while I clean the house, what do you want to do? Watch me or play?

—I want to play in my sand pile.

—Where is it?

—In the backyard.

—Well, come on and show me.

—It's right by the fence. There it is.

—What a pile of sand. Child, you're lucky.

—Papa bought me a whole truck load of sand to play in.

—Suppose I build you a sand castle?

—Oh, that'd be fun.

—Well, let's see. First, we'll make the foundation, like this . . . Then we start the walls. That's right. Pat the walls smoothly. Take your time. Now, we'll try to make the doorway. About here, hunh?

—Oh, yes. Lucy, this is going to be a wonderful castle. I can finish it now. I know how.

—You really think so?

—Sure.

—Well, I'll get inside and start my work on the house.

—Lucy!

—Yessum. I'm coming.

—Come here, please!

—Yessum. On the way, ma'am.

—Lucy!

—Yessum. Where are you, Mrs. Fairchild?

—I'm here in the bathroom. Won't you come in? I want you to wash my back.

—Hunh?

—Come into the bathroom.

—Ma'am?

—Right here. I hear you. Open the door and come in. I want you to wash my back.

—Yessum.

—Lucy, can't you hear me?

—Yessum.

—Then open the door and come in.

—Er . . . Er, yessum.

—Well, what's the matter, Lucy? Why are you poking your head like that around the door? Come in. I want you to wash my back with this brush. Come on in. I haven't got all day, Lucy.

—Yessum.

—I don't want to be late for work. Well, come on. Why are you standing there and staring like that at me?

—Er . . .

—Don't you feel well, Lucy?

—Yessum.

—Then come here and wash my back.

—Yessum.

—That's it. Scrub hard. I won't break. Do it hard. Oh, Lord, what's the matter with you? Your arm's shaking. Lucy?

—Ma'am.

—What's come over you? Are you timid or ashamed or something?

—No'm.

—Are you upset because I'm sitting here naked in the bathtub?

—Oh, no, ma'am.

—Then what's the matter? My God, your face is breaking out in sweat. You look terrible. Are you ill, Lucy?

—No, ma'am. I'm all right.

—Then scrub my back. Hard. Why, your arms are like rubber. Well, I never. You're acting very strange. Do I offend you because I ask you to wash my back? Bertha always helped me with my bath . . .

—It's just the first t-t-time . . .

—Oh, I see. Well, I don't see why I should frighten you. I'm a woman like you are.

—Yessum.

—A bit harder, Lucy. Higher, up between my shoulder blades. That's it, that's it. Aw . . . Good. That's enough. Now, Lucy, hand me that towel over there. Where're you going? You're not leaving yet. I'm not through. Oh, I must be careful getting out of this tub. Tubs are dangerous things; you can have accidents by slipping in tubs . . . Lucy, give me the towel . . . WHAT IS HAPPENING TO YOU, LUCY? Why are you staring at me like that? Take a hand towel from that rack and wipe your face. Are you well? Maybe the doctor ought to take a good look at you. My brother-in-law, Burt Stallman, is a doctor. Do you want me to call him for you?

—It's just hot in here, ma'am.

—Hot? Why it's rather cold to me. I'm cold, you're hot. What's wrong with you? HAND ME THE TOWEL! Now, that box of talcum . . . Thanks. Now, Lucy, sit here on this stool a moment. There's something I must say to you and there's no better time than now, while I'm drying myself. I want to talk frankly to you, as one woman to another.

—Yessum.

—Now, I didn't tell you when you first came here why I had to get rid of my last maid. Now, look, my husband, Dave, likes to take a drink now and then—maybe a drop more than is good for him. Otherwise, he's perfectly sober, thoughtful, and easy to get along with. You know what I mean?

—Yessum. I think I know.

—Now, Bertha too did a little drinking now and then. And, when both of 'em started drinking—well, you can imagine what happened. Understand?

—Yessum.

—Now, Lucy, tell me: do you drink?

—No, ma'am. Not a drop.

—Good. As long as you don't drink, my husband won't bother you and you can very well defend yourself. Just push him away. Now, as one woman to another, do we understand each other?

—Mrs. Fairchild, your husband isn't going to touch me.

—Well, I'm glad to hear you say it like that. Dave's not so much a problem, Lucy. He gets the way men get sometimes. Afterwards he's ashamed enough to want to go out and drown himself or something. Understand? Any strong-minded person can handle Dave when he's like that. But if you're like Bertha, then trouble's bound to come.

—Yessum. You can depend on me, Mrs. Fairchild.

—Oh, Lucy, I've just got to watch my figure. Don't you think I'm too fat?

—Ma'am, some folks are just naturally a bit heavy, you know.

—But my breasts—aren't they much too large?

—Maybe . . . a little . . .

—And my thighs, aren't they rather large too?

—Well, not especially, ma'am.

—Lucy, you are too polite to tell me what you really think. I wish I were as slender as you. How do you manage it?

—Just working hard, I guess, ma'am.

—Really, Lucy, I like you very much. Ha, ha! You're like a sixteen-year-old girl. I'm surprised that you've had two children. Listen, Lucy, what I've discussed with you about my husband is just between us, see?

—Yessum. I won't open my mouth to anybody, ma'am.

—How do you and your husband get along?

—Oh, fine, ma'am.

—Oh, yes, Lucy . . . For lunch I want spinach, lamb chops, boiled potatoes, salad, and stewed pears. Coffee. Tonight we eat out.

—Yessum. I'll remember.

—Lucy, hand me my brassiere there . . .

—Yessum.

—Lord, even when I don't eat, I get fat . . . Give me my panties, Lucy.

—Yessum.

—Well, that's all, Lucy. You can go back to your work.

—Ma'am, the coffee's still hot. You want some toast?

—I won't touch a crumb of bread. Just black coffee.

—Yessum. I'm going to see what little Lily is up to.

—That's right, Lucy. Keep your eye on her.

—Lily! Lily!

—I'm here, Lucy. Look at my castle.

—Well, you've almost finished it.

—Lucy, what's the matter? Your face is wet . . . You're shaking.

—Oh, nothing. I just want to sit here on the steps for a moment and get my breath. It was hot there in that bathroom.

—You look scared, Lucy.

—Sometimes I'm short of breath, that's all.

—Do you really like my castle?

—It's wonderful.

—Lucy!

—Yessum, Mrs. Fairchild.

—Good-by. Good-by, Lily.

—Good-by, Mama.

—Good-by, Mrs. Fairchild.

—Oh, Lily!

—Yes.

—Your lunch's ready. You must eat and then take your nap.

—I'm coming, Lucy.

—No, Lily. You must come right now, while your food's hot.

—Oh, all right.

—Did you wash your hands?

—Yes.

—Sit down. Tuck your napkin in. Here's some nice spinach.

—I don't like spinach.

—It's good for you. Eat it. There's ice cream for dessert.

—What kind?

—Chocolate.

—I like vanilla.

—All right, now. Open your mouth and eat. Let's go.

—Lucy, your face is hard.

—Hunh?

—And very rough.

—Ha, ha. I've been working hard all my life, Lily. That's why. Why are you always staring at me so? Don't look at me. Eat.

—Papa's lunch is ready?

—Yes, lunch is ready for your papa and your mama.

—Is Mama coming to lunch?

—Don't know. Now, eat your food. Stop talking.

—Lucy, are you going to be like Bertha?

—What do you mean?

—Are you going to wrestle with Papa too?

—Hunh? Ha, ha. No, not me, Lily.

—Ha, ha. Bertha was always wrestling with Papa, running from room to room.

—What happened?

—I don't know. But it was funny. I could hear Bertha hollering. They'd make so much noise I couldn't take my nap. And Papa'd give me a dime not to tell Mama.

—I won't wrestle with your papa. You'll be able to sleep.

—Aw, but Papa is quick and strong.

—I can outrun him.

—He'll catch you like he did Bertha and make you wrestle with him.

—Stop talking, Lily, and eat your lamb chop.

—I'm eating, Lucy.

—Unless you eat faster, you won't be in bed by the time they come.

—You want me in bed, when Papa comes?

—I didn't say that.

—Bertha always made me eat fast so I would be sleeping when Papa came.

—Hummnnn . . . Say, tell me a bit more about how Bertha wrestled with your papa.

—They just wrestled.

—Did it happen often?

—Almost everyday. Then Bertha left.

—Why?

—Mama said it was not nice for a lady to wrestle with a man.

—That's right, Lily.

—Lucy, don't you ever wear lipstick, like Mama?

—Oh, when I need to. Come on, Lily. Open your mouth and eat. Stop playing around. Oh, what's that whistle?

—That's the mailman.

—Now, you just eat. I'll go to the door and get the mail.

—He's Bertha's friend. He's colored, you know.

—Oh.

—Bertha used to invite him in. Are you?

—No. Now, you eat. I'll get the mail.

—Any mail, Lucy?

—Just one letter for your father.

—Did you see the mailman? Talk to him?

—No. He was leaving the door and I didn't call him.

—Bertha always did.

—I'm not Bertha.

—But isn't he your friend too?

—No.

—Don't you know his name?

—No, Lily. What is it?

—His name is Kirkby Rickford.

—Oh, yeah. I've heard of him.

—Bertha used to invite him in.

—Well, I won't.

—And Bertha used to give him a drink out of Papa's bottle.

—Now, Lily, here's your dessert. While you're eating it, I'll set the table for your mother and father, hear?

—O.K., Lucy. But you're not at all like Bertha—

—Hello! Hello! Anybody in?

—Oh, Papa! Lucy, Papa's come home.

—Hello, Lily. Are you still eating?

—I'm almost through, Papa.

—I always told you to be in bed when I came—

—I was talking to Lucy, Papa.

—Oh, hello there, Lucy.

—Hello, Mr. Fairchild.

—Is everything all right, Lucy?

—Yessir. Everything's fine, sir.

—Did she eat all right, Lucy?

—Oh, so-so, Mr. Fairchild.

—Here, Lily, let me feed you this ice cream.

—I don't want it. Papa, is Mama coming to lunch?

—I don't know.

—You're going to eat by yourself?

—Maybe.

—Papa, where did Bertha go?

—I don't know. And stop talking about Bertha. Finish your ice cream.

—Ooowwa . . . Papa, don't be angry with me . . .

—Aw, come on, Lily. It's bedtime, *now*.

—You always want me to go to bed when you come home. I know. You want to talk to Lucy.

—Will you shut your mouth and eat! Now, let me see where in hell did Anne hide my bottle. She's always trying to keep it from me. Have you seen my bottle around, Lucy?

—What kind of a bottle, sir?

—You know. My bottle of whisky. I need a little nip.

—No, sir. I haven't seen it.

—Oh, here it is. I hid it so well that I hid it from myself. Say, Lucy?

—Yessir.

—Would you like a little nip?

—Oh, no, sir. I don't drink at all.

—That's a shame. A nip never hurt anybody. There's nothing better than a good drink before lunch to get your food down.

—No, sir. It's for those who like it, sir.

—Whisky's a lot of fun, Lucy.

—I wouldn't know, sir.

—I like my whisky, Lucy.

—Papa, did you bring me something?

—Hunh? No, darling. I never bring you anything at noon. I'll bring you something tonight. Now, finish eating.

—What'll you bring me?

—Oh, that'll be your surprise. Aw, that was a good shot . . . Lily, finish eating. Say, Lucy, Lucy! Where'd she go?

—She's in the kitchen, Papa.

—Lucy!

—Yessir.

—What're you doing there in that kitchen?

—Putting the lamb chops on, sir.

—Sure you won't have a nip?

—No, sir. Thank you, sir.

—Too bad.

—I'm through now, Papa. Do I take my nap?

—Yes, right away. Lucy, come and put Lily to bed . . .

—Yessir. Come on, Lily. Go right into your room and get your dress off. That's it.

—You're going to play with Papa, Lucy?

—Shut up and take off those sandals.

—O.K.

—Lucy, did Lily obey you?

—Oh, yessir. Now, Lily, climb right into bed. That's it. Pull the blanket over you lightly. That's right. Now, take a nice nap. I'm closing the door.

—You sure know how to handle people, Lucy.

—Oh, I manage, Mr. Fairchild.

—Lucy, come on and have a drink with me.

—Never drink, Mr. Fairchild.

—Where're you going now?

—I've got to tend to the lamb chops, sir.

—Lucy, you're such an A-1 cook, I want to see how you do it.

—Just ordinary cooking, sir.

—Aw, Lucy. Huumnnnn . . .

—Take your hand away, Mr. Fairchild.

—Aw, come on.

—Take your hand off, Mr. Fairchild.

—Is your old man good to you, Lucy?

—Mr. Fairchild, you're going to make it impossible for me to work here.

—Lucy, I bet your old man's no good to you.

—Mr. Fairchild, don't touch me. Let me work.

—Gosh, you're cheeky. Not like Bertha, hunh? I just want to make you feel good.

—Take your hand away!

—Don't shout, Lucy. I'm only playing—

—If you touch me again, I'll grab you, Mr. Fairchild.

—Look who's threatening. You're going to grab me, hunh? Baby, that's just what I want. Aw, come on . . .

—I told you to stop.

—Goddamn, you're a strong bitch, eh? I can't hold you, hunh?

—Leave me alone, Mr. Fairchild!

—Goddamn, you're as strong as a man. Well, we'll see who's the stronger. I'll set my drink down and test you out, gal.

—Keep away, Mr. Fairchild.

—Damn, you've got guts. You're spry, like a spring chicken. Come here.

—I've got hold of your arm, Mr. Fairchild. If you move, I'll twist it!

—Goddamn, this nigger woman says she'll lick me. We'll see!

—Oooow! Mr. Fairchild, it's your fault. You made me push those dishes over.

—Keep still, Lucy. You're crazy if you think you can handle me.

—I'm warning you, Mr. Fairchild!

—Damn, if you're not like steel. Let my hands go. I'll teach you.

—Stop, Mr. Fairchild. I'll pick you up and throw you.

—Godammit, I dare you, I double dare you!

—I'm asking you once more to get away from me!

—You're a sassy nigger bitch, aren't you?

—Let me go, Mr. Fairchild. Your chops are burning!

—Papa, what's happening?

—Go back to bed, Lily!

—Oh, Papa's wrestling Lucy like he wrestled Bertha.

—Lily, I said go back to bed.

—Yes, Papa. But—

—Get away, Mr. Fairchild.

—I'm going to teach you a lesson, Lucy.

—Oh, Papa! You knocked the table over!—Oh, Lucy, you!—

—You black bitch, you hit me!

—Papa, you're hurt? Lucy, you knocked Papa down.

—I got you, Mr. Fairchild. I'll let you up if you promise to leave me alone.

—I'll get up from here and break your neck. Turn my hands loose! Turn me loose or I'll kick you in the stomach!

—Promise you'll leave me alone?

—O.K., Lucy. Let me up.

—You'll let me cook?

—Yeah. Let me up.

—There, Mr. Fairchild. Now, leave me alone.

—Lily, get back to bed.

—Yes, Papa. You're hurt, Papa?

—No. Goddamn, Lucy, I don't believe you're that strong. I'm coming after you.

—Mr. Fairchild, you're crazy. Stay away from me. I'll hit you!

—Haw. We'll see.

—I'm warning you. Stay away.

—Now, I got you!

—Turn me loose, Mr. Fairchild.

—Give up, Lucy.

—I'm telling you but once.

—Arrrrk! Jesus . . .

—Don't kill Papa, Lucy!

—I told you, Mr. Fairchild. Now, I'll hit you again if you— No, no! Turn my leg loose! If I hit you again, I'll knock you out.

—Naw, Lucy! Goddammit, you're as strong as a mule!

—Oh, there's Mama!

—Dave! Oh, my God! What's happening here?

—Mama, Papa's wrestling Lucy . . .

—Mrs. Fairchild, it's not my fault. Mr. Fairchild was drunk and he kept bothering me.

—You bitch! You're lying . . . Pay no attention to her, Anne.

—Mrs. Fairchild, he got drunk and kept making passes at me.

—You got drunk on my whisky, Lucy. It was you who kept—

—That's not true, Mr. Fairchild.

—I tried to get you off me and you scratched me . . . Anne, I swear, it wasn't my fault.

—Dave, oh, Dave . . . You drive me crazy! Every time I turn my back this happens! And you swore to me it'd never happen again! And I thought I could trust you, Lucy! I'm sick and tired of this! This is the end!

—Mama, don't cry . . .

—O.K., Anne. Send this bitch away, right now. Let's send her packing.

—No. Don't speak to me, Dave. I've got a better idea. Just wait.

—You see, Lucy. My wife saw what you were doing.

—You goddamn rotten white man.

—Lucy, get your damned things together and get the hell out of here. Be gone before my wife comes back in.

—O.K. I go. Let me pass—

—Aw, no! You're not getting off that lightly, Lucy.

—Aw, Mama's got a gun!

—Anne, put that gun down!

—Get out of my way, Dave. I ought to kill the both of you.

—Anne, I said put that gun down! Don't be a fool!

—Get out of my way, Dave. I'll be made a fool of no longer. For all I know, you might have sent this black bitch here to work . . . No wonder she came so early in the morning. Now, I'm going to kill her.

—Mrs. Fairchild, I didn't do anything. I swear before God. I couldn't. You don't understand.

—Yes. That Bertha said the same thing. Dave, get away. I'm going to shoot. I'll hit you, if you don't move!

—Anne, Anne, don't be a fool! Put that gun down!

—Stay away from me, Dave.

—Anne, give me that gun!

—No!

—I'll take it from you! Oh, God! No, no . . . Anne, you shot her . . .

—Mama! Papa, Lucy's been killed . . .

—Go away, Lily! Don't go near your mama.

—Oh God . . . Dave, what did I do? I shot her . . . Oh, Dave, it's all your fault. You promised you'd never let me find you doing that again. Now, I've killed somebody. Oh, Lord! Dave, you made me do it. I'm sure I've killed her.

—Mama, there's blood on the floor . . .

—Anne, drop that gun.

—I want to kill myself . . . Dave, you've spoiled my whole life . . . I'll kill us all . . . Then my misery is over . . .

—Anne, drop that gun! Don't pull that trigger again. You'll hit me or Lily if you do!

—Here, Dave . . . Take the gun . . . Oh, God, Dave . . . Look what you made me do! You've driven me crazy with your drinking . . . What can I do now?

—Anne, get into your room. Take Lily with you. We've got to talk. We're in trouble now.

—Mama, don't cry. Please, Mama . . .

—Dave, is she dead?

—I don't know . . . Lily, stop crying. Listen, Anne . . .

—Oh, Dave . . . What can we do? I want to kill myself . . . They'll take me to jail, won't they?

—Oh, Jumping Jesus . . . Anne, get hold of yourself and listen. I'm sorry. Honey, I was only fooling around.

—But, Dave, you promised me . . .

—I started drinking this morning. I didn't know what I was doing.

—You always say that.

—Mama, is Lucy dead?

—Hush, Lily. Anne, we must call a doctor. We've got to do something.

—Oh, God. I guess so. This is the end for me. Dave, see if she's dead.

—I'll call Burt Stallman. He's your brother-in-law. He's our friend. Maybe he can advise us. A bullet wound has to be reported. Perhaps he'll find a way out for us, hunh? I'll call now. I'll dial . . .

—See if she's dead first, Dave.

—No. I'll phone Burt.

—Dave, I'm so sorry, but it's all your fault. I didn't mean to shoot her.

—Hush, Anne. Sh, Lily . . . That you, Burt? This is Dave speaking. Listen, Burt, you've got to get over to the house at once. Something awful has happened. I can't say it over the phone. Somebody's hurt bad. You got to come and help us. We're in trouble. Somebody's been shot, Burt. Yeah. It's a woman. A colored maid. She's bleeding. It just happened. I shot her, Burt. She's lying on the kitchen floor. I don't know if she's dead or not. Yes, Anne's all right. Sure. Lily's fine. You're coming right away? Good. Thanks, Burt. Ohhh . . . Anne, he's on the way. I told 'im I shot her, Anne.

—No, Dave. We must tell 'im the truth. If you don't, I will.

—Honey, let me handle this. It's all a mistake.

—Mama, is Lucy dead?

—Dave, see if she's still breathing.

—O.K., stay here, both of you.

—Mama, why did you kill her?

—Oh, Lily, I'm so sorry that you have to see and hear all of this. But it's not poor Mama's fault. If I get you out of this, I'm taking you and we're going far, far away. Er, ooaww . . .

—Anne, she seems in a bad way. She's still lying there and there's blood all over the kitchen floor.

—Oh, God . . . I hope she doesn't die . . . Dave, what happened to your hands?

—Oh, that gal scratched 'em. I hadn't noticed . . .

—Dave, how could you do this to me? I want to die . . . I should've shot myself, rather than that poor fool of a gal!

—Take it easy, Anne. Look, I did the shooting, see? I'll take the blame. I found her stealing and I asked her to halt. She ran. I shot her.

—No, no. I won't lie, Dave. I've been lying for you for years. Now, I stop, no matter what happens.

—Anne, don't be a fool. Let's get our story straight. We can depend on Burt to help us. Now, look, I shot her, see?

—I won't lie again, Dave. I shot her, I killed her . . .

—Anne, maybe one of us'll have to go to jail. I'll go. Then you look after Lily.

—Oh, God, I don't know. I want to die. You made me murder. I ought to have shot you, you fool! You rotten, low-down fool! You drunk—

—Sh. Here's Burt. Anne, remember, I shot her, see?

—Hy, Anne. Hy, Dave. Hey, what's going on?

—Come in, Burt. So glad you came. Look, we caught the maid stealing, see? I shot her . . .

—My God!

—It's a lie, Burt. *I* did it.

—Shut up, Anne.

—But where's the maid?

—She's lying on the kitchen floor, Burt.

—Let's take a look at her. Stay here. I'll do it. This is serious.

—Anne, why in hell can't you let me handle this?

—I'm not going to lie, Dave.

—Mama, will we all go to jail?

—Don't talk, Lily.

—Anne, forgive me. I was drunk. I didn't know what I was doing.

—Don't talk to me, Dave.

—Mama, is Lucy dead?

—We don't know, Lily. Be quiet, darling.

—Sh. Here comes Burt.

—I'm phoning my office to bring material for a blood transfusion.

—Is she hurt bad, Burt?

—Don't really know, Anne. There's been a terrific loss of blood.

—O.K., Burt. Do what you can for her. But remember I shot her.

—Er . . . You shot *her?*

—Yeah, Burt.

—Why, Dave?

—It's a long story, Burt. But try to save her.

—He's lying, Burt. I shot her. And I'll tell why in any court-
room.

—Aw, Anne, keep your mouth shut! Let me do the talking
here, will you!

—Listen, you all . . . Let me attend to that transfusion.
Stay here. I must talk to you. I don't understand this . . .

—Will she die?

—Don't know, Anne. Maybe not, if we work fast.

—Thank God. If anybody deserves to die, it's me.

—Anne, I beg you to keep quiet. I'll handle this.

—Dave, don't talk to me!

—Come in.

—Anne, Burt, the transfusion has been given.

—Is she living? Will she pull through?

—Er . . . The patient has a chance.

—Where is she?

—I put the patient on your living-room couch.

—Burt, what do we do now? Remember it was all my fault.
Anne had nothing to do with shooting her . . .

—Don't lie, Dave! Burt, I shot her—

—Listen, I must ask you two a few questions.

—Yeah. I'm responsible, Burt. Not Anne.

—Where did you find this servant?

—She came this morning in response to an ad we put in the
paper.

—Had either of you ever seen her before?

—No.

—Oh, Burt . . . Listen, I wouldn't put it past Dave to have
asked her to come here for that job. He wants a black mistress.
Aw, maybe that was why she came so early.

—Anne, don't be a goddamn fool! Shut your mouth!

—Listen, Burt . . . It's no longer a secret. Dave has been
drinking. For ever so long . . . We can't keep a maid because
of it.

—Anne, for God's sake. Think of our child . . .

—Let me talk, Dave.

—Stop, both of you. This is far more complicated than you think. The bullet wound is not so serious. A flesh wound in the thigh. A great loss of blood, but, with care, the patient will be all right.

—Thank God.

—You see, Anne, everything'll be all right.

—But there's something wrong here . . .

—What do you mean, Burt? Give it to us straight. Anne and I can take it. I'm responsible for everything that's happened.

—Well, did you, for some reason, *make him wear that dress?*

—What are you talking about, Burt?

—I don't understand, Burt.

—Didn't you know that . . . that . . . Well, hell, dammit, it's a man you shot.

—Good God, Burt! What are you talking about?

—Burt, I don't get you.

—Who shot that servant is up to you two. But what I'm trying to tell you is that your female servant is a man wearing a woman's dress.

—You're kidding.

—No, Dave. This is straight.

—Lucy is a man?

—Yes, Anne. A man.

—Ooww!

—Don't scream, Anne. Good God, Burt, is this true?

—It's true. He admits it.

—Oh, Dave . . . How is that possible? Aren't you mistaken, Burt?

—Ha, ha. Look, I'm a doctor. The most elementary thing I know is the difference between a man and a woman. That servant lying in your living room is a man—

—Oh, that is why she was so scared this morning in the bathroom . . .

—What're you saying, Anne? Was he with you in the bathroom?

—She . . . he . . . She was sweating, trembling . . .

—Jesus! This makes it simple . . . Did he bother you, Anne?

—Anne, Burt, listen . . . I've got it solved. It's simple. This nigger put on a dress to worm his way into my house to rape my wife! Ha! *See?* Then I detected 'im. I shot 'im in self-defense, shot 'im to protect my honor, my home. That's our answer! I was protecting white womanhood from a nigger rapist impersonating a woman! A rapist who wears a dress is the worst sort! Any jury'll free me on that. Anne, that's our case.

—Anne, did this man molest you in any way in that bathroom?

—No, Burt. I'm tired of lying. No, he didn't touch me. If she is a man, she was scared to death, could barely move. Oh, I see it all now . . .

—What?

—That's why she was so scared . . . I told her to wash my back and she could scarcely—

—Then he did touch you! Burt, here's our defense!

—No, Dave. I'll not lie about this. You can't make me lie.

—Burt, can we find a way of keeping this quiet? Anne won't help me to do this thing right. Help us to get out of this. You're our friend. This scandal'll ruin me at the bank.

—I'm a doctor. Normally, I'm required to report things of this sort.

—But, Burt, this is kind of in the family, see?

—But suppose he reports that he was shot, Dave? Where does that leave you, and me, and Anne?

—Of course, Burt. You must report it.

—Anne, goddammit, keep your damned mouth shut! Burt, this nigger came into my house under false pretenses.

—That's true.

—And I defended myself against him!

—Dave, listen. I'm only a doctor. If this man talks to the police, then you're in a scandal. And I'm in trouble because I failed to report a gunshot wound. See?

—Burt, talk to 'im. Find out why he's running around in a woman's dress.

—You want me to try and make a deal with 'im?

—Right. Do that. See how he reacts.

—No, Burt. I'll not lie.

—Shut up, Anne. Let Burt see what he can do.

—O.K., you two stay right here. But, listen, this means my career if it gets out that I did not report it, see?

—Rely on us, Burt.

—Anne, for Christ's sake, stop sobbing like that. Bear up and help me to bail us out of this jam.

—Dave, it's all such a sordid mess. That's all my life's been with you. I don't want to pretend any longer.

—Mama, I'm scared. Will the police come for us?

—Hush, Lily. I wish I had somebody to take you away from all this.

—If you stopped crying, Lily'd be all right, Anne. Burt's doing all he can for us.

—Settle it any way you like, Dave. But I'm not going to lie if anybody asks me any questions. I'M TIRED OF LYING!

—Anne, honey, I'll never touch another drop of whisky.

—You've said that a thousand times, Dave.

—This time I mean it, so help me God.

—Mama, will Lucy die?

—No, thank God.

—Mama, why did you shoot her?

—Lily, don't ask poor Mama any more questions, please . . .

—No, Lily. The police are not coming for anybody. Lucy is all right. Papa was just playing. Anne, stop being morbid with the child.

—Papa, Uncle Burt's knocking at the door.

—Come in, Burt.

—Well, I've tried. Don't know if it'll work or not. Now, you two sit down and listen to me. I don't know if I'm a good judge of character or not. Now, I've talked to this boy. He seems straight, if a man wearing a dress can be described as straight. Now, here's the story he tells me and he tells it in a way that makes me believe 'im. It seems that his wife has just had a baby. He was out of work. The wife could not work because she was sick. They were about to lose their home. He was desperate. He saw your ad. He put on his wife's dress, her shoes, took her purse, assumed her name, and came here. Then this happened.

—But he violated the law when he did that, Burt.

—True, Dave. But you said that you didn't want any publicity, didn't you? Anne says that she's not going to say that he bothered her.

—Right, Burt. I won't lie.

—O.K., Burt. I'm reasonable. Burt, what would that nigger take to forget all this?

—I've already asked him that. He says if you pay his doctor's bill and give him two hundred dollars, he'll forget it. That is, if Anne doesn't wish to prefer charges against him.

—I don't. He did not touch me.

—Burt, will that nigger sign a paper to that effect? Will he accept two hundred dollars for being shot?

—He's signed it. Here it is. But I'll not give you this paper unless you give me your check.

—Hell, yes. Right now. I'll write it out. See, Anne? It's all over.

—It's not over for me.

—Aw, honey, don't be like that . . . Here, Burt, give 'im that check and get 'im out of the house, quick. That settles it, hunh?

—Right. But he insists on borrowing a suit of your clothes to go home in. He can't walk. His suit is hidden in his coal house.

—Oh, O.K. Give 'im something from my clothes closet. But get 'im out of here quick.

—Right. Be right back, in about an hour. I'm taking him to his house.

—Thank God, Burt. Anne, it's all over. Baby, forgive me. I'm sorry.

—Dave, I can't go on like this.

—Aw, hell, Anne. Come on; be a sport.

—I've been a sport for eight years with you. I'm tired. This is the end.

—Anne, darling, I need your sympathy now. We weathered it. Everything came out all right. Think of the danger you were in with a nigger man wearing a dress in the house.

—Nothing's all right, Dave. I'm going to my mother. I'm taking Lily.

—Anne, you just can't leave me like that.

—I'm leaving, Dave.

—No, oh, God, no, Anne. Don't say that.

—I can't help it, Dave.

—If you leave me, I'll get plastered and stay plastered for a month.

—Oh, Dave.

—Say you'll stay, Anne.

—Oh, God . . . I'll have to stay, I guess.

—Good girl. I'll change. You'll see. Sh. Look, there's Burt leading that nigger to his car. He looks pretty weak to me. Hope he doesn't die. There. They're driving off. Thank God, it's over, Anne.

—It's not over for me, Dave. Not as long as you drink, it'll never be over.

—Baby, I swear I'm on the wagon from now on.

—You always say that.

—Who is it?

—Open the door. We've got your husband here.

—Oh, God! What happened? CARL! CARL! You're sick . . .

—Now, Lucy, take it easy. I'm all right.

—You're hurt. What happened?

—You'd better get your husband in bed right away. He's been wounded.

—Who did it? How'd it happen?

—He'll tell you about it. First, let's get him to bed.

—Come in, come in.

—Oh, Papa.

—Hi, Henry.

—You're sick, Papa?

—No, Henry. Just hurt a bit. Nothing to worry about.

—Right through that door, sir.

—O.K. Now, let's ease him onto the bed. That's it. O.K., boy?

—I'm all right.

—Have you any pain?

—No, sir.

—Now, keep in bed for at least a week. And if you get any temperature, have your wife phone me, see?

—Yes, sir.

—Now, my friends are depending upon you to do what you promised. I'll come whenever it's necessary. You'll be up and about soon.

—Yes, sir. Thank you, sir.

—If you can't sleep, then here's some pills. Take one every two hours.

—Thank you, sir.

—I'll pass by and take a look at you tomorrow.

—Yes, sir. Thank you, sir.

—And, boy, never do that again. This time you were lucky.

—No, sir. It'll never happen again. Lucy, go to the door with the doctor.

—Yes, Carl. Do we owe him anything?

—You owe me nothing. Just keep your husband quiet.

—Yes, sir.

—You feel better, Papa?

—Sure, Henry. I'm fine. How're you?

—All right, Mama was crying—

—I know. How's the baby?

—She's sleeping, Papa. Are you hurt bad, Papa?

—No. It's nothing, son. Have you been helping Mama?

—Sure. We—

—Carl, I *told* you not to do it.

—What did Papa do, Mama?

—It's none of your business, Henry. Now, Carl, what happened?

—Listen, Lucy, don't ask me any questions. I'm not going to tell you anything. I'm all right. Everything's all right. Look. Here's the money to pay for the house. Our problem's solved. Two hundred dollars.

—Oh, God! But, Carl, where'd you get it from?

—It's a gift.

—You robbed something or somebody? You can tell me . . .

—No, no. Lucy, for once, I'm asking you not to ask me any

questions. I gave my word I wouldn't talk. So don't ask me anything. In the morning, you take that check to the bank and get it cashed.

—I don't understand.

—You don't need to. The house is saved. We can eat.

—What did you do?

—I said not to ask me anything!

—But the police will come for you!

—No, they won't.

—I knew something bad would happen when you left—

—Nothing bad's happened. I just hurt my leg, that's all.

—But how did you hurt it? Where? When?

—Lucy, shut up now.

—Did you really wear my dress?

—Er, yeah. But forget that.

—Then where is it?

—Oh, I don't know. I lost it—

—What happened?

—Stop hammering at me, honey. I'll buy you another dress.

—Carl, is this check real? Is it good?

—It's as good as gold. Now, what are you crying for? Aw, Lucy . . . Now, Henry, stop that bawling. Look, you've gone and awakened the baby and she's crying too. Goddammit, everybody's crying. Stop! I tell you, stop! Aw, Lucy . . . Goddammit, I can't help but cry too if all of you are crying . . . Oooouaw . . .

—I'm sorry, Carl. Henry, see about the baby and stop crying. We'll make Papa sick like that.

—Y-yessum, Mama.

—Carl, why did somebody give you two hundred dollars?

—I worked for it.

—Cooking?

—Lucy, it was all kinds of work.

—In a home?

—Yeah.

—The wife was there?

—Lucy, don't ask me any more questions!

—Was she pleased with your work?

—Oh, hell, Lucy! Yes, yes! Everybody was pleased! . . . That's why I got those two hundred dollars! Now, stop questioning me.

—Well, if you don't want to tell me, what can I do? But there's one thing I know: wearing that dress got you into trouble, didn't it?

—Yep. In a way, yeah.

—Carl, never—Promise me you'll never do anything like that again.

—Ha, ha, Lucy, you don't have to ask. I was a woman for almost six hours and it almost killed me. Two hours after I put that dress on I thought I was going crazy.

—But, Carl, I warned you. It's not easy for a man to act like a woman.

—Gosh, Lucy, how do you women learn it?

—Honey, it's instinct.

—Guess you're right. I didn't know it was so hard.

—Carl, never let me see you in a dress again. I almost died when I awakened and found you gone.

—You don't have to beg me, darling. I wouldn't be caught dead again in a dress.

—I was on the verge of going to the police to tell 'em.

—Oh, God! Glad you didn't do that.

—Mama, Tina's crying for her bottle.

—Carl, you could've been killed.

—Lucy, now don't go crying like that again!

—Papa, why is Mama crying so?

—Henry, don't you go crying now. Aw, God! The whole bunch of you are crying . . . Lucy, Henry . . . Aw, Christ, if you all cry like that, you make me cry . . . Oooouuwa!

ALICE WALKER

The Temple
of My Familiar

"**M**y father was not so gay as my mother," Mr. Hal said.
"She was all the time laughing; giggling really. She
just couldn't help it. Everything was funny to her. Over my
daddy's head, though, there was always a cloud. Now you might
not want to believe this, but you do live in California, after all. I
read the newspapers from time to time, so I know that a lot of
the men who go with other men are dying. Every time I read
about it I think of my father, because I think he would have
been glad. He was not an evil person—don't get me wrong—but
he just hated that kind of person and that was the only kind of
person I ever heard him express any hatred of. Even about white
people in general he never carried on the way he would about
'funny' men. While he was on his deathbed himself, he told me
why.

"He grew up on the Island on a plantation that was owned by
some white folks from the mainland and run by a black overseer.
This wasn't slavery time—the slaves had been legally freed a
long time ago—but it seemed a lot like it, the way things were
still being run. Anyhow, on some holidays like Christmas and
Easter and always during the summer, these white people came

out to their place on the Island. It was cooler on the Island in summer, much more pleasant than on the mainland. They'd sail over on their yacht—they were rich people—and bring everybody from the house on the mainland: the cook, the maids, the horse handler, even the gardeners. My father used to work for them as odd jobber and gofer, and he used to help unload the yacht, and they paid him in oranges, which we almost never had on the Island and which were the taste equivalent of gold. Anyhow, these people had a son, Heath, and he began to tag along with my father. The two boys liked each other right away, but it chafed my father that he always had to stay in his place. Heath had the run of my father's house, for instance, and during the summers would often eat there, right in the kitchen with the rest of them, but my father, whose name was David, by the way, after little David in the Bible, could never get closer to Heath's house than the back doorsteps. If you were black and you didn't work in the house, you weren't permitted. That's just the way it was.

"Heath's father and mother seemed cordial with each other rather than warm, and neither of them talked much to Heath. Still, the father seemed glad that Heath and my father were friends; the mother never appeared to notice it. She drank.

"Heath and my father were boyhood friends, seeing each other for holidays and summers, for many years. Then Heath went off to college and my father married. Eventually Heath also married, and he and his wife came to settle on the Island in the big house that Heath loved and that now belonged to him through his parents. My father was happy enough in his marriage. I don't know that he ever expected any kind of skyrockets from it. On the Island you married young, you raised a mess of kids, you and your family worked hard, you ate and slept and worshiped as well as you could. You died. That was about it. And that was plenty to most people. Excitement? The stories and rumors you heard about other people, way over there on the mainland, was your excitement.

"Having Heath around again and for good was exciting, and as well as they could manage it, now that they were more than ever unequal in the eyes of society and the law—in other words, they were grown men—they carried on their friendship. Heath, though, had started to drink, and he really didn't like black people. He was one of those whites who, drunk, would say to a black person he had his arm around: 'You know, So-and-so, I don't like nigras, but I like you!' So you can imagine how this so-called friendship between him and my father had to walk that fine line between anger and fear. Naturally my father hated Heath's racism. Just as he feared him as a white man, even as they laughed and joked together. My father had no idea—and I don't think Heath himself knew—that Heath was drawn to him in love. I mean love of that most peculiar kind. It was an understanding that sort of crept up on them both, I imagine, as they saw how much time Heath put in at our house, and how much he and my father, in spite of everything, enjoyed it.

"I can even remember him. A heavyset, stocky, rather than fat, red-faced guy, with his high color sometimes seeming to come and go in his face. Hair that bleached almost white in the sun. Substantial teeth and a minty breath. A Teddy Roosevelt sort of guy.

"It was Heath who encouraged my father to get out of farm laboring and become a furniture maker. He'd seen and admired the things my father carved in his spare time: mostly toys and the children's beds and cradles. I don't think he could bear seeing his friend working in the fields like a slave. He didn't care about the rest of the people, you understand; he thought that working like slaves on his plantation was no more than they deserved. But not David, with his thoughtful expression and always pregnant wife and his houseful of barefoot kids. He helped my father build a shop and bought the very first pieces he made, a table and some chairs. He found a market for my father's work on the mainland, and we lived very well. Much better than we had on stoop labor, digging potatoes and picking beans.

"He wanted my father.

"Even on his deathbed this was a hard concept—no joke meant—for my father to get ahold of. It was curious, too, how no matter what words he found to tell me about the situation, they always made me laugh. Even he was finally able to laugh, a hollow cackle though it was. He wasn't laughing at Heath, but at this possibility of a way of life that just seemed totally out of the realm of nature to him. Two men together, like a man and a woman? It was just too much. What would my father have made of San Francisco?

"The long and short of it is, the friendship was soon ruined. There was nowhere for any of their best feelings about each other to go. They couldn't even sit down at a hot-dog stand somewhere to discuss the problem. They would have been arrested just for that. Heath became more drunken, nigger-hating, and sullen. He talked a lot about how his father had treated him as a boy, ridiculing and beating him for being slow to understand things said to him and slow to learn to read. He spoke of this to explain his ability to understand how 'the nigras felt,' but what it really seemed to explain was why he so often tried to make those he knew feel as bad as he'd once felt himself. Around him, my father retreated into what he called his old-time know-nothing niggerisms. Scratching his head and muttering under his breath. 'Feelin' like a damn fool.' And of course you realize he called him 'Mr. Heath' from the time they were in their teens. But my father's pretense of ignorance did not protect him. One day Heath came into the shop, and before my father knew anything he was being hugged drunkenly and, as he put it, 'cried on from behind.' My father felt pretty safe, though, because he could see my mother and some of the children playing a few yards away from the open door. Heath had been drinking heavily and fighting with his wife. It would soon blow over. It always did. My father would make coffee, lay on an ice pack, and scramble up something for Heath to eat. But this time, maybe because my father felt so safe, he really let himself feel the weeping body draped around him. Let himself feel the misery and feel the shame. Maybe he felt the love. Anyway, without ever dreaming it was possible, and looking down at himself as if someone had stuck a stick up his pants leg while he wasn't looking, he responded to Heath, who had begun to fondle him.

"It was a moment that changed his life. Without understanding how it could be possible, my father wanted to be wanted by this man holding on to him, and he wanted to want. He says he saw my mother through the door and called to her, but his voice was so weak it didn't carry. Then, a few minutes later, as if she felt something was wrong, and he was in trouble, she started briskly toward the door herself. Heath, caressing my father and feeling his response, watched my mother approach, over my father's shoulder, and said, 'Tell her not to come in.' Which my father did.

"He was never the same person after that. He was gloomy. He seldom smiled. He continued to see Heath, though, and I can still remember the sullen bitterness of the fights they had. Fights that were full of a few well-chosen cruel and cutting words, and much drinking. Because, with time, my father drank as much as Heath. Whenever my father read about a lynching of a black man by whites and that they'd cut off the man's privates and stuck them in his mouth, he said he understood the real reason why. Whether he ever did so or not, I'm sure this is something he must have wanted to shout at Mr. Heath. That he understood there was something of a sexual nature going on in any lynching.

"For the rest of his life he hated anything he thought was gay. He detested art, and the carvings by which he made his living he eventually did with disgust. He was the perfect carver for the heavy barbarous furniture that became the rage during that period before the Great War. His carved lions were snarling, his griffins were biting, his ravens were shrieking. Claws and teeth and drops of blood were everywhere. The stuff made me shudder as a child, and my mother failed to find in it anything to encourage her famous giggle, but white people bought it; pretty soon, black people did, too. It appeared even in the houses of poor people right there on the Island. Generally they liked their furniture and everything else to be straightforward and simple; God only knows what they really thought of it.

"My father hated my painting. It made him think there was something wrong with me. All my life he tried to keep me from doing it. When Heath finally died, of a heart attack, my father, the only black person permitted at the funeral, was still bitter. My mother, generally merry to the last, never acted as though she knew anything about any of this, beyond the fact that Heath was a nice if drunken white man that liked her husband, David, and sometimes ate dinner—which he always praised—at our house.

"My father wouldn't have cared if the plague killed off all the gays in the world. He hated Heath because Heath had forced him to look at the little bit of Heath there was in himself. Nobody had prepared him for that vision. Nor could he pretend he hadn't seen it. I've often thought of the battle my father must have had with himself when Heath was embracing him in the shop. What happened to him that day remained a burden on his soul. He died many unhappy years later of liver failure. There was a terrible smell, so terrible that painting over the old paint on his walls wasn't enough. After he died, we had to scrape the paint off the walls, and burn it, then paint the bare walls many times to cover it up. This stench, I felt, must be the rotten smell of that part of my father that he murdered and tried to bury away from other people and from himself.

"When I told Lissie about my daddy's prejudice against 'funny' men and hatred of that part of himself, and told her about what had happened that first time between him and Heath, the first thing she said was that my father had been treated like a woman; that was one of the reasons he felt so bad; and that the way he had responded only made him feel worse. His whole existence was compromised by what was happening, yet he could not prevent an erotic response. She also said he was wrong to think queers are unnatural. She said queers have been in every century in which she found herself—and she giggled when she said it—and claimed to have seen queer behavior even among the cousins, always the epitome of moral behavior where Lissie was concerned. One of them, she claimed, not only taught her *how* to dress, but *to* dress."

Heartache

BROOKE M. STEPHENS

❧

Just Friends

June 7, 1980

Pouring rain, and I left my umbrella on the subway. A whole damn morning and $45.00 for a fresh cut, wash, and set almost wasted. I waited in a storefront for it to let up, and in a couple of minutes this not too tall, pleasant-looking young brother in a bright blue dashiki and thick glasses came along, carrying a big umbrella. A congenial face, sort of a preacher-in-training type from down home. He didn't look like he was in a hurry. I did my black Scarlett O'Hara number, all smiles and breathless, and waved him over and told him right off that no, I didn't know him, but if he didn't mind, I wanted him to do me a big favor if it wasn't too much trouble and walk me home, please. After I got silly enough to bat my eyelashes, I offered to pay him.

He gave me a weird look like maybe I was crazy and speaking Sanskrit or Urdu. I was ready to say to hell with it when this strange sound came out of his mouth like something between a hyena's howling and a kid's giggle. He said yes, took my arm, and asked me which way. By the time we got to my door, I found out he was from Savannah and his name was Dr. Melvin Patterson— deep emphasis on the doctor part. Then came this very convo-

luted explanation about how his father used to tease him about
being tiny and one day he would grow up to be monster-size like
Dino, the dino, so all his friends call him Dino, and I could too.
Okay, whatever that's supposed to mean! So "Dr. Dino" is a
shrink, clinical psychologist (he made a big deal out of that); he
teaches at Brooklyn College and sees some patients and groups
at a clinic in Cobble Hill. He's just left his wife, a social worker,
in New Jersey after six years of mutual misery—sounds like one
of those we-had-to marriages. Has a six-year-old daughter,
Jamila. I bit my tongue to keep from telling him that that was
Arabic, not African, like most of those phony African-sounding
names everybody is giving their children these days. After working in West Africa, I knew no authentic African would recognize
it. He looked harmless (but so did the Boston Strangler, stupid!),
so I gave him my phone number and invited him back for tea
one day.

June 15, 1980

Dino called and stopped by to take me up on tea. I almost said
no but decided to explore the possibility. He wasn't boring. At
least he didn't come up with that same tired line black men use
about me fixing dinner. He's not much bigger than I am, and
with all my dance classes and working out at the gym, I could
demolish him with a quick knee to the groin if I had to. But I
didn't have to. Any ideas he had about getting seductive evaporated when the thick odor of my incense hit him and he saw the
small *puja* with Baba's picture and the flowers on the mantel-
piece.

He spent three hours asking about Siddha yoga—my pagan
heathenism, as Mother calls it; what it is like to have a guru, how
meditation works, how long had I been studying and teaching
meditation, what is my mantra and why isn't it a secret like in
TM, and how soon could he meet Baba? I couldn't get rid of
him till I promised to take him up to the ashram. Damn! I've
heard Baba say that when the seeker is ready the teacher appears, but this is the first time I've seen somebody get hooked so
fast. Maybe he's the right one to answer a halfhearted wish to

find somebody to fill the vacancy in my own life, but after Michael, Greg, Glen, David, and Bob, I ain't looking for nobody no more. If God wants me to get married again he's gonna have to put his foot on my neck, grab me by the hair, and say, This one over here—and I'll still ask him, Are you talking to me? Maybe I'll introduce Dino to Sharon. He's just the kind of nice, educated, civilized southern black boy Mother would like as a son-in-law. We'll see. I've been celibate so long, I've lost interest in anything that'll turn into a complicated emotional mess just for the sake of an orgasm.

June 23, 1980

Took Dino up to South Fallsburg, and he fell in love with the whole routine, especially the Indian vegetarian thing. Now he wants to go up every weekend, loves the idea of jumping out of bed at four in the morning, chopping vegetables, working in the garden, and especially sitting, rock still, in the meditation hall for two hours. He said it was the only time his mind was clear enough to know what really mattered to him. That's what it's all about, really. Finding that one clear moment when your existence makes sense and you begin to understand why the cosmos works the way it does, how you fit into it, and how, even when you don't understand everything, the world is really a perfect place just the way it is. I'm happy for him that he got it and I could show him how to get there. This might develop into something yet. At least he's got some sensitivity and is willing to explore deeper issues where his definition of self doesn't start and end with his dick.

July 13, 1980

Dino invited me to his place in Fort Greene for Sunday dinner and to show off how he could cook. He can't believe that I don't even bother. Any man can win my heart by turning on the grill, and I'll pull up a chair and applaud. He's got a nice big floor-through with a view of Washington Park, which looks more like a war zone after a race riot. This is my first time out of Brooklyn

Heights to that side of Flatbush Avenue since I've been in New York.

He's got thirty-seven unopened boxes in his living room, so I thought he'd just moved in but he said he's been there since last year. Says he's waiting for the little elves who leave the dust bunnies under the bed to take them away. But he's not sure if he's going to stay in NYC much longer, so he'll just leave them in the middle of the floor like that. This boy has a problem. His uncle Alex from Philly came by. He calls Dino "Teddy." Dino, Dr. Patterson, Melvin, Teddy—how many names does this guy have? A shrink with an identity problem! Put a red flag on this play, honey. I am not going through any more of that "getting him ready for the next woman" thing I did last year with Sam E. after his divorce. Men just are not acceptable human beings for the first two years after they leave somebody, no matter whose fault it is. Seems like a nice guy, but I smell some complicated shit underneath and I don't want to know about it. Too bad, 'cause he's kind of cute, but he'll have to find his healing mother someplace else. For now, I think I'm better off if we're just spiritual buddies and hang out together at the ashram or the meditation center.

July 27, 1980

Dino and I went to the Wednesday-night program at the ashram, and he got off the train at Clark Street to walk me home. The soft night air, the crowd on the promenade, the lights on the water—a relaxing picture that needed no conversation and nothing else to be a pleasant end to a fulfilling evening. We didn't need to talk to enjoy each other's company. The quiet comfort of his presence was enhanced by a strong connection in our silence.

August 10, 1980

Sunday morning. Dino called to say he's taking a job teaching at Egg Harbor City State College in South Jersey (where the heck is Egg Harbor City?), and did I know if there were any Siddha yoga meditation centers in South Jersey. I went over to say good-bye and met his daughter, this being a daddy's weekend. She's his kid, alright. Same nose, eyes, and forehead. She got silent and possessive real quick, trying to figure out where I fit in. I told her we're just friends—which is true—but what does that mean to a six-year-old? Two of his army buddies from Vietnam—he never told me until now that he was a medic and a lab technician in Saigon—Joe Somebody and Phil Whoever, were there hauling stuff down to a truck. Before I left he told me he was having his thirty-eighth birthday on September 29 and since I was too far away to come to the party, all cards, gifts, and money could be sent to his new address. So he's a Libra and a shrink, which is a contradiction in terms in itself. Maybe that's why he's nuts—one side of him analyzes everything, trying to make it neat and orderly and precise, and the other side feeds on free-floating anxiety and the chaos of the mind. I'm a Capricorn, so we're supposed to have some kind of earth sign connection. Maybe that's why we get along so well. I'm going to miss having him around.

September 17, 1981

I finally had to write him and send a birthday card, since I misplaced the phone number and he disconnected the old phone and left no forwarding number. Maybe he's going to Jersey to hide out from himself or to avoid bill collectors? He told me his wife left with a ton of credit card bills.

November 5, 1981

Thinking about Dino a lot today. I miss us coming home together from the ashram, taking long walks on the promenade, sitting and watching the Staten Island ferry and the tugboats and talking for hours about everything. It's so easy to talk to him, even though he's got some silly ideas about women or maybe he's just scared of them, but I've been celibate so long I feel safe with him, knowing I don't have to worry about having to fuck him to keep his friendship. Mostly we talk about meditation and what's behind the spiritual search, how that relates to the world around us as we experience it every day. What's the karma-destiny-cosmic meaning behind the situations we find ourselves in? Why did I meet him when I did? Did we have a past life together as man and wife? Is that why we feel so comfortable and trusting with each other now in this lifetime? He's got a thousand and one questions, and if nothing else, trying to answer him makes me examine what I think I know, but I'm not ready to tell him some of my deeper experiences. I wonder when I'll see him again.

November 29, 1981

I got a long Thanksgiving /Christmas / New Year's / Happy Birthday/how's-life-treating-you, here's-the-dirt-on-what's-been-happening-with-me letter from Dino. He finally included a phone number, and I called him for a good cursing out. In between me laughing and calling him a tacky turkey and him insisting that I was just trying to hide how much I miss him, all he did was give me that hyena laugh of his, and it was nice to hear it. I do miss him and the nights we would take a bottle of cheap red wine and paper cups down to the promenade and watch the sun go down. I brought him up to date on the new job at the bank, since I had stopped working in television. Then I told him about dating Mark C. When I told him Mark C. is white, he got nasty and said that maybe if I hadn't gotten so lazy and fat and took better care of myself I wouldn't have to settle for that. He evidently thinks going out with somebody white who treats me the way I want to be treated is settling for less.

He's beginning to sound like Mother, ready with some nasty comment every time I tell her about something new I am trying that I might enjoy. She finds some perverse delight in the failure of every project I undertake that doesn't meet her approval. Most of all she wishes I'd give up going to the meditation center and find my way back to Jesus, her form of Jesus—praise the Lord and send a check to Oral Roberts! And this woman wonders why I don't have a good relationship with her.

I ignored his nastiness, telling him he was just jealous since he had missed his chance to have me and asking him what I should do about Mother's meanness. He came back with one of his classic postmodern New Age shrinky-type Siddha yoga answers—"It's your karma to accept her the way she is and learn how to love her anyway, with all her faults." Why can't she accept me the way I am—with all my faults? I swear if nothing else, getting to know him makes me glad I decided to save the money and stop seeing my shrink.

January 8, 1982

Dino remembered my birthday (!) with a funny, silly card about turning thirty-three and still no kids! That was very sweet of him, but I can do without the reminder about getting old.

April 18, 1982

6:00 A.M. Sunday morning, and out of nowhere this fool calls me up with that ridiculous laugh of his, asking, "How come you ain't up with the sun and meditating, honey, or have you given up the spiritual path now that you finally got a man back in your bed again?" Nobody else could get away with talking to me like that! He's back in town, his old '74 Chevy died on him on the BQE in the rain, he's bored with South Jersey and coming back to his old teaching job at Brooklyn College and looking for an apartment again, could I help him with that? I told him about buying my uncle's old brownstone near his old neighborhood, and he was in luck if he wanted to take over the top floor. I can't believe I let him have the place so quick and so cheaply, but at least I know him and don't have to go through the tenant screening process. He at least tries to function from the same set of spiritual ethics, I think. Maybe living together will help us figure out what we mean to each other.

July 31, 1982

He's got animals and didn't tell me! A dog and a cat! And not just any old dog that fits in an apartment! A huge white Russian malamute named Tareshia and an ornery gray Russian blue cat—what's the deal with these Russian animals? I don't care how rare and sweet and quiet they are. They bark and smell, and the damn dog is bigger than I am. But I didn't have the heart to say he couldn't keep them here. We'll see.

August 10, 1982

He moved into the empty apartment on the top floor last weekend, hauling those same thirty-seven boxes again. He says they're all books. We had Sunday breakfast together. I cooked, since he can't find anything in the mess he brought with him. We picked up right where we left off, as if it had only been a day or two since our last conversation. It'll be so good to have him around to talk to again when I start getting my strange spiritual hits. Mark C. thinks the ashram is too creepy and wouldn't go there with me after the first time, so I don't see him anymore. He wanted me to choose between God and him. At least Dino doesn't think I'm nuts when I talk about past lives and karma and Shakti and prefering meditating to screwing. He showed me a stack of meditation books he's been reading for the past year, and we swapped stories about the little miracles we witness in our lives every day. Having him back also means I'll get back to being more vegetarian and save some money. It will be so comforting to have him around again. He gave me a referral for a teaching job at the College of New Rochelle. I can use the money. When I told him about breaking up with Mark C., he got such a satisfied smirk on his face I would have loved to slap it off. Now that I'm back into the sex game, maybe I'll think about fucking Dino (what am I saying?) and find out what he's really about, but he looks too small to be satisfying. He'd die, like any black man with the proverbial ego trip about his dick size and stamina, if I ever told him that dick size was not Mark C.'s problem.

August 31, 1982

It's like having my own resident shrink on the premises. I call him upstairs about anything, and the last few weeks we've been eating dinner together two or three times a week in his apartment. Neither one of us has a scintillating social life right now since I decided not to see Mark C. for a while, so we've become each other's dates/escorts even on weekends. Now everybody thinks we're sleeping together. I got that from two people at the meditation center. Since they know he lives in my house they think he lives with me, so we're having fun playing the miscommunication games—but I don't want to ruin a good friendship until I'm sure we have something that will last a lot longer than a good lay. He's teaching me healthy cooking. I can now make a decent curry when we get together on Sundays. A couple of Sunday mornings we've gotten together in my apartment to chant and meditate together. The house is beginning to feel more like a dormitory, instead of each of us living our separate polite lives at a distance. It's rather nice.

September 3, 1982

Mark C. called to say he missed me and would like to go out again. I said I'd think about it and see how I felt in a month or so. He thinks Dino and his friends are all gay. I don't agree, but what does he know? That's an issue that I can't think of right now. White men always come up with negative images of black men who don't act like them. So does this make me a fag hag if I like hanging out with them? Who gives a rat's ass if his friends are gay? They're interesting guys, and I like talking to them.

September 17, 1982

I've watched him up close enough now so I can catch him when his mind shifts from casual attentive friend into professional listening doctor. A body move, a tone of voice, a tilt of the head. When I told him how I got a look at his habits, he laughed and told me to stop paying such close attention, I might see something I don't want to see. The only strange habit I see so far is with the damn dog. He picks her up and hugs her like she's human sometimes!

September 29, 1982

I surprised Dino for his birthday with a big carrot cake with four huge candles, since he's turning forty. He had three guys over from his school for dinner. An interesting group but strange vibes. One showed off jewelry he makes and sells on the street, and one is into tailoring and is making a suit for Dino. And the other one, Malik or something African, just sat in the corner looking serious and silent and nodding to jazz. I left after an hour.

October 3, 1982

Baba died yesterday. I called Dino, Martin, Eric, Gena, and anybody else I could think of to come to the ashram for the chant before I sat in a corner and cried for the three hours. They all came and we sat together huddled on the floor, chanting, until two in the morning, when Martin gave us all a ride home. Nobody had anything to say; what's there to say when we all feel like God abandoned his children in the wilderness of New York? I feel so awful and lazy as a devotee. I put off going on to India twice because I didn't think I could take the intense Shakti and the heat of the place. God was offering absolution, but I was busy trying to get the new bathroom done. Now I feel like God died and left me with my life in a mess 'cause I was picking out tile when I should have been praying. I couldn't find my passport, anyway.

October 15, 1982

We've been meeting at the ashram every day after work. The chant has been going on round the clock for the last two weeks. The power of the music and the sweetly devoted voices are taking away some of the shock and grief. Now it's going to end tomorrow, and I feel like I'll lose my connection to a quiet space of comfort and wholeness I'd found inside. Dino is as quiet as everybody else, and for once he doesn't try to offer one of his pat little shrinky answers. I have to go to India now, but I just don't have the money. When has that ever stopped me before?

November 12, 1982

We worked out a deal. Dino is getting me a plane ticket to go to Bombay and charging it on his Amex account, and he will take $100 a month out of the rent to pay off the card. Blessings to the spirit that brought him to me.

December 2, 1982

I feel bad that Dino had to work and couldn't come to see me off. I couldn't have done this without him. I'll have to bring him something special.

April 5, 1983

Thank God he got my telex and met me at the airport. I'm happy it was him so I didn't have to talk. Four months in an Indian village and twenty-three hours on a plane—the last thing I want is some well-meaning motormouth with lots of mundane questions. He isn't shocked to see that most of my hair is gone; I shaved my head the month after I got there. Wearing white saris and getting up at 3:00 A.M. to sit in a cave and fast for a week made perfect sense to me as a lifestyle. Just getting off the damn plane (sorry, God, I swore I would stop cursing!) and walking through Customs made me want to run all the way back to Ganeshpuri if I could. The lights, the noise, such different people. New York is so clean compared to Bombay, but with a desperately unnecessary frenetic energy and otherworldliness in a wild kind of way, an electrified hell where everything works. We have the bizarre illusion that this is perfect, this is real, this insanity matters, it is the center of the universe, and it's all such an illusion. I'm too numb to ask or answer anything. Thank you,

God, that he was there to just hug me and get me out of there. I can't talk to anybody.

April 17, 1983

Jet lag. Ten time-zone changes. Feeling like I'm trying to keep myself separate from an atmosphere of free-floating anxiety. Two weeks of still waking up at 3:00 A.M. gazing into a candle flame, feeling like I'm roaming in the stars, losing touch with the world around me, blissfully absorbed in a space inside me that is unfathomable yet draws me in each morning and will not let me go. It has no name and no reason to explain itself. I still can't talk. I'm creeping around like an invalid. Dino is bringing food down to me, but I can't eat either. I finally unpacked and gave him the shawl and statue of Ganesh that I brought back for him. He makes it bearable to wake up in the morning when he knocks on my door and kids me about living like a yogic nun. The correct title would be monk—Hindus don't have nuns. I half listen while he chatters on about meeting somebody new and going to Jersey City for conjugal visits. How can anybody think about sex now?

April 20, 1983

My Divya Diksha day, the five-year anniversary of my spiritual initiation, the beginning of this inner struggle that makes me wonder whether I'm ready to be committed and whether anything in my life is real and of significance now. I still couldn't talk when I went upstairs to his apartment and sat on the floor in the kitchen watching him correct papers and pay bills. I finally tried to explain about the nameless space I had found inside, the hollow feeling of having touched something in me that I could not explain. He got what I meant about wondering if death was real, and the true meaning of love. Most relationships between people are emotional business deals where people strike wordless bargains fraught with impossible expectations and unspeakable anticipations—offering loyalty, fidelity, and a guarantee to laugh in all the right places at each other's tired stories and support each other's public lies in exchange for regular sex, credit cards, nice cars, fur coats, and maybe a house in the country. But we were lucky enough now to know better. I crawled into his bed just to be hugged for a while, and he let me stay and cry for an hour.

May 17, 1983

Called Mark C. to see how he was and asked if we could meet to talk, have dinner. He still has my letters from India and says he got so much insight from them about what the trip meant to me. I think I want to be back with him just to feel anchored to somebody, to get grounded in something simple. Trying to figure out anything in my life now—job, Mother, Dino—none of this is simple. Mark C. is simple, easy, uncomplicated, sort of shallow sometimes, but he's gentle and well-meaning and he cares about me and is willing to pay attention to my needs. I need someone to focus on bringing me back outside myself into the mundane outer world since this is where my life is supposed to be now.

June 2, 1983

Haven't seen Dino in a couple of weeks. He says it's summer school and he's got a second job to prepay Jamila's child support. He wants to go to India too. I warn him that his mind will be turned inside out when he gets back. I miss our dinners and the talks we used to have, but I'm busy too, with a new job at the bank and seeing more of Mark C. again.

July 5, 1983

We had a "Tar Beach" party on the roof last night to watch the fireworks. It was Mark C.'s idea, so I made him haul all the stuff up those narrow little steps. Dino brought this scuzzy-looking little tramp I never heard of named Gloria. She looks half his age, acts dumber than a housecat, and comes off like a real street creep from a bad neighborhood where he never should have been. She can't keep her hands off him, and he can't stop grinning at all the attention. When I asked what rock he found her under he reminded me that his conjugal life is none of my damn business. It must be some black middle-class guilt trip about not being some kind of ignorant thug that makes him need to get it on with a pitiful excuse for a woman like this. He told me I'm trying to undermine his manhood (what manhood? this stupid little fart doesn't seem to know what manhood is all about if the best he can do when it comes to women is this lobotomized child he's got hanging around his neck!) and not let him have any fun in life. We didn't speak to each other for the rest of the night. Mark C. still says he always thought Dino was gay, and I was offended at the suggestion, but I can't deny it struck a chord. This is the first time I have seen him with a woman in the years that I have known him. Maybe he's bi and can't make up his mind what he wants, which I think is truly the ultimate mind-fuck. It sounds like a great way not to commit to anybody but play around with everybody. Then who was he fucking in Jersey City? Maybe he's just experimenting with her to see if he still likes women. If he was really into women, he probably could have had me.

July 20, 1983

That pathetic little slut has a key to his apartment! Poor child parades in and out as if she belongs here. How can a man who spends three months studying the Mahabarata and gets high from reading Seth or Rilke or the Bhagavad Gita get turned on by some no-class hussy whose idea of a conversation is to vary the way she giggles? But what he's after doesn't require verbal communication. Mark C. tells me to stop interfering in Dino's life—it's none of my business, and men make different decisions according to which head they are thinking with at the time.

August 2, 1983

Dino avoids me now by putting notes under my door and leaving messages on the answering machine when I'm out. I truly do not understand men, and this one less than any. How long is it

going to take for him to get burned out on her? From the noises
I hear up there, it sounds like they're killing each other. But does
he care about the bad karma he's creating by hurting someone
who's too dumb to know how she's being used? He damn sure
isn't seeing her just to save her soul and teach her how to meditate. I guess that's what he wants—somebody who just lies there
and doesn't talk back.

August 13, 1983

Gloria seems to have faded from the scene, but now Dino wants
to sublet the apartment and go to India for nine months. Seems
he's got a sabbatical or leave of absence and his father left him a
few thousand, which he doesn't want his ex-wife to get her
hands on, so he wants to spend it on something educational and
enlightening. India qualifies for both. I think he's trying to
outdo me and come home more brain-fried than I was. I'm
happy for him. I wrote out a long list of all the places he should
go, shrines he should see, and places to stay. God, it would be
perfect if I could go with him. A trip like this could really bring
us back together, like we used to be. Rekindle the deeper trust
and affection we had when we first met, before we got involved
with other people.

September 16, 1983

The turkey went off to the airport and left my list and some
books and his traveler's checks in the hallway. Somebody better
meet him and take care of him. It'll take ten days for him to get
this stuff by mail. He thinks he's just going to Boy Scout camp.
Ha!

January 5, 1984

Dino remembered my birthday, even from Delhi, which is more
than Mark C. managed to do. I've gotten one letter from him so
far, and it sounds so sweet and familiar to hear about what it
feels like to be sitting on that stone floor eating with your fingers

off a banana leaf for a plate, watching the moon go down and seeing the sun come up while chanting the Vedic mantras with the Brahman priests in the temple courtyard. It takes me back to my own blissful space, where the supercharged world I'm stuck in now is totally out of place. Where the biggest events of the day are the mail delivery, dinner, and a smile from Gurumayi at the evening program. I know what he means, how it felt like the perfect thing to be doing then. Why couldn't we have worked it out to do the whole thing together? No, I guess God decided that we would just get in each other's way.

March 18, 1984

His second letter makes me know he is truly out there. He went off to that new swami that Baba had mentioned and sent some people to in Gujarat, near Yeola. Prakashananda. A smaller temple, really somebody's house, where twelve of them ate and slept together. He said it felt like back in the olden days with Jesus and the disciples on the side of a mountain where the tops of the mountain would appear and disappear, in and out of the clouds on a bright day. Like God was playing a now-you-see-it-now-you-don't game with them. I wish I had been there when the swami left him in a cave for three days to fast and meditate with only water, a papaya, and a chapati once a day. And how he had gotten to the edge of reality and turned back from the chance to break through to a new experience of reality on the side of the mountain, when the swami told him he was not pure enough yet to come any farther on the path with the older disciples and then disappeared in front of him into a white cloud. "Star Wars" games for real he calls it, with sudden insights outside of normal consciousness. Experiences he could not deny, but his mind would not accept so he ran away, back to Bombay for a night at the Oberoi Hotel and a few stiff shots of Jack Daniel's to clear away the pictures in his head. Yep, now he knows why I was a mental vegetable when I got home.

May 19, 1984

Dino got off the plane looking blissed out, burned out, and gone native, wearing white leggings and a Nehru cap, glasses still down his button nose. He has a new friend from Bombay named Hari Patel. They're both broke, so I let them stay in the empty room downstairs until the woman he sublet his apartment to can find another place. He's in no hurry to move back in since he doesn't have a job and can't pay rent. Yeah, he has that spaced-out culture-shock look on his face. He stayed in bed for a week staring at the ceiling and readjusting to being back. All I could do is laugh. I recognize my own brain-fried state of transition in him. It is so good to have him back again! But will he know who he is when he finally lands?

June 9, 1984

Dear God in heaven, help us. Hari is driving a cab to support them both. He's fresh off the plane from Bombay and already loose on the streets of New York in a taxi. At least he can read and speak English, but don't ask him to take you anyplace unless you have directions. They're both good cooks and have wonderful stories to tell about where they went, how they met, etc. I just wonder, how deep is this friendship? Indian men are the worst chauvinists in the world and have "special" relationships that appear to be homo as hell—icing women out completely. Hari comes upstairs and calls his wife twice a week, shows me pictures of her and his new baby, and gives me $20 every time he uses the phone. I don't think they're fucking. He and Dino are sharing the same bed, but are they having sex? Men and their relationships are too damn bizarre for me sometimes. If I was sick enough to care I would creep downstairs at night and listen at the door. Like Mark C. says, stay out of it, sweetie, and you won't get your feelings hurt!

July 21, 1984

Aunt Sarah died yesterday, and I was glad that Hari and Dino were around to comfort me and help me get prepared for the horror of having to go home and face my mother.

July 29, 1984

I came back from the funeral relieved to be back in New York, away from the cloying madness of my demented family. Hari is gone and Gloria, the poor thing, is back. Like Mark C. said, it's none of my business. Dino has no answer about why Hari left or what really happened for the four months I didn't hear from him while he bummed around South India. He also hasn't said anything about coming up to the ashram for a while. I'm going to the ashram for August to forget this mess, and Mark C. is coming with me for a week. I didn't tell him about Dino or what I think happened with him and Hari. I wish the two of them could be friends. They are like the bookends of my world, propping me up so I can get through life every day.

September 29, 1984

I deliberately ignored Dino's birthday this year.

November 4, 1984

We've fallen into a pattern of silence and avoidance, and I don't know why, but frankly, I don't care anymore. I've had it with this on-again, off-again friendship, where I do all the work. It makes me wonder what the hell he really wants. Why are we going through this growing separation? I don't think I have anything to apologize for. Or do I?

December 6, 1984

I made one last attempt to talk to him, to get past whatever this barrier is he's put up, and asked why we can't talk anymore, why is he changing so much? He bit my head off as if I was trying to mug him.

May 25, 1985

Dino announced that when his lease expires next month he will be moving back to Jersey. He has a new job as director of a juvenile shelter/clinic/treatment center in Newark and is teaching at Fairleigh Dickinson University. It's time for him to leave my house anyway. The silences are painful, his nastiness is getting worse, and I'm getting sick of pretending not to see and hear some of the stuff that's going on up there. I don't know who he is anymore. Gloria's gone (she's gonna need a therapist one day to figure this one out) but there's a new crowd of crazies traipsing in and out—students, he says, young boys from a juvenile shelter where he is doing group counseling volunteer work. I don't think I want to know more than that for now. He needs a shrink to figure out who he is, what he is, and what he wants.

August 29, 1986

Raw unmitigated rage! That sick little pervert is finally out of my house. Maybe I should go up and fumigate the place; burn lots of incense, do some special mantras to get any trace of his degenerate insanity out of here before I paint and rent it again. So why am I crying, knowing I probably won't see him again? I'm as nuts as he is!

January 12, 1986

He sent me a birthday/Christmas/ New Year's card. I wrote and told him I was pregnant and scared to death and didn't understand how all of this happened to me. I'm thirty-seven! What the hell am I doing having a baby now? He laughed that stupid laugh of his and told me to get Mark to explain the birds and bees to me. I asked if he would be the godfather and the executor of my will and come to see me after the baby is born and reassure me that I wouldn't be a terrible mother like mine is.

Mark C. hates it when I say that and keeps trying to make me feel better about this parenthood trip, but at least Dino tells me the lovely lies I need to hear so I don't lose my mind over the prospect of being a mother. Yeah, I think I'm stupid enough to give him my child if something ever happened to Mark C. and me.

March 10, 1986

Dino's called every night this week from Savannah. His mother is dying, and I can hear him talking himself into letting her go. All I can do is listen while Dino talks himself through waiting for her to die. I have no answers that will help him to make it hurt less.

May 26, 1986

Mark C. is excited about going off to Europe to his medical conference for a week, and I feel like a bloated watermelon sitting here in this horrible heat, still feeling like death eating soda crackers. Whoever said pregnancy was wonderful was a liar and a man! Dino offered me the use of a beach house he rented for the season to get away, but I feel too sick to move. I want Mark C. back here to let him know how miserable his little bastard offspring is making me. I had the amnio but asked not to know. It kicks like a quarterback and moves like a feisty little monster of a boy.

July 1, 1986

If I didn't have Dino and Sharon to talk to I know I would have killed myself by now. I keep telling myself that God never gives us what we aren't ready for, but this is unfair! How the hell can I be ready to lose Mark and the baby all in the same month? Every Sunday morning, whenever he's away from me for the weekend, he has called. But this time I missed him, and all he left is a message on Saturday saying he was excited to be flying off on some private plane to play golf with some doctor friends and meet some biochemist he admired. Sunday night his boss called me, crying, to say the plane was sixteen hours late. I knew he was dead when they didn't call me back.

I never got to say good-bye to him. His mother hated me so much, she said she would call the sheriff if I came to the funeral. I was too stunned and sedated to try to fight with her. Two weeks later, to the day, I woke up in the middle of the night hemorrhaging. It was like Mark reached back from the grave to take the baby with him. He didn't even trust me to keep his son. I still sit here, thinking he's going to call and say he'll be late at the lab or come in the door from the hospital, too exhausted to eat, complaining about some paperwork problem. I smell him on the sheets, my pillow, the closet The dent of his body in the mattress is still next to me. How can he be gone?

November 11, 1987

Sitting on a mountaintop in New Mexico and staying with Katherine and Bob for a few days before going out to Abiquiu. Wishing I could lose myself under a rock in the desert; workaholic me, pretending that the therapeutic busyness of the job is enough. I had everything under control until I lost it in the office when I was invited to a baby shower. This is like climbing out of my own grave and pretending to have a life, avoiding facing how lonely and lost I feel, trying to talk myself into believing that there is a reason I am still alive; trying to figure out why I still wake up every morning when Mark C. and my son are dead, how God can be so cruel as to let me still be alive. No mantra in the world can make this stop hurting. I want to scream at the universe, so that's what I do from the top of Mt. Wheeler, looking down on the white silence of Angel Pass, shouting every curse word I can think of until I am hoarse and drained. I called Dino from a pay phone and talked for about an hour, knowing he would listen and understand. It made me feel better just to hear his voice after a year of not talking. I feel bad that I cut him off to try and forget. We talked until he told me he wasn't alone. Maybe now I can sleep tonight—without the double shot of bourbon.

June 25, 1989

Michael from Atlanta, my ex of twenty years ago, shows up out of nowhere on the telephone one night. I called Dino to tell him about this bad case of ugly karma reappearing. He gives me his standard shrink-type answer: "Mark C.'s dead, so maybe this is a way for you to get out there and start being alive again. Deal with him if you think it's worth it, stay detached, try to talk out the bad stuff that's happened so you can clear the air, but you don't have to fuck him to forgive him." I hung up on him, pretending to be insulted, but laughed because he'd read my mind. I went to bed thinking this was the first time we had mentioned Mark C. I can't talk about him to anybody but Dino. When I woke up, I realized that I still sleep in one of Mark C.'s old T-shirts.

September 29, 1989

I called to wish Dino a happy birthday but Lionel, I guess that's his new love, said Dino is in the hospital with the flu but doesn't want visitors. Typical. Here we go with this on-again, off-again stupidness. He makes it really hard to be a friend.

January 24, 1992

Dino is dying, and I'm mad at him. Not because he's dying, but because he's being silly and pretending that he isn't sick. Kenny called and told me about him being in the hospital again. This time he says he has pneumonia, but I think he has AIDS. How else do you explain the flu that never goes away, the forty pounds he's lost, and the lie about being on a fast to purify his body? God, please don't do this to me. I'm so sick of losing people I love.

April 2, 1992

I've been calling Dino for over a month to finish his taxes or get an extension, and all I get is that damn machine. Joe and Craig say they're both getting the same let's-pretend nonsense, too. It's wearing me down to cooperate in this lie. He's a psychotherapist, so he knows well how to play the manipulation game. Getting to know him showed me that shrinks have no answers. They're just good at asking questions. Respecting his privacy is one thing, but why must he treat me like I'm stupid? What kind of friendship is this when he is too paranoid to trust me to know what's wrong with him?

June 15, 1992

The letter came from Albany, and I thought it was from his tax audit so I opened it. They said he made too much money for state-assisted medical aid. I couldn't reseal it and forward it to him. I finally called Albany and told them to send another one.

He's testing every spiritual and moral principle I've ever learned. Baba used to say, "Greet another person with great respect and love." The respect always comes first. This is the highest worship, the greatest gift we can offer another human being, which means I have to respect his rights and keep my hands off his life and my opinions to myself, but that is very hard. He's being the ultimate asshole in my opinion, but my opinion doesn't count since I'm not the one dying. Maybe I'm also mad at him because of my own ego needs to feel like I'm racking up a few Brownie points with God by playing the hovering nursemaid and caring friend, trying to hold back the inevitable for just a few more minutes.

September 12, 1992

Now Dino wants to leave New Jersey and gives me this litany of lies and ridiculous excuses he's made up to justify it. Crime, air pollution, the cold weather won't let him get well, and the doctors don't know how to take care of him. I'm insulted by this stupid pretense.

September 29, 1992

He says he's not celebrating his birthday this year, since he's fifty and wants to stop the clock there. He makes a joke about counting backward and trying to guess how much time he has left. I can't laugh. Now he wants me to believe that he has diabetes mixed with this new strain of TB that they can't treat. I have to nod and agree and listen, wishing I could go through the phone and gleefully choke him while he is testing out this new lie on me, seeing if I will buy it. I feel like shit for putting up with this garbage. He calls that young boy, Ronald, who's living with him, his "adopted son," and he wonders why his daughter won't speak to him! Since when do you adopt a twenty-two-year-old that you met while doing volunteer work in a juvenile shelter? He says he wants to try being a daddy again, and maybe he can try to get it right this time.

I finally had to tell him I wasn't buying this crock of bullcrap he was trying to float past me. I told him I understood all too well the fear of growing old alone and how we all want to feel like we made a difference to somebody, that we'll be missed, that someone will be there to cry and hold our hands as we make the transition out of this body, to stand over our grave and mourn us, but this is the ultimate ego trip he's on, taking this kid who needs a friend and maybe a big brother and turning him into his pallbearer. Naturally, he hung up on me. Fuck the bastard. I'm wrung out on this one and have to stop caring about him anymore. Just knowing him now is too heavy a drain on my spirit, but I'll still send him a birthday card. It might be his last one.

October 1, 1992

Dino called to thank me for the birthday card and tell me he plans to commute between Newark and North Carolina, where he has sent Ronald off to college. He'll move when he can find a job and an apartment down there. Meanwhile he's been back in the hospital, but he won't tell me which one. I think we're both crazy. Him for creating this game and me for participating in it.

Why won't I just let it go? Why do I still think I can have some impact on him and his life?

December 17, 1992

I called Dino to tell him I finally took the plunge and resigned from the bank and let him know I wanted to go out and celebrate my liberation from corporate insanity. Just like a mother hen, he reminded me what a good job I was giving up for the chance to be poor and creative. We're going to meet at the Alvin Ailey Gala. He and Lionel have tickets for the same night.

December 22, 1992

I got there late and sat in the balcony. I found them at intermission; Dino had tears in his eyes and kept hugging me. Lionel stood behind him, embarrassed. I haven't laid eyes on Dino for about two years, and he looks awful—so thin, hair falling out, skin discolored and dry from the AZT treatments Kenny told me he was taking. He talked about the last time we were together up at Shanti Mandir—when Nityananda had the opening ceremony for the new ashram and a sacred *yagna* (fire pit) to invoke the blessings of the Lord Ganesh, Dino's spiritual name. We had spent the night sitting outside under the stars in the chill by the fire trying to chant away some karma and make up a *swaha* (surrender) list of all of our bad habits and bad thoughts that we wanted to get rid of by tossing them into the fire. My list was longer than his. I'd like to give up missing Mark C. When we got to the fire I didn't stand close enough, and mine missed the flame and got caught on a ledge inside the pit. Dino laughed, rolling on the ground, and said, "I guess God wants you to keep your shit to yourself." Then he went and got a long garden rake to dig my list off the ledge.

April 10, 1993

He phoned at 7:00 A.M. to ask if I could come over. Lionel is away on a business trip, there's no food in the apartment, and he feels too weak to go out. I drove over, praying he wouldn't die on me yet, scared of what I would find. The place was a mess, smelled of garbage, dirty laundry, and an unemptied cat box. I spent the afternoon cleaning, cooking, and shopping for him. I tried to talk about how life had changed so much for both of us since we came back from India, keep his spirits up, let him know I was okay with whatever he was and whatever it was about. By late afternoon I couldn't do anything but sit by his bed and try to get him to talk—about anything, how he felt, what he wanted next, Jamila, his mother, Ronald, whatever would make him feel better and get his mind off the pain and make him eat something. He kept napping and waking up and said I should wear a mask to protect myself from the TB. When I left, he just smiled and asked me to put on a chanting tape. I can't imagine what he must be feeling. I reminded him how I met him that summer afternoon in Brooklyn Heights, never imagining it would come to this one day, and how we had joked that one day when we were eighty we would be sitting in our rocking chairs on a front porch somewhere and he would be showing me pictures and bragging about what his grandchildren were doing. He was asleep as I slipped out.

May 12, 1993

I came back from D.C. and Dino had left the message that he had found a great apartment and a part-time job in Charlotte, where Ronald is in school. By the time I called him back the phone was disconnected and gave no forwarding number. His usual trick for hiding and breaking ties. I sent a note to the old address, hoping he would phone me and tell me where to reach him, but knowing him, he won't. He's going down there to die. To get away from all of us, like the old people I heard about in Eskimo country who take themselves out on an ice floe and hack it off until they can drift away, unseen, and get lost from their family and their village when they decide they are no longer useful to the community. But that isn't how it has to be here. This is the one time when, if he were in arm's reach, I would try to slap him back into some semblance of sanity; kick him from one end of the planet to another until he got some sense in him. As mad as I am at him, I know I'll find a way to forgive him. I realize now that I know his heart and soul in a way that I will never get to know anything about his life. He's so scared, and I understand every bit of that, but it really pisses me off to have to play this illusion game with him.

April 9, 1994

Got home from doing laundry and found the note in the door from Fred Maxwell. The police had phoned Fred from North Carolina to say Dino was in the morgue. They had found him dead, probably for about a week, when the landlord saw the mail piling up and noticed the smell coming from the apartment. Ronald has disappeared. I called down there, and the detective on the phone was very nice—he thought I was a relative. He said they had gone through the apartment looking for an address book, trying to find his family. At his job the two names he had listed in his file for emergency contact were Fred and me. I forgot his wife's name, and the last I heard his daughter, Jamila—she should be about twenty now—was in college up in New England somewhere. Dino had said she was dating some white boy he didn't even want to meet who thought she should change her name since Jamila was too weird. He had two sisters and a brother in Atlanta, but I never knew his first name. His uncle Alex from Philly had a different last name, which I don't remember.

April 10, 1994

Jesus Christ, if he weren't dead I'd wake him up and beat him to death for leaving me this shitty mess. Why do I have to be the one to spend my weekend like a bereaved wife phoning all of his friends, telling them the news, and trying to make funeral arrangements? This is the final thrust in one of his irresponsible asshole games he liked to play, especially since he knew he was dying! The sleazy little bastard chose to go off somewhere and hide, avoiding all contact with everyone who cared about him and then asking us to literally wipe his ass and clean up his crap after the body is cold. I guess you would call this the ultimate act of passive-aggressive hostility or just your average sick mind reaching back out of the grave to slap you across the face and say, Why didn't you pay more attention to me?

April 12, 1994

I had to get out a copy of his tax return and call the V.A. using his Social Security number and finally found Lois, the ex-wife, and Jamila, who now calls herself Janice. His two sisters who lived right in Charlotte with him are moaning, Oh, ain't it awful and why didn't somebody tell us how sick he was, conveniently forgetting how nasty they were when he left his wife.

April 17, 1994

I hate being here for this atrocious little drama. Lord, please help me get through this. It's like losing Mark C. all over again. I talked to Uncle Alex and his brother Felix on the phone but avoided the whole mess until I got there for the service. B.K. from the bookstore told me when you go to a funeral, you can always count on the one who makes the most noise being the one who has the most guilt about neglecting the deceased. This funeral is the most bizarre exercise in hypocritical posturing and pure bullshit that I have ever seen. Lois, his ex-wife, took over and stood up there like the newly bereaved widow, going on and on about what a bright, intelligent, funny guy he was and how deeply loved he was and how much he will be missed. She confronted me in the ladies' room to find out why somebody didn't tell her what was happening and how he got the disease. Until now it hadn't occurred to me to even wonder where and when or how he got sick. She stood there with this self-righteous attitude, eyes burning at me with misplaced retribution as if I should be accountable for his life and how it all came to be this way. I just walked away and said nothing. I'm mad at him, too, but that's my problem. I never told him how much I loved having him in my life.

I feel like I have a hole in my heart that won't ever close up. I didn't look at the body until the last minute before they closed the casket. I never saw Mark C.'s body, so I guess that's why it is still hard for me to believe that he's gone. I finally looked at Dino, and I'm sorry I did. That shrunken shell of dead flesh isn't him, that's not my Dino. No smile, no vitality, no quirky comment or sneaky little insult to crack me up. They left off his glasses. He looked strange without his glasses. This fool could barely see to eat without his glasses.

April 20, 1994

My Divya Diksha day, and I go out for an Indian dinner with Sharon. I smell curry and I think about Dino sitting there making a fool of himself, trying to be native and eat with his fingers like an Indian, showing off his talent for being a jerk in public. I'm too upset and can't eat and end up crying in my napkin, making a fool of myself.

May 25, 1994

I met Craig and Bill Taylor at the Black Shrink's Spring Conference for their version of a short memorial service. Bill called and asked me to speak about Dino. I wandered around the group eavesdropping on conversations, listening to some of them talk about him. They called him Melvin or Doc, relating strange little tidbits about their version of a person that I didn't recognize. We all seem to become the repository for separate special parts of each other's soul as we share life experiences—knowing one another in strange little ways that are unique to the person and the moment. Like the boxes sitting in Dino's living room for two years. As each of us passed through his life we were given a box holding some part of him that he reserved for each of us, individually. To know the whole person, each of us would have to come together to open and share our boxes of memories, experiences, and dreams. Apart we sit and contradict each other, wondering who the other person is speaking of. I'm trying to feel some sympathy and remorse, but I'm just feeling pissed and drained from the stupidness of it all.

June 21, 1994

Every time I reach for the pickled Indian peppers to put in the masala, I think about him and get tears in my eyes.

July 14, 1994

I called some of the old Siddha yoga family, and we met at the Harlem center to have a short memorial for him the way he would have wanted—full chant, incense, and the mantra playing.

Now I'm suddenly jealous of him. Almost. He's on the other side of the veil, gone beyond the void without me, discovering answers to so many of the immortal secrets we always talked and wondered about. And he'll get to see Mark C. before I will. I like to think that I will always have a special little piece of his soul inside me, like with Mark C., along with some irreplaceable memories of our times together. When my time comes to leave this body and cross over that threshold, I'd like to imagine he'll be one of the first to greet me, broken-toothed grin and all, with that silly laugh of his, and I will be oh, so glad to hear it one more time.

September 29, 1994

It's Dino's birthday. Happy Birthday, Dino! Lord, you have no idea how much I miss you. I almost sent yellow roses to his grave in Charlotte, but I didn't. He was allergic.

CARY ALAN JOHNSON

◎⁄◎

Obi's Story

At seven A.M. he looked upon her, a fantastic bas-relief against a sea of smarting blue. Brown, open, a thrush of mountains plying down her spine, into a crack, a gully of darker. He had risen from a wet July night in New York, solid black and white with the genies of rising steam on JFK's tarmac, and broken through to a clear African morning. Through the porthole he watched the coast of Mauritania transform itself into the groundnut sand of Mali, only to be replaced by the lush Nigerian bush. The plane fell east and south.

The only black passenger in the first-class section, Stu had expected at least an African diplomat or two, or a businessman flying Air Afrique back home to Doula or Libreville after parlaying gold, diamonds, or oil into VCRs and expensive cars. He was alone with the Burkinabé flight attendant and felt a strange guilt each time one of the coach passengers, overwhelmingly black Africans, would wander into the first-class cabin by mistake or curiosity.

As the Belgian woman in the aisle seat slept, a haughty nasal buzz came from her mouth. Back in New York, he had thought her French as they attempted the ad hoc friendship eight hours of flight necessitated. During the night she had spoken in her sleep, an ugly Flemish Afrikaans sound, he had thought, and he remembered how frightened she was when the plane took off, crossing herself repeatedly, gripping her crucifix, the divider between their seats, and finally his arm as they lifted high above Long Island.

"*Pardon, Monsieur.* Flying makes me so nervous."

"*De rien, Madame,*" he responded with the magnanimity he always felt at the beginning of a long trip.

"Oh, you speak French? I thought you were *noir américain.*"

"Yes, I'm an American."

She shrugged. "But you speak so well. You've lived in Europe?" she stated her question.

"No, in Africa . . . and Haiti." He added the last for emphasis, though he'd never been to the Caribbean. It was just the next deepest, darkest, blackest place he could think of.

She clucked to herself and smiled. "But you speak so well," she repeated. "You are a diplomat, perhaps . . . no, no, no. A journalist." She had decided.

He debated momentarily about which answer would most likely shut her up. Both opened a can of worms particularly savory to expatriates in Africa when they have a captive audience. He had already determined that this woman had lived in Africa for many years and was probably more at home on the verandas of private clubs in Kinshasa than in a Paris boutique. He knew her type, hated it, therefore hated her.

"Yes, journalist."

She smiled comfortably. He signaled the handsome Burkinabé to bring him more champagne. Journalist was as good as anything. What was he after all? A tourist, an invader? What had he ever been here?

Now, several hours and bottles of Moët later, he turned back to the unfolding map below. It had been too long since his eyes had feasted on this sight and he'd grown weary and red-eyed from a night of expectation and twisting in anticipation of this particular arrival. Five years since he last set foot on the continent, since that wonderful and vicious summer with Kate and Obi on the coast and all that had happened since.

He wondered if anyone would be at the airport to meet him. He imagined Kate, drinking tea, her tanned face and red hair amidst the crowd of fiercely turbaned heads and crisp robes on the observation deck. He imagined Obi, a black mountain of a man, calm and imposing in the sea of activity that always reigned at Ntala Airport, its red and black flags flapping in the harmattan. The images disquieted him, and two Valiums and the alcohol could not dispel them. Now as the earth approached the plane, miles at a time, his anxiety turned to fear.

God, she must hate him. The years of no words had methodically grown into a wall of dispassion built to shield him from the pain of that summer, of losing Obi, then Kate's friendship, and finally himself. But in New York, and then later in Washington, the losses, the liquor, and finally the drugs had come crashing down on him, leaving him with no choice but to return to the scene of this crime, to Ntala, to the coast, and to what was left of that summer's memory.

Five years ago it had been so different. It was he on the observation deck sipping not tea but Mbusa, the national beer, the "water of champions," as its advertising proclaimed. The sun was a cruel slash in the sky that day, its rays releasing the copper in his skin. Ruddy, it had turned him, tanned just like a white boy he remarked when passing reflective shop windows in the capital. He wore a safari suit: Khaki and large, it hung comfortably on his thick shoulders, a gold chain lying casually among the hairs of his chest. His short, well-oiled Afro picked up flecks of intense light and shot them back. He was twenty-nine at the time and unremarkably handsome. It was his eyes that set him apart. They had an intensely sad quality to them, as if they'd witnessed too many bitter scenes already at that young age, as if they belonged to a small child who'd been left out of too many games. It was this pain in his eyes that lit his face when he smiled, making his joy all the more important for its viewer.

At the table with him, Obi sat drinking a bottle of the same. Among the handsomely dressed and well-bred Africans in the terrace café, Obi was a commanding figure, tall for an Ntalan, with skin so dark it approached true black in its reflection of light. He did not appreciate the sun in the same way Stu did and sported a blue cap with a visor to shield his eyes. He wore a pair of plaid walking shorts, very fashionable at the time among the *"jeunes premiers,"* the West-looking youth of the capital. Hairless, muscled legs ended in clean white Nikes. A small brown tanned leather pouch hanging from around his neck seemed to be the only vestige of the traditional in his image. He quietly hummed along with the crackling radio tuned to Gabon and Africa Numero 1 until a fast track came on.

"Papa Wilo." His eyes brightened. "He's in town tonight."

"I know, I know. Best high life on the continent. We'll be there if Kate wants to go. She may be tired after the flight. Damn, must this thing always be late?"

Obi looked at his watch, a black face with tiny silver chips where the numbers might have been, a gift from Stu only last week. Stu wagered it was the nicest watch Obi had ever owned. Obi downed half the bottle of beer and leaned back in the white wire mesh chair. The sight of his body unfurling flipped a switch in Stu; he summoned the waiter. The man came, dressed in a clean white coat and beach sandals. Stu ordered more beers in Kindoma, the words falling easy and light off his tongue.

Obi smiled. "You still speak Kindoma with an American accent."

"How many Americans do you know can speak Kindoma?"

"Just you and the Great White Fathers." Obi laughed loud and killed what was left of his beer. "They're Americans, aren't they?"

"Of a sort."

"But you know more curses."

"You're damn right. That's 'cause I hang around you and Zamakil too much. Too many high-life concerts."

Obi straightened in his seat. "Does Kate speak Kindoma?"

"No, she's never been here, but her French is fantastic. She's great. I can't wait to see her."

Obi reached across the table and pulled the pack of Okapi from the pocket of Stu's shirt. "I think you like her."

"Of course I do. We've been friends for a long time."

"That's not what I mean." He lit two cigarettes, handed one across the table and returned the pack to Stu's pocket.

Stu smiled at the boldness of his lover's actions, amazed at how comfortable Obi had grown over the past six months. "Now Obi," he lowered his voice, "if I didn't know you better, I'd think you were jealous. You know I'm not thinking about anyone else, okay, homeboy? Kate is an excellent engineer. We work well together. I need her on this project if I'm gonna get that water pumped in before the river goes down. We want to be in the States by Christmas, right?"

"Right."

"So we'll work together. We're a team, okay? Okay, chief?"

"Yeah, okay, Stu." He answered this last in English. Stu slapped him lightly on the face, letting his hand linger imperceptibly while the noisy chatter on the terrace was broken by the sound of the DC-10 approaching the city.

Dear Kate,

Hey sweetheart! Trust this letter finds you well. I sure hope, however, that you've had a lousy winter and want to totally change your lifestyle, 'cause I've got a proposition. The engineer on the water project just quit and we need a replacement fast. I've been doing such a damn good job on these quickies that I've got the Minister of Works eating out my back pocket, so to speak.

So the other day, we're sitting around talking about how to get a top-notch, crackerjack engineer with small irrigation experience to spend the summer on the beautiful coast of Ntala. Well, hon, we thought and thought and couldn't come up with anyone. So I decided to ask you (ha ha).

No, but seriously, you've got to come out. We'll be in the middle of the short rainy season, and Katie, you've never seen anything like this coastline. It'll blow you away. I've really fallen in love with this country. So different than the years we spent in the Peace Corps. Do you remember how frustrated I was? Loving my work, but hating the rest. My God, I couldn't wait to get out of our village, but do you remember how I cried like a baby on the truck? But I seem to have worked things out. Or they've worked out for me.

Most of the reason is probably this gorgeous mothafucka lying in bed next to me. I swear, Katie, I'd given up all prospects of falling in love over here and had resigned myself to taking some desk job with AID in Washington. But meeting Obi has changed everything. He's just so honest and genuine. He really cares about me as a person. You'll see. If you come out we'll be working together. He's the liaison man. Most of the projects I've worked on, that means glorified interpreter and chauffeur, but I swear, Katie, the guy is so bright. I'd never get these folks working so fast if it weren't for him. And now everything else seems to be falling into place, too. I'm going to bring him back to the States for a few months, spend Christmas in Detroit. My parents will love him. And then we'll see. See how he adjusts to life in the States. Or maybe back out here. Or, there's a job with Catholic Relief in Harare.

Anyway, I'm going on as usual, letting my imagination run away with me. Let me stop. I really hope you'll consider the job. You need to be out by first July. Cable me as soon as you get this. My love to your dad.

> Best love,
> Stu

"Katie, you look great. How's Washington?"

"Same old bullshit. Summer was hot as hell. Thanks for the rescue." Kate was a modest and attractive woman in her early thirties, with angular features and a full frame. She had a playful quality that at times made her seem much younger than she was, and at other times her up-front brashness made her seem years older. Her no-nonsense, down-to-business attitude sometimes alienated people, particularly the staff under her, but she was easy to respect, a hard worker, and committed. The last ten years of her life had been divided between graduate school in engineering and work in India and Bangladesh. "Something about the faces of the children," she had confided in her letters, "I just can't stay away."

On the drive from the airport, Obi removed the top off the Jeep. Kate's hair caught the wind and rose. "It's dry as a bone out here." She pulled from her bag a pair of punk black sunglasses, hanging on an old-fashioned silver link chain, and surveyed the dusty maize fields sprawled along the road. Single huts and larger compounds, all washed a sandy brown, dotted the landscape.

"Two years. No rain." They were the first words Obi had spoken since the initial introductions on the terrace. He seemed to be brooding.

"The U.S. and France are doing some famine relief in the North. Soviets mostly in the South," Stu filled in. "Most of the grain's been going to the cities, but what else is new?"

"That's stop-gap shit. What's the solution?"

"That's what we're here for. The government decided a few years ago to dam this great big monster of a river, change the whole ecosystem, and then tell folks to dig irrigation canals. You've seen the plan."

"Yeah, I read through the stuff you sent. It's not hopeless. Water table's high enough. How many teams have we got?"

"Ten. Locally trained engineers on every one."

"Who's your anthropologist?"

Stu shook his head. "Ain't got none."

"Sociologist?"

"Couldn't get anyone on such short notice."

"So you're gonna go in and tell people to stop eating millet, start growing rice, and sell half of it to the government, all by your lonesome." She looked at him over the top of the glasses. "You're cute, dear, but not that persuasive."

Stu smiled, put his hand on Obi's shoulder and squeezed it. "No, I've got a little help." Obi stirred uncomfortably under Stu's grip, raising his eyes slightly to catch Kate's reaction to the small gesture in the rearview mirror.

"So, Obi, you're the man with the plan," Kate quipped. "Care to share it?"

He returned his eyes to the road. "No plan. The land is dry. People have no food. You will come with pipes and canals and pumps and help grow food. People will welcome you. You want them to grow rice. They'll grow rice."

"That simple?" Kate looked doubtful.

Obi sighed almost imperceptibly and continued, "Years ago, the French told us to grow peanuts. We grew peanuts. Everywhere peanuts. You took them. The land died. Peanuts killed the land. Now you want us to grow rice. We'll grow rice. What do you want us to do?"

The crush of the gravel underneath the wheels of the Land Rover and the turn of the motor Obi had tuned to mechanical perfection underscored the silence. An ancient Mercedes truck, loaded to twice its height with bags of imported grain, lumbered by. Perhaps this was food on its way to government soldiers squelching the bush warring guerrillas in the interior. The truck, leaning dangerously to its side, kicked up a great cloud of smoky stinging dust as it headed to the airport.

"Here, Obi, you need these more than I do." She removed the Greenwich Village specials from around her neck. Obi hesitated, then looked hard at her reflection in the rearview mirror. Finally he turned to Stu for a reaction. Stu provided his most encouraging smile, lighting his face with eyes that had found their way into Obi's heart at other times, trying now to break that wall that Obi was carefully constructing. With a slight release of breath, Obi put on the shades, his dark face opening into a wide gulf of white teeth as he laughed appreciatively at what he saw.

"You look great." Kate smiled with him through the mirror.

Cameroon John Little was a large, affable, blue-eyed man. He lived in an opulent villa on the peninsula where the river turned its mighty attention to entering the city. Stu had grown to tolerate Cami, probably because he had come to understand him. It was not easy to be a man who liked men on this continent, he reasoned, though being white made it easier. Cami had learned early in his life as a businessman in Africa that he could have almost anything he wanted for the right price. He participated gleefully in the free market economy of the capital, filling his home, its manicured gardens, poolside, and numerous bedrooms with the most attractive young men Ntala had to offer.

There Stu had met several law students from the university, Mohammed, a friendly military parachutist visiting from the north, and Zamakil, the goalkeeper for the national football team. The men Cami kept in rotating residence were always obliging, most quite openly. A few begrudgingly relented, but these were never invited to return. All were in need. The university and high school students were mostly poor fellows struggling through an academic and social system hard-pressed and unwilling to meet their most basic needs. The soldiers were living mean lives with large families on meager government salaries that were always late and occasionally never came. Some, like Zamakil, came out of no particular financial need, savoring only the pleasures that Cami's house offered.

Many found that they could live their sexual lives openly within the walls of Cami's compound. For some, the sex, with each other or with the various expatriates who also passed through, was an amusing addition to the life of decadence and excess lived there. For others, it was what they were forced to give in payment for the relief from difficult lives, or for the few dollars Cami would slip into their pockets when they left.

Cami's had originally been a refuge for Stu, who had lived in enough countries to know that such people were necessary, that to be befriended by the Camis of Africa meant entrée into a world it might take a man months or even years to discover on his own.

Stu's life as a gay man in Africa swung violently between the poles of the erotic and the neurotic. It swung between the attraction he felt for most of the intensely sure men he saw on the streets and in villages and his mistrust and hatred of the power they had over him. He was quite clear that the men of Ntala had the ability to validate him, to make him feel totally at home and accepted in this foreign land. But he knew all too well their willingness to reject him, to cripple him as a man, and even worse to betray him to a society that tolerated only silent difference. He knew that any unwise act, the wrong man approached, a pass unsuccessfully completed, could be his downfall, could mean in fact the end of his career abroad. When he first arrived in a new post, he would live a life of abstinence, carefully surveying the sexual landscape until he felt safe enough to venture out. Nevertheless, his future often hinged on the whims of his dick, not a healthy prospect for a man of his sexual appetite.

But he knew that Cami could, if he so desired, change the entire nature of his time in Ntala. So just as he'd done in Botswana, Togo, and then Zaire, he subjected himself to the scantily cloaked racisms, the thin jokes, the greedy stingy generous use of men as objects in this city that Cami and his expatriate friends called temporary home, one they hated with a passion and could not wait to leave when their fat contracts came to an end. In the meantime, they ate, drank, and fucked heartily at the villa on the peninsula.

Cami's place was known for its orgies. Stu would sometimes arrive after several weeks in the bush, stopping only to drop his bags off at the InterCon. He would find parties in full swing: Ntalans ranging in age from sixteen to thirty, in various states of undress, would be lounging by the pool, entertaining Cami's friends in tangled liaisons of two, three, or more.

Mostly people seemed to be having fun. These were the times when Stu could enjoy himself the most. Other times the commerce was too visceral. Cami would call a new invitee over.

"Isn't he a beautiful boy? Look at him." Cami would run his hand over the boy's head, under his shirt and finally, always end by stroking his crotch. The boy would invariably smile, knowing what was expected. Stu's skin would crawl, he would struggle to maintain composure as he vicariously felt Cami's hand on his own body, as he felt a chain tug at his neck. But Cami knew better than to try it. Stu was, after all, his equal in every way. An honorary white by these twisted standards.

Yes, the boy was beautiful. Cami entertained nothing but the best. "What's his name?" Stu would ask and then regret. He did not wait for a reply from the white man. "What's your name?"

The boy had a name. He was from a place. Had a history which Stu tried to discover in between bouts of lovemaking, at dinner, or while frolicking in the pool at his hotel where he sometimes took them after leaving Cami's house. The boy was most often not a boy at all, but a man with children, or a wife, or both. With dreams. And at the end of the day or the week in the capital the boy/man always wanted money from Stu, cab fare to go back to his place, to pay his kids' school fees, once even to buy a taxi. Stu gave what he could, took a furtive kiss (he had after all paid for it), and crawled back to the project site, back to whatever distant village he was working in, feeling alone and betrayed, but never knowing exactly by whom.

It was Zamakil who brought Obi to the house. Zamakil was the only African who seemed to approach Cami as an equal. And Zamakil and Obi were friends. They had gone to primary and secondary school together and separated only when the athlete's fate turned him into a national hero. Obi, too poor to continue on to the university, had taken up carpentry and then finally had become a mechanic for a large transport company in the capital. He'd always been good with his hands. Now, both nearing thirty, their memories of childhood games on beaches, of shadowy touches as boys, brought them together as men with hardened bodies and adult needs. They were fast friends once again, two men who shared an intimate past.

On the day Stu met Obi, he was in a difficult mood. The trip into the city had been particularly annoying. He'd been stopped seven times by knuckleheaded soldiers demanding bribes to tide them over through the first of the month. It had been hot, a day that had desperately needed a strong rain which never came to break the sun's anger. He was exhausted when he rang Cami's doorbell.

"You look a mess, man." Cami ushered him in. "Rough trip?"

"Exceedingly."

"Well, put on some trunks and come for a swim, old man. I've got something out back I think will perk you up a bit." He smiled lasciviously and slid out the back into the yard.

Stu found Cami and Zamakil downing Scotch and soda by the pool. They were enjoying a good laugh about Zamakil's recent trip to Kenya for the Africa Cup finals. Zamakil stood up when he saw Stu. They had always liked each other very much, had even had an affair which ended when Stu realized that the athlete liked fresh trade as much as Cami did and could never be tied down to one man.

"Stuart, where have you been so long? Out working in the field from the looks of it." They embraced and kissed one, two, three times on the cheek. "We've missed you."

"Zamakil was just telling me about the coach of the Kenyan football team," Cami said.

"Not the coach, the manager."

"Coach, manager, whatever. You probably had them both, knowing you, whore."

"I tried." They both laughed. "But the coach was sleeping with the goalkeeper and that bitch wouldn't let me near him. Stuart, what are you drinking?"

Stu headed to the poolhouse. "Whatever's wet, and mix it with something cold."

"Don't hurt yourself," Cami called from his lounge chair and chuckled.

"Huh?" The door to the poolhouse opened and a black man walked out wearing only a bright white bikini and a smile that matched in color and brilliance and left Stu speechless. The seconds before either of them spoke seemed both few and long.

"Excuse me," Stu said finally, "I just wanted to change."

The fine young man, tall, muscular, twenty-five or twenty-six at the most, moved away from the door to let Stu pass. "Yes, sure. How are you?" The voice was earnest and warm.

"Fine," Stu responded, feigning nonchalance, but his voice clearly matched the warmth. He entered the poolhouse and shut the door slowly behind him. Carefully sliding on his trunks, he counted backwards from one hundred in threes, thought about tombstones, asparagus, and car wrecks, waiting for the bulging nylon to recede.

He found Zamakil and Cami smiling conspiratorily. The tall perfect one with the hair a bit too long for his round face was doing laps in the pool. Stu decided to say nothing in response to the obvious plot.

"What's new?" he asked Cami.

"Your reticence, for one," Cami, always master of the sharp tongue, answered.

"Okay, okay. I'm impressed. Who is he?"

Zamakil laughed and pulled off his shirt. "Who is who? Oh, you mean him there swimming. Just someone. Just a boy." He slipped out of his shorts and dove naked into the deep end of the pool. Cami followed suit, playfully wrestling with Zamakil in the warm chlorinated water. Zamakil fought off his opponent and swam to the shallow end, where he hiked himself up and sat on the edge.

The tall one got out of the pool and sat on the grass under a shaded palm, near Stu who watched him watch Zamakil as Cami's head bobbed methodically between the goalkeeper's legs. The stranger's face, a nearly impassive mask, broke only at the corners, which twitched uncomfortably. Was he excited? Should Stu move on him? He was here, he knew the game, the unwritten rules of the house. Stu made what seemed like an interminable trip over to where Obi sat in the shade. He reached his hand out to touch the water beading on the taut chest. A black hand darted out and encircled his wrist. The man looked at him confused, betrayed. The warm look of invitation was gone. A shield had gone up. He let go Stu's hand and pulled on his pants over the wet suit. He stood and shook the water from his thick hair, then walked around the side of the house onto the path which led to the street.

Stu rubbed his wrist. It did not hurt nearly as much as his ego, newly bruised. He felt small and ashamed. He cut through the house to the front yard, racing to catch the man at the wrought-iron gate.

"Wait a minute. I'm sorry, okay?" The other was silent. "I didn't know."

"Didn't know what, nzuma?" He used the Kindoma word which had come to signify foreigner, stranger, but translated literally as white man.

Stu felt as if he'd been slapped. "Is that what you think of me?"

"Is that how you behave?" He threw open the gate.

"Wait, I'll give you a ride."

"I'll walk."

"It's a long way to town. Lots of hungry soldiers. Let me give you a ride. I'm sorry, okay. Okay? What's your name?"

Perhaps it was the earnestness of Stu's voice. Or the memory of the first few moments of their meeting. Or perhaps merely the fear of soldiers on the long road to town, but Obi relented. Stu drove.

That night at the hotel, when Obi took him, he felt warm and full, safe in a forest of circling lions. As the momentum mounted, Obi built a fire of black logs for protection. In the morning, so much later, when he took Obi, the fire was replaced by clear white light as he gasped at the shock of entrance, an entrance so tight and fitting, so perfectly unforetold that he came before he could pump or slide or ride. These would come later, of that he was sure, from Obi's sighs, from the relax in his body, from the wet he felt running down now over Obi's hard black belly.

"Are you married?" The room was lit only by dawn creeping through Venetian blinds, under doors, and across pillows.

"No, are you?" Obi propped himself up on his elbow, slid his other hand slowly down the long of Stu's body.

"I'm gay."

Obi laughed. "I, too, am sometimes very happy."

Stu scanned his face in the scattered light for a trace of sarcasm and found none. "I'm trying to understand your country. How to be happy here. I would like to find a friend. A special friend."

"I will be your friend. Zamakil says you will go to work on the coast. It is very beautiful. My oldest nephew will be baptised there during the short rainy season. I will take you to meet my family. They have never met a *noir américain*. Would you like to go?"

"Of course, I would love to meet your family. You aren't afraid they will suspect?"

"They could never suspect such a thing. And your family . . . will I meet them?"

"They're in America. Do you want to go to the States?"

"What do you tell us? It's the biggest, the best. What fool would not want to go?"

"I mean what's in this for you, Obi, before I let myself go? What *do* you want from me?"

Obi seemed to consider, lay down on the bed, raised himself up again, took Stu in his arms, and held him. His hand was hot and moist on Stu's thigh. "Your ass, right now, would make me very happy."

Outside the hotel grounds, at the port, market women waited impatiently for the arrival of the barge from up-country. They tied and retied silk wraps over rotund bellies and generous hips, dreaming of dried fish, french perfume, and moonlit nights unalone. They stared intently north, shielding their eyes from the sun's riverdancing glare.

All day the sun had burned white-hot in an unbroken sky. The evening had fallen slow without cloud cover. Stu had spent the afternoon working budget figures in the small hut they used as an office. The last canals had been dug, the pipes were laid, and two business-class tickets to Detroit via Frankfurt lay in the safe. The visa had been simple. Marc, a friend at the embassy, had made all the arrangements and now Obi's new passport lay on top of Stu's old one. All that was left was to close out the accounts and Kate could do that in a pinch.

Obi's absence that afternoon weighed on him. Late in the day, Cissé, the night guard just coming on duty, had informed him that Obi and Kate had taken the Jeep and gone to the baptism on the hillside.

"Great, just when I need him, she's got him traipsing all over the goddamn bush." Cissé smiled uncomfortably. Stu slammed the door and immediately regretted revealing so much of himself to the man, an elder from Obi's tribe. He returned to his desk and looked at the papers in disarray: figures, elevations, men and their salaries, debits ran together in black lines, red dots. His head swam.

Shutting and locking the bamboo door behind him, he took the back roads that led to the beach, down behind the small *pailotte* Obi had had the crew build for himself. Pretenses had, after all, to be maintained. The path, like the hut, was mainly unused. Milky thornbushes cut shallow grooves in his bare legs. He didn't care. The beach was empty except for a group of a dozen or so fishermen returning with the day's catch.

In this part of Ntala, the coastline was a study in natural drama. Within a half-hour's walk, the fine yellow sand lifted to tenuous cliffs and then hilly bluffs at the mouth of the river where the interior of the country drank its thirsty fill and opened itself up to weary passage.

He sat on the sand, wet with the approach of evening, and watched the fishermen. Night fell in patches around him; bits of sky turned themselves in, gave themselves over to higher powers. He could hear the drums from the baptism, urging but not urgent. What was ever pressing in this land of uncountable yesterdays and impossible tomorrows? The wind itself seemed to scoop percussion from the hillside where Kate and Obi surely danced and deposited it on the beach where Stu watched the sea alone now, the fishermen gone.

Tonight, he was waiting for a sign, a word telling him to go on. He got this way sometimes, lethargic, no motives. Earlier in the season, Obi's presence had kept him moving, prodded him to work the teams at twice their normal speed. Kate had set up evening training sessions for the Ntalan engineers, sharing techniques she'd learned from local crews in Asia. Obi was a native of this region; he was related somehow to everyone. He used his contacts to speed up the delivery of supplies for the canals and spare parts for the Jeep and pumps. The three of them worked like a well-oiled machine, turning to each other at the end of each day, falling steadily into the arms of a growing friendship. Most evenings they sat out by a fire, dodging mosquitoes and sharing stories, smoking and feeling the vastness of the night consuming them.

On a mid-season trip to the capital, they had danced all night to a band at an outdoor club. Kate was arrhythmic and knew it, swallowed it with a laugh and a beer. Obi had guided her across the floor through a sea of black faces with one sure hand on her waist and the other supporting the lifted curve of her spine. In his arms she appeared capable and weightless. To Stu, at a table in the corner, methodically getting sloshed on dark rum, the song seemed interminable.

Slowly, through the course of the season, something had been changing. Stu felt this instinctively before he ever admitted it. There was a resistance developing between him and Obi. Despite Stu's admonitions, curses, cajoling, Obi would not allow him to caress, hold, or even touch him when Kate was around. Kate's presence brought out a shame in Obi which Stu could not penetrate, as hard as he tried. When Stu demanded more time alone with him, Obi resisted. "What will the workers think? Some suspect now. We are too much together alone. They want to know why you have no children at your age. No wife."

Stu became angry. "But you're only five years younger than me."

"They begin to ask me the same questions."

"You never cared before!"

But Obi seemed to care now. "Perhaps in the city I am more free. But here, in my place . . . and around Kate . . ."

"Kate is my friend. She wants us to be happy."

Obi smiled slightly and looked him square in the eyes. "Be patient with me, Stu."

Leaving the beach, he headed back up the path. Things would be better once they were in Detroit. Once they left the country of dying soil for the city of dying steel. Obi would be overwhelmed by the strangeness, Stu would be there to comfort him, to be relied upon, to translate their new lives into English, into American. Stu would be there.

Coming up behind Obi's unused hut, his eye caught on a flicker of light from inside, and then a sound of something hard hitting something soft. Robbers, he thought, as he stopped in his tracks. Where were the guards? The sound again, only this time it was more human, a groan, perhaps a moan of pleasure or pain. He crept up to the windowless cabin and with a push of its door exposed its two occupants to the night air.

What he saw seemed cloaked in a smoky gauze. His life was

in fact smoldering around him. Obi and Kate lay tangled in each other's arms, legs, and twisted white sheets. Heat gushed from the room, it overwhelmed him. Obi stood up, the words coming quickly from his mouth were incomprehensible, his sex was still hard and wet.

"Shut up," Stu cried. Kate tried to cover herself with the sheet which was caught up in her legs. Obi continued talking, explaining what could not be explained. "Shut up," Stu roared and felt his fist make contact with the soft squish of the man's eye. He was suffocating and the room became a blur. He had to get out, but to go where and to do what, he did not know. He left the door agape, swinging on broken hinges.

"Stuart." Kate came into his room after several minutes, wrapped in a flowered green pagne covered with jungle beasts. "Stu." He started packing, savagely throwing his belongings into a suitcase. Carvings from the region, carefully chosen, a woman's head in bronze, fell at his feet.

"Stu, look at me. I know you're upset."

He stopped and looked at her, slowly focused on her blue eyes, her tanned, healthy complexion, skin still gleaming with sweat.

"You bitch." He hated her completely, there was no question, no holds barred. He wanted to hit her, the way he had hit Obi, to pummel her to the ground, permanently to mar the beauty— female, Caucasian—that he knew had drawn Obi to her.

"I don't know how it happened. It just did."

"Save it, okay. I don't understand you, Kate. You've got your choice of whomever you want. These men would do somersaults for white pussy." He glared at her.

"Stop it."

"Even back in Botswana, you got whatever you wanted. Why do you have to take the only piece of this damned country that ever loved me, the only thing that's ever mattered to me?"

"Obi is not a thing, damn you. He's a man with feelings just like you or me. He has a right to make choices. You don't own him."

"Oh, don't make yourself sound so innocent." Her

seminudity seemed to weigh on her now. The pagne looked light, as if it were nothing. "Look at you."

"Oh, so you can sleep with half of Africa and you call it getting in touch with your roots."

"Just what the hell do you know about it?" He slammed the suitcase shut and hoisted it toward the door.

She glared at him, looked into his eyes, and then softened as the years of their friendship came back to her. "Enough to know that you're better than this. Stu, you're not going to find yourself this way, running from one country to another paying for affection."

"Obi loves me." He stopped. "He loved me. It's not about money." He sat down on the bed, confused, his hand still smarting from the blow he'd struck to his lover's face. Kate sat down next to him and tried to take his hand. He recoiled from her touch. "I'm going. I can't stay here. This hurts too much."

She took his hand and held it. He didn't draw back. "Do you want me to leave, Stu? I'll leave. Our friendship means more to me than—"

"Than Obi's love? I don't think so. It doesn't to me. I love you, Kate. But I needed him."

The numbers of the combination lock fell silently into place and the safe clicked open. He immediately erased the numbers from his head. He would need them no longer. He retrieved the two airline tickets and shoved them into the side pocket of his overnight bag. He picked up both passports. He fingered the brilliant red and black of the Ntalan flag embossed on the cover of Obi's. He wondered how the thick raised paper would look burning in a fire, how neatly the seal of the country would tear into two, ten, twenty pieces and then scatter onto the floor of the hut. He wondered of the possibilities. He placed it on the table.

Outside, the fresh of night evaporated the sweat on the back of his neck, dried the wet streaks on his face. Obi stood in front of the Jeep, his eye swollen. He'd been crying but Stu knew that it was not from the physical blow he'd struck. As Stu approached the Jeep, Obi reached out and gripped the handle of the suitcase. Stu resisted, holding on, their hands touched; Obi won, taking the suitcase and tossing it deftly into the back seat.

"Where are you going so late? You know the road is dangerous this time." Obi got into the driver's seat.

"The city. What are you doing?"

"I'm driving you. I'm the chauffeur, remember?"

"The project is finished. Your services are no longer required."

"I'm driving. I'm your friend."

"You're fired." He replaced Obi in the driver's seat and shut the car door. "Give me the key." He turned it in the ignition and the motor began coughing, spitting, and then finally hummed its familiar tune.

"Be careful, Stu." Obi touched the back of his neck and rubbed it lightly.

"Be careful, homeboy." Stu shifted the car into first and rolled out the compound toward the main road. At the gate the ever-dozing guard woke up. He opened the gate and waved bewildered as Stu passed. He did not wave back.

On the road, the Ntalan sky opened before him. It struck him as serenely beautiful, untouched. Perhaps he'd never thought of Africa as anything more than a life-sized postcard, a moving breathing tourist brochure. And even the years he'd spent living and working in the villages, towns, and major cities, crossroads of black life, were nothing more than stepping into (and then out of) still life. There was never a sense of belonging, only of tolerance, mutual, guarded, and temporary.

He was glad it was night. He knew that in each of the tightly knit villages scattered along this main artery lived young black men with big chests and open shirts. In the light of day, they tantalized him with smiles and the aroma of dust and work and hidden, dark places on the body, their physical closeness deceptive in its inaccessibility.

If he made good time he'd be in the capital by morning. It was Tuesday. He could catch a flight to New York on Thursday. And then? And then. The wind whistled past his ears. His hair caught it. It did not rise. It did not move.

The plane touched down heavily and after a series of runs and turns came to a definitive stop in Ntalan soil. The Belgian dowager sighed, relieved, and crossed herself again. Stu reached into his travel bag for a mirror. He brushed his hair forward, the slight thinning in the front hardly noticeable. He looked out the window to the terrace.

He spotted them amidst the crowd. They had come. Kate and the beautiful little redheaded boy he recognized from the photos she'd sent year after year (despite his lack of response), a walking replica of his father in everything except color. The scene on the terrace was familiar. Waiters in white coats darted between tables to catch the fleeing customers running to meet their cousins, brothers, lovers coming from America, from the land of plenty. Only one person was missing.

It was the Fever that had taken Obi, the four-letter thing that had come to mean death and destruction in the States, that had ravaged Stu's circle of friends and left his address book bleeding with gaping white sores, victim of Wite-Out, numbers remembered but disconnected, no longer needed. It was the thinning disease that had taken Obi. That had left Kate an uncertain widow and had left this beautiful caramel-colored boy fatherless. And now Stu had come back to turn a new page in his life, to help his best friend, a white woman, raise a black boy to manhood, to perhaps rediscover his own manhood, lost somewhere between the coast of Africa and his youth.

The Burinkabé stood at the door of the first-class cabin, saying goodbye to the passengers. "Welcome home," he said to Stu and smiled, engaging, promising with teeth and a decidedly warm handshake.

"Thank you." Stu returned the warm press of flesh. But this was not the time. On the tarmac, Ntala buzzed with languages he'd not heard for years. He listened to the world as he walked to meet those who awaited him.

Asphalt

Do you hear that, boy? The chords and strings. All them
instruments?

Yes, Mama. Yes.

Planted where we are, planted deep. Deeply rooted . . .

Yes. I hear it.

Close your eyes and dance, boy. Listen to the orchestra in your
head. I never dream of Paris. No faraway places in my dreams. I
dream of hibiscus and lys. I dream of Petronia and voices echoing
underneath the mango tree. Perfumes and cakes and wines for
Erzuile. Erzuile ya ga ga gaaza. Erzuile ya ga ga gaaza. Erzuile ga
ga gaaza . . . Erzuile oh . . .

Yes, Mama. I hear it. Yes.

On concrete cots, there are abandoned vaginas and pagans
choked by umbilical nooses. The sounds of wilderness are these:
red river flow from blackened skies, and Stolichnaya gush from

pierced sides. There are brick and mortar mountainscapes that offer eyes and hands and lower depths. This is where the future leads him. This is where God sits on high *from* him. And no one can see Heaven from an asphalt yard.

He was a boy first, and then he was a man. The world gave him music and Jesus, but nobody gave him room for redemption. He gleaned the healing virtue from Cassandra Wilson's anointing, and sang idea and metaphor on page. He needed to re-create himself, though nobody offered him tools for invention. He was a boy first, then without much assistance, he was a man. Nameless.

The language of yesterday was about kickin' ass; about punk ass muthafuckas; about parents who conceived from interviews. The conversation of before was about coulda shoulda woulda to Brothers Johnson's "Strawberry Letter 23." All the while, fire was a late-night reoccurring theme. Haunting dreams and images of a Goddess dancing by riversides, and the grown men who tossed pennies at her feet. It was all he remembered. Her: vanishing in and out of rooms, up and down tenement stairwells, slight fingers tracing the curves and cracks of dull walls in need of painting. Beautiful tenement doors and long corridors and marble floors, chipped and dark from years of being touched and walked on. Unnatural habitats. There was a skylight or a window that lit up the hallway's final staircase to the roof. The final staircase to God. Names. Numbers. Proverbs. Torn streamers taped to doorways, dirty dishes, yellowing photographs. Rooms full of intelligible silences. She had an understated beauty that needed careful discerning. Her mind was leaking through her fingers. She was trying to hold on, but she was letting go letting go letting go. What was once a woman of flesh and blood had become a faceless Goddess in a lilac gown, alive only in his memory. There were vague recollections of Yankee Stadium, Archie Shepp, and talk of Bahama Village. Oceans. A woman's sorry hands rocking her child to Roberta Flack—*But these are trying times/trying times.* This was *all* he remembered, and he was longing to return to childhood.

There were lifelong dreams of convalescence as the child, the man, fought his way through schoolyards, other countries, bars, and emergency rooms. He lived long enough to become a sex symbol in parks at night, a savior with arms stretched wide offering his breast to hungry ghosts. His nipples gnawed religiously by sinners looking for the Holy Spirit in his ejaculations. He lived hard enough to imitate Odetta's wail behind bushes, and syncopate exacerbated rhythms up the anuses of faggots and track ho's. Love connections were made in dance halls and deconstructed over pay phones. All-night fellatios were equivalent to years of tormented marriages for intolerant pagans like him. Memory and metaphor merged between foreign blankets. Dreams were made in bus terminal bathrooms, and funerals for dreams convened on stalled subway cars. He sang elegies through cigarette smoke on harbors, laughing at the cliché of it all, and made confessionals in peep show booths. Curtain drawn, quarter tithe. *Plié*-ed pussies receiving penance for unreconciled sins. There were disagreements with sidewalks and murky recollections of dismembered maidens in the mire. The moon was a voyeur masturbating beneath a sheath of sky as he recorded his nocturnal ongoings. A bitter seed planted on paper.

He sought council in the people who advertised salvation. Usually soothsayers had to be reminded not to console with familiar phrases. Prophets were warned against foretelling. Conjure men were allowed to summon only the gods good for unexpected money, and psychotherapists were not paid at all if their livelihood relied on the dollar and not the redemption of the sin-sick soul.

Secret told into the breasts of a transvestite alien in a parking lot, ciphered on a brown paper bag: *There is a labyrinth west of here, where a blues singer's lilac gown is burning, and I want to know what key she is hollering in. I want to get there, where lilac sequins are quickly becoming orange embers.*

Response of the Rainbow on a maudlin afternoon: *Take the nearest turn from here to there and live.*

He was thirty-five or so. Not sure. The city rented his first family for him when he was nine, naked and without a name. He was found in an abandoned tenement near water, came without introduction papers or certificates of authenticity. And then there were people rented by the city to feed the child dead things on paper plates, and scrub his flesh raw red to avoid contamination. And they all gave him names. New names. Nicknames. Expletives. Sweet names whispered in dark corners. He was broad featured, with an olive-shaped mole on his ass, and his skin remained one shade of clay dust.

"Must have some Rican or somethin' up in you," one of the rental women suggested.

All rental people theorized about who the boy must have come from, and they all discarded the toys and clothes and things given him by his previously rented families, and gave him new names. The child was to grow up without the continuity of place or possession of object, so desperately needed by all adults to define identity. The boy developed like a street cat on dangerous avenues. Fever fell over him at thirteen. Diagnosed orchitis. There would be no procreation. Fever had folded its palm between his legs and fashioned a smooth bald place. His skin, soft. His manner, elegant. Only the adolescent's penis was intact, spitting clear semen from its stiffness. Tomorrow would die with him today.

He knew this much about the day before his existence: there was a cool breeze coming up from a river, and somewhere a woman sang from a rooftop, listening to Big Bill Broonzy do the Pigmeat Strut. He knew this much about the woman: Etta James and her lay open to the same dreams most nights. Riffing, wailing, turning themselves from side to side, catching the sweet crack in the harmonica's squeal. Snatching it, then pushing up, arching their backs, nails digging into the wall as if it were satin skin, then picking lint from their crotches. Complaining to the shadows that nothing but a cotton blanket had spent the night between their thighs. This he knew from something suggested to him by the pulse of the city, and the unnatural scent of hibiscus that passed whenever he saw the lilac gown burning behind his eyes.

New York City tenements tell stories. All old buildings give testimony. Cobblestone streets chatted with the clack of his heels and front stoops beckoned him to sit and stay awhile. *"Can you dance with a halting pulse?"* Everybody in the city wore veils draped over head and shoulder, and suggested past lives in their gait. The year of what could have been his twenty-ninth birthday, he surveyed his days and realized he had also lived many lives: a stickball player on South Bronx streets, an usher in a storefront church, and a high school dropout sketching charcoal and pencil portraits on sidewalks. Isolation taught him at the age of four to speak to the figures he drew. By twelve he added shades of plum to the full mouths of charcoal-grey and pencil-black women sketched on construction paper, holding erect beer cans between mammoth thighs and bare breasts. And he added hints of vermilion to the orange skin tones of geometric-shaped men who watched these women from corner shadows. He called them self-portraits. By twentysomething, the petit mal seizure of the hand would no longer produce pernicious people on paper, so he absorbed the tones and possessed the spirit of full thighs in his own narrow hips. For the rest of his life he embodied the delectability of beautiful women and dangerous men inhabiting shadow spaces. World travelers were attracted to his androgyny and the incredulity in his eyes. Six years gone by. Six years in other countries, performing for hungry ghosts looking for a revelation in his caressing. Six years singing,

> *Hit me/fuck me/*
> *Dig me Daddy dig me.*

He had been the *Beau Brun* of someone's Mapplethorpe fantasies on the Rue St. Germain. Caught staring glances on a gray day reflecting ugly pictures of himself behind the Louvre. With a little bit of magic and make-believe, he became a ballerina in Rome and a drag queen on Mainstein Strasse. And by what must've been his thirty-fourth birthday, he found himself void of tricks and travelers. Finally, back in this city, he was a car washer, a construction worker, a prostitute on the Duce, a numbers runner, a court jester, a dime-bag pusher on Ninth Street and First Avenue, a prima donna in ecstasy doing *pas de bour-*

rée's down St. Mark's Place, a go-go dancer at private parties getting dollar bills folded into his crotch, something from a Cassavetes film tipping across the globe of his own decadence. Back in the city. Searching for himself and some rite of passage that only existed here. And even though many buildings had died since he'd grown up, and many streets had been converted into something new and foreign, he believed he had known this metropolis in many ways. Had known it beyond the erection of South Bronx bodegas, Bed-Sty numbers spots, and the towers of Babel lining Wall Street. He had known the cool calm of ocean waves and the sweet of sugar waters, the tang of palm wine sipped from gourds. He could sense the shores in summertime fire hydrant falls. The dead were calling from the waters surrounding this island, and there was something to understand in the telling of the waves. Something about the asphalt. Something about other places he had not yet been, but could somehow recall.

His days were visceral upon return to this city. Some days were thick stool that he needed to push out of his system. Other days were virgin vulva on the tip of his tongue. Painted a thick sugary coat on lips and chin. A sweet odor resigned to live on his face and the tips of his fingers. There were certain things he needed to know. Questions about his own history that lived on the dryness of his scalp and burrowed its way through to the brain. He needed what he believed every human owned: names of mothers and fathers; clear recollections of himself; smells connected to the people who produced him. He took these questions to bed with him and slipped them under his pillow, resting his head on all of the possibilities.

He woke up at a quarter past three every morning in need of something to drink or plunge into, and was greeted each time by an old woman baring her breasts in the face of sin. Sometimes she metamorphosed into a coat hanging above a pair of shoes, or a curtain moving a certain way. Sometimes she became the bit of light bleeding through hallway doors ajar. But she was there. Always there. Several times that year. Ashen skin, ancient face as old as forest trees, dry tits as long as the night had been, screaming silently. She showed up wherever he slept, even in other people's apartments. He'd come to expect her visits. Usually she was summoned by six or eight cocktails, or Marvin Gaye singing "Wholy Holy." She could be invited by the furious percussion pounding from the walls of dance clubs, where he was animated in cinemascope, slave to the rhythm. Reduced to howling and nudity on the dance floor. Once it was the way Abdullah Ibrahim played "Ishamel" at Sweet Basil, and another time it was the sweet crack in the falsetto of a young girl in cotton stockings singing at a Sunday evening service, that summoned the naked woman to come to his sleep. The old woman came to him, invited by the spirits the day had conjured, sat on his chest, revealed her breasts, a sweet liquor dripping from the center of her nipples around his mouth and cheek, then screamed silently. Said nothing. He was trapped by the lock of her thighs, choking on her pungent breath. Only his eyes were able to move freely. And then the exit. If a boy or girl slept beside him during the old woman's visit, they lay sober and still. He would become drunk by her perfume. The scent of funeral bouquets in small village parlors. And then she would exit into a shadow or fold of cloth. But neither boy nor girl, when asked, remembered old naked women who disturbed the night.

He'd caught his first glimpse of the witch the day he discovered lumps behind his ears and at the base of his groin.

Her visits sent him spiraling into an abyss of incredulity and sensual living. It was not fear he felt the third time she came. Just a certain numbness that stills the quick of the eye. It was not peace he felt the fifth time. Just an immobility that halts the sudden dance of the stomach, and a tingling of fingertips playing *incy wincy spider* up and down the spine. She was a needle scratching across Shirley Horne's breath and whisper. An evening song long forgotten. The surprise of bitter bile in his sugar bowl. Her visits left the taste of crotch sweat in his mouth, rolling over his tongue. Passionate and nasty visits. Each morning, after she'd come and gone, he was forced to go out into the world and receive healing in someone's record pile from Morgana King. Holy Mother Santa Lucinda, the palm reader on

Fulton Street, told him it was Erzuile, the goddess of love, who had "come to calm your troubling."

The eighth time she came, he realized her visits were no longer restricted to depressed bedrooms. She stood just outside the glass of a coffee shop window, and sang open voiced to gridlock and precipitation. And then the temporary interruption of cigarette smoke rising. And then the quick turn of cheese eggs in his stomach. Empty sacks of breasts illuminated in the wind. And then the exit. She had not been seen or heard by still-life patrons slumped over mochaccino and morning-glory muffins. She had been his private dancer. A sweet and sour odor resigned itself to live on the tips of his fingers until the check was paid. Today was a dramatic musical and he was the Mikado of a fugue, doing *chassés* up boulevards. Chasing himself on wet asphalt, seeking money for some magic mixed with tonic and lime slices. Anything to help him hear the rhythm. A year passed and he had not seen her. He invited her into his dreams. She did not show. Eight times last year she came uninvited. One year passed, and the presence he had learned to revere had abandoned him. A metaphor, perhaps, for the mother he wanted to know. The mother whom he imagined tilted shoulder and thigh to concrete and offered her invasion back to the world on pernicious pavement channels.

Having lost his third apartment in six months, he'd taken up residence with squatters in a warehouse in the Williamsburg section of Brooklyn on Wythe Street. A middle-aged prophet named Nahum presided over the constant shift of the down and trodden, and offered his floor, his wine, his smoke, to anyone who wanted to invent sonatas on broken plates with forks and bottles. Nahum read Old Testament Scripture out loud like poetry and often listened closely to the nameless man's stories of the naked old woman, and the Goddess dancing by water. The rapture in the prophet's eyes advised "Draw it. Paint it. Make it into a song. That'll get you there."

But I'm gonna die soon . . . before I can conceive image and commit it to paper . . . I'm gonna die.

Sometimes, when Nahum slept, the pagan admired the dangerous nudity of the aging muse, and realized it was not the first time he associated paternal love with sexual sensuality. On a Wednesday, just after the third joint was passed around, while Nahum coughed and groaned into the air, his filthy blond hair violent and distressed like his eyes, the moon excused itself from the night and hurried up Bedford, vanishing above the landscape of inept buildings and lonely streets. The child, the man fell to sleep, before light could interrupt the darkness, and a salty sea sigh was breathed onto the back of the neck. She had come back. She was beckoning him to dance. Their bodies bent and crossed each other. She moved in slanted angles, rising and falling, dancing gingerly on the deaf ears of Nahum's head and bundled body. The stench of Jack Daniel's was fading with the potpourri of hibiscus and what might have been fresh mango.

Do you know something? Tell me what you know.

His tears were hungry for answers. Her dancing only hinted at information.

The woman where? The mother who? What is my name?

He wanted to see the birth canal he'd traveled through to get here, the last stop, on Wythe and South Sixth. Seeing it could help prepare him for the death canal he would have to navigate one day in order to leave.

She pushed her black lips against his, closed and tight. Her nipples cut into his stomach, and then the sun returned with light and trains and the noise of cars passing by. And then the exit. When asked, Nahum knew nothing of old women dancing in the hollow derelict room. They partook in an unholy communion, and the nameless man left Nahum folding himself into the Scriptures, inquiring truth of the pages, embracing the night's metaphor.

He wanted an epiphany. A vision. A drink. He wanted to know why she didn't sing this time. Why she'd waited a year before visiting him. Why he understood vague references to *mother* and *woman* in her silences. He frequented bars for the next few days, but his anxiety produced rapid weight loss and loose bowels. He held court with bar patrons. Talked languages he had never spoken before. He wanted to encourage the voices of angels to respond to him, through drunken strangers. He wanted them to be conduits for ghosts without suffering through the labor of explanation.

Dos Equis—$3.75. Golden Anniversary—$3.00. International Coffees. Freedom.

There were tiny Christmas lights strung haphazardly across the black walls and ceiling of this corner bar, nowhere as beautiful as the constellations. The first drink was offered by a roving hand. The rhythm of the drum, the bass, emanated from a colorful jukebox against the wall where he was groped. *"She must be ready for the telling."* Bacardi burned his throat and tried to live comfortably in the chest before nestling its way through to the stomach. The third drink was offered by crooked teeth peeking from behind purple lips. The eight ball was trying to get the side pocket the same way he was trying to get high, with just a little push. By the fourth drink, offered by the bartender, people began to notice small seeds visible beneath the epidermal layer of his skin. Germinating seeds. *"She knows . . ."* And by the sixth drink, dark rosebuds blossomed on his shoulders, his nose, his empty scrotum. Flowers the color of Concha y Toro sprung up on his cheek and chin. "You awright?" the bartender whispered into his bowed head. No response. No words could be formed from his mouth, his eyelids fainting, his drooling lips ajar. His fingers lost their strength, and his glass was broken, slicing open sections of his thighs. He bled grenadine onto himself. People moved away, afraid of the liquid pouring from his lap, afraid of his dark rouge blossoms. Catching a glimpse of himself and his flowers in the back bar mirror, he explained to judgmental eyes, "They're from her. It's our anniversary."

He left the bar facing the music, unable to say good-bye to the rhythm, his back pushing the door open, his mouth mumbling lyrics like soma mantra he wanted to remember. Traveling up the streets, he realized his garden was in full bloom. Red wine flowers grew freely from the folds of cotton and denim. Grew wildly in the lawn of hair on his scalp and groin. He thought of the recent infrequency of late-night lovers who had discovered the dunes behind his ears. And now the flowers. The flowers would surely turn the vipers away. *"They're from the old woman."* He thought, *"Rejuvenation."* He believed the old woman would rejuvinate him.

His fertile flesh wrapped itself around a skeletal frame, and changed colors from sand to soil. On the corner of Christopher and Sixth Avenue, a rapturous wind wrestled with his weakness, as his arm reached toward the third heaven, summoning the chariot of headlights down the avenue. Yellow cabs slowed down and sped off as the silhouette of this drunken nameless man and his garden came into full view. He caught the F train and curled in a corner seat. A mumbling woman sitting across from him peed on herself, and reeked of stale scotch vomit. She watched his eyes, not his flowers, and sang a gospel hymn (though she seemed to have forgotten the words) to her God (though she seemed to have forgotten His name). Crossing over to the M, he resisted the pull of his eyelids, then girded himself against the pole on a complacent subway car somewhere between the bar and home. As it pulled out of suspension, a Latino boy with glassy eyes passed out fliers for Holy Mother Santa Lucinda, and screamed above the roar of locomotion.

There's a labyrinth west of here, where the maiden is melting in the mire.

The seeds. The flowers. The vanishing flesh clinging to skeletal frame. Absent lovers conjured behind closed eyes, realized with a fist soaked in oils massaging his erection. The economics of time and existence. It would all be all right, if she would return to his ugliness and deliver him to the glass and wood frame of vague memory. *"Near water,"* he reminded the spirits while searching for indication of his station. *"Frequented by people dancing."* The images slowly crystallized in his eyes as he climbed the stairs and headed up the asphalt toward Wythe. *"There's a woman in copper bells . . . I think . . . yes . . . she reigns . . . yes . . . and the court jesters have all lived my death before."* History was not far off. Information was near. As close as the vacant loft where Nahum sleeps. Near living water, and an omniscient bridge. His whispers asked for the face of a woman, not Jesus. His trembling requested certain concrete channels where he'd been before, not streets of gold he would never know. The taste of breast milk in exchange for milk and honey. It would be all right. It would *all* be all right, if the witch could come again. His laughter sent knives pushing out of his belly and caused him to halt.

Gin straight . . . Absolut truth . . . Names . . . Faces . . . Hers . . . Mine . . . I . . . I . . . I . . .

.The asphalt shifted violently beneath him. Drooping eyelids veiled his pupils, searching for South Sixth. Toes attempted to push the pavement back beneath the ball of the foot, and then swiftly kick each long block back further with the heel. But the concrete resisted with the motion of ocean waves. And now there was light. He thought it was night. Remembered that darkness had closed the soft flesh petals on his shoulders when he emerged from the subway. But suddenly, harsh light revealed that Wythe had turned into a street called Petronia, where looming palm trees bejeweled in sun-orange fruit stood at attention on each side of a narrow path. In the heat of what was now day, his skin was moist. The rouge blossoms opened up and drank the sweat he secreted from his pores. A maddening sun gave no mercy. This street was familiar. Evening was gone. Williamsburg was gone. Brooklyn was gone, or uprooted or something. Something in the bank of his memory told him this was Bahama Village, Key West. The place the woman traveling through tenement corridors had described. The place where she said she'd kissed many mouths in an opera of crowing cocks and hairy-backed foreigners cruising Thomas Street for dark dealers of something strong and good. The woman who never got used to tired hallway marble floors, and rooftops and urban living.

—*Cool breeze comin' up from the ocean . . . feel it, boy? Bright rays on warm days . . . Some people can't hear the music mixed with the sun mixed with the sweet, sweet fragrance of honey melon . . . do you hear it?*

—Yes . . . yes, Mama, I hear it . . .

An onyx-toned man lay drunken at the bottom of a salmon wall, his arm extended beneath his ear, knees curled up to his stomach like a solo position of a modern ballet. In the sun, the black shiny skin, the pinkish wall, the white pubic hair revealed from open soiled yellow trousers, barefoot and shirtless, the old man looked like a collage.

Any minute, she'll come. I remember this place . . . I'll catch a glimpse of her . . . any minute, he thought. He expected the old woman to greet him, because she must have planned this gala. She must have. She must have costumed him in rose blossoms, and redirected the turn of the avenues, decorating a Brooklyn night with Floridian sun shower. The man, who slept at the bottom of the wall, spoke without lifting his head, or opening his eyes, or moving his lips.

—*You got rose blossoms comin' out yo' skin . . . Whatchoo know about that, huh? Whatchoo know about that?*

—A gift, that's all. That's all I know.

—*You fellin' poorly?*

—The sun is too much here, I think . . . I'm not sure if I was ever part of this landscape. But I know it . . .

—*Dere's a labyrinth west o' here. Maiden meltin' in the mire. Lilac gown goin' up in flames. Whatchoo know about that, huh, whatchoo know about that?*

—The woman who comes to my dreams, is she—

—*Dere's a city west o' here. A urban space. Vacant lots fo' prayin' 'n dancin'. A totem bein' built o' everythin' you carryin' around.*

Fire escapes on harsh horizontals. Lovers leanin' outta windas.
The night is a scrim 'n the people move in silhouette. Whatchoo
know about that?

—I . . . I'm feeling weak. The sun is too much here . . . I
think . . .

—*Lotsa songs fo' you to remember. You best sing. Geneva, she*
there. Soft as them mangos you standin' under. Cain't touch 'em.
Cain't pick 'em. Cain't do nufin' but smell that fragrance in the
rainy seasons. You best sing, if you fellin' poorly. She down there,
singing Erzuile ga ga, Erzuile ooh! Erzuile ga ga, Erzuile ooh!
Cain't peel the skin or suck the pulp. Jus' like them mangos you
standin' under . . .

—I . . . I'm wet . . . and I . . . I'm weak . . . my blossoms
are growing from my nostrils . . . and down my throat, I
think . . . yes . . . growing from my pancreas . . . my
liver . . . I . . . I can feel them . . . and I'm finding it . . .
very . . . hard to talk to y— . . . vines . . . thorny . . .
climbing down my thr— . . .

—*Erzuile ga ga, Erzuile ooh! Erzuile ga ga, Erzuile ooh!*

—The name, what? The maiden, where is she? The woman,
when will she come again? What is my name?

Palm tree leaves absorbed the sound of the old onyx man's singing, and the old woman limped by in disguise. Her flip-flops
scatted up Petronia. She wore a bonnet and big sunglasses that
would not reveal her face. Strangling on thorny vines lodged in
his throat, he watched her pause on the corner of a street called
Thomas, at the base of a blue wall. Johnson's Grocery. A couple
of bare-chested men and bare-legged women propped on crates
shared a beer from a brown paper bag. They smoked cigarettes
while gathered around a radio and lost themselves in the harmo-
nies of the Stylistics. The old woman unfolded a beach chair and
sat fanning herself with newspaper. He stood motionless. She

caught a glimpse of his fear, and revealed her breasts, the areolas as large as fists. And then she stood up and screamed silently into the humid air. He headed toward her, saliva gathering at the corners of his mouth as vines moved down his throat. The flat surface of the street turned into a steep hill and resisted his pursuit. She walked down Thomas, to a street called Angela, and hung a right toward the poured-concrete industrial green houses waiting for redemption. When he got close enough, his eyes bulging, a thick vein running down the middle of his forehead, she pulled back the drape of hibiscus-patterned polyester and revealed her breasts once more. A sugary substance leaked from the nipples, and the pedestrians, all dark and red eyed, surrounded him. They threw burnt orange-feathered roosters into the air and danced around him. A rosebush entwined in vine and new blossoms. Moist.

Erzuile ga ga! Erzuile oh!

The pedestrians demonstrated a wondrous ballet. The orchestra began in his ears. Music vibrated up through the nasal passages and settled behind the eyes. A violin. A cello. A "Dig Me Daddy" composition. The rapid gallop of horses racing through a marsh. Lights fade to black. And then the sudden circle of blue. Laughter. Chickens twirling on diagonals across cobblestone. The old woman screamed above the roar of locomotion, like the Latino boy on the train, and the dancers held their palms facedown, traveling around him in grand mal kicks. Dangerous encounters in circles of blue light. Brush of the hand. End of the moment. Then faster movement until the body of one drops and rolls away, ushered by distant stares and sullen glances. "Dig Me Daddy." And then the 2nd Opus of disillusion, and the anticipation of overcoming. Leaping legs wrapped around onyx waists and separations forming fusions. The vines down his throat melted like sugar squares in happy mouths. He could breathe. The pedestrians danced. Porcelain ornaments of children riding merry-go-rounds. Dolls orbiting into the abyss. Jump-rope songs abounding. "What is my name?" He could once again taste the texture of the day. Of all of his days. Of someone else's days. Conch fritters and Marlboro butts and inner-thigh sweat coated his tongue. The pedestrians sang as they danced.

Yo' name was Racine 'fore it was anythin' else. Yo' name? Ra-
cine, 'fore it was anythin'.

The orchestra in his head lost its place. The violinist, the cellist resounded like trains running off the track, off the cleft, off the page. Music racing through tunnels, missing stops. The pedestrians were gypsy dancers calling out his name.

Yo' name Racine 'fore it was anythin' else . . .

Racine. A high prayer, going up like incense. They engaged in the dance of fragile hearts a go-go. Of lost days and uncertainty. Finger to mouth. Cheek to palm. Shaking off all the in-between years. All of *his* in-between years. He obeyed the choreography, taken by the spirit of sagging tits and cobblestone. Racine stepped into the circle, accepting the baptism of name. *Racine.* Tilted plains rolled beneath his tipped toes. Crescendo. Elevator up. Gasp. Breath. Rose blossoms turning a shade of night, falling off his shoulders as he danced.

"Can you dance with a halting pulse and tired tongue? Can you dance on the brink of knowing?" The old woman's laugh lines asked the questions as she reached for his hand. "This is a sacred place to meander." Pornographic demigods were of no use to him here. Roses and hair removed themselves from his scalp. Two worlds existed in his memory, and they were worlds that were worlds apart. His feet had come to rest in a place called here. Not Petronia and Thomas, a place longed for by a woman captive with child and deconstruction of mind in urban tenements. Not Wythe and South Sixth or Christopher and Sixth, where he'd been something of nothing for everyone's desires. Not even Mainstein Strasse or the Rue St. Germain, but here. A place where he'd been given a name and a context.

—My name is Racine.

The pedestrians resolved the dance carrying one another on their backs. Moving. Quietly. Away. Mother and child. Alone. And then they switched places. Child bearing the burden of mother. The silent screams and abandonment and the fetus in somber solitude, starving for spirit. Growing wild and thorny and beautiful in an asphalt yard. Rose petals heaped beneath his feet as he cried. He was hairless . . . delectable . . . defenseless . . . definitive. His feet planted on another planet, in another space. The dancers had all been Racine for a moment, and placed themselves beneath his skin. The old woman gestured toward water, where a young girl in a lilac gown danced on pennies and sang to Etta James for the Goddess Erzuile.

—Racine. Racine. You hear that? You hear the sweet crack in the falsetto? You hear the music?

—My name was Racine before it was anything else.

From the lower vestibule of the vacant building, he could hear the prophet Nahum's cadence accompanied by glass shattering beneath feet and objects moving violently. His stomach was swelling, soon to erupt liquor and food, and the burnt orange foreshadowing bled through the broken windowpanes. It was Brooklyn. It was Sunday. It was morning.

Nahum turned to the man, thin, wounded, and covered in blossoms. Ripped pages from Deuteronomy carpeted the floor with fragments of tinted bottles and shared needles and matchbooks. Nahum's arm was torn. They were facing each other, bleeding rapidly. Stolichnaya gushed from Racine's pierced sides.

"Cursed shalt thou be in the city!"

Nahum had been looking for answers in needles and Scriptures and fragmented bottles.

෧෨

". . . and cursed shalt thou be in the field!"

God used fallen prophets to deliver revelations to pagans.

"Cursed shall be thy basket and thy store—"

Nahum pushed his open hands into the face of the disciple. Slapped him from brow to buttock, pulled bunches of hair and bouquets of flowers from the scalp in his fists.

"Cursed shall be the fruit of thy body—"

Nahum caressed the empty scrotum and pulled. Licked the weary shoulder and bit. Fingered the cavern of the ass and rent the veil twain. Entered the inner sanctuary. The holy of holies. Entered and overturned the tables. Disrupted the calm. The temple had been defiled.

"Cursed shalt thou be when thou comest in and cursed shalt thou be when thou goest out!"

Glass fragments were stuck into the throat, the lower back, the eye. What a beautiful sculpture, of glass and flowers, emerged from the dying body. A cooling board of torn pages. Deuteronomy. Winding sheets. Nahum embraced the metaphor, and climbed a fire escape to hear God from a high place . . . Racine's lips smiled, and his head laughed before the flesh went cold. The chest heaved, the stomach relaxed, the muscles untightened before the eyes went dark. The maiden danced near water. Pennies at her feet. Sweet liquid from her nipples moistening the fabric of a lilac gown. She'd lived his death before, and together, mother and child danced beneath a voyeuring moon.

—Yes . . . yes, Mama. I hear . . . yes . . . yes . . .

WALLACE THURMAN

Infants of the Spring

It was Raymond's last night in Niggeratti Manor. Lucille had spent most of the evening with him, aiding him to pack. The studio was bare and cheerless. The walls had been stripped of the colorful original drawings contributed by Paul and Carl Denny. They were now stark and bare. The book shelves were empty, and yawned hideously in the more shaded corners. The middle of the room was filled with boxes in which his books had been packed, and in the alcove his trunk and suitcases stood at attention in military array. The rest of the house was also in a state of dishevelment. Painters and plasterers had been swarming over the place, leaving undeniable evidence of their presence and handiwork. Niggeratti Manor was almost ready to suffer its transition from a congenial home for Negro artists to a congenial dormitory for bachelor girls.

Amid the gloom and confusion Raymond and Stephen sat, fitfully conversing between frequent drinks which had little effect. There was more bad news. Stephen had been called back to Europe. His mother was dangerously ill. There was little hope of his arriving before she died, but they insisted that he, the eldest son, start for home immediately. He was to sail the next day.

"You know, son, family is a hell of a thing. They should all be dissolved. Of course I'm perturbed at the thought of my mother's death, but I can't stop her from dying, nor can I bring her back to life should she be dead when I arrive. And yet I am dragged across an ocean, expected to display great grief and indulge in all the other tomfoolery human beings indulge themselves in when another human being dies. It's all tommy-rot."

"Assuredly," Raymond agreed, "dying is an event, a perversely festive occasion, not so much for the deceased as for his so-called mourners. Let's forget it. You've got to adhere to the traditions of the clan to some degree. Let's drink to the day when a person's death will be the cue for a wild gin party rather than a signal for well meant but purely exhibitionistic grief." He held his glass aloft. "Skip ze gutter." The glasses were drained.

"And after you get in Europe?"

"I will be prevailed upon to stay at home and become a respectable schoolmaster. Now, let's finish the bottle of gin. I've got to go. It's after three and as usual we've been talking for hours and said nothing."

Raymond measured out the remaining liquor.

"O.K., Steve. Here's to the fall of Niggeratti Manor and all within."

Stephen had gone. Raymond quickly prepared himself for bed, and was almost asleep when the telephone began to ring. He cursed, decided not to get up, and turned his face toward the wall. What fool could be calling at this hour of the morning? In the old days it might have been expected, but now Niggeratti Manor was no more. There was nothing left of the old régime except reminiscences and gossip. The telephone continued to ring. Its blaring voice echoed throughout the empty house. Muttering to himself, Raymond finally left his bed, donned his bathrobe and mules, went out into the hallway, and angrily lifted the receiver:

"Hello," he grumbled.

A strange voice answered. "Hello. Is this Raymond Taylor?"

"It is."

"This is Artie Fletcher, Paul's roommate. Can you come

down to my house right away? Something terrible has happened."

Raymond was now fully awake. The tone of horror in the voice at the other end of the wire both stimulated and frightened him. He had a vague, eerie premonition of impending tragedy.

"What is it? What's happened?" he queried impatiently.

"Paul's committed suicide."

Raymond almost dropped the receiver. Mechanically he obtained the address, assured Artie Fletcher that he would rush to the scene, and within a very few moments was dressed and on his way.

The subway ride was long and tedious. Only local trains were in operation, local trains which blundered along slowly, stopping at every station, droning noisily: Paul is dead. Paul is dead.

Had Paul the debonair, Paul the poseur, Paul the irresponsible romanticist, finally faced reality and seen himself and the world as they actually were? Or was this merely another act, the final stanza in his drama of beautiful gestures? It was consonant with his character, this committing suicide. He had employed every other conceivable means to make himself stand out from the mob. Wooed the unusual, cultivated artificiality, defied all conventions of dress and conduct. Now perhaps he had decided that there was nothing left for him to do except execute self-murder in some bizarre manner. Raymond found himself not so much interested in the fact that Paul was dead as he was in wanting to know how death had been accomplished. The train trundled along clamoring: What did he do? What did he do? Raymond deplored the fact that he had not had sufficient money to hire a taxi.

The train reached Christopher Street. Raymond rushed out of the subway to the street above. He hesitated a moment to get his bearings, repeated the directions he had been given over the telephone, and plunged into a maze of criss-cross streets. As he neared his goal, a slender white youth fluttered toward him.

"Are you Raymond Taylor?"

"Yes."

"Come this way, please. I was watching for you."

Raymond followed his unknown companion into a malodorous, jerry-built tenement, and climbed four flights of creaky stairs to a rear room, lighted only by burning planks in the fireplace. There were several people in the room, all strangely hushed and pale. A chair was vacated for him near the fireplace. No introductions were made. Raymond lit a cigarette to hide his nervousness. His guide, whom he presumed to be Artie Fletcher, told him the details of Paul's suicide.

Earlier that evening they had gone to a party. It had been a wild revel. There had been liquor and cocaine which everyone had taken in order to experience a new thrill. There had been many people at the party and it had been difficult to keep track of any one person. When the party had come to an end, Paul was nowhere to be found, and his roommate had come home alone.

An hour or so later, he had heard a commotion in the hallway. Several people were congregated outside the bathroom door, grumbling because they had been unable to gain admittance. The bathroom, it seemed, had been occupied for almost two hours and there was no response from within. Finally someone suggested breaking down the door. This had been done. No one had been prepared for the gruesome yet fascinating spectacle which met their eyes.

Paul had evidently come home before the end of the party. On arriving, he had locked himself in the bathroom, donned a crimson mandarin robe, wrapped his head in a batik scarf of his own designing, hung a group of his spirit portraits on the dingy calcimined wall, and carpeted the floor with sheets of paper detached from the notebook in which he had been writing his novel. He had then, it seemed, placed scented joss-sticks in the four corners of the room, lit them, climbed into the bathtub, turned on the water, then slashed his wrists with a highly ornamented Chinese dirk. When they found him, the bathtub had overflowed, and Paul lay crumpled at the bottom, a colorful, inanimate corpse in a crimson streaked tub.

What delightful publicity to precede the posthumous publication of his novel, which novel, however, had been rendered illegible when the overflow of water had inundated the floor, and soaked the sheets strewn over its surface. Paul had not foreseen the possible inundation, nor had he taken into consideration the impermanency of penciled transcriptions.

Artie Fletcher had salvaged as many of the sheets as possible. He handed the sodden mass to Raymond. Ironically enough, only the title sheet and the dedication page were completely legible. The book was entitled:

Wu Sing: The Geisha Man

It had been dedicated:

To
Huysmans' Des Esseintes and Oscar Wilde's Oscar Wilde
Ecstatic Spirits with whom I Cohabit
And whose golden spores of decadent pollen
I shall broadcast and fertilize
It is written
Paul Arbian.

Beneath this inscription, he had drawn a distorted, inky black skyscraper, modeled after Niggeratti Manor, and on which were focused an array of blindingly white beams of light. The foundation of this building was composed of crumbling stone. At first glance it could be ascertained that the skyscraper would soon crumple and fall, leaving the dominating white lights in full possession of the sky.

Hemorrhaging

ORIAN HYDE WEEKS

Dissimulations

W hat in the end silenced Star was his incongruous calm:
the restrained smile that sat guardedly on his lips like a
toddler forced to sit upon the knee of a blood relation it has
never seen but whom, the child suspects, adores him. The GI
Joe charm. Yes, Angel knew perfectly what she intended to do.
But he had made no effort since her arrival to sequester her, not
even to threaten her. Instead, he sat there looking directly at her
in utter innocence, hypnotized by the Christmas feast of food
and family in the nest in which they, as children and now as
adults, were suffered and sustained. What could possibly happen
among thirty relations? his attitude asked cockily. Moreover, if
you had known that my orders would be suddenly changed so
that I could stay home for the holidays, you, Star, wouldn't be
here right now! It was true; she had planned to tell their parents
while he fought for the United States and the world in the
Persian Gulf, and she hadn't known that he was still in Washington until she arrived home from L.A. He ate in a communion of
love: their father was so ecstatic to have him there among them
that he bestowed upon Angel the honor of carving the turkey.
Carmilla, Angel's white wife of twelve years, sat beside him, on

his right; Grandma, the matriarch of the Close family, and their mother's mother both to his left. At the head and foot of the table their parents—George and Eunice—were enthroned. To Star's right sat Uncle Harris and his wife, Theodora; their uncle Herbert and his wife, Flora, were to her left. In the living room was a long table occupied by ten other family members, all cousins and uncles and aunts. In the family room thirteen children squealed playfully, three of them Angel's. His eyes seemed to take them all in, but more often than not they were focused on Star. She disliked Angel watching her. The sensation was familiar, like the memory of her body before breasts.

"It's too bad you couldn't go to Somalia instead," said Uncle Herbert, chewing on Virginia ham. "Safer there."

Angel smiled proudly. "The Persian Gulf is where the action is. If I've got to go, I'd rather go where the time will pass quickly. Besides, my first tour there went pretty well. We bombed them to hell." His plate was clean, and Carmilla, ever the dutiful wife, a large breeder, asked him if he wanted it restocked. She was up before his answer was given.

"Those poor people," Flora said.

"Thank God you here with us right now!" their mother said. She had been close to tears ever since Angel arrived.

"Like the Germans," said Grandma Close. Grandpa Close, who'd died two years ago, had been in a tank brigade in World War II that was the first to see concentration camps. The horrifying stories he'd told the family lived on through Grandma Close, who recycled them with an attitude not so much sepulchral as excited, adding what few German curse words she had learned in 1914.

"The CIA should just kill that son of a bitch Hussein, that would solve the problem right there," said Uncle Herbert.

"Maybe they, or somebody, will," Angel said. "It's clear that the only way Iraq will comply with the UN's demands is if someone gets rid of him."

He was an intelligence officer with the army, presumably in on clandestine goings-on, so everyone was visibly awed, moreso by his knowledge itself than by the consequences of what he knew. He had always had an intimidating aspect. Since his graduation from West Point, no one ever doubted that what he said was true, and no one—excluding his father, who had served in Korea—really believed that anything would happen to such an extraordinary man. Thus they did not see oversunned people with zealotry in their blood as a hazard to him. This was not Vietnam: there was no swamp, just endless fields of boiling, naked desert. This war would be easy, a bloody video game the entire world could watch. No one would have been surprised if Angel went to the moon; in fact, they expected such extraordinary things of him.

His gifts were apparent early in childhood, as was his confidence, when at nine years of age he wrote a letter to the mayor expressing why bussing as a means to end segregation was important. The mayor was so taken by Angel's argument that he invited the family down for what was ostensibly an informal visit at his office but was in fact more like a press conference. Even Star remembered what Angel, standing beside the blue-eyed mayor, had said on television, fearlessly facing all those reporters and blinding, flashing lights: "I want to be so proud of this country that I would die for it. Everybody should have the opportunity to be a model citizen. My father had that opportunity—but only on the battlefield; when he came home he had to ride the back of the bus. His father was a sharecropper. And his father's father was a slave. No doubt they were proud Americans, too. But America was not proud of them."

"Star, did you know your brother rescued a little girl from a burning car in Iraq?" their mother suddenly piped up. "Why don't you tell us what happened, Angel." Star had already heard this story at least three times.

"Go on, son," urged their father.

"Well—" Angel looked around him satisfied that all were paying attention. "A cab bomb exploded on the street and set everything near it on fire. A little girl and her older sister were trapped in a car near the one that exploded. Their mother was crossing the street; she was decapitated by the blast in front of her daughters' eyes. Anyway, we ran into the fire to rescue the kids. But the fire was burning out of control and we couldn't figure out a way to rescue them without casualties. All I saw was those two little girls, screaming and banging on the car window. They were suffocating. So I climbed on top of the car. It had one of those sun roofs. I kicked it in and pulled the girls out. I just did what I had to do."

"He was given a medal, weren't you, Angel?" their mother boasted.

The conversational tone whenever Star was at home—moderate to heavy bragging about Angel's accomplishments—was now established. And to it was added a leitmotif: the denigration of Star. Star believed that her mother never for a second looked at her without remembering the monstrous outrage and embarrassment she had felt when a then-anonymous "friend of the family" had sent her a sex videotape featuring Star. After graduating from college and moving to Hollywood, Star had done a few pornography films. She was a professionally trained actress, she needed the money, and sex wasn't a big deal. One of her girlfriends had suggested the idea. At first Star had recoiled; she didn't need the work since at the time she had a role in a legitimate film (ironically, she played a prostitute in it). But that film was never released, and she found herself once again destitute. Frustration over her desire to act, on top of her poverty, made the idea of pornography less and less repulsive.

Her friend Charita had already signed on and was working on a film, loving the work more than she did the money, she claimed. After all, there were no lines to worry about forgetting. Star was twenty-two years old, burning for an ephipany after four years of boredom in college in Sandusky, Ohio, and the dullest life imaginable in Annapolis. Pornography seemed a means to an end. What stunned her, she later realized, was that she enjoyed it. She enjoyed the fantasy, the black beauty of the men, and later the women with strap-on dildos, the extraordinary odor of lust, like wisteria blossom in stagnant air. It was not a performance: her passion was real, beyond her control even, and when it was over she recognized neither herself nor the body dismounting her. "Fuck that pussy," the voices would say to her, digging deeper into her, and beneath the swirl of pleasure, beneath the shudder of muscles and after the spill of lava, was pain—nameless and deep. Once the center was reached, excavated were shame, degradation, humiliation—they rose in her eyes as she looked into the eyes of the stranger. And she would remember.

By the time she'd started her third pornographic film, the legitimate film was released, and she was suddenly getting calls for projects. That first pornographic film—the unforgettable one—was called *Fantasia*. The role required her to paint her body green, wear a white wig, and use a pseudonymn. Long after she'd left porn, she remembered that film, the pleasure, the pain. Every time she spoke to her mother, the film was playing in her mind. She could see her mother watching it.

"Star, honey, you've hardly touched your food," Flora said. "You on a diet?"

"No," said Star, glancing quickly at Angel. Their eyes met.

"You look fabulous, chile. Just like a movie star. And the weave looks so natural."

"Thank you," Star said. She scratched her thigh and closed her eyes. When she opened them, he was looking away from her, a righteous, Republican sternness to his profile, exactly as she imagined him. She had not seen him since he graduated West Point over fourteen years ago, when he was perfect. He was still perfect. When he and his family arrived, over an hour before, she had been hiding upstairs, wondering how she would get through this meeting. Dinner was being served early because Sergeant Angel Close was being shipped out at five the next morning. He had driven his family up from Quantico, Virginia, where they lived, and they still had to drive out to Baltimore, to say Merry Christmas to Carmilla's family.

When they arrived at the house, she could hear from her bedroom his children talking to each other and stomping down the stairs. She was briefly happy; she'd never seen them before, except in photographs her mother sent to her. When she finally did go downstairs, sweat bled under her arms. His voice when he greeted her was high and excited, and his body felt hard when he embraced her. She did not look at him. She would not have come home had she known to expect him—her mother and father had at first thought that he was leaving on December 21, and decided for some reason not to tell her of his change of plans. She arrived Christmas Eve assured that he would be gone, and now she was angry. Seeing her reaction, her mother had said, "I don't know why you two never talk to each other, but I'm sick of it. You used to love each other so much—my God, you were Siamese twins—and now you hardly speak to each other. You haven't seen him in years. Please, Star, please talk to him."

Flora persisted. "I saw Luther Vandross on TV. He looks terrible, like he got AIDS or something." She paused, turned her head in the direction of the living room, and shouted, "Tawanda, Luther Vandross got AIDS?" Tawanda shouted she didn't know. The conversation turned to the enormous job ahead of President-elect Clinton. Star had campaigned for him in Hollywood, and was sure that Clinton would do a far better job than Bush.

"They're all alike," Aunt Theodora said.

"They sure as hell are, as far as black people are concerned," added Uncle Herbert.

"Star always was political," their mother added, causing the conversation to stumble. "She even campaigned for Clinton. But I guess y'all do that in Hollywood."

"Clinton's a fool. The morality of this country is going to pot, and at least if the Republicans stayed in office, there wouldn't be faggots in the military," Angel said, his jaws clenched. Herbert and Flora agreed.

"Which is more of a national tragedy than AIDS, black-on-black violence, fascism, and incest," Star said hotly. I hate you, she thought. "Morality is a relative thing, Angel." They stared at each other while the table fell silent around them.

Their mother tried again, "Isn't it nice to be with your brother again?"

Tell them! Now was the time to give everyone a lesson on morality. She looked around the table, wondering who among them knew that she had done pornography. She wanted to catch them all up, smash the illusions of their impunity in their own deceit, in the country's deceit, in the world's deceit. But her mother's last remark—"This is the first time both my children have been together in fourteen years, and I'm so thankful"— silenced her.

"So Star, what's happening in L.A.?" Carmilla said. Star turned away from Theodora, glanced at Carmilla, then met Angel's eyes.

"Rain," she said, looking around tentatively at her parents, who were watching them as the other relations kept talking. "It's the rainy season." His eyes were brown, lighter than his dark skin. They watched her. "It rains a lot."

Flora suddenly chimed in, "I don't know how you can stand those earthquakes. I'd be scared to death."

Looking at Star, Carmilla said, "I saw you on *Santa Barbara*." Then, "I told you that, sweetheart," she said to Angel, whose eyes never left Star. "Remember, she was in *Malcolm X* too. He hasn't seen the movie yet, he's been away so much."

Really. That's not why he hasn't seen the film, is it, Angel? Star glared at him suddenly, then forced herself to relax. She felt herself moving inexorably forward in this conversation, and she would follow it to its end. "I've got a couple television spots upcoming," she said.

"That's terrific," Carmilla said. "What shows? Angel won't be able to see them, but I will."

"*L.A. Law* and the show with Carl Weathers, *Street Justice*."

"Thank God things is better for her out there," their mother said.

"Yes," said Angel.

"She's a fine actress," said Uncle Herbert. "And prettier than Whitley. Did you see her in *Harlem Nights*? Wadn't she something?"

"I always knew you would succeed," Angel said, an expression on his face she thought was smug until he smiled.

Angered anew, she said, "When we spoke on the phone, did I tell you I'm being considered for a role on *Star Trek: Deep Space 9*?" She looked at him firmly when she said this, then glanced quickly at her mother, then turned back to Angel.

"When who spoke on the phone?" her mother asked.

"When Angel and I did," she said, coyly. "Angel called me. We had something to discuss."

"Oh," said her mother, apparently relieved that they were talking but confused as to why and how she didn't know about it.

"Remember *Star Trek?*" Star asked, watching him. In the letter she'd written to him in September, she had described the game they used to play, based on the show—discovering new frontiers. Her letter had finally provoked Angel to call her.

"Don't you ever write no shit like that and mail it to my house again! Suppose my wife had seen it. Or one of my children got hold of it," he had hissed.

"But it's all true," she said, coldly. "Your wife should know. Your daughter is the same age I was when you molested me."

"Molested you?" he roared. "Funny word to use. I guess you molested me when you came knocking on my door in the middle of the night wanting me to 'molest' you? Putting your pussy in my face like a fucking prostitute."

I didn't go to his door at night! She was confused. "I was only a child," she cried. "Twelve fucking years old, Angel. I admired you. You were my big brother. You took advantage of me."

"We were both kids," he said brutally.

"You were sixteen," she shouted. "You should have known better."

"So should you," he said, flatly.

I shouldn't have had to know better! I am not responsible for this. I was a kid, I didn't know. I didn't know. Suddenly she was crying. "I should have told everybody a long time ago. You should've been locked up. You wrecked my life. You fucking dog."

"This ain't the Oprah Winfrey show," Angel had snapped back at her. "There is no audience to condemn me. Just a family that's ashamed of you. I've got a respectable life. You're the one who's in porno flicks. How many abortions have you had? Mom's always complaining about the way you live—your girlfriends—and I saw *Sistuhs*—you bull dyke. You know what, nobody'd believe you anyway. And they'd hate you. You make me sick."

She laughed, or screamed. "You're wrong about her believing me, Angel. She knows. I'm the 'friend of the family' that sent that video. And you know what I told her when she asked me how I could do such a thing? I told her I just pretended it was you."

"You are disgusting," Angel spat, and hung up.

Star crashed the phone to the floor. She was ready to call her mother and have it out all over again, even call the police, somebody to put down the riot ravaging her right now. But she didn't. She couldn't. She even wanted to call him back, demand that he apologize for what he had done. It was all she had wanted, all these years. She was thirty years old, oppressed by something nameless and haunting and wanting back an innocence she wasn't even sure she'd ever had. In even her most lucid moments the lurid details were inlaid with lust and she was not sure who had done what to whom. She was not sure that she hadn't enjoyed the "special" bond between them. And she was not sure whether, in the end, what devastated her the most was not his molestation but his abandonment and the vortex of guilt into which she had been thrown.

Yes, he was there, at sixteen, at midnight in her bedroom, having quietly slipped in through the door that separated their rooms. Yes, she was under him, allowing him to slide in and out of her. She wanted to believe that she was innocent, that she didn't know that what she was doing was wrong, that curiosity and trust had brought her to this position with him between her legs. He was and had always been her best friend. She loved him more than anyone else alive; he could do no wrong in her eyes. How could what they did together be wrong? How could making each other so happy be wrong?

But it was wrong. He made her know that as soon as he came home from his first semester at West Point. He was cold to her, coldly embraced her. She slipped into his bedroom and climbed into his bed, as she had done so many times. He woke up, told her to grow up and get back to her bed before their parents overheard them. How she hated him. But not then, not at that crucial moment, she couldn't. She loved him too much.

"Don't you love me? You didn't even write to me once," she

said, purring, with eyes like a woman. With her hand she touched his penis; it was not erect but indignantly flaccid.

"You're acting like a little whore. Now go to bed," he exclaimed. The memory of that scene had stalked her ever since. When Charita suggested that they do porn to make money, the first thing that came to her mind was Angel, and just as she was about to lower her mouth to a black man's penis, she saw Angel's. At home that night, she cried herself to sleep. With the video copy she sent to Angel, she enclosed a note: "I bet you didn't know you were a prophet. My performance in *Fantasia* was inspired by you." She'd always wondered if he watched it. Now, staring at him, waiting for his response, she felt certain that he had. And he understood.

"We used to love *Star Trek*," he said, after clearing his throat, with a challenging smile.

"Star what?" said Uncle Harris.

"*Star Trek*," Angel repeated, looking at Star. "A science-fiction show Star and I used to watch when we were kids."

"I know, I know, Spock, right?" Uncle Harris leaned into Star's face, blocking her view of Angel.

"Star," Angel said.

"Yes—"

"Do you remember. . . ?"

"Yes," she said.

"Damn, we must have seen every episode at least ten times," he mused, chuckling.

"Y'all sure did watch a lot of that program," their mother chimed in. "Didn't they, George?"

Angel said, "Do you remember that episode called 'Mirage or Illusion'—about a race of people that had destroyed the surface of their planet and had to go underground? They were pure intellect. They captured the *Enterprise* and tried to mate the captain with this woman they held as hostage. There was a scene where she was painted green and had blonde hair. You remember, Star?" His face was hard, brutal, challenging. Perfectly white teeth revealed themselves in a vivid, dangerous smile. He was a trained killer. He stared at her, and this time she did not look away.

"I'll never forget it," she said.

Conversation between Carmilla and their mother paved over the strange pause between them, and shortly Angel stood up and said that he hated to eat and run but they must be going. He summoned the children, who came with great discipline from the other room, presents in tow, while he and Carmilla went to kiss the family good-bye. Their parents stood near the front door, ready to launch the family off, their mother finally surrending to the tears that had threatened all afternoon. Angel took her into his arms as gently as he might his children, promising that he wouldn't be killed in the Persian Gulf.

As she watched this scene, something he said in that hysterical phone conversation struck Star. That they, the family, would hate her. Why would they hate me? she had wondered. The answer lay in the tears streaming down her mother's face, the proud pain in her father's. Everything they believed in was embodied in him; they couldn't afford not to love him, to believe in him, because there was nothing without him, not even each other. They expected her to hug him, and she hesitated just long enough to hear her mother cry, "Stop carryin' on like a child, Star. You might not never see your brother again." Before Star could even submit to the command and this odd feeling about him and, yes, her own outrage, his arms reached for her and pulled her close. So that everyone could hear, he said, "Let's not be such strangers. I'll write you from Iraq." He pushed her away far enough so that their eyes could see deeply into what was in memory too familiar, too lush, too painful, and yet was now strange and scabbed. Something like longing stirred in her, friction distilled into an essence. *Oh baby, does it feel good?* She suddenly remembered his voice, burning in her ear, as wet seismic sensations spasmed inside her and a lost happiness bloomed in her heart. "Oh, yes," she cried, pulling his mouth onto hers. *I love you. Yes.*

GLORIA NAYLOR

The Two

At first they seemed like such nice girls. No one could remember exactly when they had moved into Brewster. It
was earlier in the year before Ben was killed—of course, it had to
be before Ben's death. But no one remembered if it was in the
winter or spring of that year that the two had come. People often
came and went on Brewster Place like a restless night's dream,
moving in and out in the dark to avoid eviction notices or neighborhood bulletins about the dilapidated condition of their fur-
nishings. So it wasn't until the two were clocked leaving in the
mornings and returning in the evenings at regular intervals that
it was quietly absorbed that they now claimed Brewster as home.
And Brewster waited, cautiously prepared to claim them, because you never knew about young women, and obviously single
at that. But when no wild music or drunken friends careened out
of the corner building on weekends, and especially, when no
slightly eager husbands were encouraged to linger around that
first-floor apartment and run errands for them, a suspended sigh
of relief floated around the two when they dumped their garbage, did their shopping, and headed for the morning bus.
    The women of Brewster had readily accepted the lighter,

skinny one. There wasn't much threat in her timid mincing walk and the slightly protruding teeth she seemed so eager to show everyone in her bell-like good mornings and evenings. Breaths were held a little longer in the direction of the short dark one—too pretty, and too much behind. And she insisted on wearing those thin Qiana dresses that the summer breeze molded against the maddening rhythm of the twenty pounds of rounded flesh that she swung steadily down the street. Through slitted eyes, the women watched their men watching her pass, knowing the bastards were praying for a wind. But since she seemed oblivious to whether these supplications went answered, their sighs settled around her shoulders too. Nice girls.

And so no one even cared to remember exactly when they had moved into Brewster Place, until the rumor started. It had first spread through the block like a sour odor that's only faintly perceptible and easily ignored until it starts growing in strength from the dozen mouths it had been lying in, among clammy gums and scum-coated teeth. And then it was everywhere—lining the mouths and whitening the lips of everyone as they wrinkled up their noses at its pervading smell, unable to pinpoint the source or time of its initial arrival. Sophie could—she had been there.

It wasn't that the rumor had actually begun with Sophie. A rumor needs no true parent. It only needs a willing carrier, and it found one in Sophie. She had been there—on one of those August evenings when the sun's absence is a mockery because the heat leaves the air so heavy it presses the naked skin down on your body, to the point that a sheet becomes unbearable and sleep impossible. So most of Brewster was outside that night when the two had come in together, probably from one of those air-conditioned movies downtown, and had greeted the ones who were loitering around their building. And they had started up the steps when the skinny one tripped over a child's ball and the darker one had grabbed her by the arm and around the waist to break her fall. "Careful, don't wanna lose you now." And the two of them had laughed into each other's eyes and went into the building.

The smell had begun there. It outlined the image of the

stumbling woman and the one who had broken her fall. Sophie and a few other women sniffed at the spot and then, perplexed, silently looked at each other. Where had they seen that before? They had often laughed and touched each other—held each other in joy or its dark twin—but where had they seen *that* before? It came to them as the scent drifted down the steps and entered their nostrils on the way to their inner mouths. They had seen that—done that—with their men. That shared moment of invisible communion reserved for two and hidden from the rest of the world behind laughter or tears or a touch. In the days before babies, miscarriages, and other broken dreams, after stolen caresses in barn stalls and cotton houses, after intimate walks from church and secret kisses with boys who were now long forgotten or permanently fixed in their lives—that was where. They could almost feel the odor moving about in their mouths, and they slowly knitted themselves together and let it out into the air like a yellow mist that began to cling to the bricks on Brewster.

So it got around that the two in 312 were *that* way. And they had seemed like such nice girls. Their regular exits and entrances to the block were viewed with a jaundiced eye. The quiet that rested around their door on the weekends hinted of all sorts of secret rituals, and their friendly indifference to the men on the street was an insult to the women as a brazen flaunting of unnatural ways.

Since Sophie's apartment windows faced theirs from across the air shaft, she became the official watchman for the block, and her opinions were deferred to whenever the two came up in conversation. Sophie took her position seriously and was constantly alert for any telltale signs that might creep out around their drawn shades, across from which she kept a religious vigil. An entire week of drawn shades was evidence enough to send her flying around with reports that as soon as it got dark they pulled their shades down and put on the lights. Heads nodded in knowing unison—a definite sign. If doubt was voiced with a "But I pull my shades down at night too," a whispered "Yeah, but you're not *that* way" was argument enough to win them over.

Sophie watched the lighter one dumping their garbage, and she went outside and opened the lid. Her eyes darted over the crushed tin cans, vegetable peelings, and empty chocolate chip cookie boxes. What do they do with all them chocolate chip cookies? It was surely a sign, but it would take some time to figure that one out. She saw Ben go into their apartment, and she waited and blocked his path as he came out, carrying his toolbox.

"What ya see?" She grabbed his arm and whispered wetly in his face.

Ben stared at her squinted eyes and drooping lips and shook his head slowly. "Uh, uh, uh, it was terrible."

"Yeah?" She moved in a little closer.

"Worst busted faucet I seen in my whole life." He shook her hand off his arm and left her standing in the middle of the block.

"You old sop bucket," she muttered, as she went back up on her stoop. A broken faucet, huh? Why did they need to use so much water?

Sophie had plenty to report that day. Ben had said it was terrible in there. No, she didn't know exactly what he had seen, but you can imagine—and they did. Confronted with the difference that had been thrust into their predictable world, they reached into their imaginations and, using an ancient pattern, weaved themselves a reason for its existence. Out of necessity they stitched all of their secret fears and lingering childhood nightmares into this existence, because even though it was deceptive enough to try and look as they looked, talk as they talked, and do as they did, it had to have some hidden stain to invalidate it—it was impossible for them both to be right. So they leaned back, supported by the sheer weight of their numbers and comforted by the woven barrier that kept them protected from the yellow mist that enshrouded the two as they came and went on Brewster Place.

Lorraine was the first to notice the change in the people on Brewster Place. She was a shy but naturally friendly woman who got up early, and had read the morning paper and done fifty sit-ups before it was time to leave for work. She came out of her apartment eager to start her day by greeting any of her neighbors who were outside. But she noticed that some of the people who had spoken to her before made a point of having something else to do with their eyes when she passed, although she could almost feel them staring at her back as she moved on. The ones who still spoke only did so after an uncomfortable pause, in which they seemed to be peering through her before they begrudged her a good morning or evening. She wondered if it was all in her mind and she thought about mentioning it to Theresa, but she didn't want to be accused of being too sensitive again. And how would Tee even notice anything like that anyway? She had a lousy attitude and hardly ever spoke to people. She stayed in that bed until the last moment and rushed out of the house fogged-up and grumpy, and she was used to being stared at—by men at least—because of her body.

Lorraine thought about these things as she came up the block from work, carrying a large paper bag. The group of women on her stoop parted silently and let her pass.

"Good evening," she said, as she climbed the steps.

Sophie was standing on the top step and tried to peek into the bag. "You been shopping, huh? What ya buy?" It was almost an accusation.

"Groceries." Lorraine shielded the top of the bag from view and squeezed past her with a confused frown. She saw Sophie throw a knowing glance to the others at the bottom of the stoop. What was wrong with this old woman? Was she crazy or something?

Lorraine went into her apartment. Theresa was sitting by the window, reading a copy of *Mademoiselle.* She glanced up from her magazine. "Did you get my chocolate chip cookies?"

"Why good evening to you, too, Tee. And how was my day? Just wonderful." She sat the bag down on the couch. "The little Baxter boy brought in a puppy for show-and-tell, and the damn thing pissed all over the floor and then proceeded to chew the heel off my shoe, but, yes, I managed to hobble to the store and bring you your chocolate chip cookies."

Oh, Jesus, Theresa thought, she's got a bug up her ass to-night.

"Well, you should speak to Mrs. Baxter. She ought to train her kid better than that." She didn't wait for Lorraine to stop laughing before she tried to stretch her good mood. "Here, I'll put those things away. Want me to make dinner so you can rest? I only worked half a day, and the most tragic thing that went down was a broken fingernail and that got caught in my type-writer."

Lorraine followed Theresa into the kitchen. "No, I'm not really tired, and fair's fair, you cooked last night. I didn't mean to tick off like that; it's just that . . . well, Tee, have you no-ticed that people aren't as nice as they used to be?"

Theresa stiffened. Oh, God, here she goes again. "What peo-ple, Lorraine? Nice in what way?"

"Well, the people in this building and on the street. No one hardly speaks anymore. I mean, I'll come in and say good eve-ning—and just silence. It wasn't like that when we first moved in. I don't know, it just makes you wonder; that's all. What are they thinking?"

"I personally don't give a shit what they're thinking. And their good evenings don't put any bread on my table."

"Yeah, but you didn't see the way that woman looked at me out there. They must feel something or know something. They probably—"

"They, they, they!" Theresa exploded. "You know, I'm not starting up with this again, Lorraine. Who in the hell are they? And where in the hell are we? Living in some dump of a building in this God-forsaken part of town around a bunch of ignorant niggers with the cotton still under their fingernails because of you and your theys. They knew something in Linden Hills, so I gave up an apartment for you that I'd been in for the last four years. And then they knew in Park Heights, and you made me so miserable there we had to leave. Now these mysterious theys are on Brewster Place. Well, look out that window, kid. There's a big wall down that block, and this is the end of the line for me. I'm not moving anymore, so if that's what you're working yourself up to—save it!"

When Theresa became angry she was like a lump of smoldering coal, and her fierce bursts of temper always unsettled Lorraine.

"You see, that's why I didn't want to mention it." Lorraine began to pull at her fingers nervously. "You're always flying up and jumping to conclusions—no one said anything about moving. And I didn't know your life has been so miserable since you met me. I'm sorry about that," she finished tearfully.

Theresa looked at Lorraine, standing in the kitchen door like a wilted leaf, and she wanted to throw something at her. Why didn't she ever fight back? The very softness that had first attracted her to Lorraine was now a frequent cause for irritation. Smoked honey. That's what Lorraine had reminded her of, sitting in her office clutching that application. Dry autumn days in Georgia woods, thick bloated smoke under a beehive, and the first glimpse of amber honey just faintly darkened about the edges by the burning twigs. She had flowed just that heavily into Theresa's mind and had stuck there with a persistent sweetness.

But Theresa hadn't known then that this softness filled Lorraine up to the very middle and that she would bend at the slightest pressure, would be constantly seeking to surround herself with the comfort of everyone's goodwill, and would shrivel up at the least touch of disapproval. It was becoming a drain to be continually called upon for this nurturing and support that she just didn't understand. She had supplied it at first out of love for Lorraine, hoping that she would harden eventually, even as honey does when exposed to the cold. Theresa was growing tired of being clung to—of being the one who was leaned on. She didn't want a child—she wanted someone who could stand toe to toe with her and be willing to slug it out at times. If they practiced that way with each other, then they could turn back to back and beat the hell out of the world for trying to invade their territory. But she had found no such sparring partner in Lorraine, and the strain of fighting alone was beginning to show on her.

"Well, if it was that miserable, I would have been gone a long time ago," she said, watching her words refresh Lorraine like a gentle shower.

"I guess you think I'm some sort of a sick paranoid, but I can't afford to have people calling my job or writing letters to my principal. You know I've already lost a position like that in Detroit. And teaching is my whole life, Tee."

"I know," she sighed, not really knowing at all. There was no danger of that ever happening on Brewster Place. Lorraine taught too far from this neighborhood for anyone here to recognize her in that school. No, it wasn't her job she feared losing this time, but their approval. She wanted to stand out there and chat and trade makeup secrets and cake recipes. She wanted to be secretary of their block association and be asked to mind their kids while they ran to the store. And none of that was going to happen if they couldn't even bring themselves to accept her good evenings.

Theresa silently finished unpacking the groceries. "Why did you buy cottage cheese? Who eats that stuff?"

"Well, I thought we should go on a diet."

"If *we* go on a diet, then you'll disappear. You've got nothing to lose but your hair."

"Oh, I don't know. I thought that we might want to try and reduce our hips or something." Lorraine shrugged playfully.

"No, thank you. We are very happy with our hips the way they are," Theresa said, as she shoved the cottage cheese to the back of the refrigerator. "And even when I lose weight, it never comes off there. My chest and arms just get smaller, and I start looking like a bottle of salad dressing."

The two women laughed, and Theresa sat down to watch Lorraine fix dinner. "You know, this behind has always been my downfall. When I was coming up in Georgia with my grandmother, the boys used to promise me penny candy if I would let them pat my behind. And I used to love those jawbreakers—you know, the kind that lasted all day and kept changing colors in your mouth. So I was glad to oblige them, because in one afternoon I could collect a whole week's worth of jawbreakers."

"Really. That's funny to you? Having some boy feeling all over you."

Theresa sucked her teeth. "We were only kids, Lorraine. You know, you remind me of my grandmother. That was one straight-laced old lady. She had a fit when my brother told her what I was doing. She called me into the smokehouse and told me in this real scary whisper that I could get pregnant from letting little boys pat my butt and that I'd end up like my cousin Willa. But Willa and I had been thick as fleas, and she had already given me a step-by-step summary of how she'd gotten into her predicament. But I sneaked around to her house that night just to double-check her story, since that old lady had seemed so earnest. 'Willa, are you sure?' I whispered through her bedroom window. 'I'm tellin' ya, Tee,' she said. 'Just keep both feet on the ground and you home free.' Much later I learned that advice wasn't too biologically sound, but it worked in Georgia because those country boys didn't have much imagination."

Theresa's laughter bounced off of Lorraine's silent, rigid back and died in her throat. She angrily tore open a pack of the chocolate chip cookies. "Yeah," she said, staring at Lorraine's back and biting down hard into the cookie, "it wasn't until I came up north to college that I found out there's a whole lot of things that a dude with a little imagination can do to you even with both feet on the ground. You see, Willa forgot to tell me not to bend over or squat or—"

"Must you!" Lorraine turned around from the stove with her teeth clenched tightly together.

"Must I what, Lorraine? Must I talk about things that are as much a part of life as eating or breathing or growing old? Why are you always so uptight about sex or men?"

"I'm not uptight about anything. I just think it's disgusting when you go on and on about—"

"There's nothing disgusting about it, Lorraine. You've never been with a man, but I've been with quite a few—some better than others. There were a couple who I still hope to this day will die a slow, painful death, but then there were some who were good to me—in and out of bed."

"If they were so great, then why are you with me?" Lorraine's lips were trembling.

"Because—" Theresa looked steadily into her eyes and then down at the cookie she was twirling on the table. "Because," she continued slowly, "you can take a chocolate chip cookie and put

holes in it and attach it to your ears and call it an earring, or
hang it around your neck on a silver chain and pretend it's a
necklace—but it's still a cookie. See—you can toss it in the air
and call it a Frisbee or even a flying saucer, if the mood hits you,
and it's still just a cookie. Send it spinning on a table—like
this—until it's a wonderful blur of amber and brown light that
you can imagine to be a topaz or rusted gold or old crystal, but
the law of gravity has got to come into play, sometime, and it's
got to come to rest—sometime. Then all the spinning and pretending and hoopla is over with. And you know what you got?"

"A chocolate chip cookie," Lorraine said.

"Uh-uh." Theresa put the cookie in her mouth and winked.
"A lesbian." She got up from the table. "Call me when dinner's
ready, I'm going back to read." She stopped at the kitchen door.
"Now, why are you putting gravy on that chicken, Lorraine? You
know it's fattening."

The Brewster Place Block Association was meeting in Kiswana's
apartment. People were squeezed on the sofa and coffee table
and sitting on the floor. Kiswana had hung a red banner across
the wall, "Today Brewster—Tomorrow America!" but few understood what that meant and even fewer cared. They were there
because this girl had said that something could be done about
the holes in their walls and the lack of heat that kept their
children with congested lungs in the winter. Kiswana had given
up trying to be heard above the voices that were competing with
each other in volume and length of complaints against the landlord. This was the first time in their lives that they felt someone
was taking them seriously, so all of the would-be-if-they-could-
be lawyers, politicians, and Broadway actors were taking advantage of this rare opportunity to display their talents. It didn't
matter if they often repeated what had been said or if their
monologues held no relevance to the issues; each one fought for
the space to outshine the other.

"Ben ain't got no reason to be here. He works for the landlord."

A few scattered yeahs came from around the room.

"I lives in this here block just like y'all," Ben said slowly. "And when you ain't got no heat, I ain't either. It's not my fault 'cause the man won't deliver no oil."

"But you stay so zooted all the time, you never cold no way."

"Ya know, a lot of things ain't the landlord's fault. The landlord don't throw garbage in the air shaft or break the glass in them doors."

"Yeah, and what about all them kids that be runnin' up and down the halls."

"Don't be talking 'bout my kids!" Cora Lee jumped up. "Lot of y'all got kids, too, and they no saints."

"Why you so touchy—who mentioned you?"

"But if the shoe fits, steal it from Thom McAn's."

"Wait, please." Kiswana held up her hands. "This is getting us nowhere. What we should be discussing today is staging a rent strike and taking the landlord to court."

"What we should be discussin'," Sophie leaned over and said to Mattie and Etta, "is that bad element that done moved in this block amongst decent people."

"Well, I done called the police at least a dozen times about C. C. Baker and them boys hanging in that alley, smoking them reefers, and robbing folks," Mattie said.

"I ain't talkin' 'bout them kids—I'm talkin' 'bout those two livin' 'cross from me in 312."

"What about 'em?"

"Oh, you know, Mattie," Etta said, staring straight at Sophie. "Those two girls who mind their business and never have a harsh word to say 'bout nobody—them the two you mean, right, Sophie?"

"What they doin'—livin' there like that—is wrong, and you know it." She turned to appeal to Mattie. "Now, you a Christian woman. The Good Book say that them things is an abomination against the Lord. We shouldn't be havin' that here on Brewster and the association should do something about it."

"My Bible also says in First Peter not to be a busybody in other people's matters, Sophie. And the way I see it, if they ain't botherin' with what goes on in my place, why should I bother 'bout what goes on in theirs?"

"They sinning against the Lord!" Sophie's eyes were bright and wet.

"Then let the Lord take care of it," Etta snapped. "Who appointed you?"

"That don't surprise me comin' from *you*. No, not one bit!" Sophie glared at Etta and got up to move around the room to more receptive ears.

Etta started to go after her, but Mattie held her arm. "Let that woman be. We're not here to cause no row over some of her stupidness."

"The old prune pit," Etta spit out. "She oughta be glad them two girls are that way. That's one less bed she gotta worry 'bout pullin' Jess out of this year. I didn't see her thumpin' no Bible when she beat up that woman from Mobile she caught him with last spring."

"Etta, I'd never mention it in front of Sophie 'cause I hate the way she loves to drag other people's business in the street, but I can't help feelin' that what they're doing ain't quite right. How do you get that way? Is it from birth?"

"I couldn't tell you, Mattie. But I seen a lot of it in my time and the places I've been. They say they just love each other— who knows?"

Mattie was thinking deeply. "Well, I've loved women, too. There was Miss Eva and Ciel, and even as ornery as you can get, I've loved you practically all my life."

"Yeah, but it's different with them."

"Different how?"

"Well . . ." Etta was beginning to feel uncomfortable. "They love each other like you'd love a man or a man would love you— I guess."

"But I've loved some women deeper than I ever loved any man," Mattie was pondering. "And there been some women who loved me more and did more for me than any man ever did."

"Yeah." Etta thought for a moment. "I can second that, but it's still different, Mattie. I can't exactly put my finger on it, but . . ."

"Maybe it's not so different," Mattie said, almost to herself. "Maybe that's why some women get so riled up about it, 'cause they know deep down it's not so different after all." She looked at Etta. "It kinda gives you a funny feeling when you think about it that way, though."

"Yeah, it does," Etta said, unable to meet Mattie's eyes.

Lorraine was climbing the dark narrow stairway up to Kiswana's apartment. She had tried to get Theresa to come, but she had wanted no part of it. "A tenants' meeting for what? The damn street needs to be condemned." She knew Tee blamed her for having to live in a place like Brewster, but she could at least try to make the best of things and get involved with the community. That was the problem with so many black people—they just sat back and complained while the whole world tumbled down around their heads. And grabbing an attitude and thinking you were better than these people just because a lot of them were poor and uneducated wouldn't help, either. It just made you seem standoffish, and Lorraine wanted to be liked by the people around her. She couldn't live the way Tee did, with her head stuck in a book all the time. Tee didn't seem to need anyone. Lorraine often wondered if she even needed her.

But if you kept to yourself all the time, people started to wonder, and then they talked. She couldn't afford to have people talking about her, Tee should understand that—she knew from the way they had met. Understand. It was funny because that was the first thing she had felt about her when she handed Tee her application. She had said to herself, I feel that I can talk to this woman, I can tell her why I lost my job in Detroit, and she will understand. And she had understood, but then slowly all that had stopped. Now Lorraine was made to feel awkward and stupid about her fears and thoughts. Maybe Tee was right and she was too sensitive, but there was a big difference between being personnel director for the Board of Education and a first-grade teacher. Tee didn't threaten their files and payroll accounts but, somehow, she, Lorraine, threatened their children. Her heart tightened when she thought about that. The worst thing she had ever wanted to do to a child was to slap the spit out of the little Baxter boy for pouring glue in her hair, and even

that had only been for a fleeting moment. Didn't Tee understand that if she lost this job, she wouldn't be so lucky the next
time? No, she didn't understand that or anything else about her.
She never wanted to bother with anyone except those weirdos at
that club she went to, and Lorraine hated them. They were
coarse and bitter, and made fun of people who weren't like
them. Well, she wasn't like them either. Why should she feel
different from the people she lived around? Black people were all
in the same boat—she'd come to realize this even more since
they had moved to Brewster—and if they didn't row together,
they would sink together.

Lorraine finally reached the top floor; the door to Kiswana's
apartment was open but she knocked before she went in. Kiswana was trying to break up an argument between a short light-
skinned man and some woman who had picked up a potted
plant and was threatening to hit him in the mouth. Most of the
other tenants were so busy rooting for one or the other that
hardly anyone noticed Lorraine when she entered. She went over
and stood by Ben.

"I see there's been a slight difference of opinion here," she
smiled.

"Just nigger mess, miss. Roscoe there claim that Betina ain't
got no right being secretary 'cause she owe three months' rent,
and she say he owe more than that and it's none of his never
mind. Don't know how we got into all this. Ain't what we was
talkin' 'bout, no way. Was talkin' 'bout havin' a block party to
raise money for a housing lawyer."

Kiswana had rescued her Boston Fern from the woman and
the two people were being pulled to opposite sides of the room.
Betina pushed her way out of the door, leaving behind very loud
advice about where they could put their secretary's job along
with the block association, if they could find the space in that
small an opening in their bodies.

Kiswana sat back down, flushed and out of breath. "Now we
need someone else to take the minutes."

"Do they come with the rest of the watch?" Laughter and
another series of monologues about Betina's bad-natured exit
followed for the next five minutes.

Lorraine saw that Kiswana looked as if she wanted to cry. The one-step-forward–two-steps-backwards progression of the meeting was beginning to show on her face. Lorraine swallowed her shyness and raised her hand. "I'll take the minutes for you."

"Oh, thank you." Kiswana hurriedly gathered the scattered and crumpled papers and handed them to her. "Now we can get back down to business."

The room was now aware of Lorraine's presence, and there were soft murmurs from the corners, accompanied by furtive glances, while a few like Sophie stared at her openly. She attempted to smile into the eyes of the people watching her, but they would look away the moment she glanced in their direction. After a couple of vain attempts her smile died, and she buried it uneasily in the papers in her hand. Lorraine tried to cover her trembling fingers by pretending to decipher Betina's smudged and misspelled notes.

"All right," Kiswana said, "now who had promised to get a stereo hooked up for the party?"

"Ain't we supposed to vote on who we wants for secretary?" Sophie's voice rose heavily in the room, and its weight smothered the other noise. All of the faces turned silently toward hers with either mild surprise or coveted satisfaction over what they knew was coming. "I mean, can anybody just waltz in here and get shoved down our throats and we don't have a say about it?"

"Look, I can just go," Lorraine said. "I just wanted to help, I—"

"No, wait." Kiswana was confused. "What vote? Nobody else wanted to do it. Did you want to take the notes?"

"She can't do it," Etta cut in, "unless we was sitting here reciting the ABC's, and we better not do that too fast. So let's just get on with the meeting."

Scattered approval came from sections of the room.

"Listen here!" Sophie jumped up to regain lost ground. "Why should a decent woman get insulted and y'll take sides with the likes of them?" Her finger shot out like a pistol, which she swung between Etta and Lorraine.

Etta rose from her seat. "Who do you think you're talkin' to, you old hen's ass? I'm as decent as you are, and I'll come over there and lam you in the mouth to prove it!"

Etta tried to step across the coffee table, but Mattie caught her by the back of the dress; Etta turned, tried to shake her off, and tripped over the people in front of her. Sophie picked up a statue and backed up into the wall with it slung over her shoulder like a baseball bat. Kiswana put her head in her hands and groaned. Etta had taken off her high-heeled shoe and was waving the spiked end at Sophie over the shoulders of the people who were holding her back.

"That's right! That's right!" Sophie screamed. "Pick on me! Sure, I'm the one who goes around doin' them filthy, unnatural things right under your noses. Every one of you knows it; everybody done talked about it, not just me!" Her head moved around the room like a trapped animal's. "And any woman—any woman who defends that kind of thing just better be watched. That's all I gotta say—where there's smoke, there's fire, Etta Johnson!"

Etta stopped struggling against the arms that were holding her, and her chest was heaving in rapid spasms as she threw Sophie a look of wilting hate, but she remained silent. And no other woman in the room dared to speak as they moved an extra breath away from each other. Sophie turned toward Lorraine, who had twisted the meeting's notes into a mass of shredded paper. Lorraine kept her back straight, but her hands and mouth were moving with a will of their own. She stood like a fading spirit before the ebony statue that Sophie pointed at her like a crucifix.

"Movin' into our block causin' a disturbance with your nasty ways. You ain't wanted here!"

"What have any of you ever seen me do except leave my house and go to work like the rest of you? Is it disgusting for me to speak to each one of you that I meet in the street, even when you don't answer me back? Is that my crime?" Lorraine's voice sank like a silver dagger into their consciences, and there was an uneasy stirring in the room.

"Don't stand there like you a Miss Innocent," Sophie whispered hoarsely. "I'll tell ya what I seen!"

Her eyes leered around the room as they waited with a court-room hush for her next words.

"I wasn't gonna mention something so filthy, but you forcin' me." She ran her tongue over her parched lips and narrowed her eyes at Lorraine. "You forgot to close your shades last night, and I saw the two of you!"

The silence in the room tightened into a half-gasp.

"There you was, standin' in the bathroom door, drippin' wet and as naked and shameless as you please . . ."

It had become so quiet it was now painful.

"Calling to the other one to put down her book and get you a clean towel. Standin' in that bathroom door with your naked behind. I saw it—I did!"

Their chests were beginning to burn from a lack of air as they waited for Lorraine's answer, but before the girl could open her mouth, Ben's voice snaked from behind her like a lazy breeze.

"Guess *you* get out the tub with your clothes on, Sophie. Must make it mighty easy on Jess's eyes."

The laughter that burst out of their lungs was such a relief that eyes were watery. The room laid its head back and howled in gratitude to Ben for allowing it to breathe again. Sophie's rantings could not be heard above the wheezing, coughing, and backslapping that now went on.

Lorraine left the apartment and grasped the stairway railing, trying to keep the bile from rising into her throat. Ben followed her outside and gently touched her shoulder.

"Miss, you all right?"

She pressed her lips tightly together and nodded her head. The lightness of his touch brought tears to her eyes, and she squeezed them shut.

"You sure? You look 'bout ready to keel over."

Lorraine shook her head jerkily and sank her nails deeply into her palm as she brought her hand to her mouth. I mustn't speak, she thought. If I open my mouth, I'll scream. Oh, God, I'll scream or I'll throw up, right here, in front of this nice old man. The thought of the churned up bits of her breakfast and lunch pouring out of her mouth and splattering on Ben's trouser legs suddenly struck her as funny, and she fought an overwhelming desire to laugh. She trembled violently as the creeping laughter tried to deceive her into parting her lips.

Ben's face clouded over as he watched the frail body that was so bravely struggling for control. "Come on now, I'll take you home." And he tried to lead her down the steps.

She shook her head in a panic. She couldn't let Tee see her like this. If she says anything smart to me now, I'll kill her, Lorraine thought. I'll pick up a butcher knife and plunge it into her face, and then I'll kill myself and let them find us there. The thought of all those people in Kiswana's apartment standing over their bleeding bodies was strangely comforting, and she began to breathe more easily.

"Come on now," Ben urged quietly, and edged her toward the steps.

"I can't go home." She barely whispered.

"It's all right, you ain't gotta—come on."

And she let him guide her down the stairs and out into the late September evening. He took her to the building that was nearest to the wall on Brewster Place and then down the outside steps to a door with a broken dirty screen. Ben unlocked the door and led her into his damp underground rooms.

He turned on the single light bulb that was hanging from the ceiling by a thick black cord and pulled out a chair for her at the kitchen table, which was propped up against the wall. Lorraine sat down, grateful to be able to take the weight off of her shaky knees. She didn't acknowledge his apologies as he took the half-empty wine bottle and cracked cup from the table. He brushed off the crumbs while two fat brown roaches raced away from the wet cloth.

"I'm makin' tea," he said, without asking her if she wanted any. He placed a blackened pot of water on the hot plate at the edge of the counter, then found two cups in the cabinet that still had their handles intact. Ben put the strong black tea he had brewed in front of her and brought her a spoon and a crumpled pound bag of sugar. Lorraine took three heaping teaspoons of sugar and stirred the tea, holding her face over the steam. Ben waited for her face to register the effects of the hot sweet liquid.

"I liked you from first off," he said shyly, and seeing her

smile, he continued. "You remind me lots of my little girl." Ben reached into his hip pocket and took out a frayed billfold and handed her a tiny snapshot.

Lorraine tilted the picture toward the light. The face stamped on the celluloid paper bore absolutely no resemblance to her at all. His daughter's face was oval and dark, and she had a large flat nose and a tiny rounded mouth. She handed the picture back to Ben and tried to cover her confusion.

"I know what you thinkin'," Ben said, looking at the face in his hands. "But she had a limp—my little girl. Was a breech baby, and the midwife broke her foot when she was birthed and it never came back right. Always kinda cripped along—but a sweet child." He frowned deeply into the picture and paused, then looked up at Lorraine. "When I seen you—the way you'd walk up the street all timid-like and tryin' to be nice to these-here folks and the look on your face when some of 'em was just downright rude—you kinda broke up in here." He motioned toward his chest. "And you just sorta limped along inside. That's when I thought of my baby."

Lorraine gripped the teacup with both hands, but the tears still squeezed through the compressed muscles in her eyes. They slowly rolled down her face but she wouldn't release the cup to wipe them away.

"My father," she said, staring into the brown liquid, "kicked me out of the house when I was seventeen years old. He found a letter one of my girlfriends had written me, and when I wouldn't lie about what it meant, he told me to get out and leave behind everything that he had ever bought me. He said he wanted to burn them." She looked up to see the expression on Ben's face, but it kept swimming under the tears in her eyes. "So I walked out of his home with only the clothes on my back. I moved in with one of my cousins, and I worked at night in a bakery to put myself through college. I would send him a birthday card each year, and he always returned them unopened. After a while I stopped putting my return address on the envelopes so he couldn't send them back. I guess he burned those too." She sniffed the mucus up into her nose. "I still send those cards like that—without a return address. That way I can believe that, maybe, one year before he dies, he'll open them."

Ben got up and gave her a piece of toilet paper to blow her nose in.

"Where's your daughter now, Mr. Ben?"

"For me?" Ben sighed deeply. "Just like you—livin' in a world with no address."

They finished their tea in silence and Lorraine got up to go.

"There's no way to thank you, so I won't try."

"I'd be right hurt if you did." Ben patted her arm. "Now come back anytime you got a mind to. I got nothing, but you welcome to all of that. Now how many folks is that generous?"

Lorraine smiled, leaned over, and kissed him on the cheek. Ben's face lit up the walls of the dingy basement. He closed the door behind her, and at first her "Good night, Mr. Ben" tinkled like crystal bells in his mind. Crystal bells that grew larger and louder, until their sound was distorted in his ears and he almost believed that she had said "Good night, Daddy Ben"—no— "Mornin' Daddy Ben, mornin' Daddy Ben, mornin' . . .' Ben's saliva began to taste like sweating tin, and he ran a trembling hand over his stubbled face and rushed to the corner where he had shoved the wine bottle. The bells had begun almost to deafen him and he shook his head to relieve the drumming pain inside of his ears. He knew what was coming next, and he didn't dare waste time by pouring the wine into a cup. He lifted the bottle up to his mouth and sucked at it greedily, but it was too late. *Swing low, sweet chariot.* The song had started—the whistling had begun.

It started low, from the end of his gut, and shrilled its way up into his ears and shattered the bells, sending glass shards flying into a heart that should have been so scarred from old piercings that there was no flesh left to bleed. But the glass splinters found some minute, untouched place—as they always did—and tore the heart and let the whistling in. And now Ben would have to drink faster and longer, because the melody would now ride on his body's blood like a cancer and poison everywhere it touched. *Swing low, sweet chariot.* It mustn't get to his brain. He had a few more seconds before it got to his brain and killed him. He had to be drunk before the poison crept up his neck muscles, past his mouth, on the way to his brain. If he was drunk, then he could let it out—sing it out into the air before it touched his brain, caused him to remember. *Swing low, sweet chariot.* He couldn't die there under the ground like some animal. Oh, God, please make him drunk. And he promised—he'd never go that long without a drink again. It was just the meeting and then that girl that had kept him from it this long, but he swore it would never happen again—just please, God, make him drunk.

The alcohol began to warm Ben's body, and he felt his head begin to get numb and heavy. He almost sobbed out his thanks for this redeeming answer to his prayers, because the whistling had just reached his throat and he was able to open his mouth and slobber the words out into the room. The saliva was dripping from the corners of his mouth because he had to take huge gulps of wine between breaths, but he sang on—drooling and humming—because to sing was salvation, to sing was to empty the tune from his blood, to sing was to unremember Elvira, and his daughter's "Mornin', Daddy Ben" as she dragged her twisted foot up his front porch with that song hitting her in the back.
Swing low
"Mornin', Ben. Mornin', Elvira."
Sweet chariot
The red pick-up truck stopped in front of Ben's yard.
Comin' for to carry me home
His daughter got out of the passenger side and began to limp toward the house.
Swing low
Elvira grinned into the creviced face of the white man sitting in the truck with tobacco stains in the corner of his mouth. "Mornin', Mr. Clyde. Right nice day, ain't it, sir?"
Sweet chariot
Ben watched his daughter come through the gate with her eyes on the ground, and she slowly climbed up on the porch. She took each step at a time, and her shoes grated against the rough boards. She finally turned her beaten eyes into his face, and what was left of his soul to crush was taken care of by the bell-

like voice that greeted them. "Mornin', Daddy Ben. Mornin', Mama."

"Mornin', baby," Ben mumbled with his jaws tight.

Swing low

"How's things up at the house?" Elvira asked. "My little girl do a good job for you yesterday?"

Sweet chariot

"Right fine, Elvira. Got that place clean as a skinned rat. How's y'all's crops comin'?"

"Just fine, Mr. Clyde, sir. Just fine. We sure appreciate that extra land you done rented us. We bringin' in more than enough to break even. Yes, sir, just fine."

The man laughed, showing the huge gaps between his tobacco-rotted teeth. "Glad to do it. Y'all some of my best tenants. I likes keepin' my people happy. If you needs somethin', let me know."

"Sure will, Mr. Clyde, sir."

"Aw right, see y'all next week. Be by the regular time to pick up the gal."

"She be ready, sir."

The man started up the motor on the truck, and the tune that he whistled as he drove off remained in the air long after the dust had returned to the ground. Elvira grinned and waved until the red of the truck had disappeared over the horizon. Then she simultaneously dropped her arm and smile and turned toward her daughter. "Don't just stand there gawkin'. Get in the house—your breakfast been ready."

"Yes, Mama."

When the screen door had slammed shut, Elvira snapped her head around to Ben. "Nigger, what is wrong with you? Ain't you heared Mr. Clyde talkin' to you, and you standin' there like a hunk of stone. You better get some sense in you head 'fore I knock some in you!"

Ben stood with his hands in his pockets, staring at the tracks in the dirt where the truck had been. He kept balling his fists up in his overalls until his nails dug into his palms.

"It ain't right, Elvira. It just ain't right and you know it."

"What ain't right?" The woman stuck her face into his and

he backed up a few steps. "That that gal work and earn her keep like the rest of us? She can't go to the fields, but she can clean house, and she'll do it! I see it's better you keep your mouth shut 'cause when it's open, ain't nothin' but stupidness comin' out." She turned her head and brushed him off as she would a fly, then headed toward the door of the house.

"She came to us, Elvira." There was a leaden sadness in Ben's voice. "She came to us a long time ago."

The thin woman spun around with her face twisted into an airless knot. "She came to us with a bunch of lies 'bout Mr. Clyde 'cause she's too damn lazy to work. Why would a decent widow man want to mess with a little black nothin' like her? No, anything to get out of work—just like you."

"Why she gotta spend the night then?" Ben turned his head slowly toward her. "Why he always make her spend the night up there alone with him?"

"Why should he make an extra trip just to bring her tail home when he pass this way every Saturday mornin' on the way to town? If she wasn't lame, she could walk it herself after she finish work. But the man nice enough to drop her home, and you want to bad-mouth him along with that lyin' hussy."

"After she came to us, you remember I borrowed Tommy Boy's wagon and went to get her that Friday night. I told ya what Mr. Clyde told me. 'She ain't finished yet, Ben.' Just like that—'She ain't finished yet.' And then standin' there whistlin' while I went out the back gate." Ben's nails dug deeper into his palms.

"So!" Elvira's voice was shrill. "So it's a big house. It ain't like this shit you got us livin' in. It take her longer to do things than most folks. You know that, so why stand there carryin' on like it mean more than that?"

"She ain't finished yet, Ben." Ben shook his head slowly. "If I was half a man I woulda—"

Elvira came across the porch and sneered into his face. "If you was half a man, you coulda given me more babies and we woulda had some help workin' this land instead of a half-grown woman we gotta carry the load for. And if you was even quarter a man, we wouldn't be a bunch of miserable sharecroppers on someone else's land—but we is, Ben. And I'll be damned if I see the little bit we got taken away 'cause you believe that gal's lowdown lies! So when Mr. Clyde come by here, you speak—hear me? And you act as grateful as your pitiful ass should be for the favors he done us."

Ben felt a slight dampness in his hands because his fingernails had broken through the skin of his palms and the blood was seeping around his cuticles. He looked at Elvira's dark braided head and wondered why he didn't take his hands out of his pockets and stop the bleeding by pressing them around it. Just lock his elbows on her shoulders and place one hand on each side of her temples and then in toward each other until the blood stopped. His big callused hands on the bones of her skull pressing in and in, like you would with a piece of dark cloth to cover the wounds on your body and clot the blood. Or he could simply go into the house and take his shotgun and press his palms around the trigger and handle, emptying the bullets into her sagging breasts just long enough—just pressing hard enough—to stop his palms from bleeding.

But the gram of truth in her words was heavy enough to weigh his hands down in his pockets and keep his feet nailed to the wooden planks in the porch, and the wounds healed over by themselves. Ben discovered that if he sat up drinking all night Friday, he could stand on the porch Saturday morning and smile at the man who whistled as he dropped his lame daughter home. And he could look into her beaten eyes and believe that she had lied.

The girl disappeared one day, leaving behind a note saying that she loved them very much, but she knew that she had been a burden and she understood why they had made her keep working at Mr. Clyde's house. But she felt that if she had to earn her keep that way, she might as well go to Memphis where the money was better.

Elvira ran and bragged to the neighbors that their daughter was now working in a rich house in Memphis. And she was making out awful well because she always sent plenty of money home. Ben would stare at the envelopes with no return address, and he found that if he drank enough every time a letter came, he could silence the bell-like voice that came chiming out of the open envelope—"Mornin' Daddy Ben, mornin' Daddy Ben, mornin' . . ." And then if he drank enough every day he could bear the touch of Elvira's body in the bed beside him at night and not have his sleep stolen by the image of her lying there with her head caved in or her chest ripped apart by shotgun shells.

But even after they lost the sharecropping contract and Elvira left him for a man who farmed near the levee and Ben went north and took a job on Brewster, he still drank—long after he could remember why. He just knew that whenever he saw a mailman, the crystal bells would start, and then that strange whistling that could shatter them, sending them on that deadly journey toward his heart.

He never dreamed it would happen on a Sunday. The mailman didn't run on Sundays, so he had felt safe. He hadn't counted on that girl sounding so much like the bells when she left his place tonight. But it was okay, he had gotten drunk in time, and he would never take such a big chance again. No, Lord, you pulled me through this time, and I ain't pressin' your mercy no more. Ben stumbled around his shadowy damp rooms, singing now at the top of his voice. The low, trembling melody of "Swing Low, Sweet Chariot" passed through his greasy windows and up into the late summer air.

Lorraine had walked home slowly, thinking about the old man and the daughter who limped. When she came to her stoop, she brushed past her neighbors with her head up and didn't bother to speak.

AUDRE LORDE

✺

Zami: A New Spelling of My Name

*T*hings *I never did with Genevieve: Let our bodies touch and tell the passions that we felt. Go to a Village gay bar, or any bar anywhere. Smoke reefer. Derail the freight that took circus animals to Florida. Take a course in international obscenities. Learn Swahili. See Martha Graham's dance troupe. Visit Pearl Primus. Ask her to take us away with her to Africa next time. Write THE BOOK. Make love.*

Louisa's voice on the phone at 3:30 P.M., tight and unbelieving.

"They found Gennie on the steps of the 110th Street Community Center this morning. She's taken rat poison. Arsenic. They don't expect her to live."

That wasn't true. Gennie was going to live. She'd fool all of us again. *Gennie, Gennie, please don't die, I love you.* Something will save her. Something. Maybe she's run away, maybe she's just run away again. Not to her relatives in Richmond this time. Oh no. Gennie'll think of someplace nobody'll think of looking, and then eventually she'll come sauntering in with a new outfit she got someone to buy her and that quick toss of her head, saying, "I was fine all the time."

"Where is she, Mrs. Thompson?"

"She's at Sydenham. Evidently she rode the subways all

night, that's what she told the police, but nobody knows where she'd been before. She didn't go to school yesterday."

Cutting through Louisa's voice is the sound of the jukebox in Mike's Food Shoppe. Yesterday, after school, hearing Gennie's favorite song these days—the richly elongated tones of Sarah Vaughan's chocolate voice repeating over and over,

> I saw the harbor lights they only told me we were parting
> The same old harbor lights that once brought you to me
> I saw the harbor lights, how could I help the tears were starting,
> > were starting,
> > > were starting . . .

Mike came over and kicked the box. "Albanian magic," he grinned, and went back to his griddle. The hateful taste of black coffee and lemon in my mouth. *Gennie Gennie Gennie Gennie.*

"Can I see her, Mrs. Thompson? When are visiting hours?" Could I go see Gennie and still get back before my mother got home?

"You can come anytime, honey, but you better hurry."

Rifling my mother's old pocketbooks for ten cents carfare. My empty stomach churning. Louisa's tears as she greets me at the door of the emergency room, as she takes my hands.

"They're working on her again, honey. They won't even admit her up in the ward. They say she won't last 'til night."

The hospital bed in the glass cubicle behind the emergency room in Harlem Hospital. Her mother and grandmother and I clutching each other for comfort. Louisa smelling of Evening in Paris that always made me sneeze. My head an endless kaleidoscope of numb images, jumbled, repeated.

Speech class, the only class we ever had together.

> Jenny come tie my, Jenny come tie my, Jenny come
> tie my bonny cravat.
> I've tied it behind and I've tied it before
> and I've tied it so often, I'll tie it no more.

Miss Mason's monotonous voice drilling us through the exercise over and over. "Nice wide i's, now. Again, class." Gennie's grandmother, her insistent southern voice looking for meaning. "She didn't talk about it this time. Nobody knew. If only she'd said something. I'da believed her this time . . ." The young white doctor, "You can go in now, but she's asleep."

Gennie Gennie Gennie I never saw you asleep before. You look just like you awake except your eyes are closed. Your brows still bend down in the middle like you frowning. What time is my mother coming home? Suppose I get on the same bus as she does coming uptown from the office? What shall I tell them when I get home?

My mother was home when I got in. An unwillingness to share any piece of my private world, even the pain, made me lie. I said Gennie was in the hospital because she had swallowed poison, by accident. Iodine, from the medicine chest.

"But what kind of house is that for a young girl to grow up in? How could she make such a mistake, poor thing? Wasn't her stepmother home?"

"I don't know, Mother. That's all her father told me." Under my mother's curious gaze I kept my face carefully blank.

Early early the next morning. Using my church collection for carfare. The hospital odor and the muted sound of the p.a. Nobody around, nobody to stop me. The hospital bed in the glass cubicle. *You can't just die like this, Gennie, we haven't had our summer yet. Don't you remember? You promised.* She can't die. Too much poison, they say. She stuffed rat poison into the gelatin capsules, ate them, one by one. We had bought two dozen capsules on Friday.

A crumpled flower on the hospital bed. Arsenic is a corrosive. She lingered, metallic-smelling foam at the corners of her mouth, blackened and wet. Her Gennie braids askew, unraveling. The last five inches of them revealed as a hairpiece. How could it be that I never knew? Gennie had plaited false hair into her braids. She was so proud of her long hair. Sometimes she wound them around her head like a crown.

Now they were unraveling on the hospital pillow as she tossed her head from side to side, her eyes closed in the emptiness and quiet of the early Sunday morning hospital light. I took her hand.

"I'm supposed to be at church, Gennie, but I had to come see you." She smiled, her eyes still closed. She turned her head towards me. Her breath was foul and shallow.

"Don't die, Gennie. Do you still want to?"

"Of course, I do. Didn't I tell you I was going to?"

I bent close to her and touched her forehead. "Oh why, Gennie, why?" I whispered.

Her great black eyes flashed open. Her head moved on the pillow in a parody of her old arrogance. Her brows came down in the center. "Why what?" she snapped. "Now don't be silly. You know why."

But I did not know why. I scanned her face turned toward me, eyes closed again. The wrinkle-frown still between the thick brows. I did not know why. Only that for my beloved Gennie, pain had become enough of a reason not to stay. And our friendship had not been able to alter that. I remembered Gennie's favorite lines in one of my poems. I had found them doodled and scrawled along the margins of page after page of the notebooks which she had entrusted to my care in the movies that Friday afternoon.

> and in the brief moment that is today
> wild hope this dreamer jars
> for I have heard in whispers talk
> of life on other stars.

None of us had given her a good enough reason to stay here, not even me. I could not escape that. Was that the anger behind her great closed eyes? The skin of Gennie's cheek was hot and rough under my fingers.

Why what? You know why. Those were the last words Gennie ever said to me.

◎∕◎

Don't go, Gennie, don't go. I mustn't let her go. Two dozen empty capsules. Sitting through the movie twice. Standing on the corner waiting for the 14th Street bus. I should never have left her. But it was getting dark already. Scared of another whipping for getting home too late. Come home with me, Gennie. Not caring anymore what my mother would say to that. Gennie, angry with me. Telling me to go away. I went. Don't go, Gennie, don't go.

By Monday afternoon Genevieve was dead.

I called the hospital from Hunter. I walked out of the building and went home, leaving my books behind, wanting to be alone. My mother opened the door. She put one arm around me as I walked into the kitchen.

"Genevieve's dead, Mother." I sat down heavily at the table.

"Yes, I know. I called her father to see if there was anything we could do, and he told me." She was looking into my face.

"Why didn't you tell us it was suicide?"

I wanted to cry—even that little piece was gone.

"It's her father himself said so. Do you know anything about it? You can tell me, I'm your mother, after all. We won't say anything more about your lying this time. Did she talk to you about it?"

I put my head down on the table. From there I could see out the kitchen window, slightly open. The woman across the air shaft was fixing food.

"No."

"I'll fix you some tea. You mustn't be upset too much by all this, dear heart." My mother turned, rubbing the edge of the tea strainer dry, over and over again. "Look, my darling child, I know she was your friend and you feel bad, but this is what I been cautioning you about. Be careful who you go around with. Among-you children do things different in this place and you think we stupid. But this old head of mine, I know what I know. There was something totally wrong there from the start, you mark my words. That man call himself father was using that girl for I don't know what."

The merciless quality of my mother's fumbling insights turned her attempt at comfort into another assault. As if her harshness could confer invulnerability upon me. As if in the flames of truth as she saw it, I could eventually be forged into some pain-resistant replica of herself.

But all this was so beside the point. Across the darkening air shaft Mrs. Washer pulled down her window-shade. *Gennie was dead. Dead dead dead, a nickel a rabbit's head.*

When my father came home, he knew, too. "Next time, don't lie to us. Was your girlfriend in trouble?"

Days later, I sat on the low bench beside Louisa's window, newly opened after its end-of-winter untaping. It was an early spring afternoon. The season had begun unusually warm. The street outside was runny with old rain, the still slick pavement reflecting oily rainbows.

Louisa perched upon her window ledge. One high hip nudged against the wooden window frame, her stockinged leg moving back and forth ever so slightly. The other drooped down over the edge of the bench where I was sitting.

"You and Gene were such good friends." Louisa's tones were clipped and longing. "Matter of fact, she saw you more than . . ." she fingered the spirals of Gennie's notebook which I had just given her, keeping the diary for myself. Louisa's eyes were dry and desperately conversational. I suddenly remembered Gennie saying her mother had once been a schoolteacher down south and prided herself on proper speech. ". . . than she saw anybody else." Louisa finished abruptly. I savored this piece of information in silence. *Gennie's best friend.* "You looked enough alike to be sisters, people said." *Except Gennie was lighter and thinner and beautiful.*

Something about Louisa's eyes warned me and I stood up quickly. "I gotta go, Miz Thompson, my mother . . ." I reached for my coat on the couch. It had once been Louisa's daybed, the one where Gennie and I lay laughing and talking and smoking. When Gennie left, Louisa had redone the tiny apartment and taken over the bedroom. I suddenly saw again Gennie's scratched face and tired eyes as she snapped at me that night, "I can't go back, there's no room for me anymore . . . I can't talk to my mother about Phillip . . ."

I buttoned my coat hurriedly. "She's waiting for me to go marketing, because my sisters have a rehearsal at school." But swift-moving Louisa caught me, one hand on my arm, before I could open the door.

Louisa took off her rimless glasses and she did not look like anybody's mother at all. She looked too young, and too pretty, and too tired, and her red-rimmed eyes were full of tears and pleading. She was thirty-four years old and tomorrow we were going to bury her only child, a sixteen-year-old suicide.

"You-all were best friends," insistent, less proper, her fingers tight through my coat sleeve. "Do *you* know why she did it?"

Louisa had a mole on her face beside her nose, almost exactly the same place as Gennie's had been. It was magnified by the tears rolling down her cheeks. I looked away, my hand still on the doorknob.

"No, ma'am." I looked up, again. I remembered my mother's words, resisting them, "That man call himself father was using that girl for I don't know what."

"I have to go now."

I opened the door, stepped over the floor-anchored metal rod upon which I had tripped so many times before, and closed the door behind me. I heard the metallic clang of the police lock rod as it slid back into place, mingled with the muffled sounds of Louisa's sobbing.

Gennie was buried in Woodlawn Cemetery on the first day of April. The *Amsterdam News* story about her death announced that she was not pregnant and so no reason for her suicide could be established. Nothing else.

The sound of dirt clods flying hollow against the white coffin. The sound of birds who knew death as no reason for silence. A black-clad man mouthing words in a foreign tongue. No hallowed ground for suicides. The sound of weeping women. The wind. The forward edge of spring. The sound of grass growing, flowers begin-

ning to blossom, the branching of a far-off tree. Clods against the white coffin.

We drove away from the grave, down a winding hill. The last thing I saw of that place was two large gravemen with unshaven faces pulling the lowering straps from the grave. They tossed the still living flowers into a waiting bin, and shoveled earth into the grave. Two grave-hands, putting the finishing touches on a raw mound of earth, outlined against the suddenly grey and lowering April sky.

CATHERINE E. MCKINLEY

Afro Jew Fro

A small, weathered Cape sits on the Hill on a shaded street that sharply bends and crosses into rush-hour traffic. The house is enshrined by gnarled and flamboyant trees. Wild rose bushes, thorns mauling the fence on which they grow, seal one's view of the house from the street. From a treetop a trumpet blares. A boy stands on wooden planks wedged between the tree's limbs, warming up to reveille.

A woman leans over a sink, scrubbing beets, whistling, marking time to his battle call. A gin and tonic rests on the window-sill before her, the *Sun Chronicle* is spread on the drainboard at her side. She looks first at the obituaries and then for her students' names in the police blotter.

Below the trees' fortress is a small shed. Chickens shift nervously at the trumpet's squawk. They flutter from their roost there on the gracious wooden spine of a kayak hand-hewn by the woman, the boy, the father, stretched over with yellow tarpaulin. The woods run out from there, stumbling into swampland. A river runs through it.

It is almost an idyllic place. The fantasy of life interrupted only by the evening traffic. The factories let out at five o'clock.

The cry of a well-greased horn, the clink of a gin tumbler, muffle a girl's cry. She is running home from the river, frothing, terrorized by the smell of hot tar and the sting of blackberry vines.

RACE

Last week we won the junior category in a kayak race. My big brother and I. The littlest competitors to finish the Bungay 10K. Our photo appeared on the front page of the *Sun Chronicle*. Newsworthy. Morgan and Zarah. Against the neon orange of life vests, I appear as dark as he is white light. And now the joke is everyone thought coons were afraid of water.

First it was an acid burn. A flailing of arms. A grasping for roots.

Today I venture back to the river. I climb onto a rock not far from its edge and lift my shirt. The heat of the rock burns into my back, and the coolness of the pocketknife swinging from my neck hollows out my chest. I stretch across the rock until the ends of my braids dangle in the water, become soaked to the bright plastic beads on elastic that bind them two inches before their ends. Fighting the resistant, rubbery stem of a water lilly, I lay its shiny wetness across my chest, then howl at the slip of tiny egg sacks clinging to the leaf's underside.

Rush-hour traffic screeches on the overpass not far down the river. My father is moving in its tide. My mother will soon be ringing her cowbell, announcing dinner. I will cut back through the woods instead of navigating the stretch gully facing oncoming traffic. I head home, guided by the power lines. A boy appears before me. A boy. Only big like a man. Smoke curls out from the palm of his cupped hand. He is an undistinguished face from the headshop; the cemetery; the Commons; the schoolyard; leaning against the memorial statues in town. My terrorist wears a brown suede vest over a Big Al's T-shirt. His long, stringy hair is covered by a wide-brimmed, weathered leather hat. Big Al's or Harley. Torn jeans or blue Dickies. Indistinguishable. His hatred so plain. So ordinary. You see him all over town. In the movie house; McDonald's; at the public pool; by the duck pond. He becomes what keeps me from those places. He is the fear that tucks you into small corners and shrinks your soul.

I had learned to court the fear of what might be around each corner of the trail cut into the earth by minibikes. It became a trick of breathing. But my breath stopped as I was shoved onto hard dry ground. Nose to the tar on the telephone pole reaching above me. Remembering only a twisted laugh and the sting of vines.

QUADROON BALL

The rhythm of Sabbath. It goes like this: slowly measured, quadrille time.

One

Set the dinner table. Ring the dinner bell. Morgan retires his trumpet and empties his pockets on a corner of the kitchen counter by the door. Roots, bottle caps, owl droppings, rusted nails, and paper scraps track the day's course. At the sink he hurtles his hands into a can of Boraxo soap. Industrial size. His hands leave fresh tracks of dirt that turn to gray scum on its top. He sits down to eat under the glare of our mother's eyes. They will fight about his dirty hands.

I suck on the anger that disrupts their quiet camaraderie. He will one day suck back, gleefully it seems, the stench of Lestoil mixing with the heat from the armpits of my sweat-stained shirts, scrubbed under her schoolteacher's eyes. Our dirt is our pungent resistance.

Two

Eight o'clock. I linger over a plate of cold peas, burned or undercooked chicken, depending on the rhythm of our mother's day. Morgan runs outside to begin the baseball game our mother will later join. She can bring out the whole neighborhood. I wait for the family to leave the table. I scrape the remains of my dinner in a napkin to be flushed down the toilet—no bones—as I draw my bath.

Steam encases me, makes me sweat. "Crack the window! Crack the window!" my father commands in our fight against proliferating mildew. Tonight is not a good night for peas. I will have to flush continually so the peas will not float back up from the drain for my mother to witness how they were consumed. The flushing turns my bath from hot to cold to scalding.

I sit on the cool enamel toilet lid and slowly unbraid my hair. I wear two braids. Always two braids. For six years now since I outgrew Afro-puffs. Mickey Mouse ears. Perpetually braided in the same fashion at the same place on my head. The style cannot be outgrown as long as there is hair to groom and her hands to do it. It leaves a permanent cleave in the center of my head that lays open no matter the style. Even as a woman I will comb against two cowlicks that mark the base of each braid.

Three

This is a ritual bath. A game of water torture. I peel my clothes from my thin brown body. My brother's voice rises from the street. My mother greets a knock at the back door. *She can come out later. She's having her hair done. Remember, every other week. No, she didn't have it done last week.*

Every other week is enough. This ritual requires too much to be performed each Sunday. It is too painful, too consuming, too much a reminder of our failings.

I step into the tub and kneel into the water, allowing it to scald my feet and thighs and forearms. I clench my teeth and watch for the redness to appear. I survey my small body. I enjoy its brownness, the long froglike thighs, the spoon-shaped birthmark on my belly. My brother pinches the skin on my kneecaps and calls it chocolate pudding. I have a favorite washcloth. It is crimson colored. I can lay it diamond-shaped across my body and stretch its four corners to cover my tiny mocha nipples, which gently push up against it; my belly; my pussy. I let my hair fall down around my shoulders and become engorged by the water. Its kink is restored.

The phone rings. It is her sister. Telling her they will come
north this summer. And Jimmy will come too. Our new cousin,
seven years old. Black Jew. "He's just like you!"

I soak and wait and imagine myself dead. A drowning. Maybe
suicide. I fantasize. My mother one day finally coming upstairs
to find my body floating lifeless in six inches of bathwater. Prell
shampoo leaking green into the tub. Ruby blood clouding me.
The water begins to cool, my nipples tighten. The skin tightest
around my bones is becoming ashen and wrinkled. Her feet are
on the stairs.

She kneels beside me with a plastic cup. Rolls up the sleeves
of her denim shirt and kicks off her Adidas. She barely looks at
me. We do not speak. She lathers and rinses, lathers and rinses.
Distractedly. Two weeks of dirt is flushed out of my scalp, coloring the bathwater Bungay River brown.

Four

She pulls the stopper from the drain and turns to leave. I remain
motionless under the rush of water disappearing into the pipe. I
stand and court myself in the mirror until she has yelled to me
for the third time and is moving toward the second landing on
the stairs. I go to her in purple Toughskins, shirtless, kneeling at
her feet while she runs her fine-toothed comb through my hair,
separating each strand, ripping free each snarl. She is impatient.
She resents the time this steals. She is reminded that this is not
an easy motherhood. That this is not a three-minute child. That
this child is angry: this is what makes her tired.

*Hot tears. Hot tears. The slap of a plastic brush handle on my
neck. The dog licks my feet. The kids playing outside make sport at
the window. They will cue Monday schoolyard taunts.* She tears
into my head. I do let her see me cry, my hair falling over my
face. I want my mother's hard hands to stroke and stroke me,
but she responds with hurried irritation. "Shut up! Shut up!"
yells old Mrs. Zeenie from her porch next door at the dog's
barking, at my brother and his friends' skidding across the yard.

Outside, they know I will not join the game. Every other
Sunday I will go to bed early. Alone upstairs I cry until my head

splits and seeps into the pillow, mingling with the dampness from my braids. Much later my mother will come and gently press her face to mine, tracking my breathing while I pretend to sleep.

In the morning I hear her go out to the chicken shed. I hear the shower and the squeal of the old Volvo turning out onto the street. I wait in bed listening for Morgan to leave. Then for our father to join the 7:30 factory tide. Only then will I go downstairs. Eggs sit on the counter beside a copper frying pan, still warm and spiked with feathers clinging to shit. She has left me the blue egg from her little Rock Island hen. The one most cherished.

We do this dance until I'm turned out into other arms.

MY EDUCATION

She stands at my door with her box of plastic designer comb pieces. A pair in every primary color, plus silver, gold, and one pair with gold sparkles set in clear plastic. Those I will never wear. I don't have the clothes for all that.

Every black girl in our dorm has the same box, except Kirsten, whose Afro is so matted Roz is certain it would have to be shaved before her head could ever see a comb again. Kirsten and I are both from Massachusetts. Not north, not from the woods like the ones that surround us. Not from Boston. Or New Bedford, where the Cape Verdeans live. And not from Trenton like Roz. We have no comb pieces. We do have white girl names, fucked-up hair. Her parents are Antiguan. She was born in Oslo. I am someone's crime of miscegenation. Some throwaway child. We are aberrations. An unbelonging.

I have Izod shirts in every color and Roz's borrowed comb pieces to match. I have a jar of Vaseline on my dresser for what I imagine is ash; jars in three colors of Afro-Sheen; pink sponge curlers. I have cut pictures of brown girls from *Essence* to cover the walls. The other girls read *Jet*. I have a ghetto box and Grandmaster Flash and other fresh jams. For two weeks before I left home, I sat vigil to the airwaves to record from the only black radio station aired forty miles away in Boston. I waited for a light to shine in the attic window of the house across the street. There Mr. Huffy would sit down at his shortwave station, sharing precious airwaves. And for a time our house would settle into the hum of oldies; disco; Bach concertos; BBC and foreign news as we each sat in separate rooms tuned in to our longings.

Mr. Huffy died that spring while I was away, struck down on his bicycle by a car racing the blind curve at the end of our block. That summer the shortwave tower was dismantled, our parents were given the sign, GO CHILDREN SLOW, they had fought the city for, and I lost my socialization. That summer I burned the wires to Trenton, lying on the living room floor and playing old tapes over and over, holding tight to the memory and smell of Roz.

In September Roz comes each morning to do my hair. We have become instant allies. The boys call her an "old ugly black crow." Last week she fought a boy who called me "oreo." I cuss them weakly, trying to match her show.

Roz is beautiful. Like the girls in *Essence* or *Ebony*; what I imagine them to smell like, move like. She is everything I want to be. I've became obsessed with her ass, her strong arching back. Ant's waist. And skin whose darkness I want to be my own.

I live for the mornings. For breakfast, where I will see Derrick. Roz gets me ready for him, her hands in my head. The gentle scratch of a comb on my scalp. She knows what Derrick likes. She lives just a few houses from him. She scratches. Her tiny high breasts brush against my shoulder. This begins my education. Lessons in desire.

FREEDOM SUMMER

This was the long-anticipated meeting. A gathering of tribes. I could see the Flames from the driveway as my father steered the old Volvo in from the road. When I opened Grandma's front door, one pinched, freckled face peered out from under a sheath of red hair. "We have a new brother! He's a nigger, well, sort of. Just like you! Right, Billy?" Billy is off like a spark, yelling.

"Mommy, Amanda said the N word! And he's Jewish too, he ain't really black!"

We went to greet the sort-of nigger. Jimmy. The new member of the family. The one to round it out. Jimmy stood before us, as skinny as a wharf dog. His meager body only exaggerated the largeness of his head, his face flat and broad from the front sloping upward into a gracious mole. His thick hive of black hair was kinky here and curly there, with a few fine, bone-straight hairs poking out for mercy. His eyes were set wide on his face like an obiji. Spiritlike. His eyes appeared punched out—two bluish holes rimmed with long, excruciatingly lovely black lashes to relieve the vision's pain. Beautiful-ugly. What someone once called me. His eyes relaxed into black when you faced him head-on. They were eyes like our neighbor's malamute.

His skin was no darker than mine. But where I am shit-yellow, as people have said, he was white. Not white like white people. Jimmy had white melanin. Flat latex white. Matte finish. Primed so no other color could bleed through.

We had a new cousin to occupy our summer, to keep Fairfield County, my middle-class white-trash cousins, and us yelling and fighting and tearing across our grandmother's carefully tended lawn. Grubby and cussing. The honey-and-wheat-colored brother, the two red devils, and two awkward white cockroaches: Jimmy and me. We ran and fought and tumbled past our grown-ups. My mother spent the summer roaming the woods or perched on the wall by the rock garden. She shed her overalls for slacks but kept her engineer's cap tightly pulled down over her head. A glass of gin always nearby. The others favor beer and sherry. The men faded into the greenery. Grandma sewed and caught up on news. The Pussy-Don't-Stink Ph.D. talked to those who would listen. Child psychology.

Jimmy spent the whole summer beside me, not saying much but sticking close. He would bring me Grandma's nail polish and we would sit under the damp basement stairs hoping mold would not grow on our shoes. Mold that covered the toys and books stored there at the end of each summer, to be wiped off and set out in the sun once again if we could not bear to claim that we had outgrown them. Mold that covered the shoeboxes full of canceled checks and photos: things Amanda pulled out each summer with pride. "Our grandma is rich!" Passing over sorority shots of Grandma in blackface.

I would sit Jimmy between my legs and pull from his head the varied hairs to lay out before us. "What kind of child are you?" I would ask. "You'll look okay when you get older." That summer I loved him and hurt him, my skills well-honed, as much as anyone had ever done to me. Freedom Summer. The season of pink nail polish and Jimmy's blue holes for eyes. My hair now cut into a low Afro. His braided and teased and untied.

Cousin Billy called Jimmy a faggot once. This was a little better than nigger. But still it made me kick his ass when I caught him out of hearing range of the house. Butch queen and drag king supreme. Two queer niggers crawling out of America's woodpile. Shaking heads and quiet outrage into the wind.

Bashers

TONI MORRISON

Song of Solomon

The women's hands were empty. No pocketbook, no change purse, no wallet, no keys, no small paper bag, no comb, no handkerchief. They carried nothing. Milkman had never in his life seen a woman on the street without a purse slung over her shoulder, pressed under her arm, or dangling from her clenched fingers. These women walked as if they were going somewhere, but they carried nothing in their hands. It was enough to let him know he was really in the backwoods of Virginia, an area the signs kept telling him was the Blue Ridge Mountains. Danville, with its diner/bus station and its post office on the main street was a thriving metropolis compared to this no-name hamlet, a place so small nothing financed by state funds or private enterprise reared a brick there. In Roanoke, Petersburg, Culpeper he'd asked for a town named Charlemagne. Nobody knew. The coast, some said. Tidewater. A valley town, said others. He ended up at an AAA office, and after a while they discovered it and its correct name: Shalimar. How do I get there? Well, you can't walk it, that's for sure. Buses go there? Trains? No. Well, not very near. There is one bus, but it just goes to . . . . He ended up buying a fifty-dollar car for seventy-five dollars out of a young man's yard.

It broke down before he could get to the gas station and fill the tank. And when he got pushed to the station, he spent $132 on a fan belt, brake lining, oil filter, gas line filter, two retreads, and a brand-new oil pan, which he didn't need but bought before the mechanic told him the gasket was broken. It was a hard and bitter price to pay. Not because it wasn't worth it, and not because it had to be in cash since the garage owner looked at his Standard Oil credit card like it was a three-dollar bill, but because he had got used to prices in the South: socks two pairs for a quarter, resoled shoes thirty cents, shirt $1.98, and the two Tommys needed to know that he got a shave *and* a haircut for fifty cents.

By the time he bought the car, his morale had soared and he was beginning to enjoy the trip: his ability to get information and help from strangers, their attraction to him, their generosity (Need a place to stay? Want a good place to eat?). All that business about southern hospitality was for real. He wondered why black people ever left the South. Where he went, there wasn't a white face around, and the Negroes were as pleasant, wide-spirited, and self-contained as could be. He earned the rewards he got here. None of the pleasantness was directed at him because of his father, as it was back home, or his grandfather's memory, as it was in Danville. And now, sitting behind a steering wheel, he felt even better. He was his own director—relieving himself when he wanted to, stopping for cold beer when he was thirsty, and even in a seventy-five-dollar car the sense of power was strong.

He'd had to pay close attention to signs and landmarks, because Shalimar was not on the Texaco map he had, and the AAA office couldn't give a nonmember a charted course—just the map and some general information. Even at that, watching as carefully as he could, he wouldn't have known he had arrived if the fan belt hadn't broken again right in front of Solomon's General Store, which turned out to be the heart and soul of Shalimar, Virginia.

He headed for the store, nodding at the four men sitting outside on the porch, and side-stepping the white hens that were strolling about. Three more men were inside, in addition to the man behind the counter, who he assumed was Mr. Solomon himself. Milkman asked him for a cold bottle of Red Cap, please.

"No beer for sale on Sunday," the man said. He was a light-skinned Negro with red hair turning white.

"Oh. I forgot what day it was." Milkman smiled. "Pop, then. I mean soda. Got any on ice?"

"Cherry smash. That suit you?"

"Fine. Suit me fine."

The man walked over to the side of the store and slid open the door of an ancient cooler. The floor was worn and wavy with years of footsteps. Cans of goods on the shelf were sparse, but the sacks, trays, and cartons of perishables and semiperishables were plentiful. The man pulled a bottle of red liquid from the cooler and wiped it dry on his apron before handing it to Milkman.

"A nickel if you drink it here. Seven cents if you don't."

"I'll drink it here."

"Just get in?"

"Yeah. Car broke down. Is there a garage nearby?"

"Naw. Five miles yonder is one, though."

"Five miles?"

"Yep. What's the trouble? Mebbe one a us can fix it. Where you headed?"

"Shalimar."

"You standin in it."

"Right here? This is Shalimar?"

"Yes, suh. Shalimar." The man pronounced it *Shalleemone.*

"Good thing I broke down. I would have missed it for sure." Milkman laughed.

"Your friend almost missed it too."

"My friend? What friend?"

"The one lookin for you. Drove in here early this mornin and axed for ya."

"Asked for me by name?"

"No. He never mentioned your name."

"Then how do you know he was looking for me?"

"Said he was lookin for his friend in a three-piece beige suit. Like that." He pointed to Milkman's chest.

"What'd he look like?"

"Dark-skinned man. 'Bout your complexion. Tall. Thin. What's a matter? Y'all get your wires crossed?"

"Yeah. No. I mean . . . what was his name?"

"Didn't say. Just asked for you. He come a long way to meet you, though. I know that. Drove a Ford with Michigan tags."

"Michigan? You sure Michigan?"

"Sure I'm sure. Was he supposed to meet you in Roanoke?" When Milkman looked wild-eyed, the man said, "I seen your tags."

Milkman sighed with relief. And then said, "I wasn't sure where we were going to meet up. And he didn't say his name?"

"Naw. Just said to give you some good-luck message if I was to see you. Lemme see . . ."

"Good luck?"

"Yeah. Said to tell you your day was sure coming or your day . . . something like that . . . your day is here. But I know it had a day in it. But I ain't sure if he said it was comin or was already here." He chuckled. "Wish mine was here. Been waitin fifty-seven years and it ain't come yet."

The other men in the store laughed congenially, while Milkman stood frozen, everything in him quiet but his heart. There was no mistaking the message. Or the messenger. Guitar was looking for him, was following him, and for professional reasons. Unless . . . Would Guitar joke about that phrase? That special secret word the Seven Days whispered to their victims?

"The drink abuse you?" Mr. Solomon was looking at him. "Sweet soda water don't agree with me."

Milkman shook his head and swallowed the rest hurriedly. "No," he said. "I'm just . . . car weary. I think I'll sit outside awhile." He started toward the door.

"You want me to see 'bout your car for you?" Mr. Solomon sounded slightly offended.

"In a minute. I'll be right back."

Milkman pushed the screen door and stepped outside on the

porch. The sun was blazing. He took off his jacket and held it on his forefinger over his shoulder. He gazed up and down the dusty road. Shotgun houses with wide spaces between them, a few dogs, chickens, children, and the women with nothing in their hands. They sat on porches, and walked in the road swaying their hips under cotton dresses, bare-legged, their unstraightened hair braided or pulled straight back into a ball. He wanted one of them bad. To curl up in a cot in that one's arms, or that one, or that. That's the way Pilate must have looked as a girl, looked even now, but out of place in the big northern city she had come to. Wide sleepy eyes that tilted up at the corners, high cheekbones, full lips blacker than their skin, berry-stained, and long long necks. There must be a lot of intermarriage in this place, he thought. All the women looked alike, and except for some light-skinned red-headed men (like Mr. Solomon), the men looked very much like the women. Visitors to Shalimar must be rare, and new blood that settled here nonexistent.

Milkman stepped off the porch, scattering the hens, and walked down the road toward a clump of trees near a building that looked like a church or clubhouse of some sort. Children were playing behind the trees. Spreading his jacket on the burnt grass, he sat down and lit a cigarette.

Guitar was here. Had asked for him. But why was he afraid? They were friends, close friends. So close he had told him all about the Seven Days. There was no trust heavier than that. Milkman was a confidant, almost an accomplice. So why was he afraid? It was senseless. Guitar must have left that particular message so Milkman could know who was looking for him without his giving his name. Something must have happened back home. Guitar must be running, from the police, maybe, and decided to run toward his friend—the only one other than the Days who would know what it was all about and whom he could trust. Guitar needed to find Milkman and he needed help. That was it. But if Guitar knew Milkman was headed for Shalimar, he must have found that out in Roanoke, or Culpeper—or maybe even in Danville. And if he knew that, why didn't he wait? Where was he now? Trouble. Guitar was in trouble.

Behind him the children were singing a kind of ring-around-the-rosy or Little Sally Walker game. Milkman turned to watch. About eight or nine boys and girls were standing in a circle. A boy in the middle, his arms outstretched, turned around like an airplane, while the others sang some meaningless rhyme:

> Jay the only son of Solomon
> Come booba yalle, come booba tambee
> Whirl about and touch the sun
> Come booba yalle, come booba tambee . . .

They went on with several verses, the boy in the middle doing his imitation of an airplane. The climax of the game was a rapid shouting of nonsense words accompanied by more rapid twirling: "Solomon rye balaly *shoo*; yaraba medina hamlet *too*"—until the last line. "Twenty-one children the last one *Jay!*" At which point the boy crashed to earth and the others screamed.

Milkman watched the children. He'd never played like that as a child. As soon as he got up off his knees at the window sill, grieving because he could not fly, and went off to school, his velvet suit separated him from the other children. White and black thought he was a riot and went out of their way to laugh at him and see to it that he had no lunch to eat, nor any crayons, nor ever got through the line to the toilet or the water fountain. His mother finally surrendered to his begging for corduroy knickers or straights, which helped a little, but he was never asked to play those circle games, those singing games, to join in anything, until Guitar pulled those four boys off him. Milkman smiled, remembering how Guitar grinned and whooped as the four boys turned on him. It was the first time Milkman saw anybody really enjoy a fight. Afterward Guitar had taken off his baseball cap and handed it to Milkman, telling him to wipe the blood from his nose. Milkman bloodied the cap, returned it, and Guitar slapped it back on his head.

Remembering those days now, Milkman was ashamed of having been frightened or suspicious of Guitar's message. When he turned up, he would explain everything and Milkman would do what he could to help. He stood up and brushed his jacket. A black rooster strutted by, its blood-red comb draped forward like a wicked brow.

Milkman walked back toward Solomon's store. He needed a place to stay, some information, and a woman, not necessarily in that order. He would begin wherever the beginning was. In a way it was good Guitar had asked for him. Along with waiting for him and waiting for some way to get a new fan belt, he had a legitimate reason to dawdle. Hens and cats gave up their places on the steps as he approached them.

"Feelin better, are ya?" asked Mr. Solomon.

"Much better. Just needed a stretch, I guess." He jutted his chin toward the window. "Nice around here. Peaceful. Pretty women too."

A young man sitting on a chair tilted to the wall pushed his hat back from his forehead and let the front legs of the chair hit the floor. His lips were open, exposing the absence of four front teeth. The other men moved their feet. Mr. Solomon smiled but didn't say anything. Milkman sensed that he'd struck a wrong note. About the women, he guessed. What kind of place was this where a man couldn't even ask for a woman?

He changed the subject. "If my friend, the one who stopped by this morning, was going to wait for me here, where would he be likely to find a place to stay? Any rooming houses around here?"

"Rooming houses?"

"Yeah. Where a man can spend the night."

Mr. Solomon shook his head. "Nothin like that here."

Milkman was getting annoyed. What was all the hostility for? He looked at the men sitting around the store. "You think maybe one of them could help with the car?" he asked Mr. Solomon. "Maybe get another belt somewhere?"

Mr. Solomon kept his eyes on the counter. "Guess I could ask them." His voice was soft; he spoke as if he was embarrassed about something. There was none of the earlier chattiness he'd been full of when Milkman arrived.

"If they can't find one, let me know right away. I may have to buy another car to get back home."

Every one of the faces of the men turned to look at him, and

Milkman knew he had said something else wrong, although he didn't know what. He only knew that they behaved as if they'd been insulted.

In fact they had been. They looked with hatred at the city Negro who could buy a car as if it were a bottle of whiskey because the one he had was broken. And what's more, who had said so in front of them. He hadn't bothered to say his name, nor ask theirs, had called them "them," and would certainly despise their days, which should have been spent harvesting their own crops, instead of waiting around the general store hoping a truck would come looking for mill hands or tobacco pickers in the flatlands that belonged to somebody else. His manner, his clothes were reminders that they had no crops of their own and no land to speak of either. Just vegetable gardens, which the women took care of, and chickens and pigs that the children took care of. He was telling them that they weren't men, that they relied on women and children for their food. And that the lint and tobacco in their pants pockets where dollar bills should have been was the measure. That thin shoes and suits with vests and smooth smooth hands were the measure. That eyes that had seen big cities and the inside of airplanes were the measure. They had seen him watching their women and rubbing his fly as he stood on the steps. They had also seen him lock his car as soon as he got out of it in a place where there couldn't be more than two keys twenty-five miles around. He hadn't found them fit enough or good enough to want to know their names, and believed himself too good to tell them his. They looked at his skin and saw it was as black as theirs, but they knew he had the heart of the white men who came to pick them up in the trucks when they needed anonymous, faceless laborers.

Now one of them spoke to the Negro with the Virginia license and the northern accent.

"Big money up North, eh?"

"Some," Milkman answered.

"Some? I hear tell everybody up North got big money."

"Lotta people up North got nothing." Milkman made his voice pleasant, but he knew something was developing.

"That's hard to believe. Why would anybody want to stay there if they ain't no big money?"

"The sights, I guess." Another man answered the first. "The sights and the women."

"You kiddin," said the first man in mock dismay. "You mean to tell me pussy different up North?"

"Naw," said the second. "Pussy the same everywhere. Smell like the ocean; taste like the sea."

"Can't be," said a third. "Got to be different."

"Maybe the pricks is different." The first man spoke again.

"Reckon?" asked the second man.

"So I hear tell," said the first man.

"How different?" asked the second man.

"Wee little," said the first man. "Wee, wee little."

"Naw!" said the second man.

"So they tell me. That's why they pants so tight. That true?" The first man looked at Milkman for an answer.

"I wouldn't know," said Milkman. "I never spent much time smacking my lips over another man's dick." Everybody smiled, including Milkman. It was about to begin.

"What about his ass hole? Ever smack your lips over that?"

"Once," said Milkman. "When a little young nigger made me mad and I had to jam a Coke bottle up his ass."

"What'd you use a bottle for? Your cock wouldn't fill it?"

"It did. After I took the Coke bottle out. Filled his mouth too."

"Prefer mouth, do you?"

"If it's big enough, and ugly enough, and belongs to a ignorant motherfucker who is about to get the livin shit whipped out of him."

The knife glittered.

Milkman laughed. "I ain't seen one of those since I was fourteen. Where I come from *boys* play with knives—if they scared they gonna lose, that is."

The first man smiled. "That's me, motherfucker. Scared to death I'm gonna lose."

Milkman did the best he could with a broken bottle, but his

face got slit, so did his left hand, and so did his pretty beige suit, and he probably would have had his throat cut if two women hadn't come running in screaming, "Saul! Saul!"

The store was full of people by then and the women couldn't get through. The men tried to shush them, but they kept on screaming and provided enough lull for Mr. Solomon to interrupt the fight.

"All right. All right. That's enough of that."

"Shut your mouth, Solomon."

"Get them women outta here."

"Stick him, Saul, stick that cocksucker."

But Saul had a jagged cut over his eye and the blood pouring from it made it hard to see. It was difficult but not impossible for Mr. Solomon to pull him away. He left cursing Milkman, but his fervor was gone.

Milkman backed up against the counter, waiting to see if anybody else was going to jump him. When it looked as if no one was, and when the people were drifting outside to watch Saul scuffling and cursing at the men pulling him away, he slumped a little and wiped his face. When the entire store save for the owner was empty, Milkman hurled the broken bottle into a corner. It careened by the cooler and bounced off the wall before splintering on the floor. He walked outside, still panting, and looked around. Four older men still sat on the porch, as though nothing had happened. Blood was streaming down Milkman's face, but it had dried on his hand. He kicked at a white hen and sat down on the top step, wiping the blood with his handkerchief. Three young women with nothing in their hands stood in the road looking at him. Their eyes were wide but noncommittal. Children joined them, circling the women like birds. Nobody said anything. Even the four men on the porch were quiet. Nobody came toward him, offered him a cigarette or a glass of water. Only the children and the hens walked around. Under the hot sun, Milkman was frozen with anger. If he'd had a weapon, he would have slaughtered everybody in sight.

MAX GORDON

Babylon

The boy walked into the convenience store at 3:00 A.M. He wore no coat, and the cold from the snow outside made his face red. He was thin and small, with neatly cut blond hair, and he wore a blue sweater and jeans. Dave watched him as he opened the large glass door with trouble and walked past the counter.

"Hello," the boy said, and raised his hand to Dave. Dave watched him walk over to the Thunderkill game at the back of the store. The boy reached into his pocket and withdrew a quarter. He put the quarter into the machine and began to jerk the joystick.

Dave watched the boy and thought, he can't be more than eight years old. Seven. The boy could barely reach the joystick. His hand smacked at the fire button in a frenzy.

Dave looked at the clock. Three-fifteen in the morning. What was a little boy doing out at three o'clock in the morning?

He wondered if he should call the police.

A woman wearing a bathrobe under her coat asked for a pack of Merits and placed a Diet Coke and a bag of Doritos on the counter. Dave pulled down her cigarettes and punched the prices into the register.

He was putting her groceries into a bag when he saw her face, pinched with anger.

"I *said*," she said, "I need some matches."

"Sorry," he said. He reached under the counter and handed them to her. "Anything else?"

She walked away from the counter.

Dave could tell from the music coming from the machine that the boy's game was over. He watched as the boy inserted another quarter.

An older woman entered the store wearing a blue down coat and leather gloves. She took off her hat, shook out her red hair, and headed straight for the pet food section.

Dave should have been watching the man who was still lingering in the back next to cold cereals, but the boy was walking toward him.

"Can I help you?" he said.

The boy's face barely reached the counter.

"May I have four quarters, please?" The boy pushed a crumpled dollar toward Dave.

"Sure," Dave said. He hit a button on the register, and the drawer sprung open. He was almost out of quarters, so he opened a brand-new roll, cracking it hard, twice, against the side of the drawer. He dropped four of the quarters into the boy's small open hand.

"Thank you," the boy said. He walked back over to the game.

"*Hey, kid!*"

The boy turned around.

"Isn't it a little late for you to be . . . I mean. Do your parents know you're here?"

The boy nodded.

"Are you sure?"

"Yes," the boy said. "They let me."

Dave wanted to ask something else, but he wasn't sure what. The boy turned around and put a quarter in the machine.

I should call the police, Dave thought.

Dave helped himself to another cold slush, grape this time,

and a chili dog. He rang up the woman with red hair and her six cans of cat food.

"Brr. It's cold out there," she said, laughing.

"Is it still snowing as hard?" Dave asked.

"It's worse. I'm not taking any chances." She lifted up her gloves. "I wouldn't even have come out if it wasn't an emergency."

"That will be eight fifty-two."

"So expensive!" She took a twenty-dollar bill out of her wallet. "Oh well," she said. "You're the only place open at this time of night, so I guess I can't be too picky."

"And eleven forty-eight is your change." He placed the money in her hand and began stacking the cans inside a bag.

"I've got eight cats, can you believe it?" she said. "Eight. Jeremy, Jerome, Janelle, Jessop, Jerry, Jasper, Jane, and Julip." And she added, as if it needed explaining, "All their names start with J. I don't know. Just a thing I have. Anyway, I've been so busy lately, I just forgot to buy food. I had some dry food under the sink, but you know cats, they can be so finicky."

"Yes," Dave said, smiling. The truth was he didn't give a fuck about cats.

"Oh, you have one?"

"No. I just, I've heard that before."

"Well, I was grading papers tonight, I always save them for the last minute, I should know better by now because then I'm up all night and I can barely stay awake the next day, and you have to stay awake for eighth graders. Anyway, what was I saying? Oh yes, I already fed the cats earlier but you know once they start crying there's no stopping them until they get exactly what they want."

"Yes," Dave said. "Excuse me, I've got to go take care of some bottles in the back."

"Oh yes," she said. "Well, good night. Nice talking to you."

He walked out from behind the counter and into the storeroom. He watched her get into her car and drive away. He also watched as the boy walked away from his game, looked around, and took two handfuls of Burstin' Thirstin' Taffy from a jar on the rack.

Little son of a bitch. Dave put his hands on his hips, smiled, and shook his head.

The man in cold cereals finally came to the counter. He waited as Dave returned from the back. Dave wiped his hands on his orange-and-white uniform and sold him a box of Pop Tarts and a *Hustler* magazine.

The store was empty. The only sounds came from the whirl of the slush machine and the occasional roar and music from the Thunderkill game. It was the new game, based on the movie, the one that all the parents were complaining about. Now kids were in the store all the time.

Dave had to admit, it was a pretty good game. His own name was on the list of high scorers. Second from the top. Only it read "DAV" because he couldn't get all four letters in. Whenever things were slow, he'd wander back there to play a game or two.

Dave shook out his long black hair and leaned back as if he were playing electric guitar. He moved his fingers up the guitar strings to the theme of the video game. He watched the boy stand back and do the Thunderkill victory dance and then rush back to the screen as the game started again.

Dave could tell from the music that the kid was pretty good. He was already at the twelfth level. It had taken Dave almost six weeks of solid playing to get to the twelfth level.

The boy's game was over. He walked back over to the counter. "I need four quarters, please."

Dave pushed a button on the register. The drawer opened. "Isn't it past your bedtime, kid?"

"No."

"Don't you have school tomorrow?"

"Yes."

"You sure your parents know you're here?"

"Yes. May I have my quarters please?"

What a fucking smart-ass, Dave thought, handing him the quarters. Parents today. They ought to be shot in the head. He dropped the quarters into the boy's hand and noticed that he was chewing hard.

"By the way, you want to pay for that?"

"I brought this with me," said the boy. He could barely chew all the candy he'd crammed into his mouth. A thin string of saliva slipped down his jaw onto his shirt.

"Bullshit," Dave said.

The boy walked back to the game, and Dave thought, maybe I should leave him alone. He used to run in the street with his friends, stealing shit, getting caught, skipping school, drinking beer, smoking pot, fucking around. Everybody did it. And eventually they came around. Not only did he have a job, he was even taking classes at the community college. Leave the kid alone. But seven or eight years old?

"Hey," he called to the back of the store. "How old are you anyway?"

The boy didn't answer. He was too involved in the game.

At four o'clock Dave was leaning against the counter, half asleep. He was thinking about Ian, who was supposed to relieve him at six. He was always late with some excuse. Dave rubbed his stomach; the chili dogs had made him sick. To help it settle, he sipped from a beer he kept stashed away under the counter.

The music from the game ground down to a mechanical belch. The boy walked up to the counter.

"I can't give you any more quarters," Dave said.

"I want to buy this." The boy placed a pack of Thunderkill cards and a box of Lemonheads on the counter. He took another crumpled bill from his pocket and pushed it across the counter.

Dave rubbed his eyes, put the dollar in the register and the change on the counter. The boy had already opened the cards and was shuffling through them.

"Don't you like the gum?" Dave asked.

"Tortureboy, the Grabber, Slaughterman, the Bandit. Hey! I got it!"

"What did you get?" Dave leaned over the counter.

"The Throatcutter! I've got almost all of the others, except Throatcutter and the Brutalizer. I can't believe I got it! Wait till I show Chris!"

"Let me see that." Reluctantly, the boy handed Dave the

card. On the back was the familiar picture from the movie; the bolt of lightning and the Thunderkill Avenger. Dave flipped the card over. There was a picture of a very big man with a purple face, holding a severed head in his hands.

The boy held out his hand.

Dave gave him back the card.

"How old are you, kid?"

"Seven."

"What's your name?"

"Peter."

"Peter what?"

"Peter Johansen."

"You live around here?"

"I live in Parvale Court." The boy stuck the card in his pocket. "I have to go now," he said.

Parvale Court. "Wait." Dave looked out the window. It was still dark outside.

"Let me tell you something," Dave told him. "It isn't safe for you to be walking around at night, I don't care what your parents let you do. This neighborhood isn't safe. It isn't like Parvale. Do you understand what I'm saying?"

The boy nodded.

"Did you really walk over here from Parvale?"

The boy nodded.

"I can't let you walk home now," Dave said. He rubbed his chin. "Shit."

"I've got to go." The boy stepped away from the counter.

"Wait!" Dave glanced out the window again. "You want that Brutalizer card, don't you?"

"Yes," said the boy.

"Well, you see all these cards we got out here?"

The boy nodded.

"We've got ten times that much in the back. I mean we've got tons. I'm going to give it to you, if you just wait right here, okay? I'll be right back."

The boy didn't respond. He opened his box of Lemonheads and dropped a few into his hand.

"Be right back," Dave said.

He went into the office and took the phone book out of the metal drawer. He tried to avoid the smell of the mildewed mop in the corner by the file cabinet. He ran down the list of names. Jigund, Jirribiak, Johansen. Parvale Court. Carrietown was big, but not that big.

He dialed quickly. The phone rang eight times. He tried to look out and see what the boy was doing, but the cord wouldn't reach.

"Hello." It was a man's voice, dry and irritated from interrupted sleep.

"Yes, uh, my name is, uh, Dave, David Brackert, and I'm down here at the Stop and Shop over on Lexington Road, and there is a little boy over here, I think he may be your son."

"Our son is in bed asleep."

"Is his name Peter and does he like video games?"

There was a short pause on the other end and a sigh. "Hold on a second."

Dave twisted the cord and waited.

There was a jumbling at the other end as the phone was dropped and picked up again.

"I don't know if this is some kind of joke or something, but our son is in bed asleep. Good night."

"But—"

The man hung up the phone. Dave held it in his hand for a moment and finally set it down.

He walked out of the office, furious. "All right, kid. You want to tell me who the hell you really are?"

The store was empty.

The boy entered the house using the same key he used each day when he got home from school. He climbed the stairs. Each carpeted stair was soft and fluffy, like walking up stacks of freshly baked bread. He went into his room, undressed, and closed the door. Before he went to sleep, he could hear the sounds of his father and mother in their bedroom.

"Don't you touch me, I mean it."

"Fucking bitch."

"You're a fucking bitch, Alan. Get off me."

It seemed only minutes had passed when he felt two hands on his shoulder. His mother was standing beside the bed in her nightgown.

"Good morning, sweetheart," she said. "It's seven o'clock. Hurry, I don't want you to be late for school."

He put on some fresh clothes from his drawer and went downstairs to have breakfast. He ate two bowls of cereal and two of the maid's waffles. His father had some eggs, and his mother didn't eat anything. She wiped her mouth on a napkin and stood up from the table.

The maid fastened his coat and handed him his lunch.

"Come on, Corbin," his mother said. "We have to hurry or your father and I will be late."

He realized that his backpack was still upstairs and went to get it. He ran to his window and saw his parents waiting for him in the car. Watching them, he felt as if he were looking at something very small from the window of an airplane.

His father honked the horn.

He ran downstairs and outside. When he reached the car, his mother opened the door and leaned forward, making room for him to get in the backseat.

"Next time we're leaving," she said. She was putting her lipstick on in the mirror. His father slipped on his sunglasses and backed out of the driveway. The school was six blocks away. Corbin fell asleep in the backseat of the car.

Dave was opening a second beer and a bag of salted cashews when the boy walked in, wearing a red jacket and a white dress shirt. His shoes were untied. Dave looked at the boy as if he were a ghost and then at the clock. Three-twenty.

"Hello," the boy said, lifting his hand. He walked back to the Thunderkill game.

Half an hour later, when he came to the counter for quarters, Dave said, "You left yesterday without saying good-bye."

"You were going to tell on me," the boy said.

"So who's Peter Johansen?"

"A kid from my school."

"So you lied. You don't even live in Parvale, do you?"

The boy didn't respond. Dave sighed, opened the drawer, and handed him the quarters.

"Go play your game," he said.

The boy played eight games. On his last game, Dave walked up behind him. He watched as the boy maneuvered Thunderkill around a building. Thunderkill leaped over a trash can, dodged six bullets, and rolled underneath a police car, all while firing at the man across the street. Thunderkill shot the man four times and made his way into the restaurant, where he surprised the owner by coming in through the back. Thunderkill cut his throat.

"Good job," Dave said softly. He was in awe. He had never seen this board before.

"Thanks," said the boy.

Thunderkill escaped from the restaurant and ran down the street into a house. Inside, a family was sleeping. Thunderkill climbed the steps and entered each bedroom. He cut off the heads of the children, two boys and a girl, then of both their parents. There was a grandmother in the house too, but she jumped out of the window and broke her neck as Thunderkill ran to get her.

"Shit, that was five hundred points!" the boy yelled. "I knew she was in there!"

"But you got the others," Dave said, amazed. "Look at that." He watched as the boy's score whirled with points. Chopped heads, especially when caught by surprise, were five hundred each.

Thunderkill leaped out the window. He ran down an alleyway and was met by a woman carrying a purse and screaming for help. She opened the purse and shot at Thunderkill twice. Thunderkill shot her dead, but a small boy running down the street stabbed him in the leg. As he tried to get up, another child ran over from a nearby alley and crushed his head with a rock. The game was over.

"Shit," the boy said. "The Twins. They always get me."

"Good game," said Dave.

"I guess so." He moved the joystick and hit the button at each letter, putting them at the top of the screen.

K, I, L.

"Those are your initials?"

"No. I just like to write kill, that's all."

"Hey, you beat my high score, you little motherfucker. I was DAV."

The boy giggled.

"Hey!" Dave said. "Free banana slush on me." He walked back over to the counter.

"I have to go," the boy said.

"I'm not going to call the police or your parents or anything," Dave said. "I don't care if you come here all night."

"I have to go," the boy said. He put a pack of Thunderkill cards on the counter and a box of Milk Duds.

Dave took the money and looked out the window. He needed to get back into the office so that he could call the police. He considered pulling the five-dollar bill that was attached to the alarm system, but wondered if his boss would consider a boy out on his own at four o'clock in the morning emergency enough.

Dave handed the boy his change and rushed over and poured him a banana slush. He watched the boy open the pack of cards.

"Anything new?"

The boy didn't answer. He went through the cards twice.

"Knifethrower, Bloodraid, Rapelord, Skullcrusher, and Throatcutter. I've got all these."

"If you want," Dave said, "I'll play you a game. Things are slow anyway. How about that?"

"I can't."

"If I win, nothing happens, but if you win, I'll give you a free pack of cards. On me. Maybe you'll get the Terrorizer."

"Brutalizer."

"Sorry, Brutalizer."

The boy seemed to be considering it.

"I can't," he finally said.

"How about two packs?" Dave was coming from behind the counter slowly. He wasn't sure what he was going to do. Run to the office or grab him.

The boy stepped back. "I can't," he said, and then quickly added, "Good-bye." He walked out of the store.

Dave started to go after him, but a man in a trenchcoat came in and walked over to frozen foods.

The snow outside was coming down harder. Dave watched as the boy was swallowed into the darkness. He saw a blurry square of red waiting to cross the street, and then even that disappeared.

The man bought a six-pack and left. Dave wondered what he would do now. He could call the police, run after the kid, or close the store, get in his car, and find him. He wanted to do something. He had a strange feeling inside that he was never going to see the boy again.

An hour later he still hadn't done anything and finally accepted the fact that nothing was going to be done.

He said a prayer for the kid. Then he opened another beer and a *Hustler* magazine and tried to imagine what Ian's excuse would be this time.

Corbin walked the blocks toward home. There were exactly twenty-nine of them, and he counted each one as he passed it. He walked fast, to protect himself. No one would stop him if he walked very fast, and snow was coming down harder. Good thing.

He walked briskly past a few lit stores along Lexington Avenue, all closed for the night. He kept his mind on walking and looking out for cars, but he couldn't stop thinking about the game he'd played and about going back to get the free Thunderkill cards. Tomorrow, he decided. His parents would be awake soon.

He had turned down Melbourne Avenue when a car rushed past him. It stopped, inched back, and stopped again.

The window rolled down and a face emerged.

"Hey, little boy," the woman said. She had blond hair and red glasses and was fat. She leaned across the seat. "What are you doing out at this time of night? Are you lost?"

He ran away from her voice and across to a nearby parking lot. He wasn't quite sure where he was running, but he heard the car drive off behind him. He watched from the corner of his eye as the car came around the corner and followed him.

He ran past the bank, past the shopping mart with the pharmacy next door, past PriceRite Shoes and Donovan's Doughnuts, past the plant store and the church on the corner. He ran back to the shopping mart.

He heard the car behind him, or some other car. When he turned around, he could see the woman coming through the parking lot directly toward him. He slipped in the alley between Publix and Carrietown Drugs.

He watched her get out of her car. He heard a sound behind him, but he didn't move. The woman started toward the alley, and then decided against it and got back into her car. Corbin didn't stand up until he was sure she'd driven away.

He waited in the alley, just in case she came back with the police. It stopped snowing. He heard the noise behind him again.

When he turned around, he saw four round faces in the darkness, and a smaller fifth one.

"What the fuck is that?" one of them whispered.

"It's a kid," another said.

"What the hell is a kid doing around here?"

"Fuck if I know," said the first.

Corbin's feet were ready to run again when he recognized the noise he'd heard before. Like someone kicking a sack. There was a low moan, then gasping, and Corbin heard a crack.

"Please God." It was a different voice. Corbin's eyes were finally adjusting. He could see the shapes of the five bodies. One was on the ground.

"Please."

"Shut up. Fucking faggot."

"What is the kid doing still standing there?"

"Get him out of here. He can see us!"

"He can't see shit. Come on."

One body lifted a foot and stomped down on the one that was on the ground. The body on the ground let out a long wheeze, like the rolled-up things they gave out at birthday parties.

Corbin laughed.

"Oh, you think that's funny, kid?" The tall man did it again. He stomped his foot against the man's chest. Corbin laughed again.

"This kid's sick."

"I like him."

The man continued to stomp the man on the ground, the man on the ground continued to make the wheezing sounds, and Corbin continued to laugh. Eventually the three of them got bored with the stomping game. The man on the ground got bored with the wheezing sounds because he coughed and reached for the tall man's leg with slippery hands. The tall man kicked him in the face.

Corbin took out his Milk Duds.

The tall man was pulling the pants off the man on the ground while the others held him. The man on the ground said no, but he didn't move.

"You like it up the ass, don't you?" the tall man whispered.

"Please God," the man said.

Corbin's mouth worked the candy. He never should have gotten Milk Duds. Hot Tamales were better. At least you could chew those, when they were fresh. But Milk Duds weren't as bad as Jujubees. Jujubees stuck to the back of your teeth and you had to pull them off with your fingers.

"You're not going to fuck him in front of the kid, are you?" One man was smoking a cigarette beside the wall and laughing.

"Hell no! I'm not going to fuck this piece of shit at all." He pulled the man up off the ground and dragged him farther away from the light.

The tall man stood up very straight. He was breathing hard like he was tired. Corbin stepped in closer so he could see.

"Run," the man on the ground said. "My name is—" His head fell. He reached out a hand, and that fell too. Corbin chewed his candy.

"My name is Kyle," the man on the ground finally said. He coughed, and blood ran over the side of his mouth. Corbin jumped back. He didn't want the blood to touch his shoes.

The tall man standing reached into his pocket. He pulled out a knife. Light from the moon winked off its edge. Corbin thought it looked beautiful held up like that. Sparkly.

"You ever see somebody get killed?" the tall man asked Corbin.

Corbin shook his head.

"You like faggots?"

Corbin thought a moment. "I don't know," he said. Then he remembered and shook his head. He didn't know exactly what they were, but he knew he didn't want to be one. He knew that it had something to do with boys who kissed other boys. Shawn Martin had called him one in gym class during kickball. He'd almost caught the ball, but it had slipped out of his hands just as the bell rang and the other team won. It had been an accident.

"Is it okay if I kill him, kid?"

"No!" the man on the ground screamed. "Please! I'm not a fag!"

"That's why you came out of that bar, right?"

"Oh God!"

"If you say it's okay, kid," the tall man said, "I'll kill him."

Corbin didn't know what to say. He shrugged. The four men laughed, and the man against the wall put out his cigarette. The tall man standing was laughing so hard he was holding his knees and started coughing. Corbin laughed too.

"All right," the tall man said. "It will be light soon. Enough of this bullshit."

He snatched the man from the ground again and pulled him up until he was almost standing. The man from the ground's legs made Corbin think of noodles. The tall man standing had to hold him up with his arms around his waist. When he lifted him, the man's head rolled back against his shoulder and for a moment their eyes met. "No, please," he whispered. It was almost tender, the way the tall man standing held the man from the ground. At one point, their cheeks touched. Then the tall man standing held the man from the ground's head back.

Corbin reached into his box of candy. It was empty. He dropped the box.

Then something happened. The man from the ground began

to kick and twist, like some kind of spasm had taken over his body. The tall man standing tried to hold him up, but he bucked and leaped as if he was chained to a wall. "No. No. No. No. No," he said, clawing at the air with desperate hands. He almost slid through the tall man standing's arms, but the tall man hoisted the man from the ground up, jerked his head back, and sliced straight across his neck. The dancing arms dropped like the cut strings of a puppet. That was when the tall man standing opened up his arms and the man from the ground slid through them. The man from the ground went down, slow motion like. His cheek hit the ground with a final solid smack, and his eyes slammed open, shocked. They stared at Corbin's candy box.

"Let's get the fuck out of here," said a voice.

"What about the kid?" said another.

Corbin began backing up. He stepped out of the alley and lost the four faces in the dark as they ran in the opposite direction. He waited for the footsteps, for them to run back toward him, but there were none.

He stood outside the alley for several minutes. The only sound was the buzzing from the fluorescent lights outside Publix supermarket. Occasionally, out by the street, a car swished by. He started to go home but turned around and walked back into the alley.

It was getting lighter out. The sky had turned from black to dark blue. He walked over to the man on the ground and stood above him. The man's right hand was flat beside his mouth as if he might start doing push-ups at any moment.

"Get up," Corbin said.

When the man on the ground didn't respond, Corbin nudged him with his shoe.

"Get up," he said, again.

The man on the ground continued to stare at Corbin's shoe, his eyes wide and defiant.

"Fine," Corbin said. "I don't care." He lifted his shoe and gave the man's head a stomp. The man's head bounced once against the hard ground and one eye closed, slowly.

"I don't care," Corbin told him.

He ran the whole way home, entered the house and his bed,

and heard the toilet down the hall flush. There was no time to undress. He jumped into bed fully clothed and pulled the covers up to his neck.

The door opened.

"Corbin?"

He didn't answer.

"I can tell you're not asleep, silly, your eyelids are fluttering."

He opened them.

"Good morning, Mom."

"Good morning, sweetheart. Time to wake up for school."

"I'm coming."

She winked and shut the door.

He stepped out of bed, changed clothes quickly, and went downstairs. The maid sent him back upstairs to wash his face. He came back down, ate two full breakfasts, and was standing at the car all ready to leave when his parents left the house.

"Well, my goodness!" his mother said. "Look who's here, Alan!"

"I see," his father said, biting into an English muffin.

"I'm very proud of you. You're becoming more responsible, Corbin. That's the sign of a young man."

In the car, he leaned forward and said over her shoulder, "Last night I saw a man get killed, Mom."

"Sit back, Corbin, and put on your seat belt."

"But I did! I saw him get his throat cut by these guys!"

"I said sit down!" His mother was screaming. "Such a beautiful morning, and you were doing so well. Now lies. I don't want to hear another word about any of that nonsense. Do you understand me?"

"Yes," he said, because he did. He hadn't told her to convince her. He just needed to say it once, out loud. To make it real. He would never mention it again.

ALICE DUNBAR NELSON

A Carnival Jangle

There is a merry jangle of bells in the air, an all-pervading sense of jester's noise, and the flaunting vividness of royal colors; the streets swarm with humanity—humanity in all shapes, manners, forms—laughing, pushing, jostling, crowding, a mass of men and women and children, as varied and as assorted in their several individual peculiarities as ever a crowd that gathered in one locality since the days of Babel.

It is Carnival in New Orleans; a brilliant Tuesday in February, when the very air effervesces an ozone intensely exhilarating—of a nature half spring, half winter—to make one long to cut capers. The buildings are a blazing mass of royal purple and golden yellow, and national flags, bunting and decorations that laugh in the glint of the Midas sun. The streets a crush of jesters and maskers, Jim Crows and clowns, ballet girls and Mephistos, Indians and monkeys; of wild and sudden flashes of music, of glittering pageants and comic ones, of befeathered and belled horses. A madding dream of color and melody and fantasy gone wild in an effervescent bubble of beauty that shifts and changes and passes kaleidoscope-like before the bewildered eye.

A bevy of bright-eyed girls and boys of that uncertainty of age that hovers between childhood and maturity, were moving down Canal Street when there was a sudden jostle with another crowd meeting them. For a minute there was a deafening clamor of laughter, cracking of whips, which all maskers carry, jingle and clatter of carnival bells, and the masked and unmasked extricated themselves and moved from each other's paths. But in the confusion a tall Prince of Darkness had whispered to one of the girls in the unmasked crowd: "You'd better come with us, Flo, you're wasting time in that tame gang. Slip off, they'll never miss you; we'll get you a rig, and show you what life is."

And so it happened that when a half hour passed, and the bright-eyed bevy missed Flo and couldn't find her, wisely giving up the search at last, that she, the quietest and most bashful of the lot, was being initiated into the mysteries of "what life is."

Down Bourbon Street and on Toulouse and St. Peter Streets there are quaint little old-world places, where one may be disguised effectually for a tiny consideration. Thither guided by the shapely Mephisto, and guarded by the team of jockeys and ballet girls, tripped Flo. Into one of the lowest-ceiled, dingiest and most ancient-looking of these disguise shops they stopped.

"A disguise for this demoiselle," announced Mephisto to the woman who met them. She was small and wizened and old, with yellow, flabby jaws and neck like the throat of an alligator, and straight, white hair that stood from her head uncannily stiff.

"But the demoiselle wishes to appear a boy, *un petit garcon?*" she inquired, gazing eagerly at Flo's long, slender frame. Her voice was old and thin, like the high quavering of an imperfect tuning fork, and her eyes were sharp as talons in their grasping glance.

"Mademoiselle does not wish such a costume," gruffly responded Mephisto.

"*Ma foi,* there is no other," said the ancient, shrugging her shoulders. "But one is left now, mademoiselle would make a fine troubadour."

"Flo," said Mephisto, "it's a daredevil scheme, try it; no one will ever know it but us, and we'll die before we tell. Besides, we must; it's late, and you couldn't find your crowd."

And that was why you might have seen a Mephisto and a

slender troubadour of lovely form, with mandolin flung across his shoulder, followed by a bevy of jockeys and ballet girls, laughing and singing as they swept down Rampart Street.

When the flash and glare and brilliancy of Canal Street have palled upon the tired eye, and it is yet too soon to go home, and to such a prosaic thing as dinner, and one still wishes for novelty, then it is wise to go in the lower districts. Fantasy and fancy and grotesqueness in the costuming and behavior of the maskers run wild. Such dances and whoops and leaps as these hideous Indians and devils do indulge in; such wild curvetings and great walks. And in the open squares, where whole groups do congregate, it is wonderfully amusing. Then, too, there is a ball in every available hall, a delirious ball, where one may dance all day for ten cents; dance and grow mad for joy, and never know who were your companions, and be yourself unknown. And in the exhilaration of the day, one walks miles and miles, and dances and curvets, and the fatigue is never felt.

In Washington Square, away down where Royal Street empties its stream of children and men into the broad channel of Elysian Fields Avenue, there was a perfect Indian dance. With a little imagination one might have willed away the vision of the surrounding houses and fancied one's self again in the forest, where the natives were holding a sacred riot. The square was filled with spectators, masked and unmasked. It was amusing to watch these mimic Red-men, they seemed so fierce and earnest.

Suddenly one chief touched another on the elbow. "See that Mephisto and troubadour over there?" he whispered huskily.

"Yes, who are they?"

"I don't know the devil," responded the other quietly, "but I'd know that other form anywhere. It's Leon, see? I know those white hands like a woman's and that restless head. Ha!"

"But there may be a mistake."

"No. I'd know that one anywhere; I feel it's him. I'll pay him now. Ah, sweetheart, you've waited long, but you shall feast now!" He was caressing something long, and lithe, and glittering beneath his blanket.

In a masked dance it is easy to give a death-blow between the shoulders. Two crowds meet and laugh and shout and mingle almost inextricably, and if a shriek of pain should arise, it is not noticed in the din, and when they part, if one should stagger and fall bleeding to the ground, who can tell who has given the blow? There is naught but an unknown stiletto on the ground, the crowd has dispersed, and masks tell no tales anyway. There is murder, but by whom? For what? *Quien sabe?*

And that is how it happened on Carnival night, in the last mad moments of Rex's reign, a broken-hearted woman sat gazing wide-eyed and mute at a horrible something that lay across the bed. Outside the long sweet march music of many bands floated in in mockery, and the flash of rockets and Bengal lights illumined the dead, white face of the girl troubadour.

E. LYNN HARRIS

Just As I Am

I love the fall. It stirs a great many fond memories. Vibrant September, golden October, and brilliant November. It was in the fall that I scored my first high school touchdown against North Central. A twenty-three-yard reception between two defenders who were much bigger than I was. It's a feeling I will never forget. It was also in the fall when I first made love to another man, another feeling that I will never forget. And it was in the fall when I discovered the pleasures oral sex brought, not only to my female partner, but to myself as well.

I love fall weather. Cool, crisp nights watching the summer try to hold on until fall's colorful foliage forces its hand and sends it packing. But there was something different about the beginning of this fall that led me to believe this year's would not be the same. They say winter is the season of discontent, but sometimes discontent comes early.

One of my fondest memories of the fall was my initiation into KAΩ, my college fraternity. I pledged during the time when black fraternities *really* pledged, hazing and all. It was hard to believe it had been close to fifteen years since I and nineteen other line brothers crossed the sands into ΚΑΩ, so it was only natural that all twenty of us planned to meet to commemorate this important event in our lives and to enjoy the brotherhood of those who would follow us.

Before heading to Tuscaloosa, I stopped at my parents' home. I'd been so upset by my night in Jersey City with Basil that I'd decided against going to my family reunion. My mama would have been able to detect that something was wrong and wouldn't have let up until I confessed. I still couldn't lie or tell half truths to my mama face to face, so I just called and said I was having problems with a former client. They were disappointed but Jared did show up so I guess he took my place. I cut short a conversation with my parents when they were going on and on about how Jared helped and how all the relatives thought he was a member of the family. The phone call and my own jealousy ruined my day. I wondered how Jared felt being at my family reunion without me. I missed Jared something terrible. He and I still weren't talking, but I was seriously considering initiating a truce. As it was, I wasn't talking to much of anybody these days. Basil still hadn't called me to explain or apologize and I definitely wasn't calling him. (I must admit, though, one of the reasons I didn't go to the family reunion was because I was afraid I might miss his phone call.) It looked like Basil was off to a super year with the Warriors if the sports pages were correct. He was getting an awful lot of press. Maybe he had visited the sportswriter after all.

I wasn't talking to Kyle as much either. At first it was because his phone was out of order but then whenever I did get through, I got his answering machine or else he was asleep. Kyle seemed to be cooling out. I hoped he wasn't harboring any hard feelings regarding my representing Basil and sleeping with him. He'd changed his mind at the last minute about coming to Atlanta for Labor Day weekend, saying he had just picked up two new clients and had a shot at doing some of the costumes for Nicole's new Broadway show. I worried some that our lack of communication was due to Kyle's drinking and doing drugs again. He'd been disappointed when I'd chosen not to go to Los Angeles for the beach party on the Fourth of July weekend. It surprised me when he'd decided against going to Los Angeles alone.

I stopped at my folks' home before heading back to campus because I wanted to help with the problems developing with my little brother Kirby. My parents had decided Kirby was going to spend his first year of high school at a prep school and had gotten him into the exclusive Andover Academy in Andover, Massachusetts. They were cashing in savings bonds they'd had since I was a little boy. Prep school was an opportunity I would have jumped at, but Kirby wasn't feeling it. Pops had spoken and so my little brother was on his way East whether he liked it or not.

My parents had made a deal with him. If he made good grades and showed more responsibility, then he could choose where he went to school during his sophomore year. Come home with anything less than a B average then it was back to prep school or possibly a tougher military school. I guessed my parents were attempting a more politically correct method of child rearing with Kirby. Making deals and talking things out. When I was growing up the only talking that occurred was after I had gotten my ass whipped.

I talked with my little brother the day before he and Pops planned to leave on their long drive to Andover. He was becoming quite a handsome young man, looking more like Pops than even me. Kirby had a basketball player's build and shared my pops's brownish-green eyes that were even more distinguishable because of Kirby's slightly darker skin tone.

"What do you think about this prep school stuff?"

"I ain't got no choice," Kirby said.

"I don't have a choice," I corrected.

"Whatever you say," Kirby retorted.

"It won't be as bad as you think," I said.

"You think so. It's co-ed, you know," Kirby said.

"Oh, you like that, huh?"

"Damn betcha," Kirby said as he playfully threw a boxer punch toward me.

"Cool out, little boy, before I have to lay you out. Come here.

Do you know what this is?" I asked Kirby as I showed him a gold condom wrapper.

"Shoot, yeah, it's a rubber. I got one in my wallet," Kirby boasted.

"Do you know what it's for and how to put it on?"

"Come on, Ray-Ray, chill. I know that stuff," he answered bashfully.

"Do you know about AIDS?" I asked.

"Yeah," Kirby said, hanging his head.

"Okay, then make me a promise. You won't put your piece anywhere without one of these on. Deal?"

"Yeah, yeah. I won't, Ray-Ray," he laughed, and playfully punched my shoulders.

"I'm serious, Kirby. Don't play around with this shit. Understood?"

"Yes, big brother. I understand," Kirby said.

I don't know why but I got the feeling my little brother wasn't a virgin. I'd noticed the change in him last Christmas. The boyish charm was gone and was replaced by a cockiness, which was one of the reasons he found himself headed for Andover. From the questions he asked and the posters in his room—Olympic gymnast Dominique Dawes and the little girl from the "Fresh Prince of Bel-Air"—I assumed he was heterosexual. I hoped I was right. I didn't want my little brother going through all the pain and turmoil I had and I didn't think Pops could stomach both his sons not being totally heterosexual. I also realized adolescent heterosexuality was not an indicator of what might happen in the future. My main concern with Kirby going to Andover was that I didn't want him to come back talking and acting like a white boy.

I was happy I'd stopped off to see my little brother before he left home for his first extended stay. Not only for Kirby and myself but my mom as well. She broke out into a loud cry when Pops and Kirby pulled out. I thought maybe she would be happy about having Pops all to herself finally. Mama's quiet tears turned to loud sobs and I held her tightly in my arms until she had gotten everything out. I waited until she'd turned in for the night before I left for campus, turning on the alarm, and locking the door. I'd left her a nice note telling her Christmas was just around the corner and Santa was going to bring her two handsome young men. As I pulled out of the driveway I thought about how it seemed as though it was only yesterday I'd left for college for the first time. I'd begged my parents to let me drive alone and I'd sneaked out during the wee hours of the morning to avoid my mother's tears.

Nothing could have prepared me for what would happen at my fraternity reunion. It was great seeing everyone I had pledged with. All of my line brothers had returned for the reunion, the vast majority with wives and children. Everyone wanted to know why I wasn't married and why I let Sela get away. Luckily there was no hard court press on the marriage question since five of my line brothers were also single.

Everyone met at the fraternity house, reliving memories of the past and creating new ones with the undergrad brothers who now ran the frat. I had grown up so much through my association with KAΩ, and it was still one of my most treasured associations, but things seemed a bit different with the new frat brothers.

All of the major black Greek organizations, both sororities and fraternities, had instituted something called risk-free pledging. In other words it was walk right up, sign up, and you're a frat brother. Gone were the days of nine-week pledge periods, complete with physical and mental hazing. In a lot of ways this was good. Pledging had gotten out of hand all across the country with brutal beatings and accidental deaths touching all the fraternities. The sororities didn't have the deaths but word was out that the ladies were almost as physical as the men. So in a rare agreement, the heads of all the sororities and fraternities got together and decided to implement rules by which the groups would abide.

KAΩ had always been selective in the past, but this was soon to change. People used to say the hardest thing about pledging KAΩ was getting on line. That's the way I thought it should be. Some fraternities accepted guys just to be able to kick their asses during the pledge period—not that I hadn't kicked a little ass during my undergrad years—but risk-free pledging had its own problems. There didn't seem to be the brotherhood that we'd shared. After you went through a pledge period in the old days you really felt like brothers and the fraternity meant a great deal to you because you had worked so hard to become a member. The current pledge period was nonexistent; once you were accepted as a pledge you became a member a few days later. There was a marked difference between the new brothers and the old ones. This new risk-free process was even less rigorous than when guys used to pledge in graduate chapter, which was always looked down upon, because it was a lot easier than pledging in undergrad.

After everybody got together, we started breaking off into groups just like the old days. They weren't exactly cliques but the people who hung out together in undergrad migrated toward those people now. So I ended up with my former roommate Stanley and his wife Lencola and Trent Walters, president of my pledge class, who was surprisingly still single and was much better-looking than I remembered. Matter of fact, Trent had been pretty square-looking as an undergrad—braces and thick glasses. He'd been an ROTC man, always in the books. I had never really thought about Trent's looks when we'd first met pledging. Trent Walters had gone through a major makeover.

We left the frat house and went to the bar at the Hilton Hotel for drinks before heading back to the house for an evening meeting of the alumni and undergrad brothers.

Stanley was a professor at the University of Kansas and the proud father of two little girls. His wife—one of his former students—was a little frumpy-looking, but really nice.

Trent was an architect working for a Chicago design firm. He boasted about living on Chicago's Gold Coast. Stanley and I kidded each other about being the odd couple because Stanley was so meticulous and I was so messy. We reminisced about how we'd come home late at night or early in the morning and raid the icebox, usually eating Captain Crunch, lemon creme cookies, and fried egg sandwiches after a night of drinking KAΩ punch. Stanley asked me if I still talked with Sela and said he'd heard I had come pretty close to marrying a movie star. He had even heard it was Robin Givens. I smiled at the thought of Nicole and how she did look like Robin Givens but only better.

"Ray, the frat's pretty boy with all the pretty girls," Stanley remarked.

"Yeah, Ray was the lady-killer," Trent chipped in.

Boy, if they only knew, I thought, as I accepted their compliments with a guarded smile.

"I knew he was a motherfuckin' faggot. I told y'all," the deep voice said from inside the house. Trent, Stanley, and I walked back into the fraternity house in the middle of a chapter meeting. The brothers were discussing one of the new pledges who was about to become a full member after Sunday's ceremony.

The three of us leaned against the back wall listening to the frats talk about the pledge whom they had set up to find out if he was gay. From what I could gather from the meeting conversation, the current members had been looking for a way to keep the guy, whose name must have been Miller, out of the frat. So they'd convinced one of the guy's line brothers to try to entice the pledge into meeting him for a sexual escapade.

It appeared their plan had worked. The guy'd evidently taken the bait and one of the members laughed and said, "He had fallen to his knees just about to get busy on Terry when we broke in and cold-busted his punk ass."

"You should have seen the look on that motherfucker's face," another member chimed in.

"But do you think national is going to let us keep him out?" a voice quizzed.

"Damn straight. I don't think that punk ass Miller Thomas will even show up around this frat house again. If he does we ruin his faggot ass," the presiding officer stated.

Shocked at the proceedings, I continued to stand against the wall. There had always been rumors about gay members in all the fraternities. They were supposed to be service organizations, but that was just a cover. Sure we did a couple of service projects a year but the majority of the activities centered around the social. I still didn't understand what a person's sexuality had to do with his ability to serve the fraternity, provided he didn't force himself on other members or do anything to embarrass the fraternity. In theory that should be the only question, but deep down I knew better. It just hadn't hit me how homophobic fraternities were and continued to be.

Trent seemed to be annoyed at the ongoing dispute and pulled one of the current members over to find out more information about the situation. I stood close to Trent and listened as the current rush chairman explained that Miller had been accepted as a pledge because he had a 3.88 grade point in Chemical Engineering and was the number-one tennis player on the university tennis team. In addition his father was a judge in New Orleans and a KΑΩ alum, making Miller a legacy. We always accepted legacies. It seemed all the guys in the fraternity were crazy about Miller until the rumor got started.

Only a few current members had come to his defense and when they did their own sexuality came under question. Since Miller had already been accepted, they couldn't just kick the guy out. So instead the plan was to blackmail him into quitting before the formal induction service.

My stomach churned. I was thinking about this young guy whom I didn't know and what would have happened to me if people had discovered my doubts about my sexuality before pledging KΑΩ. Or, more important, if I had been found out after my affair with Kelvin during my senior year. What would have happened had I defended somebody I didn't know; what shadows would it have cast on my reputation as one of the better-known and better-liked members of KΑΩ?

"It sounds like this guy would be great for the chapter. I mean with his father and all. And he's on the tennis team," Trent said.

"Yeah, you're right, frat, but he's a punk. We can't have no punks in KΑΩ. After a while they'll be taking over," a guy who identified himself as Dale said.

"Yeah, but if he's the number-one player on the university tennis team then he's very likely to go pro," I said, trying to interject a business perspective.

"I think it's a dead issue. He ain't gonna show his face around here again," one of the ringleaders of the protest said.

It seemed as if Trent's and my arguments were falling on deaf ears. The members seemed to have already made up their minds and since we were not active members of the chapter, our opinions were just that, opinions.

I did take note of Trent's posture toward the case. It seemed he was really bothered by the entire situation and that made me feel good. The more I thought about it, Trent had seemed openminded and levelheaded for as long as I'd known him. He always had a girlfriend, but he was always so quiet. Could my line brother and fraternity brother be in the silent frat too?

The rest of the weekend went according to plan, at least until the end: beer drinking, barbecue eating, and re-creating the past with men who were like family. But like a family reunion, there were relatives I wasn't as excited about seeing and new relatives I was sorry I ever met. The weekend also made me realize I could still love and be close to Jared and not have to sleep with him. I mean I loved the majority of these guys. Maybe not the way I loved Jared, but I still loved them. It also helped me understand how important my friendships with men were. Saturday night after the football game I got a little full of the spirits and, I guess, emotional. So emotional that I called Jared to tell him how sorry I was for being such an ass wipe and to tell him I had to see him once I got back home. Jared, being Jared, was quite receptive and told me over the phone he'd missed me and looked forward to renewing our friendship. He warned me not to drink too much and to drive safely back to Atlanta. Right before I hung up there was an awkward silence and then before saying good-bye, I said, "Jared, you know I love you. I mean like a brother."

"Yeah, I know, Ray. That's why I put up with you. 'Cause I love you too. Stay strong," Jared said.

"Talking to one of those sweet Atlanta peaches, frat?" Derrick Hall asked. Derrick was the current president of the fraternity and leader of the gay witch hunt. He was probably also a cardcarrying member of the all-body, no-brain club.

"Naw, just talking with a good friend," I said. I wondered

if Derrick had overheard my conversation and was just being nosy.

"So tell me, Ray. You're not married. From what I've heard you always had the finest girl in the frat," Derrick said.

"Yeah, but things change, Derrick. You'll learn that as you get older," I said coldly.

"Okay, frat. Well, I just wanted to thank you for coming up and for the checks you send. They really help out," he added.

"Sure, no problem, Derrick. Nice talking with you," I said as I looked to see if Trent was in the area.

I thought about how cold I was toward Derrick and how he really didn't have a clue that I was treating him coldly. Nor would he have known why if he'd been aware of my feelings. I thought about the checks I sent in support of the fraternity and the house and how my money was helping to perpetuate this hate. For the first time since I knew about KAΩ I felt embarrassed about being a member of one of the most prestigious organizations for black men.

Sunday arrived and before leaving, Trent and I had breakfast at the Hilton Hotel. We talked about what a wonderful weekend it had been and promised to do a better job of keeping in touch. The evening before somehow managed to end on a good note even after my stoic conversation with Derrick. After seeing KAΩ perform at a jamming step show and singing the fraternity hymn with over one hundred brothers all in perfect pitch, I realized it wasn't KAΩ I was ashamed of, just some of the members. Just as I knew you couldn't diss your entire family because of a few relatives.

While Trent and I ate toast and eggs I asked him what he thought about the "gay issue" within the frat. Trent pulled his coffee mug up to his lips, took a sip, and slowly placed it on the saucer.

"Well, it's like this, Ray. I say to each his own and if homosexuality was wrong then why did God make so many people gay? I mean why would anyone choose some shit like that?" he said as he looked me directly in my eyes as though he were looking right through me.

"Well, I guess you're right," I said as I glanced around the restaurant for our waitress, trying to avoid Trent's eyes.

We decided to stop at the fraternity house one last time before heading out. When we walked in it was like a morgue. Brothers were lying around looking as if somebody had died. Initiation, which was to take place that evening, was a solemn occasion but not this morose.

"What up, frat?" I asked a brother with whom I had chatted over the weekend but whose name escaped me.

"Bad news, frat. Real bad news," the frat brother said.

"What?"

Just as he was getting ready to answer, Derrick walked into the library of the frat house.

"Ain't no reason for you niggers to be all depressed. We didn't do it. Besides being a fag, the boy was weak too," he said as he looked around the room at all the long faces.

"What happened, Derrick?" I asked.

"That guy, Miller. Fool motherfucker tried to kill himself last night. The other fraternities and his girlfriend are saying it's our fault."

"What? What did he do?"

"Slit his wrists," Derrick said with no visible emotion.

"How is he?"

"Don't know. They won't give us any information. His family flew in this morning and I heard his father is coming by the house. That's why we need you older brothers to stay," Derrick said.

"What the fuck for?" I shouted. "To save your asses for being so motherfuckin' stupid?"

"Ray, cool down," Trent said as he pulled me by the arms.

"I'm cool, frat. I'm getting my ass out of here. It smells like shit in here to me," I said as I walked out the door and to my car. I didn't turn around to see who was calling my name. I just wanted to get back to Atlanta and to make my peace with Jared.

I couldn't believe what had just transpired. I was upset over some guy whom I had never laid eyes on. A young black guy paying for being different. I thought how this could have been me. I recalled how I once considered suicide while living in New York because my secret life had been discovered. I laid my head on the steering wheel of my car and did something I rarely did. I cried and prayed Christ would see fit to give Miller and me another chance.

Go the Way
Your Blood Beats

Undressing Lady J.

I t was her nails that caught my attention first. They were painted a burnt orange and extended a half inch beyond the pink pad of each finger. Faintly age-spotted hands. Elegantly mature hands that made me consider the possible contradiction of age and vanity.

I carried her framed photograph to be rung up by the dusty owner of Isabel's Antiques along with the lavender ribbon-bound stack of love letters addressed *To Lady J.* Isabel fingered the stack of letters fondly before placing them and the picture into a brown paper bag.

"I was wondering when these would go. She must have been a real lady," she said with a snapping wink of her right eye.

Lowering my head, I fumbled in my pocket for the eight dollars that the register requested, and grabbed the bag with a quick thank you.

"Have a nice night, and enjoy them, sweetheart," she called to my back as I waded through clotted dust motes to the door.

Out on the dusk-lit street, I thought about the picture of Lady J. and about my own personal signposts, those signals that guide others in and out of my life; contemplating how adept I had become at hiding the truth.

My paranoia made the casual looks of strangers grow harder and deeper, devouring my black coat with its torn lining and my rakishly angled velvet hat, nipped by moths. Contradictions. I thrust my free hand, which had become suddenly cold, deeper into my pocket.

Memories of my past lovers assailed me as soon as I pressed the keys into my apartment door. I had fallen into the habit of forgetting their faces as quickly as I could, only remembering them as a rapid succession of coats that I could barely tell apart. I fought the thoughts of a waitress, who sported an orange-spotted leopard skin and encouraged me to carry my breast to her waiting lips. A student, in a navy-blue cashmere, who would only allow me to ride his waist with one arm tied behind my back.

With a shiver I dropped the photograph of Lady J. onto my bed, with the hope that this delicately wrinkled, brown-faced, silver-haired matriarch would be the one to finally help me understand myself. I had read her love letters over the course of a month, carefully unfolding the delicate onionskin paper that seemed to hold so few secrets. The letters all ended the same way, *Your dearest one.* The writing hand was heavy. The hand of someone who had wanted nothing more than to accompany her on weekend visits to the city. To devour her lips in the rooms of expensive restaurants, and later, those of cheap hotels.

Despite this adoration, Lady J. had refused to be held down; the pleading words of the letter writer testified to that. Like Lady J., I wanted nothing more than the backbone to be able to stand alone.

The best spells are the most simple. Those that require more faith than materials. The pages tore easily between my fingers and settled noiselessly atop my bathwater. Settling myself beneath the water, I began to scrub the fragments of Lady J.'s life against my skin until the words filled my body. Then, stepping from the water, I rubbed myself vigorously with towels still stiff with the dried fluids of past lovers.

In awe I watched the Lady unfold before me and fix her gaze on my face with a satisfied grin.

"Baby, don't stand there with that look on your face. You got what you asked for."

I managed to control my instinctive desire to recoil from her naked form.

"It's a bit chilly in here. A simple frock will do for now," she said with a raised eyebrow. I mumbled a confused apology for not immediately considering her comfort, and turned to rummage frantically through my closet for something appropriate.

Once settled with a glass of wine in her hand, she began to outline *her* plans. "Let's get things clear," she said imperiously, pointing a well-manicured nail at my face. "This little adventure is all about what I need and how you are going to fulfill those needs."

It took less than an hour after her appearance for me to realize my grave error. The smiling Lady J. had duped me. She had answered my invocation all too willingly, informing me that she had been waiting years to hear it, as she appendaged herself to my back, turning us into a two-faced biological coin.

"Oh love, what took you so long? I have been watching your feeble attempts, and just wishing I could have a hand in your exploits, and show you how it's really done."

I could not reconcile this Lady with the face I had come to trust. There was no peace in this middle-aged incubus eager to ride my back. No hint of innocence in the way she wrapped herself around me with a hunger even I had never experienced before.

Somehow, she had gotten it into her head that I had called her down because I felt the need for some competition, and I could not convince her otherwise. She was quick to let me know that she was not a lady at all. As proof, she told me stories of her many loveless encounters, which made my skin ripple with embarrassment and disgust. When the tales were no longer entertaining enough, she came up with the idea of having me relive her fantasies for her own entertainment.

One night she dragged me into a bar and within minutes had me talking to a well-heeled philistine with slick-backed hair and smoke-stained fingers. His camel hair coat looked like it had not been cleaned since he bought it five years ago.

"Dahling, you're in for a treat. He has endurance and creativity written all over his lascivious face."

On another occasion she forced me to turn out a thirty-five-year-old mother of two. "You are the answer to her fantasies. Now pay for her groceries and let's snap to it, girlie! Oh, how I used to love those protesting, begging types." I focused my attention on the woman's plaid wool back, already trying to forget the scene that would follow once in my apartment.

Each day we spent together strengthened her hold on me. Every day, with her prodding, I lured another stranger into my bed, none of them aware of her constant presence behind me. My hips were a rumbling motor that never idled. My world became a stark white room, my bed the axis on which it revolved. I lost all sense of free will. Each escape attempt was thwarted by Lady J. over the shoulders of our latest conquest, whispering my worse fears into my ear: "We are sisters. This is what we were made to do, and you know that you can't live without it." Through my body's pleasure I repeated, "No, I can't live without it."

Her spit-dripping cackle would shock me back to reality and I would fight a little harder against the army of bodies that crawled across my bed sheets. Until one day—while rubbing wrists chaffed from the handcuffs of an actor who had entered my apartment with a full-length black leather Mack coat draped over his arm—I decided that this charade had to end. Lady J. would have to go.

I would give her fair warning. After all, I had been the one to call the she-devil out of hiding. I tried to force her to remember the time she had spent with her "dearest one," to recollect some decent emotion, even though at this point I questioned her companion's sanity more than hers. Still she refused to hear me out. "Shut up. I've already been dead once, and nearly evaporated from the forced abstinence. Oh no, there will be no going back."

I decided that the only way to get rid of Lady J. was by the same method I had employed to bring her into my life. I stole moments while she slept to work on my own series of letters. On paper I explored the reality that here was an individual more off-center and hungrier than I. Someone who had also felt compelled to wear a mask of false innocence. I was convinced now that I could search for this elusive "innocence" in a hundred photographs of little old ladies, only to discover some aspect of my own desires in each one.

I chose a night thirty days from the night on which I had first called the Lady down. I tore my letters silently as she snored loudly across my back. She woke up screaming and cursing me as I settled myself beneath the ritual waters for the second time.

"You spineless wretch, how dare you deprive me of our pleasure!"

Determined, I pressed my back harder against the edge of the bathtub until I felt her body dissolve beneath me. Draining the tub, I picked up the limp photograph, all that remained of her, and flushed it down the toilet. A purity of emotion suffused my body as I stood up. I felt lighter, as though all of the cloaked strangers of my past had been sucked down with her. I smiled at my reflection in the mirror as I dressed to go out that night. Licking my lips happily, I realized that I had a sudden taste for a pea-green swing coat, who lived right next door.

REGINALD SHEPHERD

〇╱〇

Summertime, and
the Living Is Easy . . .

I am sitting in the library of Marshall's parents' house reading a book about beauty: another sentimental education. The book isn't mine, but I want it. The house is huge, three floors of rooms tastefully decorated with ormolu clocks and reclining bronze figurines on mantels: things I will never own. I envy Marshall the rows of pristine hardcovers lined up shelf over shelf, dustcovers unmarred by the indignities of hasty packing in stolen milk crates, the two circular staircases made of banded Siena marble, one with Venetian cut-glass chandelier, the guest bedrooms and small rooms in the back that were once servants' quarters (now they hire people with my skin to do things and leave). I envy him the luxury of hating it. None of it is mine, not even Marshall.

Marshall is my best friend. We had a brief affair, before we became friends. Marshall would say we slept together, once, twice (we've put all "that stuff" behind us, he says), but I say it's all in how you look at things. Marshall says I am out of touch with reality, but I am the one who grew up in a housing project and he is the one who grew up here; we have different notions of what constitutes reality. He doesn't like me to talk about things like that, his money, for example, but as far as I'm concerned that is as good a reason as any. Our relationship relies upon a certain degree of mutual annoyance. I am annoyed that Marshall is rich and white and beautiful, and he is annoyed that I constantly remind him of it. He'd like to enjoy his abundance of blessings without feeling it is anything out of the ordinary. He wants to feel normal. I, on the other hand, want him to feel guilty.

The book doesn't say much about any of this, though it does talk about longing. The author finds beauty in strange places: Czechoslovakia and northern Minnesota. The book is about the beauty disease. What the book doesn't say is that beauty costs money.

I am lying in my room, one of the guest bedrooms, listening to the Smiths. It's ninety-five out and muggy, and I want to go swimming, but it's thundering and a deceptively blue plastic tarpaulin covers the pool. So it won't attract lightning, Marshall says. Marshall's parents are vacationing on some Caribbean island (one of the Grenadines, I think, or Guadeloupe), and I have yet to see anyone but a gardener (his skin like mine, like that of the smiling people left behind on that vacation paradise when the tourists have gone home for the season), but this house is full of invisible presences stripping and making beds, stocking the pantries with heat-and-serve meals, and rolling protective tarpaulins over the pool. Marshall is asleep; he finds thunderstorms relaxing. Yet another way in which we're not alike.

Marshall's family has two dogs, some mix of terrier and golden retriever. The family rescued them from the pound as puppies; this house takes in all kinds of waifs.

The dogs are Marshall's excuse for being here; he will take care of them, avoiding an expensive and probably incompetent kennel. Marshall's family has known people whose dogs died in kennels; Bob Barker's cat received a permanent bald spot while in the care of Pets of the Stars. I, on the other hand, have no excuse. Or Marshall is my excuse. Though the incidence of first-born sons dying while their parents are on vacation is doubtless lower than that for dogs.

I understand that golden retrievers are among the stupidest of dogs. Marshall told me that as well; he finds it funny. He loves his mutts.

Marshall calls them mutts.

The dogs are afraid of thunder. They are probably afraid of lightning. One of them noses his way into my room, where I am lying on the floor trying to make the most of the air conditioner's artificial breeze, and I take great satisfaction in kicking the door closed. I can hear the dog paw at the door, then stop. He has probably climbed into the bathtub, but the air-conditioning filters out the scratch of nails on porcelain. It rained last night also, and the dog was cowering in the tub after midnight when I went to pee. I yelled at him until he left; I never touch these dogs.

Marshall was far away, dreaming of dusty softball games in spring, or damp soccer matches in fall. I will never do those things.

Life is an affair of places, isn't it? I love it here. There is the pool and there are the books and there are the kinds of food the titled rich are served in Proust, whom I refuse to read. For dessert there is invariably ice cream: kumquat-currant, persimmon-lime, macadamia-poppyseed-yam. Marshall is a connoisseur of ice cream, an emperor. There is the central air-conditioning and the home entertainment center that takes up half a wall. There is the VCR and the videotape library (that is what they call it) of all the classic films I have ever promised myself to see, the ones that play Tuesday matinees at revival houses in Somerville. And there is the illusion that I have Marshall to myself.

We go for walks and for drives in the country, to the beach, to town with its three-block-long main street, and to the mall ten miles from town, where I wonder whether I am imagining the strange looks we get together (can they be wondering if we are lovers, or adopted brothers?), the lingering glances when I enter a store alone. When I meet their eyes the proprietors always smile and look away. At home Marshall and I play chess and

Parcheesi and backgammon and Chinese checkers, and Marshall always wins; he is the one who grew up with hundreds of well-scrubbed friends with whom to play those games. I had black-and-white TV. I endure the humiliations of losing stoically, since it is I who like to sit for hours watching his face scrunched in concentration. But I always win at Scrabble, and in general I am much the better cheater. We argue about the economy and whether socialism in one country could work, we watch music videos with the sound off while I massage his shoulders, sore from a morning's game of racquetball. We play old Smiths albums as the soundtrack to *Imitation of Life*. The remake featuring Lana Turner, and a white actress as the tragic mulatto Troy Donahue beats up when he discovers the girl he's been dating is a nigger's daughter. To be honest, I prefer to hear the dialogue.

I am bored all the time, and luxuriate in my boredom. It's not often I have the opportunity to lie by a pool for weeks at a time and ponder the utter pointlessness of life. It's quite pleasant to know that when I wake up near noon (I prefer to read at night) and can't think of a reason to get out of bed, I don't have to. My melancholy is as cool as the fresh orange juice I drink quarts of each day, as warm as the azure skin of the pool when I break the surface tension with my toe, just playing, really, not quite ready to commit myself to the colder water waiting beneath that glittering canopy. I can take all day to decide. I can postpone decision until the end of the summer, when my life will begin again.

Marshall is full of plans to improve himself. He is not wondering how he will make September's rent on a stifling apartment with a window opening onto a brick wall. Come fall he won't have to ask himself each morning how to ignore the pimply-faced kids with greasy blond hair and Metallica T-shirts who shout epithets from the playground across the street whenever I come home or leave. It really doesn't matter what they call out, "Hey Mike! Hey Michael Jackson!" or "Get the Vaseline out of your ass yet?," whether they make fun of my skin or my clothes or the way I walk: it's one of the only neighborhoods I can afford. Those kids are too old to be hanging around in playgrounds.

Marshall will not be looking for another job staring at a computer screen for eight hours a day plus an hour's unpaid lunch, because it pays better than retail and sometimes includes partial health insurance. He is always proposing rounds of tennis, squash matches; maybe we can go riding. I tell him I don't feel like it. I don't know how to do those things, I don't want to learn how to do those things, I would prefer not to. I'd rather lie here beside the pool and think about my problems, knowing that for the immediate future I need do nothing about them.

One afternoon Marshall goes on one of his outings without telling me. He knows I hate to be disturbed when I am reading, or sleeping, or masturbating. "Where did you go?" I ask accusingly when he returns, well after dinnertime. "Why didn't you ask me if I wanted to go with you?"

I ask myself, "If Marshall didn't love me, why would he invite me here?" and respond, "If he loved me, he would sleep with me." Marshall always says, "Of course I love you; you're my best friend." We're not speaking the same language at all.

I put on "Parade" by White and Torch, another English duo, moody like all the music I love, and close my eyes, listening. I keep the blinds drawn tight. Wearing nothing but one of Marshall's old madras shirts, too big for me, I like to pretend I am reclining on a divan in the atrium of a stone house in Marrakech, protected from the desert sun by a maze of fine latticework shutters, lazy dust motes floating on the few stray threads of light that infiltrate the cool enclosure, the silence perturbed only by the singer's thin, almost broken voice, a barely discernible English accent filtered through an adolescence in a provincial northern town spent listening to American soul music. A boy I like to think is gay (all pretty English pop singers are, you know), whose records no one in America buys but me, singing of love abandoned, false love once imagined to be true. *Looking through your eyes, you won't even notice me.*

When Marshall knocks on the door I don't answer. I don't carry a torch for anyone.

I condescend to Marshall only to keep him in his place. If he were not so wealthy, so handsome, if only he were not so white, I could afford to be kinder. But he is, so it must be understood that I am the more intelligent.

In deference to my host, my obscure object of desire, my muse and nightmare Marshall, shall I describe him, imagine him as if he led some life beyond my desire-filled resentment, my resentful desire? Marshall lifting a tennis racket to test the heft of it before his serve, Marshall tilting a glass of milk to barely parted lips while an unruly curl pokes from beneath the plastic snaps of a backward blue corduroy baseball cap, or biting into a half-peeled pomegranate, licking the tart juice and a pulp-cased seed from his lower lip with his tongue. Marshall browsing the ethnic snacks section of the local grocer's with his Brooks Brothers chinos and untucked pink button-down Oxford, or checking his "goddamn cheap Rolex" with a scratch on the face. Marshall shaking the sweat from his hair after he has come back from running, his gray tank top clinging to the skin that sheathes his sternum and covered with a fine sheen of dust.

By the standards of one who has been the same height since the seventh grade, Marshall is quite tall. He has a slim muscular build, a swimmer's body they call it (in high school he was captain of the team), and a great devotion to keeping fit. Marshall has always been what our college catalogue called a scholar-athlete. He has a thin line of fine hair between his pectorals, and large pink nipples that stand out from his chest. Very sensitive nipples, I recall. He has black curly hair and green eyes and his ears are small and almost translucent. The left side of his mouth doesn't quite match the right, and his face looks a little lopsided when he smiles. I like to see him smile; it makes me hate him less. His teeth are perfectly even, and obscenely white.

I'm sorry I ever started this.

Most of my love goes to the pool, which has been for the past week unwrapped, unrolled, uncovered, revealed in all its hyaline glory. This is an affection Marshall and I share. He does laps; I float.

There is, apparently, someone who cleans the pool. I have never seen him.

Marshall is driving through the country and I am lying by the pool reading Jean Rhys. It's comforting to read about the sufferings of the first Mrs. Rochester on an island where people whispered that she must be part black, an island like the one on which Marshall's parents are summering a thousand miles away, with ivory beaches I can see myself lying on if I close my eyes. Jean Rhys smashed up her life and I have no life to smash up, but we both have our islands and that is what matters. Through the speakers I have carried onto the back patio Dionne Warwick insists I make it easy on myself, and I am taking her advice.

After all, in a week Kyle will be here.

I'm under no illusions. Kyle's presence will bring discomfort and anxiety. Like everything, I suppose. To Marshall, of course, it will bring someone to sleep with every night.

Kyle and I do not like one another. Kyle dislikes me because I am snide to him and often rude. I dislike Kyle because he is Marshall's lover.

Ever since I have known him, and before, since our freshman year, when he was just a Homeric myth I watched play volleyball on the Green out the windows of the dining common, Marshall has had a succession of boyfriends named Travis or Justin or Shane; I'm sure there must have been a Lance, but I can't recall him just now. With each succeeding one I have simultaneously asked myself, "How could Marshall go out with someone as stupid as Trent?" and "Why couldn't Hugh be interested in *me?*" Few of Marshall's boys (that's what we called them, I and my small band of bookish young men who never got laid, who never thought of sleeping with each other) had IQs larger than their waist sizes, but they all knew how to carry themselves. Marshall was always valiant in praise of their hidden virtues, though as far as anyone could see (and anyone could, even I), their virtues were only too apparent. But then, I can vouch for intellect's lack of allure. One of Marshall's boys was named Cameron; he rowed crew. "Call me Cam," he always said; I never did.

Each had his own distinctive charm. None of the relationships worked out, not for long, but all of those boys did. Trent played rugby, Shane was a wrestler. (Discretion, when required, has always been one of Marshall's virtues. I leave that sort of thing to him.) Late at night in my dorm room, Marshall would ask me what he should do about Skip or Ashley, while I played Echo and the Bunnymen and diffidently rested a damp open palm on his knee while gazing empathetically into his eyes. Our relationship was not off to an entirely healthy start, but I always gave excellent advice.

Marshall slept late after our talks, and I got up to work the breakfast shift at the snack bar. Cameron always ordered four eggs, and extra butter on his toast.

Kyle is the worst of a bad lot. He and Marshall have been dating for a year.

I'm Marshall's best friend. I'm allowed to say such things. He laughs good-naturedly and agrees.

When Kyle is gone, I will still have Marshall. I don't know if that comforts me.

Kyle has just returned from a month in Europe, a birthday present from his grandmother. At dinner he tells me about his trip; he's trying to open up to me. He wants me to be on his side. He was mugged in Amsterdam, Nice was filthy and noisy, and the water in Marseilles made him sick. I hate people who complain about their trips to Europe. What Kyle doesn't understand is that there is only room for one on my side.

I am floating in the pool listening to Marshall and Kyle argue. It's their main activity when together: that, and having sex. I suspect it's only the fighting that maintains the attraction; the fights make them feel different from one another. Every bout of raised voices and mutual recriminations is followed by a lengthy silence; I keep the air conditioner turned up.

As far as I can tell, they argue about nothing, who's been unfaithful to whom in whose absence, even if only in his unspoken desires the other can read like a Dr. Seuss primer. Did Kyle sleep with Jonathan in Zurich? Was Marshall in Disneyland with

Evan on Kyle's birthday? (I tell Kyle he's being silly, why would Marshall do that? I show him the 101 *Dalmatians* souvenir figurine Marshall gave me, but can't remember when.) Marshall always turns to me for counsel, as he has for years. I eagerly prise out every detail; it makes them seem more real, the two of them. Marshall tells me, "We have our best sex after we've fought. Sometimes we won't speak for almost a week, but still have incredible sex two or three times a day. You don't think that's too weird, do you?" I try to explain to him that healthy relationships are based on more than just sex.

Marshall tells me Kyle is jealous of us. "Sometimes I think he doesn't really understand what friendship is." I tell him he's being hard on Kyle; Kyle can't help being who he is.

I try to imagine them in bed, the ways their bodies fit together: what Marshall's body does to Kyle's, what Kyle's does to Marshall's. At times, I confess, I've listened at the door of Marshall's bedroom, desperate at least to hear. At times I'm sure Marshall must know. At times I think he likes it.

I can imagine the bodies, but never the people. When the shouting stops I decide to swim some laps. I have never swum a lap in my life, but there's a first time for everything.

Downstairs, they are quarreling again, but I never see either of them anymore. When I'm not in the pool I'm in the library, and when I'm not in the library I am sleeping. Thunder doesn't comfort me, but the calm steady hum of the air conditioner does. I turn it up high, then bury myself in blankets, sinking into a white linen pillow of sleep to a soundtrack of white noise. I read profiles of the hot young writers and actors in the Hip Issue of *Interview* and tributes to Marilyn Monroe and Dr. King in *Life*, I keep myself an informed voter with *Time* and *Newsweek*, and then my fingers slacken and my head lolls back. When I wake up the magazines have slipped between the bed and the wall, or dropped behind the headboard. I don't look for them. There is no shortage of magazines.

This afternoon I am reading, out of sequence because that leaves more room for me, a series of letters I found just after graduation in the room next door to mine. A tall blond boy who people whispered was Edie Sedgwick's cousin, and half insane, lived there; he should have graduated too, but he went to Italy instead. Each letter is a tortured demand for love from someone who had spent the year traveling over Europe, and when she returned had given the letters all back, because she'd decided she was a lesbian. I imagine myself that girl, probably foreign, perhaps even Italian (he'd gone there in search of her ghost), sitting by the cliffs on Corfu or at a sidewalk café in Budapest with a sad smile because all the quotes from Baudelaire in the world could not make me love this man again, could not make me love any man. That boy spent the last month of school throwing knives at the wall we shared, but the letters were beautifully written.

Marshall comes to see me, sitting on the edge of the bed as if I were a sick relative he is obliged to visit once a day. Affecting not to notice the stale smell of semen hanging in the room, he says he worries he's neglecting me. He knows I'll always be here when he knocks. He can indulge me when I sulk.

Sometimes we laugh and he hugs me; sometimes we hold hands. It makes Marshall uncomfortable to know that underneath the covers I am naked.

It seems that Marshall and Kyle are not speaking again. I pretend to be busy packing my clothes and my records and my favorite books from the downstairs library, tokens of this summer of playing house, consolations for my imminent return to life. I can keep myself occupied with this for years. Every night for the past week, Marshall has come to my room to tell me the latest twists of their arguments, to ask me what he should do. Every night I tell him I don't know, I've never had a relationship like theirs, and every night after he leaves I dream of his large pink nipples. Once I dreamt I was kneeling in front of him and he detached his penis and handed it to me, walking away. It was made of wood and very hard and I held it in my hand for a long time before I woke up.

I ask Marshall why he and Kyle can't at least be civil. I tell him it's not fair that the two of them should ruin the last days of the only real vacation I have ever had. I know they're not sleeping together and I'm glad.

All my things are finally packed and I am rewarding myself with a final afternoon in the pool; as I have for almost three months, I am wearing one of Marshall's bathing suits. Kyle is leaving for California this afternoon; he and Marshall have agreed to patch things up before his flight. I allow myself to be carried by the pool's vague eddies; I'm memorizing every movement of the warm, clear water.

I can hear them yelling and then doors slam. A cab honks and before long takes off; Kyle is gone. Marshall is standing on the patio, shading his eyes against the glare. I wave slowly and he waves back. Like in a movie, there is no sound. I don't move. I have to go back in the morning and look for a job, but now I smile and close my eyes, floating on nothing at all, and wish again this place were mine. I feel happier than in months.

CAROLIVIA HERRON

❧

Epithalamion

SURPASSING THE LOVE OF WOMEN

Now after you and Joseph speak love, and after you demand that Joseph take heart to comply with the strict orders of Pharaoh, that Joseph caress you and give you his kisses—now, after Joseph leaves you trembling with pleasure in the library, now your mind lingers much upon passion and desire. The walls lean toward your fingers and touch you with desire, the balconies, the bowls of figs and pomegranates. The dust sifts from carved stones against your body, and from the waterfall the cool water by the white curtains in the room of Pharaoh sweetens you, all is love, desire. It is thus with you, you are a fire without a flame, a bush burning without being consumed.

You turn in the room, turning as if to enter the leaves of your portfolio, as if to turn within the carved words of the stone tablets. Warm dusty love you find in the words. History. Herstory. Yourstory. Ourstory. You turn the leaves, you pull engraved stone words to yourself here in the library of the Pharaoh Akhenaten in Saïs. You read until you feel the innumerable desires of many lovers pass against you and fondle you in your own desire. You imagine a kiss on the street, persuasion upon stairs, a run toward the bed of love. You feel sea walks and night urgings, the moment of looking up at a window from outside. Beyond that window is your desire. Awe and earthquake and errantry and heat and curiosity and sweetness and embarrassed silence and comfort and touch touch touch of the body, the body, you imagine.

Desire flows between Saïs and On. Desire flows between West Cambridge University and the University of Pen Forest. Desire lifts desire and swirls one desire after another into bodies. Desire thrusts man toward man toward woman toward woman brings you to the Pharaoh Akhenaten to Joseph to Asenath to Nefertha to Madame Center Director to Steward Currant to Ruland Witly to the Skerett. Bright desire.

In which you become Joseph. By night, by day, awaiting your marriage, you are Joseph sleeping alone in the library, you lie down and awaken to desire.

For you hear your interpretations of dreams awaken love in the courtiers throughout the halls of the king surrounding you, throughout the city of Saïs there is the imagination of love. And each awakened dreamer rises up to seek a beloved. The Pharaoh Akhenaten rises, he is aroused to urgent love for you, interpreter of dreams. You are tall and your full features are soft, there is softness in your dark hair that causes it to curve and lift in the slight wind where your locks are bound with gold bands.

Yes, desire brings the touch of a man to a man, desire calls out to history to fill the loved, the beloved, the lovemaking bodies with satisfied desire. You seek each other. And find.

For as Pharaoh continues to wonder in his mind concerning all you have said, the nature of god, the nature of love, the nature of freedom, he broods about love in his apartments. He broods and meanders in his halls until he comes to the library and finds you who have now become the beloved of Ruland, you, Steward Currant, sweet. And you hear the Pharaoh Akhenaten call upon himself to be Ruland seeking you, Steward his beloved in the library where he comes in desire.

For you, Steward Currant of the University of Pen Forest, spend your days here in the library of the Pharaoh Akhenaten in the city of Saïs. Here you write upon papyrus the plans and the philosophy of the Pharaoh Akhenaten. You write the Pharaoh Akhenaten's thoughts of art and poetry and love and life and freedom and desire. You and the Pharaoh Akhenaten desire to build a house of romantic poetry in a great city, a citadel for the delight of the Pharaoh Akhenaten to play with Steward, his viceroy and his beloved.

And this is the Song of Ruland who loves you, the Song of the Coming of Ruland to be the Pharaoh Akhenaten in great desire for you, the comely viceroy of the king. Ruland loves you and wants to touch you, to make love to you. Pharaoh is caught into the music of his heart as he walks his hallways and courtyards in desire for you.

You listen for a sound beyond the tapestry, the woven figures of the pool and the tree. Desire lowers the eyes of the Pharaoh Ruland Akhenaten, desire with which he desires to touch you. Will he never come to you? Will he brush his body against your body in desire? Tender the thought of it, tender the blush and the tingling flesh in great desire. Desire holds you in your place then sets you walking toward him, a man walking toward a man with desire kissing the flesh of your thigh and brushing your eyelids. Desire reaches into your heart and fingers the blood in your veins, you, Steward, a beautiful man, desire Ruland, a beautiful man who desires to lie down in a bed with you. You long he longs to brush your lips his lips along his chest your chest and his neck your neck and his sex your sex in desire.

Desire brings exodus, brings genesis, desire holds your hand uplifted toward the tapestry the pool the tree. You move toward him longing. What configuration of interconnecting bodies and loves, what aspiration toward union, what desire brings conflagration, departure, diaspora? Desire, how great is the desire with which you desire Pharaoh, O that he might lift the clothes from your body and touch you with the rising hardening sex that calls your sex to rise and harden. O that this might be.

Desire is the name of the tapestry beyond which you have passed, desire of human life for human life. Bodies urging one toward another with sweetness the trembling in the flesh covering the stomach, the rising accentuating sex, the trembling chest all echoing there upon cloth the tapestry of your desire.

Desire brings the Pharaoh Ruland into the inner room beyond the tapestry where you, Steward the viceroy, sit longing. And the Pharaoh Ruland fears to reach forth his hand to touch you. And you, Steward, stand before the presence of the Pharaoh, who cannot so much as lift his eyes to gaze upon your face because you are so comely, comely and well-favored. But in desire you move toward the Pharaoh, who moves toward you, compelled. He cannot, you cannot hold away from your beloved but Ruland comes to you, Steward, as you come to him. The robes of Pharaoh touch in desire the robes of the viceroy in desire, you.

And the Pharaoh Ruland moves behind you. And the Pharaoh Ruland sways his hips softly against your hips, you touch. Your head droops as your sex rises and he holds his arm around your chest from behind. Here you stand and receive the caress of Ruland, standing by the tapestry.

You turn to him and place your hand upon his shoulder and gently turn him who sighs a soft whimper. You touch the front of his body, softly rubbing with the back of your body, and that touch is soft and hard and lovely in desire.

"You are my garden full and growing, my beloved, my chosen one, from you I receive lavender and gladioli, with you I taste the honey with the honeycomb, drink your wine and your liqueurs of sweetness."

Desire lay you together, Steward with Ruland, drinking up the sweetness of your bodies, your sex, in loveliness in desire do you hold one to the other. The Pharaoh Ruland and Steward the viceroy, in desire one with the other touching kissing drinking in the bed behind the tapestry desire. Take your fill of love, dear lovers, eat and drink of love, deep, deeply your bodies close one upon another in love.

Desire gazes down upon you from a high window, two men in love, from a balcony. Desire gazes upon enfolding arms, your chest against his back. Your back against linen sheets with his kisses upon your thigh, desire. The curved globes of the buttocks in the curved palms of hands and his sex kissed and tasted and sucked in your mouth. He fondles you and his thighs urge toward you his sex in desire that gazes upon you from on high. It is desire looking down from the verandah the balcony the windows upon your desire.

Ah, love, love in my bed, who can sleep when the heaviness of your body calls from the gate, from the door, from the tapestry, from the pool and tree? Is it you, my beloved, have you come to me, my heart? I hear you upon the tiles, your footsteps, your fingers tapping the walls on your way to me, to me. Come in to me, come in, I have bathed and sweetened myself in preparation for you. I have undressed myself in waiting, beloved, move not away from my door but come in to me, come in. How my heart trembles at your coming, in delight for you. I rise toward you, to let you in to me, come, come in. My hands are soft with ointments, my arms with fragrant oils, as I rise toward you, rise, and undress myself for you, O where are you, why do you not come? Will you turn away from me? Will you delay? I faint for desire of you. I long for you but you do not yet come. I call for you to be in me, with me. Go not to the watchmen of the night seeking the light of your coming. Come to me, to me, my longing follows wherever you go, my beloved, through your nights and your days, to be with you in love. I long to undress you and to touch your body in all the places of love, to carry you away from all else, being my love being with me, beloved of mine. Let me undress you for love. I adjure you, O young men of Karnak, of Washington, of Saïs, of Philadelphia, if you see my beloved tell him I faint with love for him.

Desire holds you still in the room. Beyond the tree that is woven into the tapestry is the pool of desire, desire, damp bodies together, desire pistil and stamen, desire peak and promise and fulfillment. Place your hand here yes and your tongue here stroke me here caress me hold me here and here again beloved. Come to me come hard and soft and full and melting. Ah you are better you are best of all others, most delightful of men let the peoples know how full and delightful you are.

This is your lovesong. Your lovesong is of freedom, your lovesong is of freedom from the gods, the great gift of the creator god is freedom from gods. Your lovesong is of freedom. Your lovesong is our lovesong of our freedom, that freedom that moves the love that moves the earth and the stars and the other planets. Love. Freedom. To have love, freedom, divinity in one, one, to be always on the way there, not with the many gods but with the unspoken one who has promised not eternal joy but eternal discussion, argument, contention with divinity, seeking of the divine, eternally requiring goodness of god. Shall not the judge of all the world do right? You contend with divinity.

You desire to honor only the highest, only the best. You desire a surpassing love, the imagined home, the homecoming, the love of a man for a man surpassing the love of women. Unity, union, one, highest, farthest, best orgasm, the self as one, ecstasy, the god, god as one, as unity, desire for high higher. You desire the peace that follows creation union orgasm rest it is the seventh day, rest, it is the seventh week, rest, it is the seventh chapter, rest, rest you are beautiful and good, rest in requited attained consummated desire. Desire.

My beloved is a pearl among men, his hair black and shimmering as onyx, curls and caresses surrounding his ears and his cheeks, his head high and strong. He has velvet deep eyes, as deepest waters, dark and wise, his face is gentle before my face I behold him with sighs, his lips are of sweetness, hyacinth and lilies of the valley. I long to rub my cheek against his chest and his belly, strong and soft he is as of topaz and sapphire and fine linen. My beloved, my beloved, have you not seen him? His legs are pillars of marble crested with ebony and gold, his form is high and wondrous, I love him, I love him. O you full hearts, all you lovers dwelling in On, in Karnak, in Washington, in Philadelphia and Thebes, all you sweethearts of Saïs, see you not how full of delight he is for me, I love him so.

SURPASSING THE LOVE
OF MEN

Now after you and Asenath speak love, and after Asenath complies with Pharaoh's strict orders, to have you lie upon your couch patiently while she undresses you for her delight, and Asenath leaves trembling with pleasure when you remain in the library, then your mind lingers much upon desire and passion.

The walls lean toward your fingers and touch you with passion, the balconies, the bowls of figs and pomegranates. The dust sifts from carved stones against your body, and from the waterfall the cool water by the white curtains in the room of Pharaoh sweetens you, all is love, passion. It is thus with you, you are a fire without a flame, a bush burning without being consumed.

You turn in the room, turning as if to enter the leaves of the portfolio of Asenath, as if to turn within the carved words of the stone tablets. Warm dusty love you find in the words. History. Herstory. Yourstory. Ourstory. You turn the leaves, you pull engraved stone words to yourself here in the library of the Pharaoh Akhenaten in Saïs. You read until you feel the innumerable desires of many lovers pass against you and fondle you in your own passion. You imagine a kiss on the street, persuasion upon stairs, a run toward the bed of love, you feel sea walks and night urgings, the moment of looking up at a window from outside. Beyond that window is your passion. Awe and earthquake and errantry and heat and curiosity and sweetness and embarrassed silence and comfort and touch touch touch of the body, the body, you imagine.

Passion flows between the Aegean and On. Passion flows between West Cambridge University and Saïs. Passion lifts passion and swirls one passion after another into bodies. Passion thrusts woman toward woman toward man toward man brings you to Madame Center Director to the Skerett to the Pharaoh Akhenaten to Steward Currant to Ruland Witly to Joseph to Asenath to Nefertha. Bright passion.

In which you become Nefertha. By night, by day, reading blackwomansong in the library, you are reading blackwomansong that was gathered from Zaïre and Ethiopia by Asenath in her travels. You are Queen Nefertha resting alone in the library, you lie down and awaken to passion in the days before the great wedding.

And from the library you hear the echoes of Joseph's interpretations of dreams as they awaken love in the attendants throughout your chambers. Throughout the city of Saïs there is the imagination of love as each awakened dreamer rises to seek a beloved. You are aroused in love, your head is high and straight, there is cool motion in your skirts, linen falling back from your fingers because you feel the passion of Asenath gaze up at you from the papyrus and the dust that she has touched.

And passion brings the touch of a woman to a woman, passion calls out to history to fill the loved, the beloved, the lovemaking bodies with fulfilled passion. You seek each other. And find.

For as you linger over the webs of the Lingala women, the blackwomansong now held in the library, you desire that she to whom you are beloved may seek and find you. You want her to come.

Passion rises from the root of your body stirring your sex, your womb trembling toward her womb. There is heat and warm passion between your thighs opening, loosening. There is passion in your breasts tipping up outward toward your beloved who does not come. Passion moves one passion after another into receptive human bodies, one after another quickly. Troubling passion trembles your cheeks in love, you, Nefertha, princess of Lesbos, queen of Egypt, wise Skerett of the desert, beloved of Madame Center Director, you tremble at the sound of a step in the hallway beyond the library.

Passion moves you from the library table toward the tapestry toward the passageway here in the library of the palace of Pharaoh. Passion. Neither the playroom of the lions, nor the words gathered here by Asenath, no, nor even all blackwomansongs collected here are full to satisfaction for you. You want her. You, Nefertha, barbarian of Lesbos, you patterned Skerett of the desert and wise, you Professor Skerett want Madame Pharaoh Center Director to come to you. You whisper toward the sound of her footsteps, "O that I might touch the whole of your body, have you whole with me, I would undress you and kiss your body. I would touch every place of your body with passion, with great passion."

You lift your eyes as you lift the tapestry to look beyond, and she is there, Pharaoh, Madame Center Director, stepping toward you, Nefertha, for you are the passion of her heart.

Passion is the name of the cloth, the tapestry, the curtain beyond which the Pharaoh Director walks with passion for human life, for the thought of lying down with you, playing on the floor with passion. Your bodies urge one toward another with sweetness the trembling in your flesh covering your stomach, the searing fire of flesh between your thighs and then trembling breasts. This flowing cloth was made, was created as a love place for Madame Pharaoh and you, sweet woman, her beloved.

You meet here at the sill of the library, at the curtained tapestried door, where passion lowers your eyes. She wants to touch you, Nefertha, her passion brings her to brush her body against your body. Tender the thought of it, tender the blush and the tingling flesh and great passion. Passion holds you before her trembling. Passion leans you upon her between the tables of papyrus and the curtained door, passion kisses the flesh of your thigh and brushes the eyelids of Madame Center Director. Passion reaches into your heart, fingers the blood in your veins. In your passion for Madame Director you want to lie down in a bed with her, woman with woman in passion to brush lips along her breasts and the neck and the dark hidden sex of your woman in passion.

"Nefertha. Come to me. I would have you now."

The two of you are in the library. Nefertha Skerett and Pharaoh Director making love beside carved stone, among the webs of blackwomansong. There shall be a blackwomansong about blue eyes. There shall be a blackwomansong about purple flowers. There shall be a blackwomansong about the purification of the soul through the twelve zodiac signs of Africa. There shall be a blackwomansong about the descent of two black poets through hell. There shall be black womansong. Passion is calls its object and intersects itself. You want lovemaking want blackwomansong want blackwomansong.

Passion fondles your body, your body's flesh in her hands, gentle along your back. Your bodies touch and turn and touch again in passion, passion, sweet her hand on your thigh, sweet your mouth on her breast, you rub your breasts together, in passion.

O my beloved, would that you might stay with me for all time forever not letting go. Beloved, I seek all the places of delight upon, within your body, you my dearest, by garden and by fountain, by tree and by pool, you among callalilies and bougainvillea, you beneath drooping vines, we are each the love of the other. O walk with me, come with me, be with me in our garden upon grass and lilies, let us lie down one for the other.

You are beautiful, my darling, as the bright leaf of autumn, as the banners of welcome, I am undone, my darling, by the flash of your eyes.

Passion come to stillness. Passion finding its object its culmination. Passion rippling and urging and finding a way. Finding its way home. They lie, damp bodies together, passion peak promise fulfillment, place your hand here yes and your tongue here stroke me here caress me hold me here and here again beloved come to me sweetheart and gentle and soft and full and melting. Ah you are better you are best of all others, most delightful of women and you also of women most delightful let the peoples know how full and delightful you are.

Ah love, love in my bed, your hair is a flock of sheep from the hills of Lebanon, your teeth as pure as neat as rows of aspen after purifying rain, your face is smooth and clear, you are perfect my darling your body against my body is the fulfillment of all delight you are the blessed one of she who bore you, all the women of Lesbos praise and adore you beloved, my beloved.

Passion gazes down upon you, woman and woman lying together from a high window, a balcony, passion gazes upon your enfolding arms and your breasts. You turn and stretch upon linen sheets with kisses upon, between your thighs, passion. Your curved breasts, buttocks in curved palms her hands and your sex kissed and tasted and sucked in your mouth fondled. Your thighs opened by her lips in passion that gazes upon you from on high, passion from the verandahs the balconies the windows passion.

Ah, my beloved, you are the brightness of morning, the clear warm darkness of night, lovely as day and night together holding all beauty in yourself. You are all loveliness.

Passion to honor only the highest, only the best. Passion a woman with a woman to hold and to keep and to rest surpassing joy, surpassing all imagined conclusion of joy, of home, of homecoming, surpassing the love of men, unity, union, one, highest, farthest, best orgasm, the self as one, the god as one, as unity as desire for high higher, passion for the peace that follows creation union orgasm rest it is the seventh day, rest, it is the seventh week, rest, it is the seventh chapter, rest, rest you are beautiful and good, rest in requited attained consummated passion. Passion.

And you, Asenath, you who look down from the high windows, balcony, verandah, you who step into the corridor of the future from the palace above the library, you know that there are always many songs, many stories, many lyres, many webs, many voices, many personalities. There are circles. Stories. One song will pretend there is only a beginning, another that there is only an end or a line, a line with a place to go, they are each another a way of getting there, straight hair, curly hair, nappy hair, images on tapestry.

Ehad, Asenath, ONE. You have returned with the idea of one, returned from the mountains of Ethiopia and the Nzadi River of Zaïre. One. Ehad. One. This story of the choices you have lived in your travels returns to you again and again here in the high places of the library as you look down and see your day your night of love.

You keep saying freedom. O freedom over me. Freedom. African webs. Freedom. Grecian urns. Freedom. Roman togas. Freedom. You are walking toward the future for freedom, setting sail for the past for freedom. Freedom. Singing about freedom. Songs in groups of three lines and four lines there, but infinite. Infinity. Like freedom. Like divine freedom given by that unspoken one god who has promised not eternal joy but eternal discussion, argument, contention with divinity, seeking of the divine, eternally requiring goodness of god. Shall not the judge of all the world do right? You contend with that god.

Was it a setup for slavery? Did Joseph know that when he invited the house of Jacob to Egypt to save them from famine, it was a setup for slavery? It was a defeat. Those who were fed through the diligence of the children of Israel did not love those who fed them. Those who were fed through the diligence of the children of Africa did not love those who fed them. It was defeat. You and Joseph were to understand each the people of the other. And you were to love Joseph was to love you. A new

people. A serpent magic people. Freedom then slavery then freedom. Listen. Your people shall survive. You have always contended. The questioner and the god. You have always fought
toward understanding. You, the questioner whose name is sup-
planted and supplanter, you rest upon the stone of heaven by
starlight. You struggle and wrestle with god until you discover a
new name.

You are returning from the future for freedom. You know the
way. You are on your way. You are not afraid. You are coming.
You can find the road. The road is good. You are almost here.
This is your lovesong. Lovesong. This lovesong. This lovesong is
of freedom. This lovesong is of freedom from the gods. Freedom
from the gods, the gift of the one god is choice, is freedom from
gods this lovesong is of freedom. This lovesong is our lovesong.
Our lovesong of our freedom. Our freedom, that same freedom
that moves love. The freedom that moves love that moves the
earth and the stars and the other planets. Love.

Freedom.

O my beloved, I have sought you in the pastures and the
woodlands, beside streams and fountains under lilac and rose,
my beloved, and with the sweetness of honeysuckle I come to
you and my great longing places me with you, delight of my life
for you I have struggled and wept, for you I have defied all the
powers of slavery and death, for you, you, my beloved, to be with
you.

ONE

Lotus and water lily. Sycamore and grape and myrrh and fig and
papyrus and pomegranate and mango. Between On and Saïs the
festival days end. You return to Joseph to Saïs for the consum-
mation of the wedding, grape and pomegranate. It is a celebration with great joy, your marriage to the viceroy of the king,
Joseph.

Akhenaten is aroused to love, Nefertha is aroused to love,
Joseph is aroused to love, you are aroused to love. Desire is the
tapestry tree pool beyond which you have passed, desire of human life for human life. It is you, Asenath, you longing for

touch. You imagine his full body and desire. A male body. Too strange. Joseph. Joseph. Joseph comes to you cedar woven cloth a wand of ribbons, you walk together.

You stand before the round window in the palace of Pharaoh in Saïs, there down in the garden are the wild pets, lions and leopards. You are with Joseph. Not with lions and leopards. With Joseph. Rugs and silks and pillows and the sun, the sun from heaven lies down in your bed and you undress him and kiss him and suck on him.

Who can believe our report?

Hovering in the archways of the bedrooms with frozen moonlight, the answer is freedom, it is always the same, you are dizzy with the memory of freedom, collapses upon love, upon the others. All things come from love. Stillness of love, stop running, hear who sings lovesongs to us.

Come to the high garden beyond the window. We are a quatrain of infinitely decreasing sound. Come beyond the room of white curtains where you discovered love for Joseph in your heart, for Joseph, the shepherd's son from Canaan, the son of the goatherd Israel, the sun from heaven. Come to the palace rooms set aside for play and ease. Pink stone speckled with gray and pale blue. Brown marble, black with pink. Blood mixed with light wicker copper wood tile glass bronze clay pottery plants palms and the sycamore standing pools pillows.

You come together to bed in the palace of the king with Joseph. With love. You have turned your back on heaven for love.

You have come to the door and passed over. You have lain yourselves upon a sacred bed. A tapestry tree pool covers the wall behind the bed, there is a sycamore before the tapestry tree pool. Tumbling each into the arms of other, you read the signs of the tapestry tree pool.

Love, O love, turn your body toward my body, sweet man of the Hebrews, I bring myself to you through desire through passion, through love. O love, turn your body toward my body. I would look upon you to my pleasure. Will you linger away from me forever? Will you not come to me? We are in the midst of love seeking love, seeking a new word and a true story, O Joseph,

I am black and beautiful and I love you, let us lie together in love.

O daughter of this bright world, how lovely your feet smooth and curving and your head your fluffed hair, deep and thick as purple, as crimson wool, the adornment of queens. You enrapture me in the tangle of your locks, O daughter of the hands of love, your thighs are round and full and pleasant to my touch, blessed by the thought the art that made you. Your navel is a dimple of blushing sweetness upon your belly, I drink your wine, your belly stretching, bending trembling toward me while your eyes turn away in blushes from the passion that fills you fills me. My beloved brown and golden lover, you are as fruited wheat and ripened barley, as the loam of earth watered by the Nile, your brown brown eyes, were they not steeped in the deep waters of the Anatho, toward the gates of Busiere. Your breasts, dark and light, tan beige, tremble as newborn gazelles, my beloved, your neck is as stately as the towers of cedar coming down from the hills of Lebanon. How deep, how lovely dark, how wonderful you are, beautiful, my beloved, O love, tall and firm as the cedar. Let me, O love, let me climb upon the cedar of your body, and fondle and kiss your breasts, and hold myself close against you, in rapture, in loving desire. How fond I am of the turning of your eyes, the flash of your smile, your shortened breath, yes, let my lips touch upon the soft nipples of your breasts. Let me climb upon you or beneath you as you will, my beloved, let me hold close to your branches and feel your breasts tremble against my body, taste your lips, your breath, your fragrance. If you will, my beloved, I would taste of you as of wine flowing, turning and rolling with you we lovers who cannot yet sleep.

Sleek as a gazelle in his arms you turn and sigh for the thought of love, listening seeking love, finding a way to love. You love the sunshine who is Joseph penetrating the upper stories of this room of play. You love your limbs tangling in sweet limbs. Hot bright lovers you are as your eyes tangle with the threads of the tapestry tree pool beyond the edge of the bed. You have seen and known that story, but Joseph gives you enough now. And enough. And enough again. Joseph lover kisses and kisses and you cannot remember that the beautiful one above whom you stretch your thighs was sold a slave by his brothers, but you find in him not a slave, this son of a sheepherder of Canaan, but the very sun, the very light of the sun has come from heaven into this bed. Now create the world now, when there is freedom to love afterward there will be other ways other stories other tellings of this tale the telling will change from story to story forever in many webs.

And in this web your open body is filled up with Joseph pressing into you his sex hot son of life you dripping over him helpless, helping yourself from this love dish who is Joseph.

I give myself freely to be loved and to love this one I have chosen. He has my desire and his desire is for me. We come to our bed as imperial guests, let us lie together upon the scented sheets, lilac and rose, henna and violet, we are the flowers of the vineyard, we blossom as the first fruits, we open each to each, fig and palm and plum. Now I give you my love. Now, while the turtledove awakens the land, and the sweet fruits of the earth are brought to our courtyard and our door, here, my beloved, here is my love.

There is a sound of rustling in the bed, you lie in your union. Like the trembling before rain at the center of the world. And new races arising with new songs to be stolen by old peoples, Babylonians and Saxons look what you done to my song, there where we sat down and there where we wept when we remembered. Remember? Don't remember! Run! Run and forget! Or lie about it! Lie! Why not lie in the culmination of love passion desire forever? Why accept rebirth if you must come at last to the smoky room on the right of the corridor of the future, the room of slavery? No, rest in the arms of the beloved, the beloveds, turn and sigh in the passion of that love. But even as your orgasm comes upon you you lift your eyes to the uncanny tapestry tree pool, whispering, O let me not, let me not worship the wrong god.

Yes you lie at last beside Joseph and love him whose feeding of the people was the preface to the slavery of his own. Joseph, comely and well-favored, the son of the sun, who walked out of the sun so great was his beauty, Joseph Nathan, the Increaser, the Gift of God. The gift of the god who created the world, who casts human souls back into the human mind again and again.

I love you, O how I love you, my darling. If only I could be with you for all time and times forever. I want ever to be close to you and near to your heart. I want to kiss you and kiss deeply and lie resting with your arm about me. I want my closeness with you to be within this room and beyond it, never to end, never to break, my beloved. I would call you toward me forever. I would bring myself toward you forever. And I would call my mother and my father, they who engendered me, to bless all that is between you, my beloved, and me. Let us drink of the cup of union together, O let me take you in my arms and hold you forever.

You and your beloved entwined in erotic passion in a bed beneath a high clear window breast and thigh and kiss and pubis and penis and fingers and soft skin beneath soft touch and come to me, hold me. Let my trembling be for your arms, your sweetness, let me open my thighs and my lips for you for you, my beloved, for you. And the fragrance of human bodies a new people beautiful, stepping light, a circle and a god among them. And you, brushing your sex against the sex of Joseph whispers keeps whispering, freedom, O freedom O neverending ending O love.

Joseph holds you at last, one hand twining your nappy hair, one hand caressing your breast. O beloved, O lovers of On, and Karnak, and Washington, and Thebes, and Philadelphia, and Saïs, do not, I pray thee, do not awaken love until it is pleasing to thee. And Joseph was of a strange new people, who called their mother Sally and their father Avyam, they were a people apart, this is one ocean.

They have love, they each come toward other, they each tremble toward other, they are two they are one. They are making love in the bed of the king beneath the tapestry tree pool the sycamore. They are impassioned they touch they know each the body of the other they are in love. And love after so much waiting and desiring is easy, easy, as if one should seek the world over for a unique gold mask, and grow weary with the searching, and collapse in a place of brooding and rest and quiet murmuring, and look just above the head, and see the mask and the face of love behind the mask. The mystical beloved, the desired one, a mirror who is not a mirror. Run, run toward love, taste it and know it. It is food and drink. You come together in the making of blackwomansong you, Asenath, you, sitting up on your marriage bed singing into the tapestry the song of human life, the freedom song of human life. You cornerstones, you in freedom, you, beloved, you seekers of the imageless creator god.

Daffodil and crocus, lily of the valley, rose of Sharon, I have found thee I have known thee here in the land of your birth this blessed place where thy mother bore thee, O my darling, I am thine by thy desire.

With discussion with argument with contention eternally through the halls the corridor of the future, ah sweet, my sweetness, you are, come beneath me lean upon me, my beloved. I have returned from the desert and I have found thee sweet, my sweetness.

You contended with divinity in the Nubian desert as you read the portfolio and watched the path of the Skerett through sand and as you brooded the temptation of Aapet. And you contended with divinity in the Ethiopian mountains as you talked with the sorcerer and as you studied the pastel maps. And you contended with divinity as you came to the rain forest of Zaïre, and as you moved along the Nzadi River, and as you spoke with the sorceress. You contended with divinity as you listened to Anansi, as you looked down upon the lost dead child of Zaïre in the basket in the bulrushes. And you contended with divinity as you linked yourself to the son of Israel, land of god wrestling. It is god who does battle. I shall not release thee, I shall not release thee my beloved save thou bless me, wrestling, turning, they turn one toward other.

My darling, my darling, hold me, I would be with you, you are my love. Wildfire storm of love, gentle peace burning love, stunning stroking precious love, love arising from waters, love descending as fires, flames, rivers, springs and candlelight, love, I love, I do love, I do love you, freely I love, freely I choose, freely I choose to love you, I love you.

You are racing for the future for freedom you are returning from the future for freedom. You cannot be lost. You cannot be diverted. You know where you are. You cannot be fooled. You know the way. You are on your way. You have begun. You are not afraid. You are coming. You are going. You know what you are coming for. You know what you are going for. You have stepped upon the boat. You have stepped into the corridor. Your boat is sailing swiftly. Your feet are walking quickly. You can find the road. You call that road good. You have charted the sea. You know what is most to be honored. You understand the tapestry tree pool. Someone has been lost. You recognize the green figures. Someone has been lost. You call that which is most to be honored the divine. What is lost? Who is lost? You have seen the divinity. You are almost here. You are almost there. You have fallen in love. This is your lovesong. Your first lovesong. Lovesong. This final lovesong. This lovesong is of freedom. Your freedom. This lovesong is of divine freedom from the gods. Freedom from the gods, the gift of the one god is choice, is freedom from the gods this lovesong is of freedom. This lovesong your lovesong is our lovesong. Our lovesong of our freedom. Our difficult original originating freedom, the freedom that founded creation, that same freedom that created the world and founded it in freedom so that of necessity it knows freedom with that same freedom that moves love. The freedom that moves love that moves the earth and the stars and the other planets. Love. Freedom.

They rest their bodies together, one is awake. One is awake holding Joseph. You. Joseph holds you hold Joseph. One consciousness, one wakefulness, one vision, one. Love O love I rise I lean up I see above thee the tapestry tree pool the tree the green figures the future. I know. You know. You. You are lovely awake and seeing beyond the bed into the tapestry tree pool through the future, the corridor of the future is coming in love. Silver and wood, an open door, eyes that see beyond walls beyond battlements. Cedar and silver, your shoulders your breasts above the sleeping, resting, satiated eyes, beloved, a vineyard full and growing. A song of the song of peace, protected now, enclosed, comforted for this season. You are a rich and fruited vineyard of peace, given in love, O love. O peace, more precious than ten thousand, linger, linger here in my garden in love. Hear me, hear my love, light of my heart, and speak to me, speak, answer my beloved,

I am coming now, swift as the gazelle, I am coming for and from your love, for and from your sake, for the fruit of love.

Come back, come back to the garden, tend the flowers and live. The flamboyant trees of the Virgin Islands look back over the unconsciousness of the sea, toward Africa, if you are ever in Saint Croix, go to the East End by boat, disembark, and climb up the path, following the line of the sea, an arch, and a strange air. Look toward Africa and see many epic songs arising from the Middle Passage, the great epic songs of the Africans of the Americas, we who endured, survived and triumphed to tell the tale. Now there are moments of rest where once it only took us seven years to die. There was no time. Now there are moments of rest, now there are jewels in the coral and a great power to restore life.

And yet even in this love you know something is lost, someone is dead. What is lost? Is it a story, a song? Human life.

You are lovers from two peoples who stake and create your consciousness upon divine release from slavery.

You lean up from the bed of love, look into the tapestry tree pool at the end of the bed of love and sing—

> *O you who linger in the garden,*
> *A lover is listening;*
> *Let me hear your voice*
> *Hurry, my beloved,*
> *Swift as a gazelle or a young stag,*
> *To the hills of spices*

Author Bios

JAMES BALDWIN is the author of many works of fiction and non-fiction, including *Go Tell It on the Mountain, Giovanni's Room, Notes of a Native Son, Just Above My Head, Tell Me How Long the Train's Been Gone,* among others.

AMIRI BARAKA, a.k.a. Leroi Jones, is a poet, social critic, jazz critic, and an award-winning dramatist. His works include *Dutchman, Tales, Blues People,* among others.

BECKY BIRTHA is the author of two collections of short stories, *Lover's Choice* and *For Nights Like This One: Stories of Loving Women,* and a collection of poetry, *The Forbidden Poems.*

BENNETT CAPERS has published stories in *Gettysburg Review, South Carolina Review, Poughkeepsie Review, Crescent Review, Fiction,* and other magazines. He currently resides in Brooklyn, New York, where he is working on a novel.

SAMUEL R. DELANY has written several novels, including *The Jewels of Aptor, The Fall of the Towers, Nova, Babel 17, The Ein-*

stein Intersection, and *Dhalgren*. Mr. Delany teaches at the University of Massachusetts at Amherst.

MAX GORDON is a writer and performer. His work has appeared in *Inside Separate Worlds: Stories of Young Blacks, Jews, and Latinos*. He lives in New York City.

E. LYNN HARRIS is the author of *Invisible Life, Just As I Am*, and *And This Too Shall Pass*. He resides in Atlanta, Georgia.

CHARLES W. HARVEY has had works published in *Story, The Ontario Review, The James White Review*, and others. He is completing a novel. Mr. Harvey lives in Houston, Texas.

CAROLIVIA HERRON is the author of *Thereafter Johnnie* and a forthcoming novel, *Asenath*. She has held professorial appointments at Harvard University and Mount Holyoke College. She lives in Brighton, Massachusetts.

CARY ALAN JOHNSON has appeared in *The James White Review*, the *Amsterdam News, Christopher Street*, among others, and has published a chapbook, *Surrender*. He is currently at work on a novel. He lives in Brooklyn, New York.

GAYL JONES is the author of two novels, *Corregidora* and *Eva's Man*, and several books of poetry, including the narrative poem *Song of Anninho*.

RANDALL KENAN is the author of *A Visitation of Spirits* and *Let the Dead Bury Their Dead*. Currently he teaches writing at Sarah Lawrence College and Columbia University. He lives in New York City.

AUDRE LORDE, internationally recognized activist and artist, is the author of ten volumes of poetry and five works of prose, including *Undersong: Chosen Poems Old and New, Our Dead Behind Us*, and *Sister Outsider*, and the autobiography *Zami*.

CATHERINE E. MCKINLEY is the editor of *Afrekete: An Anthology of Black Lesbian Writing* and is currently working on a novella. She lives in Brooklyn, New York.

TONI MORRISON, winner of the 1993 Nobel Prize for Literature, is the author of several novels, including most recently *Jazz*, *Beloved*, and *Song of Solomon*. She has also written two books of nonfiction, *Playing in the Dark* and *To Come*. She teaches at Princeton University.

BRUCE MORROW has appeared in *The New York Times* and *Callaloo*, among others. He is the co-editor of an anthology of short fiction by gay men of African descent and an advisory editor of *Callaloo*. He lives in New York City.

GLORIA NAYLOR received the American Book Award for *The Women of Brewster Place*. Ms. Naylor is the author of three other novels: *Linden Hills*, *Mama Day*, and *Bailey's Cafe*.

ALICE DUNBAR NELSON was the wife of poet Paul Laurence Dunbar. *The Works of Alice Dunbar Nelson* is a collection of her writings, edited by Gloria T. Hull.

RICHARD BRUCE NUGENT was the enfant terrible of the Harlem Renaissance. His work has appeared in *The Crisis* and *Fire!!*, which he founded with Langston Hughes, Zora Neal Hurston, Wallace Thurman, Aaron Douglas, John Davis, and Gwendolyn Bennett.

MAUDE IRWIN OWENS was published in *The Crisis*.

SHAWN STEWART RUFF is the editor of a forthcoming book, *Beautifully Furious: Profiles of Lesbian and Gay Writers of Color Around the World*. He is also the editor of *aRude Magazine*, and lives in New York City.

CARL HANCOCK RUX has been published throughout the United States, Europe, and West Africa in several journals, periodicals, and anthologies, including *Aloud: Voices from the Nuyorican Poets Cafe*. He has been commissioned to write poetry for several dance companies including the Alvin Ailey American Dance Theater. He lives in Brooklyn, New York.

SAPPHIRE is the author of *American Dreams* and a forthcoming novel, *Push*. She lives in Brooklyn, New York.

REGINALD SHEPHERD has published in *The Antioch Review, Callaloo, The Iowa Review, The Kenyon Review, The Paris Review, Ploughshares,* and *Poetry,* to name a few. His poetry collections include *Some Are Drowning* and *Angel, Interrupted*. He currently lives in Chicago and teaches at Northern Illinois University in DeKalb.

BROOKE M. STEPHENS has published in *Black Enterprise, Essence, Ms., Quarterly Review of Books, Sage,* and *Rosebud*. She is currently writing a historical novel. She lives in Brooklyn, New York.

WALLACE THURMAN is author of two novels, *Infants of the Spring* and *The Blacker the Berry*. He was co-editor and founder of *Fire!!*

ALICE WALKER won the Pulitzer Prize for the novel *The Color Purple*. Other works include *Meridian, In Love and Trouble, The Temple of My Familiar, Possessing the Secret of Joy,* and *Warrior Marks,* an examination of genital mutilation.

ORIAN HYDE WEEKS has published in *aRude Magazine*. She lives in Vienna, Austria.

ARTRESS BETHANY WHITE has published in *Callaloo, River Styx, The Village Voice,* and *Quarterly Review of Books,* among others. She teaches at New York University and lives in Brooklyn, New York. She is currently working on a novel.

JOHN EDGAR WIDEMAN is the author of several works, including *Sent for You Yesterday,* which won the PEN/Faulkner Award in

1983, *A Glance Away, Hurry Home, The Lynchers, Damballah, Hiding Place, Rueben,* and *Brothers and Keepers*. He lives in Amherst and teaches at the University of Massachusetts.

JACQUELINE WOODSON is the author of *Autobiography of a Family Photo* and five young-adult novels. Her work has been widely anthologized. She lives in Brooklyn, New York.

RICHARD WRIGHT is the author of *Native Son, Eight Men, Black Boy, The Outsider, The Long Dream,* and *Uncle Tom's Children.*

Permissions